"SPELLBINDING!"
—*The New York Times*

"Do you know what I always thought I would do," Tonio whispered, "when this moment came?" He held the knife before Carlo. It gleamed with the grease of the fowl and the ebbing light.

Carlo shrank back against the chair.

"I always thought it would be your eyes I would take," Tonio whispered, lifting the knife carefully, "so that you who have loved as I shall never love, you who have fathered sons as I shall never father sons, you would be shut out of life as I was shut out of it, yet living as I lived!"

CRY TO HEAVEN

ANNE RICE

PINNACLE BOOKS
WINDSOR PUBLISHING CORP.

PINNACLE BOOKS

are published by

Windsor Publishing Corp.
475 Park Avenue South
New York, NY 10016

Fifth Pinnacle Books printing: October, 1990

Printed in the United States of America

This book is dedicated with love to
Stan Rice
and
Victoria Wilson

CRY
TO HEAVEN

PART I

1

GUIDO MAFFEO was castrated when he was six years old and sent to study with the finest singing masters in Naples.

He had known only routine hunger and cruelty among the large peasant brood to which he was born the eleventh child. And all of his life, Guido remembered he was given his first good meal and soft bed by those who made him a eunuch.

It was a beautiful room to which he was taken in the mountain town of Caracena. It had a real floor of smooth stone tiles, and on the wall Guido saw a ticking clock for the first time in his life and was frightened of it. The soft-spoken men who had taken him from his mother's hands asked him to sing for them. And afterwards rewarded him with a red wine full of honey.

These men took off his clothes and put him in a warm bath, but he was so sweetly drowsy by that time he was not afraid of anything. Gentle hands massaged his neck. And slipping back into the water, Guido sensed something marvelous and important was happening to him. Never had anyone paid him so much attention.

He was almost asleep when they lifted him out and strapped him to a table. He felt he was falling for an instant. His head had been placed lower than his feet. But then he was sleeping again, firmly held, and stroked by those silken hands that moved between his legs to give him a wicked little pleasure. When the knife came he opened his eyes, screaming.

He arched his back. He struggled with the straps. But a voice beside him came soft, comforting in his ear, scolding him gently: "Ah, Guido, Guido."

The memory of all this never left him.

That night he awoke on snow white sheets that smelled of crushed green leaves. And climbing out of bed in spite of the small bandaged soreness between his legs, he came up short before a little boy in a mirror. In an instant he realized it was his own reflection, which he had never seen before save in still water. He saw his curly dark hair, and touched his face all over, particularly his flat little nose which seemed to him like a piece of moist clay rather than the noses of other people.

The man who found him did not punish him, but fed him soup with a silver spoon, and spoke to him in a strange tongue, reassuring him. There were little pictures on the walls, brightly colored, full of faces. They came clear with the rising sun, and Guido saw on the floor a pair of fine leather shoes, shiny and black, and small enough that they would fit on his feet. He knew they would be given to him.

It was the year 1715. Louis XIV, *le roi soleil* of France, had just died. Peter the Great was the czar of Russia.

In the far-off North American colony of Massachusetts, Benjamin Franklin was nine years old. George I had just taken the throne of England.

African slaves tilled the fields of the New World on both sides of the equator. A man could be hanged in London for the theft of a loaf of bread. He could be burned alive in Portugal for heresy.

Gentlemen covered their heads with great white wigs when they went out; they carried swords, and pinched snuff from small jeweled boxes. They wore breeches buckled at the knee, stockings, shoes with high heels; their coats had enormous pockets. Ladies in ruffled corsets fixed beauty marks to their cheeks. They danced the minuet in hooped skirts; they held salons, fell in love, committed adultery.

Mozart's father had not yet been born. Johann Sebastian Bach was thirty. Galileo had been dead for seventy-three years; Isaac Newton was an old man. Jean Jacques Rousseau was an infant.

Italian opera had conquered the world. The year would see Alessandro Scarlatti's *Il Tigrane* in Naples, Vivaldi's *Narone fatta Cesare* in Venice. George Frederick Handel was the most celebrated composer in London.

On the sunny Italian peninsula, foreign domination had made great inroads. The Archduke of Austria ruled the northern city of Milan and the southern Kingdom of Naples.

But Guido knew nothing of the world. He did not even speak the language of his native country.

The city of Naples was more wondrous than anything he

3

had ever beheld, and the conservatorio to which he was brought, overlooking town and sea, seemed as magnificent as a palazzo.

The black dress with its red sash he was given to wear was the finest cloth he'd ever touched, and he could scarcely believe he was meant to stay in this place, to sing and play music forever. Surely it wasn't meant for him. They would one day send him home.

But this never happened.

On sultry feast day afternoons, walking in slow procession with the other castrati children through the crowded streets, his robes immaculate, his brown curls clean and shining, he was proud to be one of them. Their hymns floated on the air like the mingled scent of the lilies and the candles. And as they entered the lofty church, their thin voices swelling suddenly amid a splendor he'd never before seen, Guido knew his first real happiness.

All went well for him over the years. The discipline of the conservatorio was nothing. He had a soprano voice that could shatter glass; he scribbled melodies every time he was given a pen, learning to compose before he could read and write; his teachers loved him.

But as time passed, his understanding deepened.

Early on, Guido realized that not all the musicians around him had been "cut" as little boys. Some would grow up to be men, to marry, to have children. But no matter how well the violinists played, no matter how much the composers wrote, none could ever achieve the fame, the riches, the pure glory of a great castrato singer.

Italian musicians were wanted the world over for the church choirs, the court orchestras, the opera houses.

But it was the soprano singer whom the world worshiped. It was for him that kings vied and audiences held their breath; it was the singer who brought to life the very essence of the opera.

Nicolino, Cortono, Ferri, their names were remembered long after the composers who'd written for them were forgotten. And in the little world of the conservatorio, Guido was part of an elect, a privileged group who were better fed, better dressed, and given warmer rooms as their singular talent was nourished.

But as the ranks swelled, as older castrati left and new

4

castrati came, Guido soon saw that hundreds were submitted to the knife each year for a handful of fine voices. They came from all over: Giancarlo, lead singer of a Tuscan choir, cut at twelve through the kindness of the country maestro who brought him to Naples; Alonso, from a family of musicians, his uncle a castrato who arranged for the operation; or the proud Alfredo, who had lived so long in the house of his patron he did not remember his parents or the surgeon either.

And then there were the unwashed, the illiterate, the little boys who didn't speak the language of Naples when they came—boys like Guido.

That his parents had sold him outright was now obvious to him. He wondered had any maestro properly tested his voice before it was done. He could not remember. Perhaps he was caught in a random net, sure to ensnare something of value.

But all this Guido perceived from the corner of his eye. Lead singer in the choir, soloist on the conservatorio stage, he was already writing out exercises for the younger pupils. By the age of ten he was taken out to hear Nicolino at the theater, given a harpsichord of his own, permission to stay up late to practice. Warm blankets, a fine coat, his rewards were more than he would ever have asked, and now and then he was taken to sing for delighted company in the dazzle of a real palazzo.

Before the doubts of the second decade of life, Guido had laid for himself a great foundation in study and regimen. His voice, high, pure, unusually light and flexible, was now an official marvel.

But as happens with any human creature, the blood of his ancestors—despite the mutation of his castration—continued to shape him. Of a people swarthy and stocky of build, he did not grow into a reed of a eunuch as did many around him. Rather his form was heavy, well proportioned, and gave a deceptive impression of power.

And though his curly brown hair and sensuous mouth lent a touch of the cherub to his face, a dark down on his upper lip made him appear manly.

In fact, his would have been a pleasing appearance had it not been for two factors: his nose, broken by a childhood fall, was flattened exactly as if a giant hand had squashed it. And his brown eyes, large and full of feeling, glinted with the wily brutality of the peasants who had been his forefathers.

5

Where these men had been taciturn and shrewd, Guido was studious and stoical. Where they had struggled with the elements of the earth, he gave himself violently to any sacrifice for his music.

But Guido was far from crude in manner or appearance. Rather, taking his teachers as models, he imbibed all he could of gracious deportment, as well as the poetry, Latin, the classical Italian taught to him.

So he grew into a young singer of considerable presence whose stark particularities lent him a disturbing seductiveness.

All his life some would say of him, "How ugly he is," while others would say, "But he is beautiful!"

But of one thing he was quite unaware; he exuded menace. His people had been more brutal than the animals they tended; and he had the look of one who might do anything to you. It was the passion in his eyes, the squashed nose, the lush mouth—all of it put together.

And so without his realizing it, a protective shield enveloped him. People didn't try to bully him.

Yet all who knew Guido liked him. The regular boys liked him as much as did his fellow eunuchs. The violinists loved him because he became fascinated with them individually and wrote music for them that was exquisite. And Guido came to be known as quiet, no-nonsense, the gentle bear cub, not one to be afraid of once you came to know him.

Reaching his fifteenth year, Guido woke one morning to be told that he must come downstairs to the office of the Maestro. He was not anxious. He was never in any trouble.

"Sit down," said his favorite teacher, Maestro Cavalla. All the others were assembled around him. And never had they been so informal with him before, and something about this ring of faces was unpleasant to him. He knew at once what it was. It reminded him of that room in which he had been cut, and he shrugged it off as meaning nothing.

The Maestro behind the carved table dipped his pen, scratched large figures in ink, and handed the parchment to Guido.

December 1727. What could it mean? A slight tremor ran through Guido.

"That is the date," said the Maestro, drawing himself up, "upon which you will appear in your first opera in Rome as *primo uomo*."

*   *   *

So Guido had done it.

It would not be the church choir for him, nor the backcountry parishes, nor even the great city cathedrals. Not, not even the Sistine Choir. He had soared past all that, right into the dream which inspired them all, year after year, no matter how poor they were, no matter how rich, no matter from where they came: the opera.

"Rome," he whispered as he stepped out, quite alone, into the corridor. Two students stood near, as if waiting for him. But he walked past them into the open courtyard as if he did not see them. "Rome," he whispered again, and he let it roll off his tongue, that thick explosion of breath that men have said with awe and terror for two thousand years: Rome.

Yes, Rome and Florence, and Venice, and Bologna, on to Vienna, and Dresden and Prague, to all the front lines where the castrati conquered. London, Moscow, back again to Palermo. He almost laughed aloud.

But someone had touched his arm. It was unpleasant to him. He couldn't shake loose the vision of the tiers of boxes, and audiences roaring.

And when his vision cleared he saw it was a tall eunuch, Gino, who had always been ahead of him, a blond and willowy northern Italian with slate eyes. And beside him stood Alfredo, the rich one, who had money always in his pockets.

They were telling him to come into town; they were telling him the Maestro had given him the day for celebrating.

And he realized why they were here. They were the conservatorio's rising stars.

And he was now one of them.

2

WHEN TONIO TRESCHI was five years old, his mother pushed him down the stairs. She hadn't meant to do it. She had only meant to slap him. But he had slipped backwards on the marble tile, and fallen down and down, a panic engulfing him before he reached the bottom.

Yet he might have forgotten that. Her day-to-day love for him was full of unpredictable cruelty. She could be full of desperate warmth one minute, and savage to him the next. In fact, he lived torn between appalling need on the one hand, and on the other, pure terror.

But that night, to make it up to him, she took him to San Marco to see his father in procession.

The great church was the Ducal Chapel of the Doge and Tonio's father was Grand Councillor.

It was like a dream to him afterwards; but it was no dream. And all his life he remembered it.

He had hidden from her hours after the fall. The great Palazzo Treschi swallowed him. The truth was, he knew the entire four storeys of the crumbling Renaissance house better than anyone else, and familiar with every chest and closet in which he could hide, he could always get away for as long as he wanted.

Darkness meant nothing to him. Being lost here or there didn't bother him either. He had no fear of rats. Rather he watched their quick passage through the corridors with vague interest. And he liked the shadows on the walls, the ripples of light from the Grand Canal flashing dimly on ceilings painted with ancient figures.

He knew more of these moldering rooms than of the world outside. They were the landscape of his childhood and all along his labyrinthine path lay landmarks of other retreats and pilgrimages.

But being without *her*, that was the pain for him. And anguished and shivering, he crept back to her finally as he always did when the servants had despaired of finding him.

She lay sobbing on her bed. And there he appeared, a man of five years, bent on revenge, his face red and streaked with dirt from his crying.

Of course he was never going to speak to her again as long as he lived. Never mind that he could not stand being without her.

Yet as soon as she opened her arms, he flew into her lap and lay against her breast as still as if he were dead, one arm around her neck, the other hand clutching her shoulder so tightly he was hurting her.

She was little more than a girl herself, but he didn't know it. He felt her lips on his cheek, on his hair. He melted into her gentleness. And deep within the pain that for the moment

8

was his mind, he thought, If I hold her, hold her, then she'll stay as she is now, and that other creature won't come out of her to hurt me.

Then she drew herself up, stroking the stiff unruly waves of her black hair, her brown eyes still red but brimming with sudden excitement. "Tonio!" she said impulsively, rocking like a child. "There's still time, I'll dress you myself." She clapped her hands. "I'm taking you with me to San Marco."

His nurses said no. But there was no stopping his mother. A gaiety pervaded the room, candles dipping and trembling as the servants followed them about, his mother's fingers deftly buttoning his satin breeches, his brocade waistcoat. She took the comb to his softer curls with the old chant, they were black silk, and kissed him twice abruptly.

And all the way down the corridor, he heard her singing softly behind him as he skipped ahead, thrilled with the click of his fancy slippers on the marble.

She was radiant in her black velvet gown, a blush suffusing her olive skin, and in the light of the lantern as she sank back into the dark *felze* of the gondola, her face with its slanted eyes resembled perfectly those Madonnas in the old Byzantine paintings. She held him on her lap. The curtain closed. "Do you love me?" she asked. He teased her. She pressed her cheek against his, mingling her eyelashes with his own, until he gave way to uncontrolled laughter. "Do you love me!" she clasped his shoulder.

And when he said yes, he felt her melting embrace, and for a moment became motionless, as if paralyzed, against her.

Across the piazza he danced on the leash of her arm. Everyone was here! He made bow after bow, hands reaching to tousle his hair, to press him to perfumed skirts. The young secretary to his father, Signore Lemmo, tossed him high in the air seven times before his mother said stop it. And his beautiful cousin Catrina Lisani, with two of her sons in tow, threw back her veil and, picking him up, smothered him against her fragrant white bosom.

But as soon as they set foot into the immense church Tonio was silent.

Never had he witnessed such a spectacle. Candles everywhere wreathed the marble columns and in the gusts from the open doors, the torches roared in their sconces. The great

9

domes blazed with angels and saints, and all around arches, walls, vaults pulsed with gold in millions upon millions of tiny twinkling facets.

Without a word, Tonio scrambled into his mother's arms. He climbed her like a tree. She rocked backwards under his weight, laughing.

And then it seemed a shock passed through the crowd like the rustle of burning kindling. Trumpets blared. Tonio turned back and forth frantically, unable to find them.

"See!" his mother whispered, squeezing his hand. And above the heads of the crowd the Doge appeared in his great chair under a swaying canopy. The sharp heavy scent of incense filled the air. And the trumpets rose in pitch, shrill and brilliant and chilling.

Then came the Grand Council in their brilliant robes. "Your father!" said Tonio's mother with a spasm of girlish excitement.

The tall bone-thin figure of Andrea Treschi came into view, sleeves down to the floor, his white hair the shape of a lion's mane, his deep-set pale eyes fixed like those of a statue before him.

"Papa!" Tonio's whisper carried sharply. Heads turned, there was muffled laughter. And when the Councillor's gaze wavered and fixed his son in the crowd, the ancient face was transformed, its smile almost rapturous, those eyes brilliantly enlivened.

Tonio's mother was blushing.

But suddenly from out of the air it seemed a great singing burst forth, voices high and clear and declaring. Tonio felt a catch in his throat. For a second he could not move, his body perfectly rigid as he absorbed the shock of this singing, and then he squirmed, eyes upward, the candles for the moment blinding him. "Be still," said his mother, who could hardly hold him. The singing grew richer, fuller.

It came in waves from either side of the immense nave, melody interwoven with melody. Tonio could almost see it. A great golden net thrown out as if on the lapping sea in shimmering sunlight. The very air teemed with sound. And finally he saw, right above, the singers.

They stood in two huge lofts to the left and right side of the church, mouths open, faces gleaming in reflected light; they appeared like the angels in the mosaics.

In a second, Tonio had dropped to the floor. He felt his mother's hand slip as she went to catch him. He dashed

10

through the press of skirts and cloaks, perfume and winter air, and saw the open door to the stairway.

It seemed the walls around him throbbed with the chords of the organ as he climbed, and suddenly he stood in the warmth of the choir loft itself, among these tall singers.

A little commotion ensued. He was at the very rail and looking up into the eyes of a giant of a man whose voice poured out of him as clean and golden as the clarion of the trumpet. The man sang the one great word, "Alleluia!" which had the peculiar sound of a call to someone, a summoning. And all the men behind him picked it up, singing it over and over again at intervals, overlapping one upon the other.

While across the church the other choir returned it in mounting volume.

Tonio opened his mouth. He started singing. He sang the one word right in time with the tall singer and he felt the man's hand close warmly on his shoulder. The singer was nodding to him, he was saying with his large, almost sleepy brown eyes, Yes, sing, without saying it. Tonio felt the man's lean flank beneath his robe, and then an arm wound down about his waist to lift him.

The whole congregation shimmered below, the Doge in his chair of golden cloth, the Senate in their purple robes, councillors in scarlet, all the patricians of Venice in their white wigs, but Tonio's eyes were fixed on the singer's face as he heard his own voice like a bell ringing out distinct from the singer's clarion. Tonio's body went away. He left it, carried out on the air with his voice and the singer's voice as the sounds became indistinguishable. He saw the pleasure in the singer's quivering eyes, that sleepiness lifted. But the powerful sound erupting from the man's chest astonished him.

When it was over and he was placed in his mother's arms again, she looked up to this giant as he made her a deep bow, and said:

"Thank you, Alessandro."

"Alessandro, Alessandro," Tonio whispered. And as he snuggled next to her in the gondola he said desperately, "Mamma, when I grow up will I sing like that? Will I sing like Alessandro?" It was impossible to explain it to her. "Mamma, I want to be one of those singers!"

11

"Good Lord, Tonio, no!" She burst out laughing. And with a foppish gesture of her wrist to his nurse, Lena, she looked to heaven.

The entire household was clattering and groaning up to the roof. And gazing towards the mouth of the Grand Canal, anticipating that infinite spell of darkness that was the lagoon, Tonio saw the sea ablaze: hundreds upon hundreds of lights bobbing on the water. It was as if all the flickering illumination of San Marco had been spilled out, and in a reverent whisper his mother told him that the men of state were going to venerate the relics on San Giorgio.

All was still for a moment, except the whistling wind that had long ago torn the fragile lattices of the ruined roof garden. Dead trees lay here and there on their sides, anchored still by their overturned pots of root and earth, their leaves snapped by the wind, crackling.

Tonio bent his head. He gave the tender stretch of his neck to his mother's warm hand, and felt a wordless and terrifying dread that pushed him close to her.

Late that night, covered to the chin in bed, he did not sleep. His mother lay back, lips slack, her angular face softened as if against her will, her close-set eyes, so unlike his own, drawn to the center of her face in a frown that seemed the very opposite of sleep, more accurately preoccupation.

And shoving back the covers (his father never slept with them; he was always in his own apartments), Tonio slipped to the cold floor, barefoot.

There were street singers out in the night, he was certain of it. And wrenching open the wooden shutters, he listened, head cocked, until he picked up the faint strains of the distant tenor. There came a basso underneath, the raw dissonance of strings, and round and round the melody rising higher, wider.

The night was misted, without forms or shapes save for the aureole of a single resin torch below that lent its heavy smell to the salt from the sea. And as he listened, his head against the damp wall, knees drawn up in a loose clasp, he was still in the choir loft of San Marco. Alessandro's voice eluded him now, but he felt the sensation, the dreamy sweep of the music.

He parted his lips, sang a few high notes in time with those

12

distant singers in the street, and felt again Alessandro's hand on his shoulder.

What was nagging at him suddenly? What came like a gnat to the eye? His mind, ever so sharp and unclouded as yet by written language, felt again the palm of that hand resting so gently at his neck, saw the billowing sleeve rising and rising to the shoulder above it. All the other tall men he had ever known had to bend to caress a boy as little as Tonio. And he remembered that even in the choir loft, in the midst of that singing, he had been startled to feel that hand rest so easily on him.

It seemed monstrous, magical, the arm that scooped him up, the hand that had caught the bones of his chest as if he were a toy and brought him higher into the music.

But the song was tugging at him, pulling him out of these thoughts as melody always pulled him, making him feel desperate for the harpsichord that his mother played, or her tambourine, or only the mingled sound of their voices. Anything to make it go on. And suddenly, shivering on the sill, he was sleeping.

He was seven years old before he learned that Alessandro and all the tall singers of San Marco were eunuchs.

3

AND BY THE TIME he was nine years old he knew just what had been cut away from these spidery beings and what had been left them, and that it was an accident of the knife, their height and their long limbs, for after that terrible cutting their bones didn't harden like those of men who could father children.

But it was a commonplace mystery. They sang in all the churches of Venice. They taught music when they were old. Tonio's tutor, Beppo, was a eunuch.

And in the opera, which Tonio was much too young to see, they were celestial wonders. Nicolino, Carestini, Senesino, the servants sighed as they said the names the next day, and even once Tonio's mother had been lured out of her solitary

13

life to see the young one from Naples, whom they called The Boy, Farinelli. Tonio cried because he couldn't go. And waking hours after, saw she'd come home, and sat at the harpsichord in the dark, her veil sparkling with rain, her face as white as a porcelain doll as in a faint uncertain voice she echoed the threads of Farinelli's arias.

Ah, the poor do what they must for food and drink. We will always have these miraculous high voices. Yet every time Tonio saw Alessandro outside the church door, he could not help but wonder: Did he cry? Did he try to run away? Why didn't his mother try to hide him? But there was nothing in Alessandro's long face but that sleepy good humor, his chestnut hair a lustrous frame for skin that was as pretty as a girl's, and that voice slumbering deep inside, waiting for its moment in the choir loft, waiting for the backdrop of hammered gold that seemed to make him one—for Tonio—with the angels.

But by this time, too, Tonio knew he was Marc Antonio Treschi, the son of Andrea Treschi who had once commanded the galleys of the Serenissima on foreign seas, and after years of service in the Most Serene Senate, had just been elected to the Council of Three, that awesome triumvirate of inquisitors whose power it was to arrest, to try, to pronounce sentence, and to carry out that sentence—even if it were death—upon anyone.

In other words, Tonio's father was among those more powerful than the Doge himself.

And the name Treschi had been in the Golden Book for a millennium. This was a family of admirals, ambassadors, procurators of San Marco, and senators too numerous to mention. Three brothers of Tonio, all long dead—the children of a first wife gone to the grave, too—had served in high places.

And on reaching his twenty-third birthday, Tonio would certainly take his place among those young statesmen promenading that long strip of the piazzetta before the Offices of State known as the Broglio.

It would be the University of Padua before that, two years at sea, a tour of the world perhaps. And for now, hours spent in the library of the palazzo under the gentle but relentless eyes of his tutors.

*　　*　　*

Portraits hung on these walls. Black-haired Treschi with fair skin, men cut from the same mold, delicate-boned but tall, with broad foreheads that rose straight to the full hair that grew up and back from them. Even as a little one Tonio perceived his resemblance to some more than others: dead uncles, cousins, those brothers: Leonardo who had died of consumption in an upper room, Giambattista drowned at sea off the coast of Greece, Philippo of malaria in some distant outpost of the empire.

And here and there appeared a face that was more perfectly Tonio's own, a young man with Tonio's wide-set black eyes and the same full but long mouth always on the verge of smiling; he peeked only from great clusters of richly clad men in which Andrea might be yet young with his brothers and nephews around him. But it was hard to fix a name for each face, to distinguish one from another among so many. A communal history absorbed them all in wonderfully wrought tales of courage and self-sacrifice.

All three sons with their father and his somber first wife peered from the grandest of gilt frames in the longer supper room.

"They're watching you," Lena, Tonio's nurse, teased as she ladled the soup. She was old but full of good humor and more a nurse to Tonio's mother, Marianna, than she was to him, and she only meant to amuse him.

She couldn't guess how it hurt him to look at this spectacle of ruddy and perfectly painted faces. He wanted his brothers alive, he wanted them here now, and he wanted to open doors on rooms filled with gentle laughter and commotion. Sometimes he imagined how it would be, the long supper table crowded with his brothers: Leonardo lifting his glass, Philippo describing battles at sea; his mother, her narrow eyes, so small when sad, grown wide with excitement.

But there was an absurdity to this little game that made itself known to him over the years. It frightened him enormously. Long before he knew the full import, he'd been told that only one son of a great Venetian family marries. It was custom so old it might have been law, and in those days it had been Philippo, whose childless wife had gone home after his death to her own people. But if any of those shades had lived long enough to produce a son of the Treschi name, Tonio would not be here! His father would never have taken a second wife. Tonio would not even exist. And so the very

15

price of life for him was that they were swept away without issue.

He couldn't grasp it at first; but after a while, it was an old truth; he and those brothers, they had never been meant to know each other.

Yet he played his fantasy out; he saw these yawning rooms brilliantly lit, heard music, pictured soft-spoken men and women who were his own kin, a swarm of nameless cousins.

And always his father was about, at supper, on the ballroom floor, turning to catch his youngest son in his arms with a wealth of spontaneous kisses.

As it was, Tonio seldom saw his father.

But on those occasions when Lena came for him, whispering anxiously that Andrea had sent for his son, it was absolutely marvelous. She would outfit him in his best, a coat of rust-colored velvet he loved, or maybe the darker blue that was his mother's favorite. And brushing his hair to a lively luster, she let it fall softly without a ribbon. He looked like a baby, he would protest. Then out would come the jeweled rings, the fur-lined cloak, and his own little sword, studded with rubies. He was ready now. His heels made that delicious click on the marble.

The Grand Salon of the main floor was always the setting. It was an immense room, the largest in a house of large rooms, furnished only with a long heavily carved table. Three men could have lain end to end on that table. The floor was a pattern of tinted marble that made up a map of the world, while the ceiling was an endless vista of blue where angels hung suspended, unfurling a great winding ribbon of Latin lettering. The light was uneven, coming as it did through open doors from other chambers. But it was often full of morning warmth as it fell on the slight, almost wraithlike figure of Andrea Treschi.

Tonio would make his bow. And as he looked up, never once had he failed to see the awesome vitality of his father's gaze, eyes so young they appeared disconnected from the skeletal face, and brimming with irrepressible pride and affection.

Andrea bent to kiss his son. His lips were powdery soft and soundless, and they lingered on Tonio's cheek, and once in a while, even as Tonio grew taller and heavier with every year,

Andrea would sweep him up in his arms and crush him for a moment to his chest whispering his name as if the word, Tonio, were a little blessing.

His attendants stood about. They smiled, they winked. There seemed in the room a ripple of soft excitement. Then it was over. Rushing to his mother's window upstairs, Tonio watched his father's gondola move down the canal towards the piazzetta.

No one had to tell Tonio he was the last of them. Death had worked such a devastation on all branches of this great house that not even a cousin remained who bore the name. Tonio "would marry young," he must be prepared for a life of duty. And on those few nights when he was ill, he shuddered to see his father's face at the door; the Treschi lay with him on the pillow.

It thrilled him; it frightened him. And he would never remember the precise moment he perceived the full dimensions of his universe. All the world, it seemed, rode the broad green waters of the Grand Canal at his doorstep. Regattas all year long with hundreds of sleek black gondolas gliding by, lavish Saturday evening parades in summer when the great families decked their *peotti* with garlands and gilded gods and goddesses; the day-to-day procession of patricians on their way to affairs of state, their boats lined with richly colored carpets. If Tonio stood on the small wooden balcony over the front door, he might see the lagoon itself, with the distant ships at anchor. He could hear the soft thunder of their salutes, the blare of trumpets outside the Palazzo Ducale.

There were the endless songs of the gondoliers, lilting tenors echoing up the olive green and rose-colored walls, the rich sweet strum of floating orchestras. At night lovers cruised under the stars. Serenades carried on the breeze. And even in the early hours, when he was bored or sad, he might gaze down on the endless throng of vegetable boats heading noisily for the markets of the Rialto.

But by the time Tonio was thirteen, he was sick of watching the world through the windows.

If only just a little of this life would spill through the front door, or better yet, if he could only get out into it!

* * *

17

But the Palazzo Treschi wasn't merely his home; it was his prison. His tutors never left him alone if they could help it. Beppo, the old castrato who'd long ago lost his voice, taught him French, poetry, counterpoint, while Angelo, the young and serious priest, dark of hair and slight of build, taught him his Latin, Italian, and English.

Twice a week the fencing master came. He must learn the proper handling of the sword, more for fun it seemed than for ever seriously using it.

And then there was the *ballerino,* a charming Frenchman who put him through the mincing steps of the minuet and the quadrille, while Beppo pounded out the appropriate festive rhythms at the keyboard. Tonio must know how to kiss a lady's hand, when and how to bow, all the fine points of a gentleman's manner.

It was fun enough. Sometimes when he was alone he tore up the air with his blade, or danced with imaginary girls beautifully constructed from those he saw from time to time in the narrow *calli*.

But save for the endless spectacles of the church, Holy Week, Easter, the routine splendor and music of mass on Sunday, Tonio's only escape on his own was into the bowels of the house, when he fled to the neglected rooms of the lowest floor where no one could find him.

There, with taper in hand, he sometimes probed the heavy volumes of the old archive, marveling at these moldering records of his family's congested story. Even the raw facts and dates, pages crackling dangerously to the touch, fired his imagination: he would go to sea when he grew up, he would wear a senator's scarlet robes; even the chair of the Doge was not beyond a Treschi.

A dull excitement coursed through his veins. He went to further prowling. He tried latches that hadn't been turned in years, lifting ancient pictures from their damp corners to peer into alien faces. Here old storage rooms still smelled of spice, once brought from trade with the Orient when in olden times boats came to the very doors of the palazzo itself, unloading a fortune in rugs, jewels, cinnamon, silks. And there was the hemp rope, still in damp coils, bits of straw and those mingled fragrances pungent, enticing.

He stopped from time to time. His eerie little flame danced uneasily in the draft. He could hear the water beneath the

18

house, the dull creak of the pilings. And far above, if he shut his eyes, he could hear his mother calling.

But he was safe from everyone here. Spiders tiptoed on the rafters, and with a sudden turn of his candle, he made a web appear, intricate, golden. A broken shutter gave to his touch, the gray light of the afternoon shone dingy through barred glass, and peering out he saw the rats swimming steadily through the debris that littered the sluggish water.

He felt sad. He felt afraid. He felt a misery suddenly, for which he didn't know the name, a dread that made the scheme of things devoid of wonder.

His father was so old. His mother was so young. And at the very core of all this, there seemed some unknown horror awaiting him. What was it he feared? He did not know. Yet it seemed he sensed secrets in the very air about him. Sometimes a name whispered and afterwards denied, some soft reference among the servants to past conflicts. He was uncertain.

And maybe in the end it was only that all of his life his mother had been so unhappy!

4

ONCE GUIDO HAD BEEN CHOSEN for the stage, it was grueling work from then on, with the dazzle of the opera house night after night where he observed, sang in the chorus if there was one, and left with a head full of applause and the scent of perfume and powder.

His own compositions were forgotten, shoved aside for endless exercises, and other men's arias of this season and the one after.

But these years were filled with such splendid intensity that not even the awakening of Guido's passion could turn him from his course.

And Guido had long resigned himself that he could feel no passion.

The celibate life actually attracted him. He believed the sermons preached to him. As a eunuch he would never be permitted to marry, as marriage was for the begetting of children. And the Pope had never granted a dispensation for a castrato. So he would live like a priest, the only life of goodness and grace allowed to him.

And seeing eunuchs as the high priests of music, he accepted this completely.

If he ever pondered for a moment the sacrifice he had made for this priesthood, it was with the mute confidence he would never comprehend the extent of it.

What's all this to me, he shrugged. He had an indestructible will, and singing was all that mattered to him.

But one night when he had come home late from the theater, he fell into an eerie dream in which he saw himself caressing a woman he'd glimpsed on the stage, a plump little singer. It was her naked shoulders he saw in the dream, the curve of her arms, and the point at which her pretty neck rose up from the sloping fullness. He awoke sweating, miserable.

In the following months he was to dream this twice more. He found himself kissing this woman, crooking her arm and kissing the tender fold there. And one night on awakening, he thought he heard sounds about him in the darkened dormitory, whispers, the padding of feet. There was a thin, recurrent laughter.

He pushed his head into the pillow. A series of pictures presented themselves to him: voluptuous eunuchs were these, or women?

In chapel after that he could not take his eyes off Gino's feet, as the boy stood beside him. It was the leather cutting into the high instep of Gino's foot that made Guido feel an odd catch in his throat. He watched the muscles move under Gino's tight stockings. The curve of the calf was beautiful to him, inviting. He wanted to touch it, and he watched in misery as the boy went up to the communion rail.

On the afternoon of one day late in summer, he could not sing at all, he was so distracted by the tight-fitting black coat of a young maestro who was standing before him.

This was a married teacher, with wife and children. He came by day to teach the poetry and enunciation all singers must learn thoroughly. And why, Guido growled to himself, am I staring at his coat like this?

But each time the young man turned around, Guido would look at that cloth pulled taut over the small of the back, the snug fit of the waist, and then the gentle flaring over the hips,

20

again wanting to touch it. He felt something akin to a sound-less and invisible wallop with every tracing of the pattern.

He shut his eyes. And when he opened them again he thought the teacher was smiling at him. The man had seated himself, and shifting in his chair, made a darting motion with his hand to arrange the burden between his legs more comfortably. His gaze was full of innocence when he looked at Guido. Or was it?

Again at supper their eyes met. And at the evening meal hours after that.

When darkness fell, slowly, languidly over the mountains, and the stained-glass windows were drained to a lusterless black, Guido found himself walking down an empty corridor past rooms long deserted.

As he reached the maestro's door, he saw the dim figure of the man out of the corner of his eye. A silvery light from an open casement fell on the man's folded hands, his knee.

"Guido!" he whispered from the dark.

This was dreamlike. Yet it was more pungent and clumsy than any dream had ever been, the sharp scrape of Guido's heels on the stone floor, the soft shutting of the door behind him.

Lights twinkled on the hill beyond the window, lost in the shifting shapes of the trees.

The young man stood up and snapped the painted shutters closed.

For a moment Guido saw nothing, and his own breath was hoarse and pounding, and then he saw again those luminous hands, gathering what was left of the light from everywhere as they opened the front of the man's breeches.

So the secret sin he had imagined was known and shared.

He reached out, as if his body wouldn't obey him. And dropping down on his knees, he felt the smooth hairless flesh of the maestro's belly before he drew the mystery of it all, that organ, longer, thicker than his own, into his mouth immediately.

He needed no instruction. He felt it swelling as he stroked it with his tongue and his teeth. His body was becoming his mouth, while his fingers pressed into the flesh of the maestro's buttocks, urging him forward, Guido's moans rhythmic, desperate, over the man's deliberate sighing.

"Ah, gentle . . ." breathed the maestro, "gentle" But with a thrust of his hips, he pressed against Guido all the

21

mingled scents of his body, the damp curling hair, the flesh itself, full of musk and salt. Guido gave a guttural cry as he felt the dry, raw pinnacle of his own passion.

But at that moment, as he clung, weakened and reverberating from the shock, to the maestro's hips, the man's seed flowed into him. It filled his mouth, and he opened to it with an overpowering thirst as the bitterness of it, the deliciousness of it, threatened to choke him.

He bowed his head; he slumped down. And he realized that if he could not swallow it, in an instant, it would revolt him.

He had not been prepared for this so abruptly and totally to finish.

And then sickness did constrict him, causing him to pull away, struggling to keep his lips sealed against it.

"Here . . ." whispered the maestro. He tried to take Guido by the shoulders. But Guido had lain down on the floor. He had crawled under the harpsichord, his forehead pressed flat against the coldness of the stones, and the coldness was good to him.

He knew the maestro had knelt beside him. He turned his face away.

"Guido . . ." the man said gently. "Guido . . ." as if scolding him. When had he heard that same beguiling tone before?

And when he heard his own moan now, it was filled with such anguish it surprised him.

"No, no, Guido . . ." The maestro crouched by him. "Listen to me, young one," he coaxed.

Guido pressed his palms to his ears.

"Listen to me," the man persisted, his hand scratching the hairs of Guido's neck. "You make them kneel to you," he whispered.

And when there was only silence, the maestro laughed. It was low, soft, not mocking. "You'll learn," he said. He gathered himself to his feet. "You'll learn, when you hear those Bravos in your ears, when they're pelting you with tributes and flowers."

MARIANNA RARELY STRUCK Tonio anymore. At thirteen, he was as tall as she was.

He hadn't inherited her dark skin, nor her slanting Byzantine eyes; he was fair, but he had the same rich black curls and spry, almost feline, figure. When both of them danced, which they did all the time, they were twins, the light and the dark, she swinging her hips and clapping her hands, Tonio tapping the tambourine as he moved in rapid circles about her.

They did the *furlana*, the frenzied dance of the streets which the maids of the house taught them. And when the ancient church behind the palazzo held its annual *sagra* or fair, they hung out the back windows together to see the servant girls whirling in their short skirts, so they might learn to dance all the better.

And in their shared life, whether it was dancing or singing, games or books, it was Tonio who had become the leader.

Very early, he'd come to realize she was much more the child than he was, and that she'd never meant to hurt him. But she was helpless in her darker moods; the world collapsed upon her, and when he had clung to her, crying and afraid, he had terrified her.

Then had come the hot slaps, the growls, even objects pitched across the room at him as she raised her hands to her ears not to hear his wailing.

He learned now to mask his fears at such times, and strive to soothe her, distract her. He would draw her out if he could, he would entertain her.

The one infallible way was through music.

She's grown up on music. An orphan shortly after birth, she'd been placed in the Ospedale della Pietà, one of the four famous convent conservatorios of Venice, whose choir and orchestra, made up entirely of girls, astonished all Europe. No less a man than Antonio Vivaldi had been the Maestro di

Cappella there when she was small, and he had taught her to sing and to play the violin when she was only six and already exquisitely talented.

Vivaldi's scores lay in stacks in her rooms. There were vocalises in his own hand which he'd written for the girls, and she always sent out for the scores of his recent operas.

And from the first moment she'd realized Tonio had inherited her voice, she had showered him with a desperate and bitter affection. She taught him his first songs, and to play and sing anything by ear so his tutors could only marvel. And now and then admitted, "Had you been born tone deaf, I would have drowned you. Or drowned myself." And when he was little he'd believed it.

So even when she was at her worst, her breath rank from wine, her eyes glazed and cruel, he would appear light, whimsical, and lure her to the harpsichord.

"Come on, Mamma," he would say gently, as if nothing were amiss. "Come on, Mamma, sing with me."

Her rooms were always so pretty in the early sun, the bed draped in white silk, a procession of mirrors reflecting a wallpaper of cherubs and garlands. She liked clocks, all kinds of painted clocks, and they tinked on tables and chests, and on the marble mantel.

And there she was in the middle of it, her hair undone, the sour-smelling glass in her hand, staring at him as if she didn't know him.

He didn't wait. He uncovered the double row of ivory keys at once and began to play. It was Vivaldi often enough, or Scarlatti, or the more subdued and melancholy patrician composer Benedetto Marcello. And in minutes, he felt the soft crush of her on the bench beside him.

As soon as he heard her voice mingling with his he felt an exhilaration. His strong bright soprano rose higher, but hers had a richer, more fascinating color. She shuffled impatiently through the old scores for the arias she loved or, having him recite any bit of poetry he'd recently learned, made up a new melody for it.

"You're a mimic!" she'd say when he followed an intricate passage perfectly. She'd swell a note slowly, skillfully, only to hear his flawless echo. And clasping him suddenly with her warm and very strong hands, she whispered:

"Do you love me!"

"Of course I love you. I told you yesterday and the day before, but you forget," he teased. It was her most poignant, soulful little cry. She bit her lip; her eyes grew uncommonly wide, then narrowed. And he always gave her what she wanted then. But inside, he was suffering.

He knew every morning of his life when he opened his eyes whether she was happy or sad. He could feel it. And he reckoned the hours of study by how soon he might slip away to be with her.

But he didn't understand her.

And he was beginning to realize that his loneliness as a child, these silent and empty rooms, this vast and shadowy palazzo, was as much due to her shyness and her reclusiveness as to the age and old-fashioned severity of his father.

After all, why had she no friends when the Pietà was full of ladies of quality as well as foundlings, and so many married well into good families?

Yet she never spoke of the place; she never went out.

And when his father's cousin Catrina Lisani came to call, Tonio knew she made her visits brief out of kindness. Marianna was like a nun behind the grille. She wore black, kept her hands in her lap, her dark hair sleek as satin. And Catrina, in gay printed silk with a great many yellow bows, made up the whole of the conversation.

Sometimes Catrina's "escort" was with her, a very proper and handsome cavalier servente, and a distant cousin, too, though Tonio could never remember the connection. But this was fun, because he wandered out into the Grand Salon with Tonio, chatting of what was in the gazettes, and what was happening at the theater. He wore shoes with red heels and a monocle on a blue ribbon.

But though a patrician, the man was an idler, spending his time in the company of women. And Tonio knew Andrea approved of no such person for his wife, and Tonio didn't approve of it either.

Yet, still, he thought if Marianna had an escort she would go out, she would meet others, and they would come home with her now and then, and the whole world would be different.

But the thought of a cavalier servente so near to her, in the gondola, at table, at mass, repelled Tonio. He felt a hot and

25

agonizing jealously. No man had ever been close to her save Tonio.

"If I could be her cavalier servente. . . ." He sighed. He looked in the mirror to see a tall young man with the face of a boy. "Why can't I protect her?" he whispered. *"Why can't I save her!"*

6

BUT WHAT DO YOU DO with a woman who, more and more often, prefers her bottle of wine to the light of day?

Illness! Melancholia! Those were the words they used for it. By the time Tonio was fourteen, Marianna never rose before late afternoon. Often she was "too tired" to sing, and he was glad to hear it, because the sight of her stumbling about the room was almost more than he could bear. She had sense enough most of the time to stay in bed, against a nest of white pillows, her face gaunt, her eyes bulbous and glittering, and listen to whatever concerts he wanted to make for her.

By twilight she was often quarrelsome and bizarre. Of course she didn't want to go out to the Pietà. Why would she want to go there? "Do you know," she said one evening, "that when I was there everybody knew me. I was the talk of Venice. The gondoliers said I was the best singer of all the four schools, the best they'd ever heard. 'Marianna, Marianna,' people knew that name in the drawing rooms of Paris and London; they knew me in Rome. One summer we went on a barge down the Brenta; we sang in all the villas; we danced afterwards if we wanted to; we had wine with all the guests. . . ."

Tonio was shocked.

Lena washed and combed her as if she were a baby, pouring out the wine to calm her, and then took him aside.

"All the girls of the conservatorios are praised like that; it was nothing, don't be so foolish," she said. "And it's the same today. You talk to Bruno; the gondoliers love the girls, whether they are fine ladies destined to marry patricians, or merely nameless little girls. It's not the same at all as being on the stage, for the love of heaven, why do you look this way?"

"I should have gone on the stage!" Marianna said suddenly. She threw back the covers, her head wagging forward, her hair spilling in rivulets over her sallow skin.

"Hush now," Lena said to her. "Tonio, go out for a while."

"No, why should he go!" Marianna said. "Why are you always sending him away! Tonio, sing. I don't care what you sing, sing things you make up. I should have run away with the opera, that's what I should have done. And you would have lived out of trunks, playing with the scenery backstage. Ah, no, but look at you, His Excellency, Marc Antonio Treschi—"

"This is utter lunacy," Lena said.

"Ah, but what you do not know, my dear," Marianna cried," is that lunatics are made by asylums!"

These were terrible times.

When Catrina Lisani came to call, Lena put her off with vague diagnoses, and on those rare but regular mornings when Andrea Treschi came to his wife's bedroom, Lena stopped him with the same excuses.

For the first time, Tonio was severely tempted to sneak out of the palazzo.

The city was in a frenzy of preparation for the grandest of all Venetian holidays—the Feast of the Ascension, or the Senza—when the Doge would go out in the magnificently gilded barque of state called the *Bucintoro* to cast his ceremonial ring into the sea, signifying his marriage with it and the dominion of Venice over it. Venice and the sea, an ancient and sacred wedding. It sent pleasant chills over Tonio, though he would see no more of it than what he could glimpse from the rooftops. And when he thought now of the two weeks of carnival after it, seeing the maskers in the *calli* and on the quais—even little children with their masks, babes in arms with masks, all rushing to the piazza—he was sickened with expectation and resentment.

More diligently than ever he gathered little gifts to throw down to the street singers at night so they would stay under his window. He found a broken gold watch, wrapped it in a fine silk handkerchief, and tossed it out to them. They didn't know who he was. Sometimes in song they asked.

27

And one night when he felt especially reckless, and the Senza was only two weeks away, he sang a reply: "I'm the one who loves you tonight more than anyone in Venice!"

His voice resounded off the stone walls; he was thrilled almost to laughing, and he went on, weaving into his song all the flowery poetry in praise of music that he knew until he realized he was being ridiculous. Yet it felt so marvelous. He didn't even note the silence below. And when the applause came, the wild clapping and shouting up from the narrow sidewalk, he blushed in shyness and silent laughter.

Then he tore all the jeweled buttons off his coat to give to them.

But sometimes it was very late when the singers came. And sometimes they didn't come at all. Maybe they were serenading ladies by commission, or singing to a pair of lovers on the canal. He didn't know. Sitting at the window, with his arms folded on the damp sill, he dreamed that he had found some cellar door no one knew and gone out with them. He dreamed he wasn't rich, wasn't a patrician. Rather he was some urchin boy free to sing and play the fiddle all night to the four corners of this dense stone fairyland that was his city rising tightly all about him.

Yet there was a mounting sense in Tonio that something must happen.

Life couldn't get any worse for him, as he saw it.

And then one afternoon, foolishly, Beppo brought Alessandro, the chief singer from San Marco, to hear Tonio sing with his mother.

It seems some time before, Beppo had hovered on the edge of Marianna's bedroom to ask when she might allow such a visit. Beppo was so proud of Tonio's voice, and he adored Marianna as something of a seraph.

"Why, bring him anytime," she'd said gaily. She was on her second bottle of Spanish sack, and wandering about in her dressing gown. "Bring him in. I should love to see him. I'll dance for him if you like. Tonio can play the tambourine; we'll have a regular carnival."

Tonio was mortified. Lena put her mistress to bed. Of course Beppo should have understood. But Beppo was old. His little blue eyes flickered like uncertain lights, and several days after, there stood Alessandro in the main parlor, looking

28

very splendid in his cream-colored velvet, and green taffeta vest, obviously delighted by this special invitation.

Marianna was sound asleep, the blinds drawn. Tonio would sooner waken the Medusa.

Running a comb through his hair and putting on his best coat, he went alone to welcome Alessandro to the house as though he were master of it.

"I'm at a loss, Signore," he said. "My mother is ill. I'm ashamed to sing for you alone." Yet even at this little unexpected company, he felt elated. The sun was streaming in on the carved mahogany and damask that made up the room. And there was a pleasantness to it all, despite the faded carpet and the soaring ceilings.

"Bring some coffee, please," he said to Beppo. And then he opened the harpsichord.

"Forgive me, Excellency," Alessandro said softly. "I never expected to trouble you." His smile was gentle and dreamy. He looked far from ethereal without his choir robes; rather he was a giant of a gentleman, on the very edge of gawkiness though a gliding rhythm rescued his every gesture. "I hoped only to sit to the side somewhere while you and your mother were singing, not to disturb you," he said. "Beppo has told me so much about your duets, and I remember your voice, Excellency. I've never forgotten it."

Tonio laughed. He knew if this man left now, he would burst into tears, he was so lonely. "Sit down, please, Signore," he said. He was relieved to see Lena appear with a steaming pot, and Beppo right behind her with a sheaf of music.

Tonio felt desperate. A lovely vision sprang full blown into his head of entertaining Alessandro so purely he would come back over and over again. He took up Vivaldi's latest operatic score, *Montezuma*. The arias were all new to him, but he couldn't risk something old and tiresome, and within seconds he was in the middle of a sprightly and dramatic piece, his voice warming quickly.

He'd never sung in this place. There was more bare marble here than tapestry or drapery. A glorious amplification occurred, and when he finished suddenly the silence chilled him. He didn't look at Alessandro. He felt a curious emotion welling up in him, an uneasy happiness.

And then turning on impulse he beckoned to Alessandro. He was almost amazed to see the eunuch rise and take his place by the harpsichord. And then as Tonio pounded quickly

29

into the first duet, he heard that magnificent voice behind him lifting and carrying his own, that strident power.

There came another duet, and another after that, and when they could find no more they made duets of the arias. They sang everything in the score that they liked, some of what they didn't like, and then went on to other music. Finally Alessandro was persuaded to share the little bench, and they had their coffee brought to them.

And the singing went on and on, until all formality had left them. They were merely two people; even their speaking voices were different. Alessandro pointed out little aspects of this or that composition. He stopped now and then, insisting that he must hear Tonio alone, and then his compliments came in a warm rush as if he must make Tonio understand the greatness of his gift and that this was no idle flattery.

When both of them finally stopped it was because someone had just placed a candelabrum in front of them. The house was dark; it was late, and they had forgotten everything.

Tonio was quiet, and the shadowy look of things oppressed him. The room seemed to yawn about him, and the lights from the canal flickering in the glass made him want to light up the entire chamber with every candle he could lay hands on. The music was still throbbing in his head, and pain was throbbing with it, and when he saw the soft smile on Alessandro's face, a musing, a look of awe, he felt an overwhelming affection for him.

He wanted to tell him about that long ago night when he'd first sung in San Marco, how he had loved it, how he had never forgotten it. But it was impossible to put into words that first childish wish to be a singer, impossible to say of course I cannot be that, impossible to tell him the humor in it, that he didn't know Alessandro was . . . what? He stopped his thoughts, suddenly humiliated.

"Listen to me, you must stay to supper," he said, rising. "Beppo, please tell Angelo I should like him to dine with us also. And tell Lena right away. We'll sup in the main dining room."

The table was quickly laid out with all the appropriate linen and silver. He asked for more candelabra, and seating himself at the head of the table as he always did when alone, Tonio was soon deep in conversation.

Alessandro laughed easily. His answers were long. He

30

complimented the wine. And soon he was describing the Doge's more recent banquet.

These were monstrous affairs, hundreds sitting down to table, and the people came in through the open doors from the piazzetta to watch everything.

"Well, one silver plate was missing"—Alessandro smiled, raising his heavy dark brown eyebrows—"and imagine, Excellency, all the heads of state waiting patiently for the silver to be counted yet again and again. I could hardly keep from laughing."

But there was no real disrespect in the way he told the story, and he was quickly launching into another. He had a languid refinement to him; his long face in the candlelight looked slightly unearthly in its smoothness.

And Tonio couldn't help realizing in the very midst of this that Angelo and Beppo were sitting quietly to his right, doing everything that he told them to do. A second bottle of wine, Tonio suggested, and immediately Angelo sent for it.

"And dessert, you must," he said. "If we have nothing in the house, send someone out for chocolate, or ices."

Beppo was gazing at him with admiration in fact, and Angelo seemed ever so slightly intimidated.

"But tell me what is it like when you are singing for a king, the king of France, the king of Poland. . . ."

"It's the same singing for anyone, Excellency," Alessandro said. "You want it to be flawless. For your own ears, you cannot bear to make a mistake. That is why I never sing when I'm alone in my rooms; I don't want to hear anything that is not . . . well, perfect."

"But the opera, didn't you ever want to sing on the stage?" Tonio pressed.

Alessandro put his fingers together to make a little steeple. He was obviously absorbed in his answer.

"It's different before the footlights," he said. "I wonder if I can explain it. Well, you've seen the singers at the—"

"No, not yet," Tonio said and he felt a sudden flush. Alessandro would realize how young Tonio was, and how curious was this whole little occasion.

But Alessandro was merely going on, explaining that on the stage one impersonated another; one had to *act*, to be there in space, to be seen. It wasn't the same at all in church; it was the voice soaring above everything.

Tonio took another sip of wine, and just as he was going to

say that he wanted so much to see an opera, he realized that Angelo and Beppo had hastily risen. Alessandro suddenly looked down the length of the table. Then he too was on his feet. Tonio followed before he actually picked out of the thin bluish gloom the figure of his father.

Andrea had just come into the room, his heavy purple robes catching the light, while behind him there stood a host of others. Signore Lemmo, his secretary, was near, and those young men who were always about to learn rhetoric and political grace from their revered elder.

Tonio's fear was so immediate all thought left him.

What had he been thinking to invite a guest to supper? But Andrea was right before him. He bent to kiss his father's hand with no notion of what was about to happen.

And then he saw his father was smiling.

Andrea took a chair beside Alessandro, as Tonio watched in absolute amazement. Some of the young men were invited to remain. Signore Lemmo told Giuseppe, the old valet, to light the sconces on the walls, and the blue satin paneling came to life suddenly and beautifully.

Andrea was talking, making some witticism. And supper was being brought in for him and the young men, and more wine was being poured into Tonio's glass, and when his father glanced to him there was nothing in his eyes but a lively warmth, a gentleness, a boundless love that showed itself deliberately and generously.

How long did it go on? Two hours, three? Tonio lay in bed later clinging to every syllable, every bit of laughter. Afterwards they had gone into the parlor again, and for the first time in his life, Tonio had sung for his father. Alessandro sang, too, and then they had shared coffee and slices of fresh melon, and a lovely elaborate ice was brought in to be divided on little silver plates, and his father had offered a pipe of tobacco to Alessandro and even suggested that his young son sample it.

Andrea looked ancient in this company, the translucent skin of his face so drawn that the skull showed its shape through it; yet the eyes, timeless, softly radiant, were as ever in sharp contradiction to the picture. Nevertheless, his mouth moved at times with an uncertain quiver, and when he rose to bid Alessandro farewell, he did so as if the exertion were painful to him.

32

It must have been midnight before the company was gone. And with the same slow and careful movement, Andrea followed Tonio to his rooms, where he had never been save when Tonio was ill. And standing almost ceremoniously in the bedchamber, inspected all with obvious approval.

He seemed too immense for this place, too grand, and hovered like a pool of shimmering purple light in the midst of it.

The candle made a melting glow of his thin white hair that seemed to float about his face as if there were no weight to it.

"You are quite the gentleman, my son," he said, but there was no reproach in it.

"Forgive me, Father," Tonio whispered. "Mamma was ill and Alessandro—"

His father stopped him with a very slight gesture.

"I'm pleased with you, my son," he said. And if there were any other thoughts in his mind, he concealed them.

But as Tonio lay on the pillow, he felt an agonizing agitation. He could find no place to rest his limbs. His legs and arms tingled.

This simple supper had been so like his dreams, his fantasies in which his brothers came to life. Even his father had come to the table. And now that it was over, he was aching inside, and nothing could soothe him.

Finally, when the clocks struck the hour of three thoughout the house, he rose, and slipping a taper and a sulphur match into his pocket, neither of which he would really need, he went to roaming.

He wandered through the upper floors, into Leonardo's old rooms where his bed stood like a skeleton, and to the apartments where Philippo had lived with his young bride, leaving behind nothing but faded patches on the walls where there had been pictures. He went ino the small study where Giambattista's books still stood on the shelves, and then, out past the servants' rooms, he went up onto the rooftop.

The city lay under a mist, rendering it visible but touched with a special beauty. The dark tile roofs glistened with the damp, and the light of the piazza glared against the sky rosy and even in the distance.

Odd thoughts came to him. Who would be his wife? The names and faces of cousins in convents meant nothing to him; but he envisioned her lively and sweet, and throwing back her veil to give out a secretive and passionate laughter. She would never be sad; melancholy wouldn't touch her. And together they would give great balls; they would dance all night; they would have strong sons, and in the summer they would go with all the great families to a villa on the Brenta. Even her old aunts and unmarried cousins could come to live in this house, her uncles, brothers; he would make room for them. And the wallpaper would go up and the new draperies. And the knives would scrape at the mold on the murals. And never would there be any place empty or cold, and his sons would have friends, dozens of friends forever coming and going with their tutors and nurses. He saw scores of such children poised for the minuet, their coats and frocks a medley of splendid pastel silks, the house tinkling with music. He would never leave them alone, his children. No matter how busy he was with affairs of state, he would never, never leave them alone like this, in this vast empty house, he would never. . . .

And these thoughts were still in his head as he wandered back down the stone steps and entered the chill air of his mother's apartments.

Now he lit his match, with a sharp strike on the sole of his shoe, and touched it to the little candle.

But she lay so sound asleep nothing could disturb her. Her breath was bitter when he drew near, yet her face was so perfectly innocent in its miraculous smoothness. He stood for the longest time watching her. He saw the point of her small chin, the pale slope of her throat.

And blowing out the candle, he climbed into bed beside her. She was warm under the covers. She drew close to him, her hand working around his arm as if to cling to it.

And as he lay there, he dreamed dreams for her.

He saw the fashionable ladies at mass; he saw the cavalieri serventi. But it was no good.

And with a vague horror he conceived of the whole of her life passing slowly before him. He saw its loneliness without hope, he saw its gradual ruin.

After a long time, she gave a little moan in her sleep. And it deepened slowly.

"Mamma," he whispered. "I'm here. I'm with you."

She struggled to sit up, and her hair fell down around her in a nasty veil of glinting light and tangles.

"Hand me the glass, my darling, my treasure," she said.

He took the cork from the bottle. And then he watched her drink and settle back. And wiping the hair from her forhead, he rested a long time on his elbow just looking at her.

The next morning, he could scarcely believe it when Angelo announced that from now on they would take an hour's stroll every day in the piazza. "Except when the carnival comes, of course!" he added crossly. And then he said with a little uncertainty and belligerence as if he didn't quite approve: "Your father says you are old enough for that now."

7

AFTER HIS BRIEF MOMENTS with the young maestro, Guido had either put on a badge for all to see or the cataracts had been removed from his eyes, for the world was alive with seduction. Each night, lying awake he could hear the sounds of lovemaking in the dark. And at the opera house women plainly smiled at him.

Finally one evening as the other castrati prepared for bed, he retreated to the far end of the attic hallway. The night concealed him, as fully dressed he sat with one leg on the deep windowsill. An hour passed, it seemed, or perhaps less, and then shadowy figures began to emerge, doors opened and shut, the moonlight showed him Gino with a finger crooked in invitation.

In the snug clean alcove of the linen closet, Gino gave him the longest, the most lush embrace. It seemed all night they lay on a bed of folded sheets as pleasure came in dizzying surges that were over and over again allowed to wane, then resurrected to be protracted forever. Gino's skin was creamy and sweet; his mouth was strong and his fingers afraid of nothing. He played gently with Guido's ears, he hurt the nipples of his chest just a little, and kissed the hair between his legs, only working with the greatest patience towards the more brutal emblems of passion.

35

In the nights after, Gino shared his new companion with Alfredo and then Alonso; and sometimes in the dark, they lay tangled two or three together. The embrace of one above and another underneath was not uncommon, and as Alfredo's sharp jabs pushed Guido to the edge of pain, Alonso's hard, ravenous mouth drew him into ecstasy.

But the day came when Guido was lured out of these exquisitely modulated encounters for the more violent and unloving thrusts of the "regular" students. He was not afraid of whole men, never guessing how much his menacing looks had always kept them at a distance.

Yet he did not like these hairy and grunting young men very much either.

There was something brutal and simple about them that was finally uninteresting.

He wanted eunuchs, toothsome and delicious experts of the body.

Or he wanted women.

And as might happen, or might not, it was with women he found the greatest approximation of satisfaction. It was approximate only because he did not love. Otherwise it was engulfing. Little girls of the streets, poor, never clever, these were his favorites, girls delighted with the golden coin, and very fond of his boyish looks and thinking his clothes and his manner splendid. He stripped them quickly in lodgings let for the purpose over local taverns, and they never cared he was a eunuch, hoping for a little tenderness perhaps; and if not, he never saw them again for there were always others.

But as his fame increased, doors opened to Guido everywhere. After suppers at which he'd sung, lovely ladies spirited him upstairs to secret chambers.

He grew accustomed to the silk sheets, the gilded cherubs cavorting above oval mirrors and frothy canopies.

And by his seventeenth year, he had a lovely contessa, twice married and very rich, for a secret and sometime mistress. Often her carriage collected him at the stage door. Or after hours of practice he would throw open the windows of his attic room, to see it lumbering below beneath the heavy tree branches.

She was old to him then, past her prime, but hot and full of tantalizing urgency. In his arms, she blushed scarlet to the nipples of her breasts, her eyes half mast, and he felt himself transported.

36

These were rich times, blissful times. Guido was almost ready for Rome and his first lead role there. At eighteen, he stood five feet ten inches tall, with the lung power to fill a vast theater with the chilling purity of his unaccompanied voice.

And that was the year he lost his voice forever.

8

THE PIAZZA, it was a small victory, but for the next few days Tonio was ecstatic. The sky seemed a limitless blue, and all up and down the canal the striped awnings were aflutter in the warm breeze, and the window boxes crowded with fresh spring flowers. Even Angelo seemed to enjoy himself, though he looked frail in his thin black cassock, and slightly uncertain. He was quick to point out that all Europe was pouring in for the coming Senza. Everywhere they turned, they heard foreign voices.

The cafés, sprawling out of their small shabby rooms into the arcades, were aswarm with rich and poor alike, the serving girls moving to and fro in their short skirts and bright red vests, their arms deliciously naked. One glimpse and Tonio felt a hardening passion. They were unspeakably lovely to him with their ribbons and curls, their stockinged ankles well exposed, and if ladies dressed like that, he thought, it would mean the end of civilization.

Each day he pushed Angelo to stay a little longer, to roam a little farther.

Nothing, it seemed, could match the piazza itself for common spectacle; there were the storytellers under the arches of the church gathering their attentive little crowds, patricians in full robes, while ladies, free of the black *vesti* they always wore to feast day church, roamed about in lavish printed-silk fashions; even the beggars had their dim fascination.

But there was also the Merceria, and pulling Angelo with him under the clock tower with the golden lion of San Marco, Tonio was soon hurrying through this marble-paved street where all the trades of Venice mingled. Here were the lacemakers, the jewelers, the druggists, the milliners with their extravagant hats full of fruits and birds, the great French doll got up with the latest Paris creation.

But even the simple things delighted him, and he pushed on into the Panetteria full of bakeries, the fish markets of the Pescheria, and reaching the Rialto bridge, wandered among the greengrocers.

Of course Angelo wouldn't hear of stopping in a café or tavern; and Tonio found himself famished for cheap meats and bad wine, simply because it all looked so exotic.

He was trying, however, to be clever.

Everything would come in time. Angelo never seemed so much the dried husk of a young man as he did now that he was shorter than his impetuous charge and easily led, when he didn't have time to think, into some new devilment. Snatching a gazette from a hawker on the street, Tonio was able to read a considerable amount of gossip in it before Angelo realized what he was doing.

But it was the bookseller's that held the strongest lure for Tonio. He could see the gentlemen gathered inside, with their coffee and wine, hear the occasional eruptions of laughter. Here the theater was discussed, people were debating the merits of the composers of the coming operas. There were foreign papers for sale, political tracts, poetry.

Angelo tugged him along. Sometimes they wandered to the very middle of the square, and Tonio, turning round and round, felt himself delightfully adrift in the shifting crowds, now and then startled by the flapping of the rising pigeons.

If he thought of Marianna at home behind the closed draperies, he would start crying.

They'd been going out for four days of this, each more entertaining and exciting than the one before, when they glimpsed Alessandro, and a small event occurred that was to pitch Tonio into consternation.

He was delighted to see Alessandro, and when he realized Alessandro was heading right for the bookseller's, he saw his opportunity. Angelo couldn't even catch up with him, and in minutes he was inside the cluttered little shop itself in the thick of tobacco smoke and the aroma of coffee, lightly touching Alessandro's sleeve to get his attention.

"Why, Excellency." Alessandro embraced him quickly.

38

"How fine to see you today," he said. "And where are you going?"

"Only following you, Signore," Tonio said, suddenly feeling very young and ridiculous. But Alessandro, with a fluid courtesy, immediately told him how much he'd enjoyed their recent supper. And it seemed the conversation went on spiritedly around them so Tonio felt comfortably anonymous. Someone was talking of the opera, and this Neapolitan singer, Caffarelli. "The greatest in the world," they said. "Do you agree with that?"

Then someone very distinctly said the name Treschi, and again, Treschi, but coupled with the first name Carlo.

"Aren't you going to introduce us?" came the man's voice again. "This is Marc Antonio Treschi, it must be."

"Just like Carlo," said someone else, and Alessandro, turning Tonio gently to the gathering of young men, gave a litany of their names as there came the nods, and then someone asked did Alessandro think Caffarelli was the greatest singer in Europe?

It seemed marvelous to Tonio, all of it. Yet Alessandro's attentions were wholly turned to him, and in a sudden burst of exuberance he invited Alessandro to a cup of wine with him.

"A great pleasure," Alessandro said at once. He'd scooped up two London papers, and paid for them quickly. "Caffarelli," he said over his shoulder. "Well, I'll know how great he is when I hear him."

"Is this the new opera? Is this Caffarelli coming here?" Tonio asked. He loved this place, and even the fact that everyone had wanted to know him.

But Alessandro was guiding him to the door; several people had risen with a nod.

And then the meeting took place, which was to change the very color of the sky, the aspect of the snow white clouds, and make the day take on a dark resonance.

One of the young patricians followed them into the arcade, a tall, blond man, his hair streaked with white and his skin darkly burnt by the sun as if he had been in some tropical land and was much the worse for it. He did not wear his ceremonial robes, but only the loose and sloppy *tabarro,* and there was about him an almost menacing air, though Tonio could not imagine why as he glanced up to him.

"Would you choose the café?" Tonio was just saying to Alessandro. This had to be done just right. Angelo was quite

39

intimidated by Alessandro. And quite intimidated by Tonio, too, of late. Life was getting better and better.

But the man suddenly touched Tonio's arm.

"You don't remember me, do you, Tonio?" he asked.

"No, Signore, I have to confess, I don't." Tonio smiled. "Please forgive me."

But an odd sensation passed over him. The man's tone was polite but his eyes, faded and blue, and slightly tearing as if from illness, had a cold look to them.

"Ah, but I'm curious to know," said the man, "have you heard much of late from your brother Carlo?"

For a protracted moment, Tonio stared at this man. It seemed the noises of the piazza had fused into a dissonant hum, and that a throbbing in his ears had suddenly distorted everything. He wanted to say hastily, "You've made some mistake—" But he heard the halting of his breath, and he felt a physical weakening so unusual it made him feel slightly dizzy.

"Brother, Signore?" he asked. Carlo. The name had set up a positive echo in his head, and if the mind had a shape at that moment, the shape was that of an immense and endless corridor. Carlo, Carlo, Carlo, like a whisper echoed in the corridor. "Just like Carlo," someone had said only moments ago, only it seemed to have happened years and years ago. "Signore, I have no brother."

It seemed an age passed in which this man drew himself up, the watery blue eyes narrowing deliberately. And there was to his whole manner a conscious and dramatic outrage. But he was not surprised, though he wanted to seem so. No, he was bitterly satisfied.

And even more astonishing than all this was Alessandro telling Tonio they must come now, with urgency. "You'll excuse us, Excellency," he said, and his pressure on Tonio's arm was just slightly unpleasant.

"You mean you know nothing of your brother?" said the man, and there was a scornful smile then, a lowering of the voice that again created an air of menace.

"You've made a mistake," Tonio said, or so it seemed he was saying. He was having all the discomfort of a debilitating headache save the pain itself, and an instinctive loyalty was collecting in him. This man meant him harm. He knew it. "I'm the son of Andrea Treschi, Signore, and I have no brother. And if you would make yourself known . . ."

"Ah, but you do know me, Tonio. Think back. As for your brother, I was with him in Istanbul only recently. He is hungry for news of you; he asks are you well, have you grown tall. Your resemblance to him is nothing short of remarkable."

"Excellency, you must excuse us," Alessandro said almost rudely. It seemed he would stand between the man and Tonio if he could.

"I'm your cousin, Tonio," said the man with that same conscious look of grim indignation. "Marcello Lisani. And it saddens me to have to tell Carlo you know nothing of him."

He turned back to the shop, glancing over his shoulder to Alessandro. And then he said under his breath: "Damned insufferable eunuchs."

Tonio winced. It was full of contempt, like saying "sluts" or "bitches."

Alessandro merely lowered his eyes. He appeared to freeze, and then his mouth moved in a slight, patient smile. He touched Tonio's shoulder, gesturing to a café under the arcade.

Within minutes they were seated on the rough benches right near the edge of the piazza, the sun cutting under the deep arch to make them warm, and Tonio was only vaguely sensible that this had been his dream, to sit and drink in a café where gentlemen and ruffians rubbed elbows.

At any other moment the exquisite little girl approaching them would have shaken him deliciously. She had that brown hair streaked with gold which he found inexpressibly beautiful, and eyes it seemed of the same dark and light mixture.

But he hardly noticed her. Angelo was saying the man was a lunatic. Angelo obviously had never heard of him.

And Alessandro was already making a polite conversation about the lovely weather. "You know the old joke," he said to Tonio confidentially and lightly, just as if this man had not insulted him, "if the weather's bad, and the *Bucintoro* sinks, the Doge might be thrown right in bed with his wife for once to consummate the marriage."

"But who was the man and what was he talking about!" Angelo said under his breath. He mumbled something about patricians who didn't wear their proper robes.

Tonio was staring straight forward. The lovely little girl drifted into his view. She was coming right towards him with the wine on the tray, and she chewed a little wad of taffy right in rhythm with the swing of her hips, and smiled at the

41

same time with a natural good humor. As she set down the cups, she bent over so far that under the soft ruffle of her low-cut blouse he saw both her pink nipples! A little riot of passion broked out in him. At any other moment, at any other time . . . but it was as if this were not even happening; her hips, the exquisite nakedness of her arms, and those pretty, pretty eyes. She was no older than he was, he reasoned, and there was about her something that suggested she might suddenly, for all her seductiveness, start giggling.

"And why would he concoct such foolishness!" Angelo was going on.

"Oh, we should leave it, don't you think?" said Alessandro softly. And he opened the English papers and asked Angelo whether the opera had ever held any attraction for him.

"Wickedness," Angelo murmured. "Tonio," he said, forgetting the proper address as he often did when they were alone, "you didn't know that man, did you?"

Tonio stared at the wine. He wanted to drink it, but it seemed quite impossible to move.

And for the first time, he looked up to Alessandro. His voice was small and cold when it came out:

"Do I have a brother in Istanbul?"

9

IT WAS PAST MIDNIGHT. Tonio was standing in the vast damp hollow of the Grand Salon, and having closed the door by which he had entered, he could see nothing. Far off, a score of church bells tolled the hour. And he held in his hand a large sulphur match and a candle.

Yet he was waiting. For what? For the bells to stop? He wasn't certain.

The evening up until this moment had been an agony for him.

He couldn't even remember much of what had happened. Two things imprinted themselves on his mind, having nothing to do with each other:

The first, that the little girl in the café, brushing up against him as he rose to go, whispered on tiptoe: "Remember me, Excellency, my name is Bettina." Piercing laughter; pretty laughter. Girlish, embarrassed, and utterly honest. He wanted to pinch her and kiss her.

The second was that Alessandro hadn't answered his question. Alessandro had not said it wasn't true! Alessandro had merely looked away from him.

And as for the man whom Angelo discounted a dozen times as a dangerous young lunatic, he *was* Tonio's cousin. Tonio did remember. And for such a person to make a mistake like this was virtually impossible!

But what was it that disturbed him above all else? Was it the fact that in him there was some elusive and dim sense of recognition? Carlo. He'd heard that name before. Carlo! Someone saying those very words, "just like Carlo." But whose voice, and where did it come from, and how could he have grown to the age of fourteen years without ever knowing he had a brother! Why had no one told him this? Why didn't even his tutors know it?

But Alessandro knew.

Alessandro knew and others knew. People in the bookseller's knew!

And maybe even Lena knew. That was what lay behind her sudden crossness when he had asked her.

He'd meant to be sly. He had come in merely to see to his mother, he said, and his mother looked like death itself to him. The tender flesh under her eyes was blue, and her face had a hideous pallor. And then Lena said for him to go, that she would try to get the mistress up for a while later. What had he said? How had he put it? He'd felt such a rush of humiliation, such a scalding misery. "One of us . . . ever heard . . . the name Carlo."

"There were a hundred Treschi before my time, now go on." That would have been simple enough if she hadn't come after him, "And don't you go bothering your mother about those others," she'd said, meaning the dead ones, of course. His mother never looked at their pictures. "And don't you go asking foolish questions of anyone else either!"

That was her worst mistake. She knew. Of course she did.

Now everyone was in bed. The house belonged to him and him alone, as it always did at this hour. And he felt invisible

43

and light in this darkness. He didn't want to light the candle. He could hardly endure the echo of his slightest footfall.

And for a long moment he stood quite still trying to imagine what it would be like to call down upon himself his father's anger. Never had his father been angry with him. Never.

But he couldn't endure this a moment longer. Grimacing at the sound of the match, he stood breathless watching the candle flame grow, and a weak light suffuse all of this immense chamber. It was so far-flung it left a dim waste of shadows at the edges. But he could see the pictures.

And he went, at once, to examine them.

His brother, Leonardo, yes, and Giambattista in military dress, yes, and this one of Philippo with his young wife, Theresa. He knew all of these, and now he came to that face, the one for whom he'd been searching, and when he saw it again, the resemblance was terrifying.

"Just like Carlo . . ." The words were a veritable din in his ears, and he pushed the flame right up to the canvas, moving it back and forth until it lost its maddening reflection. There was his own thick black hair on this young man, his high broad forehead without the slightest slope, the same somewhat long mouth, the same high cheekbones. But what particularized it, what removed it from the general flow of resemblance among them all was the set of the eyes, for they were wide, wide apart as were Tonio's. Large and black, these eyes gave one looking into them the feeling of drifting. Of course Tonio had never known it, though others had known it looking at him. But he felt it now as he stared intently at this tiny replica of himself lost among a dozen similar blackclad men, staring gently back at him.

"But who are you?" he whispered. He went from face to face; there were cousins here, ones he didn't know. "This proves nothing." Yet he could not help but see that this strange duplicate of himself stood right beside Andrea. Between Leonardo and Andrea, in fact, and Andrea's hand rested upon the shoulder of this double!

"No, it's not possible," he whispered. Yet it was precisely the evidence he'd sought, and he went on and on to the other pictures. Here was Chiara, Andrea's first wife, and there he was again, that little "Tonio," sitting at her feet with the other brothers.

But there were more certain proofs.

He realized it as he stood fixed there. There were pictures

44

where the brothers with their father and mother stood alone; no cousins, no strangers.

And going quickly, and as silently as he could, he opened the doors of the supper room.

There was the large picture, the family gathering, directly behind the head of the table, that had always so tormented him. And even from where he stood he could see there was no Carlo in it, and a sinking feeling came over him. He didn't know whether it was relief or disappointment, for perhaps he had not grounds enough yet for either.

Yet something struck him about the picture. Leonardo and Giambattista were on one side of the standing figure of Andrea, and the seated figure of his dead wife, Chiara. Philippo was all by himself on the other.

"But that's natural enough," he whispered. "After all, there are only three brothers, what are they going to do but put two on one side. . . ." But it was the spacing that was peculiar. Philippo did not stand directly beside his father. And the backdrop of darkness made a gulf there into which Andrea's red robe rather crudely spread out making his left side considerably broader than the other.

"But that's not possible. It's not likely," Tonio whispered. Yet as he moved closer and closer, the impression of imbalance became stronger.

Andrea's robes on the left were not even the same color! And that blackness between his arm and the arm of his son, Philippo, it did not appear solid.

Tentatively, almost unwillingly, Tonio lifted the light and rose on his toes so that he might stare right at the surface.

And coming through that blackness, peering through it, as if through a veil, was the unmistakable figure of that one, that one who looked exactly like him.

He almost cried aloud. The tremors in his legs caused him to rest back on his heels and even to stready himself against the wall with his left fingers. And then again he narrowed his eyes, and there it was, a figure bleeding through as so often happens in an oil painting when it has been covered over. For years, nothing shows. Then the figure begins to rise to the surface with an aspect that is almost ghostly.

And it was happening here. And there was the young man with that same agreeable face; and in this nether world in which he lived, the ghostly arm of his father was crooked to embrace him.

10

WHEN HE CAME HOME the next afternoon, his mother was asking for him.

"She awoke while you were out," Lena whispered to him by the door. "She was furious. She broke her perfume bottles, she threw things. At me, she threw things. She wanted you here with her, and you were out stolling in the piazza."

He listened to all this, almost incapable of following it or caring about it.

He had only just seen Alessandro in the piazza, and Alessandro had excused himself quickly, affectionately, rushing off before he could be asked again.

And Tonio did not know whether or not, even given the opportunity, he would have risked another question.

One thought only was obsessing him: This brother lives. He is in Istanbul, now, alive. And whatever he did to be sent out of this house was so terrible that his image as well as his name has been obliterated. And I am not the last of this line. He is there; he shares this with me. But why didn't *he* marry? What did he do that was so terrible the Treschi must wait upon an infant in a cradle?

"Go in, and talk to her. She is better today," Lena said. "Speak to her, try to get her to stay up, to bathe and to dress."

"Yes, yes," he murmured. "All right, in a little while."

"No. Tonio, go in to her now."

"Leave me alone, Lena," he said under his breath. But then he found himself staring at the open door, the room draped in shadow.

"Ah, good . . . but wait," Lena whispered suddenly.

"What is it now?" Tonio asked.

"Don't ask her about that other . . . that other you mentioned yesterday, do you hear me?"

It was as if she'd read his mind, and for one long instant he stared fixedly at her. He studied her simple face, so heavily

46

lined and drained of color by old age, her eyes small and expressionless without the openness of Beppo's eyes. On the contrary, they were closed and hard like rounded pebbles.

And eerie feeling was stealing over him. It had been with him for two days, actually, only now it was gaining a powerful momentum. It had to do with fear, it had to do with mysteries, it had to do with some dark suspicion in childhood of things unspoken in this house, some slowly mounting apprehension of his mother's youth and his father's age and his mother's misery. He did not know what it all meant. He feared, positively feared, it was all connected. Yet maybe the horror of it was that it was *not* connected. That it was just life, this house, they way life was, and everyone felt alone and frightened from time to time of nameless things, and saw others beyond the windows caught up in an illusion of preoccupation and frenzy.

But life for each of us was this dark place.

He did not say all this to himself clearly. He felt it; and he felt in himself impatience and rage against his mother. She cannot help herself. She is breaking things, is she? She thrashes about in this glorified closet.

Well, he must help himself. He must find the answer. Some simple answer as to why all his life he had thought he was the only one, why he lived among ghosts while this defector lived and breathed in Istanbul.

"What is the matter with you?" Lena whispered. "Why do you look at me like that?"

"Go away now, I want to be with my mother."

"Well, set her straight, get her up," she pressed. "Tonio, if you do not do it, I don't know how long I can keep your father out of here. He was at the door again this morning. He is weary of my excuses. But oh, to let him see her like this!"

"And why not!" Tonio said with a sudden anger.

"You don't know what you say, you pitiful child," she said. And as he stepped into the bedroom, she shut the doors behind him.

Marianna was at the keyboard. She leaned on her elbow, the glass of wine and the bottle right beside her, and with one hand she played little tinkling notes rapidly.

The afternoon was closed out by the draperies and she had for light three candles.

They made a triple shadow of her on the floor and on the

keys, three translucent layers of darkness moving in concert as she moved.

"Do you love me?" she said.

"Yes," he said.

"Then why did you go out? Why did you leave me?"

"I'll take you with me. From now on, every afternoon we'll go walking."

"Where, walking?" she murmured. She played the notes again. "You should have told me you were going out."

"You would never have heard me. . . ."

"Don't say anything ugly to me!" she screamed.

He settled down on the padded bench beside her. Her body felt cold to him, and there was about her a stale odor so unnecessary and in such contradiction to her waxen beauty. Her hair had been brushed. It made him think of a great black cat clinging to her.

"You know that aria," she murmured, "the one from *Griselda*, will you sing that for me now?"

"You can sing it with me. . . ."

"No, not now," she said. He knew she was right. The wine made her voice completely unmanageable.

He knew the song by heart and he started, but singing only in half voice, as if for her ears alone, and he felt her weight collapsing against him. She gave a little moan, the way she did in her sleep.

"Mamma," he said suddenly. He stopped playing. And turning, he gathered her up and looked at her dim profile. For an instant he was distracted by the tangle of triple-layered shadows they made on the floor beyond her. "Mamma, I must ask you to listen to a little story, and tell me what you know about it."

"If there are fairies in it, and ghosts, and witches," she said, "I might like it."

"Maybe there are, Mamma," he said.

And while she was still looking away, he described to her exactly Marcello Lisani and all he had said, and his search for the picture.

He described to her the portrait in the dining room, and the ghastly pentimento.

And very slowly, while he was talking, she turned to face him. He did not notice anything strange about her at once, only that she was really listening to him.

But gradually her face began to alter. It seemed her expres-

48

sion changed indefinably, and that the heavy mantle of lassitude and ebbing drunkenness lifted from her.

There was almost a distorted quality to it, her sharpening as she listened, her pointed fascination.

And gradually he grew frightened.

He stopped talking. And staring at her as if he couldn't believe his eyes, he felt she was changing into another person.

It was subtle, it had been slow, but it was complete, and for a long moment it silenced him.

He saw her all of a piece: her lace dressing gown, her bare feet, and her angular face with its slanted Byzantine eyes and her mouth, small, colorless, and quivering as was all the rest of her.

"Mamma?" he whispered.

Her hand burned his wrist as she touched him.

"There are pictures of him in this house?" she asked. There was a blankness to her face. It made her look young and utterly absorbed and curiously innocent. "Where are they?"

And she rose immediately as he did. She pulled on her yellow silk wrapper and waited right beside him as he took a candle from the sconce and then she followed him.

There was a mindless quality to her. And he was halfway to the supper room when he realized she was still barefoot and did not seem to know it.

"Where?" she asked. He opened the doors and pointed to the great family portrait.

She stared at it and then looked at him in confusion.

"I'll show you," he said quickly, reassuring her. "It's the clearest image of him when you look very close. Come." And he guided her to it.

There was no need for the candle. The late afternoon sunlight was flowing through the mullioned windows and the backs of the chairs were warm as he touched them.

He brought her up close and said, "Look, *through* the blackness."

And then he lifted her, surprised at how light she was, and how her body shook with an invisible tremor. Suspended in the air, she laid her hand flat on the picture, the fingers closing in on the shape that was hidden, and then at once she saw it. He could feel her shock, a slow absorbing of every detail as though the figure, rising as it had for so many years, were actually striving forward.

49

It seemed a moan came out of her, starting low, and then rising to be suddenly strangled. She had her mouth tight shut, and all at once she moved so violently, he let her drop quickly to the floor and she staggered backwards.

She moaned again, her eyes growing wider.

"Mamma?" He was suddenly afraid of her. And gradually, he realized her face had become that perfect mask of rage he'd seen so often in childhood.

He raised his hands almost before he meant to do it, and yet her first blow caught him square on the side of his face and the shock of pain instantly infuriated him.

"Stop it!" he cried out. She hit him again, and then came her left hand, as from behind her clenched teeth she let out one shrieking moan after another.

"Stop it, Mamma, stop it!" he cried, his hands crossed before his face, his fury growing stronger and stronger. "I won't stand for it now, stop it."

But again and again, the blows assaulted him and she was screaming now, and he never in his life so hated her.

He caught her wrist and, forcing her back, felt her left hand grabbing at his hair and pulling it cruelly. "Don't do this to me!" he shouted "Don't do it!"

And he embraced her, sought to crush her against his chest and hold her helpless. She was sobbing; her nails had drawn blood. And he realized with a scalding shame that the doors to the Grand Salon were being opened.

Before she knew it, he saw his father was there and, with him, his secretary, Signore Lemmo. Signore Lemmo backed away, vanished.

And as she slapped at Tonio again, screamed at him, Andrea came towards her.

It was his robe she must have seen first, the great sweep of color, and she weakened all at once, falling backwards. Andrea took her in his arms; he opened himself to her and slowly enfolded her.

Tonio, his face burning, stood helpless watching it. Never before in his life had he seen his father touch his mother. And she coiled against her husband as if she would not blemish his robes, as if she wanted to hide herself in her own arms as she was crying hysterically.

"My children," Andrea whispered. His soft hazel eyes moved over her loose clothes, her bare feet, and then he looked at his son slowly, sadly.

"I want to die." She shuddered. "I want to die. . . ."
Her voice was coming deep out of her throat. His hand
touched her hair delicately. Then the white fingers spread
themselves out, closing on her small head and pressing it to
him.

Tonio wiped at his tears with the back of his hand. He
lifted his head and said softly:

"This is my doing, Father."

"Your Excellency, let me die," she whispered.

"Go out, my son," Andrea said gently. Yet he motioned
for Tonio to come to him, and he clasped his hand firmly.
The touch was cold and dry, but ineffably affectionate. "Go
now, and leave me with your mother."

Tonio stood still. He was staring at her, her narrow back
heaving with her sobs, her hair that sleek mass falling over his
father's arm. He pleaded silently with his father.

"Go on, my son," said Andrea with infinite patience. As
if to reassure Tonio, he took his hand again and crushed it
softly with his powdery dry fingers before letting it go and
motioning to the open doorway.

11

IT WAS THAT STAGE of life at which, had Guido been a
normal boy, his voice would have "changed" dropping
down from the boy's soprano to a tenor or basso. And this is
always a dangerous time for eunuchs. No one knows why, but it
seems the body is trying to work the magic for which it no
longer has the power. And the voice is threatened by that vain
effort, so that many singing teachers do not allow their castrati
to sing during these months. The voice, it is hoped, will all
the sooner recover.

And in general it does.

But sometimes it is lost.

And in the case of Guido, this tragedy happened.

Half a year passed before anyone could be certain. And these
were months of inexpressible agony for Guido. Again and

again, he could offer only hoarse and lame sounds. His maestros were grief-stricken. Gino and Alfredo could not look him in the eye. Even those who had envied him were dumb with horror.

But of course no one felt this loss as Guido did, not even Maestro Cavalla, who had trained him.

And one afternnon, gathering all the money he had from fetes and suppers where he'd sung, gold he hadn't had time to waste, Guido dissappeared with the clothes on his back without a word to anyone.

No one guided him. He had no map. He asked a question now and then, as for ten days he walked the steep and dusty roads that led him deeper and deeper into Calabria.

Finally he came to the village of Caracena. And from there he went out at dawn, his coat matted with straw from the inn where he'd slept, and climbing the slope, found the house in which he'd been born on his father's land, exactly as he'd left it twelve years ago.

A woman stood by the fire, squat, heavy, the lines of her mouth sunken in her rounded face for want of teeth, her eyes milky. Her skin gleamed with the cooking fat. And for a moment, he was uncertain. Then he knew her perfectly. "Guido!" she whispered.

Yet she was afraid to touch him. And bowing low, she wiped the place for him to sit.

His brothers came in. Hours passed. Dirty children huddled together in the corner. And finally his father appeared, standing over him, the same hulk, to offer a crude cup of wine with both hands. And his mother placed a great supper before him.

All stared at his fancy coat, his leather boots, the sword he wore at his side, with its silver scabbard.

And he sat staring at the fire as if he were not surrounded by them.

But now and then his eyes would move as if turned by a handle.

And he would look at this dark assemblage of burly men, their hands black with hair and dirt, their clothes of sheepskin and rawhide.

What am I doing here? Why did I come?

He rose to leave them.

"Guido!" his mother said again. Wiping her hands quickly, she came forward as it to touch his face. It was only the second time that anyone here had addressed him.

And something struck him in her voice. It was the same tone of the young maestro in the darkened practice room, echoing back to the man who had held his head at the castration.

He stared at her. And his hands commenced to move, searching all of his pockets. Out came the gifts he'd received for so many little concerts. A brooch, a gold watch, snuffboxes inlaid with pearl, and at last gold coins which he gave up to all of them. Their hands felt so dry, exactly like dried dirt on a rock. His mother was crying.

He was back in the inn at Caracena by nightfall.

As soon as he reached the bustling center of Naples, Guido sold his pistol for enough to rent a room over a tavern. And ordering a bottle of wine, he cut his veins with a knife, and sat drinking the wine as the blood flowed, until he lost consciousness.

But he was found before he died. He was taken back to the conservatorio. And there, his wrists bound up, he awoke in his own bed with Maestro Cavalla, his teacher, weeping over him.

12

WHAT WAS HAPPENING? Was everything actually changing? Tonio had lived so long with the hideous notion that nothing ever would, he could not now get his bearings.

His father had been in his mother's room off and on for two days. A physician had come. And Angelo shut the doors of the library each morning and said, "Study." They weren't going out in the piazza anymore, and in the night he was certain he had heard his mother crying.

Alessandro was in the house; Tonio had caught a glimpse of him. And he was certain that he'd heard the voice of his cousin Catrina Lisani. Comings, goings, yet his father did not send for him. His father required no explanations. And when he went to his mother's door, he was shut out as once his father had been shut out. Then Angelo would take him back to the library.

Then came the word that Andrea had stumbled on the dock while getting into the gondola. Never a day in his life had he missed the convening of the Senate or the Grand Council, but this morning he had fallen. And though it was only a sprain, he would not be going out behind the Doge on the Senza.

But why do they talk of this, Tonio thought, when he is as indestructible and powerful as Venice herself? Tonio could think of nothing but Marianna.

But the worst was this: throughout these hours of waiting, he felt an undeniable exhilaration. That feeling came back to him from earlier in the year: something was going to happen! And when he thought of her screaming and hitting him in the supper room, he felt like a traitor!.

He had wanted her to be caught; he had wanted his father to see to the core of her illness. Take away the wine, make her give it up, bring her out of this darkness in which she languished like a sleeping princess in a French fairy tale.

But he hadn't led her to the supper room for this to happen! He had not meant to betray her. And why was no one angry with him? What had he been thinking to take her there? When he thought of her alone now, with physicians, and with cousins who weren't of her blood, he couldn't endure it. His face felt hot. The tears were right behind his eyes. And this was worse than anything.

Yet somewhere embedded in all this, and quite beyond his reach, was the mystery of why she had changed so, why she had screamed, why she had struck him. Who was this mysterious brother in Istanbul?

It was the second night after the incident that he was to learn the answer to everything.

As he took his supper alone in his room, he had no inkling of it. The sky was a lovely deep blue, full of moonlight and spring breeze, and all up and down the canal, it seemed, the boatmen were singing. A verse flung out here to be answered there; deep bassos, high tenors, and someplace far away the violins and flutes of his street singers.

But as he lay on his bed, fully dressed and too tired to ring for his valet, he thought certain he heard within the labyrinth of the house itself his mother singing. And when he dismissed that as foolish, there came the high and remarkably powerfull soprano of Alessandro.

When he closed his eyes and held his breath, he could hear the thin rapid notes of the harpsichord.

It had just become real to him when there came a knock on his door, and his father's elderly valet, Giuseppe, told him to come: his father wished to see him.

He saw his father first among the assemblage. He was in his bed, and even against his pillows, he appeared regal. He wore such a heavy dressing gown, it had the shape of patrician robes and it was made of deep green velvet.

But there was a frailty to him, a remoteness.

The little group in the room was at a distance from him, and when Tonio entered, his mother stood up from the keyboard. She wore a dress of pink silk, and her waist was frighteningly small, and her face had a pallor. But she was restored to herself, and her eyes were clear and brimming with some wondrous secret. Her lips were warm on his cheek; and it seemed she wanted to speak, but knew she must wait.

As he bent to kiss his father's hand, she was very near him.

"Sit there, my son," said Andrea. And then at once he commenced to speak, his voice having something of that timelessness that characterized his lively expression. It made his obvious age seem just a slight injustice.

"Those who love the truth more than they love me have often said I don't belong to this century."

"Signore, if that is so, then this century is lost," said Signore Lemmo immediately.

"Flattery and nonsense," said Andrea. "I fear it is true and the century is lost but there is no connection. As I was saying before my secretary rushed to give me unnecessary comfort, I am not of this time and have not bent easily with it.

"But I won't bore you with a litany of my failings, as I trust they would prove more tiresome than instructive. I've come to a decision that your mother must see more of this world, and you must see more of it with her. And Alessandro, having long wished a leave from the Ducal Chapel, has consented to become a member of this household. From now on, he will give you your music lessons, my son, as you have a great talent; and perfection in that art can teach you much about the rest of life if you let it. But he shall also escort your mother whenever she goes out, and it is my wish that you take time from your studies to accompany both of them. Your mother is pale from seclusion; but you suffer none of her inveterate shyness. You must see she enjoys the carnival this year, you must see she enjoys the opera. You must see she accepts those invitations she will shortly be receiving. You must see that she allows Alessandro to take you both everywhere.''

Tonio glanced at his mother. He couldn't help it, and in an instant he saw her irrepressible happiness. Alessandro was gazing at Andrea with admiration.

''It will be a new existence for you,'' Andrea said. ''But I trust you'll meet its demands somewhat gladly. And you commence by going out day after tomorrow during the Senza. I cannot go. You go to represent this family.''

Tonio tried to hide his excitement. He tried not to look too overjoyed, yet his face was working into a smile, even as he bit his lip and bowed his head and murmured a respectful assent to his father.

When he looked up, his father was smiling. And for one protracted moment it seemed his father was enjoying some special vantage point on this room and its occupants. Or perhaps he was lost in a memory. But then the pleasure melted from his face, and with a touch of resignation he dismissed the gathering.

''I must be alone with my son,'' he said, taking Alessandro's hand. ''And it will be quite late before I release him. So you must let him sleep in the morning. Oh, and yes, lest I forget. Find some important questions to ask of his old tutors; make them feel they are needed here, assure them in small ways they won't be dismissed without ever raising the question.''

There was a quiet graciousness to Alessandro's smile, to the way he nodded to this without the slightest surprise.

''Take the candles into my study,'' Andrea said to his secretary.

He rose from bed with difficulty. The doors were shut; the rooms were almost empty.

''Please, Excellency, stay here,'' Signore Lemmo said.

''Go away,'' said Andrea, smiling. ''And when I'm dead please don't tell anyone how cross I've been with you.''

''Excellency!''

56

"Good night," Andrea said. And Signore Lemmo left them.

Andrea moved towards the open doors, but he motioned for Tonio to wait behind him. Tonio watched him pass into a large rectangular room which Tonio had never seen before. He had never seen this one either, for that matter, but the other held a greater fascination. He saw books to the ceiling between the multipaned windows that looked on the canal. He saw maps on the walls that showed all the great territories of the Venetian Empire. And even from where he stood he perceived this was the Venice of long ago. Hadn't many of these possessions been lost? But on this wall, the Veneto was still a vast dominion.

He realized his father was standing on the other side of the threshold, looking back at him with an expression of almost private reflection.

Tonio started forward.

"No, wait," said Andrea. It was such a spiritless murmur he might as well have been talking to himself. "Don't be so quick to enter here. At this moment, you're a boy still. But when you leave this room, you must be prepared to become master of this house as soon as I leave it. Now reflect on your illusion of life for just a little longer. Savor your innocence. It's never appreciated until it's about to be lost. Come to me when you are ready."

Tonio said nothing. He lowered his eyes and was conscious of a deliberate obedience to this command, in which he allowed his life to pass before him. He found himself in his imagination standing in the old archive of the lower floor; he heard the rats; he heard the movement in the water. The house itself, anchored for two centuries in the marshland beneath it, seemed to be moving. And when he looked up again, he said quickly, in a small voice, "Father, let me come in."

And his father beckoned to him.

13

TEN HOURS PASSED before Tonio again opened the doors of his father's study. A pure morning sunlight seeped in around him as he walked into the Grand Salon and towards the front doorway of the palazzo.

His father had told him to go out, to stand alone for a while in the piazza, to gaze on the daily spectacle of the great statesmen moving back and forth on the Broglio. And Tonio wanted this now more than anything. It seemed a delicious silence surrounded him which strangers could not conceivably break.

And as he stepped onto the little dock before the door, he hailed a passing gondolier and proceeded to the piazzetta.

It was the day before the Senza, and the crowds were as great as ever, the statesmen in their long line before the Palazzo Ducale, receiving respectful kisses on their deep sleeves, making their ceremonial bows to one another.

Tonio gave little thought to the fact that he was alone and free, as this no longer had the same meaning.

The tale told to him by his father was full of shocks, and shot through with the blood of reality and immense sadness. And the story of the Treschi was but a part of it.

All his young life Tonio had believed Venice to be a great power in Europe. He had been brought up with the sterling concept that the Serenissima was the oldest and strongest government in Italy. The words empire, Candia, Morea, were connected in his mind with vague and glorious battles.

But in this one long night, the Venetian State had grown old, decadent, teetering on her foundations, all but crumbling to a lustrous and glittering ruin. In 1645 Candia had been lost, and the wars in which Andrea and his sons had fought had not recovered it. In 1718, Venice had been driven once and for all from the Morea.

Nothing remained of the empire, in fact, except the great city herself and her holdings on the mainland which surrounded her. Padua, Verona, small towns, the great stretch of magnificent villas along the Brenta River.

Her ambassadors no longer wielded significant power in courts abroad, and those sent to Venice came less for politics than for pleasure.

It was the vast rectangle of the piazza, thronged with the bacchanalia of carnival for three different periods during the year, that drew them. It was the spectacle of jet black gondolas gliding through flooded streets; it was the incalculable wealth and beauty of San Marco; it was the orphan singers of the Pietà. Opera, painting, gondoliers who sang in verse, chandeliers from the glassworks of Murano.

This was Venice now; her allure, her power. In sum, it was all that Tonio had seen and loved ever since he could remember; but there was nothing more to it.

Yet this was his city, his state. His father had bequeathed it to him. His ancestors were among those dim protagonists of heroic history who had first ventured into these misty marshes. The Treschi fortune had been built on Eastern trade as had so many great Venetian fortunes.

And whether the Serenissima ruled the world or merely prevailed against it, she was Tonio's destiny.

Her independence lay in his keeping as it lay in the keeping of all those patricians who were yet at the helm of the state. And Europe, craving this magnificent jewel of a city, must not ever be allowed to clasp her to its bosom.

"You will, with your dying breath," Andrea had said, his voice then as disembodied and energetic as those glittering eyes, "keep our enemies beyond the gates of the Veneto."

That was the solemn charge of the patrician in a day and age when fortunes made in Eastern trade were now dissipated in gambling, pomp, and spectacle. That was the responsibility of a Treschi.

But finally had come the moment when Andrea must unfold his own story.

"I know you have learned of your brother Carlo," he said, divorcing himself from the greater scheme of things, the measured voice for the first time giving way to a slight quaver of emotion. "It seems that you but step out this door and the world hastens to disillusion you with that old scandal. Alessandro has told me of your brother's friend, only one of his many confederates who yet oppose me in the Grand

Council, on the floor of the Senate, wherever they wield influence. And your mother has told me of your discovery in the supper room portrait.

"No, don't interrupt me, my son. I am not angry with you. You must be told now what others will twist and use for their own purposes. Listen and understand:

"What was left to me when I at last came home from sea, after so many defeats? Three sons dead, a wife lost after lingering and painful illness. Why did God so choose that it would be the youngest who would survive the lot, a son so rebellious and violent of temper that his greatest pleasure came from defying his father?

"You've seen his image, and you have seen the likeness to yourself; but there the resemblance ends, for you have the unmistakable stamp of character. But I tell you the worst of these times was embodied in your brother Carlo. Pleasure-loving, swept off his feet by prima donnas, an idler, a reader of poetry, and a lover of gambling and drink, he was that perennial child who, denied glory in the service of the state, has no taste for quiet courage."

Andrea paused as if unsure how to proceed. Wearily, he continued: "You know as well as I do that to marry without the permission of the Grand Council is extinction for a patrician. Take a bride without family or fortune and the name Treschi is stricken from the Golden Book forever; your children are nothing but common citizens of the Serenissima.

"And yet he upon whose passion this line depended spent his life in the company of wastrels, spurning the alliances I attempted to forge for him!

"At last he chose a wife for himself as he might choose a mistress. A nameless and dowerless girl, child of a mainland noble, with nothing but her beauty to recommend her. 'I love her,' he said to me. 'I will have no other!' And when I refused his suit, seeking to direct him as was my duty, he left this house blind with drink, and going to the convent where she was lodged, took her out of it by lies and trickery!"

Andrea grew too heated to continue.

Tonio wanted to put out his hand, to still his father. It gave him physical pain to see his father suffering, and the tale itself appalled him.

Andrea sighed. "Can you at your tender age understand this outrage? Greater men have been banished for such an action, hunted throughout the Veneto, imprisoned."

60

Again Andrea stopped. He had no spirit, not even in anger, for the telling of the story. "A son of mine did this," he said. "The devil in hell he was, I tell you. It was only our name and our position that held back the hand of the state, while I begged for time to use reason.

"But on the Broglio itself at high noon, your brother appeared before me. Drunk, wild-eyed, mumbling obscenities, he vowed his undying love for this ruined girl. 'Buy her into the Golden Book!' he demanded of me. 'You have the wealth. You can accomplish it!' And there as Councillors and Senators gazed on, he declared: 'Give your consent or I shall marry her now without it.'

"Do you comprehend this, Tonio?" Andrea was now beside himself. "He was my sole heir. And for this scandalous alliance, he sought to *extort* my permission! Buy her into the Golden Book, make her a noble, and consent to this marriage I must, or see my seed scattered to the winds, see the end of a House that was as old as Venice!"

"Father." Tonio was unable to keep quiet. But Andrea was not ready to be interrupted.

"All Venice turned its eyes to me," Andrea went on, his voice tremulous. "Was I to be the dupe of my youngest son? My kinsmen, my fellow statesmen . . . all waited in shocked silence.

"And the girl . . . what of her? I in my rage took it upon myself to see this woman who had turned my son from his duty. . . ."

For the first time in the span of an hour, Andrea's gaze shifted to Tonio. For a moment it seemed he had lost the drift and was perceiving something for which he had been prepared. But then he continued:

"What did I find?" he sighed. "A Salome who worked her evil spell upon my son's degraded senses? No. No, she was an innocent child! A child no older than you are now, and boyish of limb, and sweet, and dark and wild with innocence as creatures of the wood are innocent, knowing nothing of this world except that which he had chosen to show her. Oh, I had not expected to feel for this fragile girl, to feel for her lost honor.

"And can you measure then the rage I endured against the man who'd so rashly corrupted her?"

A wordless panic seized Tonio. He could not keep still any

longer. "Please believe me, Father," he whispered, "when I tell you that in me you have an obedient son."

Andrea nodded. Again his eyes rested on Tonio. "All these years I have watched over you more closely than you know, my son, and you have been the answer to my prayers more fully than you can realize."

But it was clear nothing could soothe him now; he pressed on as if that were the wiser course and there were little alternative.

"Your brother was not arrested. He was not banished. It was I who had him apprehended and placed on the ship for Istanbul. It was I who obtained his appointment there, giving him to know that as long as I lived he would never see his native city.

"It was I who impounded his wealth, withholding all support until he had bowed his head and accepted the post offered him.

"And it was I—it was I who then took a wife in my old age who gave me that child upon whom the life of this family is now dependent."

He stopped. He was weary, but he had not finished.

"Much harsher punishment might have befallen him!" he declared, looking again directly at Tonio. "Perhaps it was the love of his mother that restrained me. He'd been her joy since the day he was born, everyone knew it." And Andrea's eyes misted suddenly as if for the first time his thoughts were not clear to him. "He'd been so loved by his brothers. His frivolity was no irritant to them. No, they loved his jests, the poems he wrote, his idle chatter. Oh, how they all doted upon him. 'Carlo, Carlo.' And by the grace of God, none of them lived to see that irrepressible charm turned to the seduction of an innocent girl, that impetuosity sharpened to defiance.

"Dear God, what was I to do? I chose the only honorable course before me."

His brows came together. His voice was thinned with weariness, and for a moment he was communing with himself. Then he regained his power.

"I dealt with him lightly!" he insisted. "Yes, lightly. Soon he accepted his duties. He has done well with the allowance granted him. And laboring obediently in the services of the Republic in the East, he has petitioned again and again to be allowed to return. He has begged my forgiveness.

"But I will never allow him to return home!

"Yet this state of affairs will not endure forever. He has his young friends in the Grand Council, the Senate, boys who shared his youth with him. And when I die, he will return to this house from which he has never been disinherited. But you, Tonio, will be master here, you in the years to come will take the wife I have already chosen for you. Your children shall inherit the fortune and the name of Treschi."

The morning sun exploded on the golden lion of San Marco. It drenched in sparkling white light the long graceful arms of the arcades which disappeared into the motley shifting crowds, the great spear of the Campanile rising abruptly to heaven.

He stood before the glittering mosaics above the doors of the church. He gazed at the four great bronze horses on their pedestals.

He let himself be jostled by the crowd; he moved in an unconscious rhythm now and then, but his eyes remained fixed on the immense scheme of porticoes and domes that rose around him.

Never had he felt such love for Venice, such purified and painful devotion. And he knew in some way he was much too young really to grasp the tragedy that had befallen her. She seemed too solid, too substantial, too full of the magnificent.

Turning to the open water, the gleaming motionless sea, he felt himself for the first time in full possession of life itself as he stood in possession of history.

But a drawn and exhausted figure had left him only an hour before with an air of resignation in the face of old age that only filled him with dread. And there came back to him now his father's concluding words: "He will come home when I die. He will make this house a battleground again.

"Not six months passes that I do not receive some letter from his hand pledging he will marry the wife I choose for him, if only I will allow him to see his beloved Venice again.

"But he shall never marry!

"Would that I could, with my own eyes, see you at the altar with your bride, see your sons, see you put on your patrician robes for the first time and take your rightful place in the Council.

"But there isn't time for this, and God has given me clear signs that I must prepare you for what awaits you.

"Now, do you know why I send you out into the world,

why I take your childhood from you with this fairy tale that you must be the escort of your mother? I send you out because you must be ready when the hour comes, you must know the world, its temptations, its vulgarity.

"But remember when your brother is under this roof again, I will not be here, but the Grand Council and the law will be on your side. My will shall fortify you. And your brother will lose the battle as he lost it before: you are my immortality."

14

A FLAWLESS BLUE SKY arched over the rooftops, with only a score of perfectly white clouds sailing inland. The servants hurried through the house announcing the sea was calm and surely the *Bucintoro* could safely carry the Doge to San Nicolo del Lido. All the windows over the canal stood open to the balmy breeze, and brilliantly colored carpets streamed from the sills under flapping banners. It was a spectacle repeated everywhere along the banks, as grand as Tonio had ever seen it.

And when he and Marianna and Alessandro, all of them gaily dressed, descended to the little dock, he caught himself whispering aloud, "I am here, this is happening!" It seemed impossible he'd passed into the panorama he'd so often witnessed from a distance.

His father waved from the balcony above the main door. The gondola was lined with blue velvet and garlanded with flowers. The great single oar had been gilded, and Bruno, in his bright blue uniform, guided the boat out into the flow as all around them came the other great families. Tossed in the wake of a hundred before them, they poured downstream to the mouth of the canal and the piazzetta.

"There it is," Alessandro whispered, and as the gondolas pitched forward and rocked back, seeking to hold their place in waiting, he pointed to the glare and flash of the *Bucintoro* itself at anchor. A giant galley resplendent in gilt and crimson, it carried the Doge's throne and a throng of golden statues. Tonio lifted his mother by her small waist so she might see, and glancing up, he smiled to see Alessandro's muted wonder.

64

He himself could hardly endure the excitement. All his life he would remember it, he thought, this moment when the trumpets and fifes let loose shrill and magnificent in the air to announce that the Doge was being carried from the Palazzo Ducale.

The sea was littered with flowers; petals everywhere rode the faceted waves so it seemed the water became solid. The golden boats of the chief magistrates were moving out, then came the ambassadors, and the papal nuncio behind them. The great warships and merchant vessels that spanned the lagoon gave off their salutes with flags unfurling.

And finally all the fleet of patricians advanced towards the lighthouse of the Lido.

Cries, waving, chattering, laughter, it was a great lovely roar in his ears.

But nothing surpassed the cry that went up when the Doge had cast his ring into the water. All the bells of the island rang, the trumpets blasted; thousands upon thousands cheered at the top of their voices.

It seemed the whole city was afloat, roaring in one great communal cry, and then it broke up, boats turning back to the island by whichever way they chose, great trains of silk and satin spread out behind them to float on the water. It was chaotic, it was mad, it was dazzling. The sun blinded Tonio; he raised his hand to shield his eyes as Alessandro steadied him. The Lisani came alongside, their gondoliers in rose-colored garments, their servants pitching white blossoms into their wake, as Catrina threw kisses with both hands, her dress of silver damask ballooning out behind her.

It was enough in itself. He was spent and almost dizzy and felt he wanted to retreat to some little shady corner of the world just to savor it.

What more could happen? And when Alessandro told them they were now going to the Doge's feast at the Palazzo Ducale he was almost laughing.

Hundreds were seated at the long white-draped tables; a fortune in wax blazed over the heavy silver carving of the candelabra while servants streamed through the doors carrying elaborate dishes on giant trays—fruits, ices, steaming platters of meat—and along the walls the common people poured in to observe the never-ending spectacle.

Tonio could scarce taste anything; Marianna was whispering every moment of what she saw, who was this, who was that, Alessandro's low voice giving her all the news of the world that was splendid and full of friendly marvels. The wine went at once to Tonio's head. He saw Catrina across a great pale and smoky gulf, beaming at him, her blond hair a mass of thick and perfectly formed little curls, her heavy bosom adorned with diamonds.

She had a painterly blush to her cheeks which made the ideal beauties of paintings seem real to him suddenly; she was overblown, glorious.

Alessandro meantime was so at ease; he cut the meat on Marianna's plate, moved the candles when they blinded her, never turning completely away from her. Perfect cavalier servente, Tonio was thinking.

But watching him, Tonio felt the old mystery of eunuchs return. He hadn't thought of it in years. What did Alessandro feel? What was it like to be him? And even as he felt himself magnetized by Alessandro's languid hands and half-mast lids, that miraculous grace with which he managed the smallest gesture, he felt an involuntary shudder. Does he never hate it? Is he never consumed with bitterness?

The violins had started again. A great roar of laughter had broken out at the head table. Signore Lemmo passed, nodding quickly.

The carnival was beginning. Everyone was rising to go into the piazza.

Magnificent paintings were mounted for all to see, the wares of the goldsmiths and the glassblowers flashed and glittered in the light that flooded from the open cafés where people crowded to take chocolate, wine, ices. The shops were aglow with frothy chandeliers and splendid fabric exhibited for sale as the people themselves made up a gleaming mass of the most dazzling satin, silk, and damask.

The giant piazza stretched into infinity. The light glared as if it were high noon, and over all, the round arched mosaics of San Marco gave off a dim sparkle as if they were alive and bearing witness.

Alessandro kept his charges close and it was he who led Marianna and Tonio into the small shop where they were at once outfitted with their bautas and dominoes.

Tonio had never actually worn the bauta, the birdlike mask of chalk-white cloth that covered not only the face, but the head as well in its black mantle. It smelled strange to him, closing over his eyes and nose; he gave a little start to see himself a stranger in the mirror. But it was the domino, the long black garment that hung to the ground, that made them all truly anonymous. You could not tell who was man or woman now; nothing of Marianna's dress showed beneath; she was a little gnome giving off a sweet, mercurial laughter.

Alessandro appeared a specter beside her.

And emerging into the blinding light again, they were but one trio now among hundreds of such nameless and faceless ones, lost in the press, holding tight to one another as music and shouts filled the air, and others appeared in wild and fantastical costumes.

The giant figures of the commedia dell'arte rose above the crowd. It was like seeing puppets overblown with monstrous life; painted faces flashed grotesquely under torches. Tonio realized suddenly Marianna was all but doubled over with laughter. Alessandro had whispered something in her ear as he supported her on his arm. She clung to Tonio with the other hand.

Someone shouted to them: "Tonio, Marianna."

"Shhh, how do you know who we are!" Marianna said. But Tonio had already recognized his cousin Catrina. She wore but a half mask and her mouth was a little crescent of red beneath, naked and delicious looking. He felt an embarrassing rush of passion. Bettina, the little serving girl, came to mind; was it possible for him to find Bettina? "My darling!" Catrina drew him close. "That is you, isn't it?" She gave him such a kiss that he felt almost dizzy.

He stepped back. The sudden hardness between his legs was maddening him; he would rather die than have her know it, but when her hand slipped about his neck, finding the one place that was not draped, he felt himself on the verge of some humiliating shock he couldn't conceal. She was pressed against him; the friction was defeating him.

"What's come over your father that he let you out, both of you?" Catrina said. And now, thank God, she turned her rich affection on Marianna.

Tonio suddenly saw the house; the dark rooms, the shadowy passages; he saw his father standing alone in the center of that dimly lit study as the morning sun made solid objects of the candle flames, his skeletal frame bearing the weight of history.

He flung open the windows. The rain was coming in fragrant gusts, nothing strong enough to clear the piazza. It had been packed still when they finally slipped away, Alessandro guiding them through the tight little *calle* to the canal and signaling for a gondola. And now, as Tonio peeled off his moist and wrinkled clothes, he put his elbows on the sill and looked up above the close wall to the smoky sky to see no stars in it, but the thin silver rain silently falling.

"Where are my singers?" he whispered. He wished he could feel sad; he wished he could feel the loss of innocence, and the burden of life, but if he felt sad that emotion was a luxurious sweetness. And without thinking, he raised his voice and let out a long call to his singers. He felt his voice pierce the darkness. He felt this throat open; he felt the notes like something palpable cutting free, and from somewhere in the dark and tangled world beneath came another voice, lighter, more tender, he thought, a woman's voice calling to him.

He sang nonsense to her. He sang of springtime and love and flowers and the rain, his phrases full of florid images. He grew louder and louder and then he stopped, holding his breath, to the last bit of echo.

There were singers all around him in the dark. Tenors picked up the melody he had commenced; a voice came from the canal; and there was the tink of tambourines, and the strum of guitars, and dropping to his knees he put his hand on the sill and laughed softly even as sleep threatened to close over him.

A vagrant image passed before his mind's eye. Carlo in his scarlet robe in the embrace of his father; and it seemed all of a sudden he was someplace else, lost in an endless commotion, his mother screaming.

"But why did she scream?" His father's voice came rapid, intimate, yet the answer eluded him. In reality he had never dared to ask that question.

"But was she the bride Carlo refused? Is that it? Was she the one Carlo would not marry? And why? Why? Did she love him? And was she then married to a man so old. . . ."

He awoke with a start. And in the warm damp felt a shudder. Ah, no, he thought, never, never again mention it to her. And sliding into dream again he saw his brother's face rising slowly to the surface of that picture.

15

ANGELO AND BEPPO were confused; Lena was fussing with his mother's dress though she said over and over, "Lena, I'm wearing a domino, no one will even see it!"

Alessandro, however, was coolly in charge. Why didn't Angelo and Beppo go out and enjoy themselves? It took approximately five seconds for them to bow, to nod, and to vanish.

The piazza was now so crowded they could scarce move. Trestle stages had risen everywhere with jugglers, mimes, wild animals snarling in their cages as tamers cracked the whip. Acrobats somersaulted over the heads of the throng, the wind bringing warm rain that dampened no one.

It seemed to Tonio that over and over again they were caught in a living stream that forced them towards the jam-packed cafés or thrust them out from under the porticoes; they gulped brandy and coffee here and there; sometimes they flopped at a table, just long enough to rest, their voices sounding strange to them piping up from their masks.

Meanwhile the extravagant maskers were cropping up everywhere. Spaniards, Gypsies, Indians from the wilds of North America, beggars in tatters of velvet, young men got up to be women with painted faces and lofty wigs, and women turned out as men, their lovely little bodies inexpressibly enticing in silk breeches and close-fitting stockings.

It seemed there was so much to do, they could make up their minds to none of it. Marianna wanted her fortune told but would not stand in line at the fortuneteller's table where the woman whispered secrets through a long tube right into the victim's ear so no one need share the revelation of his destiny. More wild beasts; the roar of the lions was thrilling. A woman snatched Tonio by the waist, turned him twice, three times in a wild dance, and then let him go; it was impossible to tell if she was a scullery maid or a visiting princess. He fell back at one point against the pillars of the

69

church, his mind swept clean of all thought as it had seldom been in his life, and let the crowd merge into a magnificent spectacle of color. The commedia was being enacted on a distant stage, the actors' cries piercing the din, and quite suddenly he wanted to dissolve and rest in the quiet of the palazzo.

Then he felt Marianna's hands slip out of his, and turning he could not find her.

He glanced back and forth. Where was Alessandro?

It seemed a tall figure straight ahead must surely be he, but the figure was moving away from him. He gave a loud shout, and couldn't even hear it himself; and glancing back saw a little figure in bauta and domino in the arms of another masker. It seemed they kissed, or whispered to one another, the stranger's mantle concealing both their faces. "Mamma." He went towards the tiny one, and the crowd intervened before he could reach her.

Then he heard Alessandro behind him. "Tonio!" He had been saying the proper address, Excellency, over and over and getting no answer.

"Ah, she's disappeared!" Tonio said desperately.

"She's right there," came Alessandro's reply, and again there was a little figure, bird-faced, eerie, peering right at him.

He tore off his mask, wiping at the sweat of his face, and closed his eyes for a moment.

They did not go home until two hours before they were to be at the theater. Marianna let down her long black hair and stood with her glassy eyes to the side as if enchanted. Then seeing the serious expression on Tonio's face, she stood on tiptoe to kiss him.

"But, Mamma . . ." He drew back suddenly. "When we were near the church door, did someone . . . did someone . . .?" He stopped, positively unable to continue.

"Did someone what? What's the matter with you?" she asked warmly. She shook out her hair. Her face was all angles, her mouth drawn back in a dazed smile. "I don't remember anything by the church door. When were we at the church door? That was hours ago. Besides"—she let out a little laugh—"I have you and Alessandro to protect my honor."

70

He was staring at her with something that was very near horror.

She seated herself before the glass as Lena undid the snaps of her gown. All of her movements were swift, yet uncertain. She lifted the glass stopper of her cologne and held it before her lips. "What shall I wear, what shall I wear, and you, look at you, you who all your life have begged to go to the opera. Don't you know who is singing tonight?" She turned with her hands on the edge of the cushioned bench looking up at him. Her dress had fallen down and her breasts were almost bare, yet she didn't seem to know it. She looked childlike.

"But Mamma, I thought I saw. . . ."

"Will you stop it!" she screamed suddenly. Lena moved back, startled, but he did not move.

"Take that look off your face," she said, the voice still high in pitch, and her hands on her own ears as if to blunt the sound of it. She started to gasp, and it seemed the taut flesh of her face was being cruelly twisted.

"No, don't . . . don't," he whispered. He stroked her hair, patted her until she gave a deep breath and seemed to become limp. Then looking up at him, she made that smile again, glittering and beautiful and frightening him. But it lasted only a moment. Her eyes were wet.

"Tonio, I've done nothing wrong," she pleaded as if she were only his younger sister. "Don't you dare spoil it all for me, you can't do it. All these years, only once in my life before have I ever been out in it. Don't you, don't you . . ."

"Mamma!" He held her face against his coat. "I'm sorry."

As soon as they stepped into the box Tonio knew he would not be able to hear anything.

It was no surprise. He'd heard enough stories of what went on, and he knew that with three different performances tonight, there would be a constant shifting among the theaters. Catrina Lisani, in a white satin mask, was already seated with her back to the stage, at a hand of cards with her nephew Vincenzo. The young Lisani were waving and hissing to those below, and the old senator, Catrina's husband, dozed in his gilded chair, waking suddenly to grumble that he wanted his supper.

"Come here, Alessandro," said Catrina, "and tell me if all this is true about Caffarelli." She dissolved into laughter before Alessandro could kiss her hand. But she motioned for Marianna to sit beside her.

"And you, my dear, do you know what it means to me to see you here at last, having some fun, behaving as if you were human?"

"I am all too human," Marianna whispered. There was something irresistibly girlish in the way she almost snuggled to Catrina. That anyone could be mean to her, that he could be mean to her, seemed impossible to Tonio. He felt like crying suddenly; he felt like singing.

"Play, play," said Vincenzo.

"I don't see why," said the old senator, who was much younger than Andrea, "I must wait for all that music to start before I have my supper."

Liveried servants moved in and out offering crystal glasses of wine. The old senator spilled a red stain on his lace ruff and stared down at it helplessly. He had been a handsome man and was impressive still, his gray hair growing in tight waves back from his temples. He had eyes of jet black and a hook of a nose of which he seemed proud when he lifted his head. But now he looked like a baby.

Tonio stepped to the front. The parterre was already jammed and so were the three tiers above him.

Masks everywhere from the gondoliers in the pit to the sober merchants high above with their wives in such proper black, the hum and tinkle of talk and drink seeming to rise in waves of no discernible rhythm.

"Tonio, you're too young for this," Catrina said over her shoulder. "But let me tell you about Caffarelli. . . ." He did not look at her because he did not wish to see that deliciously animalian slit of her mouth, naked and red, beneath the white mask that made her eyes look so feline. Her arms in her burgundy satin appeared so soft he gritted his teeth with a little vision of himself squeezing them mercilessly.

But he listened intently to all this foolishness about the great castrato who was to sing tonight, that he had been discovered by his mistress' husband while in bed with her in Rome. In bed, Catrina said. His face smarted to think of his mother and Alessandro listening to this! And forced to flee, Caffarelli spent a damp night hiding in a cistern. For days after that, the man's bravos pursued him everywhere, but the lady gave Caffarelli bravos of his own who followed him all around until he threw everything up and left the city.

Andrea's words came back to Tonio in confusion, something about the world, being tested by the world. The world . . .

72

But he could keep his mind on nothing now but Caffarelli. He was going to hear a great castrato for the first time in his life, and all else could wait, for all he cared, and it was beyond him anyway.

"They say he'll fight with everyone before he's finished, and if the prima donna's pretty he won't leave her alone for a second. Alessandro, is it all true?"

"Signora, you know a great deal more than I do," Alessandro laughed.

"Well, I'll give him five minutes," said Vincenzo, "and if he hasn't captured my heart or my ear, I'm off to the San Moise."

"Don't be ridiculous, everyone is here tonight," said Catrina. "This is the place, and besides, it's raining."

Tonio turned his chair around, straddling it, as he looked at the distant curtained stage. He could hear his mother laughing. The old senator had said they should all go home and hear her sing a little song with Tonio. Then he could have his supper. "You will sing for me soon, my dear, won't you?"

"Sometimes I think I married a stomach," said Catrina. "Bet your clothes piece by piece, then," she said to Vincenzo. "Start with that vest; no, the shirt I like the shirt."

Meantime a fight had broken out in the rear of the house below. There was shouting and stomping, and quickly everything was restored to order. Beautiful girls moved through the chairs hawking wine and other refreshments.

Alessandro rose up against the wall of the box like a shadow behind Tonio.

And just then the musicians began to appear, slipping into their padded chairs with a great fidgeting of lamps and rustling of papers. In fact, librettos were being thumbed everywhere; there had been a brisk sale of them in the lobby.

And when the young unknown composer of the opera stepped to the front, there were loyal cheers from up above and a rash of clapping.

It seemed the lights dimmed, but not enough. Tonio rested his chin on his hands against the back of the chair. The composer's wig didn't fit and neither did his heavy brocade coat and he was miserably nervous.

Alessandro made a disapproving sound.

The composer flopped awkwardly at the harpsichord. The musicians raised their bows, and suddenly the house was filled with a rush of festive music.

It was lovely, light, full of celebration with nothing of tragedy or foreboding, and Tonio felt an immediate enchantment. He bent forward as the crowd chattered and laughed behind him. Just where the balcony curved, the Lemmo family was already at dinner, steam rising from the silver plates before them. An an angry Englishman hissed in vain for silence.

But when the curtain rose there were oooh's and aaah's from everywhere. Gilded porticoes and arches rose against an infinite backdrop of blue sky in which the stars twinkled magically. Clouds passed over the stars, and the music, rising in the sudden silence, seemed to reach the rafters. The composer was pounding away, his powdered curls flopping all of a piece, as grandly dressed women and men appeared on the stage to engage in the stiff but necessary recitative that began the opera's all too familiar and utterly preposterous story. Someone was in disguise, someone else kidnapped, abused. Someone would go mad. There would be a battle with a bear and a sea monster before the heroine found her way back to her husband who thought she was dead, and someone's twin brother would be blessed by the gods for vanquishing the enemy.

Tonio would memorize the libretto later. He didn't care right now. What maddened him was his mother's laughter and the sudden cries of the Lemmo family, who had just been presented with an elaborate broiled fish.

"Excuse me." He pushed past Alessandro.

"But where are you going?" Alessandro's large hand folded easily and warmly over Tonio's wrist.

"Downstairs, I must hear Caffarelli. Stay with my mother, don't let her out of your sight."

"But, Excellency . . ."

"Tonio." Tonio smiled. "Alessandro, I beg you, I swear on my honor, I will go no farther than the parterre, you can see me from here. I must hear Caffarelli!"

Not all of the chairs were taken. Midway through the performance many more gondoliers would come, admitted free, and then it would be mayhem. But now he was easily able to get close to the stage, pushing through the rougher, cruder crowd until he sat only a few feet from the raging, storming orchestra.

Now all he could hear was the music and he was ecstatic.

74

And at that moment there appeared on the stage the tall, stately figure of the great Caffarelli.

This pupil of Porpora was definitely claimed by some to be the greatest singer in the world, and as he advanced to the footlights in his enormous white wig and flowing carmine cape, he appeared a god rather than the great king whose part he played in the performance. Delicately handsome, he allowed all eyes to drink him in. Then he threw back his head. He commenced to sing, and at the first immense swelling note the theater fell silent.

Tonio gasped. The gondoliers beside him let out soft moans and cries of pleasant astonishment.

The note swelled and soared as if even the castrato himself could not stop it. And then bringing it to a close, he rushed into the body of the aria, without seeming to pause for breath as the orchestra raced to catch up with him.

It was a voice beyond belief, not shrill but somehow violent. In fact, the castrato's almost exquisite face seemed quite disfigured with rage before he had finished.

It was a face that had been painted, powdered, rendered as civilized as anyone could imagine in its frame of white curls and yet those eyes smoldered as he strode back and forth now, bowing indifferently to those who waved and clapped and nodded from the boxes, glancing to the pit, and now and then to the higher tiers as if with some remote calculations.

But the prima donna had commenced to sing, and it seemed the opera was falling apart around her. Or was it simply that now Tonio could see all the commotion in the wings, ladies with brushes and combs, a servant who darted out now to puff more white powder on Caffarelli.

Yet the prima donna's thin little voice continued bravely over the continuo of the composer at the harpsichord. And Caffarelli stood in front of her, his back to her, as if she didn't exist, affected a yawn in fact, and the hum of conversation rose again, a dull wave taking the edges off the music.

Meanwhile around Tonio all the real judges of the performance gave off their coarsely stated but very shrewd estimations. Caffarelli's high notes weren't so good tonight; the prima donna was dreadful. A girl offered Tonio a cup of red wine, and feeling for his coins, he glanced at her masked face and thought surely this was Bettina! But when he thought of his father, and the trust he'd been so lately given, he dropped his eyes, flushing deeply.

75

Caffarelli again stepped to the footlights. He tossed back the red cape. He was glaring at the first tier. And then came that magnificent first note again, swelling, throbbing. Tonio could see the sweat glistening on his face, his immense chest expanding beneath the glittering metal of his Grecian armor. The harpsichord faltered. There was confusion in the strings.

Caffarelli was not singing the right music. But he was singing something that sounded immediately familiar. Suddenly Tonio realized—just as everyone did—that he was recreating the prima donna's aria which had just finished, and making merciless fun of her. The strings tried to fall in, the composer was dumbfounded. Meantime Caffarelli crooned the notes, he ran up and down her trills with such appalling ease that he made her gifts utterly meaningless.

Mocking her long swelling notes, he pushed with monstrous power into the ridiculous. The girl had burst into tears but she did not leave the stage, and the other players were crimson with confusion.

Hisses sounded from the gallery, then shouts and catcalls from everywhere. The lady's supporters began to stomp their feet, shaking their fists wildly, but the supporters of the castrato were rocking with laughter.

At last having the full attention of every man, woman, and child in the house, Caffarelli ended this burlesque with a flat and nasal parody of the prima donna's tender little close, and commenced his own *aria di bravura* with a volume that was annihilating.

Tonio slumped in his chair, a smile spreading over his face.

So this was it, and it was all that everyone had ever said it would be, a human instrument so powerful and perfectly tuned that it rendered all else feeble in comparison.

Applause rang out from every recess of the house as the singer finished. Bravos roared from top to bottom. The loyal champions of the girl attempted to combat the swell but it soon vanquished them all.

And all around Tonio, there rose those hoarse and violent cries of praise:

"Evviva il coltello!"

Evviva il coltello, he was shouting it too. "Long live the knife" that had made this man into a castrato, carving out the manhood so as to preserve forever this glorious soprano.

*　　*　　*

He was dazed afterwards; it hardly mattered that Marianna was too tired to go to the Palazzo Lisani. Let these splendors come one at a time. This night would live in him forever; his head would teem with Caffarelli in his dreams.

And it would have been perfect, all of it, were it not for the fact that just as they were pushing their way through the doors, he had heard behind him the words, ". . . just like Carlo," spoken crisply and clearly at his ear. He turned; he saw too many faces, and then he realized it was Catrina talking to the old senator, who said now, "Yes, yes, my dear nephew, just saying you look so much like your brother."

16

EVERY NIGHT for the remainder of the carnival Tonio went back to see Caffarelli to the exclusion of every other temptation.

One opera played each house in Venice over and over for the entire season, but nothing could lure him off to witness even a part of the performances elsewhere. And the bulk of society returned here again and again, to witness the same witchcraft that held Tonio captive.

No aria was ever performed by Caffarelli in exactly the same way twice, and his boredom between these sterling moments seemed something more desperate than a mere pose to irritate others.

There was a dark quality to his eternal restlessness. A despair underlay his continuous invention.

And over and over by sheer personal power, he created this miracle:

He stepped to the footlights, he threw out his arms, he took over the house, and murdering the score of the composer, confounding the players who hastened after him, he created, alone and without the help of anyone, a music that was in fact the heart and soul of the opera.

And damn him as they might, all knew that without him it might have come to nothing.

The composer was often frantic when the final curtain

came down. And Tonio often hung in the shadows to hear him cursing, "You don't sing what I've written, you pay no attention to what I've written."

"Then write what I sing!" snarled the Neapolitan. And once Caffarelli drew his sword and actually chased the composer towards the doors.

"Stop him, stop him or I'll kill him!" shouted the composer, running backwards up the aisle. But everyone could see he was terrified.

Caffarelli howled with contemptuous laughter.

He was a vision of outrage as he pushed the tip of his rapier into the composer's buttons, nothing but his beardless face marking him the eunuch.

But all knew, even the young man, that Caffarelli made the opera what it was.

Caffarelli pursued women all over Venice. He drifted in and out of the Palazzo Lisani at all hours to chat with the patricians who hastened to pour him wine or fetch him a chair, and Tonio, ever near, worshiped him. He smiled to see the flush in his mother's cheeks as she too followed Caffarelli with her eyes.

But then she was having such a marvelous time, he loved to watch her, too. No longer keeping to the corners, her eyes sharp with suspicion, she was now even dancing with Alessandro.

And Tonio, taking his own position in the majestic chain of brilliantly dressed men and women that spanned the Grand Salon of the Casa Lisani, went through the precise steps of the minuets, thrilled by the vision of ruffled breasts, exquisite arms, cheeks that looked as soft as kittens' fur. Glasses of champagne on silver trays sailed through the air.

French wine, French perfume, French fashion.

Of course everyone adored Alessandro. He seemed simplicity itself in his fine clothes, and yet so grand and so full of grace that Tonio felt an immense love for him.

Late at night they talked together alone.

"I fear you'll find our house dreary after a while," Tonio had said once.

"Excellency!" Alessandro laughed. "I did not grow up in a magnificent palazzo." His eyes had swept the lofty ceilings of his new room, the heavy green curtains of the bed, the carved desk, and the new harpsichord. "Perhaps if I'm here a hundred years, I will begin to find it dreary."

"I want you here forever, Alessandro," Tonio had said.

And in a quiet moment he had some inarticulate and wondrous sense of how this man, beneath all the hammered gold of San Marco, had spent his life striving for perfection. No wonder he possessed such unobtrusive seriousness, such soft sureness of self; he reflected the wealth and breeding and beauty that had always surrounded him.

Why shouldn't he move through Catrina's salon with an easy elegance?

But what did they really think of him, Tonio wondered. What did they think of Caffarelli? And why was it so tantalizing for Tonio to conceive of Caffarelli in bed with any of the women who hung about him? It seemed he need only beckon in order to be followed.

But it was fast occurring to Tonio, What would *I* do with any of them, because there were quite enough who gave inviting looks to him over their lace fans. And in the pit of the theater he'd smelled the sweet aroma of a thousand Bettinas.

Time, Tonio, time, he said to himself. He would have died before he would have failed his father. All before him flashed and glimmered in the magic light of new responsibility and new knowledge. And at night, he knelt down before the Madonna in his room and prayed: "Please, please, don't let it all come to an end. Let it go on forever."

But the summer was almost here. The heat was already stifling. The carnival would soon collapse like a house of cards, and then would begin the villeggiatura, with all the great families retiring to their villas on the Brenta River. No one wanted to be near the stench of the canals, the never-ending swarm of gnats.

And we'll be here alone again, oh, noooo, please!

But when he could count the final days on one hand, Alessandro came to his room one morning with the servants who brought the chocolate and the coffee, and sat down by Tonio's bed.

"Your father is very pleased with you," he said. "All report to him you conduct yourself like the paragon of a gentleman."

Tonio smiled. He wanted to see his father. But twice Signore Lemmo had told him it was quite out of the question. It seemed an uncommon number of people came and went from his apartments. And Tonio knew some of these men were attorneys, others old friends. He did not like it.

But what made him think that long night of intimacy would produce a new existence of frequent discussion? His father belonged to the state as surely now as ever. And if his ankle had failed to heal and he could not go out as he chose, then the state must come to him. And so it seemed to be happening.

But Alessandro had something else on his mind.

"Have you ever seen the Villa Lisani near Padua?" he asked.

Tonio held his breath.

"Well, pack everything. And if you have no riding clothes, send Giuseppe for the tailor. Your father wants you there for the whole summer, and your cousin is delighted to have you. But, Tonio," he said (he'd long ago dropped the formal address at Tonio's insistence), "think of some questions to ask your tutors. They feel superfluous; they're afraid of being dismissed. And of course they won't be. They're coming with us. But you know, make them feel important."

"We're going to the Villa Lisani!" Tonio leapt up and threw his arms around Alessandro.

Alessandro had to take a step backwards, but his large languid hands moved gently over Tonio's hair, smoothing it back from his forehead.

"Don't tell anyone," he whispered, "but I'm as excited as you are."

17

AFTER THE CUTS in his wrists healed, Guido remained at the conservatorio where he had grown up, devoting himself to teaching with a rigor that few of his students could bear up under. He had genius, but not compassion.

And by the age of twenty, he had produced several remarkable pupils who went to sing in the Sistine Chapel.

They were castrati whose voices, without Guido's training and instinct, might have amounted to nothing. And grateful as they were for the instruction which had elevated them, they were nevertheless terrified of the young maestro and glad to leave him.

In fact, all of Guido's students at one time or another, if not always, hated him.

But the masters of the conservatorio loved him.

If it were humanly possible to "create" a voice where there had been none given by God, Guido could do it. And over and over again, they watched with amazement as he instilled musicianship where originality and talent were lacking.

To him they sent the dullards and those very pitiful little children who had been gelded long before their voices showed themselves to be nothing.

And Guido turned them out decent, skilled, and not unpleasing sopranos.

But Guido loathed these students. He took no enduring satisfaction whatsoever in their meager accomplishments. Music was infinitely more precious to him than himself, so pride was unknown to him.

And the pain and the monotony of his life pushed him deeper into his composition. This he'd neglected all the years he had dreamt of the singer's life, and others had passed him by, having already seen their oratorios performed, and even their operas.

His masters didn't look to him for anything here, but burdening him with students from dawn till dark, reproved him for working alone so long into the night hours.

But doubt was no component of his pain. He was far behind in his skills. Yet he never wavered. Rather he went without sleep, working endlessly. Oratorios, cantatas, serenades, whole operas, were spinning out of him. And he knew that if he had but one great voice among his pupils, he might bargain for time, and writing for that voice, recapture the ears that were now deaf to him. That voice would be his inspiration, and the impetus he so needed. Then others would come, ready and willing to sing what he had written for them.

As it was, his miserable little singers struggled without comprehension or grace to deliver his songs to him.

But on long summer afternoons when he could no longer endure the sweltering cacophony of the practice rooms, he strapped on his sword, found his only decent pair of paste buckle shoes, and wandered out without explanation into the bustling city.

Few capitals in Europe seethed and crackled with as much humanity as did the great sprawling seaport of Naples.

Suffused with the pomp and glamour of the new Bourbon court, her streets veritably streamed with all manner of men come to see the magnificent shore, the splendid churches, castles, palaces, the dizzying beauty of the nearby countryside, the islands. And looming over all, the great hulk of Vesuvius against the misty sky, and the vast sea spreading to the horizon.

Gilded carriages roared and rattled through the streets, liveried servants clinging to the painted doors, footmen racing. Courtesans strolled the promenades, splendidly decked out in jewels and laces.

And up and down the gentle slopes, calashes plunged through the surging crowds, the one-horse drivers crying, "Make way for my lord," and at every corner were the hawkers of fresh fruit and snow water.

Yet in this paradise where flowers bloomed in the cracks and vineyards spilled over the hillsides, poverty festered. The restless lazzaroni—peasants, idlers, thieves—roamed aimlessly about, mingling with the lawyers, clerks, lords and ladies, monks in their brown robes, or littered the steps of the cathedrals.

Pushed to and fro, Guido watched all with mute fascination. He felt the sea breeze. He was now and then almost struck by the wheels of a carriage.

Heavy of build, his shoulders massive under his black coat, breeches and stocking splashed and dusty, he did not appear the musician, the young composer, least of all the eunuch. Rather he was only another shabby gentleman, hands as clean as a nun's, with money enough to drink in the wine gardens he entered.

There at a greasy table, he would rest his back against the mat of vines that covered the wall, vaguely sensible to the hum of the bees or the perfume of the blossoms. He listened to the mandolin of a strolling singer. And watching the sky melt softly from the blue of the sea to a rosy haze, he felt the wine lull his pain. And yet the wine allowed the pain to flower.

Tears wet his eyes, giving them a dangerous gleam. His soul ached, and his misery seemed unendurable.

But he did not fully understand the nature of it.

He knew only that as any singing master might, he wanted those passionate and gifted students to whom he might give the full weight of his genius. And he heard these singers—yet unknown—bring life to the arias he had written.

For it was they who must take his music to the stage and to the world, it was they who would realize for Guido Maffeo the only chance for immortality given him.

Yet it was unbearable loneliness he felt, too.

It was as if his own voice had been his lover, and his lover had forsaken him.

And envisioning the young man who could sing as he himself could no longer sing, that pupil to whom he could confide all that he knew, he saw the end of his isolation. He would have someone who understood him at last, someone who knew what he was doing! And all the distinctions between the needs of his soul and the needs of his heart were melted.

Stars dotted the sky, twinkling through the traces of cloud that were like the mist from the sea. And far, far away, lost in the darkness, the mountain gave off a sudden glimmer of lightning.

But the voices of promise were denied Guido. He was too young a maestro to attract them. The great singing teachers such as Porpora, who had been the teacher of Caffarelli and Farinelli, drew the great pupils.

And though his masters were pleased with the operas he penned, he continued to be lost in a swamp of competition. His compositions were "too peculiar," it was said; then on the other hand, they were "uninspired imitation."

The drudgery of his life threatened at times to break him. And he realized more clearly all the time that one sterling pupil would change everything.

But to draw the good students, Guido must first produce one luminary from the slush that was given him.

Time passed. It proved impossible. He was not an alchemist, merely a genius.

And at twenty-six, despairing of anything coming his way, he drew from his superiors a small allowance and their leave to go about Italy in search of new voices.

"Maybe he'll find something." Maestro Cavalla shrugged. "After all, look what he's managed to do so far!" And sad to see him gone so long, they nevertheless gave him their blessing.

18

ALL HIS LIFE, Tonio had heard about it, this splendid summer interlude called the villeggiatura, with long suppers every night, rooms laid out in full silver plate and lace for each course, and leisurely excursions afterwards up and down the Brenta. There would be musicians coming and going all the time: maybe Tonio and Marianna would even play now and then, when the professionals weren't about, and all the families would make up their own little orchestras, this man proficient on the violin, that one on the double bass, this senator as talented at the harpsichord as any paid performer. The girls from conservatorios would be invited out; and there would be the open air, picnics on the grass, riding horseback, fencing for sport, great spacious gardens hung with lanterns.

Tonio packed all the old music, wondering vaguely how it would feel to sing for a room full of people. And Marianna, with a nervous laugh, reminded him of his fears on her account ("My bad behavior!"). Nevertheless it startled him to see her roaming about her room in corset and chemise with Alessandro sitting by with a cup of chocolate.

But on the morning they were to leave, Signore Lemmo came pounding at Tonio's door.

"Your father . . ." he stammered. "Is he with you?"

"With me, why no. Whatever made you think he would be?" Tonio asked.

"I can't find him," Signore Lemmo whispered. "No one can find him."

"But that's ridiculous," Tonio said.

Yet within minutes Tonio realized the household was in turmoil.

Everyone was engaged in the search. Marianna and Alessandro, who had been waiting with the trunks near the front door, rose immediately when he told them.

"Have you been in the archive downstairs?" Tonio demanded.

Signore Lemmo went there at once, only to report the lower floor was, as always, deserted.

"And the roof?" Tonio said. But this time he did not wait for anyone else; he had the strong feeling that was precisely where he might find his father. He did not know why, but all the way up the steps he was sure of it.

Yet when he came to the attic floor he stopped, because at the far end of the passage light streamed through an empty doorway. Tonio knew these rooms. He knew where all the servants slept, where Angelo and Beppo slept, and that room had always been bolted. As a little boy, he'd glimpsed furnishings through the keyhole. He'd tried the lock. But he'd never managed to get into it.

And now a dim suspicion came to him. He went quickly down the passage, vaguely conscious that Signore Lemmo followed him.

Andrea was in the room. He was standing at the front windows above the water, clad only in a flannel dressing gown. His shoulder bones poked through the flimsy cloth, and there came from him some low sound as though he were talking. Or praying.

But for a long moment Tonio waited, and his eyes passed over the walls, over the pictures and mirrors that still hung here. Long ago, it seemed, the roof had broken, and deep stains poured to the floor. There was everywhere the smell of mold and neglect; and he realized the bed was still covered by a damp and ruined coverlet. The curtains had never been removed; one panel had fallen away. And on a small table near a damask chair there stood a glass with a dark residue in it. A book lay open, face down, and others on the shelves had swollen to burst their leather bindings.

No one had to tell him this was Carlo's room. No one had to tell him it had been left hastily and never again entered.

With a shock, he saw the slippers by the bed. He saw the candles in their holders eaten down by rats; and askew against a chest as if it had been tossed there stood a portrait. It was fixed in the familiar oval and square of gold that lined the galleria below and the Grand Salon from which it had obviously been taken.

And there was his brother's face, more skillfully articulated than anywhere else, with those wide-set black eyes peering into this ruined chamber with perfect equanimity.

"Wait outside," Tonio said softly to Signore Lemmo.

The window was wide open over a vista of red-tiled roofs, slanting this way and that, cut here and there by little gardens and steeples, and the distant domes of San Marco.

There came a whistling sound from Andrea's lips. Tonio felt a sharp pain in his temples.

"Father?" he said as he drew close.

Andrea's head turned unwillingly. The hazel eyes showed no recognition. The face was more gaunt than ever and possessed the shimmer of a fever. Those eyes, ever so quick, if not severe, were vague as if covered with a blinding film.

Then slowly Andrea's face brightened. "I mean . . . I mean, I detest it. . . ." he whispered.

"What, Father?" Tonio asked. He was terrified. Something was happening, something dreadful.

"The carnival, the carnival," Andrea stammered, his lips trembling. He rested his hand on Tonio's shoulder, "I am . . . I am . . . I must . . ."

"Father, will you come down?" Tonio said tentatively.

Then before his eyes, the most hideous change in his father was taking place. He saw the eyes widen; he saw the mouth twist.

"What are you doing here!" Andrea whispered. "How did you get into this house without my permission?" He had drawn himself up with an immense and shattering anger.

"Father!" Tonio whispered. "It's me . . . it's Tonio."

"Ah!" His father's hand was raised. It hovered in the air.

And then there was a moment of infinite distress in which everything was realized.

Andrea was staring at his son in shame and embarrassment. A great anxiety caused his hands to quaver, the mouth to shudder. "Ah, Tonio," he said. "My Tonio."

For a long moment neither spoke. In the corridor, others whispered. Then they were silent.

"Father, come down to bed," Tonio said. He felt, for the first time, the bones of the man beneath the fabric that covered him.

So light he felt; so without vitality or strength. It was as if he could have been completely overpowered.

"No, not now. I am all right," Andrea answered. And he was a little rough as he removed Tonio's hands and stepped again to the open window.

Far below, the gondolas moved like pods on the green water. A barge inched its way towards the lagoon. A tiny

86

orchestra played brightly on deck, and the railing was twined with roses and lilies. Small figures flashed and turned as they ducked beneath a canopy of white silk, and rolling up the walls, it seemed, there came a thin laughter.

"I think sometimes that it has become an abomination against taste, to grow old and die in Venice!" Andrea said. "Yes, taste, taste, as if all of life were nothing but a matter of taste," he raged, his voice dry in his throat, almost a rattle. "You great whore!" he breathed, staring out at those distant silver domes.

"Papa," Tonio whispered.

The hand that touched him was like a claw. "My son, there isn't time for you to grow up slowly. I told you that once before. Now mark my words. You must make up your mind you are a man now. You must behave as if this were absolutely the truth, all the chemistry of God notwithstanding. Then all else falls into place, do you understand me?"

The pale eyes fixed on Tonio, appeared to sharpen and then again to grow dim. "I would have given you an empire, foreign seas, the world. But now I can only give you this: once you have made the decision that you are a man, you will become one. Everything else will fall into place. Remember."

Two hours passed before anyone could persuade Tonio to leave for the Brenta. Alessandro went back into his father's rooms twice, emerging each time to say that Andrea's order was absolute.

They were to leave for the Villa Lisani. Andrea was concerned that they were already late. He wanted them to go immediately.

Finally Signore Lemmo ordered everything placed in the gondolas, and took Tonio aside.

"He is in pain, Tonio," he said. "He does not want you or your mother to see him as he is. Now listen to me. You must not let him know you are worried. I'll send for you if there is any great change in him."

Tonio was choking back the tears as they crossed the little dock.

"Dry your eyes," Alessandro whispered, helping him into the boat. "He's on the balcony above to bid us farewell."

Tonio glanced up; he saw the spectral figure supported on

87

either side. Andrea had put on his scarlet robe; his hair had been tamed and his smile frozen as if in white marble.

"I will never see him again," Tonio whispered.

Thank God for the swiftness of the little boat, for the canal's serpentine course. When he finally sat back in the *felze*, he was crying silently but uncontrollably.

He felt the continual pressure of Alessandro's hand.

And when he did look up, he realized Marianna was gazing out of the window with the most wistful expression.

"The Brenta." She was almost humming. "I haven't seen the mainland since I was a little girl."

19

I N THE KINGDOM of Naples and Sicily, Guido found no pupils worth the journey home. Now and then a promising boy was presented to him, but he had not the fortitude to tell his parents he would recommend "the operation."

And of those boys already cut, he did not hear one worth encouraging.

But he pressed on into the Papal States, to Rome itself, and then farther north into Tuscany.

Spending his nights in noisy inns, his days in rented carriages, occasionally dining with the hangers-on of some noble family, he carried his few belongings in a shabby leather valise, his dagger clamped in his right hand under his coat against those bandits who everywhere preyed upon travelers.

He went to the churches of the small towns. He heard the opera everywhere in the villages and in the cities.

And by the time he left Florence, he had two boys of some talent boarded in a monastery until he should take them back to Naples. They were not marvels, but they were better than all he'd heard so far, and he dreaded the return journey with nothing.

In Bologna, he frequented the cafés, met with the great theatrical agents, spent hours with singers gathered there to pick up an offer for a season, hoping to hear of that ragged boy with a great voice who might be dreaming of the stage, who might want the chance to study in the great conservatorios of Naples.

Old friends now and then appeared to buy him a drink, singers who'd been in class with him. Glad to see him and feeling completely superior to him now, they proudly related their adventures.

But he found nothing.

And as spring came on, as the air grew warmer and sweeter and the large green leaves came back to the limbs of the poplar trees, Guido pushed on, north, to the deepest mystery of all Italy: the great and ancient Republic of Venice.

20

ANDREA TRESCHI DIED in the middle of the worst heat of August. Signore Lemmo's immediate communication to Tonio informed him that Catrina and her husband were now his guardians. And Carlo Treschi, having been called home by his father as soon as death was certain, had already set sail from Istanbul.

PART II

1

THE HOUSE WAS FULL of death and full of strangers. Elderly men in black robes and scarlet robes, endless whispering.

And then from inside his father's apartments that terrible sound, that inhuman roaring. He heard it commence, he heard it rise in volume.

And when at last the doors had been flung open, his brother, Carlo, stepped into the corridor and met his eyes with the palest, weakest smile. It was shy; it was defeated; it was the thin terrible embarrassed shield of outrage.

He had watched as his brother came up the Grand Canal. He had seen him standing in the prow of the boat, a cape unfurling lightly on the damp breeze, and that black hair, the very shape of the head familiar. He had watched as Carlo stepped on the dock; he had stood at the top of the staircase waiting for him.

Black eyes, black eyes exactly like his own, and that sudden start when Carlo, surely, perceived the likeness. The face, larger, darkened by the sun, suffused so suddenly with feeling. Carlo had come forward, his hands curling in the gesture of welcome, and taking Tonio in his arms, held him so close it seemed Tonio could feel the sigh coming out of Carlo before he had in fact heard it.

What had Tonio expected? Malice here, bitterness? Passion burnt to cunning? It was a countenance so open it seemed the guileless mirror of warmth. And those hands had so boldly caressed his head, those lips pressed to his forehead. There was a loving possessiveness to his touch, and just for an instant, as they stood in each other's arms, Tonio had felt the most secret and glorious relief.

"You are here," he whispered.

And his brother had said, ever so soft, so it was a rumble from his massive chest, the name:

"Tonio."

*　　*　　*

And then that inchoate roar, that appalling roar, rising, rising, that growl through clenched teeth, that fist coming down again and again on his father's table.

"Carlo!" Catrina whispered, rising behind Tonio with a rustle of silk, her mourning veil thrown back as the doors opened to release him, her face full of sadness.

Soft noises, whispers. Catrina went behind him down the corridor. Signore Lemmo rushed to and fro on soundless feet. And Marianna in her mourning dress stared before her.

Now and then Tonio saw the glint of the rosary beads moving through her hand, the glint of her eyes should she look up for an instant.

She had not even raised her head when Carlo entered the room. And he from the corner of his eyes had quietly noted her.

When he did bow, it was to the ground: "Signora Treschi," he said. He was so like his portraits it seemed the burning sun of the Levant had only deepened his color. The hair was dark on the backs of his hands, and a vague Eastern perfume, musky and full of spice, seemed to emanate from him. He wore three rings on his right hand.

And somewhere now behind yet another closed door, Catrina was pleading with him. "Carlo, Carlo."

Beppo appeared at the head of the stairs, and behind him the tall figure of Alessandro.

Alessandro dropped his arm about Tonio's shoulder. They moved swiftly and silently to Tonio's room.

Catrina's voice swelled behind the wall just for a moment: "You are home, don't you see, you are home and young yet and everywhere around you there is life. . . ."

And that lower, incomprehensible rumble of anger interrupting her.

Alessandro removed his dark blue cape as the door shut. He was speckled with rain, and his large dreamy eyes were shadowed with concern.

"So he is here, already," he whispered.

"Alessandro, you must stay on, I need you," Tonio said. "I need you for four years under this roof. I need you until I marry Francesca Lisani. It's all laid down in my father's will, in his instructions to the guardians of the estate. But for four years, Alessandro, I must prevail against him."

93

Alessandro pressed his finger to Tonio's lips as if he were the angel making the final seal at the moment of creation.

"It's not you who must prevail, Tonio. It's your father's will and those who must execute it. Is he disinherited?"

His voice dropped on this last word. This would have been a terrible thing, accomplished only if Carlo had ever laid hands on his father with the intent to harm him. That had never happened.

"The estate's undivided," Tonio murmured. "But my father's instructions are clear. I am to marry. The bulk of the assets are for my education, training, and all the demands of my life as a statesman. Carlo is allowed a pittance, and advised to devote himself to the welfare of my children. . . ."

Alessandro nodded. It was no surprise to him.

"Alessandro, he is outraged! He demands to know why he must abide by this. He is the eldest son. . . ."

"Tonio, that means nothing in Venice," Alessandro reminded him. "You have been chosen to marry by your father. You must not be frightened by all of this. It is not in your hands, it is in the hands of the law and your guardian."

"Alessandro, he demands to know why the fate of this house must wait upon a boy. . . ."

"Tonio, Tonio," Alessandro whispered. "You couldn't yield to him if you wished. Put your mind at rest. And for whatever good it will do, I am here to stay with you."

Tonio sucked in his breath. He was staring off as if these assurances hadn't penetrated. "Alessandro, if I could only despise him . . ." he started.

Alessandro had his head to one side, and his face had a look of limitless patience.

"But he does not seem . . . he is so . . ."

"It's out of your hands," Alessandro said softly.

"What did you know of him?" Tonio pressed. "Surely you knew of him?"

"*Of* him, yes," Alessandro said, and without realizing it, he moved to wipe a strand of hair from Tonio's forehead. His hand rested on Tonio's shoulder. "But only what everyone knew. He was an impetuous young man. And there was death in this house, his mother's death, the death of his brothers. There is little more that I can tell you."

"Catrina does not despise him," Tonio whispered. "She is sorry for him!"

"Ah, Tonio, she is sorry for him but she is your guardian

and she will stand by you. When you come to understand that you are powerless in this, you will have peace.''

"But Alessandro, tell me. The woman he refused. Years ago, when my father wanted to arrange a marriage . . .''

''I know nothing of all that,'' Alessandro said with a little shake of the head.

"But he refused a bride whom my father had chosen for him. He ran off with some convent girl, but the bride he refused. Alessandro, was it my mother?''

Alessandro had been on the verge of a denial when he paused, and for a moment seemed not to understand the question.

"If she was the girl Carlo refused, it will be unendurable for her here. . . .''

Alessandro was silent for a moment. "She was not the girl he refused,'' he answered softly.

Dark house, empty house, alien sounds.

He climbed the steps to the upper floor.

He knew Carlo was in the old room; he could see the uncommon daylight spilling out into the dusty passage.

That morning his brother had asked for him at table, sent his Turkish servants to invite him down, and he had sat alone in bed, his head in his hands, murmuring excuses to these alien faces.

Now he moved swiftly on the balls of his feet until he stood at the door and saw his brother moving among the ruined things, the bed a scaffold of dust and rags, a book in Carlo's hand, swollen from the rain, its pages heavy and damp still as he turned them. He was reading in a whisper, the blue sky behind him obscured by the grimed windows, and it seemed the sound of his whisper belonged to this place, and with a dull rhythm he spoke the words now, louder, yet to himself, his right hand moving in the air ever so slightly.

He saw Tonio. And that warmth came to his face, the eyes crinkled gently with his smile, and closing the book he laid his right hand open on it.

"Come in, little brother,'' he said. "You see I am . . . well, at a loss. I cannot invite you to sit here with me in my old apartments.''

There was no irony in his tone, yet the blood rushed to

Tonio's face, and sick with shame he looked down, unable to form an answer.

Why hadn't he sent the servants here at once to prepare this room? Why hadn't he thought of it? Lord God, he had been master of this house for just that little while, had he not? And if not he, who, then, might have given the order? He stared at the stained and peeling walls, at the ruined carpet.

"Ah, but you see the love for me that was lavished here," Carlo sighed. He laid the book down, his eyes moving over the fractured ceiling. "You see how my treasures were put away for me, my clothing saved from the moths, my books in dry and safe places."

"Forgive me, Signore!"

"And for what?" Carlo extended his hand, and as Tonio drew near, Carlo gathered him to himself, and again Tonio felt that kindling warmth, that strength. And in some recess of his mind, untroubled, he thought, I shall look like this when I am a man; I see the future as few ever see it. His brother kissed him gently on the forehead.

"What could you have done, little brother?"

He did not wait for the answer. He had opened the book again, and his hand moved over the decaying letters, *The Tempest*, written in English, and beneath it the twin columns of print, his voice dropping again into that rhythmic whisper: *"Full fathom five thy father lies . . ."* And as he looked up again, he seemed positively distracted by the vision of Tonio.

What is it, what do you see? Do you despise me, Tonio was thinking. And the ruin of the room seemed to press in on him, the dust suffocating him, and he could for the first time breathe in the stench of all that was spoiled and rotting here.

But his brother had not looked away, and his black eyes had lost all consciousness of their own expression.

"First child of the union," Carlo whispered. "Child born at the height of passion. Blessed with everything, so the saying goes, the first child." And now his brows knit and his mouth showed the smallest tightening at the edges.

"But then I was the last of my parents' blood," he went on, "and we two are so alike. There is no rule, then, is there? First child, last child, save the father's *feeling* for the first child!"

"Please, Signore, I don't understand what you are saying."

"No, and why should you?" Carlo said, the tone as even

as before, as gentle and without malice. Wondering, he looked at Tonio as if he liked looking at him. And Tonio beneath his gaze was wilting inside and miserable.

"Do you understand this, then?" Carlo asked. "Look around you." It was that roar threatening again, that roaring nudging at the edge of language.

"Signore, please, let me have the servants clean this place. . . ."

"Oh, will you do that? You are the master here, are you not?" And the voice was stretched ever thinner.

Tonio looked into his eyes. It wasn't anger, it was outrage. And shaking his head helplessly, Tonio looked away.

"No, little brother, it is not your doing," said Carlo. "And what a princeling you are," he said with the gentlest sincerity. "How he must have loved you. But I dare say, I would love you too if I were your father."

"Signore, show us the way now to love each other!"

"But I do love you," Carlo whispered. "But leave me in this place before I say what I will regret. You see, I am not myself here yet, but rather I have come home to this house to find myself slain here, and put to rest by others, and so I roam this place as if I were the ghost of myself, and in that state of mind come dangerously near to thoughts and words that are hellish."

"Oh, please, come out of here, then, Please . . . His apartments on the main floor, Signore, you can take them. . . ."

"Ah, do you give me those rooms, little brother?"

"Signore, I did not mean that I give them to you. I meant no such disrespect. I meant only surely you can take them."

Carlo smiled, and looking up, he let the book drop to the table. Then he took Tonio's head again in both hands almost roughly.

"Oh, why couldn't you have been some spoilt and arrogant boy?" he whispered. "And I could have damned him further for so indulging you?"

"Signore, we cannot speak of these things. If we do, we cannot abide each other."

"And wit and wisdom and courage, yes, courage, that is what you have, little brother. You come to face me and talk to me. You said, what, a moment ago, that I must show you a way for us to love each other?"

Tonio nodded. He knew his voice would break if he spoke just yet. And so close to this man that he held himself stiffly, he slowly bent forward until his lips touched his brother's cheek and he felt Carlo's sigh again as Carlo's arm enfolded him.

"So difficult, difficult," Catrina said. It was past midnight and all the house was dark save the room in which he was pacing. Tonio could hear the wine in his voice; it was erupting. There was no modulation.

"But you have come back rich, and you are yet young . . . and dear God, is there not enough in this city to content you without wife, children? You are free—!"

"Signora, I am done with freedom. I know what can be bought. I know what can be had. Yes, rich, and young, and free, for fifteen years I have been that! And I tell you while he was living it was the fire of purgatory, and now that he is dead, it is hell! Don't talk to me of freedom. Penance enough I did so that I might wed and—"

"Carlo, you cannot go against him!"

Servants with dark faces swept the corridors. Young men lingered at the doors of Andreas old rooms, Marcello Lisani came early to breakfast with Carlo at the long supper room table.

"Come in, Tonio!" Carlo gestured, rising at once, the chair sliding back on the tiles, at the glimpse of his brother passing the doorway.

But Tonio, bowing quickly, escaped him. And once inside his room, stood silently against the door as if he had found some refuge.

"Resigned, no, he is not resigned." Catrina shook her head. Her quick blue eyes narrowed just for an instant as she looked at Tonio's lessons. Then she gave them back to Alessandro. She had a score of papers in a leatherbound folio, what to pay cook, what to pay the valet, these tutors, how much food to lay in, and what else was wanting?

"But you must bear this in silence," she said, closing her hand over Tonio's hands. "You must do nothing to provoke him."

Tonio nodded. Angelo on the edge of the room, drawn and anxious, glanced up now and again from the pages of his breviary.

"So let him gather his old friends, let him see who has influence now, and who holds office"—Catrina's voice dropped as she leaned close and looked into his eyes—"and let him spend his money if he wishes, he has brought a fortune home. He complains of these dark draperies. He is hungry for Venetian luxuries, for French trinkets and pretty wallpapers. Let him . . ."

"Yes, yes . . ." Tonio said.

Each morning, Tonio watched him leave the house, seeing him rush down the stairs with the jingle of keys and the clank of the sword at his side, his boots loud on the marble, sounds so unfamiliar here they seemed to have a life of their own, while through the crack of his door, Tonio saw white wigs in a row on polished wooden heads, and heard Andrea's old whisper: foppery.

"Little brother, come dine with me tonight." He seemed at times to appear out of the shadows as if he had lain in waiting.

"Please forgive me, Signore, my spirits, my father . . ."

Somewhere Tonio heard the unmistakable sound of his mother singing.

In the late afternoon, Alessandro sat so still at the library table he might have been the statue of himself. Tramp of feet on the stairs. And her voice in that melancholy song very like a hymn drifted through the open doors, but when Tonio rose to find her, she was only just leaving.

Prayerbook in hand, she lowered her veil, and it seemed she did not want to look at him. "Lena will go with me," she answered. She did not need Alessandro today.

"Mamma." Tonio followed her to the door. She was humming something to herself. "Are you content here now? Tell me."

"Oh, why do you ask me this?" Her voice was so light, but her hand, darting from beneath the thin black mesh to pinch his wrist, startled him. He felt a tiny pain for an instant and was angry.

"If you are not happy here, you could go to Catrina's house," he said, all the while dreading that she would leave, and those rooms too would be alien, empty.

"I am in my son's house," she said. "Open the doors," she told the porter.

*   *   *

At night, he lay awake listening to the silence. And all the world outside his door seemed a foreign territory. Passages, rooms he knew, even the damp and neglected places; laughter erupted below; there was that faint, almost imperceptible sound of people moving in this house, a sound no one should have been able to hear, but he could hear it.

Somewhere in the night a woman was shouting something, caustic, uncontrollable. He turned over and shut his eyes, only to realize it was within these walls.

He had slept. He had dreamed. Opening the door, he heard them below, the old exchange again, Catrina's voice high-pitched and strident. Was he weeping?

It was early evening. The October carnival gave its faint distant din to the sounds of the night. There was a ball in the great Palazzo Trimani only yards away, and Tonio, alone in the long supper room, his hand on the heavy drape, watched the boats as they came and went, came and went, below him.

His mother stood on the dock beneath the window, Lena and Alessandro behind her. Her long black veil was down to her hem, the gauze of it blown back to make a sculpture of her face as she waited for the gondola.

And was *he* in this house?

The Grand Salon was a sea of pitch darkness.

But as he was savoring the silence and stillness of this moment, he heard the first sounds. Someone moving in the dark, and there came that musky, Eastern perfume, the creak of the door, a heel ever so gently touching the stone floor behind him.

Caught on the open sea, he thought, and the canal shimmered in his vision. The sky was ablaze above the distant Piazza San Marco.

The hair on the back of his neck rose just a little, and he felt the faint pressure of the man near him.

"In the old days," Carlo whispered, "all women wore those veils, and they had about them a greater beauty. It was a mystery they carried with them in the streets, something of the East they carried with them. . . ."

Tonio looked up slowly to see him so very close they might have touched one another. The black of Carlo's coat revealed a slash of glimmering white lace that seemed a dim mirage rather than fabric, and his wig, with its perfect curls above

100

the ears and a rise from the forehead so natural it seemed real hair, gave off a slight shimmer.

He drew near the panes and looked down, that resemblance jarring Tonio now as it did every time he perceived it. In the meager candlelight, Carlo's skin appeared flawless. And the only sign of age in him was those dry lines at the corners of his eyes which wrinkled so easily when there came his long smiles.

And such a smile softened his face now, evincing that irrepressible warmth as if no enmity could ever exist between them.

"Night after night, you avoid me, Tonio," he said. "Let us dine together now. The table is set. The food is ready."

Tonio turned to the water again; his mother was gone; the night for all its plodding little boats seemed empty.

"My thoughts are with my father, Signore," he said.

"Ah, yes, your father." But Carlo didn't turn away. And there was in the shadows the movements of those silent Turkish ones taking up the small flames and touching them to branching candelabra everywhere, on the table itself, on the chests beneath that haunting picture.

"Sit down, little brother."

I want to love you, Tonio thought, no matter what you did. I thought somehow it could be healed.

And bowing his head, Tonio seated himself as so often in the past at the head of the table. It was not even a moment before he realized what he had done, and his eyes rose immediately to confront his brother.

His heart quickened its pace. He studied this smile, this affable radiance. The snow white wig made Carlo's skin seem all the more dark and the beauty of the high-placed eyebrows was all the more marked as he sat gazing at Tonio with neither rancor nor censure.

"We are at odds with each other," Carlo said. And now his smile melted slowly to a calmer, less deliberate expression. "No matter how we pretend we are not, we are at odds, and almost a month has passed and we cannot even break bread together."

Tonio nodded, the tears standing in his eyes.

"And it is uncanny," Carlo went on, "this resemblance between us."

Tonio wondered if a man could feel love when the other gave the silent expression of it. Could Carlo see it in his

101

eyes? And for the first time, he realized, sitting here, very still and unable to speak even the simplest words, that he wanted so to rely upon his brother. Rely upon you, trust in you, seek your help, and yet that is beyond possibility. At odds. He wanted to leave this room now, and he feared his brother's reckless and strange eloquence.

"Handsome little brother," Carlo whispered. "French clothes," he observed, his large dark eyes flickering almost innocently. "And such fine bones, from your mother, I think, and her voice, too, that lovely lovely soprano."

Tonio's eyes shifted deliberately away. This was excruciating. But if we do not talk now, the agony will only grow greater.

"When she was a girl," Carlo said, "and she sang in the chapel, she moved us to tears, did she ever tell you that? Ah, the tributes she received, the gondoliers loved her."

Slowly Tonio looked back to him.

"She was a very siren," Carlo said. "Has no one ever told you?"

"No," Tonio answered uneasily. And he felt his brother observe how he shifted in his chair, and how he looked away again hastily.

"And beautiful she was, too, more beautiful even than she is now. . . ." Carlo dropped his voice to a whisper.

"Signore, best not to speak so of her!" Tonio had said it before he meant to.

"Why, what will happen"—Carlo's voice remained calm—"if I speak so of her?"

Tonio looked at him. His smile was changing, lengthening coldly. There are few things under God more terrible in a human expression than such a smile, Tonio was thinking.

But behind it lay that misery, that agitation, that rage which had found its greatest eloquence in the roar behind closed doors. So the smile wasn't really cold. It was merely desperate and fragile.

Tonio whispered suddenly, "This is not my doing!"

"Yield to me then!" Carlo answered.

So it had come to this.

This moment he had dreaded day in and day out. He would have risen to go, but his brother's hand had come down on his own, and it seemed he was almost pinioned to the table. He felt the sweat break out under his clothes, and the room seemed abysmally cold to him suddenly. He was staring at the candle flames, perhaps letting them burn his eyes, and he knew there was nothing he could have done to prevent this.

"Have you no hunger to hear my side of it?" Carlo whispered. "Children are curious. Have you no natural curiosity?" His face was swelling with anger, and yet that smile held and the voice died away on the last syllable as if fearful of its own volume.

"Signore, your quarrel is not with me. Do not appeal to me."

"Oh, little brother, you astonish me. You are never cowed, are you? I think there is iron in you as there was in him, and the sharp edges of impatience that there are in her. But you will listen to me."

"Signore, you are mistaken. I will not listen to you! You must make your case to those who are appointed to govern us both, our estate, our decisions."

And feeling an overpowering revulsion for his brother, Tonio drew his hand away from Carlo's.

But the face was magnetizing him. It was as if it were more youthful than it should have been, and filled with impetuosity and misery. It was challenging Tonio, it was imploring Tonio, and there was nothing of that "iron" in it, to use his own words, that Tonio had indeed known in his father.

"What do you want of me, Signore?" Tonio said. He had drawn himself up and now he took a slow breath. "Lay it down for me, Signore, what am I to do?"

"Yield to me, I have told you!" Carlo's voice again rose. "Do you see what he has done to me! Robbed me, that is what he has done, and now he seeks to rob me again and I tell you, it will not happen!"

"And how will it not happen!" Tonio demanded. He could feel himself trembling but there was now that exhilaration that overcomes all shrinking. "Am I to invent impediments, lie! Go against my father's will because you have *asked* me to do it! Signore, there may not be iron in me, I do not know, but there is the blood of the Treschi, and you have so misjudged me I am at a loss as to how I might make your error plain to you."

"Ah, you are not a child at all, are you?"

"Yes, I am, and that is why I am suffering this now," Tonio answered. "But you, Signore, are a man, and must know surely I am not the judge to whom you should make your appeal. I did not hand down the sentence."

103

"Ah, sentence, yes, sentence!" Carlo's voice was unsteady. "How well you choose your words, how proud your father would have been of you, young, and clever, and yes, full of courage. . . ."

"Courage!" Tonio said more softly. "Signore, you push me to rash words. I don't want to quarrel with you! Let me go, this is hell for me, brother against brother!"

"Yes, brother against brother," Carlo answered, "and what of the rest of this house? What of your mother? Where does she stand in all this?" he whispered, drawing so close that Tonio recoiled, still unable to turn his eyes away. "Tell me!" Carlo demanded. "How is it with your mother!"

Tonio was too amazed to answer.

He was pressed to the back of the chair, staring at his double. That vague feeling of revulsion returned to him. "Your words are too strange for me, Signore."

"Are they? Use your wit, it's sharp enough, you lead your tutors by the nose. Tell me, is she content to live out her life alone in her son's house, a grieving widow?"

"Wha else can she do?" Tonio whispered.

The smile came back, almost sweet and yet so fragile. There is no true malice in this man, Tonio told himself desperately. There is no malice, not even now. There is monstrous dissatisfaction. Dissatisfaction so terrible that it has not yet thought of defeat or bitterness.

"She is . . . what?" Carlo asked. "Twice your age? And what has her life been to her so far but a penal sentence? She was a girl when she came into this house, was she not? But you need not answer me, for I remember her."

"Don't speak of my mother."

"*You* tell *me* not to speak of your mother?" Carlo bent forward. "Is she not flesh and blood the same as you or I? And fifteen years entombed in this house with my father? Tell me something, Marc Antonio, do you find yourself fair when you look into the glass? Do you find in me the same handsomeness you find in yourself? In lesser or greater measure?"

"You speak abominations!" Tonio whispered. "You say one more word to me of her . . .!"

"Oh, you threaten me, do you? Your swords are toys to me, my boy, and you as yet haven't the slightest shadow of a beard on that handsome face, and your voice is as sweet as hers, or so I'm told. Don't threaten me. I shall say all the words I want of her. And how many words with her would it take to make her rue these years, I wonder!''

"She's your father's wife, for the love of God," Tonio said between his teeth. "You do your violence to me, if you will, I am not afraid of you. But her, you leave alone, do you understand, or child that I am I shall call to my aid those men who will stand by me!"

Oh, this was hell, hell, as surely as the priest or the painter had ever depicted it.

"Violence?" Carlo gave a soft laugh, seemingly sincere, and his face went smooth, his eyes widening slightly. "Who has need of violence? She is a woman still, little brother. And lonely, lonely for a man's touch if she can even remember it. He gave her a eunuch for a lover when she was all but out of her mind. Well, I am no eunuch. I am a man, Marc Antonio."

Tonio had risen. But Carlo was beside him.

"You are the devil in hell as he said you were!" Tonio whispered.

"Oh, did he say that of me!" Carlo cried out. He caught Tonio by the small of his arm and held him. But his face was constricted with suffering. It was hurt he was feeling as he confronted Tonio. "He said I was the devil, did he? And did he tell you what he did to me! Did he tell you what he took from me! Fifteen years in exile. How much can a man bear? Would I were the devil, I would have had the devil's strength in that inferno."

"I am sorry for you!" Tonio freed himself with a violent pull of his arm. "I am sorry for you." They were facing each other, the table behind them. The servants were gone from the room, and the candles gave off their blazing light everywhere. "I swear it before God, I am sorry for you," Tonio said, "but I cannot do anything, and she is as powerless as I am."

"Powerless? Is she? How long can you endure in a house turned against you?"

"She is my mother, she will never turn against me."

"Don't be so sure of that, Marc Antonio. Ask yourself this first, what was her crime for her fifteen years of exile?" He advanced as Tonio moved away from him.

"My crime was that I was born under a different star, of a different humor. He loathed me from the day I was born, and no one could show him the slightest virtue in me. That was my sin. But what was hers that he should deign to make her

105

his child bride and wall her up alive in this house with an infant her only companion?''

"Get away from me," Tonio said. He could see the dark well of the Grand Salon opening beyond the doorway. And yet he couldn't break loose though Carlo was not touching him.

"I'll tell what her sin was," Carlo said. "Are you ready to hear it? And then we will see if you can tell me I must not speak of her to you! It was that she loved me, that was her sin, and when I came for her at the Pietà, she went with me!"

"You're lying!"

"No, Marc Antonio . . ."

"Every word you say is a lie. . . ."

"No, Marc Antonio, nothing I say is a lie. And you know it. You've guessed it. And if you have not, go to that eunuch of yours for the truth, go to your beloved cousin, Catrina. Go to the streets where everyone remembers it. I took her out of that convent in bold daylight because I wanted her and she wanted me, and he, he would not so much as look at her.''

"I don't believe you!"

Tonio raised his hand as if he would strike Carlo, but he could no longer even clearly see him. He saw only a blurred shape before him, drawing ever closer, passing in front of the wreaths of candles, now dark, now expressionless.

"I begged him to let me marry her! On my knees I begged. Do you know what he said? Mainland nobility, he sneered, dowerless girl, orphan. *He* would choose my wife, and a burnt-out shrew he chose for her wealth, for her position, for his hatred of me! 'Father,' I begged. 'Come to the Pietà, see her.' I knelt on this very floor, imploring him.

"And when the worst was done, and he'd sent me away, he took her *himself* for his bride! Mainland nobility, dowerless, orphan, he married her! He bought her into the Golden Book with his wealth. And for me, he could have done that! For me, but he refused. And banishing me, took her to himself, I tell you! Weep, yes, weep, little brother. Weep for her and for me! For our rash love and rash misadventures, and for how we have both of us paid for it!''

"Stop this, I won't hear it!" Tonio clamped his hands to his ears. His eyes were shut. "If you do not stop, so help me God . . ." He reached out for the door frame, and finding it, lay his head there, unable to speak another word, unable to stop his helpless crying.

"Come tonight to her door," Carlo said softly behind him. "Listen at the keyhole if you will. She belonged to me then. She will belong to me now. If you do not believe it, ask her!"

He had no mask, no *tabarro*. He pushed his way through the wet and screaming crowd, the rain sometimes cutting his face as it came in fierce gusts, until he was inside the café, and the hot sticky air was all around him. "Bettina!" he whispered. It seemed for the moment she was uncertain, and then pushing her way through shoulders and wet capes, and horrific bauta faces, and clowns and monsters, she came forward, her little black hood standing in a peak over her head, her hands out to clutch him quickly. "This way, Excellency," she said, leading him out into the *calle* towards the nearby landing.

As soon as the gondola had left the dock, she was in his arms on the floor of the *felze*, pulling at his vest and his shirt, pushing up her skirts as her legs wrapped around him.

There was the sound of the rain teeming on the water around them; now and then it struck the hollow wooden bridge overhead, now and then it ran streaming fast, with a purpose, through invisible gutters. The boat rocked dangerously, it seemed, under his awkward weight; the *felze* smelt of dust, of warm flesh, of the smoky perfume between her naked legs where the hair was hot and wet. It made him grit his teeth as he nuzzed his head into it. He felt the silk skin of her thighs against his cheeks, and then her eager little hands tugging at him. That irrepressible giggle in his ears, her breasts so big they seemed to spill into his hands. She tore open his breeches; it seemed she flowed out of her blouse and skirt, white and sweet, her fingers stroking him, hardening him and guiding him.

He was afraid she'd laugh when she saw he was a boy and it was dry, but she only urged him again to cover her. He tumbled into her, inside of her again, that explosion in his brain wiping out all time, all loss, all horror.

Even a moment's thought would destroy him.

So his hands sought the hot flesh behind her knees, the wet warmth under her breasts, her rounded calves, and her mouth, her open craving mouth full of boldness and sucking breath and those tiny impetuous giggles. A multitude of tiny crevices, creases, secrets. The water lapped at the sides of the boat, music came and went, thin sounds, heavy sounds. He lay

107

under her at times, feeling her delicious weight, then laid her back down, his hand lifting her by the hot fold of her sex, his tongue on her smooth little belly.

And when he lay finally spent even the sea-green smell of the water was bound up in it, the dank smell of the moss-covered foundations plunging down and down into the canal and the soft earth beneath it that was Venice. It was all bound up with the sweetness and the salt, and her precious laughter, and the slanting silver rain coming through the tiny windows, falling on his face as he clung to her.

Would that it could last forever, would that it could blot out all thought and all pain and all tragedy, would that he could take her again and again, and the world would not come back, and he was not in that house, in those rooms, and listening to that voice; he snuggled down in the dark, covering the back of his head with his hands so she wouldn't hear his crying.

Voices tugged at him.

It seemed they were floating in those tiny, crowded water-ways with small windows above, where the laundry sagged from the lines by day, and the garbage lay piled against the quais, and if you looked up, you could see the rats racing along the walls, squat, agile, as if they were actually flying. Cats whined and bawled in the dark. He heard the slosh and the gurgle of the water. And he felt weightless and deliciously quiet, even as she still teased him.

"Love you, love you, love you, love you . . ."

But those voices again. He lifted his head. The tenor, he would have known it anywhere, and yes, the basso, and the flute and the violin. He rose on his elbow, feeling the boat heave and shift They were *his* singers!

"What is it, Excellency?" she whispered. She was naked beside him, her clothes a shapeless mass of darkness in her lap, her shoulders so exquisitely sloped, her eyes just two places that didn't exist in all the whiteness of her face as she looked at him.

He sat upright. He disentangled himself from her gently. I've had her, he was thinking, loved her, had her, known her. And yet it gave no savor, no wondrous thrill, and he clung to her for a moment, smelling her hair, and kissing the hard roundness of her little forehead. And the voices drew nearer and nearer. They *were* his singers! And they were on their

108

way home, most likely, and if he could just overtake them. . . . He pushed his shirt into his breeches, tied back his hair.

"Excellency, don't go," she begged.

"Dearest," he said, putting gold coins in her hands and closing her fingers on top of them. "Tomorrow night, right after dark, wait for me." He slipped her skirt over her head, pulled on her soft rumpled blouse, and laced up her vest tightly, feeling with the last bit of pleasure the way that it hugged her and bound her.

The singers were almost to the canal, and it was Ernestino—how many times had he heard that name spoken under the window? And the basso, it was Pietro, the one with the light basso that had no thickness to it, a pure sound for all its depth, and the fiddler tonight was Felix.

As the boat shot away from him under the nearby bridge and vanished into the dark, he wished just for a moment he were very drunk, that he had had the presence of mind to buy a jug of wine at the piazza. He crept along the wall towards the *calle*, the stones so slick he might easily have fallen down into the water.

What do they look like? He had seen so little of them in the dark. Would they know him?

And in the light of an open door, he caught sight of the little band immediately. The big, heavy-set one, bearded, coarsely dressed, that was Ernestino, and he was serenading a thick-armed woman who slouched on the step laughing softly at him. And the violinist pranced back and forth, his bow working furiously. The music was shrill and sweet.

And then Tonio raised his voice, an octave higher than Ernestino as he sang the same phrases right in time with him. Ernestino's voice swelled; Tonio could see the change in his expression:

"Ah, it's not possible!" he shouted. "It's my seraph, it's my prince from the Palazzo Treschi."

And when he opened his arms, catching Tonio up, swinging him off his feet and around before setting him down again, "But, Excellency, what are you doing here?"

"I want to sing with you," Tonio said. He took the jug of wine offered him. It spilled down his chin as he filled his mouth. "Wherever you're going, I want to sing with you."

109

He threw back his head. The rain was hitting his eyelids, and he sang an infinite ascension of notes, a pure and magnificent coloratura. He heard it echoed by the walls; it seemed to rise to the very margin of sky above, and in the narrow darkness lights flickered describing the shapes of small windows. Ernestino's deeper voice rose under his, buoying it, dropping back to let Tonio soar, and waiting again for the closing phrase in rapturous harmony.

A voice called out a sharp "Bravo," and there came soft explosions of compliments from the walls themselves, it seemed, dying as suddenly as they were uttered. And when the coins hit the wet stones, Felix scrambled to gather them.

Until dawn they wandered singing along the windy quais where they could find it; they went arm in arm through the spiderweb of *calli*. Sometimes the walls hugged them so tight they had to go one by one, but their voices became preternatural. Tonio knew all their favorite songs; he taught them others. Again and again he took the jug and when it was empty bought another.

Buttery windows broke open above them everywhere they went, and now and then they lingered to serenade some dim figure. Behind the big palazzi they roamed, drawing the richly dressed men and women away from their late-night gambling and supper tables. The blood pounded in Tonio's head; his feet were reckless, slipping on the slick stones, but it seemed his voice had never known such unbridled power. Ernestino and Pietro were made for him, and whenever he flagged, they taunted him into greater feats, giving their own applause for the piercing of high notes, the long tender swelling as his sons grew slower, and full of some sweet and caressing sadness. He remembered once rocking with his arms folded on his chest; Ernestino was leading him in some lullaby, and the night was without form or end, the moon now and then released from the heavy clouds to show the rain in a silent, silvery torrent.

Sadness, it was such an arresting emotion. You could almost convince yourself of the rhyme and reason of heartbreak.

It was daylight.

Garbage littered the piazza; bawling voices ran out under the arcades; little clusters of maskers danced about arm in arm, a whole population of black-draped persons with faces

110

the color of skulls, and the great church itself shimmered and wavered in the morning rain as if it were painted on a silk scrim hung from the heavens.

Bettina's face was puffy from sleep, she was pinning up her hair and rushing to wait on him.

She put hot bread and butter down, and strong Turkish coffee. She put the napkin in his lap, and when he wouldn't lift his head, she held it for him.

He ran his finger down the pale flesh of her throat and asked:

"Do you love me?"

2

I T WAS A WEEK before he even trusted himself to approach his mother's door, only to be told she'd gone to church. Then she was asleep.

And next time he knocked, gone to the Palazzo Lisani.

She was anywhere but there when he came to see her.

By the fifth morning, he was laughing out loud as he left her door.

Then lapsing into a paralytic silence in which he could not and would not pursue her.

But no matter how his head ached from lack of sleep, he washed, swallowed food, found his way finally to the library.

Catrina Lisani came to tell him that Carlo, with a substantial fortune acquired in the Levant, had cured all debts against the estate, which had been considerable, and now he meant to restore the old Treschi villa on the Brenta.

Tonio was so tired from his nightlong serenades, he could scarce pay attention to her.

"He is behaving himself, don't you think?" she asked. "He is doing his duty. Your father could not have wished for better."

Meantime Carlo had three bravos with him wherever he went. Husky, taciturn bodyguards who hung about the house, at-

111

tempting to melt into the shadows. They followed him every morning when in his new patrician robes he went to make his bows to those senators and councillors on the Broglio.

He was ingratiating himself with everyone, and that he meant to reenter civil life was now obvious.

Tonio took to coming to the piazzetta every morning after the night's roaming. And there he would watch his brother from afar; he could only imagine the content of those quick conversations. Clasped hands, bows, some subdued laughter. Marcello Lisani appeared; together they moved up and down, up and down, losing themselves in the crowd against a backdrop of the masts of the ships, and the dull gleam of the water.

And convinced Carlo would be away for a long time, Tonio would finally slip into the house and walk the endless stretch of ancient floor to his mother's apartments. No answer to his knock. The old excuses.

It didn't take Catrina long to find out what Tonio had been up to. He lived for the moment when darkness fell down around the house, dropped out of the winter sky so abruptly. He was out then. He stood in the *calle* waiting for Ernestino and the band to come for him.

Catrina was distraught. "So you are the singer everyone is talking about. But you can't carry on like this, Tonio, you must listen to me. You let his malice eat at you. . . ."

Ah, but why didn't you tell me, he thought, but he did not so much as whisper it. His tutors scolded, he looked away. Alessandro's face bore the mark of fear, unmistakably.

It was almost evening. He could stand it no longer. The house was dreary and only reluctantly invaded by the gentle spring twilight. Leaning against her door, he felt weakened at first. And then consumed with rage, he forced the double doors until the bolt splintered from the wood and he found himself staring into her empty apartments.

For a second, it was impossible for him to discern anything in the shadows, even the most familiar objects. And then gradually he saw his mother sitting quite still at the dressing table.

Here and there a bit of light gleamed along her silver brushes and combs. And then there was the gleam on her throat of pearls; and he realized that in this solitary darkness

112

she was dressed not in her black silk mourning dress but something rich and brilliant in color and strung with little jewels like pinpoints of light that sparkled and vanished as she moved her hands to cover her face.

"Why do you break my door?" she whispered.

"Why don't you answer my knocking?"

He could make out her white fingers clawing at her hair. And it seemed she crossed her breasts with her arms like a saint and bowed her head as if she were pulling herself down. He saw the white nape of her neck, her hair parting, falling in front of her like a veil.

"What will you do?" she asked suddenly.

"What will I do? What can I do?" he asked angrily. "Why do you put this question to me? Put it to my guardians. Put it to my father's lawyers. It's out of my hands, it's always been out of my hands. But you, what is it you do?"

"What do you *want* of me?" she whispered.

"Why did you never tell me!" He drew near to her face, his lips drawn back in a grimace. "Why! Why did I have to hear it from his lips that you were the girl, you and he. . . ."

"Stop it, in the name of God, stop!" she cried. "Shut the doors, shut the doors!" And suddenly rising and running past him, she closed the doors he had forced open and, rushing to the window, pulled the heavy velvet drapes so that both of them were completely enveloped in darkness.

"Why do you torture me?" she implored. "What have I to do with your rivalry? For the love of God, Tonio, for half my life I have been in this house reading you fairy tales! I was a child then. I was no older then you are now! I didn't know what the world was, and so I went with him when he came for me!"

"But tell you, how was I to tell you? After Carlo was sent away, His Excellency could have shut me up again in the Pietà or some worse place, and I would have died there! I had no honor left, and nothing else until he brought me here and married me and gave me his name. Dear God, I tried for fifteen years to be the Signora Treschi, your mother, that he wanted me to be. But tell you, how to tell you, for the love of God, I begged Carlo not to tell you! But Tonio, save for those few nights with him when I was a girl, I have lived the life of a nun in the cloister, and what did I ever do to earn this pious vocation? Do you see here the face and form of a saint! I am a woman, Tonio."

113

"But, Mamma, with him now, under my father's roof. . . ."

He felt her hands before he heard her movement. She was funbling to cover his mouth, his eyes, even though he could see absolutely nothing. Her fingers lay warm and trembling on his eyelids, her smooth forehead like a stone against his lips, her body rising and falling against him.

"Please, Tonio . . ." She was sobbing softly. "It does not matter what I do with him now. I cannot change this rivalry. You have no power. I have no power. Oh, please, please . . ."

"Stand with me, Mother," he whispered. "No matter what is past, stand with me now. I am your son, Mother, I need you."

"I do stand with you, I do. But I am now and have always been without power."

He felt her head in the crook of his neck, her breasts softly heaving against him. And lifting his right hand slowly he found the silky mass of her hair and stroked it.

"This *must* pass," he whispered.

By the end of the month, Carlo was defeated in his first election. The elder members of the Grand Council talked again of stationing him abroad. His young associates resisted it.

And the long-drawn-out clauses of Andrea's will had been clearly and once and for all unraveled.

Beneath his strong and ominous admonitions that his elder son should not marry, there was an ironclad provision that could not be broken:

Andrea had entailed his estate. That is, it could never be divided or sold. And it could be inherited only by the sons of Marc Antonio Treschi. So do what Carlo might, the future of the family belonged to Tonio.

Only if Tonio was to die without issue, or prove incapable of fathering children, could Carlo's heirs be recognized.

But Carlo did nothing now that was violent or shameful. Advised by his father's elderly friends that it was a scandal to challenge the wishes of his dead father, he appeared to accept this. His money he continued to lavish on the household, including increased salaries for his brother's tutors.

He accepted any and all menial duties he was given by the state, set himself to pleasing everyone of importance, and soon became the model patrician.

And what some did not observe, others explained to them: it took money to hold important office in the Republic, money to rear sons for future service, and of the Treschi, ironically, it was Carlo who possessed this money. So those seeking to build their influence commenced to turn to him. It was a natural political process.

Meantime, the man was enjoying himself immensely. He did nothing unseemly, but visiting everyone, dining everywhere, gambling when he had the time, and frequenting the theaters, let everyone know that he was the child of his native city.

Tonio was never at home. He slept often with Bettina, above the little tavern her father owned not far from the piazza. Twice his cousins, the Lisani, called him on the carpet for his behavior, threatening him with the anger of the Grand Council if he didn't start behaving like a patrician.

But his life was lived in the back alleys. It was lived in Bettina's arms.

And when the bells rang on Easter Sunday, Tonio's voice was a legend in the streets of Venice.

In the *calli* beyond the Grand Canal, people had begun to listen for him, to expect him. Ernestino had never seen such a rain of golden coins. And Tonio gave it all to him.

The exquisite pleasure he knew on these nights was all that he could have desired, and he himself did not fully understand its meaning.

He knew only that when he looked up at the sky full of stars, the breezes soft and salty from the sea, he could give himself to the wildest and full-throated love songs. Perhaps his voice was all that he had left of what had only a short while ago been father and mother and son and the House of Treschi. Perhaps it was that he was singing alone; he was not singing with her. She'd turned him out, so he'd taken himself to the world, and there seemed no limit to the notes he could reach, or how long he could sustain them. He dreamed sometimes of Caffarelli as he sang, imagined himself on such a stage, but all this was sweeter, more immediate, more colored with comfort and sorrow and pathos.

People wept above. They cried out vows of love as they emptied their purses. They demanded the name of this seraph soprano, footmen sent down to bring him and his little band up into fashionable supper rooms. He never went.

115

But he followed Ernestino to his favorite haunts as the hours grew smaller and the sky paler.

"In all my life," Ernestino said, "I have never heard a voice like that. God has touched you, Signore. But sing while you can, because it won't be long before those high notes leave you forever."

Through the soft caress of Tonio's drunkenness the words assumed their obvious meaning. Manhood, and the loss of this along with so much else.

"Does it happen all at once?" he murmured. His head was against a wall. He lifted the jug and felt the wine spilling again as it did too often. But he had to wash the bitterness out of his mouth.

"My God, Excellency, haven't you ever been around a boy whose voice changed?"

"No, I have never been around anybody at all, save an elderly man and a very young woman," he said. "I know nothing of boys, I know little of men. And when it's finally said and done, I know very little of singing, either."

A figure filled up the opening at the far end of the *calle* in which they stood. It seemed to touch the walls on either side, and a sudden wariness gripped Tonio.

"Sometimes it's fast," Ernestino was saying. "Sometimes it drags on for a long time with broken notes, you can't trust it. But as tall as you are for your age, Excellency, and . . . and . . ." He made a little smile, taking the jug. Tonio knew he was thinking of Bettina. ". . . Well, it may come sooner than with most." He let it go at that, and putting his heavy arm over Tonio, guided him forward.

The figure had moved away.

Tonio smiled, but no one saw it. He was thinking of his father's words to him, very nearly his last words, and suddenly an anguish deadened him and left him solitary even in this little company.

"Once you have made the decision that you are a man, you will become one." Could the mind thus instruct the flesh? He shook his head, communing with himself. Against Andrea he felt a sudden terrible anger.

And yet it seemed unforgivable that he should feel this, that he should be where he was, wandering with common singers in this mean and crooked place. Yet he walked on, leaning all the more on Ernestino.

116

They had reached the canal. Lanterns burned ahead beneath the dim shadow of the bridge where the gondoliers gathered.

And there appeared that figure again; he was sure it was the same, for the heavy build and the height, and the man stood by obviously watching them.

Tonio moved his hand to his sword, and for a moment he was fixed to the spot.

"Excellency, what is it?" said Ernestino. They were only a few steps from Bettina's tavern.

"That one, there," Tonio murmured, but the weight of his suspicion was breaking him, sickening him. Send death for me, like that, some paid assassin? It seemed he'd already been dealt the blow and this was not life any longer, rather some nightmare place where that sentinel stood on the bridge and these strangers urged him to a meaningless portal.

"Never mind, Excellency," said Ernestino. "That's only the maestro from Naples. A singing teacher come here for little boys. Haven't you seen him before? He's playing your shadow."

It was dawn when Tonio lifted his head from drunken sleep at the tavern table. Bettina sat at his side, her arm under his coat and warm against his back as if she would protect him from the coming sun, and Ernestino, beyond coherence, kept up an angry argument with her father.

And against the wall at the door stood a stocky man, brown-haired, with large menacing eyes and a nose that was pushed flat to his face as if someone had smashed it. He was young. He wore a tattered coat, a sword with a brass handle. And he was staring rudely at Tonio as he lifted his tankard.

3

IT WAS ALMOST completely dark in San Marco, only a score of scattered lights pulsing throughout the immense church to give the faintest glint to the gold mosaics. Old Beppo, Tonio's elderly castrato teacher, held a single taper in his hand as he gazed anxiously at the young maestro from Naples, Guido Maffeo.

117

Tonio stood alone in the left choir loft. He had only just finished singing, and there was a distinct echo of his last note lingering in the church as if nothing could put an end to it.

Alessandro was standing mute, his hands clasped behind his back, looking down at the two smaller figures, Beppo, and Guido Maffeo beside him. He was the first to see the distortion in Maffeo's features. Beppo did not see it, and at the first guttural blast from the southern Italian, Beppo was visibly stunned.

"From the greatest of Venetian families!" Guido repeated Beppo's last words. He bent forward slightly to glare into the face of the old eunuch. "You brought me here to listen to a Venetian patrician!"

"But, Signore, this is the finest voice in Venice."

"A Venetian patrician!"

"But Signore . . ."

"Signore," Alessandro ventured softly, "Beppo did not perhaps realize that you are searching for students for the conservatorio." Alessandro had sensed this misunderstanding almost from the beginning.

But Beppo still did not comprehend. "But, Signore," he insisted, "I wanted . . . I wanted that you should hear this voice for your own pleasure!"

"For my own pleasure, I could have stayed in Naples," growled Guido.

Alessandro turned to Beppo, and with obvious disregard for this impossible southern Italian, he spoke in the soft Venetian dialect. "Beppo, the Maestro is looking for castrati children."

Beppo was miserable.

Tonio had come down from the choir loft and his slight, dark-clad figure appeared behind the echo of his footsteps in the gloom.

He had sung without accompaniment, and his voice had easily filled the church, its effect upon Guido being almost eerie.

The boy was so near manhood now that the voice had lost its innocence. And long years of study had obviously contributed to its perfection. But it was a natural voice, singing in effortless perfect pitch. And though it was a boy's soprano which had not yet begun to change, it had a man's sentiment in it.

The performance had yet other qualities to it which Guido, angry and exhausted, refused to define further.

He stared at the boy who was almost as tall as himself. And realized it was just as he'd supposed the instant he'd heard the voice from the choir loft; this was the vagabond nobleman who roamed the streets at night, the dark-eyed, white-skinned boy with a face chiseled out of the purest marble. He was narrow, elegant, suggesting a dark Botticelli. And as he bowed to his teachers—as if they weren't, in fact, his inferiors—he showed nothing of that natural insolence which Guido associated with all aristocrats.

But there was no accounting for the Venetian patrician class. They were unlike anything Guido had ever known in their habitual courtesy to all men around them. Perhaps the fact that everyone went on foot in this city had something to do with it. He wasn't sure. He didn't care. He was furious.

But he did note that the boy's face was remote for all its politeness. He was leaving this assemblage with humble but indifferent apologies.

The door let in a blinding flash of sunshine as he left the church and the flustered group behind him.

"You must accept my apologies, Signore," said Alessandro. "Beppo did not mean to waste your time."

"Oh, no. No, no, no . . . nonono!" Beppo murmured with all the variety in tone of a regular sentence.

"And this arrogant young boy, who is he?" demanded Guido. "This patrician's son with the larynx of a god who does not even care whether or not his voice has made a favorable impression."

This was too much for Beppo, and Alessandro took the initiative of dismissing him. It was against Alessandro's nature to be rude, but he was now short of patience. And the fact was that he harbored a deep, secret, and iron-hard hatred of those who went out from the conservatorios of Naples to search for castrati children. His own childhood training in that distant southern city had been so cruel and relentless that it had obliterated all memory of the years that had preceded it. Alessandro had been twenty years old before he met one of his brothers in the Piazza San Marco, and even then he did not know the man who said, "See, the little crucifix you wore as a child. Our mother sends it to you." He remembered the crucifix but not the mother.

"If you will forgive me, Maestro," he said now, bending down to look into this fiercesome dark face (he had taken the taper from Beppo), "the boy has not the slightest doubt that

119

his voice pleases everyone who hears it, though he would never be so ill-mannered as to say so. And please understand he came here today out of kindness to his teacher.''

But this boor was not only crude, he was uninsultable. He was not even listening to Alessandro. He was rubbing at his temples, rather, with both hands as if he suffered from a headache. His eyes had the malice of an animal but they were too large to suggest an animal.

And it was not until this very moment, while standing this close, candle in hand, that Alessandro suddenly realized he was gazing down upon an unusually stocky castrato. He studied the smooth face. No, it had never grown a beard. This was yet another eunuch.

He almost let out a little laugh. He had thought him a whole man with a knife tucked under his belt, and a strange mingling of feelings took place in him. He softened slightly towards Guido, not because he felt sorry for him, but because he was a member of a great fraternity more likely to appreciate the pristine beauty of Tonio's voice than any other.

"If you will allow me, Signore, I might recommend several other boys. There is a eunuch at San Giorgio. . . .''

"I've heard him,'' whispered Guido, more to himself than to Alessandro. "Is there the slightest chance that this boy . . . I mean, what precisely does his talent mean to him?'' But before he glanced at Alessandro he knew that this was perfectly ridiculous.

Alessandro didn't even dignify the question with an answer.

A little silence fell between them. Guido had turned his back and taken a few steps on the uneven stone floor. The flame of the taper shivered in Alessandro's hand. And in this faulty light it seemed he could hear more distinctly the sigh that escaped from the singing teacher.

Alessandro saw the slump of his shoulders. And he felt emanating from the man a feeling that was almost like sorrow. Almost like sorrow. There was some violence in this eunuch that Alessandro had seldom encountered. In a momentary but sweeping recollection, he was again confronted with the cruelty and sacrifice which he himself had endured in Naples. He felt some begrudging respect for Guido Maffeo.

"You will thank your young patrician friend for me, please?'' Guido murmured, defeated.

They moved towards the door.

But with his hand on it, Alessandro paused.

120

"But tell me," he said confidentially. "What did you really think of him?"

Immediately he regretted it. This dark little man was capable of anything.

Yet to his surprise, Guido said nothing. He stood glaring at the uneven candle, and his face became smooth and philosophical. And again Alessandro felt the emotions of the other, what seemed to him very excessive and puzzling emotions.

Then Guido smiled at Alessandro, wistfully:

"This is what I think of it: I wish I had not heard it."

And Alessandro smiled, too.

They were musicians; they were eunuchs; they understood one another.

It was raining by the time he reached the palazzo. He had hoped that Tonio would be waiting for him outside the church, but he was not. And as Alessandro entered the library off the Grand Salon, he saw than Beppo was still in a turmoil. He had poured out this humiliating story to Angelo, who listened to it all as if he were witnessing some outrage to the name Treschi.

"It's all Tonio's fault," Angelo said finally. "He should give up all this singing. Did you speak to the Signora? If you don't speak to the Signora, I will."

"It has nothing to do with Tonio," said Beppo. "Why, how was I to know that he was looking for castrati children? I had no idea he was searching for castrati children. He spoke to me about voices, exemplary voices. He said, 'Tell me where I might find . . .' Oh, this is terrible, terrible."

"It is also over," said Alessandro quietly.

He had just heard the front doors of the palazzo shut. He knew Carlo's step by this time perfectly.

"Tonio should be in this library now," said Angelo emphatically, "at his studies."

"But how was I to know this? Why, he said, tell me where I might find the finest voices! I said, Signore, you have come to a city where you can find the finest voices everywhere but if you . . . if you . . ."

"Are you going to speak to the Signora?" said Angelo looking up to Alessandro.

"And Tonio was magnificent, Alessandro, you know he was. . . ."

"Are you going to speak to the Signora?" Angelo banged his fist on the table.

"About what, speak to the Signora?"

Angelo had risen to his feet. It was Carlo who had spoken as he came into the room.

Alessandro made a quick gesture for discretion. He did not look at Carlo. He would not give this man an edge of authority over his younger brother, and softly now, he said, "Tonio was off with me in the piazza when he should have been studying here. It was my fault, Excellency, you will forgive me. I will see that it doesn't happen again."

As he'd expected, the master of the house was indifferent.

"But what is all this you were talking about?" he said, rousing his interest almost stubbornly.

"Oh, a hideous mistake, a stupid mistake," said Beppo, "and this man is now angry with me. He has insulted me. And he was so rude to the young master, what am I to say to him?"

This was too much for Alessandro. He threw up his hands and excused himself, as Beppo unwound the whole tale down to the very name of the hymn that Tonio had sung in the church, and how exquisitely he had performed it.

Carlo uttered a short laugh and turned towards the stairs.

Then suddenly he stopped. His hand was on the marble railing. He didn't move. He looked precisely like someone who has suddenly suffered a sharp pain in the side and cannot move without making it sharper.

And then very slowly he turned his head, gazing back at the old castrato.

The disgusted Angelo was already reading a book between his elbows. And the old eunuch was shaking his head.

Carlo took several steps to the door of the room.

"Tell me this again?" he said softly.

122

4

THE SKY WAS mother-of-pearl. For a long while there were no lights across the water and suddenly it seemed there were many, scattered among Moorish arches and barred windows, flickering from the torches hung to light gates, doorways. Tonio sat at the dining table looking through the forty some odd panes of glass that composed the nearest window, its sky-blue drapery tied back, its surface running with rain that sometimes glinted with the gold of a passing lantern. When that happened all beyond it went dark. But then the lantern would pass away, and the dim hulks of the other side of the water would reveal themselves again, the sky as luminous and pearlescent as ever.

He was making a little poem aloud with just a little music to it, something that said, darkness come early, darkness open up the doors and open up the streets so that I can go out of here. He was tired and full of shame, and if Ernestino and the others wouldn't brave this rain, he would go it alone, he would find some place to sing, some place where, anonymous and numbed by drink, he could sing until he had forgotten everything.

This afternoon he had left San Marco with a feeling of despair. All the many processions of his childhood had come back to him in that place, his father walking behind the Doge's canopy, the smell of incense, those endless, translucent waves of ethereal singing.

Then afterwards he had gone with his cousin Catrina to visit her daughter, Francesca, in the convent where she would live until she was his bride. And then home again, in the incessant rain, to be alone with Catrina.

They had not meant to make love, surely, this woman who was older than his mother, and he. But they had done it. The room was warm, full of firelight and perfume. And she had marveled at his skill, and the vigor with which he drove between her legs, her body lush and full as he had always

123

imagined it. Afterwards, he felt appalling shame, all the scaffolding of his life giving way under him.

"But why are you behaving so?" she had demanded. He must give up these nights out, was there ever a time when it was so important to be exemplary? A strange lecture, he remarked softly, from this bower of fragrant pillows. "How can his malice eat at you like this?" she insisted.

He had no answer. What could he say? Why didn't you warn me she was the girl! Why didn't anyone warn me?

But he could not speak, for there was a fear gathering in him, growing stronger with every passing day that was too terrible for him to articulate even to himself, let alone to another. He turned away from Catrina.

"All right, my troubador," she had whispered. "Sing while you can; young men have done a lot worse; we can put up with it for a little while; it's harmless for all it's absurdity." And then teasing him gently between the legs, she said: "God knows you haven't very long to enjoy that lovely soprano."

A voice in the empty church turned round by the golden walls came back to mock him.

And he had come home. Why? To hear it from Lena that his brother had sent Alessandro out of the house saying his services as tutor to Tonio were extraneous? Alessandro was gone. His mother was somewhere lost to him behind closed doors.

And now as he sat alone at the supper table where he had not dined in months, he did not even stir when he heard steps in this great hollow shadowy house, steps entering this room, when he heard those massive doors creak shut, first one pair of them and then another.

The light changed, did it not?

I cannot avoid him forever.

The sky was darkening. From where he sat he could see yet the farthest edge of the water. And he kept his eyes fixed there, even though two figures, it seemed, had approached him. Almost desperately he emptied the wine in his silver cup. And she is come, too, he thought. This is pure agony.

A hand came out to refill the wine.

"Leave us alone now," said his brother.

He was speaking to the servant who set the bottle down and was gone with just a dry shuffle on the stones. Something like the sound of a rat in a dusty passageway.

124

Tonio turned slowly to look at these two. Ah, yes, it is she, with him. The candles dazzled him. He raised the back of his hand to shield his eyes, and then he saw what he thought he had seen, her face reddish, swollen.

His brother seemed uncommonly raw as if some quarrel had brought him to the brink. And as he leaned over with his hands firmly placed on the table before Tonio, Tonio thought for the first time: I despise you! Yes, it is true now I despise you!

But there was no smile now. There was no pretense. The face was sharpened as if by some new perception.

Tonio lifted the silver goblet, felt the bit of stone that adorned it. He let his eyes shift slowly to the water again. To the sky's last gleam of silver.

"Tell him," said his brother.

Tonio looked up slowly.

His mother was staring at Carlo as if with deliberate outrage.

"Tell him! said Carlo again. And she turned to go out of the room, but Carlo, moving faster than she, had caught her by the wrist. "Tell him."

She shook her head. She was staring at Carlo as if she could not believe he was doing this to her.

Tonio rose slowly from the table, out of the glare of the candlelight to look more closely at her, at the way that her face was being slowly infused with anger.

"Tell him now before me!" Carlo roared.

But as if infected by that very rage, she cried out:

"I will do no such thing, not now, not ever." She commenced to tremble. Her face was crumpling like that of a small child. And suddenly grabbing her in both hands Carlo started to shake her.

Tonio didn't move. He knew that if he moved he could not control what would happen. And that his mother belonged to this man was now beyond doubt.

But Carlo had stopped.

Marianna stood with her hands over her ears. And then she looked up at Carlo again and said No with her lips, her face so twisted that she was almost unrecognizable.

It seemed that roar was rising out of Carlo again, that awful roar like that of a man bewailing a death he could never accept, and with the full force of his right hand he struck her.

She fell several steps backwards.

"Carlo, if you strike her again," Tonio said, "it will be resolved between us, forever."

It was the first time that Tonio had ever called him by name, but it was impossible to tell if Carlo realized it.

He was staring straight forward. He did not seem to hear Marianna crying. Her tremors were becoming more and more violent and suddenly she began to scream:

"I will not, I will not choose between you!"

"Tell him the truth before God and me now!" Carlo roared.

"Enough!" Tonio said. "Do not torture her. She is helpless as I am. What can she tell me that will make any difference? That you are her lover?"

Tonio looked at her. He could not bear to see her in this pain. It seemed infinitely greater than all those years and years of appalling loneliness.

He wished somehow he could let her know, silently, with his eyes, with the color of his voice, that he loved her. And that now he expected nothing more from her.

He looked away, and then again, he looked up at the man who had turned to him.

"It is no use," Tonio said. "Not for both of you can I go against my father."

"Your father?" Carlo whispered. "Your father!" He spat the words, and then he seemed on the verge of some hysteria.

"Look at me, Marc Antonio." He bore down on Tonio. "Look at me. I am your father!"

Tonio shut his eyes.

But the voice went on louder, thinner, on the edge of breaking:

"She was carrying you in her body when she came into this house, you are the child of my love for her! I am your father, and I stand here with my bastard son placed before me! Do you hear me? Does God hear me? You are my son and you have been placed before me. That is what she can and must tell you!"

He stopped, the voice strangled in his throat.

And as Tonio opened his eyes, he saw through the glimmer of his tears that Carlo's face was a mask of pain, and that Marianna stood beside him, putting up her frantic hands to cover his mouth. With a great shove, Carlo sent her backwards.

"He stole my wife from me," Carlo cried. "He stole my son from me, this house he stole from me, Venice he took, and my youth, and I tell you he shall not prevail any longer! Look at me, Tonio, look at me! Yield to me! Or so help me

126

God, I declare I cannot be held to account for what happens to you!"

Tonio shuddered.

It was as if these words were striking him physically, and yet they receded so fast, he could scarce remember them, their sound, their literal meaning. There was only a relentless, muted hammering.

And all around him in this room there seemed a sadness building and building. It was like a great cloud collecting its deadly momentum. It shrouded him. It shut them away, concealing them. And it left him alone here in this shadowy place, staring mutely at the blurred lights that made their slow passage on the invisible stream beyond those windows that was the water.

He had *known* it. He had known it when this man first took him in his arms, he had heard it pressing through his dreams, he had known it when his mother ran about that darkened room whispering, "Shut the doors, shut the doors," yes, he had known it.

Yet always, *always*, there had been the chance that it was not true, that it was but some groundless nightmare, some foul connection made more of imagination than real happening.

But it was true. And if it was, then *Andrea had known it also.*

It did not matter what happened now in this place. It did not matter if he turned to go, or what he said. It seemed he had no will, no purpose. It did not matter that somewhere someone had given a voice to this sadness. It was his mother weeping.

"You mark my words," Carlo whispered.

Dimly Carlo materialized again before him.

"Oh, what is this, your words?" Tonio sighed. My father, this man. This man! "Is this your threat of death?" Tonio whispered. He righted himself peering steadily forward. "Your first council to me and we two so briefly reconciled as father and son!"

"You mark my council!" Carlo cried. "Say you cannot marry. Say you will take Holy Orders. Say the doctors have found you ill formed, I do not care! But say it, and yield to me!"

"Those are lies," Tonio answered. "I cannot speak them." He was so weary. My father. The thought obliterated all reason, and somewhere far, far beyond his reach stood Andrea,

127

receding into chaos. And he knew the most bitter, the most terrible, terrible disappointment that he was not Andrea's son. And this man, frenzied, desperate, standing before him, imploring him.

"I was not born your bastard," Tonio struggled. It was such an agony to speak these words. "I was born Andrea's son under this roof and under the law. And I can do nothing to change that, though you spread your abominations from one end of the Veneto to the other. I am Marc Antonio Treschi, and Andrea has given me my charge, and I will not bear his curse from heaven, nor the curse of those around us who do not know the half of it!"

"You go against your father!" Carlo roared. "You bear my curse!"

"So be it, then!" Tonio's voice rose. It was the greatest struggle of his life to remain here, to continue it, to answer once and for all. "I cannot go against this house, this family, and the man who knew all of this and chose to plot the course for both of us!"

"Ah, such loyalty." Carlo seemed to sigh and to tremble, his lips drawn back in a smile. "No matter what your hatred for me, your will to destroy me, you would never go against this house!"

"I do not hate you!" Tonio declared.

And it seemed that Carlo, caught off guard by the edge of this cry, looked up in one desperate moment of feeling.

"And I have never hated *you*," he gasped as if just realizing it for the first time. "Marc Antonio," he said, and before Tonio could stop him, Carlo had taken him by both arms, and they were so close they might have embraced, they might have kissed.

The look on Carlo's face was astonishment and almost one of horror. "Marc Antonio," he said, his voice breaking, "I never hated you. . . ."

128

5

IT WAS RAINING. One of the last rains of the spring perhaps. Because it was so warm nobody much minded. The piazza was silver, and then a silvery blue in the rain, and from time to time the great stone floor seemed a solid sheet of shimmering water. Draped figures darted here and there across the five arches of San Marco. And the lights in the open coffee houses were smoky.

Guido was not quite as drunk as he wanted to be. He disliked the din and glare of this place and at the same time he felt safe in it. He had just received another installment of his allowance from Naples, and was wondering if he should leave for Verona and Padua. This city was magnificent, the only place he had encountered in his roamings that was all that men said it was. And yet it was too dense, too dark, too confining. Night after night he homed to the piazza merely to see that vast stretch of ground and sky and feel that he could breathe freely.

He watched the rain slant down under the arches of the arcade. A dark shape crowded the door, but then it passed into the room. And again there was the rain swept in by the wind so that he could almost feel it on his warm face and on the backs of his hands which were folded before him. He drained the glass. He shut his eyes.

Then he opened them abruptly, because someone was seated beside him.

He turned slowly, cautiously, and saw a man with a commonplace and brutal face, his beard so roughly shaved that it left a hide of bluish bristle.

"Has the maestro from Naples found what he was looking for?" asked the man under his breath.

Guido took his time before answering. He took a swallow of white wine. Then he followed it with a swallow of scalding hot coffee. He liked the coffee cutting through the softness created in him by the wine.

"I don't know you," he said, looking at the open door. "How is it you know me?"

129

"I have a pupil who will interest you. He wishes to be taken at once by you to Naples."

"Don't be so certain he will interest me," said Guido. "And who is he that he tells me to take him to Naples?"

"You'd be a fool not to be interested," said the man. He had drawn so close to Guido that Guido could feel his breath. And smell it also.

Guido's eyes turned mechanically to the side until he was staring at the man. "Come to the point," he said, "or get away from me."

The man made a little smile that disfigured his face. "Some eunuch you are," he muttered.

Guido's hand moved very slowly but obviously under his cape until he closed his fingers around the handle of his stiletto. And he smiled, having no real appreciation of how truly appalling were the contrasts in his face, the sensuous mouth, the flattened nose, and the eyes which alone might have been swimming and pretty.

"Listen to me," came the man's slow murmur. "And if you ever tell anyone what I have to say, it would be better for you if you had never set foot in this city." He glanced to the door; then he continued. "The boy is high-born. He wishes to make a great sacrifice for his voice. But there are those who might try to dissuade him. It must be done with delicacy and very quickly. And it is his wish to leave as soon as it is done, do you follow me? There is a town south of Venice called Flovigo. Go there tonight, to the hostelry. And the boy will come to you."

"What boy? Who?" Guido's eyes narrowed. "The parents must consent to this. The inquisitors of state would—"

"I am a Venetian." The man's smile never wavered. "And you are not a Venetian. You take the boy to Naples, that's enough."

"Tell me who this boy is now!" Guido's voice had the tone of a threat.

"You know him. You heard him this afternoon in San Marco. You've heard him with his vagabond singers in the streets."

"I don't believe you!" Guido whispered.

The man showed a leather purse to Guido. "Go to your inn," he said. "Prepare to leave immediately."

For a moment, Guido stood in the rain outside his door as if it might bring him back to his senses. He was thinking with portions of his mind he had not used in all his life; he felt the unusual exhilaration of cunning. Part of him said go at once and get any ship out of here that will take you. Another said what is going to happen will happen whether you are here to benefit from it or not. But what exactly is going to happen? He was startled when he felt a hand on his elbow. He had not even seen this person approaching. But through the thin chilling veil of rain, he could not even perceive this man's expression. All he felt was the hand on his arm causing him immediate pain as the voice whispered in his ear, "Maestro, come, now."

It was in the tavern that Tonio first caught sight of the three of them.

He was very drunk. He had been upstairs with Bettina, and coming down now into the smoky public room, he had slumped at a bench against the wall, unable to move farther. He must talk to Ernestino, explain to him that tonight he could not go with him or the others. These mingled horrors could find no voice. Such music had not yet been written.

And as he peered into this dingy gloom an odd thought came to him; he should have lost consciousness by this time. He had never before drunk so much and remained awake to witness his own disintegration.

Everything flickered that was this room, heavy bodies shifting under soot-darkened lamps, and the tankard descending in front of him.

He was about to drink when he saw the faces of those men, picked them out one by one, each it seemed at an angle so that it showed him the scrutiny of a single eye.

And in that moment when he linked the three of these men together in the recognition of who and what they were, he felt the stab of panic through the drunkenness which would have pushed him to despair.

Nothing changed in the room. He struggled to keep his eyes open. He even lifted the wine and drank it down without realizing what he was doing. And then he felt himself pitched forward glaring at one of these men as if in challenge. And then his head hit the wall in back.

A plan was struggling to find its form. He could not however reason it out. It involved determining how far he was from the Palazzo Lisani and which was the surest route. He lifted his hand as if attempting to grasp the threads that led

131

him through *calli* and canals, and then all of this vanished. He saw one of these men coming towards him.

He moved his lips in the form of words but in this din he heard nothing of what he said, which was "My brother is going to have me killed." He said this with wonder. Wonder that it was in fact happening and wonder that until this very moment he had not really believed it possible!

Carlo? Carlo who wanted so desperately that Tonio *understand*? This was incomprehensible. But it was happening! He had to get out of this place.

And this demon of a bravo had settled opposite him, his hulking shoulders obliterating the entire tavern as his immense face drew closer: "Come on home, Signore. . . ." he whispered. "Your brother must speak to you."

"Ooooh, no." Tonio shook his head.

He reached up to beckon for Bettina and he felt himself drawn up as if he were weightless, his feet tumbling over tangled limbs, until suddenly he was pulled into the *calle*. He gulped for air. The rain fell down in little slaps on his face. And attempting to stand, he slipped back against the damp wall.

But cautiously turning his head, he realized he was free.

He burst into a run.

He could feel pain in his feet pushing through numbness, but he knew that he was moving fast, dashing in fact, towards the mist which was the canal. And for one instant he pitched forward to see the lanterns at the landing before he was drawn back, struggling, into the dark. He had his stiletto out and dug it into something soft. Then it was clattering on the ground. And his mouth was being wrenched open while he was held.

He convulsed his body against this with all his strength. Then gagging, struggling for breath as a wedge was forced between his teeth, he felt the first draft of wine.

Once he threw it back up with a convulsion that encircled his ribs with pain. But then it came again. He felt if he couldn't close his mouth or get loose he would go mad. Or drown.

Guido was not asleep. He was in that state which is more restful, from time to time, than sleep, because it can be savored. Lying on his back in this small monastic room in the tiny town of Flovigo, he was staring at the wooden shuttered window which he had opened to the spring rain.

The sky was lightening. It was perhaps an hour before dawn. And though ordinarily he would have been cold (he was fully dressed but the wind brought the rain into the room) he was not cold. Rather the air made an icing on his skin which didn't penetrate to the bone.

And for several hours now he had been thinking, and not thinking at the same time. In fact, never in his life had his mind seemed so empty and yet so full.

He knew things. But he did not think about them, though over and over again they passed through his mind.

He knew, for example, that in Venice the spies of the inquisitors of state were everywhere; they knew who ate meat on Friday and who beat his wife. And the officers of the inquisitors of state could arrest anyone anytime, secretly, and take him to a prison where he might be executed by poison or strangulation or drowning in the night.

He knew that the Treschi were a powerful family. He knew that Tonio was the favored son.

He knew that the laws of many a place in Italy forbade the castration of children unless there was some medical reason given for it, unless there was the consent of the parents and of the boy.

He knew that with the poor this meant absolutely nothing.

He knew that with the rich the operation was unheard of.

He knew that in this remote village, he was still in the Venetian State.

He wanted to get out of the Venetian State. He understood the corruption of southern Italy. He did not understand the corruption of this place.

And he knew too that every eunuch he'd ever known had been cut as a small boy, almost as soon as the testicles gained their first weight. But he did not know the reason for this, whether it was wise for the voice, or wise for just getting the operation done.

He knew that Tonio Treschi was fifteen. He knew that the voice generally drops three years after that. That the voice he had heard in the church was still unchanged, utterly pure.

He knew all of this. And he did not think about it. Nor did he think about the future, what might happen to him in an hour or in a day.

Then from time to time, he stopped knowing all this. And drifted into remembering—again without analysis—the first time he had heard Tonio Treschi's voice.

133

* * *

It had been a misty night, and he had been lying on his bed, just as he was now in this room in Flovigo, fully dressed with the window open. The worst cold of winter was past and it would soon be mild enough to travel without so much discomfort.

He would regret leaving Venice, which had both enchanted and repelled him. He had been awed by its prosperous merchant class, and by its secretive and elaborate government. Day after day he had wandered about the Broglio and the piazza watching all the spectacle and ceremony attached to the Offices of State. And the dilettanti here, those rich musicians who were as skilled and talented as any he had ever known, had been uncommonly gracious to him.

But it was time to leave here. Time to go home to Naples with the two boys he had left waiting for him in Florence. He could not at this time bear to think about them; they were neither of them exceptional. And he feared perhaps some reproach from his superiors.

But he didn't care. He was too weary from all this. It would be good to be teaching again, no matter what the odds. He wanted to be in Naples, in his rooms at the conservatorio where he had lived all his life.

Then he had heard this singing.

At first it seemed no more than the usual street entertainment. It was good, it was mildly interesting. But he heard plenty of it in Naples.

But then a soprano had risen above the rest, startling him with its exquisite tone and its remarkable agility.

He had gotten out of bed and gone to the window.

The walls rising before him shut out the sky. And below, circling the torches and lanterns along the canal, he saw a mist curling, rising. It was like something alive, this mist following as it did the path of water, and seeking out the light with tentacles. He did not like the sight of it.

He suddenly felt trapped in this labyrinthine place and eager for the open air, the spectacle of stars sliding down the curve of the sky into the Bay of Naples.

But this voice, this voice that seemed to be rising with the mist was causing him pain! And it was the first time in his life that he had encountered any voice he could not identify. Was this man, woman, or child?

Its coloratura was so light and flexible that it might be a woman. But no. It had that sharp, indefinable edge that was masculine. And it was young, very young. But who would have bothered to train a mere boy like this? Who would have lavished on him so many secrets?

The voice was perfectly on the note, weaving in and out of the violins that accompanied it, rising above them, dipping down, embellishing effortlessly.

And it did not have the sound of brass in it, this voice: it suggested wood rather than brass, the slightly darkened sound of a violin rather than the flatter sound of the trumpet.

It was a castrato, it had to be!

He was caught for a moment between the urge to go and seek it, and the desire merely to listen to it. That one so obviously young could sing with this feeling was simply out of the question. And yet he was hearing it. It was arresting him, transporting him, this voice with its acrobatic flexibility colored by so much sadness.

Sadness, that was it. He pulled on his boots, slipped on his heavy cape, and went in search of the singer.

What he found astonished him, but not entirely.

Following the little band of serenaders into a tavern he soon saw that this was a boy who was almost a man, a tall, lithe, angelic child with a man's bearing. He was rich: he wore the finest Venetian lace at his throat, and on his fingers were garnets set in heavily worked silver. And those around him, full of affection and doting, called him "Excellency."

I am alive, Tonio thought, I am in a room. People were moving, talking. And if he was alive, he could stay alive. And he'd been right, Carlo could not do this to him, not Carlo. With an enormous effort he managed to open his eyes. The darkness came rolling back over him, but he opened them again and saw the shadows slipping up the walls and across the low ceiling as these people talked.

That voice he knew, it was the bravo, Giovanni, who was forever at Carlo's door, and he was saying something in a low, threatening voice.

Why hadn't they killed him already? What was going on? He did not dare move until he was ready to make his move, and through the slits of his eyes he could see this gaunt, dirty man holding some sort of valise in his hands who was saying:

"I will not do it! The boy's too old."

"He is not too old." The bravo, Giovanni, was losing patience. "Do as you're told, and do it well."

What were they talking about? Do what? The bravo named Alonso was at his left side. There was a door behind the hollow-cheeked one who said now:

"I will have no part of this," and commenced backing towards that door. "I'm not a butcher, I'm a surgeon. . . ."

But Giovanni had taken him roughly and shoved him forward until his eyes fixed on Tonio. "Noooo . . ."

Tonio rose up, just as Alonso's hands came down to hold him, his momentum heaving him forward so that he knocked the gaunt man out of his path. The whole room blazed before him as he struggled, kicking out with both feet as he was lifted off the floor. He saw the valise fly open, he saw the knives dropping out of it, he heard that man mumbling some frantic prayer. Then he had a man's face in his hand and he was gouging it while his right fist pounded into the man's middle, knocking him back. Things broke around him, there was the splitting of wood, and suddenly he swung round free, falling because he hadn't expected it. The rain was coming down on him, he'd gotten away, he was running!

Moist earth gave under his feet, rocks cut through his boots, and it seemed just for an instant he might win, the night would swallow him, conceal him. But even then he heard them pounding down on him.

He was caught up again, he was growling, screaming. They were carrying him back into that room, a man's weight crushing him down on the pallet.

He sank his teeth into muscle and hair, and convulsed with all his strength, as he felt his legs forced apart, hearing the cloth rip even before the cold air touched his nakedness.

"NOOOO!" he was roaring between clenched teeth, and then the roar broke loose of all words, inhuman, immense, blinding him, deafening him.

And with the first cut of the knife he knew the battle was lost and he knew just what they were doing to him.

Guido saw that the sky over the little town of Flovigo was now growing a pale yellow. He lay as if dead, watching the rain catch just enough of this light to become a visible veil over the field that tilted away from his window.

There was a knock at the door. He was not prepared for the excitement with which he rose to answer it.

There stood that man who had spoken to him in the coffee house in Venice. He shouldered his way into the room and,

136

without saying a word, opened a leather packet that contained several documents.

Turning from right to left, he made a short exasperated sound to see there was no candle lit and, drawing near the wet window, examined each of the papers with the scrutiny of someone who can neither read nor write. Then he gave them to Guido along with another packet.

Guido recognized the packet immediately. It contained all his letters of introduction from Naples and he had not even known it was missing. He was furious.

But he turned his attention to the documents. All in Latin and signed by Marc Antonio Treschi, they declared his intention to submit to castration for the preservation of his voice, absolving anyone and everyone for complicity in his decision. The physician was unnamed for his own protection.

And in the last, addressed to his family, of which the paper in Guido's hands was only a copy, was spelled out clearly the boy's intention to enroll at the Conservatorio San Angelo in Naples under the Maestro Guido Maffeo.

Guido stared at this in stupefaction.

"But I have not instigated this!" Guido said.

The bravo only smiled. "There's a carriage waiting to take you south of here, and money enough for a change of horse and driver whenever you wish, to Naples," he said. "And this is the boy's purse. He's rich, as I told you. But he won't see another zecchino until he is enrolled at your conservatorio."

"The family must know I had nothing to do with this!" Guido stammered. "The Venetian government must know I had nothing to do with it."

The bravo uttered a short laugh. "Who is going to believe that, Maestro?"

Guido turned his back on the man suddenly. He glared at the documents.

The bravo drew up beside him like the bad angel.

"Maestro," he said, "if I were you, I would not wait until this boy awakens. The opium given him was very strong. I would take him now and get away from here. I would get as far from the border of the Venetian State as fast as possible. And, Maestro, take care of the boy. He is the only one who can exonerate you."

Guido stepped into the small house where Tonio slept. He saw the blood streaking Tonio's face, the mouth and throat livid with bruises. Then he saw that Tonio's hands and feet had been bound with the coarsest hemp rope. His face appeared lifeless.

Taking a step backwards, Guido let out a long low moan. His eyes rolled up in his head, and his lips pulled back from his teeth. The moaning went on as if he were powerless to stop it. Then it caught in his throat as if in a wave of nausea. He stared at the blood-stained mattress. He stared at the knives that lay in the straw and the dirt of the floor like so much debris, and shuddering all over, he felt the moans rising out of him again.

When at last he was quiet, he was alone in this room with Tonio, the bravo had gone, and the door stood open to a town so still that it might have been uninhabited.

He drew near the bed. The boy so resembled a corpse that for a long moment Guido could not bring himself to place his hand before Tonio's open mouth to feel his faint breathing.

But the boy was alive. The skin was moist and feverish.

Then Guido laid back the torn cloth and looked at the mutilation.

The scrotal sac had been gashed, its contents cut out, the wound crudely cauterized. But it was a small wound, the operation had been done in its safest manner, and there was no swelling. In time the sac would wither to nothing.

But as his fingers drew back from this, Guido's body convulsed with yet another and obvious discovery.

He stared at the boy's organ as it lay in repose and saw that it had gained its first inches of manhood.

A sharp terror seized him, even in the midst of the blatant horror of this room, the blood-smeared bruised boy, the leering bravo who hovered beyond the open doorway.

Guido did not understand the human body. He did not understand the mysteries that had defeated him when his own voice was lost on the very threshold of greatness. He knew only that mingled with this monstrous violence, there was perhaps another appalling injustice.

And slowly, he touched the sleeping boy's white face, probing for the slightest roughness of a man's beard.

But he found none.

Nor was there hair on the chest. And shutting his eyes, Guido invoked with faultless memory the sound of that high clear voice he had heard so magnificently amplified under the domes of San Marco.

It was clean, it was perfect.

And yet here lay the first evidence of manhood.

Behind him, the bravo stirred in the door. He filled it with his massive shoulders so the light died and nothing could be seen of the features of his face, as his voice came again low, full of menace.

"Take him to Naples, Maestro," he said. "Teach him to sing. Tell him if he doesn't stay there, he'll starve, as he will get nothing from his family. And teach him furthermore to give thanks that he left with his life, which he will surely lose should he ever return to the Veneto."

6

A T THE SAME HOUR in Venice, Carlo Treschi was being roused from his bed by a frantic Catrina Lisani, who had in her hands a long and elaborate letter from Tonio in which he confessed his intention to submit himself to the knife for the sake of his voice, and enroll himself in the Neapolitan Conservatorio San Angelo.

Messengers were at once dispatched to the Offices of State, and by noon every government spy in Venice was searching for Tonio Treschi.

Ernestino and his band of singers were arrested.

Angelo, Beppo, and Alessandro were summoned for questioning.

By sunset, news was out in all the quarters of Venice of the "sacrifice" made by the vagabond patrician for his voice, it was the talk of the town, and one physician after another was hauled before the Supreme Tribunal for questioning.

Meantime, no less than seven different patrician men and women confessed to having wined and dined the young maestro from San Angelo in Naples who had asked repeatedly about the patrician street singer.

And Beppo, in a flood of tears, finally confessed to having brought the man together with Tonio at San Marco. Beppo was at once imprisoned.

Carlo, with heartfelt tears and a raw eloquence, blamed

139

himself for this appalling turn of events because he had not curbed his brother's unwise and extreme addiction to music. He had not understood the danger in it. He had even heard of this meeting between Tonio and the maestro from Naples and foolishly discounted it.

He appeared inconsolable as he murmured these accusations against himself before his interrogators, his face swollen from weeping, his hands trembling.

And all of this was very geniune, because at this point he was beginning to wonder if all this was going to work and he was absolutely terrified.

Meanwhile, Marianna Treschi attempted to throw herself from a window of the palazzo into the canal, and had to be restrained by the servants.

And little Bettina, the tavern girl, wept as she described how neither food nor drink, nor sleep, nor the pleasure of women, could keep Tonio from singing.

By midnight, neither the maestro from Naples nor Tonio had been found, and police were in all the small towns around Venice, dragging from bed any physician who might have ever been connected with the castration of singers.

Ernestino had been freed, now to tell everyone how concerned Tonio had been over the imminent loss of his voice, and the coffee houses and taverns were alive with talk of nothing else, including the boy's talent, his beauty, his recklessness.

In the early hours of the morning when Senator Lisani finally came into his house, his wife, Catrina, was hysterical.

"Has everyone in this city gone mad to believe this!" she screamed. "Why haven't you arrested Carlo and charged him with the murder of his brother! Why is Carlo still living!"

"Signora . . ." Her husband sank wearily into his chair. "This is the eighteenth century and we are not the Borgias. There is no evidence here of murder, nor any crime, for that matter."

Catrina began to scream uncontrollably. She finally managed to articulate that if Tonio wasn't found alive and well by noon tomorrow, Carlo was a dead man. She would see to that herself immediately.

"Signora," her husband said again, "it is true that in all likelihood the boy is dead or gelded. But if you take it upon your head to relieve Carlo Treschi of his life for this, then you take upon yourself a responsibility for all eternity which no one among my fellow statesmen will share with you: the responsibility for the extinction of the House of Treschi."

PART III

1

THEY REACHED FERRARA before nightfall, and Tonio had not regained consciousness. Jolted by the carriage as it sped over the fertile plain, he opened his eyes from time to time but they appeared to see nothing.

Guido carried him at once to a bed in a small inn on the outskirts of the city. He bound his hands. And felt of his forehead.

A stand of shivering green poplars screened the small, deep-cut windows of this place. And the rain commenced to fall before sunset.

Guido got a bottle of wine. He set one candle on the stand by Tonio's head, and seating himself across from the foot of the bed, he waited.

Some time during the early evening, he dozed.

And when he opened his eyes, he did not know why he had awakened. For a moment, he thought he was in Venice. Then everything that had happened came back to him.

He squinted in the gloom at the tiny aureole of the candle. And then he let out a gasp.

Tonio Treschi was seated against the wall, his back to the corner, his eyes two glittering slits in the darkness. How long he had been awake, Guido couldn't guess.

But he felt that he was in the presence of danger. He said in Italian, Drink some wine. But the boy did not answer him. Guido saw then that the boy's hands were untied, and that the cloth sash he had used to tie them lay on the floor.

The boy's eyes never moved from Guido for an instant. They were shot with red, narrow, a deep purple bruise distorting the expression into utter malevolence.

Guido drank a swallow from the pint cup at his side. Then he drew the documents out of his valise and laid them on the rough white blanket before Tonio.

The eyes moved slowly down to gaze at the Latin lettering, but the boy did not read the documents, he merely looked at them.

142

Then he looked up at Guido.

And he moved so fast in rising off the bed that he had thrown Guido back against the wall before Guido even realized what had happened. His hands were on Guido's throat, and it took all of Guido's strength to throw him backwards. He gave him a forceful blow to the head. And the boy, obviously groggy and unable to defend himself, collapsed, resting on his hands, his body trembling, his face flushed as he shut his eyes.

He did not resist when Guido slammed him back against the wall. His lids opened so slowly that it was as if he were again losing consciousness.

Guido gripped his shoulders with both hands. He was looking into the eyes of the devil; or into the eyes of madness.

"Listen to me," he said under his breath. "I had nothing to do with what was done to you. The physician who cut you is most likely dead. Those who killed him would have killed me had I not agreed to take you out of the Veneto. They would have killed you also. They as much as said so."

The boy's mouth was working as though he were chewing the inside of it, gathering the saliva into it.

"I don't know who these men were. Do you know?" Guido asked.

The boy shot such a spray of spit into his face that Guido let him go and stood with his hands over his eyes for an instant.

When he looked at his hands he saw they were stained with blood.

Guido stepped backwards. He settled into the flat wooden chair in which he'd been sitting before, and felt the back of his head rest against the plaster.

The boy's eyes did not change, but his body which appeared almost luminous in the dark had commenced a violent trembling. Finally it was a shuddering.

When Guido rose to put the blanket up around him, Tonio drew back hissing something in the Venetian dialect which sounded like Do not touch me.

Guido shrank back again and it seemed for one solid hour he sat still watching this boy who never once altered his expression. Nothing changed. Nothing happened. And then finally the boy's weakness and sickness overcame him, and he slid down against the mattress.

He could not resist when Guido brought the cover up over him. Nor did it seem he could protest when Guido lifted his head and told him to drink the wine given him.

When he lay back down, his eyes were like two pieces of glass, and they moved only a little now and then over the ceiling as Guido talked to him.

Guido took his time. It was silent in the inn, and the stars appeared only now and then, brilliant and tiny beyond the shifting shadows of the poplars. And in a low, measured voice, Guido described the man who had approached him in Venice, the men who had taken him all but forceably to Flovigo. Then he described the papers that bore Tonio's signature.

Without comment, he explained carefully how he himself had been implicated in the matter, and how these men had played upon this to force him to take Tonio out of the Venetian State. And lastly he described to Tonio the carriage which was his, and the purse, and that if Tonio so wished Guido would take him to the Conservatorio San Angelo.

This was Tonio's choice, he explained. But then he paused, and finally in a half murmur confided the bravo's admission that Tonio would receive no further support if he did not go to the conservatorio and stay there.

"Nevertheless you are free to go with me or do as you wish," Guido said. The purse was heavy.

At this the boy turned his head and shut his eyes, and the gesture seemed such an eloquent plea for silence that Guido said nothing after that.

He stood against the wall, his arms folded, until he heard the boy's breath become even.

All madness had drained from the face; it lay softened and white against the pillow. The mouth was again a boy's mouth, perfectly molded and yet supple. But it was the faint light playing on the exquisite bones of the face that revealed its greatest beauty.

The light touched the line of the jaw, the high cheekbones, the smooth plane of the forehead.

Guido drew closer. And for a long time he looked at the boy's lean limbs, released in sleep, and the one hand that lay half closed on top of the cover.

The forehead was warm now. The boy did not even stir when he touched it.

And slipping out the door, Guido went down into the open field beneath the window.

The moon was covered with clouds. The town itself showed no lights to the sky from this vantage point.

And walking through high damp grass, Guido soon found a dry spot where he sank down to lie on his back and pick out those few starts that were now and again visible.

A terrible despair was creeping over Guido.

It was coming like the cold of winter, and he knew it from the past by the shivering that always accompanied it, and the peculiar taste in his mouth that was like sickness.

Only he was not sick. He was whole, and empty, and all of his life was simply meaningless. It had never been more than a mesh of absurd accidents, and there was in it nothing noble and nothing good and nothing that gave comfort.

It mattered not one whit that men from the Venetian State might kill him. It seemed to have no more meaning than anything else that had ever happened to Guido. And without wanting it, he felt himself drawn back to that room in Naples where long ago he had tried to end his life by opening his veins as he drank himself into unconsciousness.

He could remember everything about that room. The painted walls, the border of flowers along the ceiling. And he could remember an obsession in his last moments with the sea, and how pleasantly he had imagined it.

His eyes grew moist. He felt the tears on the side of his face, and above the heavens seemed milky and full of an unwelcome white light that he would have covered over with blessed darkness.

He was hearing now, without even wanting it either, Tonio Treschi's voice rising out of the tangled Venetian alleyways, and he felt a mingling of two places: that room in Naples where he had been so unspeakably happy when he'd thought he would die, and Venice where he had listened to that sublime singing.

And he knew suddenly what underlay this wild, fathomless darkness of soul that threatened to engulf him.

"If this boy does not survive, if he does not somehow overcome the violence done to him, then I am destroyed with him."

It was not very long after that he rose from the bed of grass and walked back to the inn. But he could not go up to the

145

room as yet, and seating himself on a stone step, his head on his arms, he wept silently.

Years had passed since he had shed tears, or so it seemed. Surely years since he had let them flow so copiously.

And what stopped him finally was that he could hear his own crying.

He lifted his face in wonder.

The sky was lighter, the first strands of blue threading its endless field of cloud, and bowing his head, he wiped his tears on his sleeve before rising.

But when he turned and looked up the stone steps that clung so narrowly to the wall, he saw at the top the slender and somewhat fragile figure of Tonio.

The boy was looking down at him. And his soft black eyes never left Guido as Guido came up to him.

"You are that maestro whom I met, are you not?" Tonio asked softly. "The maestro for whom I sang in San Marco?"

Guido nodded. He was studying the white face, the moist lips, the eyes which still had the gloss of illness.

He could hardly endure the sight of this battered and broken innocence. He offered up a silent prayer that this boy would turn away from him.

"And was it for me," Tonio asked, "that you were weeping?"

For a moment Guido didn't speak. He felt his habitual flashing anger; it colored his face and twisted the edges of his mouth, and then suddenly it came to him as clearly as if it had been spoken into his ear that yes, it was the truth, it was for this boy he had been weeping.

But he swallowed and said nothing. He was staring at Tonio in sullen wonder.

And then the boy's face which a moment before had been blank and almost angelic assumed a bitter expression that was as brittle as it was frightening. Malice slowly sharpened it, giving a menacing glint to the eyes that caused Guido to look away slowly.

"Well, we must get out of this place," the boy whispered, "we must get on with our journey. I have business which must be attended to."

Guido watched him turn and go into the room. All of the documents were laid out on the table. And the boy gathered them up now and returned them to the Maestro.

"Who were the men who did this?" Guido demanded suddenly.

Tonio was putting on his cloak. He looked up as if already in deep thought.

"Fools," he answered, "at the command of a coward."

2

TONIO SPOKE SCARCELY a single syllable until they reached that great bustling capital of the north, Bologna.

If he felt discomfort, he concealed it, and when Guido urged him to see a physician, as there was always danger of infection, he turned his head resolutely away.

It seemed his face was permanently transformed. It was elongated, the line of the mouth hardened. And the eyes retained that feverish glitter though they were wide and seemingly blind to the unfolding spring of the Italian countryside.

They seemed not to see the fountains, palaces, and teeming streets of this great city either.

But after insisting upon the extravagant purchase of a jewel-encrusted sword, a stiletto, and two pearl-handled pistols, Tonio also bought himself a new suit of clothes and a cloak to go with it. Then he asked Guido politely (he had been polite in everything so far, though never actually obedient or compliant) to find for him a lawyer who had to do with the affairs of musicians.

This was no problem in Bologna. Her cafés swarmed with singers and musicians from all over Europe come here expressly to meet with the agents and impresarios who might find them positions in the coming season. And after a few inquiries they were soon in the offices of a competent lawyer.

Tonio commenced to dictate a letter to the Supreme Tribunal in Venice.

He had accomplished his sacrifice for the sake of his voice, he said, and it was imperative that no one at Venice be blamed for his course of action.

Exonerating his former teachers and all those who had encouraged him in the love of music, he went on then to exonerate Guido Maffeo and all those connected with the Conservatorio San Angelo, who had not known of his action before it was taken.

But it was foremost in his mind that no blame for this attach to his brother Carlo.

"As this man is now sole surviving heir of our late father yet sound of body and able to marry, it is imperative that he must be absolved from all responsibility for my actions so that he may attend to his duties to future wife and children," Tonio said.

And then he signed the letter. The lawyer, never batting an eyelash at its strange contents, witnessed it, and so did Guido.

A copy was then sent to a woman named Catrina Lisani, with the request that all Tonio's possessions be forwarded to Naples immediately. And would a small dowry be paid at once to a Bettina Sanfredo, serving girl in her father's café on San Marco, so she might be properly married?

After this, Tonio retired to the monastery at which they were lodged, and fell down on his bed exhausted.

Often during the night, after that, Guido would wake to find Tonio on the edge of the room, fully dressed and waiting for the morning. And sometimes before midnight, he stirred in his sleep, even cried out, but then he would wake and his face would become as wooden and unreadable as ever.

It was impossible to know the extent of the pain which was sealed inside, though at times it seemed Guido could feel that pain emanating from the boy's still frame as it rested listlessly in the corner of the jolting carriage. At times, Guido wanted to speak, but he could not, and that same despair touched him as it had that night in Ferrara. And yet it humiliated him that this boy had heard him weeping and asked him so openly if the tears had been on his account. And Guido completely forgot that he had never given Tonio any answer.

In Florence, when they at last met those two boys Guido had left there for the return to Naples, Tonio was visibly disturbed by their presence in the carriage. And he seemed unable to prevent himself from staring at them.

Yet in Siena, he bought both children new shoes and capes and ordered them sweets at table. They were shy, obedient boys, one nine years of age, the other ten, and neither dared speak nor move unless told to do so. Yet Paolo, the younger of the two, had a humorous turn, it was clear, and could not now and then resist a broad smile that always forced Tonio's eyes abruptly away from him. Once when Guido dozed, he awoke to see this boy had nestled in beside Tonio. It was raining then. And lightning broke over the soft, deep green hills, and with each crackle of thunder the boy drew nearer so that at last, without looking at him, Tonio slipped his arm about him. A film descended over Tonio's eyes, and as his fingers clasped this child's leg to hold him firm, it seemed suddenly an uncontrollable emotion might well up in him. But then he shut his eyes, his head to one side as if his neck were broken. And the carriage jolted on under the warm spring rain towards the Eternal City.

But while Tonio seemed blind to all the somber splendor of Rome, he had by the time they reached the Porto del Populo turned his obsessive attention away from the two boys and fixed it upon Guido. His eyes, meantime, had lost nothing of their quiet malevolence. Yet mercilessly they fixed on Guido, his walk, his manner of sitting, even the scant dark hair on the backs of his hands. And in the rooms they shared at night, Tonio watched boldly as Guido removed his clothes, staring at Guido's long and seemingly powerful arms, his heavy chest, his large shoulders.

Guido bore all this in silence.

Yet it began to wear on him, and why precisely he was not certain. His body actually meant little to him. He had performed on the stage of the conservatorio since he was a small boy, costuming, painting, and otherwise draping and disguising himself so that his own peculiarities were rather routine to him. He knew, for example, his heavy frame made him look well in male roles and that his immense eyes if too lavishly painted appeared supernatural.

But nudity, scrutiny, and defects here and there meant nothing to him.

And yet this boy's stare was so bold and so relentless that it commenced to irritate him. One evening when he could endure it no longer, he put down his spoon and looked back at Tonio.

Tonio's stare was so hostile and so constant that for a moment Guido thought, This boy has been driven to madness. Then he realized that Tonio was so intent on looking *at* him that he did not even realize Guido was returning the look. It

149

was as if Guido were inanimate. When Tonio's eyes did shift, they did so in their own time, only to fix on Guido's throat. Or was it the white linen tie there? Guido had no idea. Now Tonio was staring directly at his hands, and then again right into his eyes as if Guido were a painting.

And the disregard of Guido was so total, so blatant, that Guido felt his temper rising. Guido had, in fact, a terrible temper, the worst in the conservatorio, as any of his students could have testified. And now for the first time it was loosening itself against this boy, and it collected to itself a thousand small resentments.

After all, he had been doing the bidding of this child as if he were nothing more than Tonio's lackey.

His inveterate hatred of any and all aristocracy began to surface, and he realized suddenly that he was confusing everything.

And that Tonio had laid down his napkin and risen from the table.

They were on this night, as they had been all along, provided with the most lavish accomodations the town had to offer—in this case, a wealthy monastery which let large and exquisitely furnished chambers to gentlemen who could afford it.

And Tonio had left their private dining room where the boys still scraped their plates, and had gone out into a narrow, high-walled garden.

For a long time, Guido sat thinking. He was thinking still as he led the boys to bed, and saw them under the covers.

But stepping out into the night, he still did not understand his own anger. He only knew that he resented this boy, resented his disregarding gaze, his eternal silence. He attempted to remind himself of the boy's inevitable pain, his inevitable anguish. But he could not think of this. All along he had prevented himself from thinking of it, because it was simply too terrible to think about in the first place.

And every time his mind had forced him to ask what is happening to this boy now, what does he think, what does he feel, some stubborn little voice in Guido said, Ah, but you have always been a eunuch, you can never know, and all of this with the mock tone of superiority.

Whatever the reason, he felt rage when he stepped into the garden, and saw in the moonlight an immense reclining statue

150

over a shell-shaped pool, and the slender, very straight figure of Tonio Treschi standing before it.

Rome is full of such statues, statues that are three or four times the size of a normal man. It seems they grow in every nook and cranny of the town, against walls, over gates, presiding over an infinite variety of fountains. And though one would think nothing of them in a church or great palazzo, they can sometimes be violently disturbing in a small place, when one comes on them suddenly.

Because at such a moment, one can be overcome with a sense of the grotesque. These statues are giants in these narrow circumstances, and yet they are so lifelike that it seems they might commence suddenly to breathe and then reach out with their immense hands to crush those around them.

The details of the statues impress themselves. One sees the white muscles moving under the marble, the veins on the backs of hands, the indentation on the toenail. But the whole is horrible to look at.

And Guido felt this jarring sensation when he stepped out of the cloister and into this narrow space behind Tonio.

A god reclined against the wall, its enormous bearded face hung forward. And through its fingers, open to the sky, water ran, trickling down to the moonlit surface of the pool beneath it.

Tonio Treschi was staring at its naked chest and at the broad hips that melted into a loose drapery exposing a powerfully muscled leg upon which the giant's full weight rested.

Guido looked away from this monstrous god; he saw the moonlight shattered in the surface of the rippling water. And then he saw out of the corner of his eye that the boy had turned to him. He felt those relentless and greedy eyes moving over him.

"Why do you stare at me!" he demanded suddenly, and before he could stop himself his hand had closed on the loose cloth at Tonio's shoulder.

He could feel the boy's astonishment. The moon revealed his crumpling expression, his mouth slack and then silently, stupidly working.

The hard, bright angles of his young face dissolved in helplessness, in total remorse. And it seemed he would stammer some negation if he could; he started, stopped, and left off, his head shaking.

And Guido too was helpless. He reached out again as if he

151

would touch the boy, but his hand hung in the air, and he watched in awful fear as the boy seemed all over to weaken.

The boy had looked down. He had lifted his hands and he was staring into the open palms of one and then the other. He reached out as if trying to capture something in the open air, or merely to look at his own arms. Yes, he was looking at his own arms, and suddenly there was a rattle in his throat, a groan, half strangled.

Turning to Guido he drew his breath in gasps as if he were a dumb beast that could not speak, his eyes growing wider and wider and more desperate.

And suddenly Guido understood everything.

Yet the boy still gasped, still held up his hands, staring at them, slapping them suddenly to his chest, and that half-strangled groan became a guttural cry growing louder and louder.

Guido reached out, took him in his arms, and held his stiff form with all his strength until he felt it suddenly go limp and silent against him.

The boy who lay so still against his shoulder before being led off silently to bed had uttered one word in Guido's ear. It was "monster."

3

IT WAS THE FIRST DAY of May when they entered Naples, and even the long drive through the green wheat fields did not prepare them for the spectacle of the great sprawling city itself, drenched in sunlight and cascading downhill in a blaze of pastel walls and burgeoning roof gardens to hold the panorama of the clear blue bay in its embrace, the harbor crowded with white sails, Vesuvius sending up its plume of smoke into the cloudless sky above it.

As the carriage rocked and struggled along, the tireless swarm that was the city's population surrounded it, as if brought to life by the warmth that hung fragrant in the air, carriages whipping to and fro, donkeys blocking the path, vendors crying out their wares, or coming right to the windows to offer ices, snow water, fresh melon.

The driver cracked the whip, the horses straining uphill, and with each turn of the crooked street another vista of land and sea opened magically before them.

This was Eden. Guido had suddenly not the slightest doubt of it, and he was unprepared for the sense of well-being that flooded him.

One could not look on this place with its profusion of leaf and flower, this jagged shore, and that ominous mountain, and not feel joy to the marrow of one's being.

He could see the excitement of the little boys, especially Paolo, the younger one, who leapt right into Tonio's lap, thrusting his shoulders out of the window. But Tonio had also completely forgotten himself. He was straining for a view of Vesuvius at every angle.

"But it's breathing smoke," he whispered.

"It's breathing smoke!" echoed Paolo.

"Yes," Guido answered. "It has been doing that off and on for a long time. And don't pay it so much attention. We never know when it will decide to really show off."

Tonio's lips moved as if saying some private prayer.

As the horses clopped into the stable yard, Tonio was the first to jump down, with Paolo in his arms. And letting the boy go, he followed him immediately into the courtyard. His eyes moved up the four walls that enclosed it, rising as they did over a four-cornered cloister of Roman arches, the whole covered almost entirely with an unruly fluttering green vine. It was alive with small white trumpet-shaped blossoms and the song of thousands of bees.

The din of instruments streamed out of the open doors. Tiny faces appeared at the glass. And the fountain, its worn cherubs stained by time as they clung to their open cornucopia, let loose a generous and muting spray that caught the sun.

Immediately, Maestro Cavalla came out of his office doors and embraced Guido.

A widower whose sons were long gone to foreign courts, the Maestro had a special love for Guido. And Guido had always known it, and he felt a sudden warm rush of feeling for the man now. The Maestro seemed older, was that inevitable? His hair had gone entirely white.

He sent the two little boys off with a perfunctory greeting,

153

and then his eyes settled on the elegant and remote figure of the Venetian who was wandering among the orange trees that crowded the cloister, their blossoms already turned to tiny budding fruit.

"You must tell me at once what is going on here," said the Maestro under his breath. But when he looked at Guido again, he gave way immediately to another warm embrace, holding his old pupil for a moment as if he were listening to some distant sound.

Guido was at once steamy. "Surely you got my letter from Bologna."

"Yes, and daily I am visited by men from the Venetian Embassy. They have all but accused me of gelding this princeling under this roof, and threaten to obtain the right to search us."

"Well, then, send for them," Guido growled. But he was afraid.

"Why have you gone to such lengths for this boy?" the Maestro asked patiently.

"When you hear his voice, you will know," Guido answered.

The Maestro smiled. "Well, I see you are your old self, nothing has changed there."

And after a moment's hesitation, he consented that, for the time being at least, Tonio might be given a private attic room.

Tonio proceeded up the stairs slowly. He could not stop himself from glancing back at the crowded practice rooms whose doors stood open revealing some hundred or more boys all at work upon various instruments. Cellos, double basses, flutes, and trumpets gave off their roar amid the general din, while here and there at least a dozen children pounded upon harpsichords.

And in the halls themselves the boys sat at their lessons at various benches, one even practicing his violin in a corner of the stairway, another having made the landing his desk where he bowed his head as Tonio and Guido passed, hardly missing a stroke of the pen on his staff as he harmonized a composition.

The stairs themselves were worn concave from so many feet over so many centuries, and there was about everything a barren, scrubbed look which Guido had never before noticed.

He could not guess what Tonio was thinking, and he did

154

not know that in all his life, this boy had never even for one day been subject to the rules or discipline of any institution.

Tonio knew nothing of children either. And he was staring at them as though they were quite an unusual phenomenon.

He paused, stranded, at the door of the long dormitory in which Guido had spent his nights as a boy, and turned willingly enough to be led down an attic corridor to the little slope-roofed room that would be his own chamber.

All within was neat and ready for some special occupant, a castrato who had in his last years of residency here distinguished himself. In fact, Guido himself had once slept in this chamber.

The shutters opening inward from the dormer window were painted with green leaves and soft overblown roses, while a similar border of flowers ran along the tops of the walls.

And bright enameled decorations covered the desk and chair, the dark red cabinet with its gilded edges waiting for Tonio's possessions.

The boy glanced back and forth, and then suddenly he saw through the open window the distant bluish peak of the mountain again, and he moved almost mindlessly towards it.

For an eternity he stood gazing out at that plume of smoke that rose so straight to the faint disintegrating clouds and then finally he turned again to Guido. His eyes were filled with quiet wonder. And they moved again over the furnishings of this little place without the slightest censure or complaint. It was as if, for an instant, he liked all that he saw. As if the weight of his pain were something any human being could carry, day in day out, hour by hour, without some final alleviation. He turned again to the mountain.

"Would you like to climb Vesuvius?" Guido asked.

Tonio turned with such a bright face that Guido was startled. It was the boy again enhanced by the softest natural radiance.

"We'll go up some day if you like," Guido said.

And for the first time Tonio smiled at him.

But Guido was stricken to see the light go out of the boy's face when he explained to him that he must meet with the Venetian representatives.

"I don't wish to meet with them," Tonio whispered.

"This can't be helped," Guido answered.

As they assembled in the large ground floor office of Maestro Cavalla, Guido understood Tonio's reticence.

These two Venetians, unknown to the boy obviously, entered the room with all the pomp one associated with the last century. Or rather, in their great wigs and frock coats, they resembled galleons at full sail proceeding into a narrow harbor.

It was with undisguised contempt that they examined Tonio. Their questions were rapid, hostile.

There was a slight quiver to Tonio's eyes; he had gone dead white, and the hands clasped behind his back were working against each other. Yes, he replied, he had decided upon this course of action on his own, no, no one from this conservatorio had influenced him, yes, the operation had been performed, no, he would *not* submit to an examination, and no, he could not reveal the name of the physician. Again, no one of this conservatorio had had any knowledge of his plans. . . .

And here Maestro Cavalla interrupted, furious, his Venetian dialect as rapid and sure as Tonio's, to state that this conservatorio was made of musicians, not surgeons. Boys were never operated on here! "We have nothing to do with it."

The Venetians sneered at this.

And Guido almost sneered at it himself, but he managed to conceal his feelings.

The interrogation was obviously over. And now an uneasy silence fell on all present and it seemed that the elder of these two Venetians was wrestling with some latent emotion.

Finally he cleared his throat, and in a low, almost rough voice, he asked:

"Marc Antonio, is there nothing more to this!"

Tonio was caught off guard. His lips whitened as he pressed them together, and then obviously unable to speak, he shook his head, his eyes moving off to one side where they widened slightly as if deliberately blurring their focus.

"Marc Antonio, you did this of your own will!" The man took another step forward.

"Signore," Tonio said in a voice that was hardly recognizable, "it is an irrevocable decision. Is it your purpose to make me regret it?"

The man flinched as if what he had to say to this were better unsaid. And then he lifted a small scroll in his right hand which had hung all this time at his side. And in a lackluster voice, he said quickly, bitterly:

"Marc Antonio, I fought with your father in the Levant. I

156

stood on the deck of his ship at Piraeus. It gives me no pleasure to tell you what you must already know, that you have turned your back on your father, on your family, and on your homeland. You are henceforth and forever banished from Venice. As for the rest, your family commits you to this conservatorio, in which you must remain, or you will receive no further support from them.''

The Maestro was beside himself. He was furious. He stared stupefied as the doors closed.

Then he seated himself at his desk, gathered up Tonio's papers into a black leather folio cover, and shoved them to the side angrily.

Guido gestured for a moment's patience.

Tonio had not moved, and when he did finally turn to face the Maestro, his face had a studied look of sheer emptiness. Only the red glimmer of his eyes betrayed him.

But Maestro Cavalla was too insulted, too outraged, too perfectly angry to sense anything around him.

He regarded the Venetians as utterly ridiculous and was muttering as much under his breath, with the sudden outburst that their lofty statements meant next to nothing. "Banishment! A child!" he stammered.

He emptied Tonio's purse on the desk, noted the contents, dropped the whole into the top drawer which he locked as a matter of course, and then drew himself up to address Tonio.

"You are now a pupil of this institution," he commenced, "and due to your advanced age I have consented that you shall for the time being have your own private quarters on the attic floor away from the rest of the castrati. But you shall at once put on the black tunic with the red sash that is worn by all castrati children. In this conservatorio we rise two hours before dawn, and classes are dismissed at eight o'clock in the evening. You will have an hour's recreation after the noon meal as well as two hours of siesta. As soon as your voice is tested and—"

"But I do not intend to use my voice," Tonio said quietly.

"What?" The Maestro stopped.

"I do not intend to study singing," Tonio said.

"What?"

"If you will look at those papers again you will see that I intend to study music, but nowhere does it say that I must

157

study singing. . . ." Tonio's face had hardened again, though his voice was quavering.

"Maestro, allow me to talk to this boy . . ." Guido started.

"Nor do I intend to wear any costume," Tonio continued, "that advertises that I am a . . . a castrato."

"What is the meaning of this!" The Maestro rose, his knuckles white as he pressed them to the desk.

"I shall study music . . . keyboard, string, compositon, whatever you put me to study, but I will not study singing!" Tonio said. "I will not now, nor will I ever sing! And I will not be costumed like a capon."

"This is madness!" The Maestro turned on Guido. "Is there no one from that marshland in the north who is not out of his senses! Why in the name of God did you consent to have yourself castrated! Get the physician!" he said to Guido.

"Maestro, the boy's been cut, please allow me to reason with him."

"Reason with him!" The Maestro glared at Tonio. "You are under my care and my authority," he said, and reaching out for the neatly folded black uniform that lay on the desk beside him, he thrust it at Tonio. "And you will put on the official dress of a castrato."

"I will never, I will obey in all else, but I will not sing and I will never wear that costume."

"Maestro, dismiss him, please," Guido said.

As soon as Tonio had left, the Maestro slumped back in his chair.

"What is happening here?" he demanded. "I have two hundred students under this roof, I do not intend to—"

"Maestro, let the boy enroll in the general program, and allow me please to reason with him."

The Maestro said nothing for a while. Then when his temper had cooled, he asked, "You have heard this boy sing?"

"Yes," Guido answered. "More than once."

"And what sort of a voice is it?"

Guido was considering. "When you are alone, and you are reading a new score, and you shut your eyes for a moment to hear it sung perfectly . . . it is that voice which you hear in your head."

The Maestro absorbed this. Then he nodded. "All right, reason with him. And if that fails, I shall not be ordered around by a Venetian patrician."

158

THIS WAS A NIGHTMARE, yet it was impossible to wake up or get out. It went on and on, and every time he opened his eyes he was still there.

Two hours before dawn, the first bell sounded. He sat upright as if jerked by a chain, sweating, staring out into the black sky with its wealth of stars drifting slowly down into the sea, and for a moment—for a moment—there was that ineffable beauty like a hand laid on his head.

It was not possible that this was happening to him, that he was in this low-ceilinged room five hundred miles from Venice, that this had been *done* to him.

He rose, washed his face, staggering into the corridor, and with the other thirty castrati filing out of the dormitory descended the stone stairway.

Two hundred pupils moved like termites through these corridors, somewhere a little child was crying—little whimpering, despairing cries—and all found without a word their place at harpsichords, cellos, study tables.

The house came alive with shrill sounds, each fragment of melody caught up in the general dissonance. Doors slammed. He struggled to listen to the Maestro, his vision blurred, the man's words ripping fast through concepts he could barely grasp, the other students dipping their pens; he plunged into the exercise on the barest faith that it might yield itself to him as he scribbled.

And seated finally at the keyboard, he played until his back ached, the day's pressures and miseries alleviated for these few sweet hours when he was doing what he knew how to do, and had always known how to do, and just for this little while he was on a par with those boys his age who, if they had not been here since early childhood, had been admitted late only on account of their immense skill and talent.

"You do not even know how to hold a violin? You have never played a violin?" He struggled to draw the bow across the strings without that dissonant screech. His shoulder ached so badly, he hunched forward from time to time, no matter how sharp the tongues that ate at him, the switch coming down on the music stand before him.

If he could only for one minute fall into the music, feel it uplift him, but this is not part of the nightmare; in this nightmare music is noise, music is penance, music has become two hammers at the temples. He felt the sharp cut of the switch across the back of his hand and stared at the welt, the feeling reverberating throughout his body, the welt seeming to have a life of its own as it rose.

Then the breakfast table. Bowls of steaming hot food that nauseated him. All had turned to sand on his tongue as if the slightest pleasure must be denied him. He refused to sit with the other castrati; he asked politely, softly, for another place.

"You will sit *there*." He stepped back in the face of the advancing figure, the fist nudging his shoulder, the peremptory "You will sit there."

He felt his face burning, burning. It was impossible for flesh to contain this fire. All the eyes of this silent room dusting him gently—"the Venetian prince," he understood that much of their Neapolitan dialect—everyone knowing exactly what had been done to him, *that he was one of them*, these bowed heads, these mutilated bodies, these *things* that were not and would never be men.

"Put on the red sash!"

"I will not!"

This is not happening. None of it is happening. He wanted to rise suddenly and go out of doors, into the garden, but even that simple freedom of motion was forbidden here, silence locking each boy to the bench in his proper place, though beside him there came that contemptuous whisper, "Why don't you take the sash and wad it into your breeches, Signore, then no one will know!" He turned suddenly. Who had spoken those words? Those mocking and devious smiles gave way suddenly to blank faces.

Guido Maffeo's door opened. He stepped inside. Blessed silence, if even for two hours he had to stare at that cold unfeeling face, those vicious eyes! The gelded master of the gelded. And worst of all, he *knew*, he *knew* exactly what had been done, that this is nightmare. He knows behind that insensible mask of anger.

"Why do you stare at me?"

Why do you think I stare at you, I stare at you because I

am a monster and you are a monster and I want to see what it is I will become!

Why didn't he strike Tonio? What was he waiting for? What lay behind that fixed expression of cruelty, all about the man being so much a mixture of fascination and allure, why is it that I cannot stop looking at him, though I cannot endure looking at him? Once when he was a child, Tonio's mother had slapped him over and over again, stop crying, stop crying, what in God's name do you want of me, stop! Looking at Guido Maffeo, he thought, I understand this for the first time. I cannot endure your questioning of me, leave me alone!

In this room for now, please, God, leave me alone.

"Sit quietly then. Watch. And listen."

He brings this white-faced eunuch monster into the room. I do not even want to hear this, this is torture. And he commences with his instructions, he is no fool, this one, he is better perhaps than all the rest put together, but he will never, never teach me.

And at eight o'clock when the last bell sounded, going up the stairs so tired he could scarce lift one foot in front of the other, he fell down, down, down, into the nightmares within the nightmare. Please, just this one night, let me not dream. I am so tired. I cannot do battle in my own sleep, I will go mad.

There is someone outside the door again. He rose on his elbow. Then snatched it open so that the boy, surprised, could not get away. And there are two of them. They press forward as if they would come into this room. "Get away from me," he snarled.

"We only want to see the Venetian prince who is too good to wear the red sash."

Laughter, laughter, laughter.

"I am warning you, back away."

"Oh, come now, you are not very friendly, it is not very gracious of you to let us stand at the door. . . ."

"I am warning you. . . ."

"Oooh? And how is that?"

Both of them were staring at the stiletto. The taller one, already monstrous with those thin dangling arms, laughed nervously. "Does the Maestro know you have that?"

He shoved hard against this one with his left hand suddenly, and the two of them, off balance, scuttle out of the room with

161

that same eerie laughter. Even the sound of the speaking voice is not natural, it has a shrillness to it if you do not control it, pitch it down. So there is that too. He can envision a time, suddenly, when he will not even speak aloud.

He pulled at the heavy frame of the bed. At first it didn't move, but then, as if ripped free, it slid on the bare floor, so that he might shove it up against the door, and only then fall down again into sleep.

But the sky was red suddenly, he'd seen it from the corner of his eye, and imagination told him there had been a faint sound. It seemed he heard movement throughout the building, and then advancing to the window, he saw it was the mountain in the distance on fire.

There are always two nightmares:
    The first.
    You are running in that *calle* and you get away. When the hands go to draw you back, you throw yourself forward and hit the quais, but then you roll into the water and you are safe. You are swimming like a rat, silently, swiftly, through the water as they run helplessly on the bank. You are terrified. But you get away! You are throwing everything into trunks and packing cases, and rushing down the steps out of the palazzo, out of Venice, you have gotten away.

And then that awful realization, that slow dawning that cracks through the darkness of the dream, that you are asleep, this is not real, it is the other that is real, you are dreaming!

This has really happened, and oh, how you played into their hands! Singing, singing, singing, it is almost possible for a moment to hear your voice echoing up those damp walls, amplified beyond your wildest expectations, almost possible to hear it without deafening rage.

    The second dream:
    They are still there. You've still got them between your legs because they have grown back. Or is it that they did not cut them away properly? A little part of it was left and from that the whole has grown back. They have made a terrible error. On any account *they* are still there, and a physician is explaining all this to you, matter of fact, yes, it does happen in these cases where it was not cleanly done, yes, they have completely come back, examine them for yourself if you like.

He sat in the dark. He did not remember having left the warm cleft of the bed, but he is at the window, feeling the salt breeze from the sea as it stirs the heat which is trapped beneath this low-slung ceiling. It horrified him suddenly that he could touch the roof over his head, but then he collapsed with his arms folded on the sill, the tumbling-down lights of the city a blur. Listen. Listen. There was some distant rhythm as if from a tavern. Or street singers here, wandering these low slopes. He opened his mouth as if gulping for air, and closed his eyes.

Dreams again.

It is summer and a heat like this hangs in all the great empty rooms of the palazzo. He counts the panes in the windows, there are some forty panes to a window, and he is lying naked with his mother, she having stripped off everything above her waist so that her lovely breasts are exposed, the heat tracing her damp tresses against her forehead and her cheek. She stirs, she turns over towards him, the down mattress giving with a groan, and she lifts him on his side, and draws him in so that he feels the very definite heat of her breasts against his naked back, her lips raising the hairs on the nape of his neck.

Ooooooh, God, nooooooo, you are dreaming!

The bell sounds.

It begins again.

"Put on the red sash!"

"I will not!"

"Do you want to be whipped for this?"

I do not want anything.

Why is there never a dream like this:—that I have him in my hands, that he cannot get away from me, and that I may do to him what he has done to me, *done to me*—where is that dream?

"What is it you hope to gain by this?" Guido Maffeo was walking back and forth. "Talk to me, Tonio! Speak to me. You have admitted yourself to this place, I did not admit you! What is it you must accomplish by this, this silence, this. . . ."

I cannot bear this. I cannot stand still for this, these faces puffed with anger. *I beg you not to whip him, if you will only leave this to me. But I've left it to you and he has stubbornly refused*. . . .

"Put it on."

"I will not."

163

The first lash, this is a pain you must defend yourself against, but you cannot defend yourself, and the second, this is more than anyone can endure, and the third, and the fourth, and fifth, do not think about it, think of anything else, anywhere else, anything else, anything else.

"Put it on."

"I will not."

"Tell me, since you are so learned, my fine little Venetian, what becomes of a eunuch who does not sing?"

They are all in a row at the front gate. They move in double ranks, hands behind their backs, the red sashes dividing the soft black fabric of the tunic perfectly in half, black ribbon at the nape of the neck, all with the right foot out as the gates open. Is it possible that I will pass through this gate with them, that I will walk in this procession with these, these eunuchs, these capons, these gelded monsters?

This is more miserable than being stripped naked, and yet I am moving, I am putting one foot in front of the other, and it seems the very world is made of human beings, walls of people pressing in to get a closer look, and their voices rising, mingling, for the first time they are so beautiful and so sure, these voices rising up, up, in the open air, the very advertisement of it, and everyone who looks at us knows, knows, red sash or no, they know exactly what I am.

This is unendurable, yet it is happening. It is like descriptions of those barbarous executions, you cannot imagine the thoughts or feelings of that one at the center of it, led forward into the crowd, his hands bound so that he cannot even shield his face. All that you are belongs to this world around you, and yet you stare forward as if this were not happening to you, you pick out the clouds overhead moving so swiftly on the sea breeze, you gaze up at the facade of the church.

Who are these southern Italians, who are they but the world, the entire world!

Leave this place, leave it.

"If you leave here"—that vicious Guido Maffeo, that dark one who knows all about it—"where will you go?"

"I will *not*."

"Do you want to be expelled!"

And this time as the lashes come, try to think *about* the pain, instead of against it, because there is not one single aspect of life, past, present, or future, that does not tear your reason from you, to think on it. So think about the pain. This

164

pain after all has its limits. You can chart its passage through your body. It has a beginning, middle, end. Imagine if it had a color. This first cut of the lash is what, red? Red, spreading into a brilliant yellow. And this one again, red, red, no yellow, and then white, white, white, white.

"I beg you, Maestro, leave him to me."

"You will sing or you will be expelled from this school. . . ."

"Where will you go . . ."

That's it. *Where will you go?* Why have you incarcerated yourself in this palazzo of torture chambers, why do you not leave this place? Because you are a monster and this is a school for monsters, and if you leave here, then you will be completely, completely alone! Alone with this!

Don't weep in front of these strangers. Swallow it down. Don't weep in front of these strangers! Cry to heaven, cry to heaven, cry to heaven.

5

WHAT IS IT you are attempting to accomplish? Do you even know *yourself* what it is you want to do!"

Guido strode back and forth, his face convulsed with anger. He locked the door of his practice room and put the key in his belt.

"Why did you stab this boy?"

"I did not stab him. He is merely gashed a little, he will live!"

"Yes, this time he will live!"

"He forced his way into my room. He was tormenting me!"

"And what of the next time? Do you know the Maestro has taken away your sword and your stiletto and those pistols you bought, but that won't stop this, will it?"

"Not if I am tormented, not if I am surrounded by tormentors, no, it will not stop!"

"Don't you understand? You cannot continue like this. You will be put out of the conservatorio, if you continue like this! Lorenzo might have died from the wound you gave him!''

"Leave me alone."

"Oh, so that brings tears to your eyes, does it? Say it again, I want to hear it.''

"Leave me alone!"

"I will not leave you alone, I will never leave you alone, not until you sing! Do you think I don't understand what it is that prevents you? Do you think I don't know what has happened to you! Good God, are you mad not to realize I risked my life to bring you here when it would have been better for me if I had gotten clear of you and your tormentors? Yet I took you out of the Veneto, I brought you here, where the emissaries of your government could have sent their bravos to tear me limb from limb out there in the street if they chose.''

"And why did you do it? Did I ask you to do it! What do you want of me, what have you always wanted of me!''

Guido struck him. Before he could stop himself, he had slapped him so forcefully that Tonio staggered backwards, reaching for his head as if he could not see. Guido struck him again. And then with both hands he grabbed hold of him and swung his head against the wall.

Tonio let out a short, guttural gasp. And again Guido's hand caught him, twisting his head around on his neck.

Guio drew back away from him, his right hand clutching at his left wrist as if he meant to prevent himself from striking Tonio again. He stood with his back to Tonio, leaning over slightly as if trying to close into himself.

Loathing himself, in silence, Tonio could not prevent the tears from flowing, and finally with a slow resignation he withdrew his handkerchief and wiped them roughly away.

"All right, then," came Guido's voice, barely audible over his shoulder. "Sit there. Again. And watch."

The afternoon sun was hot on the stone floor, and on the wall, and moving the bench to where he might rest in the sun, Tonio sat back and shut his eyes.

The first pupil was little Paolo, whose strong voice filled the room like a bright golden bell. He ran up and down the arpeggios with ease, and swelling the notes he infected them with what seemed to be almost joy.

Tonio opened his eyes to see the back of the boy's brown

head. He was drifting into sleep as he listened, and he felt some vague surprise at Guido's admonitions, and the keen grasp of what the boy had done wrong. Or was it wrong? Guido was saying, I can hear your breath, I can see it, now go through it again more slowly, but do not let out your breath and this time . . . this time . : . this time . . . the little voice rose and fell, those long poignant notes. . . .

And when Tonio awoke again, it was another child, older, this was the castrato voice, wasn't it, just a shade richer or perhaps harder than that of a boy. Guido was angry. He banged the window shut. The boy was actually gone, and Tonio was rubbing his eyes. Had the air become cool? The sun was gone, but it was so caressingly warm in this place, and all along the sill of this deep first-story window there fluttered the white flowers of that never-ending vine.

He stood up, his back suddenly shot with pain. What was Guido doing at the window? He could not even see Guido's head, only the hunch of his shoulders, and some vague movement in the garden beyond, children running, crying out.

Then Guido rose up and it seemed a great sigh rose with him as if it came from all of his heavy limbs, his massive shoulders, his shaggy head.

He turned to Tonio, his face dark against the brightness framed by the arch of the cloister where the sun still lingered at a different angle on the orange trees.

"If you do not change," he began, "the Maestro di Cappella will dismiss you within one week." The voice was so low and so raw that Tonio could not have said that it was Guido's voice, even as it went on. "I cannot prevent it. I have done everything that I can do."

Tonio stared in vague astonishment. He saw those voluble features that had so often seemed the perfect expression of anger softened into some terrible defeat that he could not understand. He wanted to ask, But why does it matter to you, why must you care for me? Why did you care in Ferrara? Why do you care now? He felt helpless as he had felt that night in Rome in the little monastery garden when this man had so furiously demanded, "Why do you stare at me?"

He shook his head, he tried to speak, but he could not. He wanted to argue that he had studied all else given to him, that he had obeyed rules that were crushing and relentless, why,

167

why. . . . But he knew why. They demanded only that he be what he was! And they would settle for nothing else.

"Maestro!" he whispered. The words seemed to dry in his throat. "Don't ask this of me. It is *my* voice, and I cannot give it up to you. It is not yours, no matter how long and far you traveled to bring it back with you, no matter what you endured in Venice to bring it back here for your own purposes! It is mine, and I cannot sing. I cannot! Don't you understand, what you ask of me is impossible!

"I will never sing again, not for you, not for me, not for anyone!"

It was dark in the room, though outside the cloister the sky was an even purple over the topmost gables of the house. Shadows hung down the four storeys of the building into the garden itself, where only here and there a shape distinguished itself, boughs heavy with oranges, and those lilies flickering in the dark, like waxen candles. And here and there, behind the many-paned windows was the glimmer of candles. And from recesses everywhere there came the late night sounds of the better musicians, those more pounding, constant melodies issuing from instruments on all floors.

It was not cacophony. It was just a great hum, as if this building were alive and humming, and Tonio felt the strangest sense of peace.

Was it possible that he was so weary of anger and bitterness he had let it slip away for a while? He had said, just give me this moment alone? He did not think of Venice, he did not think of Carlo, he did not pull and jerk at all the recesses of his mind where these thoughts lingered. Rather his mind was just a series of empty rooms.

And he felt this peace in this place which would have been so beautiful to him if only he could feel this for it all of the time.

Yes, just for the moment, let go.

Imagine, if you will, that life is still livable, that life is even—well, good. And that if you wanted to, you could, perhaps, approach that instrument that is still lying open, and that seated there, your fingers on the keys, you could, if you wanted to, sing. You could sing of sadness, and you could sing of pain, unspeakable pain, but you could sing. You could do anything that you wanted, really, because all that prevents it has fallen away like scales off a body that is really

168

human, and has been by some inhuman injustice rendered monstrous but is now free to return to itself.

He lay with his eyes open, on the narrow bench where sometimes perhaps Guido himself slept in between his arduous sessions, and he thought, yes, imagine all this for as long as you can.

The sky deepened. The garden changed. The orange tree beyond the arch, once full with shadow, had now lost its shape. Nothing could be seen of the fountain, nothing of the white lilies. And those lights in the windows across the yard had the only clarity now, so many beacons in the dark.

He lay still, wondering that he was being allowed to stay here, wondering that he had been allowed to linger in this empty room and fall into such deep and empty sleep.

And it occurred to him gradually that perhaps with the glass shut and the door closed, he might just go to that harpsichord and lay his hands on it, and he might. . . . But no, if he pushed this too far, he would lose all of it. And again he closed his eyes.

The very thought of his voice was unendurable to him. It was unendurable to him to think even for an instant of those nights roaming through the *calli* of Venice when, so in love with the sound of singing, he had played right into his brother's hands. And if he did not leave all this, he would be thinking of it again in that obsessive, relentless way, wondering what it was now they said of him, if anyone, anyone, believed that he had done this to himself as the lie had been told.

But that was not it. It was that if he let that voice out of him, if he let it go, it could no longer be the voice of the boy who had sung with such exuberance, it would be the voice of this creature now that would never change. The thought of it was too much; it was like giving in to them, and it was entering into the very nightmare role they had written for him as if this life were an opera, and they had given him this hideous part.

It was shame, shame that he felt at the mere sound of it in his head. Might as well tear open one's clothes and let them stare at the scars there, that withered empty . . .

He sucked in his breath and stopped. He was sitting up.

But when he heard the door open, now, he put his hands up to receive his bent head.

He knew that it was Guido who had come in, but he did

not know why he knew, and he felt the tug of the real world at him again, ready to pick him up.

He raised his eyes, resigned to surrender himself once more, and he saw that it was the Maestro di Cappella, Signore Cavalla, who was standing in front of him with Tonio's sword outstretched in both hands. "Take it," he whispered.

Tonio did not understand. He saw then the stiletto on the desk, and his pistols, and the purse which had been taken by the Maestro when he first came.

The man's face was ashen. Its anger was gone. And in the place of it was some awful emotion which Tonio could not identify. He did not understand.

"There is no reason for you to remain longer in this place," the Maestro said. "I have written to your family at Venice that they must make other arrangements. But you need not remain here any longer. You must get out."

He stopped. Even in the shadows, Tonio could see that his jaw was trembling. But this was not anger. "Yes. Your trunks have arrived. Your carriage is in the stable yard. You must go."

Tonio said nothing. He did not even take the sword.

"This is Maestro Guido's decision, then?" he asked.

The Maestro stepped to one side and laid the sword on the bed. Righting himself, he looked down at Tonio for a long moment.

"I would like . . . to speak to him," Tonio said.

"No."

"I cannot leave without speaking to him!"

"No."

"But surely you cannot forbid me. . . ."

"I can forbid you anything as long as you are under this roof!" said the Maestro. "Now leave this place, and take with you the sorrow you have brought! Go."

Tonio stared in confusion as the Maestro left the room.

He stood still.

And then buckling on the sword, arming himself again with his pistols and his stiletto, he gathered up the purse and slowly opened the door.

The corridor before the front entrance of the conservatorio was empty. The Maestro's office gaped, a dark cavern with an odd look of neglect about it because it was invariably shut up.

And there seemed no sounds now in the building. In fact

the silence was remarkable, and even the long practice room which always housed a few boys at this hour was perfectly still.

Tonio walked the length of the corridor and looked down the hallway which extended to the back of the building where lights burned beyond a door.

He thought that he saw the silhouette of the Maestro di Cappella, and then that figure commenced to come towards him with slow, rhythmic steps. It was shrouded in shadow. And there was an eerie deliberation to its approach. He watched it with some vague uncomfortable curiosity until again he and this man were standing face to face.

"Do you wish to see the results of your stubbornness? Do you wish to look with your own eyes?"

The man's hand closed around his wrist and jerked him forward. Tonio resisted, but he was yanked again.

"Where are you taking me?" he demanded. "For what?"

Silence.

He was walking fast, ignoring the pain in his wrist, his eyes fixed on the profile of the Maestro's face.

"Let go of me!" he said when they had all but reached the final door. But the Maestro gave him a furious pull and thrust him into this lighted room.

For a moment he could see nothing. He lifted his hand to shield himself from the glare of several lights. And then he saw a row of beds and an enormous crucifix hanging on the wall. There were cabinets by each bed. The floor was bare. And the smell of sickness hung over this long room, occupied as it was by two boys at one end, both of whom appeared to be asleep.

And there in the bed to the far left lay another figure, large and heavy under the coverlet, the face perfectly motionless as if in death.

Tonio could not move. The Maestro di Cappella gave him a sharp blow between the shoulders. Still he didn't move, not until he was dragged forward and made to stand over the foot of the bed.

It was Guido.

His hair was slicked away from his face as if very wet and the face itself was, even in this dim light, not the color of a living man.

Tonio opened his mouth to speak, but then he pressed his lips together, and he found himself trembling with the lightest

171

feeling in his head. It grew lighter and lighter. It was as if he were losing all his bodily weight and would suddenly be lifted right out of this room, as if on the air. He tried to speak again. He could feel his mouth opening, he could feel it making the shape of a word. And before him the vision of this deathlike figure wavered as beyond a rain-drenched glass.

There were faces all around it, faces of those young instructors who had pushed him and pulled him through all the instruction in which he'd sought over and over to conceal himself and they were staring at him with mute accusation, and suddenly he heard a terrible moaning, an inhuman moaning that he realized was coming from himself.

"Maestro," he stammered. Bile had come up in his mouth.

Then before his eyes some small miracle revealed itself. The figure in the bed was not dead. The eyes had movement, and there was the smallest heave of breath.

He realized that he was standing over it, and if he wanted to he could touch the Maestro's face. No one was going to prevent it. No one was going to protect the Maestro, and again he spoke that one word.

The eyelids fell back and those immense brown eyes stared blindly up at him. And then slowly, they closed.

Then rough hands took hold of Tonio. They forced him down the length of the infirmary and into the hall. The Maestro di Cappella was cursing him.

"It was the fishermen who saw him, saw him under the moon, swimming out to the open sea, and if they had not seen him, if there had been no moon. . . ."

The man's eyes glittered, his heavy jaw trembling.

"This child I reared as if he were my own, with a voice like the angels he could sing, and twice now from the very maw of death I've taken him back. Once when he lost that voice and nothing could give it back to him, and now again, on your account!"

He forced Tonio against the door to the cloister, and held him there, peering through the dark as if he must see Tonio's face.

"Do you think I don't know what was done to you! Do you think I have not seen it again and again?

"But, oh, it is high tragedy that it was done to *you*, a Venetian prince! Rich, handsome, on the verge of manhood with all of life before you as if it were but a series of amusements you could pluck if you wanted like fruit from the very trees!

"Oh, tragedy, tragedy!" He spit the words. "And what was it for him? And for all of those others here? Were they but ordinary monsters, severed in childhood, from that which was not worth having to begin with? Is that how it goes?

"And what were you, what was it you stood to become? A strutting peacock on the Broglio of that vain and imperious city which is rotten to its very core? A government of wigs and robes parading back and forth before its own mirrors, drunk on its own reflection, while beyond its tiny orbit the world . . . yes, the world . . . sighs and heaves and passes by.

"Well, what would you think, my proud elegant young prince, if I told you I care not one whit for your lost kingdom, for your blind and bloated nobility, for your saturnine men and painted whores. I have lain between those thighs, I have drunk my fill at that masked ball you have made of life itself, and I tell you it is not worth the dust at our feet.

"All my life I have known such idlers, arrogant, corrupt, full of nothing but vainglorious protection of the right to lives of utter worthlessness, the supreme privilege of doing nothing of any significance from the cradle to the grave.

"But your voice! Ah, your voice, your voice which has become the nightly incubus of my beloved Guido and has driven him mad, that is another matter, your voice! Because had you but half the talent he described to me, but half the holy fire, you could have made dwarfs and monsters of ordinary men! London, Prague, Vienna, Dresden, Warsaw, you give the cities to me, was there not in some forgotten corner of your stinking city a world globe? Did you not know the size of Europe, had you never been told?

"And in all those capitals you could have brought them to their knees, thousands upon thousands would have heard you, carrying your name out of the opera houses and the churches into the very streets. They would have said it like a prayer from one end of the continent to the other, as they speak of rulers, or heroes, of the immortals.

"That is what your voice could have been, had you but let it rise out of the ruin of what you were, had you but forged it out of all your suffering and all your pain to give back to God that which He had given you!

"But you are of that ancient ilk that recognizes no other aristocracy save itself, the gilded maggots feeding on the corpse of the Venetian State, brave champions of the supreme

173

privilege of doing nothing, nothing, nothing! And so you forfeit that one strength with which you could have bested any natural man!

"Well, I will not suffer you under my roof any longer. I have no pity for you now. I cannot help you. You are but a freak of nature without its destined gift, and there is nothing lower! Leave this place, go out of it. You have means to find a habitat for your misery somewhere else."

6

THE MOUNTAIN was talking again.

Its distant rumble rolled over the moonlit slopes, a faint and shapeless and horrible sound that seemed to rise out of the earth itself everywhere: a great sigh seeping from cracks and crannies in these ancient winding streets as if any moment the ground would commence to buckle and shake as it had so often in the past and bring down with it these hovels and palaces which for some reason or other, unknown to man, had survived all earlier holocausts.

Balconies and rooftops everywhere were crowded with dimly lit excited faces, turned to the lightning and smoke against the wide open sky, so brilliantly lit by this full moon that it seemed broad daylight as Tonio descended the hill, his feet leading him blindly into the wide piazzas and avenues of the lower city.

His back was straight; he walked slowly, gracefully, his heavy silk-lined cape over his shoulder, his right hand resting on the hilt of his sword, as if he knew in fact where he might go, what he might do, what might become of him.

But pain had numbed him. It had like a great blast of icy wind frozen his skin so that he was aware of every dimension of his body: cold face, cold hands, cold limbs that moved mindlessly towards the sea, and the Molo, thundering with carriages and plumed horses galloping before it.

Now and then a violent shudder swept over him, stopping him, lifting him for the moment off the balls of his feet so that he would sink down, disoriented, his unconscious moan

174

lost in the crowd that everywhere jostled him and forced him forward.

He wove his way through vendors and hawkers of sweets, men offering fruit drinks and white wine, strolling musicians, and lovely women of the streets who brushed against him, their laughter like hundreds of little bells, all it seemed in an air of noonday fest as if before this volcano finally burst and buried them all under its ash, they must live, live, live as if there were no hereafter.

But the volcano would bury no one tonight. It would roar and spit its hot stones and steam into the cloudless sky while the moon shone on the waves and those who swam in the warm sea, and those who played on the shore, in a miraculous flood of illumination.

This was merely Naples; this was merely paradise; this was earth and sky and sea and God and man, and none of it, none of it, could touch him.

Nothing could touch him but this pain, this pain like ice freezing his skin to his bones and closing the whole so that his soul lay seared and sealed within; and stumbling finally into the sand, into the waters of the Mediterranean itself, he crumpled down, bent double as if by one last fatal blow and felt this water with all its warmth wash against him.

It filled his boots; he splashed it to his face, and then he heard over the crash of the waves in the secret chamber of his own ears, his own crying.

He was there, at the foaming edge of the sea, staring back now and then at the rush of gilded wheels, those footmen dashing like specters over the stones, their feet scarcely touching down to earth, horses bridled with jingling bells, feathery plumes, fresh flowers, when suddenly out of that stream of traffic that ran the length of the wide arc of the road from one end of the city to the other, a calash came rocking towards him, its driver jumping down to shake Tonio's cape, to gesture with wild concern, to offer the little padded seat inside his carriage.

Tonio stared at him for the longest while, vaguely amazed by all of this Neapolitan jargon.

The sea rolled in at his feet. The man pulled him back with a great gesture of alarm for these fine clothes, the sand smeared on Tonio's breeches, the water sparkling all over his lace shirt front.

Tonio suddenly started laughing. Then he drew up, and over the roar of the sea and the clatter of the traffic said in the little of the dialect he knew:

"Take me up on the mountain."

The man drew back. Now? At this hour? It was best to go by day when . . .

Tonio shook his head. He had two gold coins out of his purse and pressed them into the man's hand. He had that eerie smile of one who feels he can get anything he wants because he cares about nothing. He said:

"No. As high as you can go, now. On the mountain."

They moved fast through the suburbs of the city; yet it was a long drive before they started up the gentle slope itself, its orchards and olive groves laid beautifully open by the giant moon, the rumble of the volcano growing steadily louder.

Tonio could already smell the ash. He could feel it on his face, and in his lungs. He covered up his mouth, convulsed with coughing. Little houses meantime revealed themselves in the bluish night. Their occupants, seated at the open doors, rose at the sight of the jogging lantern, only to shrink back as the driver whipped the horse onward.

But the climb was becoming steeper and more difficult, and finally they reached the point where the horse could go no higher.

They came to a halt among a tangle of olive trees, and here and there Tonio could glimpse far below the great glittering crescent of Naples.

Then there came a faint roar, so diffused and alarming that Tonio found himself clutching the side of the calash, and the sky lit up revealing an immense column of smoke rent perfectly in two by a glaring flash as the roar culminated in a deafening bellow.

Tonio jumped down and told the driver to leave him. It seemed there were protests. And as he attempted to get away, two other dark figures emerged from the tangled growth of the rocky slope. These were the guides who took men by day to the cone, and they were now ready to haul Tonio up behind them.

The driver didn't want him to go; and one of the guides himself seemed reluctant. But before an argument could ensue, Tonio paid one of these men and, taking the stick offered him as a crutch, grabbed onto the leather thong that hung from the

176

back of this man's belt and, thus braced, commenced to be drawn up into the darkness.

Another bellow sounded from the earth, and again that flash of light that brought midday to the straggling trees, and in it a small house above distinguished itself. Yet another figure appeared just as from above a shower of small stones filled the air, raining down with thumps and thuds everywhere. One rock struck Tonio's shoulder but with no force. He shouted for the guide to continue.

The man who had just appeared was waving his arms.

"You cannot go higher!" he declared, and drawing near to Tonio, he let the moon discover him through the olive branches. His face was gaunt, his eyes bulging as if with some wasting sickness. "Go back down. Can't you see you're in danger?" he cried out.

"Go on," said Tonio to the guide.

But the guide had stopped.

And then the man pointed to a great mound that stood before him.

"Last night that was a grove of trees as flat as this," he said. "I saw it rise and buckle within a matter of hours. I tell you, you are courting death to go higher."

He ducked as the rain of stones came flying again, and this time Tonio felt the trickle of blood on the side of his face though he didn't hear or feel the weight of the stone that had struck him.

"Go on," he said to the guide.

The guide dug in his staff. He pulled Tonio a few yards farther up the slope. Then he stopped. He was gesturing, but over the noise of the mountain Tonio couldn't hear what he was saying. Again he shouted go on. But he could see now the man was finished and nothing would make him continue. In Neapolitan, he begged Tonio to stop. He released him from the leather thong, and when Tonio started up the slope hand over hand, his fingers digging into the dirt, the man cried out in Italian that Tonio could understand:

"Signore, it spills lava tonight. Look, above. You cannot go farther!"

Tonio lay on the ground, his right arm up to shield his eyes, his left cupped loosely over his mouth, and dimly through the particles of ash that hung in the air, he could see the faint glimmer of a stream defining the slope to his right as the lava poured down and away, disappearing into the amorphous shapes of the overgrowth. Tonio stared at it without moving. More ash belched from above, and there came the stones again falling on his back and his head. He covered his head with both hands.

"Signore!" screamed the guide.

"Get away from me!" Tonio cried out. And without looking back to see if he was obeyed, he rose on all fours and ran up the incline, gaining speed as he grabbed for roots and scorched tree limbs, digging the toes of his boots into the soft crush beneath him.

Again came the shower of rocks; it was in a rhythm that these bursts were occurring, but he could not time it, nor did he care, dropping down again and again to protect his face and rising as soon as he could, the fire above lighting up the sky even through the haze of the ash which had become a veritable cloud over him.

A fit of coughing stopped him. He ran on. But now he had his handkerchief over his mouth and he was going slower. His hands were bruised, so were his knees, and when the rocks showered down on him this time, they cut his forehead and his right shoulder.

The mountain gave another roar, the rumble collecting into a greater and greater sound until it was once more that appalling bellow. The night was again fully illuminated.

And he saw beyond the half dead trees that lay ahead that he had reached the foot of the giant cone itself. He was almost to the summit of Vesuvius.

He reached out for the earth above, taking it in tight handfuls as it fell away, pebbles and rocks rolling back into his mouth, and suddenly he felt the ground itself moving! It was heaved upward. The raging bellow deafened him. And the smoke and ash swirled about the great blinding flash that showed the high barren cone slanting heavenward. Again he went forward. He groped for the tree that he could see only a few yards ahead, a last gnarled and tortured sentinel. But falling down, he felt himself thrown up again as with a tremendous crack, the tree itself split open.

Half the trunk swung to the right, seemed to catch itself. And then it crashed in a thunderous crackling. A seething steam rose from the cracks opening everywhere. And he found himself scrambling desperately backwards.

He slid against the earth. He felt the dirt in his mouth, the dead leaves caked against his eyelids. And even blinded as he

178

was, he still saw the red flash as if from an explosion. But he clung fast. The ground carried him up, shifted him to the side, but he lay motionless. The bellow rose again, shattering him. And though his throat convulsed with cries, though his hands clawed into the rubble, he heard no sound from himself, felt no life in himself as he became part of the mountain and the roaring cauldron within it.

7

THE SUN WAS WARM on his face.

Smoke hung in the air in thousands upon thousands of tiny particles. Yet far off the birds were singing. And it was not early morning. It was noon, he could tell by the slant of the sun, by the feel of it on his face and his hands. And the mountain gave off but a faint murmuring.

He had just opened his eyes. For a long moment he lay very still, and then he realized that a man was standing before him.

The figure wavered against the blue sky, and so consumptive was it, so pale, so wild of eye, it seemed the very visage of death itself, while behind it lay the lush green slopes, knotted with trees, that melted down to the fertile plain in which lay the jumbled facets of color and light that were Naples.

But it wasn't the figure of death. It was only that man who had come out of his hut the night before to warn Tonio to go no higher.

And mutely, he extended his hand. He caught Tonio up out of the dirt and led him slowly down the mountain.

As soon as Tonio reached the city, he went to one of the better *alberghi* on the Molo, and rented for himself an expensive suite of rooms in which he could bathe, after sending a servant to purchase fresh linen.

When he was finished with the bath, he had the tub taken out and he stood alone for awhile, naked, in front of the mirror. Then he put on his clean shirt, arranging the lace neatly at the collar and at the cuffs, and having had his frock coat brushed, he put that on too and his breeches and stockings and went out onto the veranda.

Fruit and chocolate were brought to him for his breakfast, and the Turkish coffee he had liked so much all his life in Venice.

And there he sat in the open air, looking beyond the morning traffic to the white beach and the blue-green water.

The sea was a swarm of fishing boats and vessels drifting into port.

And beneath him the open space called the Largo was full of all that minute and busy life he had grown accustomed to seeing here.

Tonio was thinking.

But seldom in his life had he so little need to do so.

For fourteen days, he had been at Naples. And for fourteen days on the road before that, after leaving that filthy room in Flovigo. And during all of this time, it was entirely possible that he had never once really used his reason.

All that had happened to him weighed on him *totally*. And yet he could not see it as a whole, nor see around it. Rather all its aspects beset him like so many buzzing flies come from hell to drive him out of his mind and they had almost succeeded. Torn with hatred, torn with grief for the man he would not be, he had flailed against everyone around him, even himself, without purpose, and without hope, rectifying nothing and vanquishing no one.

Well, that was over.

That had changed.

And he was not entirely sure why it had changed, either.

But after a night of lying on Vesuvius, of moving only when the mountain chose to move him, it had all of it done its damnedest to him, and now it was over.

And central to this change was the realization—not made in the heat of anger and pain, but coldly, in the midst of danger—that he was entirely alone now.

He had no one.

Carlo had done evil to him, irrevocable evil.

And that evil had separated Tonio from everyone he loved, completely. He could never live among his family or friends as he was now. If he did, their pity, their curiosity, their horror would simply destroy him.

Even if he were not banished from Venice, an inalterable

180

fact that caused him excruciating humiliation, he could never return there. Venice and all those he knew and loved were lost to him now.

All right. That was the simpler part.

Now came the harder part.

Andrea, too, had betrayed him. Surely Andrea had known Tonio was not his son. And yet Andrea had led him to believe that he was, setting Tonio against Carlo, to fight Andrea's battle after Andrea's death. That was a terrible, terrible betrayal.

Yet even now, Tonio knew what Andrea would say on his own behalf. Save for Andrea, what would Tonio have been? The first of a wretched brood of bastards, children of a disgraced nobleman and a ruined convent girl? What would Tonio's life have been? Andrea had chastised a rebellious offspring who deserved nothing, saved the honor of his family, and *made* Tonio his son.

But even the will of Andrea could not work miracles. At his death, the illusions and laws he had created in his own house had crumbled. And he had never made Tonio understand what lay before him. He had sent Tonio to fight the battle sustained only by lies and half-truths.

Was it a miscalculation of pride finally? Tonio would never know.

All he knew and understood now was that he was not Andrea's son, and the man who had given him a history and a destiny was gone from him, his wisdom and his intentions forever beyond Tonio's reach.

Yes, he had lost Andrea.

And what of the Treschi remained? Carlo, Carlo who had done this to him, Carlo who had not the courage to kill him, but the cunning to know that for the House of Treschi Tonio could never point the finger of blame.

Clever, cowardly, but very clever. This spoilt and rebellious man who, for the love of a woman, had once threatened to doom his family to extinction, would now rebuild it on the cruelty and violence done to his blameless son.

So the Treschi were gone from him: Andrea, Carlo.

And yet the blood of the Treschi ran in his veins. There persisted in him a love for Treschi who had gone before these two men, father and grandfather, a love of Treschi who would come after, children who must inherit the traditions and the strength of a family in a world that would remember

181

little or nothing of Tonio, Carlo, Andrea, this appalling tangle of injustice and suffering.

All right, that was hard.

But what comes now is the hardest.

What lay before Tonio? What emerged from this chaos? What had become of Tonio Treschi, who sat now on a veranda in the southern city of Naples, alone, staring out under the shadow of Vesuvius on the ever changing surface of the sea?

Tonio Treschi was a eunuch.

Tonio Treschi was that half man, that less than man that arouses the contempt of every whole man who looks upon it. Tonio Treschi was that thing which women cannot leave alone and men find infinitely disturbing, frightening, pathetic, the butt of jokes and endless bullying, the necessary evil of the church choirs and the opera stage which is, outside that artifice and grace and soaring music, very simply monstrous.

All his life he'd heard the whispers behind the eunuch's back, seen the sneers, the lift of eyebrows, the mock foppish gestures! All too perfectly he'd understood the rage of that proud singer Caffarelli at the footlights glaring at the Venetians who had paid to see him like the court ape perform vocal acrobatics.

And already within the confines of the conservatorio to which he'd clung like a shipwrecked prisoner to the remnants of his prison boat in alien water, he had seen the self-loathing of these neutered children, taunting him to share their degraded state. Slipping into his room at night with barbs of uncommon cruelty, "You are the same as we are!" they all but hissed at him in the dark.

Yes, he was the same as they were. And how the world took cognizance of it! Matrimony was forever denied him, his name no longer his to give to the lowliest woman nor the most needy stepchild. Nor would the Church ever receive him, save for the lowest Orders, and even then only by special dispensation.

No, he was outcast, from family, from church, from any great institution in this world that was his world, save one:

That was the conservatorio. And the world of music for which the conservatorio would prepare him.

Neither of which had the slightest actual connection with what had been done to him by his brother's men.

182

But were it not for that conservatorio, and were it not for that music, then this thing truly would be worse than death.

As it was, it was not worse.

When he had lain in that bed in Flovigo, and that bravo, Alonso, had put a pistol to his head, saying: "You have your life, take it and leave here," he had thought then it was worse than death. "Kill me," he had wanted to answer, but he had not even the will then to do that.

But on the mountain, this very day, he had not wanted to die. There was the conservatorio, and there was music that, even in the moments of his worst pain, he could hear, purely and magnificently, in his head.

The smallest ripple of feeling came over his face. He was staring at the sea where children moved in and out of the waves like a great flock of swallows.

So what would he do?

He knew. He had known when he had come down from the mountain. Two tasks lay before him.

The first was the revenge against Carlo. And that would take time.

Because Carlo must marry, Carlo must have children first, healthy strong children growing up well towards the day when they might marry and have children of their own.

But then he would *get* Carlo. Whether he himself survived the revenge did not matter. In all likelihood he wouldn't survive it. Venice would get him, or Carlo's bravos would get him, but not before he himself had gotten to Carlo and whispered into Carlo's ear, "This is between *us* now."

What he would do then he wasn't certain. When he thought of those men in Flovigo, of the knife, of the cunning of all of it, and the finality of all of it, death for his father who had lived and loved so much already in his thirty-five years seemed infinitely too simple and too good.

He knew only that some day he would have Carlo in his power, as those men in Flovigo had had him in their power, and when that moment came, Carlo would wish for death just as Tonio had wished for it when the bravo had said in his ear, "You have your life."

Then Carlo's bodyguards could take him, Venice could take him, Carlo's sons, it did not matter. Carlo would have paid.

Now the second task.

He would sing.

That he would do for himself because he wanted to, whether it was all a eunuch *could* do or no. Whether it was what his brother and those henchmen of his had destined him to do did not matter. He would do it because he loved it and he wanted it, and his voice was the one thing in this world which he had once loved that was still his.

Oh, the magnificent irony of it. Now, his voice would never leave him, never change.

Yes, he would do it for himself and he would give it everything that he had and he would let it take him wherever he might go on this earth with it.

And who knew just how splendid that might be? The celestial brilliance of the church choirs, even the grand spectacle of the theater, he dared not really think of it now, but it just might give him the only time that he would ever spend with God's angels.

The sun was high in the sky. The pupils of the conservatorio had long ago settled in for the hot, fitful sleep of the siesta.

Yet the Largo hummed with life below him. Fishermen were coming in with their catch. And against a far wall a little stage had been erected before the milling crowd on which a tawdry Punchinello was gesturing coarsely.

Tonio watched that lone figure for a short while, its rough voice now and then carrying over the din of the square, and then he rose and entered the small room to gather up his few possessions.

There was one more aspect of it all that he had taken down with him from Vesuvius.

It was perhaps the one thing of which he was most certain, and he had known it in a wordless and clear way when he had first awakened in the sunlight and seen that graceful corpse teetering over him.

He had thought in those moments of Andrea's words: "Make up your mind, Tonio, that you are a man . . . behave as if it were absolutely true and all else will then fall into place."

He strapped on his sword, lifted his cape onto his shoulders, and glanced once more into the mirror at the young form and face that were his reflected there.

"Yes," he whispered. "Make up your mind that you are a

man, and that is what you *will* be, and damn him who says otherwise."

That was the way to overcome it. That was the only way, and in this quiet moment before the mirror, he allowed himself to accept all the good that his "father" had once given him. Anger was gone. Hatred was gone. Blind rage had evaporated.

Yet a fear remained, which for all his clarity of mind he could not yet examine. He knew it was there. He felt its presence as surely as one feels the menace of a nearby flame; yet he could not turn to it and acknowledge it.

Perhaps silently, he committed it to the future; he said to himself, I will not think of it and in time, it will leave me alone. It was wound up however with powerful, throbbing memories of Catrina Lisani against the pillows of her bed, of little Bettina, his tavern girl, lifting her skirts in the dark of the gondola. And perhaps most hideously, it had something to do with his mother circling that dark bedchamber, whispering over and over, "Shut the doors, shut the doors, shut the doors."

At one moment these thoughts coagulated so that he stopped in the very act of leaving this suite of rooms in the *albergo.* He stood with his shoulders hunched as if he'd been struck an ugly blow. But then his mind emptied itself. These three women vanished.

And the conservatorio loomed above him, nestled in the hills of Naples, with something of the allure of a lover.

8

IT WAS THE STILL quiet of the siesta time when he reached the gates, and he mounted the steps without being seen, soon finding his little room almost as he had left it. He felt the most palpable calm in this place as he looked at his trunk and those few pieces of clothing that someone had so carefully removed from the cabinet and laid out to be taken away by him.

The black tunic was still there. And removing his frock

185

coat, he slipped it on, and, gathering up the red sash from the floor, he put it around his waist and, quietly passing the slumbering dormitory, made his way downstairs again to the door of Guido's study.

Guido was not resting.

He looked up from the harpsichord with the immediate flashing anger with which he greeted all interruptions. But he was dumbstruck when he saw Tonio standing there.

"Can the Maestro be persuaded to give me another chance?" Tonio asked.

He stood with his hands behind his back, waiting.

Guido did not answer. In fact, his face was so much the picture of menace that for one moment Tonio was made aware of the most violently conflicting feelings for this man. But one thought emerged: this man must be his teacher here. It was unthinkable that he study with anyone else, and when he thought of Guido walking into the sea to destroy himself, he felt just for an instant the weight of an undeclared emotion that had battered him for twenty-eight days. He closed his heart to it. He waited.

Guido was beckoning to him. He was also shuffling wildly through his music.

Tonio saw a glass of water on a small stand beside the harpsichord and he drank all of it.

When he looked at the music, it was a cantata by Scarlatti, and though he did not know it, he knew Scarlatti.

Guido plunged into the introduction, his somewhat short fingers appearing veritably to bounce on the keys, and then Tonio hit the first note perfectly on pitch.

But his voice sounded huge, unnatural to him, completely out of control, and it was with a tremendous act of will that he forced himself on, up and down the passages which his teacher had written in, the embellishments and graces which he had added to the composer's score.

Finally it seemed to him his voice was all right; it felt almost good; and when he finished, he experienced an odd sensation of drifting. It was as if a great deal of time had gone by.

He realized that Guido was looking past him. The Maestro di Cappella had come in through the open door and he and Guido were staring at one another.

"Sing this again for me," said the Maestro, approaching.

Tonio gave a slight shrug. Yet he could not bring himself

to look directly at this man. He lowered his eyes and, lifting his right hand slowly, felt the fabric of his black tunic as if he were making some casual adjustment of its simple collar. He could feel it encasing him, rendering him distinct in some way he'd never been, and he could remember in an inarticulate instant all of this man's harsh condemnation of him.

It seemed another age, and what was said was unimportant.

He looked at the Maestro's large hands, the hair on the backs of his fingers. He looked at the broad black leather belt encircling his cassock. And he envisioned beneath it, effortlessly, the man's unmutilated anatomy. And then looking up slowly, he saw the shadow of the Maestro's shaven beard darkening face and throat.

But the Maestro's eyes, confronted at last, surprised him.

They were soft and wide with awe and anticipation. And Guido was looking at Tonio with the same expression. They were both of them locked to him, waiting.

He let out his breath and started to sing. And this time he heard his own voice perfectly.

He let the notes rise, following them in his mind without the slightest effort to modulate them. The simpler, lustier parts of the song came. His voice took wing. And at some indefinable moment, the joy in all its purity was returned to him.

He could have wept then.

Had there been tears to shed, he would have wept, and it did not matter to him that he was not alone, that they would have seen.

His voice was his again.

The song was finished.

He looked out through the cloister at the light flickering in the leaves and felt a great delicious weariness overcoming him. The afternoon was warm. And in the far distance it seemed he heard the soft cacophony of children at play.

But a shadow rose before him. And turning almost reluctantly, he looked into Maestro Guido's face.

Then Guido put his arms around him, and slowly, tentatively, Tonio gave himself over to that embrace.

Yet it seemed he was remembering some other moment,

187

some other time when he had held someone in his arms, and there had been this same sweet, violent, and concealed emotion. But whatever it was—whenever it was—it was gone. He could not now recall it.

Maestro Cavalla stepped forward.

He said, "You voice is magnificent."

PART IV

1

Even as Tonio unpacked his trunk that first afternoon at the conservatorio (and his family had indeed sent him *everything* that belonged to him), filling the red and gilt cabinet with a few favorite clothes and arranging his books on the shelves of his room, he was aware that the transformation he had undergone on Vesuvius had yet to be really tested.

This was one reason he wouldn't give up this little room though the Maestro di Cappella had immediately told him he might have an unused apartment on the first floor should he want it. He wanted to see Vesuvius from his window. He wanted to lie in bed at night and see the fire of the mountain against the moonlit sky. He wanted to remember always that on that mountain he had learned what it meant to be completely alone.

Because as the future commenced to make known to him the true meaning of his new life, he needed his resolves to stand by him. There would be moments of acute pain. And he had some inkling, no matter how resigned he felt now, and no matter how appalling had been the pain of the last month, that the worst was yet to come.

And he was right about that.

The little moments of pain came immediately.

They came in the warm sunlight of the afternoon as he lifted from his trunks those brocade and velvet coats he'd once worn to suppers and balls in Venice, as he held up the fur-lined cloak he'd once wrapped around himself in the drafty pit of the theater as he sat gazing up into the face of the singer Caffarelli.

It was pain, too, that he felt when that night at the evening meal, he took his place among the other castrati, ignoring the shock on their hostile faces.

But all this he bore with the most serene expression. He nodded to his fellow students. He flashed a disarming smile at those who had ridiculed him. He reached out to touch the hair of that little one, Paolo, who had ridden with him from Florence and often approached him in the days afterwards.

And it was with the same apparent calm that he gave up his purse to the Maestro di Cappella.

And again he smiled graciously when told to give up his sword and stiletto. But trembling inside, he refused with a little shake of the head as though he didn't understand Italian. The pistols, of course, he would give them up. But his sword? No, he smiled. He could not do that.

"You're not a university student here," snapped the Maestro. "You do not carouse at will in the local taverns. And need I remind you that Lorenzo, the student you wounded, is still bedridden? I want no more quarrels. I want your sword and your stiletto."

Again that gracious smile. Tonio was sorry for what had happened with Lorenzo. But Lorenzo had entered his room. He had been forced to protect himself. He could not give up his sword. And he didn't volunteer the smaller and more useful stiletto either.

And no one could have perceived how astonished he was when the Maestro di Cappella gave in to him.

It wasn't until he was safe in the privacy of his attic room that he started to laugh over this. He'd expected the injunction "Behave as if you were a man" to be his armor against humiliation. But he had not expected it to work upon others! He was just beginning to understand that what he had brought down from Vesuvius was a mode of behavior. No matter how he *felt*, he would behave as if he did not feel it, and everything would be better.

Of course, he deeply regretted the injury done Lorenzo. It was not that the boy hadn't deserved it; it was that he might cause trouble later.

And Tonio was still thinking about this when, an hour after dark, he heard the older castrati in the passage outside, those boys who were responsible for seeing there was order in the dormitory, those who had in the past accompanied Lorenzo into Tonio's room to harass him.

Now he was ready for them. He invited them in, and offering a bottle of excellent wine which he'd brought from the *albergo* by the sea, he apologized for the lack of cups or goblets. He'd rectify that soon enough. Would they join him for a little drink? He gestured for them to be seated along the side of the bed, and he took the chair from the desk, offering

191

them the bottle again. And then again, because he saw they had enjoyed it.

Actually, they couldn't resist it.

And all was done by Tonio with such quiet assurance that they weren't sure they *should* refuse it.

Tonio was studying them for the first time, and while he did so, he commenced talking. In a low voice he spoke just enough of the weather in Naples and of a few peculiarities of the place that the silence didn't weigh on them.

Yet he was not giving an impression of being talkative because in truth he wasn't really talkative.

And he was trying to size them up, to determine who, if any, among them owed any loyalty to Lorenzo, who was still in bed because the wound had become infected.

The tallest was Giovanni, from the north of Italy, about eighteen years of age and possessed of a tolerable voice which Tonio had heard in Guido's study. This one would never perform in the opera; but he was good as a young maestro with the younger boys, and many a church choir would later want him. His limp black hair he wore severely shaped like a pigtail wig with only a string of black silk ribbon. His eyes were soft, uninteresting, perhaps cowardly.

He seemed perfectly willing to accept Tonio.

Then there was Piero, that blond-haired one from the north of Italy, too, who had hissed so many epithets at Tonio, only to turn his head afterwards as if he hadn't spoken. He had a better voice, a contralto that might even be great someday, but from what Tonio had heard of him in church he lacked something. Maybe it was passion, maybe it was imagination. He drank the wine now with a slight sneer, and his eyes were cold and suspicious. Yet when Tonio addressed him he seemed to melt immediately. When Tonio asked him questions, he preened with the answers. So what he wanted was attention.

By the end of this short visit he was attempting to woo Tonio and make an impression upon him, as if Tonio were the elder, which he wasn't, as though Tonio were his superior.

And lastly, there was the sixteen-year-old Domenico. He was so exquisitely beautiful that he might have passed for either a man or a woman. His chest having expanded from the use of his lungs in singing and the flexibility of his eunuch bones, he had in fact the shape of a woman, with a narrow waist and a flare above it that suggested a bosom. But this was so subtle it could be missed by some. His dark eyelashes and pink lips had such a sheen to them they appeared to have been painted. Of course they weren't. And on his fingers he wore an assortment of rings that caught the light as he used his hands with deliberate grace in the most languid movements. His black hair he left curled naturally at his shoulders; it was just a little too long. And he didn't talk at all, which made Tonio realize he had never heard the sound of Domenico's voice, either in song or speech. It intrigued him. Domenico was just always there looking on. He had seen Lorenzo stabbed with no change of expression.

As he took the bottle of wine now, wiping his lips first with a lace napkin, his eyes fixed on Tonio and their stare was unnerving. He was appraising Tonio in some new light. And Tonio thought, This creature knows so well he is beautiful that he is beyond vanity.

In the coming opera production on the little conservatorio stage, Domenico would play the part of the first woman. And Tonio found himself suddenly fascinated by the prospect of seeing this boy transformed into a girl. He thought of the stays of a corset closing around Domenico's waist and it actually made him blush so that he lost track of what Giovanni was saying to him.

So he stopped thinking about it. And then the thought that this was a woman in breeches began to unnerve him. He took a little uncomfortable breath. Domenico's head was slightly to the side. He was almost smiling. In the candlelight his skin looked like porcelain, and he had a little cleft to his chin that suggested a man, which made him all the more confusing.

When they had gone, Tonio sat on the side of the bed thinking. He blew out the candle and lay down and tried to sleep, and when sleep wouldn't come right away, he imagined he was on Vesuvius. He felt that trembling earth again; he felt it against his eyelids.

And this became a ritual with him every night for years, the feel of that earth and the rumble of that mountain.

2

BUT TONIO HAD no real need to induce sleep after this first evening. The next morning, though he was still bruised from the night on the mountain, he awoke in exceptional humor. He was to start his studies with Guido immediately.

Even the colors and the scents of the conservatorio rather appealed to him. There was in particular a fragrance which he associated with wood instruments that seemed to linger in the hallways, and he liked it. He liked the sounds of the practice rooms coming alive.

And enjoying a somewhat plain breakfast, especially the fresh milk, he found himself just a little entranced with the early morning stars which he could just see over the wall from the refectory window.

The air was almost silky, he was thinking. It had an inviting warmth. You felt you could have walked outdoors naked.

And it was exhilarating to him to be awake so early.

Even Guido Maffeo looked good to him.

The Maestro was at his harpsichord, making notes with his pen, and it appeared he'd been working for hours. His candle had burned low; the darkness was turning to mist outside his window; and settling back to wait at a bench against the wall, Tonio for the first time absorbed the details of this little studio.

It was a stone room, its hard floor relieved only by a rush mat. And yet all its furnishings—the harpsichord, high desk, chair and bench—were lavishly painted with floral designs and shining enamel. They seemed vibrant against the cold walls. And the Maestro in his black frock coat and small linen stock looked somber and clerical here, but as if he belonged to all of it.

He was not always so terrible to look at, Tonio was thinking, in fact, he was somewhat handsome. But his expression was so often full of rage, and those brown eyes of his were just a little too large for his face and gave the rest of it a pugnacious

194

quality. But it was altogether such a mobile and expressive face; it was so full of turbulence and caring that Tonio could not help but be fascinated with it.

Yet he could not think of this man in Flovigo, or in Ferrara, or in Rome in that garden where they had embraced. If he thought of these things, Tonio would despise him. So he did not think of them.

Finally the Maestro put down his pen, blew out the candle which had become nothing but a solid little flicker of yellow in the bluish light, and started talking without any formal greeting.

"Your voice is extraordinary. You've been told that enough," he said as if arguing with somebody, "so don't expect further praise from me until you earn it. But you have gotten by for years doing what you like and what you don't understand, singing songs well only because you have a perfect ear and you have heard others sing them properly. You shied away from anything you found difficult, taking refuge again and again in what was enjoyable to you, what was easy. So you have no real control over your voice, and you have many bad habits."

He stopped and ran his right hand back through his brown curly hair as if he hated it. It had the shape of a cherub's mop in some painting of the last century, luxuriously full and curling upward at the ends; but it looked neglected and slightly dusty.

"And you're fifteen years old, which is very late to start really singing," he continued. "But I can tell you right now that you'll be ready to perform on any stage in Europe in three years if you do everything that I tell you to do. Whether or not you really want to be a great performer doesn't matter to me. I don't care. I'm not asking you. You have a great voice, therefore I'll train you to be a great performer. I'll train you for the stage, for the court, for all Europe. And after that you can do what you want with it."

Tonio was furious. He rose to his full height and advanced on the glowering, flat-nosed figure at the harpsichord.

"You might have asked me why I came back here yesterday!" he said in his haughtiest, coldest manner.

"Don't ever speak to me like that again," Guido sneered. "I'm your teacher."

And without further explanation he presented the first exercise.

195

*   *   *

They began that day with a simple *Accentus*.

Six notes were shown to Tonio on an ascending scale, "Ut, Re, Mi, Fa, Sol, La." Then he was presented with a more complicated embroidering upon these notes, so that in singing the whole he was singing a gently ascending melody with little ups and downs, each tone having at least four notes around it, three going up, one coming back down again.

It was to be sung in one breath and each note was to be sung with equal attention. At the same time the vowel sound was to be pronounced perfectly. And the whole was to be absolutely fluid.

And it was to be sung over and over and over again, day after day, in this quiet empty room, without the harpsichord for accompaniment until it ran naturally and evenly like a golden stream from Tonio's throat with no indication of the breath he had taken at the start of it, or of any breathlessness at the end of it.

The first day Tonio thought he would lose his mind from singing it.

But commencing the second day, certain this monotony was a subtle form of torture, he witnessed a change in himself. It was as if his temper had created a bubble, and at some point in the afternoon the bubble popped. And the peeling of the bubble fell back like the petals of a bud and a great flower rose out of the center.

This flower was a hypnotic attraction to the notes Tonio was singing, a drifting with them, a slow dreamy awareness that each time he started again with the *Accentus*, he was tackling some new and fascinating little aspect of it.

By the end of the first week of this, he lost all track of various problems he solved, he knew only that his voice was changing completely.

Again and again Guido pointed out to him that he had sung Ut and Re and Mi more lovingly than the other tones. Did he love them more? He had to love all equally. And over and over again Guido reminded him "*Legato*," link them all slowly, perfectly together. Volume didn't matter. Expression of feeling did not matter. But each tone *must* be beautiful. It is not enough that it be perfectly on pitch (he told Tonio several times almost begrudgingly that he had the gift of singing on perfect pitch, but Alessandro had long ago told

196

Tonio this), the tone must be beautiful in itself like a drop of gold.

Then he sat back and said, "Again, from the beginning," and Tonio, his vision blurred, his head aching, would start that first note and then glide into it.

But then with some infallible sense, just when Tonio was tingling all over with a desperate exhaustion, Guido would release him from this exercise and send him to the high desk to work out some problems of composition or counterpoint while standing.

"You don't sit at desks anymore. It's no good for your chest to be bent over. And you never never do anything that is bad for your voice or your chest," he said. And Tonio, his legs aching, merely bowed his head, grateful for the chance to let the *Accentus* die out of his head for a little while.

But then would come some younger student to murder it.

He did not know how long he had been singing this elementary passage when Guido finally added two notes at the top and two notes at the bottom, and allowed him to sing the whole faster, and then a little bit faster. It was an event of sorts to have four new notes, and Tonio sarcastically announced that surely he ought to be allowed to get drunk to celebrate.

Guido ignored this.

But again on a hot afternoon when Tonio was on the verge of rebelling, Guido suddenly gave him several arias freshly written and full of changes and told him he might have the keyboard to accompany himself.

Tonio snatched up these songs before the thanks were out of his mouth. For him it was like plunging into the warm sea under the summer stars. And he had sung the second all the way through before he realized that of course Guido was listening to him. And Guido would tell him in a moment that he was dreadful.

He commenced consciously to try to apply what he had learned from the *Accentus*, and he realized that he had been applying it all along. He was articulating the words of these songs very distinctly but easily; and he had been singing with a new smoothness and control which made his immediate apprehension of the music infinitely easier.

He had his first real sense of power in those moments.

And when he returned to the exercises he was thinking of his voice in terms of power.

It seemed to him late that evening when he was so tired he could not think of his legs or his feet or of a soft pillow without falling over, that he had become something inhuman. He had become a wooden instrument out of which his voice rose as if someone else were playing it. He could feel his voice rising out of him; he could feel its evenness, its smoothness.

He was light-headed by the time he climbed the stairs. And turning over in bed he realized that for at least ten days he had not thought once of any of the things that had happened to him before coming here.

The next morning Guido informed him that due to his excellent progress they would begin with the *Esclamazio*. With any other new pupil, this jump would have been unthinkable, but Guido had ideas of his own about how to proceed.

This was the *Esclamazio*: the slow and perfectly controlled swelling of a note from a soft intoning of it to a louder and louder amplification of it, diminishing slowly to a soft finish. Or it might begin loud, diminish to a soft middle and then build again to a loud finish.

In either case, absolute mind control was essential. Again volume didn't matter. Again the tone must be perfectly beautiful. And again days and days would pass during which Tonio performed this exercise over and over again, first on the tone of A, then on the tone of E, then on the tone of O, before going back and back again to the *Accentus*.

And all this was performed in the quiet, echoing stone chamber of Guido's study with no accompaniment from the keyboard while the Maestro studied Tonio as if listening to sounds Tonio himself was not hearing.

At times Tonio realized that he despised this man so much that he could have struck him. It gave him pleasure to imagine that he was in fact striking Guido, and this made him ashamed afterwards.

But beneath these quiet peaks of unexpressed anger, Tonio knew that what tortured him truly was the realization that Guido despised him completely.

At first he had told himself, It is the man's manner; he is barbaric. But Guido was never pleased with him, Guido was rarely polite, and the habitual rudeness seemed always to mask a deeper antipathy and displeasure. There were moments when Tonio felt this scorn from Guido as palpably as if

198

Guido had spoken it aloud, and the past with its unspeakable humiliation threatened to press in on him.

And then, trembling with anger himself, Tonio offered to him the one thing he wanted: the voice, the voice, the voice. While surrendering to sleep afterwards, he combed the day's experiences for the scantest memory of his teacher's approval.

And without meaning to, Tonio fell into the terrible trap of trying to draw affection from Guido, some interest from Guido.

In the mornings, he would attempt conversation. Was it hotter today? What was going on in the theater of the conservatorio? Would it be years before Tonio could take part in the school performances? But surely Tonio would be allowed to see this one, wouldn't he?

Guido snarled at all this, but rather impersonally. Then he would look up abruptly from his writing and say, "All right, today we are going to hold all of these notes for twice their length and I want the *Esclamazio* perfect."

"Ah, perfection again, is it?" Tonio would whisper.

Guido would ignore this.

It was sometimes ten o'clock at night before Guido let him go, and Tonio heard the *Esclamazio* in his sleep. He awoke with these liquid notes in his ears.

Finally they moved into the first of the ornaments.

What Tonio had learned so far was the basis of control of the breath and tone, and absolute attention to what he was singing.

But the process of ornamenting a melody was more involved. It meant not only new sounds or combinations of sounds had to be learned, but he had to acquire some sense of when to add them to a melody on his own.

The first ornament he learned was called the *Tremolo*. It was simply how to sing the same note but with several repeated beats. That is, to take an A, and sing it A A A A A, again with perfect control and perfect fluidity, the sounds melting one into the other yet the beats clear like recurrent explosions.

When his mind was exhausted with that, when it issued from him with some degree of naturalness, he went on to the *trill*, which was a warbling of tone from one note to a higher note and back again over and over in one long breath rapidly, as ABABABABABABABA.

After the long weeks with the *Accentus* and the long opulent notes of the *Esclamazio*, this was great fun actually. And the challenge of control, the challenge of power over the voice, was becoming absolutely enthralling.

The hypnotic falling into the music came sooner each day and seemed to last longer. And sometimes an hour into the evening's lessons, Tonio got a second wind and was singing these exercises with an inspired grace and an inspired selflessness.

He wasn't there. He had become his voice. The little room was wrapped in darkness. The candle flickered over the scratches on the page before him, and the sounds he heard were unearthly, suggesting a great flashing of abstract form in his mind that made him almost frightened.

He would go on and on. He would push.

It was very late.

Sometimes the Maestro di Cappella came into the room and said that it was time to stop. Tonio would fall onto the bench, rolling the back of his head back and forth against the wall, and Guido might then let loose on the harpsichord. The rich, tinkling sounds flooded the room. And looking at him, Tonio felt his body and soul empty.

Then Guido would say, "Get out of here." And Tonio, a little shocked and humiliated, would go upstairs to fall asleep immediately.

It seemed Tonio was never given arias to enjoy anymore, and even his hours of composition were narrowed down so that he might spend the day in exercises.

But if he should show the slightest strain in the voice itself, Guido would stop immediately. Sometimes Tonio merely rested while other pupils went through their lessons. He would become absorbed in their mistakes, their unchangeable or slowly yielding limitations.

And sometimes watching these other sessions, it comforted Tonio that Guido seemed to despise these students as much as he despised Tonio. *Sometimes* it comforted him. Sometimes it made him feel worse, and when Guido struck his students, which was often, this incensed Tonio.

One day after Guido had beaten little Paolo, the boy who'd come down with them from Florence, Tonio lost his temper, telling Guido flat out that he was boorish, loutish, a peasant done up in a frock coat, a dancing bear.

Of all the little ones who often aroused his affection, or even his pity, it was Paolo whom Tonio could never quite forget. But that had nothing to do with the injustice of it. Paolo had pushed himself under Guido as far as he could. He was impish by nature, full of laughter and smiles, and it was that more than anything he'd actually done which had earned him the whipping and Tonio was now white with rage.

But Guido merely laughed.

He introduced Tonio to the final culmination of all earlier lessons, the singing of passages:

This was the taking of a line of music and breaking it up into many smaller notes, while at the same time keeping intact the verbal sense of the passage and its underlying thematic purity. Guido used the word *Sanctus* as an example. For it the composer might write two notes, the second higher than the first. But Tonio must be able to divide the first sound, *Sanc*, into seven or eight notes of varying length, moving up and down but eventually ascending smoothly to the second note or sound *Tus*, which must then have its seven or eight notes, but terminating with a pleasing finality on that same second note again.

Practicing these ornaments and passages as Guido had written them out would be the beginning. But then Tonio must learn to pick up the bare bones of any composition and create his own embellishments tastefully and with perfect timing. He must know when to swell a note, how long to hold it, whether to break a passage into notes of unequal time or those of equal time, and how far he might go into ascending and descending intricacies. And he must at all times articulate the words of a cantata or aria so that in spite of all this exquisite ornamentation, the meaning of the words was clear to everyone.

This was, fundamentally, all that Guido had to teach Tonio. The rest was variation, refinement.

And normally it took five years for a pupil to master it, the pupil moving on much more slowly from *Accentus* to *Esclamazio* to ornaments. But Guido had fed it rapidly to Tonio for obvious reasons: that Tonio not become bored, and because Tonio was proving that he could absorb it.

He could work on all aspects of his vocal technique at once; and so Guido began to write for him more and more complicated vocalises. He had of course many old books by teachers of the last century as well as the early 1700s. But like most teachers, he wrote his own, knowing what Tonio most needed.

And Tonio, when he saw that this was the basis of his study and that what lay ahead was the perfecting of his voice through these exercises until it was as strong, as consistent, and as beautiful as a series of perfectly cast bells struck over and over again with exactly the same force, burst into tears with his arms folded under his head at the harpsichord.

He was now so tired in brain and muscle that he felt he had never before understood either sleep or exhaustion. And he did not care if Guido Maffeo was glaring at him.

He hated Guido! As much as Guido hated him, and so be it. And all this he had vowed to do for himself, for his own pleasure! He felt terrified suddenly. If he let go of this, what was left?

He had a swimming feeling as if he were losing his balance, and he was aware suddenly of a substratum of dreams which in the mornings had always been forgotten. A little door threatened to swing open on nightmare and on nothing, and he cried on bitterly, wishing that Guido Maffeo would leave him. Leave him in disgust, go on. Get out of here!

That was what the Maestro would say in a moment. "Get out of here."

"My voice is coarse," he said finally. "It's uneven, it swells and cracks of its own accord in my throat. What I've learned so far is simply this: to hear how bad it is!"

Guido was glowering at him. Then his face went curiously blank.

"May I go to bed?" Tonio whispered.

"Not just yet," Guido said. "Go up to your room and get dressed. I'm taking you out with me to the opera."

"What?" Tonio raised his head. He could scarce believe what he'd heard. "We're going out, we're going to the opera!"

"If you stop squalling like an infant, we are. Go get dressed immediately."

3

ONIO TOOK THE STEPS two at a time. He splashed cold water on his face and commenced dragging out his fine clothes which he had not worn since Venice. In a minute he was dressed in a dark blue brocade coat and his finest white lace, with paste buckle shoes. And strapping on his sword, he was suddenly on the lower floor to Guido's apartments.

It was then he remembered that he despised Guido. And that he wasn't a child who'd never been to an opera. But he forgot that again immediately. In fact, he felt so happy he couldn't quite understand it. He was almost laughing.

Then Guido appeared, and Tonio, who was unprepared for anything but his clerical black, was astonished. The Maestro wore a coat of rich chocolate velvet perfectly the same brown as his eyes and his smoothly combed hair, and beneath it a vest of gold silk. In the lights before the door of the conservatorio, the lace at his throat, though nothing as fancy as that of Tonio, was slightly luminescent, and his eyes were so large that they were distracting. Had he evinced the slightest pleasantness, the barest little smile, he would have been handsome beyond doubt. But he was surly and brooding as always.

Tonio stiffened when he saw his nasty expression. And he followed him in silence to the first busy corner where they hailed a cabriolet to take them to the Teatro San Bartolommeo.

It was an old building, brilliantly lit and very crowded, the gaming rooms smoky and noisy, the performance already under way before a restless and chattering audience. This was the theater in Naples for heroic opera—that is, serious opera—and for the aristocracy, which filled the first of its rectangular tiers.

To Tonio it was a vision. It was as if he had never seen such simple splendors before, never grown up with chandeliers of Murano glass, never seen such a wealth of wax tapers.

And Guido had definitely acquired a new dignity and polish in his eyes; the man appeared almost a gentleman. He bought both the libretto and the score and led Tonio not up to the noisy boxes, but down to the most expensive seats of the parterre before the footlights.

The first act was only half over, so the most important arias were yet to come. And as soon as Guido was confortably settled, he drew Tonio close beside him.

This is the beast who has snarled at me for over a month, Tonio thought. He was somewhat mystified by it. And could not stop looking at Guido.

There were two castrati, Guido explained, and a lovely little prima donna, but Guido said it was the old eunuch who would outsing everyone, and not because he had a decent voice, he didn't, but because he had the skill.

As soon as the castrato began to sing Tonio was enthralled. The voice was silky, full of tenderness, and brought an enormous hand of applause. "That's not a great voice?" he whispered.

"The high notes were all falsetto because his range isn't that great. But he has such control over the falsetto you didn't notice it. Listen next time, and you'll see what I mean. As for the tempo, it was written for him, and it's slow so that he can take everything on with great care. His middle range is all that's really left to him, and all the rest is pure skill."

As the evening progressed, Tonio saw this was true. Meantime the little prima donna captivated everyone with her spontaneous and emotional singing, but she had grown up in the streets, Guido said, singing as Tonio sang, and though her high notes gave one chills, she couldn't handle lower notes at all. They got lost in the pounding of the harpsichord. You saw her lips moving and nothing coming out.

The younger castrato was yet another surprise in that he was a fine contralto, which Tonio had seldom heard in a male. His voice was lustrous; it made you think of velvet, but when he went up high, he became rough.

Both of these young people could have outsung the older man by virtue of their natural gifts, but neither of them really knew how to do it, and over and over again it was the old castrato who stepped to the footlights and silenced the audience.

But Guido didn't content himself merely with the singing. He drew Tonio's attention to the score, how various arias had obviously been added for various voices, the little contests that went on between the younger castrato and the prima donna, how the old singer held himself very still when he sang because had he gestured with his unusually long and thin arms he would have looked like a fool. The young castrato was handsome, the audience liked this, and he held himself like statues of antiquity in graceful poses. The little prima donna didn't know how to breathe, but she had great warmth.

By the time the curtain came down, Tonio had had much too much white wine between the acts and was arguing furiously with Guido about whether or not the music was just a blatant imitation of Scarlatti or something legitimately new. Guido said there was originality there, Tonio must hear more Neapolitan composers, and suddenly they were being moved through the lobby by the press of the excited crowd.

Men and women spoke to Guido; carriages were coming up one by one to the open doors.

"Where are we going?" Tonio said. He was dizzy, and when the carriage lurched forward he almost lost his balance and realized a woman opposite was laughing at him. She had black hair and a milk white throat and only the gossamer sleeves over her arms and little dimples on the backs of her hands.

Tonio did not actually remember entering the house. He was moving through an endless chain of immense rooms all of them splashed with the vibrant colors these Neapolitans seemed to love, gilt and enamel furniture against the walls, the windows draped with tasseled brocade, the chandeliers encrusted with white wax and wreathed with soft light as hundreds of musicians assembled in various orchestras, stroking their shining violins, blowing their golden horns to fill the broad marble hallways with a rippling, almost violent music

Trays of white wine floated through the air. Tonio captured one glass in his hands and drank it down, then took another, the wigged servant in his blue satin coat as still as a statue, then off again.

Suddenly he was lost. He had not seen Guido for the longest time, and he was being accosted it seemed by one woman after another who spoke to him in French or English or Italian. An elderly woman was gliding towards him, and then putting out her long arm as if it were a cane, crooked him in her hand and brought him forward until her dry lips touched his chest. "Radiant child," she said in Neapolitan dialect.

He disentangled himself, lost his balance, and felt he had to escape from this. It seemed everywhere he looked he saw perfect skin, some little mound of breast over a strip of ribbon. A woman laughing so hard she could not breathe held her ruffled breasts in her hands as if they would fall out of the seams of her printed taffeta dress, and seeing him she made her lips vanish behind a white lace fan on which there was an arc of red roses.

He was teetering over a billiard table. And then he realized that far away on the edge of that room stood a gaunt, consumptive man, so white of skin that he could all but see his bones beneath his flesh, staring at Tonio and smiling.

For one moment he did not know who this was, only that he must know. And then he realized it was that vision of death, that living corpse who had stood over him on Mount Vesuvius. He moved towards this man. Ah, yes, it was that consumptive, only done up now in a frivolous coat of gold-threaded brocade which gave him the tawdry look of one of those marble statues in a church which is dressed in real cloth garments by the faithful.

The man wore a powdered wig, and his eyes, deep-set and full of shadows, moved almost fondly over Tonio as he allowed Tonio to move closer and closer.

Again a tray of drinks, the fragile glass in his hands. He was right up against the man and they were looking at one another.

"Alive and well," said the man in a hollow, cracking voice. And instantly, as if in pain, he put his handkerchief to his lips, the rings on his fingers bound to white bones. He backed away, doubling slightly, and it seemed a whirl of skirts opened to envelop him.

"I want to get out of here," Tonio whispered. "I must get out of here." And when another woman drew close, he found himself giving her such a vicious look that she backed off, affronted. He had turned, stumbling into an empty supper room with a long table set for some hundred persons it seemed, with sumptuous plate and fresh cut flowers.

And far down the wall, in one of the deep-set arched windows, stood a lone young woman watching him.

For just one second he thought she was the little prima donna of the opera, and a wave of despair came over him. He heard the richness of her voice, its lusty peaks, and saw again those little breasts, heaving with her untrained breaths, and felt the despair agitated to panic.

But this was not the prima donna. This was another young woman with the same fair hair and blue eyes, only she was tall and slight of build and her eyes were very dark, almost smoky. She wore only a plain dress of violet-colored silk, with none of those frills and ribbons he'd seen on the stage, and this dress molded her arms and her shoulders exquisitely. It appeared she'd been watching him for a long time as he stood there, and that before he had come in, she'd been crying.

He knew he must leave this room. But gazing at her, he felt an anger mingling in him with some drunken passion. She was lithesome, this girl, her hair full of lovely little wisps that softened its calculated curls, giving her an aureole in the candlelight.

And without meaning to, he was approaching her. It was not only that prettiness that drew him, however. There was something abandoned and uncaring about her. Crying, crying, he thought, why is she crying? He stumbled. He was very drunk. Before him a candle teetered on the tablecloth and then fell over. It went out with a fragrant wick of smoke rising straight to the ceiling.

And he found himself before her, marveling that those dark smoky-blue eyes seemed to hold no fear of him.

No fear. No fear. And why in God's name should she be afraid of him! He felt his teeth clench. He had not meant to touch her. And yet he had reached out.

And all of a sudden, without reason, fresh tears appeared in her eyes. She was crying helplessly.

And it was she who laid her head against his shoulder.

It was an anguishing moment. It was full of terror. Her soft yellow hair smelled like rain against his face, and in the gaping ruffle of her dress, he saw her bosom as it rested against him. He knew that if he did not get away from her, he would strike her, do her some appalling violence, and yet he was holding her so tight surely he was hurting her.

He lifted her chin. He closed his mouth on hers, and then heard her cry out. She was struggling.

It seemed he'd fallen backwards. She was far, far away from him, and the look on her face in those shadows was so innocent and so stricken that turning he all but ran out of this

207

room until he found himself in the very middle of the ball, and its great confusion of dancers.

"Maestro," he murmured, turning this way and that, and when suddenly Guido took his arm he insisted that he had to get out of here.

An elderly woman was nodding to him. The man beside him was explaining to him that the Marchesa wanted to dance with him. "I cannot. . . ." He was shaking his head. . . .

"Oh, yes, you can," Guido's low voice rumbled in his ear. He felt Guido's hand in the small of his back.

"Damn you," he whispered. "I have to get out of here. . . . You must help me . . . get back to the conservatorio."

But he was bowing to this ancient woman, kissing her hand. There was such a sweetness in her expression, the ruin of a lovely face, and a grace even to the withered arm outstretched to him.

"No, Maestro—!" he whispered.

She turned lightly in her white slippers. He felt the room going round and round. He must not see that fair-haired girl. He must not see her! He would go mad if she suddenly appeared, and yet somehow if he could only make it known to her.

But what?

That he wasn't to blame, she wasn't to blame.

They were facing each other, the Marchesa and he, the music was full into the quadrille and by some miracle he came forward, bowed to his partner, breaking to move down the long line of couples exactly as he'd done a thousand times before, but again and again he kept forgetting what he was doing!

Guido appeared, his brown eyes too big for his face.

And then he was leaning on Guido, saying something to someone, an apology, he must leave, he must get out of this place, he must be in his room, his own room, or they should go up now onto the mountain. Yes, go up on the mountain, this was the one thing he had been unable to admit to himself, it was unendurable.

"You are tired," Guido said.

No, no, no, he shook his head. Impossible to tell anyone, but the thought that he could never again lie with a woman was unendurable. He would start roaring if he did not stop thinking of it. Where was she? He had never believed for a moment that Alessandro could really do it! He had thought

208

his mother such a child, and Beppo, inconceivable. And Caffarelli, what had he really done when he got alone with them?

Guido was lifting him up into the carriage. "I want to go up on the mountain!" he said again furiously. "You leave me alone. I want to go, I know where I am going."

The carriage was moving. He saw the stars above, felt the warm breeze on his face, and saw the leafy branches dipping down as though they meant to stroke him. If he thought of little Bettina now in the gondola, that soft nest of white limbs, that silky flesh inside her thighs, he would go mad. Banish him! He would never set foot there again, until . . . and when . . .

He fell against Guido. They were standing at the conservatorio gates, and he said, "I want to die." Confide to you my pain, I'd rather die. And that voice spoke to him again, from inside himself, saying, Behave as if you are a man, and he was walking upstairs to bed as if he felt nothing.

4

IT WAS SOON CLEAR that whenever Tonio was too tired to work, Guido would have some reward for him. They would go out to the opera, or Tonio would be given some simple arias to enjoy. But Guido could not be foxed in this. He *knew* when his pupil could do no more, and one afternoon when Tonio was unusually discouraged Guido took him out of the practice room and down the hall to the conservatorio theater.

"Sit here; watch and listen," he said, leaving Tonio in the back row of chairs where he might stretch his aching limbs unnoticed.

Tonio had been more than intrigued by the sounds issuing from this room.

And he was delighted to find it was as lavish a little theater as any he had ever seen in a Venetian palazzo. It had one tier of boxes all fitted with emerald green curtains, and its proscenium arch was aglitter with gilded scrollwork and angels.

Some twenty-five musicians were at work in the pit, an

awesome number it seemed, since the opera house had only that many for some performances, and all were working away on their private exercises oblivious to singers practicing their scales, and the student composer, Loretti, fuming that the production would never be ready for the first night two weeks from now.

Guido, pausing at the door, laughed shortly at this and told Tonio everything was going splendidly.

Tonio started, as if awakened from a dream, because from the milling cast on the boards he'd already picked out the figure of Domenico, that exquisite sylph of a boy, whom he'd seen of late only at the supper table.

He had never once thought of this room, or of the coming production, without thinking of Domenico.

But the composer was calling everyone to attention.

The rest period was over, and within minutes a silence fell over the little theater and the musicians struck up the overture.

Tonio was astonished at the richness of the sound; these boys were better than professionals he'd heard in Venice, and when the first singers appeared on the stage, he realized that these students were probably ready to perform anywhere in Europe.

Naples was surely the musical capital of Italy as everyone had always said, though Venetians sneered at those words, and in a moment of gentle calm, listening to this lovely, lively music, Tonio thought, Naples is my city.

A relief coursed through him. The pain in his legs from so many hours of standing was almost delicious. And leaning forward to the rounded back of the green velvet chair in front of him, he folded his arms on its carved frame and rested his chin there.

Domenico appeared. And though he was dressed in his simple black tunic and red sash, he seemed to have become the woman whose role he was playing. There was about every gesture a yielding and a grace that caused Tonio suddenly to feel tense, resentful.

Only the boy's voice distracted him. It was high, pure, and utterly translucent, with none of the opacity of the falsetto. His true soprano range was obviously phenomenal, and the liquid manner in which he connected his rounded tones made Tonio ashamed of his own miserable performance with the *Accentus*.

"This is a voice to reckon with," he sighed as soon as

Domenico had finished and made his exit. But this was merely a rehearsal and the boy lingered at the edge of the stage, his body forming such a languid posture that he seemed to be resting comfortably against the air as if it were a tree, and over the length of the house, his eyes appeared to be fixed on Tonio.

Tonio was so absorbed by this, by the light angular figure of the boy and those hollow cheeks and deep-set black eyes, that he did not even notice a figure was approaching him.

Then suddenly he realized a shadow had fallen over him. He looked up just as the music died away, and a silence fell over the theater.

Lorenzo, the castrato he had stabbed a month ago for tormenting him, was standing beside him.

Tonio stiffened.

He rose slowly. His eyes moved warily over this boy who was taller than he was, and dark-skinned as well as dark-haired, a somewhat rough-looking individual. Like many of the castrati, however, he had a bloom to him, though the face was plain and without contrast.

His eyes were fixed on Tonio. The rehearsal had come to a complete halt.

And Tonio had no weapon.

Yet as Tonio gave the boy a slow nod of greeting, he let his right hand rise slightly as if for something at his waist. Then he lowered it again as if he would pass it up under his tunic to reach for a stiletto. The gesture was drawn out, calculated.

But the boy appeared not to notice. His body taut, fingers curled at his sides, he acknowledged Tonio's nod with his own bow, his mouth breaking into a long ugly smile as he did so.

No one made a sound in the little theater.

And then Lorenzo, moving backwards carefully, turned and left Tonio there.

Tonio stood still, thinking. He had expected some attack from this boy. But this was worse. This boy meant to kill him.

That afternoon he left the conservatorio with Guido's permission to bring a locksmith back to his room; and slipping his stiletto into his belt, he now took it with him everywhere. No one could see it under his tunic. And wherever he went, he

211

was cautious. Climbing the stairs in the dark at night, he listened before advancing.

But he was not afraid. And then suddenly the absurdity of that caused him to flush. He was not afraid because Lorenzo was only a eunuch!

He shook his head, his brain teeming. Was that what Carlo had counted on? That Tonio was only a eunuch?

He wished he could get at his brain with his hands and squeeze the organ of thought itself, he was in such pain suddenly. He did not know what the years would do to him, or what they had done to this dark-skinned boy from the south of Italy whom he had stabbed so thoughtlessly when he felt like a cornered animal. But should he expect any less of this one than he expected of himself?

As time passed, he found himself hoping that this boy would attack him and wondering how it would go when it happened.

A slight murderous feeling came over him when he thought of it, bound up with the memory of his strength pitted against others, not the awful defeating blows that had brought him down in that room in Flovigo, but that moment when he had almost been free, and then drawing back from that pain, he thought coldly, sensibly, I will meet this when it comes to me.

But nothing happened in the following weeks except that this boy had changed his position at table so that Tonio might see him, and see that sinister smile which he never failed to offer with some gracious gesture.

And Tonio's hours with Guido deepened into fixed patterns, brilliantly illuminated now and then by wonderful little victories, though Guido was colder than ever, and taking Tonio out more and more often in the evenings in spite of it.

They attended comic operas which Tonio loved more than he thought he would (since they so seldom used castrati) and another performance of the same tragic opera at the San Bartolommeo.

Afterwards, however, Tonio would not go to any balls or suppers with Guido. Guido was puzzled by this. He seemed slightly disappointed. Then he remarked coldly that such entertainments were good for Tonio. But Tonio said he was tired, or that he would rather be at his practice in the morning. And Guido shrugged, accepting this.

212

Tonio was cold all over and sweating when these little discussions happened. He had only to think of those women around him and he felt a suffocating fear. And then he would think, without meaning to, of Bettina in the gondola; it was as if he could feel the gentle sway of the boat, smell the water around him, breathe the air that was Venetian air, and again there came the sensation of that warmth in entering her, the wetness of the little hairy cleft between her legs, and that incredible flesh on the inside of her thighs where he had sometimes nuzzled his head before taking her.

He would grow still at such times, silent, looking out the window of the carriage as if in the most peaceful thought.

And coming back one night from the San Bartolommeo, it occurred to him that he would not be entirely safe until he was inside the conservatorio. An odd thought when Lorenzo, offering his sly smile whenever their paths crossed, was obviously waiting there for the chance to harm him.

Yet the early part of these evenings out meant everything to Tonio. He was loving the theaters of Naples, and all the nuances of the performances were alive for him. There were times when after several glasses of wine he felt talkative, and he and Guido were constantly interrupting each other in their impetuosity.

And at other times, a baffling apprehension of the strangeness of it all would descend on Tonio. He and Guido behaved for the most part as if they were enemies of each other. Tonio was often as haughty as Guido was surly.

And one night when they were riding along the curve of the sea, and the air was salty and warm, and Guido had bought a bottle of wine for them, and the carriage was open, and the stars seemed especially low and brilliant in the clean sky, Tonio found himself quietly agonizing over this coldness between them. He stared at Guido's profile against the white foam that seemed to lash the black water and thought, This is the gruff tyrant who makes my days so miserable when with just a few words of praise he could make everything easier. And yet here he sits a gentleman tonight in his handsome clothes talking to me as if we were merely good friends in a drawing room. He is two people. Tonio sighed.

Guido seemed to have no awareness of Tonio's thoughts. He was describing to him in a low voice a talented composer named Pergolesi who was dying of consumption and had been so ridiculed in Rome when his opera premiered there that he had never recovered from it. "The Roman audiences are the worse," Guido sighed. And then he looked off to sea as if distracted. He added that Pergolesi had entered the Gesù Cristo Conservatorio years ago and was about Guido's own age. If Guido had given his all to composing he might have to worry now about the Roman audiences.

"And why didn't you give your all to composing?" Tonio asked.

"I was a singer," Guido murmured. And then Tonio remembered that flaming speech which Maestro Cavalla had made to him the night he'd gone up to the mountain. He was suddenly embarrassed to have forgotten it. He thought so much about himself, his pain, his recovery, his small triumphs that he had thought almost nothing about this man beside him, really, and then he thought, And so this is why he despises me?

"The music you've often given me . . . it's your own, isn't it?" Tonio asked. "It's marvelous!"

"Don't purport to tell me what is good or bad in what I do!" Guido suddenly became incensed. "I will tell you when my music is good just as I will tell you when your singing is good!"

Tonio was stung. He took a deep swallow of the wine, and without warning, even to himself, threw his arms around Guido.

Guido was furious. He pushed him off roughly.

Tonio shrugged, laughing. "You embraced me once, twice, if you remember," he said. "So I embrace you now and then. . . ."

"For what reason!" Guido snapped. He took the wine from Tonio and took a drink of it.

"Because I don't despise you as you despise me. I am not such a divided person!"

"Despise you?" Guido growled. "I don't care about you one way or the other. It's your voice I care about. Are you satisfied?"

Tonio settled back against the black leather seat, his eyes on the stars. His mood gradually darkened. Why do I care what this boor feels, he was thinking, why is it necessary that I like him? Why can't I just take what he gives me . . .? But then a coldness came over him. He felt a chill that signaled the old pain, and he found himself thinking suddenly of the

214

opera they'd heard, of this or that little musical problem to distract himself, anything but of how lonely he suddenly felt, and it was unreal to him for an instant that he had ever lived in a great house in Venice with a father and a mother and servants so much a part of life they were his flesh and blood and. . . . This was Naples, this was the sea, this was his home now.

Two days later Guido informed Tonio at the end of a particularly ragged and hot day that he might sing a very small part in the chorus of the conservatorio opera.

"But it's to be put on tomorrow night," Tonio said. Yet he was already on his feet.

"You'll only sing two lines at the end," said Guido. "You can learn them in an instant, and it will be good for you to taste the stage immediately."

Tonio had never dreamed this would come so soon.

And being backstage was the real excitement. He couldn't get enough of what was happening around him.

He peered into dressing rooms heaped with plumes and costumes, with tables piled with powder and paint, and watched in awe as a great row of ornamented arches was slowly lifted into the black void above the stage by weighted ropes that brought it soundlessly down again. It seemed an endless maze was formed in this vast open place behind the rear curtain in which the carcasses of other operas lay abandoned. He found a golden coach covered with fluttering paper flowers, and transparent scrims with only the barest trace of stars and clouds on them.

Boys ran to and fro with swords in hand, or lugging gilded cardboard urns full of cardboard foliage.

And as the rehearsal commenced, Tonio marveled to see order brought out of chaos, performers drifting in on cue, the orchestra giving forth its spirited accompaniment, the whole sharpened and fast paced and full of one delightful aria after another, the voices astonishing in their agility.

He could scarce concentrate on his usual exercises the next day, until finally Guido limited them to those lines Tonio would sing that night in the chorus.

He did not see the full cast in costume until an hour before the curtain.

The audience was already arriving. Carriage after carriage rolled through the gates. There was lively chatter in the corridors, and candles everywhere gave the building a festive warmth, bringing to life nooks and crannies that had always disappeared into evening darkness. The great drawing room was filled with the local nobility, come to see this early preview of singers and composers who might later attain celebrity.

Tonio, hurrying into the wings, found himself caught up in the frenzy. Cast as a soldier, he wore one of his more colorful Venetian coats of red with gold embroidery, and a ribbon was now fixed over his shoulder to the hilt of his sword in the manner of the last century.

"Sit down," said a voice, gesturing to a little table before a mirror, and he was quickly draped so that a great deal of powder could cover his black hair, finally bringing it up to complete whiteness. He flinched when deft hands commenced to powder his face, and he stared in fascination when all the painting was finished.

The sight of his eyes so heavily circled in black intrigued him and disturbed him at the same time.

But all around him were painted faces, complexions that seemed almost to glitter.

Peering through a small chink beyond the corner of the stage, he saw the boxes were filled. White wigs, jewels, flashing satin and taffeta everywhere. Tonio drew back feeling the oddest throbbing inside of him, the strangest vulnerability.

It could not be that he was performing on this stage before all these men and women who only six months before. . . . He stopped and shut his eyes. He must command his limbs to be still, his heart to cease its pounding. And he felt the first sting of tears in his eyes before he could prevent it.

But turning suddenly around he gave himself to the whirl of activity behind the curtain. In a distant mirror he saw a young boy who was himself looking innocent, fresh, with a serene expression like those white-wigged men who stare at you from the corner of the eye in portraits. And just the touch of a smile shaped his lips as inside of him the pain went away at his command. Each time, perhaps, he thought, it will be easier.

The fact was he loved what was happening! And if some sense of humiliation threaded him through and through it was only a bass chord thumping softly beneath a lovelier, stronger music. He touched the powder on his face; he gave that

216

distant mirror image one last deliberate glance and the smile became fuller and slower and he looked away from it.

The Maestro di Cappella strode into the wings and reached out with both hands for a young goddess who had just appeared, her white curls flowing down her back, her skin like bisque with a blush to the cheeks so subtle and beautiful that Tonio gasped to see her.

It seemed an eternity he gazed at this luxurious doll before he realized with a start that there could be no women on this stage, this was Domenico!

The Maestro di Cappella was driving home his last instructions. Domenico's dark eyes slipped to one side and opened just a little wider when they saw Tonio, and those pink lips curled with complete sweetness.

But Tonio was too stunned to give any wordless answer. He was studying the shape of this creature, the small waist, the ruffles of pink lace that grew broader and broader as they mounted to the breast, and there the barest little cleavage of the ravishing flesh pressed by the border of pink ribbon. This is impossible, he was thinking.

Then clutching the voluminous white satin skirts in both hands, Domenico moved past the Maestro di Cappella and in front of everyone planted a kiss on Tonio's cheek so that he drew back as if burnt. Everywhere there was laughter.

"Enough of that!" the Maestro said.

Domenico had become a woman! And turning now with the most graceful and subtly flirtatious air, he whispered in a husky tender voice that he was merely assuming his role already, becoming the woman he must play on the stage, of course. Again, laughter.

But Tonio had receded into the shadows. The first backdrop of painted arches had been lowered into place. Against this classic garden most of the action would occur, never mind that it was set in the ancient Greek countryside and all these frock-coated, wigged creatures were rustics!

Giovanni, Piero, and other castrati who had major roles in the performance had assumed their places ready to go on, and their attendants were brushing the powder from their lapels furiously.

Someone said that this was Loretti's big chance, the Contessa *had* come, and if this went half as well as it should, next year he'd be composing for the San Bartolommeo.

Loretti meantime had come backstage to plead with Domenico

to follow his beating of time, and Domenico had nodded graciously.

Now Loretti was back at the harpsichord. The house lights were down with only scattered attendants at the doorways holding single tapers. Someone fell in the backstage shadows, the curtain shivered on its ropes, and the orchestra commenced with all the violent brilliance of a great gathering of musicians in a royal theater.

It seemed the night was one of the longest Tonio had ever endured, with all manner of mishaps and over and over again the magic of perfection before the footlights, as the presence of an audience pulled this frantic little band of talented boys together. The arias rose and fell splendidly over the tinkling keyboard continuo, Domenico's voice soaring like the pipe of a god in a mythic forest. The spotlights bathed him in ethereal light, he made his exits with extraordinary grace, and time after time, threw his beaming smile at Tonio.

Tonio's head was aching when at last he stepped onto the stage, and swept up with the grandest excitement, felt to the marrow of his bones that he was now part of this magnificent illusion. He could hear his voice amplified by the voices around him, and seeing only the barest shimmer of the audience he felt its presence everywhere in the gloom, and the applause that followed this finale was a veritable thunder.

The elation could not have been more shared had they all locked hands before the curtain. Bows were taken again and again. Someone whispered that Domenico's fame was made. He had sung better than anyone currently on the stage in Naples, and as for Loretti, look at him!

Maestro Cavalla pushed behind the curtain embracing his singers one by one until he came to Domenico. He made as if to strike this exquisite girl who cowered with a soft husky ripple of laughter.

They were all invited to the Contessa's now, he said, to her house, now, now, all of them. The Maestro took Tonio by the shoulders and kissing him on both cheeks, took a bit of paint from his face, and said: "See, you have this in your blood now, you'll never recover from it."

Tonio smiled. The applause was still ringing in his ears.

But he knew that he must not, he could not, go with them to the house of the Contessa.

* * *

218

For a moment, it seemed he wouldn't get away. It surprised him that so many others wanted him to join them. Piero said, "You must come," and whispered that Lorenzo would not be with them.

But removing the blue ribbon from his sword, Tonio hurried off to leave by the stage door to the garden, when someone beckoned to him from a dressing room. There was only a little light. He felt in his coat for his stiletto. "Come in here!" came the whisper again.

And he advanced very slowly, pushing the door wide with his left fingers.

A candle burned on either side of a big standing mirror in this room, and all about it were elaborate dresses on hooks, wigs on their blind wooden heads, and heaps of paste buckle slippers. It was Domenico who had summoned him, and he quickly shut the door and drew the latch on it.

Tonio's fingers didn't leave the handle of his stiletto. But there was no one else in the room, he soon saw that.

"I have to leave now," he said, averting his eyes from that tiny fold of flesh that gave the perfect illusion of a woman's bosom.

Domenico appeared to lie against the door, and in the shadowy dark, his face was luminous and delicate. When he smiled the hollows of his cheeks deepened, the light played more beautifully on the bones, and when he spoke, it was that woman's voice again, husky and stroking.

"Don't be afraid of him," he whispered.

Tonio realized he had taken a step backwards. His heart was making a tumult inside of him.

"Afraid of whom?" he asked.

"Lorenzo, of course," said the roughened velvet voice. "I won't let him do anything to you."

"Don't come any closer!' Tonio said sharply. Again he took a step backwards.

But Domenico only smiled, his head falling a little to the left so that the white powdered curls spilled over his shoulder onto that flaring breast.

"You mean I am the one you're afraid of?"

Tonio looked away in confusion. "I have to leave here," he said.

Domenico let out a long beguiling breath. And then suddenly he put his arms around Tonio; he pressed the soft ruffles of his breast against Tonio. Tonio stumbled back and

219

found himself against the mirror, the candles flickering on either side of him. He reached back for the glass, his hands down, to get his balance.

"You are afraid of me," Domenico whispered.

"I don't know what you want!" Tonio said.

"Ah, but I know what you want. Why are you afraid to take it?"

Tonio was going to shake his head but he stopped, staring into Domenico's eyes. It was inconceivable that anything of a man existed under this froth, this magic. And when he saw the lips moist and parting and drawing near to him, he shut his eyes, straining away. Surely he could knock this creature to the floor with one blow, and yet he was shrinking back as if he might be burned here!

But he felt the length of Domenico against him, the curve of his thigh under the satin skirt, and then Domenico's hand reaching for the front of his breeches.

He almost struck Domenico. But Domenico's face touched his, he felt the eyelashes against him at the same moment Domenico's hand found his sex and, stroking it, brought it to life.

Tonio was so shocked that he almost killed it.

Again he let his eyes close. And when Domenico kissed him, he felt his passion collecting, and then Domenico's hand opening the cloth, freeing his sex to go its full length as Domenico appeared to look down and utter some little oath under his breath, and then turning his face up again he kissed Tonio roughly, parting his lips, drawing the breath out of him, and giving it back as his hands shaped and hardened what they held so tightly.

Tonio couldn't stop himself from going up under the dress and when he felt the hard small organ there, he drew back as if he'd touched something hot, and again Domenico kissed him.

In a moment, they were both of them on their knees, and then Domenico lay under Tonio on the stone floor and was offering himself face up as if he were a woman.

It was tight, oh, so tight, and so very like a woman, tighter even at its very mouth and rough, so that he gritted his teeth and gave an awful moan between them. He thrust harder and harder until at last he'd felt the pinnacle and then he lay there shuddering.

He was staring down at Domenico. He didn't remember drawing away, but he was sitting against the mirror, his knees

220

to one side just looking at the little girl on the floor who now rose as languidly and gracefully as she did everything else until she was standing over him.

He was too dazed to speak. And it had all happened so quickly, the same as before, there was no difference! He felt a mindless urge to rise and take the figure in his arms again, to crush it with kisses, eat at it with kisses.

To rip that little ribbon away from the breast and see what was there!

But Domenico had already pulled loose the clasps of the dress and let it fall around him. At the sight of the gossamer chemise Tonio winced. And then it too fell to the floor and the great white wig was lifted and laid aside as Domenico shook out his moist black curls, tossing them free in a rather mannish, head-forward gesture.

Tonio was staring wide-eyed at him. His body so not a woman's body, no, not at all, and yet it was certainly not the body of a man either.

The chest was flat; only the size of the lungs gave it its full shape and the skin as everywhere else was beautiful. And the sex itself was a short but rather thick penis, hard now, and eager for what it could get, obviously.

But the most mystifying thing of all was that the dark hair around it had the shape of a woman's hair, not a man's, which grows wildly up onto the belly. Rather it was straight across the top as if it had been shaved with a razor, and therefore formed a dark inverted triangle exactly like the hair of a woman.

But all of the body engrossed him, the lovely skin and the slender graceful legs, the beautiful face with its remnants of paint and the full dark hair falling down like that of those large marble angels.

This creature came down now on his knees.

Tonio turned away.

"Do you think I want of you what you don't have to give?" Domenico whispered. "Take me again, and this time on the hard floor with nothing under me but your hand," he said, and he lay down on his face, drawing Tonio on top of him.

Tonio drew up, looking at the small tight buttocks under him. He was engulfed by the memory of that tight opening, its little rough mouth that was almost too tight and the warmth inside of it. And suddenly he collapsed on the naked figure, feeling its nakedness against his rough clothes, the

221

bare flesh of the neck under his teeth, as Domenico drew his right hand down under the smooth belly and placed that thick, hard sex in it.

Tonio felt himself stiffen, gasp. He was inside of the boy again and he rode him with one vicious thrust after another. He felt his hand close on that sex, abusing it, working it as if he meant to break it off as the boy moaned against the cold floor, and when Tonio felt the climax again, Domenico shuddered beneath him.

Tonio fell to one side and lay on his back, exhausted.

When he opened his eyes, Domenico was fully dressed, with his scarlet cape over one shoulder.

"Come on, now, they're calling for us!" He smiled. "You must get the paint off your face, hurry."

Tonio scarcely heard him. It seemed he was a woman in the clothing of a man; and before he had been a man in the clothing of a woman. Rising on his arm, Tonio tried to speak but he could say nothing.

The tumult in his mind was not thought. And what he was feeling was not happiness. It was the most overpowering relief that he had ever known, and quietly he did anything that Domenico told him to do.

In the dark of the carriage, all the way to the house of the Contessa Lamberti on the road to Sorrento, he devoured Domenico with kisses. And when Domenico reached into Tonio's clothes, when he felt that scar behind his sex, Tonio stopped in the act of hitting him. He stopped because it was enough to crush him in both hands like something that wanted and needed to be crushed and to press him down again and take him again even as the carriage rocked steadily behind the thin beams of its lanterns.

It was very late that night that Tonio again saw the young fair-haired woman he'd encountered at the Contessa's house before, in the empty supper room. She was not sad now as she had been then. In fact, she was laughing as she danced, conversing with her partner. Her sharp little shoulders, so nicely rounded for all their straightness, gave her an almost jaunty grace as she moved, lifting her blue skirts all of a piece, and her yellow hair was full of neglected white flowers.

He looked away, however, when their eyes met. And wished that, tonight of all nights, she had not been here. Yet he could not prevent himself from glancing back to her.

The dance had stopped; a tall, white-wigged gentleman was whispering in her ear, and again her little face became radiant with laughter. He had not remembered she had such a lovely neck, or that her breasts had spilled so beautifully into her bodice, and when he saw that snug blue fabric shaping her little waist, he felt his teeth clench in spite of himself. He fancied he could hear her laugh through all these mingled voices. But then she looked shyly away, falling into a seemingly instant preoccupation. She looked as she had before, almost sad, and he wanted desperately to talk to her.

He at once imagined them alone again in some place he didn't know, as he told her he was neither coarse nor mean, and he had never meant to insult her. He was damned fortunate, he thought, that he did not have two men looking to do him harm, Lorenzo and this girl's father.

It seemed Domenico sought him out then, just as these thoughts were taking their worst hold, and seeing that beaming face so close to his, feeling himself in possession of this dazzling presence which others desired, he felt again the quick surge of his passion. He could have taken Domenico on the floor of this place. He wanted nothing more than some dark chamber and the danger of discovery.

But he saw that pretty girl again and again.

He saw her sometimes sitting alone on the edge of a tapestried chair, her hands idle in her lap, her face abstracted and serious.

And there was about her that negligent air he'd sensed before. It was as if you could take her up, carry her off, and she would never have the presence of mind to protest it. He saw himself raking loose all that blond hair, wiping back the loose strands from her forehead. He imagined it tumbling down around the irresistible slope of her shoulders, and then he saw himself gathering up all those curls again, the better to kiss her neck. This was maddening.

But once after a long moment, she looked up at him directly. He was a great distance away, but it was as if she'd known all the while he was watching her. He could see the dark blue of her eyes, and instead of turning away, he stood transfixed, wishing to God he had never seen her.

5

IN THE WEEKS that followed it seemed to Tonio that surely Guido knew of his little "affair" with Domenico. Yet Guido gave no real sign of it.

He was as cold as ever, but the stunning velocity of Tonio's progress absorbed him so completely that there was less time for gratuitous meanness. Both of them were lost in their work for hours at a time, and Tonio's schedule had hardened into that of a senior student.

He sang for two hours, then two hours more before a mirror, watching his stance, his gestures, just as if he were on the stage, then after the noon meal devoted himself to librettos, practicing his enunciation. More singing for one hour. Then counterpoint, and improvisation. He must be able to pick up any melody and properly ornament it on his own. He worked furiously at the blackboard, Guido correcting his work before he was allowed to sing it.

Another hour of composition, then the day ended with singing. In between there were breaks during which he sang with the conservatorio choir, or worked in the theater on the next opera that would be performed at the end of the summer.

And then there were those afternoons when the boys went out to perform at various churches, and to walk in processions.

The first time Tonio willingly joined the double rank of castrati proceeding slowly through the streets it was as bad as he had expected. Some part of him, proud and perhaps always suffering bitterly inside, could not accept that he was being paraded before these gaping crowds as a customed gelding.

But each time he conquered this misery, his will was strengthened. And when he pierced through his contempt for what he saw, he beheld all manner of new aspects of what was happening to him. He saw awe in the eyes of those who banked the streets; they looked to the older castrati with reverence, straining to hear those polished voices, even memorizing the features of individual faces.

The hymns on the summer air, the church itself full of light and perfume, all of this gave forth its sensual brilliance. And finally lulled with small thoughts, or wrapped in the perfecting of his own singing, Tonio felt some vague enjoyment of it all. In these guilded churches, full of lifelike marble saints and glimmering candles, he knew moments of serene happiness.

But the feeling persisted that Guido knew of his nightly hours with Domenico and that Guido did not approve of it.

Actually it was Tonio who did not approve of it. Night after night he came upstairs to find Domenico in his rooms, no matter what the hour. Domenico was always fresh, fragrant with some spiced cologne, his hair undone on his shoulders. He would rise from sleep on Tonio's bed, his body so warm that at times it seemed he must be in the grip of a fever. But the fever was simply desire. He offered his lips, he offered his naked limbs, he did not care what Tonio did to him.

Their coupling was always rough. It had the outward form of rape, and sometimes the language of rape, and sometimes a mock struggle beforehand. Tonio would rip away the lace shirt, the breeches. He would run his hands over Domenico's skin that had the resilience and perfection of a baby's. Then he would slap Domenico if he chose, or force him up to be raped on his knees as if he were praying.

And finally after much persistence, Domenico lured him into the most delicious play beforehand. Going down between Tonio's leg's, he suckled him, devoured him, emitting his little moans as if this act—it was inconceivable to Tonio—were enough to satisfy him.

But the rape was always the end of it, Domenico's organ roughly clasped in Tonio's hand as if Tonio meant to punish him both ways as he thrust into him without the slightest care or gentleness.

It puzzled Tonio that Domenico did not need more, demand more. But Domenico was always satisfied afterwards.

And there were wild moments during the day, mostly in the quiet siesta hours, when Domenico would beckon him into some empty practice room, and this struggle would be enacted with the added spice of risk and secrecy. Tonio could not get enough of Domenico naked or clothed; he was not sure which was the greater pleasure. And then there was that memory often pervading everything, of Domenico as a woman.

225

Once or twice, incited by the perfection of Domenico's face, those fine features, and that wealth of perfumed hair, Tonio really slapped him.

But what puzzled Tonio about Domenico's acquiescence in bed was that Domenico was cold and uncompromising to everyone. He was beyond vanity as Tonio had once surmised, and he was also beyond routine nasty behavior. But he was not friendly to others, and sometimes in a rather clever way he was mildly abusive, especially to other eunuchs.

Yet there he was night after night inviting Tonio's hot cruelty.

Tonio was more than slightly ashamed of it. Why did he fall over and over into this gentle assault, why did he feel both pride and shame that others must know of it?

When he heard quite casually from the eunuch Piero that Domenico's last "very good friend" had been one of the regular boys, a violinist named Francesco, he was surprised how much this little bit of news amused him and satisfied him. So he was performing the "office" as well as that hairy, whole, and rough-looking violinist from Milan, was he?

Yet he was ashamed. And when he thought of Guido knowing of all this, he was so ashamed that he could find no explanation for it.

It would have helped had he and Domenico ever conversed, or shared some other pleasures. But they hardly ever spoke to each other!

Domenico was out of the conservatorio more than he was in it, singing in the chorus at the San Bartolommeo, and more often than not when he and Tonio did see each other in a fully lighted room it was during some ball or supper after the opera.

Because Tonio had commenced going to these again whenever Guido invited him.

Guido was obviously pleased with this. He had remarked quietly once that he thought all of this would be a pleasure for a boy of Tonio's age. Tonio had smiled. How could he tell Guido of the life he had lived in Venice? He found himself saying simply that these southern aristrocrats did not impress him very much. "They care so much about titles," he murmured, "and they seem so . . . well, self-satisfied and idle."

He was immediately sorry. This smacked of rudeness and

226

snobbery. Guido would become furious. But Guido didn't. Guido appeared to reflect on this as if it did not occur to him to be offended.

And one night after a particularly lavish supper at the house of the Contessa Lamberti, where there had been servants everywhere—a man behind each and every seated guest, others along the painted walls, to fill a glass, touch a candle to a Turkish cigarette—Tonio had an unusual glimpse of Guido among women he obviously knew, conversing with them somewhat naturally.

Guido was dressed in red and gold, his brown eyes and hair remarkably well set off, and he was completely at ease as if absorbed in some particular question. At some point he smiled; then he laughed; and in that moment he looked as young as he was, and gentle, and full of some capacity for feeling that Tonio had never guessed before.

Tonio could not take his eyes off him. Even Domenico, who had commenced to sing at the harpsichord, didn't distract him. He watched Guido's response to the boy's voice; and he had been watching Guido for the longest time when suddenly Guido's eyes found him in the crowd, and Guido's face toughened and grew cold, and then slightly angry.

Tonio flinched before he could look away. He fixed his eyes on Domenico; and when Domenico had finished, when the room resounded with applause, he threw to Tonio one of his most gracious looks, full of the knowledge of Tonio's possession of him.

Ah, disgraceful, Tonio thought.

He hated himself and everyone around him. Why think of all this, he murmured to himself. He wandered off alone to some dark room where the stones seemed damp, perhaps because it was always shut up, and he walked there in the moonlight from the high arched windows, thinking, Why does he despise me and why do I care? Damn him.

An ugly shame overwhelmed him. That he was lovers with another boy? Ah, this was appalling. And yet he knew why he did it. He knew that every time he did it with Domenico he proved to himself that he could do it, and therefore he could do it with a woman if he wanted to.

He was surprised to hear the click of the door behind him. So some servant had found him out even here; it's a wonder every dark corner was not full of them.

But when he turned he saw it was Guido.

Tonio felt a rush of hatred for him. He wanted to wound him. Wild and stupid thoughts came to him. He'd fake the loss of his voice, just to see what Guido would say; or get ill, just to see if Guido worried. This was idiocy! Some man you are, he murmured to himself quietly.

Of course all Guido saw was this young boy standing by waiting patiently for him to speak, Tonio knew that. Good.

"Are you tired of it all?" Guido asked gently.

"Why would you give a damn!" Tonio sneered.

Guido was astonished.

"Well, I don't give a damn, particularly," he said. "It's only that I'm tired of it. I want to go down into the city, to some out-of-the-way tavern for a while."

"It's late, Maestro," Tonio said.

"You can sleep tomorrow morning if you like," Guido said, "or you can go back home on your own, too, if you like. Well, are you coming?"

Tonio didn't answer.

Sit in a public tavern with another eunuch? He couldn't conceive of it. Rough men, the jostling and coarse laughter, the women with their short skirts and easy smiles.

All the warm, crowded taverns of Venice came back to him, the café of Battina's father, and all those other places that he and Ernestino and the street singers had frequented in those last days.

He missed all of it; he had always missed it. Hearty wine, tobacco, some special pleasure in drinking in the company of men.

But above all, he wanted to be free to go, free to go there or anywhere, without this suffocating sense of vulnerability.

"It's a place the boys often go," Guido said. "They're probably there now, all those who went to the opera tonight."

This would mean the older castrati was well as the other musicians. Tonio immediately envisioned them.

But Guido was walking out of the room. He had become frosty. "Well, go back when you like," he said over his shoulder. "I can trust you to behave yourself, I assume."

"Wait," Tonio said. "I'm coming with you."

It was jammed and full of congenial noise when they arrived. And the conservatorio musicians were there, and so were a good many fiddlers from the opera house whom Tonio recognized immediately. A few actresses were there also, but by and large it was a crowd of men, broken here and there by the pretty tavern girls trying to meet all the raised hands and calls for wine that seemed to come from everywhere.

Tonio could see that Guido was perfectly at ease here and even knew the woman who waited on them. He ordered the best wine, and some cheese and fruit to eat with it, and settling back into the wooden alcove in which they were seated, he stretched out his legs towards the crowd under the dim lamps and gazed at it contentedly.

He seemed to like the taste of the wine from a tin cup. He might be alone, Tonio thought.

And I am in Venice in Bettina's tavern and if I do not get up and go out to my brother's bravos who are waiting for me, then all of this is a dream. He shook his head, gulped the wine, and wondered if to these rude men here he appeared a boy or a castrato.

The fact was, there were many eunuchs in the room, and no one took any notice of it, any more than had the crowd in the bookshops in Venice when Alessandro came in to drink coffee and listen to the theater gossip.

But Tonio could feel the warmth in his face, and when a great gathering of men at one of the long rough tables began to sing, he was relieved to see all eyes turned on them.

Tonio drank all the wine in his cup and poured another from the bottle. He looked at the splintery wood in front of him, watching the droplets of dampness here and there bubbling up in the grease that gave it a sheen like a polish. He wondered wearily just how long it would take before he and that man who had come down from Vesuvius were one being.

The song was over. Several musicians had begun a duet with a mandolin, and these might have been regular street singers. It had a wild, savage sound to it, like something out of the hills, and again very unlike the melodies of the north. Perhaps it had more of the Spanish in it.

Tonio closed his eyes, letting the tenor's voice sift through his thoughts, and when he opened his eyes again, his cup was empty. He was aware that Guido was watching him as he poured a third cup, but Guido said nothing.

When it was exactly that Lorenzo had come to the table he did not know. He only knew that for a long time he had been aware of a figure there, and then looking up he saw it was

Lorenzo. The boy's head blocked the light of the low-hanging lamps, and he could not make out his features.

"Go on, Lorenzo," Guido said coldly.

Lorenzo's body bent forward into an arc, and he roared something suddenly at Guido in the Neapolitan dialect.

Tonio was on his feet. Lorenzo had drawn out his stiletto. A silence had fallen over those nearest, and Guido in that silence was obviously ordering Lorenzo to leave the tavern. He was threatening him, that much Tonio understood.

But he understood too that it didn't matter. The moment had come. Lorenzo's face was the picture of hatred and cunning. But he was also very drunk, and he looked as dangerous as any ordinary man as he advanced slowly on Tonio.

Tonio took a step backwards. He wasn't thinking clearly. He had to get his weapon out, but he knew if he reached for it what would happen. One of the tavern girls was pulling on Lorenzo's sleeve and men had risen from that long table in the center of the room, closing in around them. Guido suddenly gave Lorenzo a vicious shove and the crowd opened, but Lorenzo had his balance.

And Tonio had his weapon out, also.

"I don't want a quarrel with you," Tonio said in Italian.

The boy was spitting curses at him in the Neapolitan dialect.

"Speak so I can understand you," said Tonio. But it was as if the wine had evaporated in his veins. He was coolheaded, speaking, but thinking something completely different. For one moment he knew true fear: he imagined that weapon going right into his flesh; but he knew in that same moment that he had no time for this fear, this fear could not defeat him. He had taken a step backwards to broaden the distance, the better to see this boy who was much taller than he was, with a eunuch's seemingly endless arm ready to thrust that deadly blade right into him.

When Guido went to shove him again, the boy whirled around and everyone knew his threat was real, he would just as soon stab Guido.

It seemed some other figure entangled itself with them in the shadows, a man who was drawing Guido out of it.

Again Guido attempted to grab at Lorenzo, and as Lorenzo spun to attack him, Tonio uttered a growl and came forward.

Lorenzo snapped back immediately.

And then it happened so fast, Tonio could never have

230

explained it to anyone. The boy came at him, that great arm plunging straight forward, and Tonio buckled coming up under it, past it, feeling his blade jammed into Lorenzo. But the blade stopped, and then Tonio with all his might forced it, past cloth or flesh or bone or whatever impeded it, feeling it sink so weightlessly that he was crushed up against Lorenzo.

Lorenzo's left fingers closed on Tonio's face; Tonio jerked the stiletto out. And then Lorenzo staggered backwards.

A gasp went up from the crowd. Lorenzo's eyes were narrow with hatred, his stiletto held aloft, and then suddenly his eyes widened.

He fell forward, dead, onto the tavern floor at Tonio's feet, and Tonio stared down at him.

It seemed the crowd all of a body took hold of Tonio, gently pushing him back out of the tavern. A woman was screaming, and Tonio did not know what was happening to him. Hands turned him, shoved him, led him through a door into a dark alleyway; someone mentioned quickly for him to get away, that way, go! And suddenly Guido was pushing him forward.

He couldn't know it, but it was merely the instinctive action of the crowd to protect him. The police would be called; they had gotten the murderer away. They did not look to the police to settle anything.

Tonio was so sickened and horrified that Guido had to drag him into a cabriolet, and then pull him through the gates of the conservatorio. He continued to look back in the direction from which he'd come, even when he was forced into Guido's darkened study.

He struggled to speak, but Guido motioned for silence.

"But I . . . I . . ." Tonio was gasping as if he couldn't breathe.

Guido shook his head. He gave a slight lift to his chin and then his face fixed in a demonstrative expression of silence. But when he saw that Tonio didn't understand, he whispered, "Say nothing!"

All the next day Tonio struggled with his exercises, marveling that he now possessed such control over his voice that he could get through them.

If there was ever a formal acknowledgment of Lorenzo's death he did not hear it. If the body was found and brought back to the conservatorio, he did not know it.

Taking no breakfast or lunch (the thought of food disgusted him), he lay in his room at various periods wondering what was going to happen to him.

The fact that Guido carried on as usual was of course the most significant indication that Tonio wasn't going to be arrested. He knew, absolutely *knew*, that if he were in danger, Guido would tell him.

But as the congregation convened for the evening meal, he began to realize there was a subtle but unmistakable current moving through the dining hall. Everyone at one time or another was looking at him.

The regular boys, whom he had steadfastly avoided as if they did not exist, were giving him the smallest and most significant nods when their eyes met. And little Paolo, the castrato from Florence who always managed to sit very close to him, could not keep his eyes off Tonio, forgetting finally to eat. His round little snub-nosed face was full of deep fascination, and not once did he break into one of his impish smiles. As for the other castrati at table, they were clearly deferring to Tonio, passing him the bread first, and the communal pitcher of wine.

Domenico was nowhere to been seen; for the first time, Tonio wanted him here, not naked in bed upstairs, but here beside him.

And when he entered the theater for the evening's rehearsal, Francesco, the violinist from Milan, came up to him and asked him politely if in all his years at Venice he had ever heard the great Tartini.

Tonio murmured assent. Yes, and Vivaldi, too, he had heard them both that last summer on the Brenta.

This was all so unexpected and strange!

At last he was in his room, and exhausted. Domenico was in the shadows, he knew, though he could not see him. And finally Tonio, unable to contain himself any longer, blurted out:

"It was stupid, rash and stupid, for that boy to die."

"Probably the will of God," Domenico answered.

"Are you playing with me!" Tonio flashed.

"No. He couldn't really sing. Everyone knew that. And what is a eunuch who can't sing? He was better off dead." Domenico shrugged with perfect candor.

"Maestro Guido is a eunuch who cannot sing," Tonio whispered angrily.

"And Maestro Guido has twice tried to take his own life," said Domenico coolly. "Besides, Maestro Guido is the best teacher in this conservatorio. He's better than Maestro Cavalla and everyone knows it. But Lorenzo? What could Lorenzo do? Croak in a country church where no one knew any better? The world's full of eunuchs like that. It was in God's hands," and again he shrugged rather wearily.

He wound his arm around Tonio's waist like an agreeable snake. "Besides," he said, "what are you so worried about? He had no family."

"And the police?"

Domenico laughed outright. "My, but Venice must be a peaceful and orderly city! Come." He started to kiss Tonio.

This was the longest conversation they'd ever had and it was over.

But late that night, while Domenico slept, Tonio sat silently at the window.

He was stunned by the death of Lorenzo. He did not want to put it out of his mind, though for long moments he merely stared at the distant peak of Vesuvius. There were soundless flashes of light, and a trail of smoke marked the path of the lava flowing down to the sea.

It was as if he were mourning Lorenzo because no one else mourned him.

And against his will, he found himself far, far away from here, in that little town on the edge of the Venetian State, alone, under the stars, running. He felt the crunch of the dirt under his feet, and then those bravos taking hold of him. He was carried back into that dirty little room. He struggled with all his strength against them while they, as if in nightmare, forced him down over and over again.

He shuddered. He looked at the mountain. I am in Naples, he thought, and yet his memory expanded with all the insubstantiality of a dream.

Flovigo melted into Venice. He held the stiletto in his hands and this time he faced another opponent.

His mother cried and cried, her hair obscuring her face, as she had cried that last night in the supper room. They had not even taken leave of each other. When would they have their farewells? In those last moments, he had never dreamed that he would be parted from her. And now she cried on and on as if there were no one to comfort her.

233

He lifted the knife. He felt its handle firmly in his grip. And then he saw a familiar expression—what was it?—horror on Carlo's face? Surprise? The tension snapped.

He was in Naples, his head on the windowsill, exhausted.

He opened his eyes. The city of Naples was waking before him. The sun set its first rays into the mist that shrouded the trees. The sea was a gleam of metal.

Lorenzo, he thought, you were not the one. And yet the boy himself was already obliterated. And Tonio felt pride in that abominable moment, the blade, the body on the tavern floor.

Stricken, he bowed his head. He understood this pride in all its miserable components. He understood all the glory, all the significance, of that appalling act.

That he had been able to do it so easily, that he would do it again!

Domenico's delicate face was smooth in sleep as he lay so easily on the pillow.

And the sight of that beauty, given over to him so much and so often, made Tonio feel absolutely alone.

Entering the practice room an hour later, he needed the music, he needed Guido, and he felt his voice rising to meet this day's challenges with a new purity and a new vigor. It seemed the most difficult and intricate problems disappeared under his persistent attack. And by noon, he felt lulled by the possibility of beauty in the simplest tone.

Putting on his frock coat that night to go out, he realized that it had been tight on him for some time. He stared at his outstretched hands. And glancing up, almost furtively, in the mirror was astonished that he had grown so much so soon.

6

TONIO'S HEIGHT WAS INCREASING rapidly, there was no doubt of it, and every time he took some notice of it, he felt a weakening, a sudden loss of breath.

But he kept this to himself. He had his new coats made

with longer arms, knowing he would soon outgrow them otherwise, and though Guido worked him mercilessly, it seemed the entire city of Naples was outdoing herself to distract him.

In July, he had already witnessed the dazzling spectacle of St. Rosalia when fireworks had illuminated the whole sea, and it seemed a thousand boats had been brilliantly lit over the water.

And now in August shepherds came out of the distant hills of Apulia and Calabria, playing pipes and stringed instruments which Tonio had never heard, and dressed in the most rustic sheepskins, they visited the churches and houses of the aristocracy.

September brought the annual procession to Madonna del Piè di Grotta. All the boys of Naples' great conservatorios walked in it beneath balconies and windows beautifully and sumptuously draped for the occasion. The weather was milder, the summer heat had lifted.

And in October, the boys were gathered morning and night for nine days at the Franciscan church, an official duty for which the conservatorios were exempt from certain taxes.

Soon Tonio lost all track of the saints' days, the festivals, the street fairs, and the official occasions on which he was appearing. While untrained, he had often kept silent in the chorus, or sung only a few bars. But he was learning more and more of the music and singing it well, as Guido kept him up late and had him rise early to go over it.

There were enormous and elaborate processions for the various guilds in which the boys sometimes rode on massive floats, and there were also funerals.

And every waking hour in between there was Guido. There was the empty stone study, the exercises, and Tonio's voice gaining new flexibility, exactness.

Early in the fall, however, Tonio had received a letter from his cousin Catrina Lisani, and he was surprised at how little it affected him.

She said she was coming to Naples to see him. He at once wrote that she must not do this. He had put the past behind him, he said, and if she appeared here, he would not see her.

He hoped she would never write again, but there was not time to think about it, too brood, to let this throw its mantle over the present.

And when she wrote again, he answered politely that he would leave Naples, if need be, to avoid a meeting with her.

Her letters changed after this. Despairing of a visit, she broke her guarded style with a new candor:

> Everyone laments your departure. Tell me what you desire and I shall send it to you. Until I had your letter in hand and matched it with your old lessons, I did not believe you were living, though I had been told otherwise.
> What do you wish to know of this place? I will tell you all. Your mother was gravely ill after you left, refusing all food and drink, but she is now recovered.
> And your brother, your devoted brother! Why, he so reproaches himself for your going away that only the fair sex in great numbers can comfort him. And this medicine he mixes with as much wine as possible, though nothing prevents his morning attendance at the Grand Council.

At this Tonio put the letter aside, the words scalding him. Unfaithful to her so soon, he mused, and does she know it? And she was ill, was she, poisoned no doubt by the lies that he had forced her to digest, and why must he read any of this? Yet again, he unfolded the parchment:

> Write to me what you wish. My husband is ever your champion in the Council, and this banishment will not endure forever. I love you, my dearest cousin.

Weeks passed before he was to answer her. He had told himself these few years belonged to him, and that he did not wish to hear from her, nor anyone from Venice, ever again.

But one evening, without warning or explanation, the urge seized him, and he sat down and wrote her a brief but courteous reply.

After that, not a fortnight passed that he did not hear from her, though often he destroyed her letters so that he would not be tempted to read them over and over.

Another purse arrived from Venice. He had more money than he could spend.

And that winter he sold his carriage, as he never used it and did not wish to maintain it. And thinking that if he was to have a eunuch's long and lanky body he should dress it well, he ordered more magnificent clothes than ever in the past.

236

The Maestro di Cappella teased him on account of it, and so did Guido, but he was ever generous, gave gold to the beggars in the streets, and brought little Paolo presents whenever he could.

But he was rich even after that. Carlo had seen to it. He might have invested his funds. But he never found the time.

And as full as life was, as crowded with event and struggle and constant work, he was still astonished the morning Guido told him he would sing a solo in the Christmas Oratorio.

Christmas. He had been in this place half a year!

For a long moment he didn't reply. He was thinking that it had been at a Christmas mass in San Marco that he had first sung with Alessandro when he was only five years old.

He saw that fleet of gondolas going out across the water to venerate the relics on San Giorgio. Carlo would be with them now.

He tried to put this out of his mind.

And he realized that Domenico would be leaving Naples for Rome soon.

Domenico would make his first appearance in Rome at the Teatro Argentina at the opening of the Roman carnival on the New Year.

What had Guido said? That he would sing, he would sing what? He murmured some apology and when Guido said it again, that he was to sing a solo in the Christmas Oratorio, Tonio shook his head.

"I can't do that," he said. "I'm not ready."

"Who are you to tell me whether or not you are ready?" Guido asked earnestly. "Of course you're ready. I wouldn't have you sing it if you weren't ready."

Tonio could not stop the vision of all the lanterns riding the black lagoon as a fleet of gondolas made the Christmas crossing to San Giorgio.

The morning sun was shining full on the conservatorio garden outside, making each archway of the cloister a picture of yellow light and fluttering leaves. No, the light was tinted green actually. And yet Tonio wasn't in this place. He was in San Marco. His mother said, "See, your father!"

"Maestro, don't put me to this test," he murmured. He summoned all his Venetian breeding. "I cannot rely on my voice, and if you force me to sing alone, I'll fail you."

This worked wonders on Guido, who was getting angry.

"Tonio," he said, "have I perhaps failed *you?* I wonder. You are ready to sing this solo!"

Tonio didn't answer. He was too surprised, because he could not remember Guido ever calling him by name before. And he was unprepared for the fact that he cared so much that Guido had done so.

He insisted again that he couldn't sing. He tried to dispel the atmosphere of San Marco. Alessandro was right beside him, and Allesandro said, "I never believed it!"

When the day drew to a close, he was exhausted. Guido had said no more about the solo, but he had given him several pieces of Christmas music to sing, and for all he knew the solo was one of these. His voice was ugly and unwieldy to him.

And as he climbed the stairs to his room, he was discouraged and anxious. He didn't want to see Domenico, but there was a thin band of flickering light beneath the door, and Domenico was dressed and ready as though going out for the evening.

"I'm tired," Tonio said and he turned his back to make this even clearer. Often he and Domenico coupled quickly before Domenico left for some engagement. And he could not do it tonight, the very thought of it oppressed him.

He stared at his hands. This black uniform was already too short; he deliberately avoided his reflection in the nearby mirror.

"But I've made very special arrangements for tonight," Domenico said. "Don't you remember? I told you."

There was a slightly timorous quality to Domenico's voice. Tonio turned to see him better by the light of the one candle. He was splendidly decked out. His slender frame supported clothing with all the grace of those figures in French fashion engravings. And for the first time, Tonio realized they were eye to eye though Domenico was two years older than he. If he didn't get rid of him, he would lose his mind.

"I'm tired, Domenico," he whispered, annoyed with himself for being so rude. "You must leave me alone now. . . ."

"But Tonio!" Domenico was obviously surprised. "I've arranged everything. I told you. I'm leaving in the morning. You can't have forgotten that. . . ." His voice trailed off.

Tonio had never seen his face so agitated. It gave a piquant

238

spice to his looks and aroused some careless passion in Tonio.

But suddenly it dawned on him what Domenico was trying to tell him. Of course, this was his last night because he was going to Rome immediately! Everyone had been talking about his leaving, and now the moment had come. Maestro Cavalla wanted him there early to rehearse with Loretti. Loretti had fought Maestro Cavalla for the opportunity to write *his* opera for Domenico, and Maestro Cavalla, whose taste was far better than his talent, had conceded.

The moment had come and Tonio had completely overlooked it.

He began to dress immediately, vainly trying to recall what Domenico had told him.

"I've got a private room for us with supper ordered at the Albergo Inghilterra," Domenico explained. This was that lavish place by the sea where Tonio had rested after his night on the mountain. He stopped for an instant when he heard the name, then he pulled on his slippers and took his sword down from its hook.

"I'm sorry. I don't know where my mind is," he murmured.

He was more ashamed when he entered the rooms. They were not those he had let before, but they commanded a full view of the sea, and through the freshly washed windows the sand was perfectly white in the moonlight.

The bed was in its own small chamber already lit with several candelabra, and the supper table was set in the main room and decked out with linen and silver.

All very pretty and he could not concentrate on a word that Domenico was saying to him.

He talked about the rivalry between Loretti and his teacher, and how unsure he was of the audiences in Rome, why did he have to go to Rome, why couldn't he have made his first appearance in Naples. After all, look what the Romans had done to Pergolesi.

"Pergolesi . . . Pergolesi . . . ." Tonio whispered. "I hear that name everywhere. . . ."

But this was an imitation of conversation. His eyes moved over the white panels of the walls, their dark green painted leaves and blue and red flowers. All appeared dusty, shadowy in this mellow light, and Domenico's taut, pale skin looked good enough to . . .

He should have bought him some gift. It was dreadful that he hadn't, and what the hell was he going to say about it?

"Will you come!" Domenico said again.

"What?" Tonio stammered.

Domenico threw down the knife in disgust. He bit into his lip, an exquisite child angry and confused. Then he looked at Tonio as if he could not believe what was taking place here.

"Come to Rome," he repeated. "You must come! Tonio, it's not as if you were some charity student. If you tell Maestro Maffeo you must go, he'll let you go. You can come with the Contessa, why there are any—"

"Domenico, I can't go to Rome! Why would I go to Rome—" But before the words were out of his mouth, bits and pieces of the conversation came back to him.

Domenico's face was so stricken that Tonio couldn't bear to look at it.

"You're just anxious and you've got no reason to be," Tonio said. "You're going to be a sensation!"

"I'm not anxious," Domenico whispered. He had turned away and was looking into the shadows. "Tonio, I thought you would want to be there. . . ."

"I would if I could, but I can't pick up and leave."

It was unbearable to see him like this. He looked so miserable. Tonio ran his hand back through his hair. He was tired; his shoulders ached, and he wanted to sleep more than anything, and suddenly the prospect of remaining in this room a moment longer seemed impossible.

"Domenico, you won't think about me when you get to Rome, you know you won't," he said. "You'll forget me and everyone else here."

Domenico would not look at him. He was staring off as if nothing Tonio had said penetrated.

"You'll be famous," Tonio said. "My God, what did the Maestro say? You could go on to Venice if you wanted to, or right to London. You also know as well as I do . . ."

Domenico put his napkin down and rose from the chair. He came round and before Tonio could stop him he had dropped down on his knees beside him. He looked into Tonio's eyes.

"Tonio," he said, "I want you to come with me, not just to Rome, but everywhere after that. I won't go to Venice if you don't want to go there. We can go to Bologna and Milan and then to Vienna. We can go to Warsaw, Dresden, I don't care where we go, but I want you to come with me. I wasn't

240

going to ask you until we were in Rome, until I saw that things go well, and if they don't go well, well . . . I can't think about that. But if they do, Tonio . . ."

"No. No, stop this," Tonio said. "You don't mean all this, and it's out of the question. I can't just drop my studies. You don't know what you're saying. . . ."

"Not forever," Domenico said, "just in the beginning, six months perhaps. Tonio, you have the means, it's not as if you were poor, you've never been poor, and you—"

"It has nothing to do with that!" Tonio said, suddenly angry. "I have no desire to go with you! What ever made you think I would do it!"

Instantly he regretted it.

But it was too late, and it had been said with too perfect a candor.

Domenico had gone to the window. He stood with his back to the room, a somewhat delicate figure partially concealed by the shadows, and he appeared to be looking up as if to the sky. And Tonio felt, I must make this up to him.

But he did not know the extent to which he'd wounded Domenico until Domenico turned and again approached him.

Domenico's face was knotted and small and stained with tears, and as he drew near, he bit his lip and his eyes glimmered and melted.

Tonio was quietly stunned.

"I never dreamed that you would want me to come," Tonio said. But dismayed by the irritation in his voice, he stopped, defeated.

How had it come to this?

He had thought this boy so strong, so cold. It was as much a part of his charm as this exquisite mouth, these skilled hands, the pliant and graceful body that always received him.

And now ashamed and miserable, Tonio felt more alone with Domenico than he had ever felt. If only he could pretend to love him just for this moment.

But as if reading his thoughts, Domenico said:

"You care nothing for me."

"I didn't know you wanted me to," Tonio said. "I swear I didn't!" But on the edge of tears himself, he suddenly became angry. That cruelty welled in him that he'd so often let loose in bed. "Good God," he said, "what have we ever been to each other!"

241

"We've been lovers!" Domenico answered in the smallest, most private whisper.

"We have not!" Tonio came back. "It's all games and foolishness, nothing but the most shameful . . ."

Domenico put his hands to his ears as if he wouldn't listen.

"And stop crying, for the love of God, do you know what you're acting like, an insufferable eunuch!"

Domenico winced. His face was very wet and white as he spoke. "How can you say that to me? How you must loathe yourself to talk this way to me! Oh, God, I wish you'd never come here, I wish I'd never seen you. Damn you into hell. I wish you were burning in hell. . . ."

Tonio sucked in his breath. He shook his head. And as he watched helplessly Domenico went to the door as if to leave him.

But he turned back. His face was so perfectly made that even in this misery he had an irresistible beauty. Passion colored it and sharpened it, and he looked as innocent and wounded as the smallest child who has just begun to understand disappointment. "I . . . I can't bear the thought of leaving you," he confessed. "Tonio, I can't. . . ." And then he stopped as if he couldn't continue. "All the time, I thought you cared for me. When you first came, you were so miserable, so alone. You seemed so to despise everyone. And at night, we could hear you when you thought everyone slept, and you were crying. We could hear it. And then when you came back and you put on the sash, you tried so hard to deceive us. But I knew you were miserable. We all knew it. Just to be with you . . . it was to feel pain. I could feel it! And I thought . . . I thought I was good for you. You didn't cry anymore, and you were with me. I thought . . . I thought . . . that you cared for me!"

Tonio put his head in his hands. He let out a low moan and then behind him he heard the door close and Domenico's steps on the stairway.

7

THE WEEK HAD BEEN UNENDURABLE. Since Domenico's departure for Rome, restless nights had worn Tonio down, and this evening as he came back from the supper table he knew he could not work any longer now.

Guido would have to let him go early. Anger and threats could not keep him here.

Domenico had left at dawn after their evening at the *albergo*. Loretti had gone with him, and Maestro Cavalla would come after. There had been laughing in the corridors, the tramp of feet.

Domenico's stage name would be Cellino, and someone had cried out, "Bravo, Cellino."

Suddenly Tonio had left his spot at the windowsill and run all the way down the four flights of stairs without stopping. He pushed through the knot of boys at the door. The cold air shocked him for an instant, but he caught the carriage just as it was starting. The coachman held the whip.

And Domenico's face appeared at the window, brightening so innocently that Tonio felt his throat tightening.

"You'll be a wonder in Rome," he said. "Everybody's sure of it. You've got nothing to fear from anyone."

And there was such a wistful, innocent smile then on Domenico's face that Tonio felt the tears rise. He stood on the cobblestones staring after the lumbering carriage, and then the cold commenced to close on him.

Now he sat very still on the bench in Guido's room and he knew he could not do any more tonight. He must sleep. Or he must lie in his little room and prepare for the missing of Domenico, for not having those warm limbs nestled close to him, that pliant and fragrant flesh ready to give him whatever he wanted, when in truth he didn't care if he ever set eyes on Domenico again.

He swallowed and made a little wish with a silent smile that Guido would beat him when he refused to practice further.

He wondered what he would have to do to make Guido beat him. He was now taller than Guido. He imagined himself growing and growing until his head touched the ceiling. The tallest eunuch in Christendom, he heard a voice announce, and incomparably the finest of those singers over seven feet by a great margin.

Wearily he looked up and he saw that Guido had finished his notations and that Guido had been studying him.

That eerie feeling came over him that Guido knew all about him and Domenico, even of that miserable scene in the *albergo*. He thought of those rooms again, all those fine wax candles. And the sea outside. And he wanted to weep.

"Maestro, let me go tonight," he said. "I can't sing any more. I'm empty."

"You're warmed up. Your high notes are perfect," Guido said softly. "And I want you to sing this for me."

His voice had an uncommon gentleness to it. He struck a sulphur match and touched its odoriferous flame to his candle. The winter night had fallen down around them suddenly.

Tonio looked up, drowsy and numb, and saw the freshly copied music.

"It's what you are to sing at Christmas," Guido said. "I've written it myself, for your voice." And then, very low, he added, "It's the first time anything of mine will be performed here."

Tonio probed the face, looking for the edge of anger. But in the soft uneven flicker of the candle, Guido was calmly waiting. And there seemed at that moment a violent contrast between this man and Domenico, and yet something united them both, some feeling that flowed from Tonio. Ah, Domenico is the sylph, he thought, and this is the satyr. And what am I? The great white Venetian spider.

His smile was bitter. And he wondered what Guido thought of it, as he saw his expression darken.

"I want to sing it," Tonio whispered. "But it's too soon. I'll fail you if I try, I'll fail myself, and all those who listen."

Guido shook his head. There was the evanescent warmth of a smile, and then he said Tonio's name softly.

"Why are you so afraid of it?" he asked.

"Can't you leave me tonight? Can't you let me go!" Tonio asked. He stood up suddenly. "I want to get out of this place, I want to be anywhere but here." He started for the door and then he turned back. "Am I allowed to go out!" he demanded.

"You went out to an *albergo* not so very long ago," Guido said, "without begging anyone's permission."

This caught Tonio off guard, and it took the wind out of him. He stared at Guido, in a moment of apprehension that was almost panic.

But Guido's face remained empty of judgment or anger.

He appeared to be reflecting, and then he drew himself up as if he had made a decision.

He looked to Tonio with an uncommon patience, and when he spoke, his voice was slow and almost secretive.

"Tonio, you loved this boy," he said. "Everyone knew it."

Tonio was too surprised to answer.

"Do you think I've been blind to your struggle?" Guido asked. "But Tonio, you have known so much pain. Can this be such a loss to you? Surely you can turn to your work as you've done before, and you can forget him. This wound will heal, perhaps more quickly than you realize."

"Loved him?" Tonio whispered. "Domenico?"

Guido's brows came together in a frown that was almost innocent. "Who else?" he asked.

"Maestro, I never loved him! Maestro, I felt nothing for him. And oh, if there were only the smallest wound so that I might somehow atone for it!" He stopped, staring at this man, caught up in this unguarded moment.

"This is true?" Guido asked.

"Yes, it's true," said Tonio. But the misfortune of it was that I alone knew it. And I had to show it to him. When he is off to Rome to the most important appointment he may ever have to keep in all his life, and God knows if ever I make that same journey how I will despise anyone who sends me off as I sent him! I wounded him, Maestro. I wounded him, and senselessly, and stupidly."

He paused.

All this he was saying to Maestro Guido? He stared before him, astonished at his own weakness. He loathed himself for this, and for the loneliness that lay behind it.

But Guido's face was unreadable as he sat waiting without a sound. And all the man's small cruelties in the past came back to Tonio.

He knew that he should leave this place, enough had been said, and he could no longer trust himself.

But suddenly, without will or design he continued:

245

"God, if you were not the brutal and unfeeling man you are," he found himself saying. "Why do you speak of all this to me! I struggle to believe that I am yet something that can be good inside, have worth, and yet I turned my life with Domenico into something that's not fit to cast into the gutter. And over nights such as those, he shed tears and I'm the cause of it."

He glared at Guido.

"Why was it you walked into the sea?" he demanded. "What was it that drove you to do that? The loss of my voice? The voice you went to Venice to bring back with you! Well, I am flesh and blood as well as a voice!" he said. "And yet I'm neither man nor woman and it makes no difference whom I lie with, and so I turn myself into carrion."

"Was it so wrong to lie with him!" Guido whispered. "Who was hurt by it, now that you are what you are, and he is what he is? Was it so wrong you sought some affection with each other?"

"Yes, it was wrong, because I despised him! And I lay with him as if I loved him, and I did not love him. And that is wrong for me. Even in this state, there are those things that matter!"

Guido stared straight forward. And then very slowly he nodded. "Then why did you do it?" he whispered.

"Because I needed him," Tonio said. "I am an orphan in this place, and I needed him! I could not do it alone! I tried, I failed, and I am alone now, and this is worse than any pain I've ever known. I have looked it in the face a thousand times and sworn to endure it. But it's sometimes more than I can bear, and he gave me the semblance of love and let me play the man, and so I took it."

He turned his back on Guido. Oh, this was fine, wasn't it? All his resolves washed away in the breaking of this dam, and all he could think of was that just for this moment he was pouring it out to another. And there was hatred here too, hatred and loathing just as surely as he'd felt it for Domenico.

"How can I endure it?" he asked. He turned slowly. "How can you endure it, every day of your life to work in such anger and such coldness! A voice that's nothing but invectives. Good God, don't you ever want just once to love those you instruct, to feel for those who struggle so hard to follow the merciless rhythm you beat for them!"

"Do you want love from me?" Guido asked softly.

246

"Yes, I want love from you!" Tonio said. "I would get down on my knees to have love from you. You are my teacher! You are the one who guides me and shapes me and hears my voice as no one else has ever heard it. You are the one who strives to make it better than I myself could ever make it. How can you ask me if I want you to love me? Can't this be done in love? Isn't that possible, that if you showed to me the slightest warmth, I would open to you like the flowers of spring, that I would strive for you until my past progress seemed like nothing!

"Sing this music you've written, if you loved me, I could do anything you believed I could do, if you would just give me love hand in hand with your harshest, truest judgments. Mingle the two, and give that to me, and I could get through this darkness, I could find my way out, I could grow in this damp, strange place where I am some creature whose name I can't bear to speak. Help me!"

Tonio stopped. This was as terrible as he could ever have imagined it, and he was lost, utterly lost, and he did not even want to look at that brutal uncaring face, those eyes that seemed always afire with rage and so full of contempt for all pain and all weakness. He closed his eyes. He remembered that once in Rome what seemed like ages ago this man had embraced him, and he almost laughed aloud at the folly of all he'd said, but as the room swam in his vision, as the candle suddenly went out and he opened his eyes on a great obliterating darkness, he thought, Oh, these are just words, not actions. And somehow this will pass as all of it has passed, and tomorrow it will be the same as before, each of us in his own hell, and I will grow stronger yet, and more accustomed to it.

Because this is life, is it not? This is life, and years of this will pass, for this is what is meant to be, "Shut the doors, shut the doors, shut the doors." And the knife that brought me here was but the cutting edge of what awaits all of us.

The scent of burning wax lingered.

And then he heard Guido's footsteps ringing on the stones, and he thought, Ah, so this is the final humiliation, he is leaving me here.

His cruelty had never seemed so exquisite, so overpowering. Ah, the hours we two have spent together, this hideous marriage of exhausting work that mounts again and again to sublime torture.

247

And what have I learned? That in this as in all else I am alone, which I knew before, and come to realize with each passing day to its fullest meaning?

It seemed he was drifting.

And then quite suddenly he realized that the iron latch had been slipped into place against the door and that Guido had not left him.

He felt his breath halt. He could see nothing. And for the moment hear nothing. But he knew that Guido was there watching him. And such a sharp stab of desire caught him he was appalled by it.

Desire radiated from him. It radiated out into the darkness and seemed to find the four walls of this enclosing place, and he turned around waiting, waiting.

"Love you?" came Guido's voice. It was so low Tonio strained forward, as if yearning for it. "Love you?"

"Yes . . ." Tonio answered.

"I am in a hell of desire for you! Have you never guessed? Have you never looked beneath the coldness? Are you so blind to this suffering? In all my life I have never wooed and suffered as I have over you. But there is love and love, and I am spent trying to separate the one from the other. . . ."

"Don't separate them!" Tonio whispered. And he reached out like a child, grasping for what he wanted. "Give it to me! Where are you? Maestro, where are you?"

There seemed a rush of air, a soft shuffling of garments and steps, and he felt the near smarting touch of Guido's hands, hands that in the past had only struck him, and then those arms enclosing him. And in this moment, he understood everything.

But that was but the last glimmer of thought, and he knew just how it had been and how it would be, and he felt Guido's chest, and then Guido's mouth tore at him.

"Yes," he whispered. "Now, yes, everything, all of it . . ." He was crying.

Guido sucked at his lips, his cheeks, his fingers digging into him as they gathered him up as though he were fit for devouring, and it seemed all cruelty was alchemized into a great outpouring that sought no parodies of hate or punishment, so much as the swiftest, most desperate union.

He sank down on his knees, pulling Guido with him. He was leading the way. He was offering himself, giving what Domenico had always given him, yet never asked of him.

The pain was no consideration in it.

Let there be pain. And though he could hardly bear to release this mouth that was opening his and widening his, and sucking even at his teeth, he lay down flat on the stones and said; "Do it. Do that to me, do it. I want it." Guido's weight came down full length above him, crushing him as he felt his clothes torn loose, and the first nudge terrified him. He gave a long gasp and then all of his body opened up, welcoming it, refusing on any account to deny it, and when it came again, short, but hard and thick and pounding, he found himself moving with it. For one instant they were bound together, Guido's lips pressed to the back of his neck, Guido's hands working his shoulders, clutching him close, and then from Guido's guttural cry he knew it was over.

But he was stunned, wiping his mouth, and charged and craving. He could not keep his hands off Guido, but it was Guido who lifted him, Guido's arms so tight around his hips that he held Tonio up in the air as his mouth surrounded Tonio's organ with a wet warmth, a delicious ravenous sucking. It was stronger, more violent than Domenico had ever been. He gritted his teeth not to cry out, and then fell back, released, turning over to bury his head in his arms, his knees drawing up as the last shocks of pleasure faded.

He was afraid.

He was alone. He could hear the silence again. And the world was coming back, and he could not even lift his head.

And telling himself he expected nothing, he felt that in this moment he could have begged for anything. But he felt Guido near; Guido's hands, so heavy, so strong, were tugging at him, and rising abruptly he thrust his heated face into the crook of Guido's shoulder. Those dusty curls brushed him, and it seemed all of Guido cradled him, even the fingers so firm and warm, and this was Guido with him in this place, Guido holding him and loving him and kissing him now with the tenderest mouth and they were absolutely together.

It seemed Tonio was dazed and did not know where he was going, only that they were walking through the clean cold streets and the glare of torches against a wall had a frightening beauty.

The air was full of the hot scent of cooking fires and burning coals, and the windows looming at every turn out of the dark were filled with lovely yellow light and then there

249

was the blackness, the rustle of dry winter leaves, and Guido and he locked together with those rough and cruel kisses, embraces that knew nothing of tenderness, only starvation.

When they reached the tavern, the swing of the door threw out an inviting warmth and they pressed together into the deepest alcove amid the noise and rattle of swords and tankards smacked to the wooden tables. A woman sang, her voice dark and full like the tones of an organ, and one of those shepherds from the hills played his pipes, and the people all around them were singing.

Shadows fell over the table. They fell with the swinging of the lamps and the swell of the crowd, and gazing across this narrow space, it seemed a sweet agony that he could not now touch Guido. And yet as he sat against the wooden wall of this small place and looked into Guido's eyes, he saw such love there that he was content to smile and hold the wine in his mouth that was full of the tart flavor of the grape and the wood of the cask from which it had been taken.

They drank and drank, and when it was that Guido began to talk he did not know except that in a low, roughened voice, that defiant whisper deep from his chest, Guido was telling him all those secrets he had never dared to tell and again Tonio felt his mouth spreading into that smile he couldn't resist, and the only words that came to his mind were: Love, love, you are my love, and then at some moment in this warm and raucous place, he said those words and saw the flame in Guido's eyes. Love, love, you are my love, and I am not alone, no, not alone, for this little while.

8

IT WAS LOVEMAKING every night, full of insatiable hunger and animal cruelty, and yet redolent afterwards of an unspoken tenderness that had shaped the whole. And they slept locked in one another's arms as if the flesh itself were a barrier that must be broken with the tightest embrace, and there were always those rough, ravenous kisses, and then in

250

the morning, the two of them rising with one mind, to get to work again in Guido's studio before the first light.

And with the lessons, all was changed.

It was not that they were any less demanding, or that Guido was any less severe or hot-tempered when Tonio fell short of the mark. It was that the whole was more intense, and suffused with their new intimacy and absorption in one another.

Tonio had promised in that gush of unwise language and emotion fused to words that he would open to Guido, but he came to realize he had always been open, at least when it came to music, and now it was Guido who opened to him. Guido for the first time acknowledged the mind that governed Tonio's body and his voice, and Guido began to confide in that mind the principles that underlay his relentless practice repetitions.

Actually this tendency to talk was nothing new in Guido, but at the opera or during their long seaside drives afterwards the subjects had invariably been other singers. And there had been an illusion of impersonality, and even something of coldness mixed in with the way that all this heat coming from Guido must be attached to other music, other men.

Now Guido spoke of the music they shared, and it seemed in these early weeks of their hottest and most eager love that this talking was more important to Guido even than their amorous embraces.

Not an evening went by that they did not go out, hiring a carriage perhaps for a coastal drive, or to seek out some quiet tavern where over the table they might talk in heated whispers until a certain taste in the mouth from the wine, a certain lightness of the head, told them to go home.

They did not take their evening meal anymore at the conservatorio. They walked arm in arm through pitch dark streets, and finding here a darkened door, there the cover of a stand of trees, they touched one another, clung to one another feeding on the danger of it, and some infatuation with the night itself, its rustling sounds, its carriages groaning uphill out of nothingness to appear suddenly with a rocking yellow beam to find them out.

But once on the long Via Toledo, they had their pick of fine taverns with the money in Tonio's pockets and were soon feasting on roast fowl or fresh fish with that wine they both loved, Lagrima Christi, and in the pleasant glow of these clean and crowded places, they would talk.

251

Guido would give Tonio the names of the old masters who'd written the exercises he was studying, and explain how Guido's own vocalises differed from these.

But the greatest pleasure now for Tonio was giving any question to Guido for an answer and having his teacher take it up at once. Had Guido ever seen Alessandro Scarlatti? Yes, certainly, when he was a boy he had in fact met him, and Maestro Cavalla had spirited him often to the San Bartolommeo to see Scarlatti at the keyboard directing his own work.

It was Scarlatti who had really brought greatness to Naples, Guido said. In the old days men looked to Venice and Rome for the new operas. But now it was Naples, and as Tonio could see all around him, it was to Naples that foreign students came.

But opera was changing all the time. The long boring recitatives that advanced the plot with all the information the audience had to know were becoming more lively instead of such tiresome interludes between the arias. And comic opera, that was the coming thing. People wanted to hear opera in the vernacular, too, not just in classical Italian. And more and more recitatives with the orchestra were appearing in operas, where before most of recitatives had been dry.

But you had always to care about what the people wanted, and no matter how long or boring the singing in between, the people would put up with it for beautiful arias, and that would never change.

That is what opera was, Guido said, beautiful singing. And no violin or harpsichord could ever do to a man what singing could do to him.

Or so Guido, at that time in that place, believed.

Some evenings when they were tired of the taverns, they went on to the continual round of balls, especially favoring the Contessa Lamberti, who was such a patron of the arts, but here their endless dialogue did not stop.

They would find some out of the way parlor, rescue a candelabrum for the clavichord or the new pianoforte, and after Guido let his fingers fly for a while, he would nestle into some high couch and once again Tonio would begin his questions, or Guido would take off on his own.

His eyes were full of some new and softening wonder at such moments; his face, relaxed, was boyish and gentle, and he seemed incapable of the bad temper of the past.

And it was on one such night in one of the Contessa's small music rooms, when they had found a round table, a deck of playing cards, and a candle and they sat opposite each other going through some simple little game, that Tonio finally said:

"Maestro, tell me about my voice!"

"But first you must tell me something," Guido said, and there was a flicker of temper that sent a shudder through Tonio. "Why is it you won't sing this Christmas solo when I've told you it's simple and that I wrote it for you?"

Tonio looked away.

He laid down the hand of cards in a small fan, and singled out for no reason the king and the queen. And then, unable to seek for the moment the obvious answer to Guido's question, he found a simple solution to this next battle he must fight. He would sing the solo for Guido, if Guido wanted it. He would sing it for Guido, even if he was not yet strong enough to do it for the young man who had come down from the mountain. Yet he was afraid.

As soon as he raised his voice alone in the chapel, he would really be a castrato. This was it, wasn't it? It was one great step beyond wearing a black tunic with a red sash. It was one immense step beyond blending his voice with others in a chorus. He would step forward in that moment; he would be fully illuminated for what he was.

It was like being stripped naked, and showing to all of them the mutilation that had been done. Inevitable, but coldly terrifying to him. And now reflecting silently on his height, on the long slender hand that was his as it lay on the table, bent slightly to move these cards on the polished wood, he thought, Will I sound like a boy anymore at all? Am I a boy? Or would I have been, by now, a man?

A man. He smiled at the brutal simplicity of that word and its great avalanche of meanings. And for the first time in all his life the word struck him as . . . as what? Coarse. Never mind. You deceive yourself, he half-whispered aloud. For all its vast abstraction, the word had but one fully understood meaning.

And he knew he was very young for that great natural change to have come about in him. But in a bedroom in another world a woman had teased him, saying that it would not be long. He had been proud then of those simple

253

endowments, so utterly certain of them, and so miserable at the same time.

But that was another world.

He was a castrato and he would be a castrato in that chapel when he raised his naked voice.

And it was but the first exposure. There would come so many others, and that final moment: when he stepped out on the stage of some vast theater, alone. If he was fortunate enough! If he was good enough, if his voice was strong enough, yes, that was what he had to look forward to: the eunuch revealed to all the world.

He looked at Guido. And there seemed in him a fathomless innocence of all these dark and continuous things. He loved Guido. He would sing it for him.

And he remembered almost suddenly, unexpectedly, that when Guido had first spoken of it, he'd said, "It's the first time anything of mine will be performed here." Good God, had he been such a child that he had not even considered what this might mean to Guido? Had he been such a fool?

He had known all along that those splendid arias given him to sing at the end of the day were Guido's own arias.

"It means a great deal to you that I sing it," Tonio said, "because you've written it, isn't that so?"

Guido's face reddened, his eyes quivering slightly.

"It's important because you are my pupil and you are ready!" he insisted.

But Guido's anger flashed and died. Guido rested his elbow on the table with his chin on his hand.

"You asked me to tell you about your voice," Guido said. "Maybe I've failed you in not telling you more about it, in being so very hard with you. Well, it was the only way I knew how to be. . . ."

One of those silent wraithlike servants had ventured into the room with a flicker of blue satin and a hand descending into the soft airy light around the candles to pour some wine.

Guido watched the glass fill, motioning for the man to wait, and then he emptied it and watched it fill again.

"I'm going to speak plainly to you," he said. "You are the finest singer I've ever heard, short of Farinelli. You could have sung this solo the first day you came to the conservatorio. You could have sung it in Venice."

His eyes narrowed slightly as he studied Tonio. And there

254

was about him an unusual combination of softness and intensity released by the wine.

"This solo was written for you," he continued. "It was written for the voice I heard in Venice, for the boy singer whom I followed there night after night. I knew your range then, your power. I knew where you faltered when no one else would have noticed it. I knew what you had managed to learn on your own with just a little prodding from your teachers and I was amazed. The accuracy of pitch, the natural sentiment." He shook his head, drawing in his breath with a hiss.

"All I'm giving you is flexibility and strength." He sighed. "In two years, you'll have the skill to pick up any aria from any opera and know just how to ornament it and deliver it perfectly anywhere under anyone's direction at any time. That's all I'm giving you. . . ." He paused. He looked away, and when he glanced back to Tonio again, his eyes were large and shadowed, and his voice was just a little deeper.

"But you have something else, Tonio, something beyond a voice," he said. "Those singers who don't have it almost never acquire it, and others who possess it haven't your purity and power of tone. It's this: some secret power that shocks people when they hear you, some power that enflames them so that they become absorbed with you and with you alone.

"When you sing in the church at Christmas, people will turn their heads to see your face, they'll be drawn out of their petty thoughts and distractions, and when they go out they'll ask for your name.

"Oh, for long years, I've tried to anatomize this, to figure exactly what it is. I had it when I was a boy. I know from within how it feels. But I cannot lay it all down. Perhaps it's some subtle sense of timing, some infinitesimal and infallible hesitation, some instinct for knowing just when to increase the swell of a note, when to stop. And perhaps it's bound up with the physical, with the eyes, with the face, with the way that the body holds itself as the voice rises. I don't know."

Tonio was engrossed. He was remembering that moment when Caffarelli stepped before the footlights in Venice; he was remembering the ripple of expectation that ran through the crowd. And how he, rushing down to the pit, had been magnetized by this eunuch even when Caffarelli was merely walking back and forth, not singing a note.

Could he do that to people? Was that possible?

"Now, there's more," Guido said. "You would have had this special fire in you even if you had been cut at the age of six as I was. But you were not cut then. . . ."

Tonio felt a tensing, a sudden violent shock.

But Guido reached out and quieted him with the brush of his hand. "You were reared," he went on, "to think and move and act like a man. And this adds its own strength to what you are, too. You haven't the softness of some eunuchs. You haven't that quality of being . . . well, neither sex."

Guido hesitated. "But of course," he went on slowly, as if speaking to himself now, "there are some eunuchs cut very young who have this power, too."

"This might change," Tonio whispered. He could feel a stiffening all over, especially in his face, and that tendency to smile coldly which had come over him at such moments in the past, but his voice went on, even, gentle. "When I look in the mirror, I see Domenico already."

Yes, Domenico, he thought. And my old double in Venice, the master of the House of Treschi, smiling behind him to see us at last grown so far apart.

He felt himself light and airy, something unnamable finally for all the names it was given, sprung from the husk of the boy he'd been.

"Yes," Guido was saying, "you will resemble Domenico very much."

Tonio could not conceal his fear, his loathing. And Guido touched his hand. But an evanescent sense of Carlo confused Tonio, some broken memory of pressing his face to that rough and closely shaven beard, of a sigh coming out of his brother, husky and muted, carrying with it sorrow and weariness and the man's inevitable and God-given strength.

"Domenico was beautiful," Guido scolded. "And he had this masculine power, too."

"Domenico?" Tonio answered. "Masculine power? He was a Circe," he said. He would never forget those caresses, and was ashamed even now of that old desire.

But Carlo was with him. Carlo had invaded this room, this moment, this intimacy with Guido which he so treasured, the sound of Carlo's laughter drifting through those hallways. He looked to Guido and felt love for him, and looking down saw that Guido's fingers were touching him still. Domenico. Power. Guido was laughing softly, too.

"Maybe Domenico was a Circe in bed," Guido was saying. "Unfortunately, I'll have to take your word on that. But when he sang, he had this other power, and his beauty gave it to him as well as his voice. Even dressed and coiffed as a woman, he was steely and formidable and made others afraid. Ah, you should have watched the faces of the men and women in the audience when he sang. It is not hair on the chest nor a swaggering posture, this power. It is something which emanates from within. Domenico had it. Domenico wasn't afraid of God or the devil. And you, my young one, have not begun to understand what a castrato can be."

"I want to understand," Tonio whispered. "But I never saw Domenico that way. I saw him as a sylph, maybe even at times an angel." Tonio stopped. "Or maybe just a eunuch," he confessed.

But this did not offend Guido.

Guido seemed absorbed in some little revelation. "A eunuch," he whispered. "So you saw in him what you would become. And he saw in you his own style of beauty and strength. He always went for those who were most like him. But he was painfully lonely the last two years. . . ."

"Was he?" Tonio asked. He would never lose the pain of disappointing Domenico, though Domenico might now have forgotten all of it.

"Yes, very lonely," Guido went on. "Because he was better than everyone around him, and that is the worst loneliness of all. Everywhere he looked he saw envy, and fear. And then you came, and he set his sights on you. It was why Lorenzo taunted you, because Lorenzo loved Domenico and Domenico did not care."

Tonio's spirit was wasted. He was staring at the cards before him, the hard-eyed king and the hard-eyed queen. The queen had a Byzantine slant to her eyes. She was black-haired. She was the queen of spades.

"But don't worry yourself over Domenico. If you wounded him as you say you did, then you taught him something which no one ever had before. It's only in your elegance you resemble him. You have his fine bones, and that same hair that women love. But you are larger all over than he is; you'll grow to greater height; and the features of your face, they are most unusual in that they are . . ." And here Guido struggled, his eyes fixed on Tonio, his own mouth soft with his absorption. "They are all just a little farther apart from one another than

257

one finds in most men. When you are on the stage you will be a blinding light; no one else on the boards will even be visible, including Domenico, your delicate shadow, if he were there.''

Tonio was silent as they returned to the conservatorio. They entered Guido's rooms. Austere as they were, with only a few pieces of heavy furniture and a worn Turkey carpet, they were lavish for this place, and Tonio felt more than ever a part of Guido when he was with him here.

The heavy bed with its coffered roof was fitted with plain dark curtains for winter, and Tonio climbed up on the coverlet, resting against the paneled headboard as Guido lit the candles on the harpsichord, which meant that love would not come so soon.

In a small voice Tonio asked:

"How tall will I grow?"

"No one knows that. It depends on how tall you might have been. But you are growing fast.''

Tonio felt a black water coming up in his mouth as though he were going to be sick. It was now or never that he ask these questions, and for so long he had wanted merely to voice them if even to the roaring sea.

"What else is happening to me?''

Guido turned. Tonio wondered, did he remember that night in Rome, in that small garden, when Tonio, choking for breath, actually choking as if he were dying, had stretched out his hands to him, to that statue which glowed in the moonlight with a white light of its own.

"What's happening to me!'' he whispered. "All over. You *know*.''

How indifferent Guido seemed. His dark figure came between Tonio and the candles so that it lost its face.

"You will continue to grow tall. Your arms and legs will increase in length, but how much, again, no one knows. But remember they will always seem normal to you. And it is this flexibility of bone which gives you such power with your voice. Every day that you practice you increase the size of your lungs; and the elastic bones let those lungs grow. So that very soon you will have power in the upper register that no woman could ever possess. No boy, for that matter. No other man.

"But your hands will hang low on your body, and your

feet will flatten out. And you will be weak in the arms as a woman is weak. You will not have the natural muscularity of a man."

Tonio's turning away from this was so violent that Guido took hold of him.

"Forget these things!" Guido said. "Yes, yes, I mean what I say. Forget these things. For every time you feel pain over them, it means you have not accepted what can never be changed! Realize where your strength lies."

Tonio nodded, full of bitterness and mockery. "Oh, yes," he said.

"Now, I have one more lesson for you," Guido said. "And you need it most of all."

Tonio nodded with a little smile. "Teach me," he said.

"You've turned away from women, and that's not a good thing."

Tonio was incensed. He was about to protest, and Guido kissed him roughly on the forehead.

"In Venice, you had a little girl. You'd go off with her in the gondola when the singers had gone home. I used to watch you. It happened night after night."

"Those things are best forgotten, too." Tonio smiled again, feeling the coldness of it suffusing his face.

"No, not so. Don't ever forget it. Cherish the memory of it, and whenever the fire gets hold of you, no matter when, no matter where, if there is some safe opportunity for reenacting that ritual, then you must reenact it again. And if the fire takes hold of you with men, with other eunuchs, whoever it is, seize it, don't waste it, don't let it go. Do all of it with honor and common sense, but don't turn your back on it, not out of love for me, not out of love for music, not out of indifference, but hearken to your desires again and again."

"Why are you saying this?"

"Because you never know when that desire will go away. Men never lose it. That is not always the case with us "

"You! You have no fear of losing it!" Tonio said.

"No. Not now. But I had all but lost it, until we were brought together. It was in the town of Ferrara when I saw you lying on that bed, feverish and in need of care, that it came back." Guido paused. "I thought it had left me with my voice."

Tonio stared at Guido without saying a word. He appeared

to weigh all this, but now Guido realized that he should never have mentioned that time, nor that place.

Tonio's face had become white and elongated, and it seemed he was not himself but some bitter and frightening image of himself.

Yet he reached for Guido's hand and drew him close.

Hours later, Tonio awoke with a start. He had been dreaming the most terrible dream of all of them, the dream of real things and real men, and that struggle that had ended in irrevocable defeat.

Sitting up in the dark he felt the peace and safety of this room surround him, laced as it was with bitterness and grief. And he realized that for a long time he had been hearing music, full of starts and stops, and then a solemn, sacred-sounding melody that was proceeding inch by inch.

Across the dim vista of the darkened room, he saw Guido at the harpsichord, his candles a handful of tongues that were solid and still in the air, Guido's scowling face beneath them seen as if through a dusky veil.

The sharp, distinct smell of the ink reached him, and then he heard the scratch of Guido's pen. Once again, Guido played that melody, and for the first time, Tonio heard Guido's own voice, low, almost empty of sound, like a man whispering a melody he cannot sing.

Tonio felt such love for him then he knew that as he lay back on the pillow he was fixing this moment in time. He would never forget it.

When morning came Guido told him that he had greatly enlarged the solo he was to sing on Christmas Eve. In fact he had written an entire cantata, and now he must get Maestro Cavalla to approve it so it could be performed.

It was noon before he returned to the practice room to say the Maestro, who had spent so much time this year with Domenico, was quite delighted with what Guido had done. Tonio would sing it. Now they must perfect it together. There was no time to lose.

260

9

ON CHRISTMAS EVE, the chapel of the conservatorio was crowded to overflowing.

The air was chill and clean and Tonio had spent the early evening roaming the city to see all around him those life-sized *presepi* or cribs which the people of Naples so love, families handing down the statues from generation to generation. On rooftops, on porches, in convent gardens, everywhere, these splendid Nativity scenes unfolded with magnificent images of the Virgin, Saint Joseph, shepherds, and angels awaiting the Infant Savior.

Never before had the pure meaning of this night been so palpable to Tonio. Since he had left the Veneto, he had found no faith in himself, no grace. Yet it seemed on this night the world would and could renew itself. Some ancient power lay behind the ritual, the hymns, these glorious images. And he could feel a quickening in him as midnight approached. Christ was coming into the world. The light would shine in the darkness. It had an eerie and heartrending power.

But when he came downstairs in his black uniform, the famous red sash tied neatly in place, he felt the first trepidation for his performance, and knowing the effect of worry on the voice itself, was doubly stricken.

Suddenly he couldn't remember a single word of Guido's cantata, or the melody. He reminded himself it was an extraordinary composition, that Guido was already proceeding to the harpsichord to conduct, and that he had the score in his hand, so it didn't matter if he couldn't remember. Then he almost smiled.

What a gift this was. If he weren't terrified for his performance, what would he be feeling? The chorus of geldings will now raise its voice to heaven!

But he was terrified, just like any other singer. And in a moment, just as Guido had told him, he would become calm, he would hear the opening bars, everything would be perfect.

Yet as he moved along the side wall and down through the

assembled boys to the front rail, he saw in the very first row of the congregation beneath him the small blond head of a young woman. She was bent over her programme, her dark taffeta dress forming a circle around her.

He looked away at once. Impossible that it be she, on this night of all nights! But as if some grim hand, some bullying brutal hand were forcing him to it, he looked down again at her. He saw the delicate wisps all about her soft curls, and then slowly she raised her eyes, and for an instant they looked at one another.

Surely she remembered those awkward moments in the Contessa's supper room, his drunken recklessness, which he himself would never forget. Yet there was no malice in her expression. It was musing, almost dreamy.

A bitterness welled up in him, poisoning him, poisoning all the beguiling beauty of this place, the sanctuary with its rows of lights, its great masses of fragrant flowers.

He attempted to steady himself. It was she who had looked away first, her small hands folding that rustling paper in her lap, and then he felt himself grow tense, only to weaken slowly and completely. He had the impression of the pain positively washing through him like water.

Only the idea that he was trapped was real to him. And that the congregation had stopped its low murmuring, and that Guido had seated himself at the keyboard. The little orchestra was lifting its instruments. The thought came clearly to him. "I cannot do it." The music was nothing but a series of inscrutable marks. And then came the opening blasts of the trumpet.

He looked out over the open space before him. He started singing.

The notes climbed, they plunged down and rose up again, the words interwound effortlessly, the scroll of music closed shut in his hands. And quite suddenly, he knew it was all right. He was not lost in it; rather it was coming strongly and beautifully and he felt the first quiet rush of pride.

When it all came to an end, he knew it had been a little triumph.

The audience, not allowed to applaud, was shuffling, coughing, moving its feet, all subtle signals of unbounded approval. And Tonio could see it in the faces everywhere. As he followed the other castrati out of the chapel, he wanted only to be alone with Guido. That need was so great in him, he could hardly endure the congratulations, the warm hand clasps, Francesco murmuring to him that Domenico would have been sick with jealousy.

When Guido took hold of him that would be praise enough, the rest he knew, and he was exhausted.

Yet he returned quite deliberately to the stream of those leaving the chapel, and when that young blond-haired girl emerged, as he knew she would, he felt his face grown warm.

The reality of her was so startling. In his memory she had paled, grown insignificant, and now here she was, her golden hair tumbled softly about her rounded neck, and her eyes, so infinitely serious, were a glimmer of dark blue. She wore a bit of violet ribbon at her throat which gave its color to her small mouth. Slightly pouted, succulent, it made him almost feel its fullness, as if he had pressed his thumb to her lips just before he kissed her, and flustered, miserable, he looked away.

An elderly gentleman accompanied her. Who was that, her father? And why hadn't she told him of that little incident in the supper room? Why hadn't she cried out?

She was directly in front of him now, and as he looked up, he looked into her eyes.

Without hesitating, he made her a correct bow. And then almost angrily, again he looked away. He felt himself strong and quieted and aware for the first time perhaps that of all the painful emotions of life, only sadness has such an exquisite luster. Now she was gone.

The Maestro di Cappella had come forward and was clasping his hands:

"Quite remarkable," he said. "And I had thought you were moving too fast."

Then Tonio saw Guido, and Guido's happiness was so palpable that Tonio felt a small catch in his throat. The Contessa Lamberti was embracing him. As soon as she had gone away, he turned to Tonio and, gently ushering him down the corridor, seemed on the verge of kissing him when he thought the better of it, wisely.

"What in the world happened to you up there! I thought you weren't going to start. You terrified me."

"But I did start, perfectly in time," Tonio said. "Don't be angry."

"Angry?" Guido laughed. "Do I seem angry?" He em-

263

braced Tonio impulsively and then let him go. "You were perfect," he whispered.

The last of the guests were gone, and the front doors were being closed, and the Maestro di Cappella was in deep conversation with a gentleman who had his back turned.

Guido had unlocked his door, but Tonio knew he would not retire without hearing what the Maestro had to say.

But as the Maestro turned and guided his guest towards them, Tonio experienced a quiet shock. This was a Venetian, he realized at once, though how he knew he could not have said.

And then, when it was too late to turn away, he saw that this blond, heavily built young man was Giacomo Lisani, Catrina's eldest son.

Catrina had betrayed him! She had not come herself, but she had sent this one! And though he wanted to escape, he realized immediately that Giacomo appeared as miserable as he was. Giacomo's cheeks were aflame, and his pale blue eyes downcast.

And how he had changed from the awkward colt whom Tonio had known in Venice, that impetuous student from the University at Padua who was forever whispering and laughing with his brother, with an elbow in the ribs.

The shadow of a beard darkened his face and neck ever so slightly, and it seemed a sense of duty weighed upon him as he made Tonio a deep, almost ceremonial bow.

The Maestro was presenting him. It was impossible to avoid this. Then Giacomo looked directly to Tonio, and as quickly he looked away.

Is it revulsion, Tonio thought coldly? Am I loathsome to him? But all consideration of himself and how he must appear to his cousin were slowly alchemized in a silent animosity that was the enemy of reason, while at the same time he felt a fascination with the workings of nature in Giacomo, workings he would never see in so many of the students who were his only real kin now.

"Marc Antonio," Giacomo began. "I've been sent by your brother, Carlo, to see you."

The Maestro was gone. Guido, too, had moved away, but he lingered just behind the young man, his eyes fixed on Tonio.

And Tonio, hearing for the first time in so long the beautiful Venetian dialect, had to disentangle the meaning of

Giacomo's words from the deep masculine timbre that seemed almost magical to him in this moment. How exquisite was that dialect, how like the gilt everywhere on the walls here, on the curlicues and the columns, on the painted doors. Giacomo's heavy, languid voice seemed composed of a dozen harmonious sounds, and each resonant word was touching Tonio like a child's soft fist pressed to Tonio's throat.

". . . is concerned about you," Giacomo continued. "He has heard a rumor of trouble here, that you had, shortly after your arrival, made a mortal enemy of another student, that that student made an attack on your person which you were forced to defend."

Giacomo's brows came together in a caricature of deep concern; his tone, so pregnant with duty, had become condescending, though there was nothing in him but a tormented sincerity. Ah, youth, Tonio found himself thinking, just as if he were an old man.

But a silence had fallen between them. And Tonio could see the sudden, clear warning in Guido's face. Guido's face said Danger.

"Your brother is very concerned that perhaps you are not safe here, Marc Antonio," said Giacomo. "Your brother is concerned that you did not write of this occurrence to my mother and . . ."

Yes, danger, Tonio thought, to my heart and my soul. For the first time since he had commenced to speak, Giacomo was again looking him in the eye.

And at some intangible little point in this exchange, Tonio saw the whole of it, what it was about, what was wanted here. Concerned for his safety! This foolish young man didn't even guess the nature of his own mission!

"If you are in any danger, Marc Antonio, you must tell us. . . ."

"No danger," Tonio said suddenly. And the coldness of his own voice astonished him, and yet he went on. "There was never any question of danger," he said, almost sneering, and his words had such an authority to them that he saw his cousin ever so slightly recoil. "The affair ended stupidly enough, but there was nothing I could do to prevent it. You must tell my brother he worries about nothing, and that he has taken too much trouble and expense in sending you here."

In the shadowy distance, Guido gave a desperate negative shake of the head.

But Tonio had reached for his cousin's arm, and taking him firmly in hand, was turning him and leading him towards the front doors.

Giacomo seemed mildly astonished. Far from offended at being dismissed, he was staring at Tonio with a vaguely concealed fascination, and as he spoke now there was almost a relief in his voice.

"Then you are content here, Tonio," he said.

"More than content." Tonio gave a short laugh. He moved Giacomo steadily down the corridor. "And you must tell your mother that she is not to worry, as well."

"But did this boy who attacked you—"

"This boy," Tonio said, "as you put it, stands now before a sterner judge than you or I. Say a prayer for him at mass. Now it's Christmas morning, and surely you do not wish to spend it here."

Giacomo stopped at the door. This was all happening too fast for him. Yet as he hesitated, he could not prevent his eyes from moving rapidly, almost greedily over Tonio, and then he gave a small but very warm smile. "It's good to see you are so well, Tonio," he confessed. And it seemed just for a moment he wanted to say more, but thinking the better of it, he looked quickly to the floor. He seemed to grow smaller, to become exactly the boy he'd been at Venice, and Tonio realized silently, without the slightest change of expression, that his cousin was feeling love for him and pain.

"You were always exceptional, Tonio," Giacomo said, almost in a whisper, and tentatively he raised his eyes to Tonio's eyes again.

"And how is that, Giacomo?" Tonio said almost wearily, as though he were bearing all of this, without, however, being the slightest bit rude.

"You were, well . . . you were always the little man," Giacomo said, and his manner invited Tonio to understand and to smile at this with him. "You seemed to grow up so quickly, it was as if you were older than us."

"I didn't know very much about children." Tonio smiled.

And when his cousin seemed lost suddenly, Tonio said:

"And you are relieved to see that I have not suffered so far away from home?"

"Oh, very relieved!" Giacomo said.

Then when they looked at each other again, neither moved to look away. The silence lengthened, and the dim wavering light of the sconces made their shadows grow large, then small.

"Goodbye, Giacomo," Tonio said softly. He held his cousin firmly by both arms.

Giacomo could only stare at him for a moment. Then reaching into his velvet frock coat, he said, "But I have a letter for you, Tonio. I almost forgot. My mother would be so angry!" He put the letter in Tonio's hands. "And your singing . . ." he started. "In the chapel. I wish, I wish I knew the language of music so I could tell you what it was like."

"The language of music is only sounds, Giacomo," Tonio answered. And without hesitation they embraced.

Guido was lighting the candles when he stepped into the room. And for a long moment, they stood locked in each other's arms.

But the letter was in Tonio's hand, and he couldn't dismiss it from his mind. And when he drew away to sit down with it at the table, he saw for the first time the mingled concern and anger in Guido's face.

"I know, I know," Tonio whispered, tearing open the parchment envelope. It bore Catrina's seal.

"Do you know?" Guido bore down on him, but despite the anger in his voice, his hands were caressing. And he pressed his lips to Tonio's head. "Your brother sent him here to see to your spirit!" he whispered. "Couldn't you have played the shy, diffident little student just this once?"

"Shy, diffident cunuch," Tonio answered. "Say it, for that is what you mean. And I will not play it for anyone. I cannot! So let him go back to Venice and tell my brother what he will. Good God, he heard me singing with children and angels, did he not? He saw the *obedient* student, the *obedient* gelding, was that not enough?"

The letter was indecipherable before his eyes in the dim light. He had vowed a thousand times never to speak of these things to any living being, not to the priest in the confessional, not anyone, but had he been a fool to think that Guido had never guessed? And sitting still, the letter flat on the table beneath his hand, he could all but feel the weight of Guido's unspoken words as he saw the shadow of Guido moving slowly back and forth across the room.

It seemed an age he sat there after he had finished.

267

Then he read it again. And when he was finished this time, he lifted it, holding it to the cool flame of the candle until the fire burned hotter, the parchment crackled, was consumed, and turned to ash.

Guido was watching him. Yet it seemed all the familiar furnishings of this room were alien to him. He felt contained and cold and part of nothing. And as he looked at Guido, it was as if he did not know this man with whom he'd only just been quarreling, this man whose lips he could still feel on his own. He did not know him, nor why they were both of them here.

He looked away, coldly aware of the effect of his expression on Guido, but he was looking now into his brother's face. No, his father's face, he thought with the thinnest smile. Father, brother, and beyond it a backdrop of unilluminated emptiness that was very simply the end of life.

And all the church bells of Naples were ringing, this was Christmas morning, and their lovely monotonous pealing came through the walls like the rhythm of a pulse. Yet he could feel nothing, he could taste nothing. He could want nothing, save suddenly that this time should come to its inevitable end.

Why had he let himself forget what lay ahead of him? How had he managed to live as others lived, to hunger, to thirst, and to love?

Guido had poured the wine. He had placed the glass at Tonio's right hand. The fragrance of the grape filled the room, and Tonio, sitting back in the chair, looked dully from the corner of his eye at the letter gone to ashes and the food that lay undisturbed, the artifact of itself, on a silver plate.

He had married her.

Married her! That was what the letter had said.

Decorous, simple, hardly more than an announcement. He had married her! Tonio felt his teeth clench until he was in pain, and he saw nothing of this room anymore. Married his father's wife, married the mother of his bastard son, married her before Doge and Council and Senate and lords and ladies of Venice. He had married her! And now he would breed those strong sons, my little brothers! Those Giacomos, those brothers, brothers, always beyond reach, as if the very idea of fraternity were some immense fiction. Others are part of it, others are locked arm in arm. Magnificent illusion.

"Tonio, whatever it was, put it out of your mind," came Guido's voice, soft, unobtrusive, behind him. "Put them all out of your mind. They reach across the miles yet to cut you. Don't let them."

"Are you my brother?" Tonio whispered. "Tell me this. . . ." He took Guido's hand. "Are you my brother?"

And Guido, hearing these simple words spoken with uncommon feeling, could only nod in confusion. "Yes."

Tonio rose and drew Guido close to him, his hand on Guido's lips as if to make him silent, just as she had reached for Carlo's lips in the supper room that last night. But Guido was speaking yet.

"Forget them, forget them now."

"Yes, for an hour," Tonio answered. "For a day, for a week, I should so like to do that," he whispered.

And yet he saw her lying in that rank and darkened bedroom; he saw her deep in drunken sleep, her face the waxen mask of death, her moans inhuman. And now it's filled with lights; it's filled with people, those halls, those rooms, that vast salon, just as I had always dreamed, and she is in his arms, and *he* has saved her. Yes, there you have it laid bare. He has saved her! He cut you down to save her. And she is not doomed, and you are doomed, and you are in that dark room and you can't get out, and she is no longer there!

"Oh, if I could just take the pain out of your head," Guido said, ever so softly, his hands on Tonio's temples. "If I could only reach in and take it out."

"Ah, but you do, and you do it as no one else can," Tonio answered.

And they are married.

Married. And little Francesca Lisani clutches the convent grille to look at me, my betrothed, my bride. Married. His mother, peering up at him from the dressing table, suddenly threw back the great mane of her black hair and laughed.

Does she dance, does she sing, does she wear pearls around her neck, and is the long supper room thronged with guests, and has she her cavalier servente now, and what does she belive happened to her son, what does she believe!

But then he kissed Guido's open mouth slowly, with all the semblance of real feeling. And then pressing Guido's hands together, he let them go as he backed away. Never, he thought, will you ever know what happened, and what must happen, and just how brief this time is that we have together, this little span we call life.

*   *   *

It was near daylight when he rose from bed and penned his response to Catrina:

> In my father's store rooms on the first floor of our house were several old, but still fine swords. Please ask my brother if I might have these weapons, and if he would send them to me here when it is convenient for him to do so. And if there is some sword which was our father's which he is willing to send to me, I should be profoundly grateful for that weapon, as well.

He signed the letter and sealed it, and sat watching the morning light appear in the little courtyard, a slow and silent spectacle that never failed to fill him with extraordinary peace. First the shadowy shapes of the trees distinguished themselves beneath the arches of the cloister; then the light broke out in patches everywhere so that he could see the tracery of limbs and leaves. The color was the last to come, and then it was morning, and the house was giving off its full vibrations like a giant instrument sending its sounds through the pipes of a vast church.

The pain was gone.

The confusion in him had subsided. And as he looked at the smooth mask of Guido's face in sleep, he found himself humming softly the hymn he'd sung the night before, and thinking, Giacomo, you gave this little gift to me; I had not known how much I loved it, all of it, until you came.

10

DOMENICO WAS A SENSATION in Rome, though Loretti was hissed and attacked by the audience, particularly the *abbati*—the clerics who always took the front rows of the Roman house—accusing him of stealing from his idol, the composer Marchesca, so that all during the performance they hissed "Bravo Marchesca! Boooo Loretti," keeping quiet only when Domenico sang.

It was enough to unnerve anyone and Loretti was back

in ,Naples, swearing never to set foot in the Eternal City again.

But Domenico had gone on to a grand court appointment in one of the German states. And the boys at the conservatorio laughed to hear that he'd enjoyed an escapade with a count and his wife, playing the woman for one and the man for the other in the same bed.

Tonio listened to all this with relief. Had Domenico failed, he would never have forgiven himself. And he still could not hear the stage name "Cellino" without shame and something of grief. Guido was distraught over Loretti's reception, muttering as always that the Roman audiences were the worst.

But Tonio was too caught up in his own life to think of much else.

Right after Christmas, he began visiting a French fencing master every chance he could. No matter what his other obligations, he managed to get out of the conservatorio at least three times a week.

Guido was furious. "But you can't do this," he insisted. "Practice all day, rehearse with the students all evening, the opera on Tuesdays, the Contessa's on Friday night. And now you want to spend these hours in a *salle d'armes*, this is nonsense."

But Tonio's face took on an elongated and determined expression, complete with an icy smile. And he won out.

He told himself that there were times when after a day of music and high-strung bickering voices, he must be away from the school and among those who weren't eunuchs, or he would go mad.

Actually the opposite was true. It was very hard for him to go to the fencing salon, hard for him to greet the Frenchman who instructed him, to take his place among the young men who were lounging about in their lace shirt sleeves, faces already glistening from earlier exertion, and quick to offer him a match.

He felt their eyes on him; he felt sure they laughed at him behind his back.

Yet coldly, he took his position, left arm crooked in the perfect arc, legs bent for the spring, and commenced thrusting, parrying, striving for ever greater speed and accuracy, his long reach giving him a deadly advantage as he moved towards an obvious ease and grace.

After others were spent, he carried on, feeling the tingle of hardening muscles in his calves and his arms, the pain melting into added strength, as with a strident energy he took the sport out of it for his partners, sometimes driving them right to the wall before the fencing master himself stepped forward to restrain him, whispering, "Tonio, come now, rest a while," in his ear.

It was almost Lent before he realized no one ever jested in his presence; no one ever spoke the word "eunuch" when he was near.

And now and then the young men made their gestures. Would he join them in drinking after? Would he care to go hunting, or riding? And always he said no. But he could see he'd won a respect from these dark-skinned and often taciturn southern Italians, who surely must have known he wasn't one of them. But that gave him scant warmth.

He shunned the company of young men, regular men, even the regular students of the conservatorio, who continued to defer to him as they had after Lorenzo's death.

But crossing blades with a man? He forced himself to it. And he was soon good enough for almost anyone he took on.

Guido called it mania.

Guido couldn't guess the cold flinty loneliness he felt in the midst of it, the relief he felt once he was back inside the conservatorio doors.

But he had to do it. He had to do it until he was so exhausted he might have dropped.

And when the awareness of his freakishness—of his increasing height and the inhuman gleam of his skin—when these things obsessed him, he took to stopping, to slowing his breath. Then he would move more slowly as he walked, or talked, or spoke; he would make each gesture graceful, languid. And that seemed to him less ridiculous, though no one had ever indicated to him that they found him ridiculous at all.

Meantime at the conservatorio, the Maestro di Cappella urged Tonio to take a small chamber near Guido's rooms, on the main floor. The death of Lorenzo obviously worried him. He didn't approve, either, of all this time spent with the sword. The students were looking up to Tonio, making something of a hero of him.

"But then I must admit," he added, "you surprised everyone with that Christmas cantata. Music is the blood and pulse of this place, and if you did not have the talent, you would not make the impression you so obviously make."

Tonio protested. He didn't want to give up the view of the mountain; he didn't want to give up that snug attic place that was his own.

But when he realized all of these apartments on the first floor were linked by connecting doors, and that his lay exactly beside Guido's bedroom, he accepted. And he went out to furnish the room as he chose.

The Maestro was appalled to see the treasures coming through the front door: a chandelier of Murano glass, silver candlesticks, enameled chests, a coffered bed fitted with green velvet curtains, carpets from the Orient, and finally a splendid harpsichord with a double keyboard and a long triangular case. It was painted with galloping satyrs and nymphs, under a mellow glaze, in ocher, gold, and olive green.

This was a present for Guido, actually, though giving it to him outright might have been indiscreet.

And at night when the draperies were pulled against the cloister windows, and the halls echoed with dim and dissonant sounds, no one knew who slept in which bed, who came and went in which chamber, and the love of Guido and Tonio went on undiscovered as before.

Guido was meantime hard at work on creating a *Pasticcio* for Easter, which the Maestro di Cappella had gladly entrusted to him as the result of his recent Christmas success. This *Pasticcio* was a complete opera in which most of the acts were revisions of earlier and famous works. Scarlatti's music would be used for the first with part of a libretto by Zeno, something suitable by Vivaldi worked into the second, and so on. But Guido had an opportunity to write the closing act himself.

There would be parts in it for Tonio, and for Paolo, whose high sweet soprano was astonishing everyone, and for another promising student named Gaetano, who had just been sent to Guido in recognition of the Christmas work.

Guido was ecstatic. And Tonio soon realized that though he could have bought out all Guido's time for private lessons here, Guido wanted recognition from the Maestro for his students and his compositions; Guido was working towards the fulfillment of certain dreams of his own.

And on the day the Maestro accepted the *Pasticcio*, Guido was so happy he actually threw up all the pages of the score into the air.

Tonio got down on his knees to pick them up and then made Guido promise to take him and Paolo to the nearby island of Capri for a couple of days.

Paolo was brimming with excitement when told he was to go. Snub-nosed, round-faced, with a mop of unruly brown hair, he was loving and easy to love; and late at night in the inn, Tonio kept him up talking, saddened to discover the boy remembered no parents, only a succession of orphanages, and the old choirmaster who had promised the operation wouldn't be painful, when in fact it was.

But as Lent came on, Tonio realized what Guido's victory meant. Tonio must now appear on the stage not in the chorus, but alone.

Why should it be any worse than the chapel? Why should it be any worse than the processions which moved right through the common people to the church?

Yet it chilled him. He could see the audience assembling, and it was almost a sensual pain that came over him when he contemplated stepping before the lights: that old feeling of nakedness, of vulnerability, of . . . what? Belonging to others? Being something to please others, rather than one who is to be pleased himself?

Yet he wanted it so badly. He wanted the paint and the tinsel and the excitement; and he remembered how, when Domenico had been singing, he had thought: Some day I will do it and better than that.

Yet when he finally opened Guido's score, he discovered he was to play a woman. He was stunned.

He was alone at the time.

He had taken the score to the empty little theater with permission to practice it there, hearing his voice fill the place.

Little sunlight leaked into the hall; the empty boxes were hollow and dark, and the stage itself barren even of its curtains, so that furnishings and props were exposed.

Sitting at the keyboard and staring at the score before

274

him, he had the instant flashing feeling that he had been betrayed.

Yet he could almost see Guido's astonished face when confronted with it. Guido hadn't "done" this to him deliberately. Guido was merely giving him the opportunities for training he must have.

He forced his hands to sound the first few notes; and letting loose the full power of his voice, he heard the opening phrases fill the little house. The whole production came to life in his mind. He felt the crowd, he heard the orchestra, he saw that fair-haired girl in the front row.

And there he was at the core of it, that splendid horror, a man in a woman's dress. No, not a man, you forget yourself. He smiled. And in retrospect, Domenico seemed sublimely innocent and supremely powerful to him.

And he felt his voice dry in his throat.

He knew that he should do it. He should accept it as it was. That was the lesson of the mountain and within the unfolding petals of this new terror there lay the seed of greater strength. He wished he could go back to the mountain. He wished he understood why it had so helped him and transformed him that first time.

But without thinking, he had risen, closed the harpsichord.

And finding a pen in Guido's bedroom, he wrote his message on the top page of the score:

"I cannot perform women's roles, not now or ever, and if you do not rewrite the part for me, I do not perform at all."

There would have been an argument when Guido came in, except that Tonio did not speak. He knew all the arguments: castrati performed women's roles everywhere; did he think he could go through the world singing only men's parts? Did he understand what he was sacrificing? Did he think he could always pick and choose?

And then finally Tonio looked up and said in a small voice: "Guido, I will not do it."

And Guido had gone out. He had to obtain the Maestro's permission to rewrite, to completely refashion the last act.

It seemed an hour that he was gone.

And there was this unusual thickness, this dryness to Tonio's throat. It was as if he couldn't sing, and all the vague images of the mountain, and his night there, brought no comfort, and

275

he was afraid. He felt he was being drawn into something that would utterly destroy him, and he had miscalculated all along. To be the simple and uncontemplative thing which could be all things a castrato must be—that would be the death of him and what he was. Always he would be divided. Always there would be pain. Pain and pleasure, intermingling and working him this way and that, and shaping him, but one never really vanquishing the other; there would never be peace.

He wasn't prepared for Guido's crestfallen attitude when he returned. He knew immediately something was wrong.

Guido sat at his desk for a long time before he spoke.

"He's given the good part to Benedetto, his pupil," he said finally. "He says you may sing the aria I wrote for Paolo at the end."

Tonio wanted to say something; he wanted to say that he was sorry, and that he knew he had disappointed Guido terribly.

"It's your music, Guido," he murmured, "and everyone will hear it. . . ."

"But I wanted them to hear you sing it; you are my pupil, I wanted them to hear you!"

11

THE EASTER *Pasticcio* was a success. Tonio had helped with the revisions of the libretto, lent a hand with the costuming, and worked backstage at every rehearsal until he was ready to drop.

It was a full house, and the first time Guido had ever played in the theater, and Tonio had bought him a new wig for the occasion and a fashionable burgundy-colored brocade coat.

Guido had rewritten the song for him. It was an *aria cantabile* full of exquisite tenderness and perfect for Tonio's increasing skills.

And when Tonio stepped to the footlights, he wanted it so badly that the old sense of vulnerability was alchemized into exhilaration, a heady awareness of the swimming beauty around him, the expectant faces everywhere, and the obvious and reliable power of his own voice.

Breathing slowly, calmly, before he began, he felt the sadness of the aria, and then moved into it fully expecting to bring the audience to tears.

But when he saw that he had done this, that those before him were actually weeping, he was so astonished he almost forgot to leave the stage.

The young fair-haired girl was there too, just as he had suspected she would be. He saw her transfixed, gazing up at him. The triumph was almost more than he could bear.

But this was Guido's night, Guido's premiere performance before an audience of sophisticated Neapolitans, and when Tonio saw him taking his bows, he forgot about everything else.

Then later at the Contessa Lamberti's house, he saw the fair-haired one again.

It was very crowded. Lent was over, people wanted to dance, to drink, and of course the performance at the conservatorio had been very fine, and all the musicians were welcome. And Tonio, roaming about, glass in hand, happened to see the girl suddenly as she came through a door. She was on the arm of a very old, dark-skinned gentleman, but when their eyes met, she nodded to Tonio. Then she went to join the dance.

Of course no one noticed it. No one would have thought it remarkable. But Tonio felt immediately light-headed. He got clean away from her as fast as he could, wondering even critically, out of sorts suddenly, why was she here? She was so young after all. Surely she wasn't married, and almost all Italian girls of that age were shut up in convents. Rarely did they ever go to balls.

His bride-to-be, Francesca Lisani, had been so thoroughly entombed that when he was told he was to marry her, he could not remember her face. But she had been so beautiful when they finally met that afternoon at her convent! He still saw her through the grille, and why was he so surprised, he thought now. After all, she was Catrina's child.

But why think of all this? It was unreal to him, actually; or rather, unreal to him one moment, and then poignantly real the next. What was overpoweringly real was that every

277

time he paused for an instant someone complimented his performance.

Sleek gentlemen he didn't know, their walking sticks in one hand, their lace handkerchiefs gathered delicately in the other, bowed to him, told him he had been delightful and that they looked to him for great things. Great things! The ladies were smiling at him, lowering those elaborately painted fans for an instant, making it quite evident he might come to sit beside them if he liked.

And Guido, where was Guido? Surrounded by people, Guido was actually laughing, the little Contessa Lamberti on his arm.

Tonio stopped, took a deep, ungraceful gulp of his white wine, and continued his wandering. More guests streamed in and there was a blast of fresh air from the front doors.

He leaned his shoulder against the fretted edge of a long mirror, and without willing it, realized it had been his last day in Venice when he had seen his future wife, oh, so many things had happened that day, he had lain with Catrina, he had sung in San Marco.

This was dreadful, and how long had he been in Naples? Almost a year!

When he saw Guido beckon, he went to him.

"You see that little man there, the Russian, Count Sherzinski," Guido whispered. "He's a brilliant amateur, and I've written a sonata for him. He may play it later on."

"Why, that's splendid," Tonio whispered. "But why don't you play it?"

"No." Guido shook his head. "Too soon. They've all just discovered I'm something more than . . ." But he swallowed the words, and Tonio, secretly, slyly, pressed his hand.

More of the conservatorio musicians had just arrived. Guido was moving away, and Piero, the blond-haired Milanese castrato, came up to Tonio at once. "You were marvelous tonight," he said. "You teach us something every time you sing."

From a distance Tonio saw Benedetto, the Maestro's new pupil, who had taken the role originally written for him. Benedetto passed them without a glance.

"It was his night," Tonio said with a resigned gesture, "and Guido's to be sure."

He had assisted Benedetto with his costume; he had placed the wig of curls and ribbons on his head. How disdainful he had been of those around him; he took no more notice of Tonio than he would of a valet; and he had long, perfectly oval fingernails, each one with its pale half moon at the root. He must have buffed them when he was alone; they shone as if they were lacquered when he was on stage. Yet there was something hard-bitten and starved-looking about him; the white lace and paste jewels never really transformed him; but he wore it all without the slightest self-consciousness. What would he think, Tonio wondered, if he knew I'd given up the part rather than put on those clothes?

"He was all right; he will always be all right," Piero said now, giving Benedetto a cold, appraising look.

He was drawing Tonio into the billiard room. "I want to talk to you, Tonio," he was saying. From here they could see the open ballroom and the long line of those performing the minuet, though the music was thin here and distorted. At moments, when the conversation roared, it seemed these brilliantly clad men and women danced to nothing.

"It's about Giovanni, Tonio. You know the Maestro wants him to stay on another year, he's determined he should try for the stage, but Giovanni's been offered a position in a Roman choir and he wants to take it. If it was the Pope's chapel, the Maestro would say yes, but as it is, he's turned up his nose at it. . . . What do you think, Tonio?"

"I don't know," Tonio said. But he did know. Giovanni had never been good enough for the stage, he'd known it the first time he'd heard him sing.

But the girl with the yellow hair had appeared in the frame of the distant archway. Was it that same violet dress she wore? The one she had worn almost a year ago? Her waist seemed so small he might have closed it easily in both his hands, and the swell of her breasts was so flawless and radiant, the flesh there as lovely as the flesh of her cheek. It seemed her eyebrows were not blond as they might have been, but dark, smoky, like the blue of her eyes, and it was what made her so very serious. He could see so clearly her expression, her slight frown, and the slight pout of her lower lip.

"But Tonio, Giovanni wants to go to Rome, that's the worst part of this. Giovanni has never enjoyed the stage, he never will, and he's always loved singing in church. He loved it when he was very little. . . ."

Tonio smiled at this. "But Piero, what can I do?"

"You can tell us what you think, Tonio," he said. "Do you think Giovanni could ever make a life for himself with the opera?"

"Ask Guido, that's what you should do."

"But Tonio, you don't understand. Maestro Guido would never contradict the Maestro di Cappella, and Giovanni really wants to go to Rome. He's nineteen, he's been here long enough, this is the best offer he's ever gotten."

A little pause fell between them. The girl turned, she bowed, she took her partner's hand and proceeded down the row of dancers, her skirts swaying.

Suddenly Piero laughed and touched Tonio in the ribs. "Oh, so it's that one you're after," he whispered.

Tonio flushed. He had to rein in his immediate anger. "Certainly not, I don't even know who she is. I was just admiring her."

He appeared as casual as he could. Motioning to a passing waiter, he took a fresh glass of white wine, holding it to the light as if the sudden wash of liquid against the crystal fascinated him.

"Go flatter her, Tonio, and maybe she'll paint your picture," Piero said. "She'll paint you naked if you let her."

"What are you talking about!" Tonio said sharply.

"She paints naked men." Piero laughed as if he were enjoying this teasing immensely. "Of course they're angels and saints, but they haven't much clothing on. Go look in the Contessa's chapel, if you don't believe me. She painted all the murals over the altar."

"But she's so young!"

"Yes, isn't she!" Piero whispered, smiling broadly.

"But what's her name?"

"I don't know, ask the Contessa. She's connected to the Contessa. But why don't you fix your attentions on a nice older lady? Girls like that mean trouble. . . ."

"Well, it doesn't really matter," Tonio said sharply.

A painter. And she painted murals on the walls. The idea shocked him; it tantalized him, giving her a luxurious new substance, and suddenly her negligent air seemed all the more seductive. She seemed concentrated on something beyond her own loveliness, and the protection of it. But she was so pretty! Had Rosalba, the Venetian painter, been so pretty? If so, then why did she paint? But that was moronic. And what did he care if she was the greatest painter in all Italy! Yet it maddened him deliciously, the thought of her with a brush in her hand.

Piero's face seemed suddenly so vulnerable, and Tonio was now looking at him as if he had only just seen him. He'd just begun to understand his words. This matter for Giovanni was crucial. It might determine the course of his life, and Piero was turning to him for a solution. It puzzled Tonio, but it was not the first time the others had come to him.

"Tonio, if you talk to him, he will do what you say." Piero spelled it out. "I think he should go to Rome, but he won't listen to me. He'll be disappointed and humiliated if he keeps trying for a life in the opera."

Tonio nodded. "All right, Piero," he said. "I'll talk to him."

The fair-haired girl had disappeared. The dance had broken up. He couldn't see her anywhere. And then he saw her from a great distance as she proceeded to the door, still on the arm of that elderly gentleman. She's leaving, he thought, and he felt a sharp regret to see her go. Of course it wasn't the same violet dress, just a dress of the same color, and it had such wide skirts, gathered with clusters of little flowers. She must love that color. . . .

But Giovanni, what was he going to tell Giovanni? He would make Giovanni express the answer for himself, and then he would urge Giovanni to follow his own conviction.

There was in him some troubling sense of the responsibility given him. But more than that, he experienced a warm feeling for all the boys who were now turning to him often as some sort of leader. It seemed he was close to so many, and not only the castrati. Not long ago, the student composer Morello had given him a copy of his recent *Stabat Mater* with the note, "Perhaps some day you will sing this." Twice recently, Guido had let him take over the instruction of the younger boys, and he had loved that too, seeing how much they looked up to him.

And what was it he had been thinking? Something about the chapel, the Contessa's chapel, where was it? He'd let the wine go to his head. And the Contessa herself seemed to have disappeared. Of course any of the servants would know where the chapel was. Guido would know. And where was Guido? But he felt he must not ask Guido. "I am disgracefully drunk," he whispered. And seeing his reflection in a glass, he said: "Your mother's son!"

It seemed he was in an empty salon and knew that he must lie down. Yet when another servant approached him with the inevitable cool white wine, he drank it and, touching the servant's arm, said: "The chapel, where is it? Is it open to the guests?"

Next he knew he was following the man up the broad central stairs of the house, and down a long corridor to a pair of double doors. A sense of intrigue quickened him. He watched the servant lift his candle to the sconces, and then Tonio stood in the dimly lit chapel by himself.

It was beautiful, rich, and full of wondrous details. There was gold everywhere as the Neapolitans loved it, etching arches and fluted columns, bordering the ceilings and the windows with gleaming arabesques. And the lifelike statues were dressed in real satin and velvet. And the altar cloth was encrusted with jewels.

Silently he went up the aisle. Silently he knelt on the velvet cushion at the communion rail, putting his hands together as if he meant to pray.

In the dim light, he saw the murals pulsing above him, and it seemed impossible that *she* could have painted these huge and splendid figures: the Virgin Mary ascending into heaven; angels with arched wings, gray-haired saints.

Robust, powerful, these figures seemed on the verge of life, and he felt a rush of love for her as he looked at them, imagining himself near to her, and in the midst of some low and passionate conversation in which he could hear, finally hear, her voice. Ah, if he could only pass close to her some night on the dance floor when she was talking to her partner, he could hear her voice. Above him, the Virgin's dark hair flowed in ripples to her shoulders, her face a flawless oval, her lids half mast. Did *she* really paint this? It seemed suddenly too exquisite for anyone to have painted it. He closed his eyes.

He held his forehead with his right hand. A torrent of feeling threatened him. He was miserable and compelled in his mind to make some explanation to Guido of why he had come to this place. "I love only you," he whispered.

And dizzy from the wine, and sick, he moved clumsily away from the altar towards the doors.

Had he not found a couch then in a small upstairs parlor, he might have been very ill.

As it was, he lay down and shut his eyes, and then he heard his mother say very distinctly, "I should have run away with the opera," and he was asleep.

It was quiet when he awoke. Surely the party was over. And getting up quickly, he went to the head of the stairs. Guido would be furious with him. Guido might even have gone home alone.

Only a few guests remained now sprinkled about the immense rooms, and everywhere below the servants moved quietly gathering up napkins and glasses onto silver trays. The air smelled of tobacco, and a lone harpsichordist, an amateur, was playing a spirited little song.

Only three of the violinists were still there, and they were chatting with one another. And when Tonio saw Francesco among them, he hurried down the stairs.

"Did you see Guido?" he asked. "Has he gone home?"

Francesco was obviously very tired, having played two engagements this evening, and at first he didn't seem to understand.

"He's going to be furious with me, Francesco. I fell asleep. He's probably been looking for me," Tonio explained.

Then Francesco smiled. "He won't be angry with you," he whispered in an oddly confidential manner. And now he laid his violin carefully in its case and, snapping the cover shut, rose to go. But seeing the blank expression on Tonio's face, he smiled again and glanced pointedly to the stairs and the floor above.

Tonio bent forward, as if straining to hear the unspoken. Francesco made the gesture with his eyes again. "He's with the Contessa," he whispered finally. "Just wait."

For a long moment Tonio merely looked at Francesco. He watched Francesco gather up his music; he watched him make his farewells to the others. He saw him go out.

And then as Tonio stood alone on the edge of the vast empty room, the little exchange made its full impression upon him, and slowly, he approached the stairs.

He told himself there was no truth to this. It meant nothing. Perhaps he had misunderstood.

Of course, Francesco couldn't know that he and Guido were lovers when no one knew.

Yet when he found himself in the mouth of the dark upstairs corridor, he was trembling in every limb.

He rested against the wall. His earlier dizziness came back to him, and suddenly he wanted to be out of this place, far, far away from it. Yet he stood perfectly still.

He did not have long to wait.

Down the hall, a door opened, and in the light that seeped out onto the flowered carpet, Guido and the Contessa appeared. Her plump little body was still done up in an elaborate ball gown, but her dark hair was flowing free. And Guido, turning tenderly to her, bent to kiss her as he took his leave.

Their bodies merged in the shadows. Then she was gone, and the light was gone with her. And Guido was coming to the head of the stairs.

Tonio was speechless as he watched this. He was speechless as he saw the indistinct shape of Guido approach.

But then he saw the look on Guido's face as their eyes met and there was no longer the slightest doubt.

12

HE WAS CRYING. He was crying exactly as if he were a small boy, and he didn't care. He could not accept that this was happening. Guido had deceived him. Guido had deliberately wounded him. And if he had spoken angry words to Guido in the beginning, it was only panic, the desperate attempt to keep the pain of this full moment away from him.

And now here was Guido speaking to him in that cold, inflectionless voice, giving him nothing! What had he expected? Excuses, lies even? And Guido had said to him that he had warned Tonio. He would take women when and where he could. And it had nothing to do with the love between them.

"Oh, but you made a fool of me!" Tonio whispered. He could not think, however. He could not keep track of a sequence of accusations.

"How made a fool of you? Do you think I do not love you? Tonio, you are my life!"

But there were no excuses, there was no remorse. There was no concession to stop. There was nothing but that coldness and that low voice repeating the same words over and over.

284

"But was it only tonight, or were there other times? Oh, there were other times."

Guido would not answer. He stood silent, his arms folded, his eyes fixed on Tonio as if he could not feel for an instant the misery he had inflicted.

"Well then, how long? When did it begin?" Tonio cried. "When was it that I was not enough for you, tell me?"

"Enough for me? You are the world to me," Guido said softly.

"But you won't give her up. . . ."

Guido said nothing.

It was no use talking any more; he knew the answers would be the same, and that this abyss could open under him, that this misery could come, drawing him back to his other earlier hurts, was stunning him. This pain seemed unendurable. It resonated with every fiber of his being, and it seemed the small world he had made for himself in this place teetered, threatened to crumble. What did it matter that he had once known worse pain? It was unreal to him, it was this moment that was real now.

He wanted to get up, to go away. He never wanted to see Guido again, nor the Contessa, nor anyone here, and yet this was unthinkable.

"I loved you . . ." he whispered. "There was no one for me but you. There was no one else ever."

"You love me now, and there is no one else for me but you," Guido answered. "You know that."

"Don't say any more. Just leave it. It only gets worse the more you say. It's over."

But as soon as he had spoken those words, he knew Guido was moving towards him.

And just when he thought surely he would strike Guido, he felt himself turning to him. It was almost as if in his misery, he could not resist Guido. Guido could yet protect him even from Guido's cruelty. And when Guido whispered again, "You are my life," it was tortured and hungry, and Tonio gave himself over to him.

Guido's kisses were slow and savoring. It seemed passion came in such clear waves, carrying Tonio up, only to slacken ever so slightly, just before swelling again.

But when it was finished and they lay close, intertwined, Tonio whispered in Guido's ear, "Show me how to understand this. How could you wound me and feel nothing? I

285

would not for all the world have wounded you so, I swear it.''

He thought he saw Guido smile in the dark. But it was not an ugly smile. Rather it was sad and his sigh seemed to come from the weight of some old knowledge.

There was in his embrace then a desperation, and as he folded Tonio yet closer to his chest, he held him as if someone else meant to take him.

"In time, beautiful one, you will," he said. "And for now, show me this gentle generosity."

Tonio's eyes were closing. He wanted to deny it, but it seemed even as he slipped reluctantly into his dreams that a vast part of this puzzle was missing and he had only just seen the size of it. There were fears stirring in him, fears he could not voice, and he knew for this moment Guido loved him and he loved Guido and if he were to press for the missing part of that puzzle, misery might overwhelm him again.

He accepted it. He felt helpless, but he accepted it. And in the days that followed he understood this had been wise, for Guido was more surely his than ever before.

Yet one bitter lesson had been learned by Tonio: it was not Guido who kept him from the blond-haired girl. Tonio's guilt in the chapel that night for so much as glimpsing her paintings mocked him in memory, because he knew now he might approach her without so much as an explanation to Guido, and yet he could not bring himself to do it, falling silent and miserable every time she crossed his path.

But his love for Guido filled him and quieted him in the months to come. It seemed at times he was tantalized by the knowledge that Guido had his Contessa. And from Guido he received an even greater measure of tenderness and submission, perhaps because Guido was at last receiving the recognition as a composer he had craved for so long.

As the warmer months came on again, with all their inevitable festivals and processions—and occasional excursions with Paolo into the countryside—it was clear that Guido was much in demand.

Advanced composition students were given to him; the beginners were taken away; and with Tonio as his star pupil, and Paolo surprising everyone, he was attracting more excellent singers than he could accept.

286

He was placed in almost complete control of the school theater, and though he drove everyone mercilessly, Tonio found him all the more alluring for it, and most impressive in the fine clothes that Tonio's purse supplied.

Yet Guido's face softened somewhat with authority; he was less angry all the time. And he had about him a more casual air of command which caused Tonio to feel a secret and debilitating pleasure at the mere brush of Guido's hand.

Maestro Cavalla cautioned Guido not to push Tonio. Yet it was through performance that Guido's real work with Tonio had begun.

Before the lights, he could better examine Tonio's weaknesses and strength. And though he drilled Tonio relentlessly with his exercises, and wrote for him a variety of arias, Guido could see it was with the *aria cantabile*—the aria of sadness and tender feeling—that Tonio excelled. Benedetto was good at tricks; he could do acrobatics with his high notes, only to plunge into the contralto range with disturbing ease. It had the audience gasping, but it didn't make them weep.

And that Tonio could do, without fail, every time he sang.

Meanwhile the Bourbon King Charles III, who had been ruling Naples for two years now, decided to build his Teatro San Carlos, and within a matter of months it was completed and the old San Bartolommeo was pulled down.

But though everyone marveled at the speed with which the house had been erected, on opening night it was the interior which drew the gasps of admiration and awe.

The San Bartolommeo had been an old rectangular house. This was a horseshoe with six tiers. But the marvel was not its impressive size so much as the way it was so lavishly lighted, each box being fixed with a mirror on the front and a candle on either side. When the candles were lighted, the mirrors amplified the tiny flames a thousandfold in all directions; it was an unbelievable spectacle dimmed only by the talent of the prima donna Anna Peruzzi, and her rival, the contralto Vittoria Tesi, who was renowned for her skill in male roles. The opera, *Achille en Sciro,* was from the recent libretto by Metastasio, with music by Domenico Sarri, whom the Neapolitans had loved for many years.

One of the greatest scene designers of the time, Pietro Righini, had been employed for the stage, and the whole was a magnificent production indeed.

Guido and Tonio had places in the front of the parterre, enormous seats with arm rests, which could be locked by the season subscriber when not in use. No one could take your place, then. It was there for you no matter how late you might come; and the rows were so broadly spaced, a man might walk to his seat without disturbing anyone else.

Of course everyone knew the monarch didn't care for opera; they laughed that he built such a spacious theater so he might place himself as far as possible from the stage.

But the eyes of Europe were more than ever turned to Naples. Her singers, her composers, her music had fully superseded those of Venice. And they had long ago eclipsed those of Rome.

Rome however was still the place for a castrato's debut, as far as Guido was concerned. Rome might not be producing singers and composers, but Rome was Rome. And Guido reminded Tonio of this all the time.

Tonio's progress amazed everyone. And though he had sung four arias in the fall opera at the conservatorio and spent his evenings out with Guido, he still took some meals with his fellow students, spent his afternoon recreation with them, and worked with them at all the menial tasks assigned to him backstage.

But some time after his second Christmas in Naples, Tonio had a clash with another fencing student which proved as dangerous as his struggle with Lorenzo the year before.

It happened on a day when Tonio's mind was heavy, and he moved through the world with an unusual sluggishness and indifference to all he heard and saw.

That morning one of Catrina Lisani's letters had informed him his mother had given birth to a healthy son. Five months ago, the baby had been delivered; he had been in this world almost half a year.

A debilitating languor came over Tonio, and he had found himself lost in an inaudible little prayer. May you be sound of limb and quick of wit, he was almost whispering. May you receive every blessing from God and from men. Were I at your christening, I would kiss your tender little forehead myself.

288

And an image drifted into his mind, of itself, it seemed, so that he saw his figure, tall and white, this spider of a creature he had become, moving through those dank and moldering rooms. He saw an endless arm outstretched to rock the infant's cradle. And he saw his mother weeping alone.

Why was she weeping? His thoughts collected themselves slowly and he realized she was weeping because he had slain her husband. Carlo was dead. And she was in mourning again and all those brilliantly imagined candles had gone out. Little bits of smoke rose from the wicks. And up and down those halls, the stench from the canal moved as if it were thick and palpable as the winter mist.

"Ah," he had spoken aloud finally, folding the stiff parchment sheet of paper, "what did you want? A little more time?"

Another step had been taken; another step. Catrina's letter said Marianna was once again, already, with child!

So when he arrived at the fencing salon, he had stupidly pushed ahead of a young Tuscan from Siena as he went through the door. Carelessness, that was all.

But as he prepared for his first bout, he could not help hearing a snarl behind him, and raising his eyes, he felt that odd sense of disorientation that had come over him in the Piazza San Marco when he had first heard of Carlo years before. He stood still; it seemed for a terrifying instant he was slipping into dream. And then he clung to the vision of the polished floor in front of him, the high windows, the long and barren room. The words penetrated: "A eunuch? I never knew capons were permitted to carry swords." Nothing unexpected, nothing very clever, and he saw capons, those emasculated birds, plucked and ready for eating, dangling from the butcher's hook. He saw the mirrors of the fencing salon all around him and reflected in them the young men in their dark breeches and white shirts standing about.

And he realized the room had fallen silent, and that he himself was turning slowly around.

The young Tuscan was staring at him. Yet the features made no impression; and it seemed he was hearing a multitude of whispers, echoes of whispers, rising from all those in this room, all those of this great ilk of young manhood with whom he had vied and struggled here and won. He was standing very still, with narrowed eyes, waiting for the whispers to shape themselves into words he could understand.

But he became vaguely sensible that the young Tuscan was unnerved. The others were uneasy, and then he positively felt the current of wariness circling the room. He could see the blank, almost sullen faces of these southern Italian men; he could smell their sweat.

And then he sensed the young Tuscan's fear. He saw it cresting in panic, and with it a desperate and self-destructive pride.

"I don't cross swords with capons!" the boy shouted almost shrilly, and even these shrewd southern Italians evinced their slight shock.

A strange thought came to Tonio then. He saw the stupidity of this boy. He saw that this boy would rather die than lose face in this small crowd. There was no doubt in Tonio's mind he could kill him. No one here knew the art of the sword as well as he. And even as he felt his own height, his own metallic anger, he felt the meaninglessness of this act. He didn't want to kill this young man. He didn't want for him to die. Yet a man should want to kill him; a man should understand that his insult was not to be borne.

It baffled him; it weighed on him. And the boy was giving him such a rich opportunity! He felt sorrow for the boy. Yet if he let this dilemma grow in him it would weaken him.

And he saw himself as from a great distance narrowing his eyes as he glared at the other and slowly lifted his sword.

The Tuscan drew his rapier; it gave a loud zing as it came loose and flew out at Tonio in the air. His mouth was twisted with fear and anger, and Tonio immediately parried, and tore open the boy's throat.

The boy dropped his blade, gasping, both hands flying to the wound.

And then all the room came to life quickly and silently, with a handful of young men rallying to Tonio to urge him to back off. He saw others surrounding the Tuscan; he saw the blood drenching the boy's shirt. The fencing master was insisting they set a time and place outdoors.

All the way back to the conservatorio Tonio was visited by flashes of those confused moments, of those young men surrounding him, of the informal and friendly touch of their hands.

Before midnight, a young Sicilian nobleman came to tell him that the boy had packed up and fled. There was a contemptuous sneer on the swarthy young man's face as he revealed this, without any other comment. And then hesitating in the stiffly decorated parlor of the conservatorio where he had been received, he asked Tonio to hunt with him some time soon. He and his friends went regularly into the mountains. They should welcome his company. Tonio thanked him for the invitation, without ever saying that he would accept.

And only a few days later Guido and Tonio went into the mountains south.

The weather was mild, and together they sought out one of those seaside towns that clung to the sheer cliffs above a water so purely blue and still it seemed the flawless mirror of heaven.

They dined on simple food in a little white piazza, and then summoned a band of rustic singers, shabby but spirited, who sang them barbarous and inventive melodies no trained musician would possibly attempt.

The night they spent in an inn, on a bed of straw, the window open to the sky.

And the next morning Tonio went out early, wandering alone into a great grassy place, sprinkled everywhere with the first spring wild flowers where once a Greek temple had stood.

Great wheels of fluted marble lay scattered in the green growth, but four columns stood yet against the sky, and as the clouds moved beyond, these columns appeared weightless and to be floating with some eerie motion of their own.

Tonio found the sacred floor. He walked its broken stones until he charted the whole, and then he lay down in the fresh grass that seemed everywhere to rise through crevices and cracks; and looking full into the blinding light, he wondered if he had ever known such serenity in all his life as he had known this past year.

It seemed the world was fragrant and full of unspoiled loveliness everywhere he looked. It held no hideous mystery for him. There was no draining tension day in and day out.

And he felt quieted with love, love for Guido, love for Paolo, love for all those who were his fast friends under the same roof, those boys who shared work and play and study and rehearsal and performance, those who were the only brothers he'd ever known.

And yet the darkness was there.

The darkness was always there. It waited only for Catrina's letter, for the insult of that rash and inept Tuscan boy. But it had been so easy for so long to shut it out!

It seemed a wonder to him that he had ever counted upon hatred, bitterness, to sustain him until the children of Carlo numbered so many that he could go back and settle the old score.

Was he so flawed that he had forgotten the wrong done him, the world denied him, that he could have fallen so easily into this strange life in Naples which now seemed more real to him than any life in Venice he'd ever known? Was it weakness that he had not wanted to kill the Tuscan? Or could it have been something wiser and finer than he felt in those moments?

He had the appalling fear suddenly that the world would never let him know.

Yet it seemed unreal to him that he had ever lived in Venice. That he had ever seen the mist steal over those motionless canals the color of lead, or the walls rise up on either side so close they threatened to swallow the very stars.

Silvery domes, rounded arches, mosaics shimmering even through the rain, *what was this place?*

Shutting his eyes he tried to recall his mother. He tried to hear her voice, to see her whirling in the dance on that dusty floor. Had there ever been a day when seeing her at the window, he had crept up crying behind her? She was singing some common street song. Was she thinking of Istanbul? His hand went out for her. She turned to strike him. He felt himself falling. . . .

Had any of this happened at all?

He was standing suddenly in the grass. The green land was laid open all around. Far off, he saw Guido's dark form stranded amid a great drift of tiny flowers that streaked this vast and beautiful place like white traces of the clouds. And the figure seemed too motionless, the head cocked to one side as if Guido were listening to the sound of the distant birds or simply to the emptiness itself.

"Carlo," he whispered. "Carlo!" as if he could not leave this spot until he had made his father real. And then he closed his eyes on the gentle sun, on these endless fields, and in that distant city he knew so well, he found himself stalking, feline, deadly until in some shadowy and unexpected place he'd come upon him, and in his face he saw the horror, the shock.

But dear God, what would I give if I could live but one day, just one day, with this cup passed from me?

13

ANOTHER SEVEN MONTHS PASSED before Tonio was to hear from Marianna herself, telling of the birth of her second son.

He was so shaken when he saw the letter that he carried it with him all day, opening it only when he was alone on the edge of the sea.

It seemed with the roar of the waves in his ears he would not hear her voice, which had for him some menace like the Sirens' song.

Not an hour goes by that I do not think of you, that I do not feel pain for you, that I do not blame myself for your rash and terrible action. You are not lost to me, no matter how you protest, no matter how reckless and spiteful the course you took.

Your little brother, Marcello Antonio Treschi, was born a week ago in this house. But no child takes your place in my heart.

Only a few days separated Tonio from his first lead role in an opera entirely written by Guido for the conservatorio stage. And he knew if he could not forget this letter, he could not perform.

He drove himself almost foolishly as the production drew near, and his will stood by him. On that night he thought of nothing but music; he was Tonio Treschi of the conservatorio, and Guido's lover, afterwards, when only a frenzied lovemaking could silence the echo of the applause in his ears.

But in the days that followed this little triumph, he was obsessed with his mother, though little of his love for her, his sense of her beauty and her sometime tenderness, remained.

She was Carlo's wife now; she belonged to him, and how could she have ever believed him! Yet believed him she had, without doubt.

Beneath this almost blinding anger, Tonio knew the answer, of course. She had believed Carlo because she *had* to, she had believed him to go on living, she had believed him to escape her empty room and her empty bed. What would there have been for her in that house save Carlo?

And at times, when these thoughts revolved in his head almost incessantly, he could not escape the memory of her old unhappiness, her loneliness, those flashes of cruelty that could even now in recollection bring the chills to the surface of his skin.

Shut up in a convent she would have died, he was certain of it, and his brother, his powerful and cunning brother, his wronged and righteous and willful brother, would have taken another wife in her place.

No, she had faced an impossible choice, and to live with the man without his love would have been as unendurable as the convent cell. She must have the man's love as well as his protection and his name. What had name and protection ever done for her in the past, after all?

"And I shall send her back to her loneliness," he mused. "I shall send her back to her cloister. . . ." And he saw her once more in a widow's black veil.

It was real to him, more real than the pictures these letters conjured of babies christened, and of a life in that house such as he had never known.

She turned on him, she railed at him. With fists clenched, she cursed him. He heard her cries over the years and the miles, and over the dim vista of the imagined future, "I am helpless," and his anger moved inexorably past her so that she became a shadow unable to affect what lay before him any more than she had ever affected the past.

She was lost from him, truly lost from him, and yet his eyes misted over again and again to think of her, and he turned sharply, his heart racing, from the everyday spectacle of those dark-clad women in the churches everywhere, widows ancient and young lighting their candles, on their knees before the altars, walking in black clusters with their old servants, through the streets.

Invitations poured in now for him to sing at private suppers and concerts. He ventured out once to the house of the old Marchesa he'd met his first night at the Contessa Lamberti's house.

But as time passed, he sent only regrets no matter when he was asked.

Guido was furious naturally.

"You must be heard!" he insisted. "You must be seen and heard in the great houses. Tonio, the foreign visitors must see you, don't you understand?"

"Well, they can hear of me and come to see me here," Tonio said, quickly blaming it upon the rigors of his schedule. "You expect too much of me!" he said with conviction. "And besides the Maestro's always complaining about how the boys get into trouble when they go out, too much drinking . . ."

"Oh, stop it," Guido said contemptuously.

But the conservatorio became the only place where Tonio would perform.

More and more he kept to it when he was not in the fencing salon, and he never accepted the invitations of the other young men there to join them in drinking or the hunt.

Again and again he was startled to see his blond-haired friend. She was in the Franciscan church when he went with the other boys for the regular performance. He saw her in the Teatro San Carlos, perched like a queen in the Contessa's box. She faced the stage as English people did, and seemed forever engrossed in the music.

And she was at the school every time that he sang.

From time to time, he returned to the Contessa's with one purpose, though he never admitted to himself what it was. He would go to the chapel and look at those delicate and darkly colored murals, the oval-faced Virgin and her angels with their stiff wings, the muscular saints. It was always late when he did so; he had always just a little too much wine. And sometimes seeing her afterwards in the ballroom, he would stare at her so boldly and so long that surely her family was bound to take offense.

They never did.

* * *

But it was his life at the conservatorio that more fully engrossed him, and nothing really disturbed his regimen, his
day-to-day happiness, except the long letters of his cousin
Catrina, who in spite of the fact that he seldom if ever
answered her, grew more and more bold.

Always delivered to him by the same young Venetian from
the embassy, the letters were clearly meant for Tonio's eyes
alone.

She, too, reported the birth of Marianna's second baby,
saying simply it was healthy as the first:

> But your brother's bastards far outnumber his legitimate
> heirs, or so I am told, as it seems not even his brilliant
> successes in the Senate and in the councils prevent him
> from an almost continuous delight in the fair sex.
>
> Your mother he worships however, have no fear on
> her account.
>
> Yet all marvel at his vigor, his robustness, his capac-
> ity for work and play from the crack of dawn to the
> chiming of midnight. And to those who express their
> admiration, he is quick to counter that exile and misfor-
> tune have both combined to make him savor the life he
> lives.
>
> Of course at the mere mention of his brother, Tonio,
> he is at once driven to tears. Oh, how grateful he is to
> hear that you are doing so well in the south, and yet for
> all that gratitude, he is nevertheless concerned to hear
> so much about your singing and your prowess with the
> sword.
>
> "The stage," he says to me, "you don't really think
> he would ever go on the stage?" And he confesses that
> he had fancied you somewhat of the temperament of
> your old teacher, Alessandro.
>
> And I observe that you are more inclined to be
> another Caffarelli, and at that you should see the look
> on his face.
>
> He would have everyone feel sorry for him! Can you
> imagine it! Don't I know what it means to him to be
> reminded so often, he says, of all this disgrace?
>
> "And the dueling!" he says to me. "What of all this
> dueling? I only want for him to be at peace."
>
> "Yes, and there is nothing so peaceful as the grave,

is there?'' I observe. Only to have him give way to great emotion again and leave my house in a flood of tears.

But he returns, soon enough, much fortified with wine, and pleasantly exhausted from the casinos. And bleary-eyed, he condemns me for my persecution, and yes, if I must know it, he has often thought it would have been better for his unfortunate brother, Tonio, if the surgeon had unwittingly caused some greater injury so that the boy were at rest.

"Why so?" I laugh. "What a dreadful thing to say. Why, he prospers remarkably by all accounts!"

"But what if he's slain in some foolish sword fight?" he demands. "I am never without worry over him night or day." He should never have sent you the swords you requested.

"Swords he can purchase anywhere," I remark.

"My little brother, my little brother," he says with such emotion it would wring tears from an audience. "Does anyone know what I have endured!" But then he turns from me as if he cannot confide in one so simpleminded and unsympathetic as myself *the full extent of his various regrets!*

But truly Tonio, I beg you to be careful and wise. If he hears more of your swordsmanship, he may well feel compelled to dispatch a pair of bravos to Naples for your protection. And I think you would find the company of such men confining, if not positively smothering. Tonio, be watchful and wise.

As for the stage, your voice, how can anyone begrudge you the gift God gave you? I hear your singing when I lie awake at night on my pillow. Would I could really hear it once again, and take you in my arms to show you how much I love you now as I have always. Your brother is a fool if he does not look to you to do great things.

This letter Tonio kept with him for a long time before he eventually committed it, as he had so many others, to the fire

He was much amused by it, and strangely fascinated by it, and his hatred for Carlo was stoked by it to a new and hotter flame.

How well he saw his brother drinking of the cup of life that was Venice! How well he imagined that figure moving from the ballroom to the floor of the Senate, to the Ridotto, to a courtesan's arms.

But all Catrina's gentle warnings were lost on Tonio. He changed nothing in his own life.

He was as dedicated as ever in the fencing salon. And he perfected his aim with the pistol at targets when he had time for it. And alone in his room, increased his skill with the stiletto as much as anyone can without the luxury of sinking it regularly into other people's flesh.

But he knew it was not belligerence or courage that had prompted him to take such a commanding manner with Giacomo Lisani, or pushed him to such obvious skill with weapons just now.

It was simply that he could not conceal from anyone what he was in any way.

More and more the glances of those he met told him they knew he was a eunuch. And the glances of the young Neapolitans told him that he had won their unqualified respect.

As for the stage—his being another Caffarelli, as Catrina had so generously put it—he wished for it and dreaded it so much that sometimes he was baffled by his own mind.

He was intoxicated by the applause, the paint, the glitter of the beautiful sets, and the moment when he heard his own voice ring clear over the others, weaving its elusive and powerful magic for all who wished to hear.

Yet to think of the great theaters filled him with an isolating and strangely exciting fear.

"Two children in two years!"

Sometimes it hit him with such clarity and force that he stopped in his tracks. Two children, both of them healthy sons!

Many a Venetian family had only that claim upon immortality.

And he wished, oh, how he wished with all his heart, that his mother and his father had given him just a little time!

as Venice! he would be imagined that figure moving from

14

TONIO WAS WALKING in the Via di Toledo amid a swarming crowd at high noon when he realized that as of this day, May 1, he had been in Naples exactly three years.

It seemed impossible. And then it seemed he'd been here all of his life, and had never known any other world.

He stopped, stranded for a moment, though the crowd was unwilling to let him stand still, and then turning around he looked up at the perfect blue sky and felt the breeze so gentle and so warm that it was like an embrace.

A little tavern opened nearby with a handful of tables outside on the cobblestones, the whole sheltered by a pair of old gnarled fig trees, and Tonio went there and ordered himself a bottle of Lagrima Christi, the Neapolitan white wine he'd come to love.

The leaves of the figs made huge hand-shaped shadows on the stones, and the warm air, caught here between narrow walls, seemed nevertheless to be always gently in motion.

In a minute he was drunk. It took no more than half a cup, and a spectacular happiness stole over him as he rested back against the rough little chair and watched the steady flow of those in the street. Naples had never seemed so beautiful to him. And despite all that he so disliked—the appalling poverty everywhere and the sheer idleness of the nobility—he felt himself a part of this place; he had come to understand it, on his own terms.

Maybe, too, anniversaries always evoked some celebratory feeling in him. In Venice there were so many and they were always festivals; it wasn't just the way to measure life; it was the way to live.

And after the morning's errands, this happiness was a quiet relief.

For hours he'd been imprisoned at the tailor's. He couldn't avoid the mirrors. And again and again the seamstresses reminded him of his increasing height. He was now six feet tall, and no one looking upon him could any longer think him a boy.

The bloom to his skin, the fullness of his hair, the innocence of his expression; these only combined with the long limbs to make it known to all the world now what he was.

And there were moments when all the compliments he received angered him; and some thin memory of an old man in an attic room came back to him, a man denouncing a world in which all was measured by taste. It was taste that kept such a shape as his fashionable; it was taste that made women send him tributes and confessions of adoration, when all he ever saw in the mirror was the ghastly ruin of God's work. There was a horror to it, watching the scheme of creation so totally wrecked. He wondered sometimes if those who were gravely ill did not feel this—when they lost the feeling in their limbs, when some fever caused them to lose the hair on their heads. The gravely ill attracted him; freaks attracted him, the midgets and dwarfs he saw sometimes on the little stages about town, cripples, a pair of human beings linked together at the hip laughing and drinking wine as they occupied the same chair. These creatures magnetized him and tortured him; he counted himself one of them, secretly, beneath this magnificent disguise of brocade and lace.

He'd bought every fabric shown to him by the tailor; he'd bought a dozen handkerchiefs, cravats, gloves he didn't need.

"All the better to render you invisible, tall one," he'd whispered to the mirror.

Now as he felt this first delicious euphoria from the wine, that immediate alchemy of the spirits and the summer heat, he smiled. "You could be ugly as well, you know," he said to himself. "You could have lost your voice as Guido did. So let it be."

Yet the little torture chamber of the tailor's shop had put him in mind of his recent arguments with Guido and the Maestro di Cappella, arguments that were not likely to stop. Guido had been very disappointed when Tonio refused the prima donna role in the school's spring opera, stating again he would never appear in women's dress. The Maestro had again sought to punish Tonio by giving him a small role. But Tonio had showed no regret.

If anything had disturbed him about the spring opera, it was that his fair-haired friend was not there. For some time

300

now she had not been in chapel either. Nor had he seen her at the Contessa's last ball. And this was disturbing him very much.

As for performing in female dress, his teachers weren't going to leave him alone. They did not share his conviction he could make a life for himself playing only men's parts. Centuries ago, the first castrati had been introduced to play women's parts; and though women performed everywhere now outside of the Papal States, the castrati were still famous for these roles. But with all major parts in the opera written for high voices, everyone had to be ready for anything, women often playing male leads, too.

Finally, the Maestro di Cappella had called Tonio in.

"You know as well as I do," he began, "that you need this experience before you leave here. And the time for your debut is almost at hand."

"But that's not possible," Tonio said. "I'm not ready—"

"Be quiet," said the Maestro. "I can judge your progress far better than you can judge it. And you know I'm right about this. I'm also right that you should perform out of the conservatorio, but you refuse this too. Invitations come in every week for you to perform in private houses, yet you refuse. Tonio, don't you realize this school has become a refuge for you?"

Tonio winced. "That's not so," he murmured with quiet anger, but he knew the Maestro was right.

"Tonio, when you first came here," said the Maestro, "when you first resigned yourself to sing, I didn't think you would endure. I thought the discipline would be much too harsh for you, and I steeled myself to see Guido disappointed again. But you surprised me. You became an aristocrat of this little place; you made it your Venice; you shone here as you might have there.

"But this isn't the world, Tonio, any more than Venice is the world. And you are ready for the world now."

After a long pause Tonio turned to meet the Maestro's gaze.

"May I confide to you a little secret?" he asked.

The Maestro nodded.

"Never in my life have I known the happiness I've known here."

The Maestro gave an affectionate and slightly sad smile.

"Does that surprise you?" Tonio asked.

"No," the Maestro said. "Not when one has a voice such as your voice, it does not." Then he bent across the desk. "That's your power, that's your strength. I promised you once that it would be if you let it. Now, it's nothing more than the truth. And now I'm going to tell you something else. Guido is ready for the world, too. He's ready to write your premiere opera for the Roman stage. He's patient with you because he cannot bear to see you suffer. So he waits. But you are both of you ready, and for Guido the work and the waiting have gone on for a long, long time."

Tonio didn't answer. He was not thinking. Rather he was merely aware that by now, in the normal course of events, he would have been a man. He would have looked and sounded like that double in Venice, and he was wishing vaguely that he could remember better the timbre of that manly voice. His own speaking voice by habit was soft, low, but he made it that way; and he never, never forgot himself, even when he laughed.

"I am going to be even more ruthless," said the Maestro. "There are others here ready to take the spotlight, ready to take your place."

Tonio nodded. But the man went on.

"Do you think I don't know what happened to you? From Guido year in and year out I've gotten only silence; from you, the same. But I know what happened to you, what you've endured. . . ."

"You don't know," Tonio said sharply, "because it has never happened to you."

"You're wrong. True evil in this world is done by those with no imagination. I have imagination. I know what you lost."

Tonio didn't answer. He wouldn't admit to this. It struck him as proud and vain, but all the rest the Maestro had said was very simply true.

"Give me a little time . . ." Tonio said finally, more to himself than to the Maestro. And the Maestro, satisfied that he had been understood, had left it at that.

So now this was the third anniversary of the day he'd come.

And in the midst of this celebratory feeling, this gentle euphoria, he knew more clearly than ever that the Maestro was right.

It was almost dark when he returned to the conservatorio.

He had gone first to the Albergo Inghilterra near the sea and let a couple of rooms. It was his plan to take Guido there tonight, and before that he wanted to stop into a nearby church to hear Caffarelli sing. Caffarelli had been in Naples over a year now, singing often at the San Carlos, but it meant something to Tonio to hear him on this special day.

Finding Guido's studio empty, he went into his room.

Guido was dressed already for the evening in a fine red velvet frock coat that Tonio had bought for him, and he was putting a jeweled ring on his left hand. His hair was neatly combed, the thick curls a glossy chocolate brown, and there was an unusual sheen to him altogether as he pulled on a new pair of white silk gloves. He wore his rhinestone buckle shoes.

"Ah, I've been asking for you all afternoon," he said. "I want you to come to the Contessa's house early," he said. "Have a light supper and don't drink any more wine. This is a special night, you must do as I tell you, and don't make any excuses, I know you don't want to come there, but you must."

"When have I not wanted to come there?" Tonio asked. Guido never looked so good to him as when he was going out.

"The last half a dozen times you've been invited," said Guido, "but you must come tonight."

"And why is that?" Tonio asked coldly. He could scarce believe the irony of all this. He was remembering Domenico's little plan of years before, the same *albergo*, rooms by the sea. He smiled. What could he say?

"The Contessa's been through an ordeal, and this is her first ball since she's been back. You know her cousin died, the old Sicilian who'd lived all those years in England. Well, she had to take him back to Palermo to be buried. I don't suppose you've ever witnessed a funeral in Palermo."

"Never witnessed anything in Palermo," said Tonio.

Guido was shuffling through the bound scores on his desk. "Well, the old man had to be placed in a chair in the church for the ceremony, and afterwards mounted in the Capuchin catacombs with all the rest of the family; it's an underground necropolis, hundreds of corpses all properly dressed, some standing, others lying down, the lot tended by the monks."

Tonio winced. But he'd heard of these places. He could conceive of nothing like it in northern Italy.

"Yes, well, the Contessa has enough Sicilian blood that it didn't make much difference to her. But the old man's bride, the young girl from England he married, she was quite hysterical when she saw the catacombs. She had to be taken out."

"Small wonder."

"Anyway, the Contessa's back. She's done her duty, her cousin's buried, and this ball is rather important to her. So be there early as I ask."

"But what has this to do with me?"

"The Contessa likes you, she has always liked you," Guido said. "Now"—he put his arm around Tonio and held him tightly—"no more wine, as I said."

The house was dark when he reached it. He had left the church as soon as Caffarelli had sung his first aria, the castrato's music thrilling him and humbling him at the same time. Nothing of Venice had come back to plague him; he had heard Caffarelli too often since; and he'd been thirsty for that perfection, that lust in the voice, that understanding of a thousand things which he seldom found in others around him anymore.

He'd tried to let Caffarelli inflame him in a special way, too. He wanted Caffarelli, without ever knowing it, to give him some courage he lacked.

Whether that had happened or not he didn't know.

But it was pleasant to come into the Contessa's house early and have the luxury of seeing all this gilded plaster by the light of the moon. He gave up his cloak to the porter, said he didn't want anything yet, and wandered off alone through a chain of empty rooms. Simple furniture became spectral in the shadows, hovering above carpets full of half-realized illuminations, and the warm air pouring in was sweet. There was no smoke yet, no burning wax, and no French perfume.

And he didn't really mind coming here as Guido thought. He had just become tired of it, particularly since some four or five months before the yellow-haired girl had disappeared. But maybe, *maybe,* she would be here tonight. The house open to the fragrant night with its hum of insects and its scent of roses seemed the very essence of the south. Even the unbelievable multitude of servants seemed particularly southern, a host of the poverty-stricken, got up in lace and satin, working for nothing, carrying their little beacons from room to room.

He wandered out into the garden. He didn't really want to see the house come alive, and glancing back through the dark gulf of the parlor he'd just left, he saw a distant procession of musicians already coming through the corridor, their huge double basses and cellos on their bent backs. Francesco came along, carrying his violin by the neck, as if it were a huge dead bird.

Tonio looked away to the half moon. Everywhere about him were neatly clipped lemon trees, and the faint glow of marble benches on the carpet of grass, and right before him a dimly discernible stone path.

He commenced to walk. And as the lights grew brighter behind him, he drifted out a gate into the large rose garden which he knew lay to the left. There were the most marvelous blooms here, the Contessa herself tending them, and he wanted that sweetness all around him for as long as he could have it. It was the first of May, everything was still pressing on him, giving him thoughts, and he wanted to be alone.

But as he entered the rose garden proper, he saw, far beyond it, a strong light coming out of a small outbuilding not very far from the back of the house. A pair of doors stood open, and as he drew nearer, taking his time, his hand gently touching here and there a particularly large cabbage of a blossom, he saw through those doors a splendid array of colors and faces, and what seemed a blue sky.

He stopped. It was a curious illusion. The doors were portals to some sort of overcrowded and tumultuous world.

He moved a little forward and made out that he was looking into a room full of paintings! On the wall was mounted an immense picture, but there were others before it on easels, and he stood for quite some time looking at these works. In the distance they seemed finished and alive: clusters of biblical faces and forms surely as perfected as those that covered all the palaces and churches in which he'd ever been. There was Saint Michael the Archangel driving the damned into hell, his cape swirling beneath his lifted wings, his face subtly illuminated by the fire below. And beside him was a picture of a saint unknown to Tonio, a woman with a crucifix clasped to her breasts. The colors pulsed in the light. And all of these pictures seemed darker, more solemn, than those he'd known at Venice when he was a child.

He could hear little sounds from the room.

The stillness of the garden, its concealing darkness, gave

him that delicious feeling of being invisible, and he drew
even closer now, picking up the fragrance of the paint and the
turpentine and the oil.

But as he reached the threshold nearest him, he realized
the artist was at work inside. It couldn't be she, he thought.
These paintings had an authority, perhaps even a virility, that
was lacking in those light and airy murals on the chapel
walls. Yet as he saw the bent figure, clothed in black, before
the canvas, he realized it was a woman who was painting, a
woman holding the brush, and down her back there fell a
wealth of glowing yellow hair.

It was she.

And I am alone with her, he thought suddenly. He stood
very still.

But the sight of her sleeves rolled back from her bare arms,
the shabbiness of her black chemise with its smears of paint,
caused him an immediate panic. She looked lovely to him in
this disarray. He stood gazing at her softened profile, the
deep rose color of her lips, the dark blue of her eye.

Just when he knew he should leave here at once, she turned
with a rustle of taffeta under her outer garments and looked
him full in the eye.

"Signore Treschi," she said and her voice penetrated him,
causing him a little contraction in the chest. It was a sweet
treble, soft at the edges, and caught off guard by it, he had to
tell himself to answer her.

"Signorina." He mumbled the word, and made her a little
bow.

She was smiling; in fact, she seemed infected with an
immediate gaiety, which gave her blue eyes a lovely glint.
And as she rose from the chair, her dark chemise, tied at the
neck, opened, so that he saw an expanse of pink flesh above
the bodice of her black dress. Her small cheeks were plumped
with her smile, and all of her seemed round and real to him
suddenly as if he'd seen her only on the stage in the past.
Now she was here.

Her hair had those eternal wisps about it, but there were no
stiff curls; it was merely parted in the middle and hung down
everywhere, and he wondered how it would feel to the touch.
The severity might have been cruel to another face, but her
pretty features did not really seem to be her face. Her face was
her dark blue eyes, and the smoky eyelashes around them and
the utter seriousness which overcame her quite suddenly now.

It was such a sharp shift of expression he felt he must have caused it. And in an instant he understood something about her. She could not conceal her thoughts and emotions as other women did.

She did not move, but he felt exactly as if she were menacing him suddenly. He was certain she wanted to touch him, and he wanted to touch her! He could already feel the smooth flesh of her neck in his hands, her cheek against his thumb; he wanted to touch the delicate little curves of her ears. He imagined himself doing terrible things to her, and he could feel himself flush. It seemed absurd that she would wear clothing at all; her soft arms, her small wrists, that glimmer of pink flesh beneath her chemise, all of it was part of a delectable being that was foolishly, unnaturally disguised.

But this was dreadful.

The blood pounded in his face, and bowing his head for a moment, he let his eyes drift over all the painted faces around her, the great flashes of magenta and burnt umber and gold and white that made up this dazzling universe that had obviously come from her brush.

Yet she was inescapable. And she terrified him. Even the black taffeta of her dress disturbed him; why should she paint in black? The gleaming cloth was streaked with color, and she was so young and so seemingly innocent, and black was very wrong for her, and at the same time there was that delicious negligence about her, that soft disregard he'd found in her every single time their eyes had met.

She was smiling again. Bravely, she was smiling at him, and he had to speak to her; he must. He was going to tell her something proper and decent, but he couldn't think what and then to his absolute terror, she extended her naked hand.

"Won't you come in, Signore Treschi?" she said in that same sweet treble. "Won't you come in and sit with me for a while?"

"Oh, no, Signorina." He made a deeper bow this time, backing away. "I don't wish to disturb you, Signorina, and I . . . we . . . I should like to . . . I mean, we have never really been introduced, I . . ."

"But everyone knows you, Signore Treschi," she said with a little nod to the chair near her, and that gaiety flashed exquisitely in her eyes before it abruptly died away.

She fell to staring at him in absolute silence when he did not move and merely stood staring in the same manner at her.

And he was doing exactly that and nothing more when he heard his name repeated behind him by the Contessa's valet, who said he was wanted upstairs.

He positively rushed to answer the summons. The house was already crackling with laughter and thin music as he hurried along the upper corridor to be shown right into the Contessa's rooms.

But then he saw Guido standing idly by with his lace shirt opened over his naked chest, and the Contessa herself just slipping into a ruffled dressing gown beside her immense and lavishly draped bed.

He was furious. He almost went out. But this woman was innocent of any attempt to wound him. She knew nothing of his bond with Guido, no more than anyone else knew of it. And when she saw Tonio, she brightened at once.

"Ah, beautiful child," she said. "Come here. Come here and listen to me." She lured him across the room with both her upturned little hands.

Tonio threw Guido his iciest smile and approached with a short bow. Her stout little figure looked warm all over as if it had only just been folded in a blanket or in the act of love.

"How is your voice tonight?" she said to him. "Sing to me now!"

He was outraged. He glared at Guido. He was being trapped.

"Pange Lingua," she intoned, melting beautifully into the full Latin phrase.

"Sing, Tonio," Guido said softly. "Your voice, is it all right tonight, good, bad, what?" His hair was all tousled and there was about him in the open shirt an almost lush look. There is your beautiful child, Tonio thought, your cherub. And this is what I get for loving a peasant.

He shrugged and let loose the beginning of the *Pange Lingua* at full volume.

The Contessa drew back and gave a little shout. And Tonio wasn't surprised as his voice sounded immense and unnatural in this cluttered domestic room.

"Now," she said, brushing aside the maids who hovered about with candles. And searching in the bedclothes produced a bound score. "You can sing this, beautiful child?" she asked. "Tonight, here?" She answered her own question with a little nod. "Here, with me?"

Tonio stared at the cover for a moment. He could not put

308

all this together. Her voice, of course, he had heard of her voice, and over and over, she was a splendid amateur, but she never sang anymore and here, in this house, before hundreds of people, when Guido knew he didn't want to do this! He turned to Guido.

Impatiently, Guido pointed to the music.

"Tonio, kindly wake from that dream in which you live out your life and look at what is in your hand," he said. "You have an hour in which to prepare. . . ."

"I won't do it!" Tonio said furiously. "Contessa, I can't do it. It's impossible, I . . ."

"Darling child, you must do it," she crooned. "You must do it for me. I have been through a terrible ordeal in Palermo. I so loved my cousin and he was such a fool, and his little wife, she suffered so and needlessly. There is but one thing which will gladden my spirits tonight, and that is to sing again, to sing Guido's music, and to sing with you!"

He stared at her. He was scrutinizing her, sensing it was all lies, all a trick. Yet she seemed perfectly sincere. And without wanting to, he looked down at the score. It was Guido's best *Serenade a duo, Venus and Adonis,* a lovely series of songs. And just for a second, he imagined himself singing it not just at practice with Piero, but here. . . .

"No, it's impossible, Contessa, ask anything else of me. . . ."

"He doesn't know what he's saying." Guido stepped in.

"But Guido, I've never rehearsed this for performance. Twice, maybe, I've sung it with Piero." Then under his breath, "Guido, how could you do this to me!"

"Darling child," said the Contessa, "there is a little parlor down the hall. Go and practice. Give yourself an hour. And don't be angry with Guido. It is my request."

"Don't you realize this is an honor!" Guido said. "The Contessa's to sing with you herself."

Tricked, tricked, he was thinking. There would be three hundred people under this roof in an hour. And yet again he thought of the score. He knew the part of Adonis perfectly, its high sweet purity, and he could see the company overflowing downstairs. They were making it easy for him, weren't they? They were sparing him the soul-searching and the long gathering of his strength. And he knew silently how it would be if he just let it happen, how the terror would be trans-

309

formed into euphoria once he saw all those eyes on him, and once he knew there was simply no escape.

"Go now and practice." Guido was shoving him towards the door. And then he whispered, "Tonio, how can *you* do this to *me!*"

Tonio made himself heavy, unyielding. But his face had taken on a blank, dreamy expression, he knew. He could feel himself softening, the battle being lost, and he knew, positively knew, this was the moment to move towards that strength he had wanted so much for himself when he heard Caffarelli tonight.

"You believe I can do it then?" He looked to Guido.

"Of course," Guido said. "You sang it perfectly the first time I gave it to you, when the ink wasn't even dry." And now, with his back to the Contessa, he gave Tonio some wordless little assurance with his eyes, some quiet passage of affection, and then he whispered: "Tonio, this is the right time."

This was the moment, there was no doubt about it, and he was too hungry for it to be frightened. He took a full hour and a half however before wiping his forehead with his handkerchief, blowing out the candles over the keyboard, and making his way to the top of the stairs.

Then just for an instant he was afraid. In fact, it was worse than that. He was terrified. Because it was that inevitable moment at such a gathering when every single invited guest is there. The early comers had not yet left; the latecomers had just arrived. The sheer volume of talk and laughter crashed gently against the very walls, and everywhere he looked there were men and women, iridescent silks and wigs as white as sails navigating this temptuous sea that flowed in and out of mirrors and yawning doors.

He rolled up the music, and without thinking another coherent thought started down the steps. But yet a greater shock came to him as he moved in towards the orchestra. Caffarelli himself had just come in, and was in the very act of kissing the Contessa's hand.

Well, that was the end of it, surely, he felt. No one would expect him to sing in front of Caffarelli. Yet even as he was trying to decide if this was good or bad, Guido appeared.

"Do you need more time?" he asked immediately. "Are you ready now?"

"Guido, Caffarelli's just come in," he whispered. His hands felt clammy. He wanted to do it, and to get clean out of all this at the same time. No, he couldn't sing in front of Caffarelli.

But Guido was sneering in the direction of the great castrato. Tonio glimpsed him for an instant as the crowd rolled back and then came together, and it seemed even here the man exuded some immense power as he had years ago on the Venetian stage. It seemed Tonio could hear him laughing.

"Now do as I tell you," Guido said. "Let the Contessa set the pace. I will follow her and you do so as well."

"But Guido—" Tonio started, and then it seemed he was powerless to speak. This was a mistake of incredible magnitude. But Guido was even now slipping away.

Maestro Cavalla had just appeared with Benedetto, and Guido, shifting back quickly to Tonio, said, "Go on to the harpsichord, now, and wait."

It seemed he did not know where to put his arms. He had the music in hand but how high should he hold it? Suddenly it dawned on him that this was the hostess herself singing and everyone would *have* to pay strict attention; what had Guido done! And there was the Maestro staring at him and of course Benedetto was looking at him also, and someone had taken Caffarelli aside. Caffarelli was nodding, ooooh God! Why did Caffarelli have to be so damned gracious tonight when he was intolerable at other times! Why couldn't he have threatened to storm out? Caffarelli's eyes caught hold of Tonio, as they had three years ago for an instant in a Venetian drawing room.

But a hush was falling over the assemblage, and servants appeared from everywhere carrying little padded chairs. The ladies were taking their seats and the gentlemen filling up the doorways as if to cut off any possible escape.

The little Contessa's small plump hand suddenly touched his wrist and he turned to see her with her hair powdered and daintily curled. She looked so very pretty. She rocked her head from side to side as she hummed the first few bars of her song which would open the serenade right after the introduction and then she winked.

It seemed then he'd forgotten something, that he must ask her some question, a thought was deviling him, but he could not think of what it was. Then he realized he had not seen his yellow-haired girl. Where was she? They couldn't begin without her, surely she would want to be here, and surely she must be, and in a moment he would see her face.

The room was silent now save for the rustle of taffeta and Tonio saw with sudden panic that Guido's hands were poised over the keys. The violinists lifted their bows. The music commenced in a lovely throbbing of the strings.

It seemed he closed his eyes just for an instant, and when he opened them again, he was visited by the most complete calm. It was warmth, gradual, infinitely comforting, in which he felt himself inhabit his body, his breaths coming regularly and with a renewed ease. Each face before him was distinct, the mass of congealing colors melting to the hundreds who in actuality were in this room. And he even peered for a moment at Caffarelli, who sat among these ordinary men and women looking remarkably like a lion.

The violins were prancing. The horns in perfect golden notes came in, then all together they pulsed with the melody so that Tonio could not resist moving with it just slightly, and when they stopped, resuming in a sadder, slower vein, he felt himself drifting, his eyes now safely blind.

What he saw next was the little Contessa as the harpsichord led her to her first notes. The cellos were behind it, so soft they sounded like low breath. And then her little head rocked back and forth again, and her whole little body rocked back and forth, and a low, lustrous voice came out of her with such richness and such intoxicating sweetness that Tonio felt himself emptied of all thought. Her eyes left the music. She looked up at him and at that moment he could not resist a long slow smile.

Now she was beaming at him, her plump little cheeks like bellows, and she was singing to him, she was singing to him that she loved him and that he would be her lover when he commenced to sing.

Then she came to the end of her opening songs. The inevitable silence had fallen, and over the thinnest ripple of the harpsichord, Tonio began to sing.

His eyes held to the Contessa's, and he saw the little press of her smile and the tiniest nod of her head. But it was the soft high flute intertwined with his voice that he saw and felt as he sang along with it, going up and down, higher and higher and then down again, and now it led him in a series of passages which he matched with ease.

Yet it was as if he wanted the Contessa's voice, and she

312

knew it, and when she answered him, he felt himself actually falling in love. With a surge of the strings he went into a stronger and faster aria to her, and it seemed even the lovely poetry he was singing to her was all of it perfectly true.

His voice was seducing her voice, not merely for its answers but for that moment when the two would come together in one song. Even his softest, most languid notes told her that, and her slow passages so full of dark color echoed the same vibrant desire.

At last they were together in the first duet with such a gentle exhilaration that he commenced that same little rocking with her, her little black eyes full of the radiance of laughter, her deep notes blending perfectly with his soaring protestations of love. A third sound seemed to emerge from the edge of the two voices, the brilliance of the instruments surging and dying again and again to let them fly free.

It was an agony when he had to back away from her, sing to her, and her voice answered him with the same exquisite pain.

Finally the strings were prancing again and a horn was leading him and this was his final summons to her, his last challenge to her to come with him, join him, be carried up with him. It seemed the Contessa leaned forward, that she rose on the balls of her feet, that every fiber of her moved with his dizzying rises, until with the fastest pace, they plunged into the final duet.

Her voice was wed to his voice. Her cheeks were flushed and her eyes had the gleam of tears. Her little body heaved with the fullness of her voice, his own winding up and up out of his immense lungs and this languid slender frame that seemed the flesh left behind in stillness and grace as the voice went free.

It was over.

It was finished.

The room shimmered. Caffarelli leapt to his feet and with a grand gesture was the first to break into the rapid thunder of applause.

The little Contessa rose on tiptoe to kiss Tonio; she put her hands to his face and then she saw the look of unspeakable sadness in him, and she threw her arms about him and laid her head on his chest.

* * *

Everything happened so quickly. It seemed Caffarelli had clasped him by the shoulder and, nodding to everyone, gestured with his right hand to bring up the applause again and again. And all around him came the soft passionate compliments—he had sung so beautifully, and he had gotten the Contessa to sing with him, which was no small feat, and his voice was extraordinary, and why had they not heard of him before, all these years at the San Angelo, where *was* the Maestro! (He couldn't have written this libretto better himself!)

But why was it so hard for him to listen to this, why did he have the irrepressible urge to get away? Guido's pupil, yes, Guido's pupil, and what a divine composition, that Guido, where was he? It was all too perfect and yet he found this almost unendurable. Maybe, if only Guido were here!

"Where is he?" he whispered to the Contessa. Maestro Cavalla loomed over him for an instant, but before Tonio could read his expression he had disappeared, and then the Contessa was pressing for his attention:

"Tonio, I want you to meet Signore Ruggerio," she insisted as if it were possible to actually converse in the midst of all this.

He bowed to the man, he accepted his hand. He felt someone tug at him, and saw it was the old Marchesa who again pressed those dry lips to his cheek. He felt a rush of affection for her, her dimly lit eyes, and that creased white skin, and even the hand with which she held him, reptilian and surprisingly strong.

Someone else had loomed up suddenly. The Contessa was talking to the other, the Signore Ruggerio, and just then, unexpectedly, they were pressed together so that she wound her arm about Tonio's waist. Something had just come clear to him:

"Contessa," he whispered, "that young woman, the light-haired one." He realized that he had been expecting every moment to see her, and she simply was not here. A sinking feeling silenced him suddenly, even as he was making lame gestures to describe that wispy hair. "Blue eyes, but very dark blue," he must have murmured, "and such pretty hair."

"Why, my little cousin, you mean, my little widow, of course," said the Contessa, pulling forward yet another gentleman for him to meet. This was an Englishman from the embassy. "She is in mourning, dearest, for her husband, my Sicilian cousin, why I told you all about it, didn't I? And now

314

she doesn't want to go back to England." She shook her head.

"A widow . . .!" Had he heard her right? He was bowing to someone else. And Signore Ruggerio was saying something of apparent importance to the Contessa and the Contessa was leaving him here!

A widow. Where was Guido? He couldn't see him anywhere. But then he saw Maestro Cavalla far far across the room, and Guido was with him and so was the Contessa and so was that little man, Ruggerio.

Someone else had hold of him, telling him earnestly he had a magnificent voice and that he should make his debut here at the San Carlos instead of going all the way to Rome. Why did everyone still have to go to Rome?

But a widow, he was thinking; was it possible to cast a more sensual light upon her? Was it possible to make her more enticing, more available, then have her married and widowed in one sentence, removing her forever from that unattainable choir of virgins to which he'd always told himself she surely belonged?

He was excusing himself now to everyone, trying vainly to get across this great expanse of marble floor, to get near to those distant figures, Guido and the Maestro.

And then he saw Paolo, looking the perfect little prince in his finery, rushing towards him through the crowd. He embraced Tonio quickly.

"What are you doing here?" Tonio asked, even as he acknowledged another greeting from the old Russian Count Sherzinski.

"The Maestro said I could come to hear you." Paolo clung to him; he was obviously so excited by the whole affair he could scarcely speak.

"What do you mean? He knew I was going to sing?"

"Everyone knew," said Paolo breathlessly. "Piero's here and so is Gaetano, and . . ."

"Ahhhh, Guido!" Tonio whispered.

But he was almost laughing.

Quickly he left the gathering this time, pulling Paolo with him just as Guido and the Maestro and the dark gentleman disappeared.

By the time he reached the corridor, they were gone into some parlor, and all the doors were shut. And he had to stop to catch his breath, and just to savor the excitement he felt.

He was so happy all he could do was shut his eyes and smile. "So everyone knew," he said.

"Yes," Paolo answered, "and you have never sung better, ever. Tonio, I'll never forget it as long as I live."

But then suddenly his little face crinkled and it seemed he was about to cry.

He pressed close to Tonio. At twelve he was a reed of a boy, and he could just push his head into Tonio's shoulder. The shimmer of pain that came out of him alarmed Tonio.

"Paolo, what is it?"

"I'm sorry, Tonio, it's only we came to Naples together. And now you're going to be leaving. And I'll be alone."

"But what are you saying? Leaving where? Just because . . ."

Yet as he was speaking he could hear raised voices coming from one of the rooms down the hall. He tugged Paolo gently, his hand firm on his shoulder to reassure him, and Paolo was obviously struggling still not to cry.

An argument was in progress.

"Five hundred ducats," Guido was saying.

"Let me handle this," said the Maestro.

Tonio pushed very gently on the door. Through the margin of light he could see it was that dark gentleman, Ruggerio, they were talking to, and the Contessa, seeing Tonio, came forward quickly:

"You go upstairs, radiant child," she said now as she came into the corridor, closing the doors behind her.

"But who is that man?" he whispered.

"I don't want to tell you until it's settled," she said. "Come with me."

15

THREE O'CLOCK Yet half the company was still in the house.

"Darling child," the Contessa had said as she shut him in, "it was only by chance Signore Ruggerio was to be here. And we were all so sure if we told you, you wouldn't sing!"

316

And for hours Tonio had waited alone in this spacious upstairs chamber over the noisy street.

Five hundred ducats, he was thinking, that's a fortune. Surely it's some sort of theatrical negotiations, but what sort?

One moment he feared everything, and the next he was terrified of disappointment. Yet Caffarelli had applauded him! No, he was merely being gracious to the Contessa. Tonio could make up his mind to nothing. What did it all mean?

Carriages came and went. Guests paused on the doorstep below to laugh and to embrace. And in the uneven flare of the torches could be seen a dim configuration of the lazzaroni on the steps of the church opposite, men who in this mild delicious night had no need of shelter and could simply stretch out under the moon.

Tonio left the window and found himself pacing the floor.

The painted clock tinked on the mantel. There were maybe three hours before dawn. And he had not undressed yet; certainly Guido must come to him.

What if Guido were in bed with the Contessa? No, Guido couldn't do that to him, not tonight. And the Contessa had promised him she would come; "as soon as it is all settled," she had said.

"This could be nothing," he told himself now firmly for the seventeenth time. "This Ruggerio, why, maybe he runs some little theater in Amalfi or someplace, and they want to take you there for some sort of trial. . . . But for five hundred ducats?" He shook his head.

But no matter how tormented he was over all of this, he could not stop thinking of the yellow-haired girl. He'd not recovered from the shock of learning she was a widow, and he had only to pause in his thoughts at any moment to see her and to see that room full of paintings, to see that mourning dress of black taffeta and that radiant little face.

No violet ribbon, no violet bows. Only her little mouth was violet this time, and she is a widow. That was the only color to her, save for that hair, and all those colors on the canvases behind her, which surely must have been her own.

He was such a fool for stammering and staring as he had done. How many times had he wanted such a moment with her, and she was a widow! When he had it finally, what did he do?

And maybe, just maybe, from some private corner somewhere in the palazzo she had heard him sing.

He saw those pictures in a blaze suddenly. It seemed quite unreal to him that it was her work. Yet she had been painting in the very midst of it. The canvas before her had been enormous, and if he could only remember the exact figures in it, then he could compare it in his memory with the rest.

It was so remarkable that she might have done all that. Yet he understood now that she had been married to that elderly man whom he had always believed to be her father, and he saw the whole of her life in a new light. He could remember so vividly their first meeting, her tears, some sense of deep suffering into which he'd blundered, drunk and careless, and tantalized by her loveliness and her youth.

She'd been married to that old man and now she was free.

And she painted not only simple Virgins and little angels; she painted giants, forests, turbulent seas.

He stood listening in the middle of this darkened bedchamber, and the church bells were ringing, it seemed, soft solemn reverberations. The little painted clock had been fast.

He buttoned his vest suddenly, smoothed his coat, and went to the door. Maybe everyone had forgotten him, and Guido was actually with the Contessa. The house was so quiet.

But a great blaze illuminated the distant stairwell. And cocking his ear for voices, he heard them. And then he turned and made his way to the inevitable back stairs.

The night was just as warm as it had been earlier, and as he stepped out into the grass, he saw countless stars overhead, uneven, some so clear they were faintly yellow or even pink, others merely tiny points of white light. And the fleeting clouds made him rock for a moment on the balls of his feet with his head back, for the whole heavens or the whole earth seemed to move.

Light streamed out from the parlor windows and when he finally went up to the glass, he saw Maestro Cavalla was still there. Guido was talking to Signore Ruggerio, and Signore Ruggerio appeared to be describing something with his finger on a bare table, while the Contessa looked on.

He turned his back, and in spite of the most intense excitement, he knew he must not go in.

He walked fast through the garden, finding his way into the patches of rose trees, and slowing his pace he made his way to that outbuilding which was completely dark. The moon shone bright for an instant, and just before the clouds passed over it again, he saw the doors were still open and he moved quietly towards them with just the crunch of the grass under his foot. Was it wrong to go in when all lay open so fearlessly? He told himself that he would merely stand in the door.

And placing his hand timidly on the frame, he saw the pictures before him, drained of color, the faces luminous and indistinct. Slowly Saint Michael materialized, and then the whiteness of that canvas on which only part of the work had been done. His foot sounded very loud to him on the slate flooring, and then he settled slowly onto the bench before the picture and made out a gathering of figures, white, and intertwined under what seemed a black mass of trees.

It was maddening not to be able to see it, and yet he felt an intruder. He did not want to touch her brushes, her little pots of paint so tightly covered, nor even the cloth that lay folded to one side. But these objects fascinated him. He remembered her when she was still bent forward. And he heard her voice again, its lovely treble and its slight opacity, and he realized that there had been a slight accent to her words.

After a moment's playing with conscience, he took one of the matches from her little table nearby and lighted the candle on his right.

The flame sputtered, grew larger, and slowly an even illumination filled the room. The great work against the wall quickly colored in, and the picture before him showed nymphs in a garden, lithesome and golden-haired, their gauzy dresses barely covering them as they danced with garlands of flowers in their tiny hands.

It was nothing as chaste and dour as her murals in the Contessa's chapel; it was more lively and immensely more skilled. And why not, he mused? In three years, what had he learned of singing? Wasn't it natural that she should have made her own progress, unknown to him, with the brush? Yet he could see now an attitude to the painted faces before him which indisputably connected them to the chapel Virgin he'd admired so many times. He found himself staring at the naked limbs of these nymphs, however, with a slight humming fascination that made him feel suddenly ashamed.

The paint was fresh; if he touched it, he would harm it, but he did not want to touch it. He merely wanted to look and to think that she had painted this.

Guido's little story of the funeral in Sicily came back to

him. So she was the little English cousin, the little widow who had been so frightened by those horrid catacombs they had to take her out. Now he could hear it in her voice in his memory, that touch of an accent, and it gave her even greater fascination, though when he thought of her alone now without her husband, he wondered if it might even be worse for her than the marriage must have been.

A sadness came over him, a sadness slow but without measure. And he realized that all the times he'd ever seen her, in any place no matter how crowded, she had always seemed alone.

But her loveliness was all the more palpable, all the more a low beating torment, and finally he reached out to extinguish the candle flame. Deliberately he let it burn his fingers and then he rose reluctantly to go. What had she to do with him, after all? What did it matter she had such skill in her, such craft, such preoccupation that it made of her a lost sprite of a girl? Somewhere in his mind there was the notion that innocence alone could have done nothing so interesting as this work for he saw in it little simpering sweetness which he associated with innocence. Rather it was massive. And it was very fine.

But again, what was this to him, and why was he sweating? Why were his palms damp?

It occurred to him as he hovered in the doorway that he wished she would leave him alone, and in an instant he realized foolishly that it was he who perpetually stared at her, so much so she had nodded finally. Well, then, why the hell hadn't she told someone how badly he behaved? He was furious with her.

And then looking up he saw her.

She was sitting in the rose garden, and her long robe was very white under the moon.

He sucked in his breath. But he was so badly shaken that he felt almost a fool. She'd been watching him! She'd seen the light in her little studio. And surely she could see him as clearly as he now saw her.

The blood was teeming in his face. And then to his gentle amazement she rose from the marble bench and came towards him, so slowly and so soundlessly that she appeared to drift rather than to move. In the grass he saw the gleam of her naked foot, and the breeze stirring the gauzy layers of her robe caused her form to be visible as if these loose garments were an eerie collection of light.

It seemed to him that for her sake he must make some nod and get gone from her as quickly as he could. But he didn't stir. He only watched her and something about her deliberation began to terrify him.

She came closer and closer until he could see her face clearly, and her eyes were full of significance, and as she looked up to him, her forehead creased with a little frown; she was speaking to him without words. And there came that fragrance from her that was the actual smell of summer rain. He was not thinking anymore. He was not seeing her rounded cheeks, or the dark pout of her small mouth. Rather he was seeing the whole of her, the pulsing thing she was beneath that sheathing of sheer linen and all that neglected golden hair: the body inside it, with its inevitable heat and damp and this fragrance so like the rain beating in full force on flowers, on pathways, on dead leaves.

He wanted her so badly it was an agony, as if all of him were starving for her and sharpened for her and paralyzed at the same time. It was a nightmare in which one cannot scream; one cannot move. It horrified him. Had she no caution, no care? This great empty garden, and beyond it the slumbering house, and here she stood alone with him. Would she have done that with any other man? A terrible violence rose in him suddenly, and it seemed she was some hideous thing and not the most lovely and delicate creature he'd ever seen.

He wanted to hurt her, to catch her up and crush her, and show her the truth of it, make her see what he was! He was trembling; he could hear his own breath.

But her face was changing. It had darkened and wrinkled in a terrible little frown. She bowed her head, and shrinking back, she turned away from him as if falling from a great height.

He was stricken watching her, seeing her recoil. And then helplessly, he saw her move away, straightening when she had covered some distance, her yellow hair a great gleaming mass just before she vanished in the dark.

Once inside his room, he rested gently against the closed door. He pressed his forehead to the hard enameled wood.

Miserable with shame, he could not believe it had come to

321

this! It had seemed over the years they had been partners in some wonderous dance, and always there had been the terrifying promise of their coming together.

And it had come only to this!

That she had offered herself was beyond question, and bitter, humiliated, he knew now just what he was, and she knew it, too. And if there was any mercy left for him, Guido and the Contessa would come soon to tell him that he was going to Rome, where he would never see her again.

He had fallen asleep, fully dressed, the blanket over his shoulder, before Guido came. He awoke to see Guido and the Contessa standing over him and the Contessa said:

"Sit up, beautiful child, you must make me a promise."

Guido didn't even look at him. He moved about the room as if dreaming, his lips pressed together and then slack in a secret monologue.

"What is it? What's happened?" Tonio said sleepily. He saw his blond-haired girl for an instant, and then she was gone.

He felt he could endure this waiting no longer.

"Tell me," he said. "Now."

"Ah, but first, beautiful child," she was saying in that measured and polite way of hers, "promise me, promise me, that when you are very famous you will tell everyone that it was in my house in Naples that you first sang."

"Famous?" He sat up, as the Contessa nestled beside him and pressed her lips to his cheek.

"My beautiful child," she said, "I have just written to my cousin, the Cardinal Calvino in Rome; he will be expecting you, and you will live with him as long as you like.

"Guido wants to leave immediately. He wants to get to know the audiences; he wants to do the work there. And I will come, too, of course, on opening night to see you both. Oh, but beautiful child, it is all arranged now; you are to make your first appearance as principal singer in Guido's opera in the Teatro Argentina in Rome on the first of the year."

322

16

I T WAS WELL OVER a fortnight before the day of departure arrived.

Everything was packed. Tonio's rooms were empty save for the magnificent harpsichord which he was leaving as a gift for the Maestro di Cappella, and the carriages, laden with trunks, were waiting in the stable yard.

Tonio stood alone at his window, looking out through the dusty cloister into the garden, for the last time.

He had dreaded the moment of parting with Paolo, and it had been as bad as he expected. Paolo had been mute, spiritless. There was no substance to the words he uttered. That Tonio and Guido were leaving him was more than he could bear, and though he was gone now, Tonio knew that he could not leave Paolo like this.

In fact, a little scheme was forming in Tonio's mind, but he was afraid the scheme would not work. And he lapsed for a moment into a confusion of thoughts just as Maestro Cavalla came into the empty room.

"Well, this is the painful moment," sighed the Maestro.

Tonio's glance was full of affection, but he didn't speak. He watched the Maestro run his fingers over the delicately painted case of the harpsichord. It gave Tonio deep pleasure to know the Maestro treasured this gift.

"Has it been easier for the little trick we played on you at the Contessa's?" the Maestro asked. "I had hoped it would be."

Tonio only smiled. Easier, yes, it had been easier.

But there was a little spasm in his face now that meant pain and he wondered if the Maestro could see it. He had an uneasy feeling about the Maestro suddenly. The Maestro was deep in thought; something more than a farewell was pressing on his mind.

"What are you thinking?" the Maestro asked him. "Tell me."

"It's nothing as complex as you might suppose," Tonio answered softly. "I'm thinking what they all think when they

323

leave you." And when he saw the question still in the Maestro's face, Tonio confessed, "I'm afraid I'm going to fail in Rome."

His eyes shifted to the garden again, and he was conscious of having said something that was not entirely true. A greater confusion was pressing on him. It had to do with life and all that life had to offer him, and how much he wanted it, and how much he would have liked to forget.

Once three years ago he'd told himself he would sing for his own pleasure, and how simple that had sounded, how simple that had seemed.

Now he wanted to be the greatest singer in Italy. He wanted Guido to write the finest opera anyone had ever heard. And he *was* afraid, afraid for both of them, and he could not help but wonder had he always feared this moment, ever since he'd known what was left to him, and had that fear been so great he had had to construct some other, darker purpose for his life?

He thought dimly of his old resolves, his hatreds, those dark vows.

But life was a magnificent snare, and now all he could think about was life. He wanted desperately to be on the road to Rome.

Guido was so excited there was no feeling to his farewells. Night and day, he'd been scribbling scenes for his opera. He was always humming to himself, and at times when they were not working, the two of them would look at each other, with that mingled fear and exhilaration that was shared by no one else.

"You won't fail," the Maestro said gently. "I would not let you go if I thought you would."

Tonio nodded. But his eyes remained fixed on the cloister and the archway filled with leaves. Others had left here with high hopes; they'd left with the Maestro's blessing, only to return in defeat.

But do any of them feel failure as *we* feel it, Tonio mused, we who are mutilated and tormented so much for that moment of success? He felt a quiet communion with those other singers; he felt a deepening of the brotherhood he had always known with those who struggled here at his side.

And yet as he heard the Maestro draw closer, as he became vaguely aware that the Maestro was troubled and brooding, another perception was just breaking in Tonio's mind.

What if it were a triumph? What if it were exactly as he imagined it? The audience on its feet, those inundations of applause. Just for a second, he imagined it over and done, an incontestable victory, and he saw a road unwinding out from that moment, a road that was life itself.

It was life he saw unwinding, and he felt such fear he was appalled.

"God," he whispered, but the Maestro didn't hear him. He didn't hear himself. He gave a little shake of his head.

The Maestro touched him on the shoulder, and turning, he allowed himself to be separated from his secret self, and he looked into the Maestro's face.

The Maestro *was* troubled.

"We must talk," said the Maestro resolutely, "before you leave."

"Talk?" Tonio felt an uncertainty. It was so difficult to say farewell. What more did the Maestro want? And then there was Paolo. Tonio knew he could not leave Paolo here.

"I told you once," said the Maestro, "that I knew what had been done to you."

"And I told you," Tonio answered suddenly, "that you did not." He felt an old anger rise, and he struggled to quiet it. He felt only love for this man now.

Yet the Maestro went on.

"I know why you have been patient all these years with those who sent you here. . . ."

"You know nothing." Tonio struggled to be courteous. "And why do you press me now when for so long you've been quiet?"

"I tell you I know, as well as others know. Do you think we are fools here, that stage intrigue is all we understand? I know. I have always known. And I know now your brother in the Republic of Venice has two healthy sons. And I know you have never sent assassins against him; there has never been a particle of gossip in the Veneto of such an attempt to trouble his sleep."

Tonio felt these words as if they were a series of physical blows. For three years he had never spoken of this to anyone; it was an agony to hear these words spoken aloud in this room.

He knew his anger was transforming him and he turned on the Maestro as coldly and harshly as he could: "Don't talk of these things to me!" he insisted. "I will not speak of them to you."

Yet the Maestro would not stop.

"Tonio, I know too this man is guarded day and night by a band of the roughest bravos he can hire. It's the gossip they are never, even in his own house, beyond the sound of his voice. . . ."

Tonio moved towards the door.

But the Maestro had caught him and gently forced him to remain. For one second the strength of the man's will was measured against Tonio's, and then Tonio, shaken and furious, bowed his head.

"Why must we quarrel like this?" he asked softly. "Why can we not embrace and say farewell?"

"But we are not quarreling," the Maestro said. "I tell you I know you mean to go after your brother on your own." His tone had dropped in a whisper. And he was so close to Tonio that Tonio could feel the Maestro's breath on his face. "But this man waits for you as a spider waits," the Maestro said. "And the decree of banishment against you has made the entire city of Venice his web. He will destroy you if you move against him."

"No more," Tonio said. He was now so angry he could not trust his voice, but he could see the Maestro had little grasp of the effect of his own words.

"You know nothing of me," Tonio said, "of what I came from, of why I am here. And I will not stand here and listen to you speak of these things as if they were common things! You will not talk of them in the same tone you take to chastise your students! You will not voice your distress as if this were merely the failure of an opera, the passing of a monarch in some distant land!"

"I don't mean to speak of them lightly," the Maestro insisted. "For God's sakes, will you hear me? Send other men to do this deed! Send men as ruthless as those who are guarding him. These bravos are trained assassins; send against them their own kind."

Tonio struggled to free himself, but he was incapable of raising his hand against this man. Bravos, this man was telling *him* about bravos and what they were! Had he not awakened enough nights to find himself still in that town of Flovigo struggling against those hardened and brutal men? He could feel their hands on him, he could smell their breath; he could remember his powerlessness in those moments and the knife that cut him; he would never in all his life forget.

"Tonio, if I am wrong," said the Maestro, "if you have

sent assassins and if they have failed, then surely you must know you cannot accomplish this yourself."

The Maestro's grip was loosened, but Tonio was for the moment spent. He was looking away; and he had seldom felt more alone since those early days. He could not now remember all that had just been said; his confusion had obliterated much of it, save the feeling that the Maestro would go on and on, understanding so little while imagining himself to understand so much.

"If you were some common singer . . ." The Maestro sighed. "If yours were not the voice they all dream of, I would say then do what you must."

He let go of Tonio. He let his hand drop to his side.

"Oh, I have been remiss," he said, "in that I have not tried to understand you before now. You seemed so content, so happy here."

"And was it so unnatural that I should be content!" Tonio demanded. "Was it so wrong that I should find happiness? But did you think they cut the spirit out of me with all the rest?

"You have ruled in this principality of geldings too long without ever being part of it. You have forgotten what life is like! Do you think all the world is made up of maimed creatures who wander forth bleeding to pursue their destiny! This is not life!"

"Your voice is your life! It's been your life since you came here! Do you want me to deny my senses!" the Maestro implored.

"No." Tonio shook his head. "That is art, that is the painted stage, and the music, and the little world we have made for ourselves, but that is not life! If you would talk of my brother to me, of what was done to me, then you must talk of life. And I tell you what was done to me *must* be avenged. Any man out there in the street would understand it. Why is it so hard for you?"

The Maestro was chastened but he did not give in.

"You're not speaking of life if you go to Venice to kill your brother," he whispered. "You are speaking of death, and that death will not be his, it will be yours. Oh, would you were but one of the others. Would you were not what you are."

"I am only a man." Tonio sighed. "That is all I am. That is what I was born to be, and what I've become no matter

327

what was done to prevent it. And I tell you, when all is said and done, a man does not stand for what was done to me."

The Maestro turned away. He seemed for the moment unable to compose himself, and in that time, a cold quiet settled over the room. Tonio, exhausted, rested his weight against the wall, seeing again the arch of the cloister and those green leaves.

It seemed he was visited by a thousand random impressions, as if the mind could empty itself of thought and see visions, and those visions were made up of concrete objects, glistening with meaning: table silver, the candles on a chapel altar, wedding veils, and infants' cradles, the soft rustle of silk when women embraced. The great fabric that was Venice was a backdrop for this vision, and there was in it mingled sounds, the cry of trumpets, the scent of sea breeze.

What did I want a moment ago, he was thinking. He tried to transport himself into that little whirlwind of excitement that existed eternally behind the curtain of a theatrical stage; he could smell the paint, the powder, hear the sharp, shrill violins beyond the curtain, hear the rumble of bare boards. What was I thinking? He heard his own voice in a succession of pure notes that seemed to have nothing to do with men and women or life and death. His lips didn't move with his thoughts.

It seemed a long time before the Maestro turned back.

And Tonio's eyes were glazed with tears.

"I didn't want to leave you like this," Tonio said softly, defeated. "You're angry with me now and I love you. I have loved you since I came."

"How little you know of me," said the Maestro. "I have never been angry with you. And the love I feel for you has few rivals here."

He approached Tonio, but he hesitated to embrace him and in that moment Tonio was conscious of the man's physical presence, that strength and roughness that was nothing but the characteristic of ordinary men.

He was conscious too of his own appearance as if he could see his own unnatural skin and youth mirrored in the man's gaze.

"I had words to say before we parted," Tonio said. "I wanted so much to thank—"

"No need for such words. I'll be in Rome to see you on the stage soon enough."

"But there was something more," Tonio said, his eyes lingering on the Maestro. "Something I wanted to ask of you, and I wish now that I had not waited so long. You might not grant my request, and to me it means the world."

"The world?" the Maestro asked. "You tell me that even if it means your death you will kill your brother, and yet you speak of something that means the world?"

He turned to look at Tonio.

"Years ago I tried to tell you what the world was, not the world you came from, but the world you might conquer with your voice. I thought you had listened to me. But you are a great singer, yes, a great singer, and you would turn your back on the world."

"In time, Maestro, in time," Tonio said, his voice sharpened ever so slightly by anger again. "All men die in time," he insisted. "I am different only in that I may name the place with certainty when I choose. I may go home to death and leave my life circumscribed behind me. In time. But for now I live and breathe as anyone else."

"Then tell me what you want," said the Maestro. "If it means the world to you, then it means time, and I would give you all the time in the world."

"Maestro, I want Paolo. I want to take him with me to Rome."

And when he saw the shock, the disapproval in the Maestro's face, he added quickly:

"Maestro, I'll care for him, you know that, and even if I should send him back to you someday, he won't be the worse for having been with me. And if there is one enemy of the rancor I feel against those who made me what I am, it is love for others. Love for Guido, and Paolo, and for you."

Paolo was in the very back of the chapel when Tonio found him. He was sitting slumped in the chair, his little snub-nosed face stained with tears. His black eyes were fixed on the tabernacle and when he saw that Tonio had come again, that one farewell was not enough, he felt betrayed.

He turned away.

"Be still and listen to me," Tonio said. He smoothed back the boy's dark brown hair and rested his hand on Paolo's neck. It felt fragile to him; the boy felt fragile. And then he was so overcome with love for Paolo that for a moment he did not speak. The warm air of the chapel was full of the scent of wax and incense, and it seemed the gilded altar drained all the sun it could from the dusty shafts of light that cut to the marble floor.

"Close your eyes and dream for a moment," Tonio whispered. "Do you want to live in a fine palazzo? Do you want to ride in fine carriages and dine on silver plate? Do you want for there to be jewels on your fingers? Do you want to wear satins and silks? Do you want to live with me and with Guido? Do you want to come with us to Rome?"

The boy turned on him with an expression so savage his breath was taken away.

"That's not possible!" Paolo said in a strangled voice as if it were an oath.

"But it is possible," Tonio said. "Anything is possible. When you least expect it, it's possible, to be sure."

And as belief and trust came into Paolo's face, as he moved to lock his arms around Tonio, Tonio drew him up.

"Come," he said. "If you have anything in this place you want to take with you, get it now."

It was noon when the carriages finally commenced to roll. Guido, Paolo, and Tonio were in the first, while behind came the servants and the great bulk of the trunks.

And as they drove down through the Via di Toledo towards the sea for one last glimpse of the city itself, Tonio could not take his eyes off the bluish camelback of Vesuvius sending its faint plume of smoke into the sky.

The carriage swayed onto the Molo. The glaring sea seemed to fuse itself with the horizon. And as they turned north, the mountain was lost.

And hours later, it was Tonio and only Tonio who was crying as night fell over the endless and beautiful wheat fields of Campania, and the carriage struggled on towards the gates of Rome.

PART V

1

THE CARDINAL CALVINO sent for them as soon as they arrived. Neither Tonio nor Guido had expected this immediate courtesy, and with Paolo hurrying after them, they followed the Cardinal's black-robed secretary upstairs.

Nothing Guido had ever seen at Venice or Naples quite prepared him for this immense palazzo right in the center of Rome, no more than twenty minutes' stroll from the Vatican in one direction, and perhaps the same distance from the Piazza di Spagna on the right. Its somber yellowish exterior enclosed corridors lined with antique sculptures, walls hung with Flemish tapestries, and courtyards virtually peopled with Greek and Roman fragments as well as colossal modern statues guarding gateways and fountains and ponds.

Noblemen were milling about in great numbers, clerics in cassocks came and went, while a long library revealed itself through one pair of double doors after another in which black-clad clerks bent over their quill pens.

But it was the Cardinal himself who proved the most interesting surprise. It was rumored he was deeply religious, having come up from the priesthood, which was not so common for a cardinal, and that he was a great favorite with the people, who were always hanging about outside to see his carriage pass.

The poor of Rome were his special concern; he was the patron of numerous orphanages and charitable institutions which he visited constantly; and sometimes, letting his crimson robes drag in the mud, his retinue waiting, he visited in hovels, drank wine with workingmen and their wives; he kissed the children. He gave of his own wealth daily to those in need.

He was almost fifty now, and Guido anticipated great austerity in him, some pious contradiction to this highly polished splendor, the floors patterned so freely in varicolored marble they rivaled the floors of San Pietro itself.

But the Cardinal exuded good humor.

His eyes crinkled with immediate cheerfulness, a vitality that seemed the fusion of grace and love for everyone he saw.

A sparely built man with hair of an ashen color, he had the smoothest eyelids Guido had ever seen. They had no indentation, no fold. And with the few lines in his face, so seemingly deliberate, he had a graven look, like those gaunt figures on very old churches who in this time appear emaciated and distorted, often grim.

But there was nothing about him that was grim.

Surrounded by brilliantly clad noblemen who gave way at his command like water, he beckoned for Guido to come in. Allowing his ring to be kissed, he then embraced Guido, saying that his cousin's musicians must live in his house as long as they desired.

His body was full of movement, his eyes narrow with gaiety.

"Do you need instruments?" he asked. "I shall be happy to send for them. You have only to tell my secretary, and he will obtain for you what you want."

He took Paolo's face in his hands and carefully ran his thumb over Paolo's cheek, and Paolo warmed to this as was his nature, drawing up instinctively as the Cardinal pressed him against his long crimson robe.

"But where is your singer?" he asked.

And when he looked up at Tonio, he appeared to see him for the first time.

There was an undisguised moment of absorption, a change in the Cardinal which Guido could almost feel. It seemed those around him must surely notice it, as Tonio stepped forward to kiss the Cardinal's ring.

Tonio was only slightly disheveled from the carriage, his dark green velvet frock coat was only a little dusty, and he had for Guido the look of an angel in mortal dress. His increasing height had never made him awkward, and the last two years of fencing had caused him to move almost like a dancer, all of his gestures seemingly hypnotic, though Guido wasn't sure why. It was that they were so slow perhaps; even the raising and lowering of Tonio's eyes was very slow.

The Cardinal's mouth was slack. He watched Tonio as if Tonio were doing something startling and unfamiliar, and then he stared at Tonio with no expression in his pale gray eyes. His eyes darkened slightly.

Guido felt an unwelcome warmth under his clothes; he

imagined the heat of this crowded room was suffocating him. Yet as he saw the expression on Tonio's face, the manner in which he regarded the Cardinal, and felt what seemed a fathomless silence around them all, he experienced more than a twinge of fear. Of course this was not at all as he was imagining it, surely.

Who would not notice a young boy of such remarkable beauty, and who would not look upon a man such as His Eminence without a certain measure of awe?

Yet the fear in Guido subsided only slowly, echoing all of his heavy thoughts during the journey to Rome; his anxiety over a thousand practical details to do with the coming opera, and most unexpectedly, his preoccupation with the loss of his own voice years before.

"I have never much enjoyed the opera," the Cardinal was saying to Tonio gently. "I fear I know little of that world altogether, but it will be very pleasant indeed to have a singer to perform for us after the evening meal."

Tonio stiffened. Guido could sense the slight but predictable injury to Tonio's pride. Tonio did what he always did when treated as a common musician; he looked down for a long moment, and then up again slowly before saying with subtle weight: "Yes, my lord?"

The Cardinal had perceived that something was wrong. It was a curious thing to witness, but he took Tonio's hand again and said: "You will be kind enough to sing for me, won't you?"

"I should be honored, my lord," Tonio said graciously, the prince talking to the prince.

Then the Cardinal laughed with infectious innocence; and turning to his secretary, said like a child almost: "This will give my enemies something to talk about for a change."

Immediately they were ensconced in a chain of vast rooms overlooking an inner garden where the grass was shaved and the trees made discrete shadows on the ground. They unpacked; they roamed about; Paolo became very excited when he saw the bed he was to sleep in, with its puce curtains and carved headboard. And Guido realized that of course he and Tonio must take separate chambers, and for Paolo's sake, sleep apart.

By late afternoon, Guido had his scores laid out, and he had reread the letters of introduction the Contessa had given

334

him. He would begin at once attending every conversazione, concert, or informal academy open to him. He must talk to people about the operas that had succeeded here in recent years; he must hear what he could of the local singers. The Cardinal's secretaries had already produced the scores and librettos he wanted. And tonight he would go to his first little concert in an Englishman's home.

So why was he not brimming with anticipation as he saw the harpsichord brought in, and the Cardinal's servants arranging his books so neatly on the shelves?

Tonio was certainly captivated by Rome, conferring with Paolo about all they'd seen on the way into the city. They wanted to go this very night to see the Pope's treasures in the Vatican museum. Off they went together on various errands, even that an adventure in itself.

But Guido, alone finally, could not shake this sense of foreboding, so akin to sadness, which had pursued him all the way from Naples to Rome.

What was it that would not leave his mind alone?

Of course, there was always that old terror that he carried within him, to do with Tonio's early life, and his last days in Venice of which he would never speak.

No one had ever had to tell Guido that Tonio's elder brother, Carlo, had been responsible for the unspeakable violence done Tonio, or why Tonio had never let this be known.

It was all clear from the papers Tonio had signed and dispatched to Venice before they ever reached Naples. This Carlo Treschi was the last male of the line.

And Guido could remember the man, dimly, a smartly dressed and somewhat genial presence at a few conversaziones into which Guido had drifted before those Venetian days came to such a dramatic and surprising close. Guido had marked him only because he was the brother of "the patrician troubador" as they called Tonio. A big man, very handsome, teller of amusing tales, and a quoter of poetry, who seemed ever desirous of pleasing others, of keeping their attention and their affection as well. He had seemed at the time only another well-bred and infinitely courteous Venetian.

Guido thought coldly of him now.

He had never explained any of it to Maestro Cavalla. But in time, that had proved quite unnecessary, the Maestro putting it all together for himself as anyone could.

But both teachers had believed, when Tonio devoted himself so completely to his singing, that time and accomplishment would heal his wounds. And the brother? They had supposed him of necessity pardoned by Tonio forever, and thanked God for that.

But this Carlo Treschi had surprised them. Not only had he married Tonio's mother ("Enough to inflame the most obedient little eunuch!" the Maestro had said, and in no sense could Tonio be described as an "obedient little eunuch"), he had fathered by her two healthy sons in three years.

And Marianna Treschi was again with child.

This had not come to his attention until he was ready to leave Naples and the Maestro told him of it, cautioning him to watch Tonio with a careful eye.

"I fear he is biding his time. He is a pair of twins in the same body, one loving music more than anything in this life, the other hungering for revenge."

Guido had said nothing: he remembered the little town in the Veneto, the boy bruised and drugged as he lay upon that filthy blood-spattered bed.

And worst of all, he remembered the role he himself had played in the entire plan.

He felt listless and almost dumb as he had gazed at the Maestro, marveling silently at that image: twins in the same body. Never did he think of such things; he did not even know the name for such talk. But he had often enough seen the face of the dark twin on his gentle and gracious lover; he had often enough seen it evince hatred, anger, and a coldness one could feel as palpably as winter in the damp walls in a northern inn.

But he knew, too, the other twin that lived and breathed inside of Tonio, the twin that wanted this first appearance at the Teatro Argentina as badly as Guido wanted it; that was the one who had a voice like no other in this world, the one who made love both fierce and gentle, the one who had become Guido's life.

"Keep watch," the Maestro had said fearfully, "and let him see what the world offers him, let him have all the pleasures he desires. Feed the one twin so the other starves, for they battle with one another, and surely one must give way."

Guido had nodded, dazzled again by the idea. But in his leaden silence, unable even to offer the Maestro the slightest concurrence, he thought only of that little town again, the mutilated child in his arms. He thought of how even in the midst of his horror, he had so wanted that voice he could not grieve for that battered innocence.

So there lived in Tonio a part of himself that wanted vengeance?

Well, how could there not!

Yes, the old terror visited him. But it had always been there. At one time, it was the fear that bitterness would destroy Tonio; so now it was that vengeance would accomplish this. It was all one and the same. It was a knowledge finally that Guido carried within him, like the awareness of his mortality, and it made him feel as helpless as that; it made him feel silent and cold.

Never had he been able to make Tonio speak of it. On those dreadful days when letters came from the Veneto, true, it was that other twin who read them, destroyed them, and went about the world as if numbed by some poisoned draft.

But it was a radiant and eager Tonio who spoke with him now about the coming opera, the theater, what they should take with them from Naples, what they should leave behind? How many people could the Teatro Argentina hold?

"I know what this means to you," he had once said to Guido. "No, no, I'm not speaking of myself now, nor you as my teacher, I'm speaking of Guido, the composer. I know what it means."

"Then don't talk about it." Guido had smiled. "Or you'll worry both of us." They had talked softly, excitedly, now and then laughing, as they packed up the music, the books, and that great quantity of goods and paste and lace, the king's ransom that was Tonio's clothes.

"Feed the one twin," the Maestro had said to him.

Yes, he would do that, because that was the only thing he could do, the only thing he had ever done; teach, guide, love, and praise this incomparably talented and beautiful singer, his lover, Tonio, who wanted now all the success that Guido had once wanted when years and years ago Guido had dreamed of his debut in Rome.

But why was it that all the way to Rome, Guido had been obsessed with that old tragedy, the loss of his voice? Never one to dwell on the past, any more than on complicated

337

images, he was always overwhelmed by it at those rare moments when it overtook him, and he found his memories unsoftened by time.

Ah, maybe when all was said and done, it was only that he could not think of his parting from Maestro Cavalla and the school where he had lived since he was six years old.

And his mind sought this old pain to protect him from the leavetaking. But he did not really believe this. He did not know.

Pain and loss continued to weigh on his mind, intermingled with his recollection of the Maestro's words regarding Tonio, "Let him see what the world offers him, let him have all the pleasures that he desires."

What was it finally that Guido was feeling? The strong sense of losing something utterly precious, of something like his voice being taken away? Tonio would never leave him now for that terrible pilgrimage to Venice, if in fact Tonio ever truly meant to make that pilgrimage at all.

Yet the feeling persisted, the foreboding, the dread.

Even now, as he sat quietly in his room in the Cardinal's palazzo, Guido was aware of it. And it was punctuated with repeated flashes of the Cardinal Calvino's face when he set eyes on Tonio. Such innocence that man had evinced! Surely he was the saint everyone said he was, otherwise he would have disguised his immediate fascination and never made such a foolish little joke.

The Cardinal had gone out after greeting his musicians.

Guido had watched the extraordinary procession leaving the gates. Five carriages made up the Cardinal's retinue, with exquisitely liveried drivers and footmen; and not five paces from the house, the Cardinal had flung to the crowd the first handful of gold coins.

Tonio came in. He'd been to the tailor's already with Paolo to outfit him as though he were destined to inherit a local throne. He had bought him a finely worked sword, a dozen or so books, and a violin because this was Paolo's favorite instrument, and Guido insisted he be proficient on an instrument just in case. . . .

Thoughts of loss; gloom. Why was Guido worrying about this? Just in case! No tragedy would visit Paolo; no tragedy would visit any of them.

Yet Guido felt heavy and weary in this vast room. Saints in

a gilded frame did nothing to comfort him. Saint Catherine amid a crowd of hundreds of onlookers identified the "True Cross."

Tonio was undressing just beyond the door.

Guido watched him peel off his limp white shirt and drop his breeches as old Nino, the valet sent by the Contessa, gathered these things and made them disappear.

Tonio stood still with his back to Guido as if he enjoyed the cooler air of this place washing over him. Then he put on a green silk robe. He tied it loosely at the waist, and as he turned, looking up slowly, there was about him something almost Oriental in its sensuousness, his hair fallen in his face, the soft fabric hanging from the angles of his tall and graceful body as if it were the proper dress in some foreign land.

"Why are you so somber?" he asked so softly Guido didn't hear him at first. The meaning of the words had to travel through the shadows of the room.

"I am not somber," Guido said. But he could see he wouldn't get off so easily. Tonio sat down close enough that he could touch the back of Guido's hand with his gathered fingers. And again Guido found himself watching Tonio, just as he had a moment ago, as if they were not talking to one another.

He'd been right in his predictions years before that Tonio would have all Domenico's grace. But Tonio had perfected a manner which greatly enhanced that grace. The languid movements natural to him now restrained his long limbs; the muted voice had a richness to it that made an eerie prelude to the singer's power when it was revealed.

His face, it seemed, had become slightly larger, all of the features even a little farther apart than those of an ordinary boy, and there was as ever that subtle mystery to the placement of the eyes. Looking at Tonio even now, Guido felt a subtle disorientation. The magic of the knife, he thought wearily. What it looses, not what it cuts away, is this surpassing seductiveness. He need not know that he has it, nor try to use it. It is there. And infused with the old Venetian manner, he is enough to drive another mad.

"Guido," he was saying somewhere very far away, "Paolo will be good. I know he will be. I'll give him his lessons myself."

Guido hated him suddenly. He wished he would go away. He looked at him but he could not speak to him. He was remembering some moment years before when he had lain on the floor of a practice room, miserable after his first act of love. The maestro he so desired then had bent down and spoken something in his ear. What was it?

"I don't mind Paolo," he said now, annoyed at this misunderstanding. "Paolo is a fine singer," he said simply. It excited him to think that Paolo would learn much more from his time in Rome than ever he would learn at the conservatorio. He had room in his heart for Paolo. He wished Tonio would leave him alone.

"I'm tired from the journey," he said shortly. "I have so much work before me. I have no time to lose."

Tonio bent close to him. He whispered something soft and slightly shocking in his ear. Guido was conscious that they were alone in these rooms. Tonio had sent the servants away.

"Be patient with me," he said angrily. He could see the hurt in Tonio's face. But Tonio gave only a little nod. It was always that way with him, that infernal Venetian graciousness. There was no rebuke in him now as he looked at Guido; with a faint smile he rose to go.

Silently shaken, Guido watched him cross the room. He pictured him on the stage, he saw the crowds at the dressing room door. Again, he saw the face of the Cardinal Calvino, that innocence, those remarkably vital eyes.

You have no idea of the adulation that awaits you, you cannot even guess. Of course they will have their compliments for the composer; if the opera is good, they might even put my name on the handbills, but then again, they might not. It is for you that Rome will crack open like an egg and give birth to itself all over again, and I want it for you, I want it for you.

So why do I feel the way I do?

Tonio was somewhere beyond the doorway. Guido could feel him near. He imagined himself striking Tonio suddenly; he saw that perfect face disfigured by red marks. He had risen from his desk before he realized what he was doing, and passing quickly into the bedchamber, he stopped when he saw Tonio at the window looking down into the yard.

"You know what these Roman audiences are," Guido said. "You know what I have before me. Be patient with me."

"I am," Tonio said.

"You must do everything that I ask of you! You must give me that!"

340

He felt sharp, eager for argument. Everything that angered him and irritated him in Tonio came to the fore. But he knew this was not the time. There was plenty of time. . . .

"I will do anything that you ask," Tonio was saying politely in that rich, measured voice.

"Oh, yes, anything except perform in female dress when you know that is what you must do. In Rome of all places, and of course you will do anything but that which it is absolutely essential that you do!"

"Guido," Tonio interrupted him. For the first time he evinced anger and impatience. The transformation of that angelic face never failed to amaze Guido. "This, I *can't* do. There is no reason to argue it any more."

Guido gave a low, scornful sound. He had what he wanted now, strife, and plenty of it, the angry words coming to his lips, and Tonio's face coloring, the eyes growing colder. But why was Guido doing this? Why on their very first day in Rome, when he did have time, a great deal of time to take Tonio to the theaters, to show him the castrati in female costume, to make him understand their great power and appeal?

Tonio turned abruptly and went to the open dressing room. He was removing the robe. He would dress now and go out, and these rooms would be empty. Guido would be alone.

A desperate feeling came over him.

"Come here!" he demanded coldly. He moved to the bed. "No, bolt the doors first," he said, "then come."

For a moment Tonio merely gazed at him.

He pressed his lips together ever so slightly and then with that small patient nod so characteristic of him, he did what he was told. He stood waiting by the high bed, his hand on the coverlet, looking serenely into Guido's eyes. Guido had opened his breeches, and he felt his passion collecting his other emotions and fusing them into one strength.

"Take off the robe," he said crossly. "And lie down. On your face, lie down."

Tonio's eyes were actually a little more beautiful than eyes should be. With the slightest betrayal of his disapproval of all this, Tonio did again what he was told.

Guido mounted him roughly; the nakedness under him, against his clothes, maddened him. He pressed Tonio's face into the bed with the heel of his hand, and took him with his crudest thrusts.

It seemed a long time he lay still beside Tonio before Tonio rose to go.

Without complaint, Tonio dressed, and when he had put on his jeweled rings and taken up his walking stick, he came quietly to the side of the bed. He bent to kiss Guido on the forehead and then on the lips.

"Why do you put up with me?" Guido whispered.

"Why shouldn't I put up with you?" Tonio whispered. "I love you, Guido," he said. "And we are both of us just a little afraid."

2

THAT STREET, the stars overhead, the ceiling of the room, his teeth biting down into flesh, and the knife, the actual slash of the knife, and that roaring sound which was his own scream . . .

Then he awoke, his hand to his mouth, realizing he had not really uttered a sound.

He was in the Cardinal Calvino's house; he was in Rome.

It was nothing really, that old dream, and the faces of those bravos whom he sometimes imagined he had seen in the streets. Of course he had never really seen them; that was a little fantasy of his, seeing one of them, catching him unawares: "You remember Marc Antonio Treschi, the boy you took to Flovigo?" and the stiletto driving between the ribs.

Just before leaving Naples, he had spent an afternoon with a bravo learning even more about how to use the little dagger. The man, paid well for his instruction, seemed to enjoy an apt pupil.

"But why attend to this yourself, Signore?" he had said under his breath as he eyed Tonio's clothes, the rings on his fingers. "I am out of work just now. My services are not as expensive as you might think."

"Just teach me." Tonio had smiled. Smiling always made him feel better at such moments. The bravo, something of a natural teacher, merely shrugged.

Remembering this dispelled the dream quickly. And before

Tonio had placed his bare feet on the delicious coolness of the marble tiles, he knew again he was in the Cardinal's palazzo, and he was in the middle of Rome. The dream was like a bad taste in his mouth, or a faint headache. It would soon, altogether, be gone.

And the city was waiting for him. For the first time in all his life he was truly free. Years ago, he'd gone from the restraints of his tutors in Venice to the care of Guido and the discipline of the conservatorio, and he could not quite get used to the fact that all this was at an end.

But Guido had made it clear. As long as Paolo had his tutors and Tonio devoted the morning to practice, Tonio had not to answer to anyone anymore. Guido never said so. It was simply the way it was. Guido would disappear in the afternoon when others were still napping and might not come back till midnight. He would ask in the manner of one man speaking to another, "And where have you been?"

Tonio couldn't help smiling. Nothing of the dream lingered now. He was wide awake and it was very early, and if he hurried he could hear the Cardinal Calvino's early morning mass.

Each day, the Cardinal Calvino said mass in his private chapel to which members of his household were welcome to come. The altar was decked with white flowers, the candelabra spreading their tiny flames in great arcs beneath the giant image of the crucified Christ, His hands and feet streaming a copious and shimmering red blood.

The glare of the candles hurt Tonio's eyes when he entered the chapel, and no one appeared to notice as he took a small chair at the very back. And he did not know why he was watching the distant figure at the altar, who turned now with the golden chalice in his hands.

A cluster of young Romans knelt to receive communion, behind them the clerics, humble, more soberly dressed. But Tonio felt good here, and his head resting against the gilded pillar behind his chair, he closed his eyes.

When he opened them again, the Cardinal had his hand raised in the last blessing, and his face appeared ageless in its smoothness, and sublimely innocent, as though he knew nothing of evil and never had. There was conviction to his every attitude and movement, and it seemed a little thought took shape in Tonio's mind, very like a pulse beating in his temple, and the thought was the Cardinal Calvino had reason more than most of us for being alive: he believed in God; he believed in himself; he believed what he was and what he did.

It was afternoon when, after several hours of practice with Guido and Paolo, Tonio entered the deserted fencing salon of the palazzo alone.

No one had used this room in years. And there was something familiar to Tonio about the polished floor shining through his footprints in the dust. Unsheathing his sword, he advanced against an invisible opponent, humming to himself, as if this battle were accompanied by great music and were actually part of a splendid pageant on a great stage.

Even when he became weary, he continued to go through his exercises until he felt the first agreeable ache in his calves.

But after an hour of this, quite suddenly he stopped, convinced that someone had been watching him at the door.

He spun round, the rapier firmly clasped in his hand.

No one was there. The corridor beyond was empty, though there were sounds of life throughout the enormous house.

Yet he had the persistent feeling someone had come and gone. And putting on his frock coat quickly and sheathing his sword, he found himself wandering about the palazzo almost aimlessly, nodding and bowing to those he passed.

He neared the Cardinal's immense office, but seeing it was shut up, moved on along a mezzanine, examining the huge Flemish tapestries, and the heavy portraits of those men of the last century who had worn such enormous wigs. White hair appeared to bubble over their shoulders. The skin, exquisitely molded, veritably glistened with life.

Suddenly there was a great clamor below. The Cardinal was just coming in.

And Tonio watched as, surrounded by his pages and attendants, the Cardinal mounted the broad white marble stairs. He wore a wig, small, pigtailed, and perfectly proportioned to his lean face, and he was talking pleasantly with those who accompanied him, pausing once, his hand on the marble railing, to catch his breath with a murmured jest.

He had the air of a monarch even in this little pause. And for all the richness of his crimson watered silk and silver jewelry, and the dignity of his carriage, there was that natural gaiety to his face.

344

Tonio stepped forward without any real purpose; perhaps only to see the man as he continued up the steps.

And when the Cardinal stopped again, catching sight of Tonio and looking at him for a definite interval, Tonio found himself bowing and backing away.

He did not know why he had let himself be seen. He stood alone in a shadowy corridor, the sun blazing in a high window at the far end of it, feeling suddenly ashamed.

Yet he was savoring the Cardinal's faint smile and the manner in which the Cardinal had let his eyes linger on Tonio before giving him such an affectionate nod.

Tonio's heart became a tiny hammer. "Go out into the city," he whispered to himself.

3

IN THE NEXT FEW WEEKS, Guido resolved not to mention the matter of a female role for Tonio again.

But he was more than ever convinced it was a necessity as he went about his work.

He visited the Teatro Argentina, talked with Ruggerio about the other singers he had set out to hire, satisfied himself that the machinery was in working order for any scenes he might write, and made some final arrangements for his percentage of the sale of the printed score.

Meantime Tonio was buying little Paolo every article of clothing a boy could possibly wear, from gold-threaded waistcoats to capes for summer and winter—though it was summer—handkerchiefs by the dozens, shirts trimmed with Tonio's favorite Venetian lace, morocco slippers.

It was provoking, but Guido didn't have time to reprimand, and Tonio was an excellent teacher, guiding Paolo through his vocalises as well as his Latin.

Paolo's bushy brown hair was now tamed into a civilized shape; he was dressed all the time to go out, and they went off to visit the museums by torchlight in the evenings, Paolo terrified by the Laocoon for the very reasons it probably terrified everyone: that the man and his two sons, caught by the serpents, must all perish at the same time.

Tonio was also teaching Paolo a gentleman's manners.

Every morning the three of them breakfasted together before one of the high windows, its garnet-colored draperies fastened back, and Guido had to admit he rather liked listening to the two of them who made no demand on him to join in; he liked people talking around him as long as he did not have to speak.

Guido had enough talking to do in the evenings. He was received everywhere, thanks to the Contessa, who wrote to him regularly, and everywhere he asked questions about the local taste and, pretending ignorance, had people describe to him all the recent operas in simple detail.

Making his way through immense ballrooms, up and down the steps of cardinals' palaces and lodgings of foreign dilettanti, he sensed a massive society here, infinitely more sure of itself and more critical than he had known in any other place.

And why should it not be so? This was Rome, this was the magnet of Europe. All came here sooner or later to be elevated, humbled, absorbed, conceivably annihilated, or repulsed and driven away.

Whole communities of expatriates lived in this place. And though it had produced no recent outpouring of composers as Naples had done, or Venice in the past, this was where reputations were made or broken. Fine singers who had won laurels in the north and south might be destroyed in Rome, famous composers driven right out of the theater.

The south seemed soft to these people. If its beauty intoxicated them when they went there, it was not enough to keep them from returning to Rome. And they ridiculed the Venetians, saying it was all *barcarola* from there, that is, the kind of music one expects from the gondoliers on the water, and they felt no compassion for those whom in the past they had ruined.

Sometimes it angered Guido, this strident snobbery, especially since Naples supplied the world with her talent. And Vivaldi, the Venetian, was as fine as any composer in Europe. But he held his peace. He was here to learn.

And he was fascinated.

By day he haunted the coffee houses, drank up the life of the thriving Via Veneto and the narrow Via Condotti, musing as he watched the young castrati come and go, some boldly done up in luxuriant female dress, others slinking about like beautiful cats in the beguiling severity of clerical black, their fresh complexions and lovely hair drawing eyes to them everywhere.

And wandering into the summer theaters where the comic opera or the plays were being performed, he studied these boys as they pranced on the stage, coming better to understand here in Rome than in any other place he'd ever been, how eunuchs had come into fashion and necessity.

Here the Church had never relented its ban on performing women, that prohibition which had once dominated the stages of all Europe. And these audiences simply never saw a female creature before the footlights, never witnessed that spectacle of womanly flesh magnified by the cheers and clapping of thousands packed in a dark hall.

Even the ballet had its male dancers frolicking in long skirts.

And Guido perceived that when the woman is taken out of an entire realm of life that must needs imitate the world itself, then some substitute for that woman is inevitable.

Something must rise to take the place of what is feminine. Something must rise to *be* feminine. And the castrati were not mere singers, players, anomalies; they had become woman herself.

And they knew it. How they swung their hips, how they mocked and taunted their hungry audiences.

Guido wondered could Tonio see it, or did it make Tonio suffer beyond endurance? Could he not recognize in this place the violent amplification of all his powers which a female role would mean?

It was a grand irony, really, Guido reflected, hearing these sopranos rise and fall. There was the skill he'd known all his life, but here it had become a divine obscenity, more fraught with the sensual than that which it so reincarnated.

"It will give my enemies something to talk about," the Cardinal had said in his unguarded moment. And he was right.

Guido sighed. He scratched a few notes on the pad he carried in his pocket. He noted the temperament, the habits, the unrestrained tastes of those he saw.

And he knew that on that stage at the Teatro Argentina on the first of the year, Tonio must appear as a woman. His voice could call the gods to attention; but in Rome, he and he alone must shine with that carnal power, and could

347

suffer no other young singer to have that advantage if he did not have it; he *must* have it. Guido must win.

And this was but one aspect of the war that lay ahead of him. Guido must triumph on all counts. He must come to understand this city, forgive it its mercilessness, or he would be too afraid to do what he must do. And making it his landscape day after day, he sought to compass it with his mind.

And he fell in love with it.

San Giovanni in Laterano, San Pietro in Vincoli, the Vatican Treasures, the moldering hulk of the antique Colosseum overgrown with weeds, the sprawling fragments of the ancient Forum, all this he pondered, letting the roaring carriages of the cardinals pass, caught up again and again in the spectacle of hooded friars in procession, cassocked priests, clerics come from all the world to hear the voice of the Holy Father echoing through the largest church on earth and out across continents and seas to the very edges of Christendom.

But what was it he felt in the air around him as he stood in the Piazza San Pietro, what was it that made this city so seemingly solid, so seemingly invincible?

It was as if he could feel a hum, a seething. It was as if this immense metropolis were itself the core of a volcanic mountain. It *was* that cauldron from which the fire and smoke belched forth, and all those living and striving here were bound up in that communal force.

Was it not fair then that all must come here finally to be tested? Let the audiences curse and shout and drive from the theaters and the city itself all those not fit for the pantheon. It was not their sport, finally, it was their right.

He went home.

He wrote until his eyes failed him and he could no longer hear the notes he scribbled. He had a sheaf of arias; he had them for all emotions, all voices.

But he did not have his story yet.

Finally the Cardinal sent for Tonio to sing.

A little supper of only some thirty-five persons, the table ablaze with light and animated faces, the flash of silver, and the harpsichord in a far corner of the room.

348

Guido gave Tonio only a simple aria that would reveal no more than a fourth of his talent and power, and with the music long committed to memory, he looked up from the keyboard to study this little audience as Tonio commenced to sing.

Tonio's notes were high, pure, and tinged with sadness. They brought the appropriate pauses in conversation, here and there the unabashed turn of the head.

The Cardinal stared at his singer. His eyes, slanted down at the corners by those strange smooth lids, gave off a slight gleam.

Yet in between the many demands upon his attention, the man devoured everything on his plate. There was an undisguised sensuousness to the manner in which he ate. He cut his meat in large pieces; he drank his wine in deep gulps.

And yet he was so slight of build, as though he burned all that he consumed, a vice transformed into necessity, even as he lifted the glistening grapes to his lips.

When he had finished the meal, he drove a long pearl-handled knife into the board, so that it stood straight up, and curling his fingers around it, there rested his chin.

His eyes were fixed on Tonio. He had the look of one musing, pleasant to those around him, but secretly absorbed.

Late at night, often, Guido sat alone at his desk too tired to write. Sometimes he was too tired to undress and go to bed.

He wished he could lie beside Tonio as a matter of course, but the time of night-long embraces was over, at least for this little while. And there came that fear again, against which he could find no defense in these alien rooms.

Yet there was an undeniable pleasure in seeking out his love, something sweet and mysterious in crossing the vast expanse of cold floor, opening doors, to approach that bed.

Now he set down the quill pen, and stared at the pages before him. Why was it all so flat, so without the slightest inspiration? Soon he must drive it towards its final shape. All evening he had been reading the librettos of Metastasio, who was now the rage, and luckily a native-born Roman, but he could not find the story yet, not until he had won that last victory which he had no chance of winning tonight.

But it was not in his mind now. He wanted Tonio.

He let his passion slowly mount.

He hummed to himself, ran his knuckles along his lip, letting bits and pieces of fantasy tantalize him.

Then he padded silently across the floor. Tonio lay deep asleep, his hair in loose strands over his eyes, his face as perfect and seemingly lifeless as Michelangelo's melting white figures. But as Guido drew close, he felt the face warm to his kiss, his hand beneath the cover to draw the body up. The eyes fluttered open. Tonio moaned, blind for a little while, struggling, his flesh so hot he seemed a child consumed with a fever. His mouth opened to let Guido in.

They lay close in the dark afterwards, Guido fighting sleep as he could not allow himself to be found here.

"Are you mine completely still?" he whispered, half expecting nothing but the silence of the room.

"Always," Tonio answered drowsily. It seemed not his own voice, but the voice of some sleeping being inside of him.

"Has there never been anyone else?"

"No one."

Tonio shifted, pressing in, winding his arm around Guido so he could nuzzle into Guido's chest and they were clamped together, Tonio's smooth hot belly against Guido's sex, Guido feeling that fine black hair that always amazed him with its texture.

"And don't you sometimes wonder what it would be like?" he asked slowly. "A man? A woman?"

He closed his eyes and had almost drifted off when he heard the answer come low as before.

"Never."

4

IT WAS VERY LATE when Guido came in.

The palazzo was absolutely quiet as if the Cardinal had retired early. Only a few lights burned in the lower rooms. The corridors stretched out in pale darkness, the white sculptures—those broken gods and goddesses—giving off an eerie illumination of their own.

Guido was exhausted as he climbed the steps.

He had spent the afternoon with the Contessa at her villa on the edge of Rome. She had come up to make arrangements for the opening of the house later in the year, and she would remain in Rome only a few days now, returning before Christmas to spend the opera season here.

It was for Guido and Tonio that she was doing this, as she much preferred the south, and Guido was grateful for her decision to come.

But when he saw they might have no opportunity to be alone together today, he had become incensed. He was almost rude.

The Contessa, surprised at this but understanding, took him with her back to the palazzo where she was stopping as a guest. And once they were in bed, his hunger for her astonished them both.

They had never spoken of it, but it was she who led the way in their couplings. Fearless and loving with her mouth and hands, she had always enjoyed teasing Guido and hardening him for the act. In fact, she treated Guido exactly as if she owned him. She caressed him as if he were a child, possessively, with little gasps, as though he were infinitely enticing to her and someone of whom she hadn't the slightest fear.

Guido liked the attention. Almost everyone else was afraid of him, and he didn't care what she *thought*.

On some inarticulate level, he knew she was purely symbolic to him. She was *woman*, and Tonio was Tonio with whom he was miserably in love.

He reasoned it was always so with men and women, and men and men, and if he ever found himself thinking about it, he dismissed it at once from his mind.

But this afternoon, he behaved somewhat like an animal. And the new unfamiliar bedchamber, his odd behavior, and their brief separation from each other, all conspired to make the love play especially rich.

They did not get up right away. They drank coffee, a little liqueur, and they talked.

Silently, Guido wondered why he and Tonio were so at war. Their quarrel this morning over the question of a female role had reached an ugly climax, when Guido had produced the contract Tonio had signed with Ruggerio in which it was plainly stated Tonio had been hired as the prima donna. Tonio, shoving it aside, felt betrayed.

But Guido saw the first signs of defeat in him, only to be angered moments later when Tonio insisted that he would never take a stage name. He would be known to the audience as Tonio Treschi. They could call him Tonio if they must have a single name.

Guido was furious. Why such an irregularity? Tonio would be accused of haughtiness. Didn't he realize that most people would never believe he was a Venetian patrician? They would think this an affectation on his part.

Tonio was clearly wounded.

After a long moment he said softly, "I don't care what people believe. It has nothing to do with where I was born, or who I might have been. My name is Tonio Treschi. That is all."

"All right, but you will perform the role I write for you," Guido had said. "You are being paid as much as or more than experienced singers. You were brought here to play a female part. Your name, whether it's Tonio Treschi or anything else, will be on the posters in big letters when you're nobody. And it's your youth and your looks as well as anything else that will bring them in. The audience expects to see you in female dress."

He could not look at Tonio after these words were spoken.

"I don't believe that," Tonio had replied softly. "You have told me for three years the Romans are the strictest critics. Now you tell me they want to see a boy in skirts. Have you ever looked at those old engravings of torture instruments? Iron masks and manacles, veritable suits of pain? That is what female dress would be to me, and you say: 'Put it on.' I say I will not."

Guido couldn't understand any of this. He had performed female roles a dozen times before he was eighteen. But the complications of Tonio's mind always discouraged him. He could only follow one path:

"You must give in."

How could anyone love singing as Tonio loved it, how could anyone love performance as Tonio loved it, and not do everything that was required?

But he did not tell the Contessa these things.

He could not confide to her the worst part of it; his coldness to Tonio, and the recrimination of Tonio's forbearance.

Instead, he listened to the Contessa, who had troubles of her own.

She had failed to persuade the widow of her Sicilian cousin, that pretty little English girl who painted so beautifully, to consider marrying again.

The girl wouldn't go home to England; she wouldn't look for another husband. She wanted to be a painter instead.

"I always liked her," Guido murmured with only a little interest. He was thinking of Tonio. "And she is skilled at it. Why, she paints like a man."

The Contessa could not understand it, a woman wishing to set up a studio of her own, a woman mounting the scaffolding in a church or a palazzo to hold a paintbrush in her hand.

"You won't turn your back on her, will you?" Guido asked gently. The girl was so young.

"Heavens, no," said the Contessa. "She isn't my flesh and blood, after all. Besides, my cousin was seventy when he married her. I owe her something for that."

And with a sigh, she observed the girl was rich enough to do anything she wanted on her own.

"Bring her with you to Rome for the opera," Guido said sleepily. "Maybe she'll find a suitable husband here."

"It's hopeless," said the Contessa. "But she is coming. She wouldn't miss Tonio's first appearance for the world."

Now as he made his way slowly down the corridor to his rooms, Guido saw light under his door. And he was half glad of it until he remembered the animosity between him and Tonio, and then he felt slightly anxious turning the knob.

Tonio was awake and fully dressed. He was sitting by himself in a corner, and he was drinking a glass of red wine. He didn't rise when Guido came in, but he glanced up and his eyes caught the light.

"You needn't have waited for me," Guido said almost sharply. "I'm tired. I'm going to bed."

Tonio didn't answer. He rose slowly and approached Guido, watching from a little distance as Guido removed his cape. Guido had not rung for the valet. He did not really like servants about him and he could easily undress himself.

"Guido," Tonio said in a cautious whisper. "can we leave this house?"

"What do you mean, leave this house?"

Guido removed his shoes, and hung his jacket on a peg. "You might pour me some wine," he said. "I'm very tired."

"I mean leave this house," Tonio repeated. "I mean live somewhere else. I have money enough."

"What are you saying?" Guido demanded caustically. But he felt the slightest twinge of that terror that had been threatening him for days. "What's the matter with you?" he said, narrowing his eyes.

Tonio shook his head. The wine made his lips glisten. His face was drawn.

"What's happened? Answer me," Guido said impatiently. "Why do you want to leave this house?"

"Please don't be angry with me," Tonio said slowly, with great emphasis on each word.

"If you don't tell me what you're talking about, I'm going to hit you. I haven't done that in years. But I'll do it now," Guido said, "if you don't come to the point."

He could see the despair in Tonio's face, and the recoiling, but he could not relent.

"All right, then I shall tell you plainly," Tonio said in a low voice. "The Cardinal sent for me this evening. He said he could not sleep. He said he needed music to quiet him. There was a small harpsichord in his bedroom. He asked me to play, and to sing."

He was watching Guido as he spoke. Guido could barely hear the words. He found himself picturing the scene, and he felt an uncomfortable warmth in his chest.

"And so?" he demanded angrily.

"It wasn't music that he wanted," Tonio said. This was terribly difficult for him, and then he added, "Though I doubt he realized it himself."

"Then how did you realize it?" Guido snapped. "And don't tell me you refused him!"

Tonio's face was blank with shock.

Guido lifted his hand in a state of pure exasperation. He made a little circle, pacing, and then he threw up his hands.

Tonio stood accusing him silently.

"How did you leave him?" Guido asked. "Was he angry? What actually took place?"

Tonio obviously couldn't bring himself to answer. He was staring at Guido as if Guido had struck him.

"Tonio, listen to me," Guido said. He swallowed; he knew that he must not betray the panic he felt. "Go back to him, and for the love of God have patience with what he wants. We are in his house, Tonio, he is our patron here. He is the Contessa's cousin, and he is a prince of the church. . . ."

"A prince of the church, is he?" Tonio said. "Have patience with what he wants! And what am I, Guido? What am I?"

"You are a boy, that's what you are, and a castrato," Guido sputtered. "It doesn't matter to you, it means nothing to you if you do it! But it means everything if you do not! Couldn't you see this was coming? Are you so blind! Tonio, you are destroying me in this place. Your obstinacy, your pride, I have no chance against it. You must go back to the Cardinal now."

"Destroying *you*!" Tonio said. "You tell me to go to him and do what he wishes, as if I were nothing but a whore from the streets—"

"But you are not a whore. If you were a whore you wouldn't be in this house, you wouldn't be fed and sheltered by the Cardinal. You are a castrato. For God's sake, give him what he wants. I would do it without hesitation if he wanted it of me."

"You horrify me," Tonio whispered. "You disgust me. There is no other word for it. They took you out of Calabria and dressed you in velvet and made you some thoughtless, soulless being with the semblance of a gentleman when in fact there is nothing you won't do for your purposes; you have no honor, no creed, no decent sentiments in you. You would take my name from me, you would take my form from me, all this in the name of music and what *must* be done, and now you send me to the Cardinal's bed in the name of the same necessity. . . ."

"Yes, yes, yes!" Guido said. "I tell you to do all those things. Make me out a demon if you will, I tell you the configurations you place on all these things are lovely and meaningless. You are not bound by the rules of men. You are a castrato. You can do these things."

"And you," Tonio demanded in the same whisper, "what does it mean to you that I lie with him?" It was as if he dared not raise his voice. "Have you no feeling in this?"

Guido turned his back.

"You send me from your bed to his bed," Tonio went on, "as if I were nothing but a gift for His Eminence, gratitude for His Eminence, respect."

Guido merely shook his head.

"Have you no understanding of honor, Guido?" Tonio pleaded softly. "Did they cut it out of you in Calabria? They did not cut it out of me."

"Honor, honor." Guido turned wearily to face him. "If it has no heart, if it has no wisdom, what is honor? What does it matter? Where is the dishonor in giving this man what he asks of you when you will not be diminished in the slightest? You are a banquet from which he seeks once, perhaps twice, to take his fill while you are under his roof. How will you be changed by it? If you were a virgin girl you could plead that, but he would never have asked it of you. He is a holy man. And were you a man, how it might shame you to admit that it was your nature to do as he asks. You could claim an aversion whether you felt it or not! But you are neither of these, and you are *free,* Tonio, free. There are men and women who dream every night of their lives of such freedom! And it's yours by your nature and you cast it away. And he, he is a cardinal, for the love of God. Is what God gave you so very precious that you must save it for one better than he!"

"Stop this," Tonio insisted.

"When I took you for the first time," Guido said, "it was on the floor of my studio in Naples. You were alone and helpless and without father, mother, kindred, friends. Was there honor then?"

"There was love," Tonio said. "And *passion!*"

"So love him then! He is a great man. People stand at the gates for hours just to see him pass. Go and love him for this little while, and there will be passion, too."

Guido turned his back again almost immediately.

The silence was unendurable and without realizing it, he was holding his breath.

He felt swollen with anger, ugly with it, and it seemed all the misery that had been threatening him since they had set out on their long journey was now fully upon him and he had no defense.

But in the midst of this anxiety, this confusion, he understood.

And when he heard the door open and close, it was as if a blow had been dealt him between the shoulders.

Abruptly, willfully, he went to his desk.

He seated himself before an open score, and dipping his pen quickly, he lifted it to write.

356

For a long time, he stared at the marks on the parchment. He stared at the quill in his hand. Then he laid it down with a careful motion, as if he did not wish to disturb so much as the dust in the air.

His eyes moved over the objects of the room. And tightening his right arm around his waist, as if to fortify himself for some terrible assault, he rested his head against the back of the chair and closed his eyes.

5

Tonio was outside the Cardinal's door.

At the heart of this lay a painful conviction that he had brought it upon himself. He did not know why exactly, but he felt it was his own fault.

Even when old Nino had first come for him, saying His Eminence could not sleep, Tonio had felt an elusive excitement that the great man was calling for him.

There was something a little odd about the servant's behavior, the manner in which he hastened to remove Tonio's frock coat, offering him another of his more richly embroidered coats to put on. There had been a furtiveness to the old man's gestures, as if he must walk on tiptoe to some purpose, as if he must hurry, as if neither of them were to be seen.

From his pocket he had drawn an old comb, uneven and broken, for Tonio's hair.

Tonio had not realized at first he was in a bedchamber. He'd seen only the tapestries on the wall: antique figures moved through the Hunt with a score of those tiny animals woven into the flowers and the leaves. The candlelight showed oddly abstracted faces, men and women on horseback, gazing into time from the corner of an eye.

Next he had seen the harpsichord, a small, portable instrument, with its single manual of black keys. The Cardinal was beyond it, a collection of soft movements and sounds, clothed in a robe that was the same color as the darkness,

357

hazy as it was from the few tapers that seemed embedded in the rich hangings of this room.

The Cardinal's words had no beginning to them, no end. And there had been a pounding in Tonio, a sense of the forbidden, though he did not know why. The middle of a statement had penetrated to him, something about song, and the power of song, and it seemed he wanted Tonio to sing.

Tonio sat down. He touched the keys; the notes were short and exquisitely delicate and in tune. Then he commenced an aria, one of Guido's sweetest and saddest, a meditation on love from a serenade which he had never publicly performed. This he liked more than the music he'd sung in Naples, more than the more tempestuous writing Guido had done for him of late. The words, from some unknown poet, used the yearning for the beloved as a yearning for the spiritual, and Tonio liked them very much.

Once as he was singing, he had looked up. He had seen the Cardinal's face, its singularity, its almost carved perfection, infused with that immediately apparent feeling that made the man so visible and magnetic wherever he was. He was not speaking a word, yet his pleasure was obvious, and Tonio found himself trying to make this song as nearly perfect as he could. Some little memory was coming back to him, or if it was not memory he was experiencing a familiar feeling of well-being as he played alone in this room for this man.

He had paused at the end, thinking, What can I sing that will delight the Cardinal most? And when the Cardinal himself set a jeweled cup of Burgundy wine in front of him, it was then he realized they were completely alone.

"My lord, allow me." He'd risen, seeing the Cardinal fill his own drink.

But when he had reached for the narrow-throated pitcher, the Cardinal had taken hold of him and brought him forward until they stood pressed against one another and he could feel the Cardinal's heart.

All was confusion in him; he'd felt the man's strength beneath his dark robe and the hoarseness of his breathing, and sensed that the Cardinal was in perfect torment as he let him go.

Tonio remembered backing away. He remembered that the Cardinal was then standing before the window looking out on distant lights. There was described there the nearby rise of a hill, little windows and rooftops thrown up against a paler sky.

Misery. Misery. And yet some terrible sense of triumph, some near intoxicating sense of the forbidden, as if it were a fragrance in the air. But when the Cardinal had turned back to him, the Cardinal was resolved. He laid his hands on Tonio's neck, his thumbs touching the front of it gently, and in a half whisper he asked ever so gently would Tonio remove his clothes?

It was said with such courtesy, such simplicity, and the mere touch of the Cardinal seemed to carry with it some power to weaken Tonio, to make him feel he must comply.

But he had not complied. He had almost stumbled away. A multitude of thoughts came between him and the desire that was awakening inside him, more powerful even than the Cardinal's soft command. He couldn't look at the Cardinal. He begged, could he be allowed to go?

The Cardinal hesitated, and then he said so sincerely and so gently, "You must forgive me, Marc Antonio, and yes, yes, of course, you should go."

What was left? That sense that somehow Tonio had willed it, that he had made it happen and inexplicably he had wronged this man.

Yet as he stood outside the Cardinal's door, shaken and bruised from Guido's angry words, he thought, For you, Guido, I do this, for you. The things he feared he always conquered for Guido, the things that humiliated him he somehow, for Guido, learned to endure.

But this, this was something altogether different and Guido didn't fully understand that difference, Guido did not know what he was doing sending Tonio here!

Tonio knew, however, and he knew suddenly that he had desired the Cardinal from the first moment ever he saw him. He had wanted him as he had wanted no others before him, locked as he had been in the warmth and safety of Guido's love. But the Cardinal, whole and powerful, yes, this was the man. It was as if he had an appointment with him towards which he had been moving for a long time.

The door gave when he knocked. It had never been bolted. And the Cardinal said, "Come in."

The Cardinal was bent over his writing desk, the room unchanged save for the light of what appeared a small antique oil lamp. And there were illuminated letters in the book before him, tiny figures fitted into the capitals, the whole gleaming as he let his hand, quivering, turn the page.

"Ah, think of it," he said, smiling as he saw Tonio, "written language the possession of those who took such pains to preserve it. I am forever entranced with the forms in which knowledge is given to us, not by nature, but by our fellow man."

He was not in his loose black garments any longer. Rather he had put on his crimson robe. A silver crucifix lay on his breast, and his face had such a curious mixture of angularity and vital humor that Tonio merely stared at him for a long time.

"My dear Marc Antonio," he said, wondering, his lips again lengthening into a smile, "why have you come back? Surely you must realize you were right to go?"

"Was I, my lord?" Tonio asked. He was trembling. Ah, it was a curious thing to tremble while giving no outward sign of it, merely to feel all the signals of panic sealed within. He drew near the desk; he looked down on the Latin phrases, lost in a schematic confusion, a wilderness of tiny beings living and dying amid curlicues of vermilion, crimson, and gold.

The Cardinal's hand was open and outstretched.

Tonio moved towards it, allowing himself to be enfolded in the Cardinal's arm. And at the touch of those fingers, he felt an undeniable awakening, though he fought it just as he had before. Free, he thought bitterly. He would even now run back and hide in Guido's arms if he could. He had the sense of something being destroyed, something that had been guarded desperately for so long. Yet he did not move away. He was looking down into this man's rapt face; he was looking into his eyes, and wanting to touch those smooth eyelids, and the colorless lips.

But the Cardinal was in quiet anguish, and his own passion was dividing him, though he could not push Tonio away.

"For me, the sins of the flesh have been too few to instruct," he murmured, halfheartedly, as though he were reflecting. There was no pride in what he said. "You put me to shame and rightly so. So why do you come back?"

"My lord, can we go to hell for a few embraces? Is this the will of God?" Tonio asked.

"You're the devil with the face of an angel," the Cardinal said, recoiling slightly, but even now Tonio could hear his breath grow heavy and uneven, and he could see that an inner struggle had commenced.

"My lord, is that really so?" Tonio went down slowly on one knee so that he was looking the Cardinal in the eye. What an amazing texture was this face, a man's face, the lines of age confined to such definite places, yet so deeply etched, the roughness of the pointed chin. There was a softness about the eyes, yet nothing alleviated the clarity of that gaze. "My lord," Tonio whispered, "since they cut so much away from me, I have often thought the flesh was the mother of all."

A defenseless confusion came over the Cardinal, and Tonio fell silent, astonished to hear such a confession from his own lips. What was it about this man that he should say such things to him?

But the Cardinal's eyes were fixed on him as if he must understand. And how wrongly Tonio had assessed this. The man *was* innocent, truly innocent, and he wanted desperately to be led.

"I've sinned enough for both of us," said the Cardinal, but it was without conviction. "Now you must go and let me win my battle for God and with myself."

"But will you be the loser for that, my lord?"

"Ah, no," the Cardinal pleaded, but at the same time, he drew Tonio closer to himself, holding him firmly in his arm.

"My lord," Tonio pressed, "may God forgive me if I'm wrong, but is it not true that this sin has already been committed? That in our passion for each other, we are already damned? You have not sent for your confessor, and I have none, and if we should die at this moment, we would burn as surely as if we had already committed the act? Well, then, if this is so, my lord, let me give you the little bit of heaven we can yet have."

He brought his lips to the Cardinal's face. He felt the inevitable shock of new flesh. A body he did not know was turning to him, opening its arms to him, and as the Cardinal rose and they stood together and Tonio embraced him, he felt against him the hardness of a body he had never known.

His hunger was weakening him. He would have begged for it suddenly had there been the need.

And this man's fire caught hold of him.

It seemed he led the Cardinal to the bed. He brought the candles there and set them down, extinguishing all but one, and looking dreamily at its little flame as his shadow leapt up and over the wall, he felt the Cardinal's fingers loosening his clothes.

He was slow about things. He did not help. He was looking into the core of what he wanted, feeling his own waning shock. From a great distance he saw his garments tumbling to the floor, and he felt the Cardinal's eyes passing over him. He heard him speaking in a barely audible confession: "It is enough."

"My lord," Tonio said, laying a hand on this firmness, this solidity, "I burn. Let me give you pleasure, or I will go mad."

He sucked at the Cardinal's mouth, astonished at its malleable innocence, and then, further astonished, he gave himself over to the powerful clumsiness of the Cardinal's hands. The Cardinal lapped at the nipples of his chest, he plunged into the dark hair between his legs, pressing his open palm right against Tonio's scars, and feeling them, convulsed with passion, unable to be quiet. He moaned as Tonio moaned, those dead seams of flesh suddenly alive with a jarring vibration, and Tonio, arching his back, felt the Cardinal's mouth on his rigid sex.

"No, my lord, I beg you. . . ." Tonio, his eyes half mast, his lips quivering as if he were in deep pain, drew back ever so gently and, sliding down to his knees at the side of the bed, whispered, "My lord, let me see it. Let me see it, please."

The Cardinal stroked Tonio's head uncertainly. He appeared dazed and mindless, and then he opened his hands almost in an attitude of discovery as Tonio removed his red robe.

It was a root, it had that strength. It was round and hard as something made of wood is hard, and suddenly, as Tonio caught his breath in his throat, he was holding the heavy silken scrotum in his hands. It was eerie, the lightness of it and the heaviness of it, the seeming fragility of what hung suspended within it, and bending down, he sought to take the whole of it in his mouth, tasting the loose hairy flesh, the saltiness of it, the deep fragrance and heat that came from this place. He drew up and took the organ itself.

It touched the back of his mouth as he went up and down on it, his teeth stroking it, and between his own legs there came the first violent explosion as his own sex sought the little friction it needed from where it did not know nor care.

But he could not stop his movements. The passion was rising in him almost from the moment it had crested, and he was devouring this brutal, unyielding thing as his hand held the soft heaviness of the scrotum, tight yet gentle at the same time. And again it reached its inevitable summit, and he rose up, rigid against the Cardinal, feeling nakedness against his own nakedness and not caring if the world heard his strangled cry. The Cardinal was writhing against him; he was mad for him, and yet so innocent as if he did not know what to do, as if he could not do anything except Tonio's bidding.

Tonio stretched out on the bed, reaching back for him as if he were a cloak to be drawn over himself as he spread his legs. He felt the Cardinal kissing his bare back, his hands massaging Tonio's buttocks, and then Tonio's hand reached for the weapon itself and showed it the place.

This was pain; this was being impaled, and yet it was irresistible, a splendid overpowering, the first thrust bringing a groan from him, and then he felt his entire body moving in the same rhythm and it seemed a throbbing circle of pleasure radiated through him from that orifice and that cruelty, and gritting his teeth, he was giving the most blasphemous assent.

When the Cardinal finished in one last excruciating series of shocks, it was with a wailing cry as if he too suffered and could contain it no longer, falling back away from Tonio, his hand out to hold onto him as if some force might tear Tonio away.

An hour later perhaps, Tonio awoke. For a moment he did not know where he was. Then he realized the Cardinal was standing by the bed and looking down at him, the Cardinal's back to the open window full of the slow progression of the stars.

The Cardinal was speaking, and now his hand lay on Tonio's shoulder, and seeing Tonio's eyes were open, he touched Tonio's cheek. "Could God damn me for this ecstasy?" he breathed. "What is the lesson in it?" It was again an astonishing innocence. And such a childlike animation to the eyes, the face as majestic as ever with its smooth, slightly slanting eyelids, the mouth turned down at the ends.

"I was damned for it a long, long time ago," Tonio whispered, and felt himself slide immediately back to sleep.

When next he awoke the sky was a deep rose color beyond the rooftops, the clouds streaking it through and through with gold. There were the faint distant cries of geese in the air, and somewhere the lowing of cows. And as a cock crowed, it seemed the warming air split this room asunder so that all its brocade and enamel tumbled into itself, as shabby as the contents of a draper's in a back room, layered with dust. Motes moved heavily in the first beams that hit the carpet, and each little gust of the warm breeze carried with it the scent of fresh-turned soil. It penetrated the fragrance of incense and wax which before had been intact.

Tonio roused himself at once. He wondered why the Cardinal hadn't sent him away. It seemed such a charitable courtesy. But the Cardinal lay asleep against his pillow, and even now reached out sluggishly for the warm cleft in the sheet that Tonio had left.

Tonio dressed silently, and made his way down the dim gray halls.

And entering Guido's bedchamber, he saw that Guido had fallen asleep at his desk. His face was buried in his arm. The candle had died in its own wax.

For a long time, Tonio stared at the bowed head, at those thick dusty curls. And then he lifted Guido, who started and then moved slowly and clumsily towards his bed. Old Nino came quietly in and raised the cover over Guido after he had had taken off his shoes.

Tonio stood staring at him, then he turned and went into his own rooms.

He shut his eyes and felt himself with his arms around the Cardinal, his face pressed to that lean and unyielding body, feeling the tumult in it, feeling that coarse though perfect skin. His mouth opened on its secrets again until he could stand this no longer and he commenced to pace the room.

A rhythm caught him up and took him in circles until finally he threw open the window and bent far out over the ledge of it so he could drink up the air. A perfectly round fountain sparkled below. And the pattern of the disruption of the water began to absorb him when he realized he could not hear the splash of it from here.

It would never be the same between him and Guido!

And surely Guido had known this; what had Guido done? He had lived in a locked room with his lover, and Guido had sent him out of it, Guido had opened the door. All that gentle complexity, that bruising tenderness had paled and left him

364

with no savor; he could invoke nothing of it suddenly to quiet him and reassure him; it was old, it was remembered already as if some limitless time had passed. He had been too scorched by the Cardinal's fire.

He would have wept now. But he was too tired and empty and full of some early morning chill for all the warmth of the brightening sun.

Rome seemed not a place so much as an idea as he knelt at the window, his forehead pressed against the sill. "What is the lesson in it?" the Cardinal had asked.

Well, for him, he knew the lesson. That he was losing Guido. And hungering for the Cardinal, hungering for that crushing passion, he knew he would do anything so that Guido would not know. The genius of it was to find Guido in the losing of him, and hold him forever in a new embrace.

6

HE HAD BECOME DROWSY since he sat down in this room. There was a fragrance here, and a quality of light that reminded him of some close place, full of fabric and paste jewels, where he had once been, and he'd been alone there and feeling some delicious warmth from the sun on his bare shoulders and his back.

But he wouldn't allow himself to remember this. It was not important. What was important was to complete what had been begun.

And this woman was waiting for him, obviously thinking that she must assist him, her maids like blackbirds clustered on the edges of the room, their small brown hands full of business, gathering bits of ribbon or thread here, straightening a wig on its wooden head. It amused him suddenly that she expected him to strip off his male attire here and hold out his limbs for her as if she were his nurse.

He was leaning on his elbow, distracted slightly by his image in the shaded glass. His face looked so curiously blank to him most of the time, no matter how grotesque were his thoughts. It was as if the soft feminine flesh that had grown over it (pinch it between two fingers, it was as resilient as a woman's) had robbed him of expression, made him eternally young.

But how am I to close this bodice, he was thinking, how am I to tie up these skirts? Take it all back to the Cardinal's palazzo and give it over to that toothless old man who, even if he has fathered a dozen children in some narrow hovel on a back street, knows nothing of women's dress?

It was hot in this room, the noises of Rome clattered and hummed beyond the shuttered windows, and light lay in bars over this immense silk skirt.

She seemed to have sensed his hesitation. She clapped her hands for attention and sent her women out.

"Signore . . ." She bore down on him, reaching for his cape. He felt its weight lifted from his shoulders. "I have dressed the most famous singers in the world," she said. "I do not merely make clothes! I am a maker of illusions. Allow me to show you, Signore. When you look in that glass again you will not believe your eyes. You are very beautiful, Signore, you are the one I dream of when I ply my needle."

Tonio gave a soft dry laugh.

He rose, unwinding his height before her, smiling down on her heavily wrinkled little brown face. Her eyes were like two small kernels in the flesh, kernels you've just taken out of your mouth so that they are still glistening and wet.

She took the frock coat from him and laid it almost lovingly aside, her hand stroking the fabric as though hinting of its value to one who would buy it. But she had saved her most adoring gesture for the clothes she would help him put on.

"The breeches, too, Signore. It is important." She gestured, sensing his resistance. "You must think of me as your mamma in these matters. You see, to carry yourself as a woman, you must feel like a woman underneath it all."

"Not a centaur, Signora?" he asked under his breath. "Ready at any moment to trample my ruffles underfoot and wreak havoc on the tender virgins of the front row?" He was trembling.

She laughed. "You have a clever tongue, Signore," she said, taking his stockings and his slippers. He took a long slow breath, his eyes half closing.

And then he stood still, feeling his nakedness as if the air were cool when it was not. And when she drew near, she

366

touched him as if he were as fine as the fabric, drawing the hooped petticoat with its wide paniers around him, and tying the ribbons in the back. He let it rock to and fro as she dropped the underskirts over it. Then came the voluminous violet silk, full of tiny pink flowers. Perfect, perfect. And then the full lace blouse, which she deftly buttoned down the front.

Now she slowed in her gestures; she seemed to sense this padded bodice, this armor, was a crucial step. It would fit over his shoulders, its darker violet sleeves coming down just to that spill of ruffle. And then she held it up, letting him pass his arms through it, and closing it first at the waist.

"Ah, but you are the answer to my prayers," she said as she fastened the hook. For the first time he felt the whalebone stays sewn into it, he felt it confine him, and yet it was cool and smooth against his skin, and as she brought it tighter and tighter up to his chest, he felt the oddest sensation, almost of pleasure, as if this thing were supporting him, as if he were being propped by it as well as shaped by it.

Her little hands hovered for a moment on the bare skin of his throat, the smooth flesh descending to the low ruffle that went straight across his chest. And then she said, "Allow me, Signore," in the most confidential whisper, and slipping these rough warm hands inside the fabric she had just tightened, she shaped the flesh there, lifting it, it seemed, until looking down he saw there the slightest flair, and the tight cleft of a woman's breast.

A bitter water came up in his mouth. He did not look in the mirror. He was standing so still he might have been entranced, his eyes staring dully to one side, as she moved the full violet skirts all around, and smoothed the bodice, before bidding him to sit down. He stared at his hands.

"Your face needs no paint, Signore," she said. "Ah, but there are women who would murder you for these eyelashes, and this hair, ah, this hair." Yet she brushed it back, flattened it, and then he felt her lower the weight of the wig onto his head. It was not so very large, all of it snowy white and studded with tiny pearls, gathered at the nape of the neck from which soft curls hung down that he could feel against his naked back. She was clasping his neck just beneath the hair, and now she turned him so that his face nearly touched her own ample breasts.

"Just a little piant, Signore, black magic"—she grimaced—"to the eyes."

"I can do that," he whispered, trying to take her brush.

"Signore, you punish me, I want to do it," she said and then laughed herself, a hoarse sexless laugh from old age. "No, don't look in the mirror," she said with her hands up as if he would try to run away. She bent down and touched his eyes with a sureness he couldn't have matched himself. He felt the tiny weight of the paint on his lashes, he felt it smooth and harden his brows. "Gilding the lily," she clucked, shaking her head, and then suddenly, as if she could not stop herself, she kissed him on both cheeks.

He bent his head to one side, thinking, When I get out of here the servant is going to have to carry my sword, and he is such an imbecile. It was as if the Cardinal preferred perfect idiots around him. Perhaps I am a perfect idiot, he was thinking. And then he bent forward and shaded his eyes with one hand. She had opened the blinds; that warm sun melted into the room; he felt the lightening all around him as surely as he saw it, and then she said:

"Darling child," her hands clasping his shoulders.

That phrase, he though again disgustedly.

"Rise, and look into the mirror. Is it not exactly as I promised you?" she whispered. "You are perfection. Men will fall at your feet."

He stood gazing in silence.

He did not know who this creature was. Lovely? Oh, she was lovely, and innocent, so sheerly innocent, her large dark eyes gazing at him as if to accuse him of some sullying thought. Her bodice narrowed so perfectly to the waist, flaring up with its row after row of cream-colored ruffles and bows to that smooth white skin that was the illusion of a breast. Domenico would have been beside himself with jealousy, and the white hair, how it rendered this face fragile and delicate, remaking its features into those of this guileless young girl.

The white hair rose from its smooth seam at the forehead and the curls fell down on the gleaming silk of the long full sleeves.

She turned him around with both hands, standing on tiptoe as if to see some fine detail, and then dipping her index finger into the rouge pot she ran it along his lips.

"Ah!" It was more an explosion of breath as she backed

away. "Now give me your leg," she said, lifting the skirts with a rustle as she sat down. He placed his foot in her lap. She had gathered the stocking into a circle and smoothed it up, up, until she bound it with a garter at the knee.

"Yes, everything inside and out must be perfection," she said as if reminding herself. She held the white leather slippers as if they were glass.

And now, finally finished, she stood back as though out of breath. "Signore . . ." She narrowed her eyes. "I swear to God Himself, that you could deceive even me." And she continued to look at him as if she did not want him to move.

"You remember what I told you," she said as he approached the hook where she had placed his coat. "You move slowly, you do not really move like a woman, for if you moved so fast and so much as a woman, the illusion would be broken, the illusion is a complete lie. You move more slowly than a human creature, and you keep your arms close to your body."

He nodded. He had already thought it out, constructed it on a grand scale, having for days watched every woman that he could find so long and with such concentration he'd risked indiscretion.

"What is it you want?" She went to take his hands away from his old clothes. But he had drawn out the stiletto, and when she saw that, she stopped.

He was smiling at her as he slipped its icy blade right down the center of his breast.

She turned abruptly, and lifting a little pink rose from a vase, she held it up to the light so that he could see its hairy stem enclosed in a glass tube. This she inserted in that same place, beside the handle of the stiletto, so that only the little bloom showed.

And then she took his fingers, fondling them, as she slipped on the paste rings, and then she placed them on this small, fragrant, and plump little rose.

"Feel that softness," she whispered. "That is what you must appear to be." And again her rough lips brushed his cheeks. She touched his lips as he smiled. "I am in love with you." Her low voice rumbled from her chest, those neat small teeth revealing themselves in her own dry smile.

The carriage was moving slowly through the Via Veneto, halted every few seconds by the procession before it, the ruts

369

from last night's rain dried to a rough and uneasy surface, the swarm of those on foot pressing right past the snorts and tosses of the impatient horses.

Tonio, with one white-gloved hand on the bottom edge of the window, kept his eyes strictly on the open coffee houses, and then suddenly he gave a rap at the top of the carriage and felt it turn awkwardly with a creak towards the rode curb.

The toothless old valet had jumped down to open the door. He held the sword as Tonio had directed him and followed his mistress now through the crowds that made way for her with guarded but admiring looks as she pushed through the open doors.

To the right, but close to the center of the room, so he might watch the endless parade on the street, sat Guido with his elbow on the table, his wine cup before him untouched. He was half-lidded and weary, his heavy face looking oddly young, as if exhaustion weakened his guard, and his disappointment and worry let him assume his more natural boyish scowl.

He did not even notice when a bench was brought up beside him; he did not see this lady sit down.

Then he sat back, startled, seeing the violet silk, perhaps, before anything else. Tonio, as still as a doll in the midst of the wide skirts, sat staring serenely at the street.

The air was warm and caressing, and he let his thin fichu slip away from his breasts. From everywhere, it seemed, came those covert glances. He had unsettled the place; even the serving boy did not know whether to approach, or to bow, or somehow to manage both, as he hovered awkwardly, his tray in hand. Tonio could feel Guido's eyes on him, and then slowly he bowed his head and turned, so when he looked at Guido he was looking up.

Guido's face looked so remarkably different to him, the expression of his eyes, the set of his mouth. And then suddenly the most luxurious private feeling came over him. Guido didn't know who he was! He lifted his fan as the old woman had showed him how to do it, and opened it fully as if revealing some splendid secret as he covered his mouth with it, looking down and then again looking up.

7

HE WAS SO RAPT in his thoughts that he did not hear anything much that Guido was saying, that lovely bubbling speech of Guido's when he was at last content. Tonio allowed it to pass over him, and now and then he would give a little gracious nod.

The heavy afternoon heat had not prevented them from hiring an open carriage for a tour of the city, the exquisite lady and her enamored companion, chided now and then for the bold-faced advance he had made before he knew he was not being unfaithful, and they had wandered arm in arm through a half-dozen churches, the lady opening her parasol now and then with a languid sigh over the heat. They had dined early in the Via Condotti, then making an obligatory trip from one end of the Corso to the other, they had come home.

But not before returning to Signora Bianchi, the seamstress, and engaging her for backstage through the entire run of Guido's opera, which he now knew would be *Achille en Sciro*, based on the fairly new libretto by Pietro Metastasio, who was so very popular now, the poet whom all along Guido had wanted to use.

"It's perfect for you," he was saying. "Achille's mother wants to keep him out of the Trojan war; she sends him to the island of Scyros, disguised as Pirra, a young girl. You'll go through part of the opera as Pirra; then tricked into revealing your true identity, you become Achille in golden armour. So you see, you're a man playing a woman even on the stage!"

"Yes, that's splendid," Tonio murmured. He smiled. But he was not even in the room, and only now and then in the present at all, to marvel maybe at how he had relished his disguise at moments when men admired him, how he had felt some dim vengeful spirit surfacing that was full of mockery and meanness, and something reckless and innocently boyish at the same time. He had the little rose in his hands which the seamstress had given him, the water having kept it very well.

And lounging back in his more comfortable shirt and breeches, his foot on the chair in front of him, he was roughly stroking its little petals, daring it to open.

"Well, you see you are tempted by others all the time to reveal who you are—"

"Guido, Sarri's version of it opened the San Carlos. We saw it together," Tonio said softly.

"Yes, but you didn't pay that much attention to the libretto, did you? And besides I'm changing it considerably. And you must blot that out of your mind. I know what the Romans want. I've seen it all. They want absolute originality with only the most cautious invention. They want a feeling of solidity and richness, and of everything being consummately performed."

It was defiance, that's what it was, Tonio was thinking, being sealed into those garments, knowing what others couldn't possibly know, watching them play the fool as they had shot him their discreet glances, sometimes their open invitations. What was the turning point, he wondered? When had he become the perpetrator of some vile impersonation rather than the victim of it? When had the old feeling of vulnerability melted into the sense of power? He could not say.

It was well after dinner that Guido roused himself from his armchair at the window to receive a letter that had been delivered to the gates.

Paolo had been sent to bed; Tonio had been drowsing, a glass of wine in his hand.

"What is it?" he asked as Guido sat down heavily, his expression unreadable before he crumpled the note and threw it away.

"Ruggerio has hired the other two castrati who'll appear with you," Guido said. He rose and with his hands stuffed in the pockets of his satin robe seemed in the act of mapping out his thoughts. He looked at Tonio. "It could be . . . worse."

"Well, who are they?" Tonio asked.

"One is Rubino, an old singer, very elegant and perhaps too antique in his style. But the Romans have liked him in the past. There's absolutely nothing to fear from Rubino; but we must pray he isn't losing his voice." He hesitated, so absorbed it was as if he'd forgotten Tonio was there.

"And the other?" Tonio coaxed.

"Bettichino," Guido said.

"Bettichino!" Tonio whispered. Everyone knew of him. "Bettichino . . . on the same stage."

"Remember!" Guido said sharply. "I told you it could be worse." But he seemed to lose his conviction immediately. He walked a few paces, made a sharp turn. "He is cold," he said. "He is imperious, he conducts himself as if he were royalty when he came up from nothing, like the rest of us . . . well . . . like some of us." He threw a humorous glance at Tonio. "And he invariably has the orchestra tune itself from his voice. He's been known to give instructions to those singers he thought needed it. . . ."

"But he is a fine singer, a great singer," Tonio said. "This is marvelous for the opera and you know it. . . ."

Guido was staring at him as if he did not quite know what to say. Then he murmured, "He has a very great following in Rome."

"Have you no faith in me?" Tonio smiled.

"All my faith is in you," Guido murmured. "But there will be two camps, his camp and your camp."

"And so I must astonish everyone," Tonio said with a playful lift of the head. "No?"

Guido straightened his shoulders. And staring forward he went directly through the room and to his desk.

Tonio unwound himself slowly from the chair. Stepping quietly, he let himself into the cluttered little chamber which was his dressing room and settled there before a table of pots and jars, staring at the violet dress.

The cabinets bulged on either side of him with frock coats and capes; a dozen swords glimmered in the open armoire; and the window which might have been golden a moment ago was now a pale blue.

The dress lay as he'd left it, over an armchair, its underskirts mussed, its placket of cream-colored ruffles open all of a piece, as if it had been slashed along one side to reveal a yawning blackness within the rigid shape of the bodice.

He leaned on his elbow, his hand moving out just to touch the surface of the silk, and it seemed he was experiencing the feel of light itself because the dress gleamed in the dark.

He could imagine it covering him again, he could feel that unfamiliar nakedness above the ruffles and the heavy sway of those skirts. At the core of each new humiliation there was this sense of illimitable power, this exhilarating strength.

What had Guido said to him, that he was free and that men and women only dreamed of such freedom? And in the Cardinal's arms he had known this was divinely the truth.

Nevertheless it puzzled him. Each layer of him that was peeled away left him trembling for just a little while. And now as he stared at this empty dress, as it became perfectly the color of the shadows, he wondered, Will I emerge from this first night with the same strength? He could see a tier crowded with Venetians, he could hear the old, soft dialect all about him like whispers and kisses, and those faces full of expectation and half-concealed horror to see this gelded patrician got up like the queen of France in paste and paint and that voice winding upwards. Ah!

He stopped.

And Bettichino. Yes, Bettichino. What about that? Forget about dresses and ribbons and Venetian carriages coming south and all the rest of it.

Think about Bettichino for a moment, and what this meant.

He had feared bad singers and all the mundane horrors they might bring: pasteboard swords glued in the scabbard when you tried to draw them, your wine lightly poisoned so you got sick as soon as you went on. Paid cohorts hissing before you even opened your mouth.

But Bettichino? Cold, proud, a lofty prince of the stage who brought with him reputation and a perfect voice? It was the ennobling challenge, not the degrading contest.

And it was just that sort of blinding light which might eclipse him totally, leave him struggling on the fringes to regain an audience which with Bettichino had already drunk its fill!

He shuddered. He had been so deep in his thoughts his body was coiling up on him, and he had hold of this dress, as if trying to cling to the last bit of violet color that the light could still reveal. He lifted it so that he might feel its cold smoothness with his face.

"When have you ever doubted your own voice?" he whispered. "What is the matter with you now?"

The light was gone. The window pulsed with the deep, luminous blue of the night. And rising with an angry air, he went out of his rooms and down the corridor, filling his thoughts with nothing but the echo of his heels on the stone

Darkness, darkness, he was whispering almost affectionately. You make me feel invisible. You make me feel that therefore

I'm not a man nor a woman nor a eunuch and that I am simply alive.

But when he reached the door of the Cardinal's study, he did not hesitate, but knocked at once.

The man was at his desk, and for just one moment this room with its high walls of books and faint candles was so reminiscent of another place that he wondered at the love and the desire he felt when he saw the quick radiance of passion in the Cardinal's face.

8

BY THE END OF SUMMER, it was obvious to everyone that the powerful Cardinal Calvino had become the patron of Tonio Treschi, the Venetian castrato who insisted upon appearing under his own name.

"Tonio," said the Contessa, who was visiting Rome more and more often, "you'll hear it to the rafters, you wait and see."

Meanwhile the Cardinal kept the nightingale in the cage, not allowing him to sing outside the palazzo from which a handful of friends carried tales of his remarkable voice.

But Guido was following another path.

To the concerts he attended, he was always sure to take with him a sheaf of his music. And when the keyboard was offered him, sometimes out of mere politeness, he accepted at once.

Now he was a regular visitor to the homes of the dilettanti, and everyone was talking about his harpsichord compositions, declaring that nothing like them had been heard since the days of Scarlatti the elder, except that Guido was more melancholy and could make you weep. This was true even in the lighter music, sonatas that were so tripping and frothy and full of sunlight you felt you were inebriated with them as with champagne.

A visiting French marquis soon sent his invitation; another came from an English viscount, and Guido was frequently summoned to the homes of those Roman cardinals who held regular concerts, sometimes in their private theaters, for which he was now gently urged to compose.

But Guido was clever. He was not free to accept any specific commission. He was preparing his opera. But any time he might step forward and take out a brilliant concerto from his portfolio of scores.

Yes, this new opera ought to be something, people murmured, if one were to judge by his shorter compositions. And Tonio, his pupil, was so remarkable to look at, so perfect in every feature, even if he did always, without exception, politely refuse to sing.

This was public life.

At home, it was relentless to work for Guido, who drove Tonio through more rigorous practice than he'd ever endured at the conservatorio, particularly with high rapid glissandos, which were Bettichino's stock in trade. After a strong two hours of morning exercises he now pushed Tonio towards notes and passages Tonio could execute only when the voice was thoroughly warm. Tonio didn't feel safe in these realms, but practice would give him the security, and though he might never use these high notes, he must be ready for Bettichino, Guido reminded him again and again.

"But the man's almost forty, can he sing this?" Tonio stared at a new set of exercises two octaves above middle C.

"If he can," Guido said, "then you must." And giving Tonio another aria, one which might not survive the day to appear in the finished opera, Guido said: "Now, you're not in this room with me. You're on the stage and there are thousands listening to you. You cannot make a mistake."

Tonio was secretly ecstatic over this new music. Never in his life at Naples had he dared utter critical judgments of Guido, but Tonio knew his own taste had been educated before he had ever left home.

It was not only Venetian music he'd known; he had heard a great deal of Neapolitan music performed in the north.

And he realized that Guido, now freed of the dreary regimen of the conservatorio and the constant demands of his old students, was astonishing even himself. He was refining his performance, as well as his compositions, and delighting in all the attention he received.

After the day's lessons were over, he and Tonio were

completely free. And if Tonio did not want to accompany him to the various parties and concerts he attended, Guido did not press.

Tonio told himself he was happy to see all this. But he was not. Guido's independence confused him. Guido took to wearing finer clothes than he had in Naples, thanks to the Contessa's generosity, and he almost always wore a wig. The white frame for the face worked its civilizing and formalizing miracle, and those odd features—the immense and challenging eyes, the flat and brutal nose, and those lips spread so generously in a sensuous smile—made Guido a magnet even in a crowded room. And the sight of a woman on Guido's arm, her breasts often pressed right against his sleeve, made quiet fury erupt in Tonio which he could only turn on himself.

It was all changing.

There is nothing you can do about it, and you as spoiled and vain as anyone ever accused you of being, Tonio thought, if you begrudge him this.

Yet he was glad to leave these social gatherings at times. He couldn't sing. The constant conversation wore him out. And with a bitterness, he reflected that Guido had "given" him to the Cardinal; he wanted still to be angry with Guido. Sometimes he wanted still to believe it was all Guido's fault.

But by the time he reached the gates of the Cardinal Calvino's house, he'd forgotten this.

He had but one thought in his mind and that was to be in the Cardinal's bed.

It commenced early on those evenings when the Cardinal did not have guests. Paolo was sound asleep, Tonio always saw to that. And then he slipped into the Cardinal's rooms without so much as a knock on the door or an exchange of words.

The Cardinal was in a fever of waiting, and his first act was always to remove Tonio's clothes. It was his wish that Tonio be like a child in his hands, and he fought buttons and lace and hooks, even when they maddened him, without Tonio's aid.

Once it had been told to him that Tonio was now and then going about in women's clothes, far from being shocked, he wanted to see them, and frequently had the violet dress with the cream ribbons brought in so that Tonio might be put into it by him, and then stripped of it, as he chose.

It seemed at times it was Tonio's skin he craved more than anything else. Pushing the fabric back, he would taste it with his tongue as well as his lips.

Tonio was as pliant in his arms as Domenico had ever been in his own. He would watch with the softest smile as the Cardinal tore away that wealth of cream ruffles merely to lay his hands on the flatness beneath it, then pinching the nipples hard until Tonio couldn't keep silent, only to kiss him then as though begging forgiveness and then push up those skirts to drive his horn between Tonio's legs. Each time that awesome length brought its pain, but he would close his mouth over Tonio's mouth as if to say, If you cry out, cry out into me.

There was a soft delight in all that the Cardinal did, his hands running through Tonio's hair, his kisses on the eyelids, this feverish adoration which moved at its own pace.

But it was not this soft kneading and kissing that made Tonio's passion burn white hot. What excited Tonio was not what the Cardinal did to him, but the Cardinal himself. And it was when he had the man's hips locked in his arms, when he could cover that root with his mouth, when he felt the Cardinal's seed flood into him, buttermilk sour and sweet at the same time, that was when his body shuddered with an ecstasy that threatened to tear him apart.

That, and the inevitable rape the Cardinal always preferred, that iron driven hard between the legs.

And so Tonio bore the rest, enthralled that it was *this man* who did it to him, thinking, Yes, it is the Cardinal Calvino, it is this prince of the church, who attends the Holy Father, who sits in the Sacred College, it is this powerful one to whom I surrender, whom I take in my arms. His hands were all too eager to hold those heavy testicles, to breathe their warmth, to feel their loose hairy sheathing, to press them ever so lightly as if in menace only to feel the Cardinal's body become one awesome and cruel shaft.

Yet he came to understand that for the Cardinal even the gentle play was its own form of rape. As surely as he wanted to pound Tonio into the sheets beneath him, he wanted to see Tonio groan with pleasure, he wanted to invade Tonio with pleasure, he wanted to enslave him with it, as surely as with any pain.

And so the hours passed between them. Tonio, his eyes glassy and unseeing, lay against the Cardinal afterwards, almost like a wrestler taking one moment to steal from his opponent a limp embrace.

* * *

But there was more to it all even than this. Because almost with the first night there had begun some other exchange.

They would dress together after lovemaking. Perhaps they would dine. The Cardinal had various wines to offer, all of them excellent. Then summoning old Nino with his torch, they would begin their regular promenade through the Cardinal's halls.

By the flickering light they would pause at various statues which for years, the Cardinal confessed, he had not enjoyed at all. "I used to so love this little nymph," he would say of a Roman work. "It was found in the garden of my villa when the men were digging out the earth for the fountains. And here, this tapestry was sent to me from Spain years ago."

Nino's torch gave off a dull roar, its heavy scent permeating the darkness around them, and Tonio, studying the Cardinal's gray eyes, his delicate but worn hand on the bronze of an ancient figure, felt the most curious peace.

He followed the Cardinal into the open gardens, full of the gentle splash of the fountains, the green smell of freshly cut grass.

And then to the library they would go, entering together a sanctum whose leatherbound volumes reached beyond the uneven light.

"Read to me, Marc Antonio," the Cardinal said, finding his favorite poets, Dante and Tasso. And he sat with his hands folded on the polished table, his lips moving silently as Tonio read the phrases softly, slowly, in a low voice.

A languor overcame Tonio. Years ago, in another lifetime, he had known hours such as these, when lulled by the sheer beauty of language, he had lost himself in a universe of exquisitely rendered images and ideas. He felt an unspoken closeness to the Cardinal suddenly; this was a realm that Tonio and Guido had never shared.

Yet Tonio was tentative in revealing himself. He was clever enough to know the Cardinal might have illusions that his lover was nothing but an urchin brought up by musicians and might want it to be so. There was anguish in the Cardinal's eyes often enough. And even more often there was sadness. He was in the grip of an "unholy" passion for Tonio. He was a man now divided against himself.

And Tonio could sense that in some way all of these pleasures—poetry, art, music, and their feverish coupling—

379

were bound up with the Cardinal's notion of those enemies of the soul: the world and the flesh.

Yet the Cardinal prodded him:

"Tell me about the opera, Marc Antonio. Tell me, what is good in it? Tell me why men go."

How innocent he seemed at such a moment. Tonio could only smile. No one had to tell Tonio of the church's long battle with the stage and its players, with any and all music that was not sacred, the horror of women performers which had engendered the castrati. All this he had always known.

"What is the value of it?" the Cardinal whispered with narrow eyes. Ah, Tonio thought, he thinks he has imprisoned here some emissary of the devil who will, somehow, guilelessly, tell him the truth. Tonio struggled not to appear defiant:

"My lord," he said slowly, "I have no answer to your question. I only know the joy that singing has always given me. I only know that music is so beautiful and so powerful that at moments it is like the sea itself, or the sweep of the heavens. God created it surely. God loosed it like the wind into the world."

The Cardinal was quietly astonished by the answer. He sat back in his chair.

"You speak of God as though you love Him, Marc Antonio," he said wearily.

His anguish was close to him.

Love God, Tonio thought. Yes, I suppose that I did love Him; all my life whenever I was put in mind of Him I loved Him, in church, at mass, at night when I knelt by my bed with my rosary in my hands. But in Flovigo, three years ago? On that night I do not think I loved Him, nor did I believe in Him.

But Tonio made no answer. He saw the misery engulfing the Cardinal. He knew the night had ended.

And he knew, too, that the Cardinal could not endure this struggle for long. Sin was for the Cardinal its own punishment. And a sorrow came over Tonio when he realized these embraces were only for a short while.

Sooner or later would come the moment when the Cardinal forswore Tonio, and pray it would be done with grace, for if it were done with unkindness. . . . But then Tonio could not conceive of that.

They left each other now in the midst of the dark and sleeping house.

380

Yet Tonio, impelled by an emotion he had never acknowledged before, stole back to catch the slight yielding figure of the Cardinal in his arms for one last lingering kiss.

And he was troubled by this afterwards, when he considered it, when he put his hand to his own lips. How could he feel affection for one who regarded him as an obscenity, one who saw a castrato as that thing upon which he might lavish all the passion he could not give to women, that thing for backstairs?

It did not matter finally.

In his heart, Tonio knew it did not matter at all.

Daily, he watched in silent awe as the Cardinal went to the altar of the Lord, to work the miracle of the transubstantiation for the faithful, while compounding sacrilege in his own soul. He watched the Cardinal on his way to the Quirinal. He watched him as he went to tend the sick and the poor.

It went to his soul that the man never faltered, no matter how great his secret passion. The man showed to all the love of Christ, the love of his brothers, as if, having conquered pride, he knew all this was eternal and infinitely greater than his own weakness, his own vice.

And soon there was not a single moment when seeing the Cardinal—either resplendent in his crimson robes or stranded in the riches of his rooms—that Tonio did not think only, Yes, for this time we have together, I love him, truly love him, and for as long as he desires me, I want to give him pleasure in every way.

If only it had been enough.

The fact was, incited by disconnected visions of the man who'd taken unavowed possession of him, Tonio belonged to whole men he did not know everywhere, strangers who passed him by day in the Cardinal's corridors, even ruffians who shot their hot single-minded glances at him in the very streets.

The fencing salons, where in the past he'd sought a soothing exhaustion, had become his torture chambers, peopled with the most tantalizing bodies, those healthy, whole, and sometimes feral young noblemen he had always kept at arm's length.

381

Now it was chests gleaming under open shirts, arms tense and beautifully muscular, the bulge of the scrotum between the legs. Even the scent of their sweat tormented him.

Pausing, he wiped his brow and shut his eyes. Only to see a moment later the young Florentine Count Raffaele di Stefano, his most enduring opponent, staring at him with an undisguised greed and fascination, his glance now guiltily turned aside.

Had it ever been simple fear of these men that goaded him? Had there always been this unacknowledged desire?

He straightened, ready for the Count's blade; in a frenzy of movement he bore down on him, driving him backwards, seeing the Count grit his teeth. His round black eyes had lashes so thick at the root the eyes seemed lined with black paint. There were no visible bones behind those smallish, rounded features; and the hair, so black it might have been dipped in ink.

The fencing master forced them apart. The Count had received a scratch and the fine linen shirt was torn from the shoulder. No, he didn't wish to stop.

And when they came together again there was enraged pride in the Count, merely his lips working in concentration as he struggled to get beyond Tonio's immense reach.

It was finished.

The Count stood panting; the dark hair of his chest rose even to the base of his throat where the razor had sheared it away. And yet that mask of flesh over his nose and face was so smooth Tonio could feel it beneath his fingers. That shaven beard was so coarse it would actually cut.

He turned his back on the Count. He walked to the center of the polished floor and stood with his sword at his side. He could feel the eyes of others measuring him. He could feel the Count approach. The man gave off an animalian scent, delicious and hot, as he touched Tonio's shoulder. "Come dine with me, I am alone in Rome," he said almost abruptly. "You are the only swordsman who can get the better of me. I want you to come with me, be my guest."

Tonio turned to look at him slowly. The invitation was unmistakable. The Count's eyes were narrowed. A tiny black mole gleamed on the side of his nostril, another on the line of his jaw. Tonio hesitated, languidly lowering his eyes. And when his refusal came it was a murmur, a stammering, as if he were in a hurry with only the time to be polite.

Almost angrily, he splashed his face with cold water,

wiping roughly with the towel before he turned to the valet to receive his coat.

When he stepped into the street, the Count, who had been dallying at the wine seller's opposite, raised his cup in a slow salute.

The richly dressed young men in his company nodded to Tonio. And Tonio, fleeing, lost himself in the milling crowd.

But that night, in a dreary ill-ventilated villa, Tonio allowed himself to be caught in a darkened alcove by hands and lips he hardly knew.

Somewhere far off, Guido played for a small assemblage, and Tonio led his pursuer farther and farther from the danger of discovery, until he could no longer keep those strong fingers at bay.

He felt the man's tongue force his mouth open, he felt the hardness against his legs. Finally he freed it from its breeches so it might make a cavern out of the crush of his thighs. He was Ganymede in those moments, carried upward with all the sweet humiliation of surrender in the shape of the young boy already fashioned for conquests of his own.

And in the nights to follow, all his conquerors were older men, men in their prime, or even streaked with gray, quick to savor young flesh, though at times he startled them as he dropped down to his knees to take into his own mouth all the force it could contain.

When it was finished, he knelt there still, his head bowed as if he were a first communicant at the altar rail, as if he were feeling the presence of the Living Christ.

Of course he shunned these partners afterwards, if partners they could be called. And he was never alone with them in any place that belonged to them. Rather he carved for himself secret meeting places out of shut-up parlors and unused chambers very near to the sounds of the dancers, the crowds. His stiletto was always in readiness, his sword at his side.

It astonished him that men and women everywhere were ready to entice him, that those stories had commenced of naïve foreign gentlemen falling in love with him, absolutely convinced he was a young woman in disguise.

He would bathe before he went to the Cardinal. He would dress carefully in immaculate or new clothes. And then, convinced that none of these encounters had ever even existed, he lost himself in the Cardinal's arms.

Yet the memory of those furtive embraces heated all that transpired.

One afternoon finally, he directed his carriage into the worst streets of Rome.

He saw children playing in doorways, people cooking in the open shops, arches hung with cheeses and meats. A fat glossy sow stopped his carriage, her piglets squealing after her. Laundry on sagging lines shut out the sky.

He sat back against the leather cushions, the windows open despite the splashes now and then, and a general stench the air from the nearby Tiber could not stir.

Finally he saw what he wanted. A young man fixed in a doorway, his shirt open to his heavy leather belt revealing a line of curling black hair. It rose up from his waist and moved out to encircle the tiny pink nipples of his chest as if forming the arms of a cross. His face, even shaven, was as rough as new-sawn lumber, and when his eyes met Tonio's, the small distance between them was suddenly closed by a current that caused Tonio's breath to halt in his throat.

He let the painted door swing back. The carriage stood listing in this tiny, all but impassable place, and Tonio in gold brocade stared forward, one hand palm up and inviting as it rested on his knee.

The young man's eyes puckered ever so slightly. He shifted in such a way it seemed his hips were thrust forward, and the bulge beneath his tight breeches grew larger as if deliberately to make itself known.

Then he moved forward into the carriage and Tonio brought down the blinds to seal them off with only the thinnest seams of light.

The horse plodded forward. The little compartment rocked slowly on its giant springs. Tonio stared at the black curling hair against the man's olive skin. And then suddenly he laid his white hand on it, opening his fingers broadly, and felt the hardness of the man's chest.

He could just see the glimmer of the eyes, the light etching the man's jaw. And very cautiously, he touched this, too, feeling the rough stubble left by the razor, and the skin beneath it so tight it moved all of a piece.

He drew back and let his head fall to one side. Turning

384

away, he let his left shoulder shut the man out, or draw him in. And as he bent forward, his hands on the seat under him, he felt the man's weight against his back. He went down, stretching out on the leather until his face touched it and his eyes closed as if in sleep.

The man's left arm came under him, gathering him up tightly as if the better to hold him for the assault. And feeling that tightness, that rough muscle against his chest, pinning him against the man above him, sent the shocks through him as much as the iron itself driving in.

For one moment the pain was almost too great. And yet the pleasure blazed with it, until they were one harrowing flame. Then he realized his captor had not let him go. He felt his anger rising as his right hand eased toward his stiletto. But with a gentle nudge, he was let to know this young Roman was only stoking the fire for the second assault.

It was over. The young man had drawn himself up coldly when offered money. He had let himself out into the street. But just as the carriage moved forward, he had caught the edge of the window in both hands, and whispered the name of the saint that was the name of the street where he lived. Tonio had smiled at him, nodding. There had been the rarest smile given back.

And then there were only those somber walls again rising on either side, full of ocher and dark green, dissolving into the first veil of rain.

Tonio's eyes misted over. He stared listlessly as the carriage neared the Vatican. And then as if emerging from a thin nightmare which was never dispelled by the waking mind, the sign of a small shop came into view, its letters spelling out for all the world:

SINGERS FOR THE POPE'S
CHAPEL CASTRATED HERE

9

BY THE FIRST of December Rome was obsessed with the new opera.

The Contessa Lamberti was to arrive any day, and the great Cardinal Calvino had taken a box for the season for the first time in his life. A great number of the nobility were solidly behind Guido and Tonio, but the *abbati* had commenced to talk.

And everyone knew it was the *abbati* who would pronounce the crucial judgment on opening night.

It was they who ruled on plagiarism with loud hisses; it was they who drove the unskilled and the unworthy scurrying from the stage.

Try as they might, the great families who governed the first and second tiers could not save a performance once the *abbati* had condemned it, and they were already voicing their passionate devotion to Bettichino. Bettichino was the singer of the season; Bettichino was better now than he had been in years past; Bettichino had been marvelous last year at Bologna; Bettichino was a marvel even before he had gone to the German states.

If they mentioned Tonio at all, it was to scoff at this upstart from Venice who let it out he was a patrician and insisted upon using his own name Who believed all this anyway? Every castrato claimed family once he'd taken on the glow of the footlights, and gave out some foolish story as to why the operation *had* to be performed.

But then Bettichino's pedigree was preposterous, too, really. Descent from a German lady and an Italian merchant, his voice preserved by virtue of an unfortunate attack in childhood by a pet goose?

Only snatches of this talk reached Guido, who was scribbling night and day. He went out only to attend affairs at the Contessa's villa, having given up all visits to the dilettanti as the day drew near.

But Tonio sent Paolo out to hear what he could.

Paolo, delighted to be free of his tutors, called on Signora Bianchi, who was hard at work on Tonio's costumes, then hung about with those men working on the backstage machines. In the crowded coffee houses, he moped about as if he were looking for someone as long as he could.

And when he at last returned, he was red-faced with anger and on the verge of tears.

Tonio did not see him as he came in.

He was engrossed in a letter from Catrina Lisani in which she told him that many Venetians had already left for the Eternal City with no other object than to see him on stage. "The curious will come," she wrote, "and those who remember you with great love."

This gave him a mild and thoroughly unpleasant shock. He was living in daily terror of the opening night; sometimes that terror was delicious and exhilarating. Other times it was torture. And now to learn that his countrymen were coming to see it as if it were a spectacle at carnival caused a coldness to creep over him even as he warmed himself by the fire.

Also, it surprised him. He tended to think of himself as having been extracted from the Venetian world as surely as if someone had lifted him out of it, the crowds closing indifferently to fill the space where he had been. And to hear that people were talking there of the opera, talking a great deal of it, gave him an odd feeling that he could not define.

Of course they were talking because Catrina's husband, old Senator Lisani, had once again tried to have the decree of banishment against Tonio revoked. The government had only confirmed its earlier judgment: Tonio could never again enter the Veneto under pain of death.

But it was the last part of Catrina's letter that cut rather abruptly to his heart.

His mother had begged to come to Rome. From the first moment she had heard of his engagement at the Teatro Argentina, she had begged to make the journey on her own. Carlo had adamantly refused, and Marianna was now ill and confined to her rooms.

"There is some truth in this matter of illness," wrote Catrina, "but I trust you know it is illness of the soul. And for all your brother's weaknesses, he has been most attentive to her; this is the first real rift between man and wife."

He put the letter aside.

Paolo was waiting for him, and he knew that Paolo needed him now. Something had frightened Paolo. But for the moment he was almost powerless to speak.

She had wanted to come! Never, never had he expected this, and it was as if a thin membrane that separated his two lives had suddenly been broken; and a soft, eerie, intoxicating sense of her was seeping through. Never in all these years had he felt such an abrupt and total awareness of her presence, the perfume of her skin, even the texture of her hair. It was as if she were at his shoulder weeping, angry, and struggling to embrace him.

His feelings were so violent and so unusual to him that he found himself on his feet before he realized it and moving across the room.

"Tonio!" Paolo tugged at him. "You don't know what they're saying in the cafés, Tonio, it's dreadful. . . ."

"Shhh, not now," he whispered. But even as he spoke the membrane was healing itself, separating her from him, putting her with all her love and misery far, far away from him in that other life that he no longer lived. What if he were some simple singer, long separated from her? What would it have meant to know she wanted to be here?

"You're a fool," he whispered. "All they have to do is reach out for you, and you bare your heart."

He drew himself up and turning back, he took Paolo by the shoulders, and then lifted his chin.

"What is it? Tell me. It couldn't have been all that bad."

"Tonio, you don't know what they're saying. They think Bettichino is the greatest singer in Europe. They say it's an outrage you should appear on the same stage."

"Paolo, they always say things like that," Tonio said softly, soothingly. He took out his handkerchief and wiped at Paolo's face.

"No, but Tonio, they say you're a nothing from nowhere, it's all a lie about your being a high-born Venetian. They're saying you were hired for your looks. They called Farinelli *il ragazzo*—the boy—when he started. And they're saying you'll be called *la ragazzina*—the girl. And if the girl can't sing, they'll get up a dowry for you so you can be shut up in a proper convent where no one has to listen to your voice."

Tonio started laughing in spite of himself.

"Paolo, that's nonsense," he said.

"But Tonio, you should hear them."

"All it means," Tonio said, brushing Paolo's hair out of his eyes, "is that the theater will be packed on opening night."

"No, no, Tonio, they won't listen to you. That's what Signora Bianchi is afraid of. They'll shriek and howl and stamp their feet. They're not going to give you a chance."

"We'll see about that," Tonio whispered. Though he wondered if Paolo could see him turning pale. He felt certain he was slightly pale.

"Tonio, what are we going to do? Signora Bianchi says when they're in a mood like this they can close the theater down, and it's all Signora Grimaldi's fault, that's what started it. She came to town and said you sang better than Farinelli. That's what made them say all that about Farinelli."

"Signora Grimaldi?" Tonio said in a small voice. "But who is Signora Grimaldi?"

"Tonio, you know who she is, she's mad for you. She was always in the front row in Naples when you sang. And now she's got them all stirred up. Last night, she told everyone at the English ambassador's that you were the greatest since Farinelli, and that she'd heard Farinelli in London. You know what the Romans are saying, who is an Englishwoman to tell them."

"Paolo, stop for a moment. Who is she? What does she look like?"

"Oh, blond hair, messy hair, you know, Tonio. She's the one who was married to the Contessa's cousin, and now she's rich and all she does is paint. . . ."

Tonio underwent such a change that Paolo was silent for a moment.

"Tonio!" Paolo tugged at his hand. "They were bad before she came, but now they're impossible. Signora Bianchi says a crowd like that can shut the theater down."

"She's in Rome. . . ." Tonio whispered.

"Yes, she's in Rome. I wish she were in London," Paolo declared. "And she's with Maestro Guido right now."

Tonio's eyes shifted to Paolo at once.

"What do you mean, she's with Guido?"

"They're at the Contessa's villa. She's getting settled." Paolo shrugged. "Tonio, what are we going to do?"

"Stop being so foolish," Tonio murmured. "This isn't her fault. Everyone's excited about the opera, that's all. If they weren't saying this, they'd be . . ."

389

Tonio turned abruptly and reached for his coat. He adjusted the lace at his throat and went to the armoire for his sword.

"Where are you going, Tonio?" Paolo demanded. "Tonio, what are we going to do?"

"Paolo, Bettichino will never let them shut down the opera," Tonio said confidently. "If he did, he'd be out of work."

It was late afternoon when he arrived at the Contessa's villa just south of Rome.

The gardeners were all about with their clippers fashioning evergreen shrubbery into birds, lions, and deer. The lawns lay green and immaculate under the receding sun, and the fountains played everywhere in rectangles of clipped grass, in the middle of pathways, under colonnades of small, perfectly round trees.

Tonio wandered into the newly papered music room and saw the shape of the harpsichord under a snow white sheet.

He stood stock still for a moment, staring at the floor, and was about to leave the room as rapidly and purposefully as he had entered it when an old porter shuffled forward, his hands clasped behind his back.

"The Contessa has not come yet, Signore," said the old man, his words whistling between his dry lips. "Any day now, any day."

Tonio was about to murmur something about Guido when he saw an immense canvas on the far wall. All its colors were familiar to him, its tiny figures, nymphs dancing in a circle, their scant clothing transparent and seemingly soft to the touch.

Without meaning to, he was wandering towards it when behind him he heard the old man mutter faintly:

"Ah, the young Signora, *she* is here, Signore."

Tonio turned around.

"She will be back any time now, Signore. She went with Maestro Guido to the Piazza di Spagna this afternoon."

"Where in the Piazza di Spagna?" he asked.

A smile broke in the old man's wrinkled face. He rocked on the balls of his feet again, never once breaking the clasp of his hands.

"Why, to the young Signora's studio, Signore," he said. "She is a painter, a very great painter," and there was a slight mockery in his tone, but it was so soft and general it might have been directed to the entire world.

"She has a studio there. . . ." It was more a statement than a question. Tonio looked again to the circle of nymphs on the wall.

"Ah, but see, Signore, she is coming now, with Maestro Guido," the old man said and for the first time gestured with his right hand.

They were on the garden path.

She had her hand on Guido's arm. And she carried a portfolio, thick and heavy, though not as large as the one Guido carried for her on his right. Her dress was flowered linen, flashing brightly from beneath her light wool cape, and the hood was thrown back to let the breeze play with her hair. She was talking to Guido. She was laughing, and Guido, his eyes down as he guided her along the path, was smiling and nodding his head.

Tonio sensed an informality between them. They knew each other. They were talking earnestly of some subject, as if they had known each other for a long time.

He was not even breathing when they came into the room.

"Well, do I believe my eyes?" Guido said ironically. "It's young Tonio Treschi, the famous and mysterious Toni Treschi, who will soon astonish all Rome."

Tonio stared at him stupidly without saying a word. It seemed the girl's soft laughter filled the air.

"Signore Treschi." She made a little curtsy very quickly, and said with a lovely lilting inflection, "How marvelous that you should be here."

There was a great animation in her, her eyes crinkled and full of light, the flowered dress adding somehow to the impression of lightness and motion that she created as she merely stood quite still.

"I have something to show you, Tonio," Guido was saying. He'd taken the heavy portfolio and put it down on the harpsichord. "Christina just finished it this afternoon."

"Oh, but it isn't finished," she protested.

Guido was lifting a large pastel sketch.

"Christina?" Tonio said. His voice sounded harsh to him, and partially strangled. He couldn't take his eyes off her. She was absolutely radiant from the outdoors. Her cheeks were flushed, and though her smile faltered for an instant, she immediately regained it.

"Oh, but forgive me," Guido said easily. "Christina, I thought surely you and Tonio had met."

"Oh, we have, really, haven't we, Signore Treschi?" she said quickly. And coming forward, she offered her hand.

He stared down at it, conscious that her fingers were enclosed in his fingers, and that her flesh was ineffably soft. It was a hand like a doll's hand, too tiny; one couldn't imagine it doing anything serious whatsoever. But he realized with a start he was standing as still as a statue and that both of them were staring at him. He bent to kiss her hand at once.

Yet he didn't really mean to touch it with his lips. And she must have seen this, for at the right moment, she lifted her hand just a little and received his kiss.

He glanced up at her. She looked unspeakably vulnerable suddenly. She was peering at him as if they were at a great distance and she had a great deal of time.

"Look at this, Tonio," Guido said with an easy manner as if he sensed nothing amiss. He was holding up a pastel portrait of himself.

It was an excellent study; Guido was alive in it; there was his brooding, even that glint of menace in his eyes. She hadn't spared his squashed nose or the fullness of his mouth, and yet she had caught the essence of him, which transformed the whole.

"Tonio," Guido coaxed, "tell me what you think!"

"Perhaps you could sit for me, Signore Treschi," she said quickly. "I'd like so to paint you. In truth, I *have* painted you," she said almost bashfully, her cheeks coloring slightly, "but only from memory and I would so much like to do a real portrait of you with care."

"Accept the offer," Guido said matter-of-factly, leaning his elbow on the draped harpsichord. "In a month, Christina will be the most popular portraitist in Rome. You'll have to make an appointment and wait your turn like an ordinary mortal, if you don't."

"Oh, you'd never have to wait your turn." She laughed almost gaily, and it seemed she was full of movement suddenly, her blond curls wispy and light in the air that stirred invisibly in the room. "But you could come tomorrow, perhaps," she said earnestly. "I'm so anxious to get started." Her eyes were darkly blue, almost violet, and so lovely! Beyond words. In his life he'd never seen dark blue eyes like that.

"You can come at noon," she was saying with that faint tremolo to her voice. "I'm English, I don't sleep in the afternoons, but you could come later if you prefer. I should

392

like to paint you before you're so wildly famous that everyone will want to paint you. It would be a favor to me."

"Ah, such modesty, these gifted children," Guido said. "Tonio, the young Signora is speaking to you. . . ."

"You're going to live in Rome?" Tonio murmured. The words sounded so feeble he was certain she would ask if he were ill.

"Yes," she said. "There is so much to study here, so much to paint." Then her expression underwent one of those dramatic alterations, and she added in a strangely simple tone, "But maybe when the opera closes, I'll follow you, Signore Treschi. I'll be one of those mad women who follows a great singer all over the Continent." Her eyes grew wide, but she was grave. "Maybe I cannot paint if I am too far from the sound of your voice."

Tonio blushed furiously. And stunned, he heard Guido laugh.

She was too young! She understood nothing of the implications of her words! She couldn't be here all alone without the Contessa! And to look at her, her exquisite white breasts flattened almost cruelly under that stiff lace border. . . .

The blood was positively stinging his face.

"That would be marvelous," Guido said. "Everywhere we go you would go, and portraits by the great Christina Grimaldi would appear, and word would get around. Very soon, we'd be summoned to sing by those who are absolutely tone deaf and merely wanted to see themselves immortalized in oil or pastel."

She laughed, her cheeks reddening, and gave her hair the slightest toss. It was moist on her white neck, and tiny ringlets clung to her cheeks. But there was the faintest edge of strain in her voice.

"The Contessa would come with us," Guido went on with feigned boredom, "we'd all travel together, a regular cavalcade."

"Wouldn't that be lovely," she whispered, but she was slightly miserable.

And Tonio realized he was staring at her as if he had lost his wits. He looked away from her; he tried to think; even the smallest sentence, what could he say? This talk was all wrong for her; she didn't understand. It was clever, and for cavalieri serventi and adulterous women, and there was something pure

393

and serious about her. Freshly widowed, she was a butterfly struggling from the cocoon.

But she seemed alien in her fragility, something exquisitely exotic. He lifted his eyes to her again because he couldn't stop it, and without ever looking at Guido, he sensed in him a slight change.

"But to answer you seriously, Signore Treschi," she said in that same simple manner, "I've let a studio in the Piazza di Spagna. I'm going to live there. Guido was kind enough to sit for me so I could make up my mind about the light."

"Yes, we had to move from place to place every five minutes or so," Guido said, feigning complaint, "and to pin dozens of pictures to the walls. But it's a fine studio, actually. And I can walk there from the palazzo and watch Christina paint when I'm tired and cross."

"Oh, you must do that," she said with obvious delight. "You must come all the time. And you must come, too, Signore Treschi."

"And my dear," Guido said, "I don't mean to rush you, but if we're to get your maids moved in, and the trunks brought up, we should leave now, or we'll be stumbling about in the dark."

"Yes, you're right," she said. "But will you come tomorrow, Signore Treschi?"

For a moment Tonio said nothing. Then he heard himself make a faint sound very much like the word "yes." But quickly he stammered; "I can't. I can't. I mean, Signora, I thank you, but I have to practice, we have less than a month before opening night."

"I understand," she said softly. And offering him that radiant smile again, over her shoulder, she excused herself and left the room.

Tonio turned at once to the door and he had reached the garden walk before Guido caught his arm.

"I'd say you were very rude if I couldn't see the reason for it," Guido said seriously.

"And what's the reason!" Tonio demanded between clenched teeth.

Guido seemed on the verge of anger. But then he pressed his lips together and his eyes puckered as if he were about to smile.

"You mean you don't know yourself?"

394

10

FOR THE NEXT THREE DAYS, Tonio practiced from early morning until late at night. Twice he started to leave the palazzo, only to abruptly change his mind. Guido had finished all his arias; Tonio must now work out his ornaments to perfection, preparing himself to vary the arias in an infinite number of ways. No encore must sound exactly like what had gone before it; he must be ready for any expediency or change of mood in himself or his listeners. So he stayed home, even taking his meals at the keyboard, and working until he fell into bed.

The servants meantime were gathering at the doors of his room to listen to him; he often moved Paolo to tears. Even Guido, who usually left him alone in the afternoons to visit Christina Grimaldi in her new studio, stayed behind to hear just a few more bars.

"When I hear you sing, when I stand in the very presence of your voice"—Guido sighed—"I'm not afraid of the devil in hell."

Tonio wasn't grateful for this comment. It reminded him that Guido was truly afraid.

Once in the very middle of an aria, Tonio stopped and began to laugh.

"What's the matter?" Paolo demanded.

Tonio could only shake his head. "Everyone is going to be there," he whispered. He shut his eyes for a moment and then, shuddering almost dramatically, laughed again.

"Don't talk about it, Tonio," Paolo said desperately, biting his lip. He was pleading with Tonio for reassurance, and then the tears sprang to his eyes.

"Rather like a public execution," Tonio said, catching his breath, "if it goes wrong." He dissolved into silent laughter. "I'm sorry, Paolo, I can't help it," he said. He tried to be serious, but he could not. "Everyone, absolutely everyone, will be there."

He folded his arms above the keyboard and shook with

inaudible laughter. Now he understood the meaning of one's first appearance: it was a grand invitation to risk the most dreadful public failure of one's entire existence.

He stopped laughing only when he looked again at Paolo's stricken face. "Come on," he said gently, opening the score of a duet, "don't pay any attention to me."

By dusk on the fourth day, however, everything sounded like noise. He couldn't work anymore. And he understood the virtue of this practice: he had not had to think; he had not had to remember anything; he had not had to ponder, plan, or worry at all.

And when the Cardinal, whom he had not visited in over a fortnight, sent for him, he rose from the keyboard with a faint exasperated sound. No one heard him. Nino was already laying out his clothes. Red velvet for the Cardinal, a waistcoat threaded with gold. Cream-colored breeches and high arched white slippers that would leave a cruel mark on his instep that the Cardinal might later lovingly touch.

It didn't seem possible to him now that he could please His Eminence. But he had gone to it wearier and more distracted even than this, and had done it well.

Not until he approached the Cardinal's door did he realize this was far too early for them to be together discreetly. The house was full of busy clerics and idle gentlemen. Yet it was to the bedchamber that he had been called.

He knew something was not right when he stepped into the room.

The Cardinal was dressed for ceremony and duty, the silver crucifix gleaming on his chest. He sat at his desk behind a pair of large candles, his hands folded on the open face of a book.

There was a rare light to his expression, an innocent exuberance to him that Tonio had not seen in months.

"Sit down, beautiful one," he said. He told his attendants to go out.

The door shut; the quiet seemed to close around them like water washing back from a shore.

Tonio looked up with just the slightest hesitation; he saw the Cardinal's gray eyes were filled with an infinite patience and wondering, and Tonio felt the first pang of warning. A dull sense of finality slowly came over him before the Cardinal spoke.

"Come here to me," the Cardinal whispered as though summoning a child. Tonio had slipped far, far away into some realm that was not even thought, and he rose slowly and approached the Cardinal, who had risen from his chair. They stood almost eye to eye, and then the Cardinal kissed him on both cheeks.

"Tonio," he said softly, confidentially, "there is but one passion for me in this life and that is the love of Christ."

Tonio smiled. "I am relieved, my lord, that you are no longer divided," he said.

The Cardinal's eyes appeared hazel in the candlelight, and he narrowed them now, studying Tonio before he answered:

"You mean this, don't you?"

"I feel love for you, my lord," Tonio said. "How could I not wish for your good?"

The Cardinal weighed this with far more care than Tonio expected, turning away for a moment and again motioning for Tonio to sit down. Tonio watched the Cardinal seat himself again at the desk, but he remained standing, his hands clasped behind his back.

The room seemed filled with gray, almost ashen light. Its objects seemed alien to Tonio and unimportant; he wished only that the candles could give a greater illumination, and not merely a dismal shape to the gloom. He turned his eyes to the high mullioned window and the first sprinkling of evening stars.

The Cardinal sighed. He seemed lost in his thoughts for a moment and then he said, "This morning for the first time in months I said my mass in the state of grace." But now he looked up at Tonio, and his face filled with trouble, and gently, as if with respect, he asked, "And what of you, Marc Antonio, what of the state of your soul?"

It was no more than a whisper, and it carried with it no judgment.

But Tonio wished for anything now but this exchange of words. He knew only that this chapter of his life had come to an end. He did not know whether or not he would weep when he left these rooms, and maybe he wanted to find out. He felt strangely vulnerable to remain here now.

"My feeling for you was evil, Marc Antonio." The Cardinal struggled. "It was a depravity that has destroyed men infinitely stronger than I. But try as I might . . ." He faltered. "Try as I might I cannot find in you the evidence of evil, I cannot find the malice and the decay that must follow the willful commission of such sin." He implored Tonio. "Help me to fathom this. Have you no guilt, Marc Antonio, have you no regret? Help me to understand!"

"But why, my lord!" Tonio answered suddenly, without thinking. It wasn't anger he felt so much as astonishment. "Anyone who has ever known you but for a little while knows you belong to Christ. When I first set eyes upon you, I said, 'There is a man who has a reason to be alive.' But I haven't your faith, my lord, nor do I suffer from the lack of it, and I do not have your guilt."

This seemed to agitate the Cardinal greatly, and he rose again and took Tonio's head in his hands. The gesture disturbed Tonio, but Tonio did not move away. He felt the Cardinal press his thumbs softly into the flesh just beneath his eyes.

"Marx Antonio, there are men who believe in no god," the Cardinal averred, "and yet would condemn what passed between us as unnatural, as calculated to bring ruin to us both."

"My lord, why should it bring ruin!" Tonio demanded. He resented all of this terribly. He wanted for the Cardinal simply to send him away. "You are speaking a tongue foreign to me," he said. "This brought pain to you because you had made your vow to Christ. But had there been no vow, what would it have mattered? Our union was sterile, my lord. I cannot procreate. You cannot procreate with me. So, what does it matter what we do with one another, the affection, the warmth we feel? It did not bring ruin to your day-to-day life. It certainly brought no ruin to mine. It was love finally, and what is the ruin in love?"

Tonio was angry now, but he was not sure why.

He was vaguely aware that once, a long time ago, Guido had spoken words to him that echoed these same sentiments in a much simpler way.

And it was such a vast question that he could not feel the dimensions of it, and he did not like this. It put him painfully in mind of the fragility of all ideas.

There lingered in him a numbing sense of his mother's loneliness, that empty bedchamber in which she'd spent her youth, paying for an exuberant passion that had brought him into the world. And there was in him a devastating anger against the old man who had shut her up there in the name of honor and right.

And it is I who paid the highest price for all of it, he thought. Yet even in his darkest moments he could not really condemn her lying in Carlo's arms. And there were times when even in clearest rage, it tore at him like a vulture's claw that he, Tonio, might one day drive her back into that empty room again. Widow's black. He felt himself shudder and strained to conceal it, moving his eyes away.

To this very day he could be driven from a room by the common sight of a moth beating against a pane. He could not even bring himself to take it in his hands and free it, that moth, for thinking of her in that bedchamber alone.

But in the arms of others, he had known a healing satisfaction so powerful it had been for him his sanctifying grace.

Sin, that was malice. That was cruelty. It was those men in Flovigo annihilating his unborn sons.

But his love for Guido, his love for the Cardinal, no one would ever convince him this was sin.

Not even in that locked carriage with the toughened and dark-skinned youth had there been sin. Nor had there been sin in Venice in the gondola where little Bettina had put her head against his chest.

Yet he knew it was impossible for him to express these sentiments to a man who was a prince of the church. He could not unite two worlds: the one infinitely powerful and bound to revelation as well as tradition; the other inevitable and irrepressible, holding sway in every shadowy corner of the earth.

It angered him that the Cardinal asked him to do it. And when he saw the defeat and sadness in the Cardinal's eyes, he felt cut off from the man as though they'd known each other intimately a long, long time ago.

"I cannot *account* for you," the Cardinal whispered. "You once told me that music was to you something natural that God had loosed into this world. And you, for all your exotic beauty, seem natural, like the blossoms on the vine. Yet you are evil to me, and for you I would have damned my soul for all eternity. I do not understand."

"Ah, then it is not from me that you seek answers," Tonio said.

Something flared in the Cardinal's eyes. He was staring at Tonio's placid face.

399

"But you are enough, don't you see," the Cardinal said between his teeth, "to drive a man mad!"

He took Tonio by the arms, and his fingers closed on the flesh with uncommon strength.

Tonio breathed deeply, attempting to let this anger pass from him, saying to himself, This little pain is not enough.

"My lord, let me leave you now," he begged softly. "Because I bear you only love, and want that you should be at peace."

The Cardinal shook his head. He was glaring at Tonio, and there came from him a low humming sound. His breath was hoarse and his face was slightly flushed. The strength of his grip increased. Tonio's anger began to mount.

It was infuriating him to be held like this, to feel the man's urgency and power through his hands.

He was helpless, he was sure of it. And he could remember well enough the strength of these arms that had turned him so easily in bed as if he had been a woman or a young child. He thought of those arms clashing with him in the fencing salon, pushing him in darkened bedchambers, imprisoning him against the leather seat of the carriage, arms that might as well have been the branches of trees, and that smoldering energy that seemed to emanate from the very poures of a man as he sought the evidence of submission in the very midst of passion over and over again.

Tonio's vision faltered. It seemed he had uttered some desperate sound. And all of a sudden he moved as if he meant to escape the Cardinal, or even to strike him, and he felt that grip infused with an incalculable force. He was as helpless as he imagined. The Cardinal held him so easily he might have broken the bones in his arms.

But the man was stunned. It was as if with this small convulsive gesture Tonio had awakened him and he was staring at Tonio as he might at a frightening child.

"Did you mean to raise your hand to me, Marc Antonio?" he asked as if he feared the answer.

"Oh, no, my lord," Tonio said in a low voice. "I meant for you to raise your hand to me! Strike me, my lord!" He grimaced, shuddering. "I should like to feel it, that force that I do not understand." He reached out and clutched at the Cardinal's shoulders. He held tight to him as if trying to weaken the lean muscularity that was there.

The Cardinal had let him go, and backed away.

"Natural, am I, like the blossoms on the vine?" Tonio whispered. "Oh, if only I understood either of you, what either of you feels. You with your limbs that are weapons against me when I am unarmed, and she with her softness, and that tiny voice like little bells ringing and ringing, and beneath her skirts that secret yielding wound. Oh, if you were not both of you mysteries to me, if I were part of one or the other, or even part of both!"

"You're speaking madness," the Cardinal whispered. He put out his hand and felt the side of Tonio's face.

"Madness?" Tonio murmured under his breath. "Madness! You have forsworn me, in the same breath called me natural and then evil; you've called me the thing that drives men mad. What could these words possibly mean to me? How am I to abide them? And yet you say I speak madness. What was the mad oracle of Delphi, but a wretched creature whose limbs had the unfortunate conformation of an object of desire!"

He wiped his mouth with the back of his hand and pressed his hand against his lips as if he meant to stop the flow of words by force.

He was aware that the Cardinal was gazing at him and that the Cardinal had become calm.

The moment lengthened in silence and stillness.

"Forgive me, Marc Antonio," the Cardinal said slowly in a low voice.

"And why, my lord, for what?" Tonio asked. "Your generosity and your patience even in this?"

The Cardinal shook his head as though communing with himself.

Reluctantly, he took his eyes off Tonio and walked a few steps towards his desk before he looked back. He held his silver crucifix in one hand, and the candlelight brightened the red watered taffeta of his robe. His eyes were a narrow gleam beneath their smooth lids, and his face was ineffably sad.

"How appalling it is," he whispered, "that I can better live with my self-denial now that I know you feel such pain."

11

THAT NIGHT, when Guido came home from the Contessa's
villa, the Cardinal summoned him to ask if he needed
any particular assistance now that the opera season would soon
begin.

He assured Guido he would be at the theater this year,
though he'd never rented a box in the past. And after the
opening performance, he would hold a ball at his house if
Guido so desired.

Guido was as always deeply touched by the Cardinal's
kindness. But then he asked in a spare and straightforward
manner if it were within the Cardinal's power to provide
Tonio with a pair of armed guards.

He explained in the same manner that Tonio had been
banished from the Veneto when he became a castrato three
years before. His was an old family; there was some mystery
surrounding it all, though Guido knew nothing about it. And
a great many Venetians were coming to Rome.

The Cardinal thought about this for a moment and then
nodded.

"I have heard these stories." He sighed. It would be no
problem whatsoever to have a pair of bravos accompany Marc
Antonio wherever he went. The Cardinal knew little of such
matters; but there were many gentlemen about him who knew
a great deal. "We will manage this without consulting Marc
Antonio," he offered. "And that way, he will not become
alarmed."

Guido couldn't conceal his relief as it was his strong
suspicion that Tonio would refuse such protection were he
asked.

He kissed the Cardinal's ring and struggled to express his
thanks.

The Cardinal was always considerate and kind. But before
dismissing Guido, he put to him this question:

"Is Marc Antonio likely to do well on the stage?"

When he saw the consternation in Guido, he hastened to

explain he knew nothing of music. He could not judge Tonio's voice.

Guido told him confidently, almost stridently, that Tonio was at this time the greatest singer in Rome.

But when Guido returned to his rooms, he was more than disappointed to find that Tonio was not at home.

He needed Tonio just now. He needed the comfort of his arms.

Paolo was sound asleep. The rooms were full of moonlight, and Guido, too weary and anxious to work, merely sat for a long time by himself.

Tonio had gone directly from the Cardinal's rooms to the fencing salon, where after a few inquiries, he learned the address of the Florentine, Count Raffaele di Stefano, who had been his fencing partner so often in the past.

It was dark when he reached the house, and the Count was not alone. Several of his friends, all of them obviously wealthy, idle, and full of recklessness, were dining with him, while a young castrato, got up as a woman, sang and played the lute.

This was one of those creatures with the breasts of a woman, and they were showed to superb advantage by the cut of a gawdy orange dress.

The table was littered with roast fowl and mutton, and the men had the belligerence of those who had been drinking for days on end.

The castrato who sported hair as long and full as a woman's challenged Tonio to sing, saying he was sick of hearing about Tonio's voice.

Tonio stared at this creature. He stared at the men. He stared at Count di Stefano, who had stopped eating and was watching him almost anxiously, and then Tonio rose to go.

But Count di Stefano came after him at once. He gave his friends leave to stay the night in the banquet hall if they wanted to, and then he urged Tonio up the stairs.

When the door of the bedchamber had been bolted, Tonio stood very still looking at the bolt. The Count had gone to light a candle and now the light swelled evenly throughout the room. It showed the massive bed with its heavily worked posts. Beyond the open windows hung the giant moon.

The Count's round face had a maniacal seriousness to it,

his glossy black curls making him look Semitic, his heavy shaven beard a veritable crust on his chin.

"I'm sorry my friends offended you," he said quickly.

"Your friends didn't offend me," Tonio answered calmly. "But I suspect that eunuch downstairs has engendered some expectations I cannot meet. I want to go now."

"No!" the Count whispered almost desperately. His eyes were glazed and strange, and he approached Tonio as if propelled to do so, drawing so close that some touch was inevitable, and then he lifted his hand and let it hover in the air, the thick fingers spread out.

He looked half mad. As mad as the Cardinal had ever looked, as mad as the eldest and most grateful of Tonio's lovers had ever appeared. He had no pride. He hadn't the haughtiness of the laborer Tonio had picked up in the streets.

Tonio reached for the door, but his passion was rising, making him reckless and as half mad as this man.

He turned around and let the breath hiss between his lips as the Count caught hold of him, and held him against the door.

It was rare, exquisitely rare, because he could not command himself.

And for so long it seemed all his passion had been at his command! Be it with Guido, or with any of those he selected for himself like so many cups of wine, and now he was lost in this, knowing full well that he was under the Count's roof, in his power, as he had never been in the power of any young and unrestrained lover before.

The Count ripped off his own shirt, and slipping his hand down the front of his own breeches broke them open as well. His dark stubble of a beard actually caused Tonio pain as he mouthed Tonio's neck, and then he pulled almost like a child on Tonio's coat, tearing loose his sword.

The weapon clattered to the floor.

But when the Count pressed his naked body against Tonio and felt the stiletto in Tonio's shirt, he left it there. He pulled Tonio to him moaning, his organ rising stout and cloven at the tip.

"Give it to me, let me have it," Tonio breathed, and going down on his knees, took the organ into his mouth.

It was midnight when Tonio rose to go, and nothing stirred in the house. The Count lay naked on the white sheets except for the gold rings on the fourth and fifth fingers of his left hand.

Tonio, looking down at him, touched the mask of silky skin that overlay his nose and cheeks, and silently went out.

He ordered his carriage to the Piazza di Spagna.

And when he arrived at the base of the high Spanish Steps, he sat for a long time gazing out of the window at those who passed in the dark. High above him against the moonlit sky were many lighted windows, but he knew no houses here, no names.

A passing lantern shone for a moment in his face before the man who carried it turned the beam politely away.

It seemed he slept for a while, he did not know. He awoke suddenly, feeling *her* presence, tried to recapture a dream in which they had been together in fast conversation, he trying vainly to explain something to her, and she saddened and threatening to draw away.

He realized he was in the Piazza di Spagna. He had to go home. And just for a moment he was not certain where that was.

He smiled. He gave the driver the word, and wondering in a half sleep why Bettichino had not come, he realized with a start the opera would open in less than two weeks.

12

WORD CAME TO THEM on Christmas Day that Bettichino had arrived.

The air was purified with the first touch of frost, and full of the ringing of all the church bells of Rome. Anthems carried from the choir lofts, and children preached from the pulpit as was the custom. And the Baby Jesus, resplendent amid dizzying tiers of candles, lay beaming from a thousand magnificent cribs.

Guido, discovering the violinists at the Teatro Argentina were masterly musicians, had rewritten all the string parts. And he only smiled when Bettichino, claiming a slight indisposition, had begged to be excused the courtesy of a visit. Would Guido merely send him the score?

Guido was ready for all difficulties. He knew the rules of the game, and had given the great singer three arias over and above those given to Tonio, with which Bettichino could well show off his tricks. He wasn't surprised when in twenty-four hours he had the score returned with all the singer's graces neatly copied in. He could now adjust the accompaniment. And though there were no compliments on the composition, there were no complaints.

He knew the talk in the cafés had reached its highest pitch. And everyone was frequenting Christina Grimaldi's new studio, where she talked of nothing but Tonio. The theater would be packed.

Guido's principal task now was to keep from Tonio his own fear.

Two days before the first night, the one and only rehearsal for the singers was called.

Tonio and Guido went in midafternoon to the theater to meet this opponent whose followers might try to drive Tonio from the stage.

But immediately Bettichino's manager appeared to say the singer was still suffering from a little indisposition and would merely walk through the part. At once the tenors insisted on the same prerogative, and Guido ordered Tonio to keep absolutely silent as well.

Only old Rubino, the elderly castrato who would play the second man, announced cheerily that he would sing. The players in the pit put down their instruments to applaud him and he launched into the first aria Guido had given him with a full heart. His high notes were long gone. This was written for and delivered by a contralto full of such polish and such clarity that everyone was almost weeping when he finished, even Guido himself, to hear his music sung by this new voice.

But it was right after this little performance that Bettichino appeared. Tonio felt himself brushed ever so gently by a passing figure and turned with a slight start. He then saw a giant of a man pass him, his throat wound in a thick wool scarf. A mass of yellow hair showed above it, so pale that it seemed almost silvery, and he had a very narrow, very straight back.

Only when he had reached the far side of the stage, passing

old Rubino, in the same indifferent manner, did he turn as if on a pivot, shooting Tonio his first decisive glance.

His blue eyes were the coldest Tonio had ever seen. They seemed full of some northern light. And fixing on Tonio, they faltered suddenly as if meaning to move away, but were caught instantly as if by a hook.

Tonio did not move or speak, but he felt a strong shudder as if the man had sent him some hideous shock like an eel found still alive on the sandy beach.

He allowed himself to look down slowly, almost respectfully, and then up again to this figure of at least six feet and three inches that would so exquisitely dwarf his own tender illusion on the stage.

And then Bettichino with a very casual movement of his right hand pulled straight down on the edge of his wool scarf. It hissed about his neck softly, and fell loose, revealing the full expression of his large, square face.

Handsome he was, majestic even, as everyone said, and full of that smoldering power that Guido had once described as the magic of only some performers, long years ago. When he stepped forward it seemed of consequence to the entire earth.

Still he stared at Tonio; and so unrelenting, so cold, was his expression that all around him seemed suddenly at a loss. Scrambling to meet some unspoken challenge, musicians coughed into their curled fingers and the impresario nervously worked his clasped hands.

Tonio did not move. Bettichino commenced to walk towards him with very slow measured steps. And then standing directly in front of Tonio, the man reached out and offered his clean, pale hand.

Tonio clasped it at once; he let out a soft murmur of respectful greeting. And the singer, turning before his eyes turned with him, gestured silently that the music might begin.

That afternoon, Paolo dragged himself from the cafés to report the *abbati* were threatening to hoot Tonio off the boards.

"Well, naturally," Tonio whispered. He was playing a little sonata to amuse himself, content to listen to the music coming up from the harpsichord rather than to make any himself.

When Guido came in, Tonio asked him matter-of-factly if Christina Grimaldi would be in the Contessa's box.

"Yes. You won't have any trouble seeing her. She sits facing the stage. She wants to hear what goes on."

"Is she doing well?" Tonio asked.

"What was that?" Guido said.

"Is she doing well!" Tonio said crossly, but loudly.

Guido gave him a cold smile. "Why don't you go see for yourself?"

13

AN HOUR BEFORE the curtain was to go up, the heavens opened a torrent on the city of Rome. However nothing, not crashing flashes of lightning nor the wind that blasted the darkened windows of the theater, could stop the press of spectators fighting their way to the front doors.

A heavy jam of carriages blocked the street, one gilded hulk after another bobbing to a halt to disgorge its bejeweled and white-haired men and women into the sputtering light. And the high galleries were already packed with pale faces in the shadows, as catcalls and shouts and lewd verses rang out over the darkened house.

With dim little flames the tradesmen led their wives to the upper boxes, quickly assuming their places to watch the parade of finery that would soon fill the tiers below them, as breathtaking surely as any spectacle of music and movement on the stage itself.

And Tonio, having just entered backstage, moved at once to the peephole beside the curtain, though he was dripping wet.

Signora Bianchi was hysterical and started at once to rub at his hair.

"Shhhh . . ." He bent forward, peering into the theater.

Liveried servants were moving from sconce to sconce of the first tier, bringing to life velvet draperies, mirrors, polished tables, and padded chairs, as if a hundred drawing rooms floated, disembodied, in the dark.

And below, in the parterre, hundreds of the *abbati* were already seated, a candle in the right hand, a score spread open in the other, their sharp argument and commentary already cutting back and forth.

A lone violinist had already taken his chair. And now came a trumpet player, his cheap little wig barely covering his dark head.

Someone in the highest gallery shouted suddenly; a missile soared through the gloom, and from the first floor came a violent curse and a figure leapt to its feet, fist flying, only to be pulled back. A fight had broken out above; there was thundering on the wooden stairs behind the walls.

"Turn around to me!" Signora Bianchi said hysterically. "Look at you, did you throw yourself into the river! Your voice will close up in an hour. I must get you warm."

"I am warm," Tonio whispered, kissing her little withered mouth. "Warmer than I have ever been." And he led the way through the clutter to his dressing room, where old Nino was stirring the brazier and the air was already like the blast from an oven.

Tonio had awakened early that morning, and felt an immediate exhilaration when he began to sing. For hours he had gone up and down his most intricate passages, until he felt as elastic and powerful as he had ever been.

He kissed Guido on both cheeks before Guido left for the theater. He gave Paolo instructions to make himself one of the audience and watch everything.

And then when the sky was still clear, and a soft lavender over the twinkling windows that dotted the hills, he had wandered into the mired streets nearest the Tiber and, gathering a group of ragged children in front of him, commenced to sing.

The stars were just coming out. For the first time in three years, he heard his voice rising between close stone walls; and his eyes wet, he pushed his melody up and up until he was hitting notes he'd never attempted and hearing them soar, rounded, perfect, into the night that was closing over him above. From everywhere people had come. They crowded the windows, the doorways, they packed the little streets on either side. They offered him wine and food when he stopped. They brought out a stool for him, and then a fine embroidered chair. And again he sang for them; any song they named, he gave voice to it, and his ears were ringing with their screams, and clapping and Bravos, all those faces around him swollen with the heat of their adoration when at last the rain had come.

Now he kissed Signora Bianchi. He kissed Nino. He let them tear away his wet clothes and rub his head with towels. He let them scold. He let them curse.

"I tell you, it will be perfect," he whispered to Signora Bianchi. "I tell you it will be perfect for Guido and for me." And in his heart, he made a little vow that he would savor every minute of it, be it triumph or debacle, and all the rest of the darkness of his life must part here so that he could cross this all-important sea.

In a wordless moment, he envisioned all those who would be in the house. He looked at the exquisite dress before him, woman's ruffles, woman's ribbon, woman's paint. Christina! He said that inaudibly so it was just a little explosion between his lips. It didn't matter to him now the pain and the fears.

What mattered was that he was at last going onto the stage, and for now, this moment, that was where he wanted to be.

"Now, darling," he said to Signora Bianchi, "do your magic. Make all your little promises come true. Make me so beautiful and so much the woman that I could fool my own father should I climb on his knee."

"You wicked boy." She pinched his neck with her soft hot fingers. "Save your silver tongue for the audience. Don't speak horrors to me."

And resting back against the chair, he felt the first soft sensuous strokes of her little brush on his face, the pull of her comb, the heat of her touch.

When he rose at last and turned to the mirror, he felt that familiar and no less alarming loss. Where was Tonio in this hourglass of dark red satin? Where was the boy behind these darkly painted eyes, these roughed lips, and this flowing white hair that ran in deep waves back from the forehead and in full long curls down the back?

It seemed he was drifting as he stared at her in the glass, and she whispered his name to him, and then drew back like some phantom on the other side who might suddenly take life away from him as he himself stood still.

He touched the bare skin of his shoulders with his gloved

fingers; he shut his eyes and felt the familiar bones of his own face.

And then he realized that Signora Bianchi had withdrawn from him as she sometimes did. It was as if she herself were startled by the final effect. And when he turned to her very slowly, he had the distinct impression she was frightened.

It seemed in some other distant world a roar had arisen from the crowd. Old Nino said they had lighted the great chandelier; the theater was overflowing. And there was yet so much time. . . .

He looked down at Signora Bianchi. Her face showed no pleasure, and her little squinting eyes darted over him anxiously as she appeared to shrink away.

"What is it?" he whispered. "Why do you look at me that way?"

"Darling one . . ." Her voice became mechanical. "You are magnificent. You could fool even me. . . ."

"No, no . . . why do you look at me that way?" he whispered again, certain no one living could have told it was not a woman's whisper.

She didn't answer.

And suddenly he advanced all of a piece like a doll gliding towards her and she backed up suddenly and let out a little cry.

He was glaring at her.

"Tonio, stop it!" she said, biting her lip.

"Then what is it?" he demanded again.

"All right, then, you are like a demon, a perfect woman who is larger, larger than life! You are delicate and beautiful all over; but you are too large! And you frighten me as if the angel of God were to come into this room, now, and fill it up with his wings, knocking the feathers out of them so that they were tumbling down through the air, even as you heard a scraping of his wings against the ceiling. And his head was bigger and his hands were bigger . . . well, that is what you are. . . . You are beautiful and perfect, yet you are a . . ."

"A monster, my dearest," he whispered. And on impulse he took her face in both hands and gave her another deep kiss.

She held her breath, her eyes closed, her mouth open, and then her heavy breasts heaved with a sigh.

"You belong out there. . . ." she murmured. And then she opened her eyes. For a long time, she just looked at him

411

and then her face crinkled with pleasure and pride and she threw her arms about his waist.

"Do you love me?" he asked.

"Ah!" She backed away. "What do you care about me! All of Rome is about to love you, all of Rome is about to fall at your feet! And you ask do I love you? Who am I?"

"Yes, yes, but I want you to love me, in this room, now."

"Oh, so soon it starts." She smiled. She lifted her hands to caress the white waves of hair, to slip a long jeweled pin in place. "The endless vanity"—she sighed—"with its endless greed."

"Is that what it is?" he asked softly.

She stopped.

"You're afraid," she whispered.

"A little, Signora, a little." He smiled.

"But, darling . . ." she started.

But the door had flown open, and a breathless Paolo, his hair wet and rumpled, came into the room.

"Tonio, you should hear them, the trash! They're saying Ruggerio paid you more than Bettichino, and they're spoiling for a fight. And the place is full of Venetians, Tonio, they've come all the way just to hear you sing. There'll be a fight all right, but, Tonio, they're not going to give you a chance!"

14

THERE WAS NO MORE TIME. Twenty-five years of trudging steadily towards this moment, then it was down to a couple of years, then month after month and day after day. Now it was actually happening. Time had run out.

Guido could hear the orchestra tuning in the pit. Signora Bianchi had told him Tonio was ready, but he must not go in. And he and Tonio, having embraced each other that afternoon with the most intimate words, had agreed on that; neither would fire the other in these last moments with his own doubts.

Guido made one last routine inspection in the glass. His smooth white wig was perfect, the gold brocade frock coat, after a series of adjustments by the seamstress, did finally allow him the free use of his arms. He struggled to flatten the lace at his throat, to shake it loose at his wrists, and now he loosened his belt just a little, certain no one would notice, and gathered up the score.

But before stepping into the pit, he stood behind the curtain and looked into the hall.

The great chandelier had just disappeared into the ceiling, taking with it the light of day.

And it seemed the descending gloom loosed a wild roar. There was stamping in the gallery, and coarse shouts coming from both sides.

The *abbati* had taken over the front of the house as he'd expected, and the boxes were positively jammed. Extra chairs had been squeezed in everywhere, and directly above him to the right it was a dozen Venetians he saw, he was certain of it, and one among them looked particularly familiar, that giant eunuch from San Marco who had been Tonio's tutor and friend.

The Neapolitans were here, too, in full force, the Contessa Lamberti with Christina Grimaldi in the very front row of the box, their backs to the supper table where others were already at cards. Maestro Cavalla was there, who had already sent his greetings backstage.

The Cardinal Calvino was only one of many cardinals present, a score of young noblemen clustering about him, all of them nodding and talking over their wine.

Suddenly a man dashed up the aisle towards the orchestra and, cupping his hands, let out some long derisive yell. Guido tensed, furious that he couldn't comprehend it, and then from the rafters it seemed there descended a fluttering white snow of little sheets of paper, with figures rising everywhere to snatch them up.

People had commenced to hoot and stamp. It was time for Guido to step out.

He closed his eyes and rested his head against the edge of the wall. Then he felt someone shaking him and he gritted his teeth, ready to demand this last moment of peace.

"Look at this!" It was Ruggerio, who had one of those pieces of paper which had fluttered from above.

Guido grabbed it, twisting it to the light. It was a crude sonnet insisting Tonio was nothing but a gondolier in his

413

native city and should go back to singing the *barcarola* on the canals.

"This is bad, this is bad," Ruggerio was murmuring. "I know this kind of house, they can shut me down! They won't listen to anything, it's all sport to them, they've got a Venetian patrician to jeer at, and Bettichino's a favorite of theirs, and they'll shut us down."

"Where's Bettichino!" demanded Guido. "He's responsible for this." He turned, his fist doubled.

"Maestro, there isn't time. And besides, they don't take orders from Bettichino. All they know is the theaters are open, and your boy's given them a perfect armory with all his airs. If he'd only taken a stage name, if he wasn't so damned much the aristocrat and more . . ."

"Oh, shut up!" Guido said. He shoved the impresario away from him. "Why the hell do you say all this to me now!" He was frantic. All the tales of injustice and debacle came back to him now, Loretti's misery when Domenico had triumphed and Loretti himself had failed, the old story of Pergolesi, embittered, never returning to Rome.

He felt a fool suddenly, and it was the most despairing feeling in the world. What had made him think this was a tribunal where anything noble or just would happen? He started for the stairs.

"Maestro, keep your head," said Ruggerio. "If they start throwing things, don't throw anything back."

Guido laughed aloud. He took one last contemptuous look at the impresario, and coming out onto the main floor, he walked towards the harpsichord as the musicians rose to greet him with a quick bow.

The house went quiet, even the shouts being hushed, it seemed, as his fingers plunged into the first triumphant theme, the strings rising jubilantly around him.

The music formed a solid volume, obliterating for the moment every fear, and he felt himself carried along in it rather than driving its rapid tempo.

The curtain had gone up. Applause had greeted the figure of Bettichino above. And one glance told him the man was the perfect image of a god, his blond hair gleaming under the lights, his fair skin brilliantly highlighted with white powder. Guido knew men were bowing to him from the boxes. He could see from the corner of his eye that Bettichino was

414

returning the bows. Rubino had come on stage, and now, and now, glancing up, he saw Tonio.

Even over the music, he heard the gasps and murmurs of the house, like the gentle roar that had accompanied the earlier spectacle of the chandelier.

And indeed it was a spectacle. An exquisite woman standing at the footlights in scarlet satin and gold embroidered lace. Tonio's eyes, etched in black, were like too shimmering pieces of glass. An air of command emanated from him, though he appeared lifeless as a mannequin, the spotlight beautifully accentuating the bones of his face.

Guido glanced up again quickly, but he could gain no recognition from Tonio who appeared to be serenely surveying the house. Only now, as Bettichino completed his little promenade of the stage, did Tonio respond to the greetings being offered him. Glancing slowly from the right to the left, he made a grand feminine bow. As he rose, his slightest movements had an immensity to them. Surely he had drawn to himself all eyes.

But the opera bore inexorably down upon Guido. They were already half through the opening recitative. Bettichino's voice was full of polish and power.

And suddenly he launched into his first aria. Guido had to be ready for the slightest change; the strings were reduced to a strumming continuo along with the harpsichord.

The singer had stepped to the front. The blue of his long coat caused his eyes to flash almost as if they were detaching themselves from his face, and his voice rose in stultifying volume.

Now ending the second part, he commenced the repetition of the first, which was the standard form of every aria, and as he must, he commenced to vary it, slowly, with more and more fanfare, yet nothing of the true power that Guido knew he would show later. But soaring to the last note, he commenced a magnificent swell, the note growing louder and louder and louder, and all executed in one long breath until the audience in the midst of it was totally silent. Guido was silent. The strings were silent. The singer, motionless, was unwinding an endless stream of sound into the air without the slightest symptom of stress, and just as he tapered it off and all thought he must conclude or die, he swelled the note again bringing it up to an even louder peak and then suddenly stopped it.

Applause rang from all quarters. The *abbati* were shouting in sharp, almost begrudging voices, "Bravo, Bettichino!" while the same cry came from the gallery and from the rear of the pit as well as the boxes. The singer left the stage as each man would do after his aria. And plunging back into the music, Guido led those assembled before the lights through the ongoing story of the opera.

Guido could feel his face aflame. He did not dare look at the stage. He had commenced, his fingers sweating so badly he felt them sliding on the keys, the introduction to Tonio's first aria. And then unable to prevent himself, afraid that in this moment he would fail Tonio if he did not, he swallowed his fear long enough to look up at the still figure of the woman standing there.

Tonio did not see him. If he needed him he did not show it. Those exquisite black eyes were fixed on the first tier as if confronting every person in it. And with a great rush of energy, he started in, his voice as clean and pure and absolutely translucent as Guido had ever heard it.

But the noise had already begun everywhere, the stomping of feet, the hissing from the back, the catcalls from the ceiling.

"Go back to Venice, to the canals!" came the strident roar from the topmost gallery.

Some of the *abbati* had risen from their seats, fists clenched at those above, screaming out, "Silence, silence."

Tonio continued to sing, unmoved, his voice never straining to drown out the din, which would have been impossible. Guido was clenching his teeth, and without meaning to, banging the keyboard as if he could draw some greater volume out of it.

The sweat fell from his face right onto the backs of his hands. He could not hear Tonio now. He could not even hear his own instrument.

Tonio had finished the song, he had made his bow, and with the same placid countenance gone into the wings.

From the whole first tier came a riotous applause that added nothing but noise to the hissing and screaming of the others.

It seemed to Guido there could be no more perfect hell for him than the moments that followed. The next scene was assembling itself on stage, and it was for this, the closing of the first act, that he had written Tonio's most magnificent aria. Every melody he'd given him was expertly tuned to show off his voice, but this was the set piece, the song that must prevent the great ladies and gentlemen of Rome from rising indifferently from their boxes and moving on elsewhere.

Bettichino's strongest aria would come right before it, but Bettichino would be heard! Guido was frantic.

The hissing had commenced again as soon as Tonio had appeared on the stage, and out of the corner of his eyes Guido saw another torrent of those little white slips of paper, covered no doubt with some malicious verse, falling everywhere.

Bettichino had come to the fore. He had now the most tantalizing and original of Guido's accompanied recitatives. It was the only part of the opera where action and song met, for he was now singing about the story itself, yet singing not humdrum narrative, but singing with feeling.

It was here Guido's strings did their finest work, and he himself could hardly hear or think or know what he was playing. The hisses had died as Bettichino began, and then the singer went from this into the grandest of his arias.

He had taken his time before giving the signal, the applause for the recitative producing for the first time a violent reaction in the audience. Guido took a deep breath. So Tonio had his own champions, thank God, and they were fighting Bettichino's with the same catcalls and protests.

Guido saw the singer signal for him to start, and alone Guido led the way into this most tender of arias. There was no other piece of music to match it in the rest of the opera, save the song that Tonio sang directly after.

Bettichino slowed the tempo. Guido followed immediately. And then even Guido felt the mastery of Bettichino's smooth and poignant beginning, his voice weaving up so delicately and yet so strongly it was like an unbreakable wire slowly uncoiling itself.

He let his head fall back. Going into the repeat of the first part, he was trilling the first note perfectly in one straight line, never deviating from it up or down, but merely punching it gently again and again, and again, as if that wire that was his voice were pulsing over and over with staccato radiance. Then he glided into the tender phrases, enunciating them magnificently, and as he came to the end, it was the swell, but this time the *Esclamazio Viva*, the note started at full volume and now diminished ever so gradually and so sweetly that it produced the most profound sadness.

It seemed that descending note, that note vanishing almost to the echo of itself, was wrapped in total silence. And then he let it rise again becoming stronger and stronger until he stopped it at full volume, with a resolute shake of his head.

His followers went wild. But there was no need for them to stoke the blaze in the parterre. The *abbati* were heralding him with a deafening stomping of the feet and hoarse exclamations of Bravo!

Bettichino circled the stage and now he came to the fore for his encore.

No one, of course, expected it to be the same—it was mandatory that it be different, and Guido at the keyboard was ready for those subtle differences—but it is doubtful anyone expected the show of tremolos and trills and then again those swells that seemed to defy human explanation. It was swells finally that were carrying the hour.

Bettichino went into the song a third and last time, and retired from the stage an unchallenged victor.

All right. Guido couldn't be sorry for this. He couldn't be sorry for an audience on the edge of their seats, but if these beasts had any decency they would realize their singer had had his moment and nothing from Tonio could now ruin it. But when were rivalries that decent? It wasn't enough their idol had just demonstrated himself invincible, they must now crush Tonio.

And again, that ravishing young woman, her face so smooth she seemed deep in thought, came to the footlights as if nothing could shake her.

From the gallery came the first cries as before, but then they were taken up from the parterre.

"Go back to the canals!" they were screaming. "You don't belong on the same stage with a singer!"

But the *abbati*, infuriated, were again hurling their own invectives: "Let the boy sing! Are you afraid he'll make a fool of your favorite!" It was war, and the first missiles descended from above, the soft rotten pears and apple cores. The police appeared in the aisles. There was a silence, only to be followed by more catcalls and yells.

Guido stopped, slamming his hands down on the keyboard.

He was about to rise from the bench when he suddenly saw

418

Tonio turn and resolutely gesture for him to stop his protest. Then came a sharp little nod: continue.

Guido commenced playing, though he could hear and feel nothing of what he was doing. The strings came in for the moment blurring those cries, but now challenged they rose louder.

Tonio's voice was rising, too, and nothing had shaken him. He was singing those first few passages with the same conviction and beauty that Guido had dreamed of. And Guido was almost in tears.

Then suddenly the great hollow of the house reverberated with an unbelievable noise!

A dog had been loosed on the first floor, and howling and barking, it scampered frantically towards the orchestra.

It seemed the entire first tier was on its feet in a roar of outrage. The Cardinal Calvino was signaling furiously for order.

Guido had stopped.

The orchestra had stopped. The *abbati* were cursing the dog, and now the police streamed into the gallery as well as the pit, and there were scuffles and cries as a score of culprits were dragged out to be whipped before being returned to the theater.

Guido sat perfectly still at the bench staring forward. He knew in a matter of seconds the theater would be cleared, not by any authority, but by the example of the lords and ladies who would start filing out of the first tier to leave this rabble to exhaust itself. He was sickened and unable to reason.

The *abbati* were one solid roar in his ears, and through a glaze of bitter tears, he looked up again to that horseshoe of infuriated faces.

But something was happening. Something was changing. The dog gave out its last piercing yelps as it was dragged away, and suddenly a deluge of orderly clapping drowned out the hoots and the stamps and the laughter.

Bettichino had returned to the stage. He had thrown up his hands for order.

His face was contorted with rage, red to the roots of his blond hair, and he shouted in full voice:

"Silence!"

An approving roar went up all around, drowning the last volley of hoots and curses.

"Let the boy sing!" Bettichino cried.

419

And at once the first tier signaled its assent in loud applause, all sinking again to their chairs, as the *abbati* settled en masse, picking up their scores and righting their candles.

Bettichino stood glaring before him.

The house went absolutely quiet.

And then, throwing his cape over his shoulder, Bettichino composed his face, and turned slowly towards Tonio. The most innocent smile blossomed on Bettichino's features; he extended his hand to Tonio. He bowed to him.

Guido stared speechless at Tonio as Tonio stood absolutely alone in this void of relentless light and perfect silence.

Bettichino clasped his hands behind his back and assumed an air of one who is waiting.

Guido shut his eyes: with an emphatic nod he spread out his hands, hearing the rustle of the musicians around him, and then all of a piece they commenced the introduction to the aria.

Tonio, placid as before, his eyes fixed not on the audience before him, but rather on that distant masterly singer, opened his mouth and right on pitch as always let loose the first gilded stream of melody.

Slow, slow, Guido was thinking, and into the second part Tonio went, only now beginning the more intricate passages, the back and forth, the up and down, the slow building of trills with ease and control, until returning again he commenced his true ornamentation.

Guido had thought he was ready for it, but instantly he adjusted himself: Tonio had chosen that very one note trill that Bettichino had done so perfectly and was now sustaining it with the very same rhythmic pace of Bettichino's aria and not his own, though to anyone else the shift would be indistinguishable. The note was limpid, sparkling and growing stronger and stronger as, trilling it all the while, he commenced now to swell it and diminish it. He was performing both of Bettichino's feats simultaneously and with perfection, but it was going on and on, that note stretched across infinity. Guido himself could no longer breathe, and feeling the hairs rise on the back of his neck, he saw Tonio's head lift ever so slightly as without a break Tonio now ascended in the most exquisite passage, rising and rising until he found that very same note again, only a full octave higher.

Slowly, slowly he swelled it, slowly he let it pulse from his throat, this very limit of what the human voice could attain,

420

yet so velvet smooth and soft it seemed the loveliest sigh of grief drawn out and out until one could not endure it.

If he breathed now, no one saw it, no one heard it, they knew only he had plunged down in that same languid pace, singing softly of sadness and pain, and taking it lower now into the full raw throb of his contralto, where he stopped with the slightest catch of his head and stood motionless.

Guido bowed his head. The boards beneath his feet shook with the obliterating roar that rose from every corner. No rabble's din would equal such a sound as these two thousand men and women thundering their shared adoration. Yet Guido waited, waitied, until from all over the first floor he heard the voices he must hear: the *abbati* themselves screaming "Bravo, Tonio! Bravo, Tonio!" and then just when he had told himself in this sweetest victory he did not care, he heard from all sides a second cry: "Bravo, Guido Maffeo!"

Once, twice, a hundred times, he heard those two cries intermingling. And then just before he rose to take his bows, he looked up to see Tonio motionless as before, his eyes not on anyone beyond the painted world that surrounded him. Rather he was looking silently to Bettichino.

Bettichino's eyes were narrow, his face distant. And then slowly he yielded to a long smile, nodding as he did so. And when that happened it seemed the house renewed its torrential clamor.

15

IT WAS PAST MIDNIGHT; the theater reverberated with the tromp of those pouring into the streets, with the laughter and shrieks of those descending the pitch-black stairwells.

Tonio slammed the door of the dressing room, quickly latching it. He pulled off the gilded pasteboard helmet, and resting his head against the door, he stared at Signora Bianchi.

Almost at once a pounding started. The door rattled violently behind him.

He stood catching his breath, and all of his exhaustion descended upon him. For four hours he and Bettichino had vied with one another, every aria a new contest, every encore full of new triumphs and new surprises. He could not quite believe now that it had happened; he wanted others to tell him it had been as he felt it was; and yet he wanted not to be near anyone, but to be alone, and he saw sleep in waves coming to bear him out of this room and away from all those who clarmored so loudly to get into it.

"Darling, darling," Signora Bianchi said. "The hinges are going to break, you must open it!"

"No, get me out of this first." He moved forward, ripping off the pasteboard shield that was fixed to his arm, and throwing aside the wooden broadsword.

But he paused, struck by the horrific figure in the mirror. A woman's painted face, crimson lips, eyes etched in black, and this Grecian garb with gilded breast plates to make up an unearthly warrior.

He removed the powdered wig, yet still it was even more hellish than the girl Pirra he'd been when the curtain first went up, this Achille with his tunic stained with sweat, his face so white it might have been a carnival mask, and just as concealing.

"Get it off, all of it," he said, his hands moving clumsily, Signora Bianchi struggling to help him.

He pulled on his regular clothes; he scrubbed at his eyes and his skin.

And at last, a frayed young boy, slightly red of face with a glossy mop of black hair fallen down to his shoulders, stood facing the door, ready to receive the first screams and embraces.

Men and women he didn't know, the players in the orchestra, Francesco the violinist from the conservatorio, a young harlot with lovely red hair—all of them beat him with their arms, lips leaving their wetness on his cheeks, as several servants crowded in, gifts in hand, waiting to present them. There were letters for him that each courier demanded he read and answer now; flowers were being carried in, and the impresario Ruggerio crushed him so hard to his chest that he almost lifted him off the floor. Signora Bianchi was now sobbing.

Somehow or other he'd been pushed into the vast open space outside his door, a great hanging backdrop creaking as he fell against it. Paolo's voice suddenly rose above the din calling "Tonio, Tonio!" and he found himself thrashing about until, seeing Paolo's outstretched arms, he caught him up and held him to his shoulder. Someone steadied him meantime. A

422

tall gentleman clasped his right hand and deposited it in a tiny jeweled snuffbox. It was impossible to bow; whispered thanks went in the wrong direction. A young woman had kissed him suddenly on the mouth, and in a panic he almost fell backwards. And no sooner had Paolo's feet touched the floor again than people were trampling him.

But Tonio quickly realized Ruggerio was pressing him back into the dressing room where a half-dozen little padded silk chairs had been arranged and the dressing tables were banks of fragrant flowers.

He fell down into a chair; another woman had appeared, surrounded by liveried gentlemen it seemed, and suddenly grabbing in her hands a whole mass of soft white blooms, she pressed them right to his face and he laughed out loud, feeling all that coolness and softness. Her blue eyes were puckered in a silent smile as he looked up. He nodded his gratitude.

And then there was Guido. Guido who had slipped in against the wall and was staring at him with the most remarkable expression. His mind shot back unerringly to that moment in the Contessa Lamberti's house when he had first sung, and there was that same brimming pride and brimming love. He rose up into Guido's arms and held him in a long moment of dark concealing silence until the room around him fell still, and no one was there, only he and Guido. Or so it seemed. And so it didn't matter.

Somewhere far off, Ruggerio was making polite excuses. A voice returned: "But my mistress is waiting for an answer." And Signora Bianchi was horrified to discover that Paolo's right hand was cut and bleeding. "Good God, a dog has bitten you!" But none of this penetrated. Guido's heart was beating against Tonio's heart, and then ever so gently Guido guided him back to the chair and, holding his arms, said:

"We must go now and pay our respects to the great singer. . . ."

"Oh, no, not through that crowd!" Tonio shook his head. "Not now . . ."

"We must, and now . . ." Guido insisted, and with a faint smile, he said, "It is very, very important that we do so."

Tonio rose obediently and Ruggerio and Guido on both sides shoved him through the crowd towards yet another mob at Bettichino's door and into the singer's more spacious, brilliantly lit dressing room. It seemed in fact a parlor where some five or six men and women were already seated with their wine, and Bettichino still in his costume and paint rose immediately to greet Tonio.

In a moment of confusion, the room was emptied at Bettichino's insistence, except for Guido, who stood just behind the singer, his face silently urging Tonio to be his most courteous.

Tonio bowed his head. He spoke softly.

"Signore, I've learned much from you tonight. I could not have learned it had we not performed on the same stage. . . ."

"Oh, stop it," Bettichino scoffed. He laughed out loud. "Spare me such nonsense, Signore Treschi," he said. "We both know this was your triumph. I must apologize for my devotees, but I doubt they ever set a better stage for a rival."

He paused. But he was not finished. He drew himself up as though he were in the midst of a little debate, his expression intensified by the paint he still wore, gold dust and white gloss.

"You know," he said, "it's been too long since I gave my best on any stage anywhere. But I gave it tonight, you saw to it that I had to give it. And for that I thank you, Signore Treschi. But don't meet me on those boards tomorrow night, or the next, or the next after that without everything God gave you. I'm ready for you now. You'll need it to stand up to me."

Tonio blushed deeply, his eyes moist. He was smiling, however, as if he couldn't prevent it.

And then as if reading Tonio's thoughts, Bettichino suddenly opened his arms. He held Tonio tight for an instant and then let him go.

Tonio was in a quiet delirium as he opened the door. But he stopped as behind him he heard Bettichino say to Guido:

"This isn't really your first opera, is it, Maestro? Where are you going after this?"

16

HUNDREDS CROWDED the Cardinal Calvino's reception, which lasted till dawn. The old Roman families, visiting nobles, even royalty, passed through his vast and brilliantly illuminated halls.

The Cardinal himself presented Tonio to many in attendance, and Tonio found it deliciously excruciating finally, the never-ending praise, the soft recounting of various moments, the gracious greetings and soft clasping of hands. He smiled at the disparaging remarks on Bettichino. Bettichino was beyond question the greater singer, no matter what anyone said.

But Tonio had made them all forget that for a little while.

Even the Cardinal himself had been moved by the performance, and drawing Tonio aside finally, struggled to describe his response.

"Angels, Marc Antonio," he said with subdued amazement, "what are they, what is the sound of their voices? And how can one who is corporeal sing as you did tonight?"

"You are too generous, my lord," Tonio answered.

"Am I wrong when I say it was ethereal? Do I misunderstand? At some point in the theater they came together, the world of the spirit and the world of the flesh, and from the fusion, your voice rose. I saw about me worldly men, laughing, drinking, enjoying themselves as I see men everywhere, and then they would hearken in perfect silence to your singing. So was it but the highest level of their sensual pleasure? Or was it rather a spiritual pleasure become, for the moment, earthbound?"

Tonio marveled at the Cardinal's seriousness. He was warmed by the Cardinal's obvious admiration, and he felt he might gladly give up the crowds now, the drink, the sweet delirium of the evening just to be alone again with the Cardinal and talk of these things for a while.

But the Cardinal took him by the hand and led him back to the others. Liveried servants opened the double doors on the ballroom and they were to be lost from each other again.

425

"But you have taught me something, Marc Antonio," the Cardinal confessed in a quick, furtive whisper. "And that is how to love what I do not understand. I tell you not to love what is beautiful and incomprehensible would be vanity, not virtue." And then he gave Tonio a small ceremonial kiss.

Count Raffaele di Stefano had his compliments for the music also, confessing the opera had never much affected him in the past. He stayed ever close to Tonio, though he did not much talk to him, watching all those around Tonio with jealous eyes.

And the sight of Raffaele tantalized Tonio as the evening wore on. It brought back the bedchamber vividly and there were moments when Raffaele seemed a creature who should not be clothed as other men at all. The thick hair on the backs of his wrists appeared incongruous under layers of lace, and Tonio had to turn his eyes elsewhere or he would have left with Raffaele right then.

If there was one disappointment, it was that Christina Grimaldi had not come.

Everywhere he looked for her. He could not have missed her, and he could not understand why she was not there.

Of course she'd been at the theater, he'd seen her! And he understood that of course she wouldn't come backstage. But why wasn't she here at the Cardinal Calvino's house?

The most abominable thoughts occurred to him. He felt himself slipping into nightmare thinking of her witnessing the spectacle of him dressed as a woman. But then he had bowed to her, and she had returned the bow from the Contessa's box, her little hands working furiously with applause after his arias, her smile quite visible to him even over the gulf that separated them.

Why wasn't she here now?

He couldn't bring himself to ask Guido or the Contessa, who was ever at his side.

Many had come this evening merely because the Cardinal Calvino was giving a ball. And the Contessa had made up her mind to see that as many guests as possible met her musicians and would come to the opera tomorrow even if they never had been to the theater before.

But the success of the opera was almost assured.

It would run every night right through to the end of the carnival, Ruggerio was certain, and both Tonio and Guido were approached several times in the evening about their future plans.

Bologna, Milan, even Venice was mentioned.

Venice! Tonio had excused himself at once.

But it thrilled him, this talk, just as it thrilled him to be presented over and over again to the royal guests.

At last he and Guido were alone together. The door was locked. And confessing a slight amazement at the heat of their desire, they made love.

Afterwards, Guido slept, but Tonio lay awake as if he could not let the night go.

Finally, the winter sun was spilling in dusty shafts onto the tiled floor, and Tonio was walking alone back and forth through these grand and cluttered rooms, staring now and then at a heap of gifts and letters as tall as himself as it rose from a round marble table.

He put the wine aside, and sent for some strong coffee.

And bringing up a chair, he commenced to shuffle through all this crisp and decorated parchment. He told himself he was not looking for anything. He was merely doing what had to be done. But he was looking for something.

Oh, the Venetian names were everywhere. A chilled and quiet person inside of him read the greetings of his cousin Catrina, realizing, against her word, she was here. Well, he would not see her. He was too happy now for that. And the Lemmo family, they too had been in the audience, and other Lisani, and a dozen others whom he scarcely knew.

So the world had seen him lost in that feminine guise uttering sounds that belonged to children and gods. Old nightmares, old humiliations, it had been as marvelous as his wildest dreams.

He took a deep swallow of the hot and aromatic coffee.

He read through a handful of little notes full of warm superlatives, reliving odd moments of the performance as he did so. And then sitting back, whistling with the edge of one stiff letter, he realized at this very hour the *abbati* were probably gathered in the coffee houses to relive it all again as well.

There were invitations here of all sorts. Two from Russian nobles, one from a Bavarian, another from a powerful duke.

427

And several were for late night suppers after the performance, and they intrigued him the most.

He knew what was expected here. And he felt the lure of it, as if a distant street band were summoning him by means of a rhythmic beat that penetrated the very walls.

He thought of Raffaele di Stefano and just how long it would take him now to dress and go to Raffaele's house. Raffaele would be asleep, the room would be warm. But then sleep nudged him ever so gently and he folded his arms and sat back, shutting his eyes.

There was nothing here from Christina. And why should there be?

Why should there be?

Yet rousing himself he took one more look. And as he fanned out those letters which remained unopened, he saw a handwriting he knew.

He couldn't place it. And opening the letter, he read the following words:

My Tonio,
What has befallen you would have defeated a lesser man. But you made it your victory. Therein lies a measure few could live up to. Tonight you made the angels take heed. May God go with you always,

Alessandro

And then almost as an afterthought, the address of his lodgings in Rome was scribbled at the bottom.

It was almost an hour later that Tonio, fully dressed, emerged from the palazzo. The air was bracing and clean, and he walked the few narrow streets that separated his house from that mentioned in Alessandro's note.

And when the door of Alessandro's room opened and Tonio lifted his eyes to that familiar face, he felt himself shaken as he had seldom been in his life. He had never felt so cold, so small suddenly, standing in that empty passage, though he had long ago met Alessandro's height.

Then he felt Alessandro take hold of him, and for the first time since he had left Naples, he was near to tears.

He stood very still, the tears stinging him slightly, but never breaking loose, and it seemed a wave of pain silently inundated him. It was Venice in this room, Venice with its

428

tangled alleyways, and those immense rooms that had once been all of Venice for so many years. And when all of this fell away in an instant, it left him naked, monstrous, humiliated.

Tonio forged the gentlest, slowest smile. And as Alessandro placed him silently in a chair, he watched that old languid grace with which Alessandro seated himself opposite, and reached for the decanter of red wine.

He filled the glass beside Tonio. And together they drank.

But they did not speak.

Little had changed in Alessandro. Even the delicate mass of lines that threatened the surface of his skin was precisely as it had been before, merely a veil through which one could see the timeless radiance perfectly.

He wore a dressing gown of gray wool, with his chestnut hair loose on his shoulders. And every movement of his delicate hands brought back with it a wealth of muted and agonizing impressions.

"I'm so grateful that you came," Alessandro said. "Catrina made me swear that I would not approach you."

Tonio nodded respect for that. God knows he'd told Catrina enough times that he would see no one from Venice.

"I had a purpose in coming to you," Tonio answered, but it was as if it were someone else's voice. He himself was locked silently inside and wondering: What is it you see when you look at me? Do you see these long arms, this height already stretching itself towards the grotesque? Do you see—? He could not continue.

Alessandro was giving him his most respectful attention.

"It wasn't only love that brought me," Tonio went on, "though love would have been enough. And that I must know how it is with you. I could have suffered the loss of all that, with never seeing you. I must admit it. Because I would have saved myself so much pain."

Alessandro nodded. "What, then?" he asked compliantly. "Tell me. What can I tell you? What can I do?"

"You must never tell anyone that I asked you this, but are the bravos of my brother, Carlo, the same men who served him when I was last in Venice?"

Alessandro said nothing for a moment. Then he answered. "Those men disappeared after you left. The inquisitors of state searched everywhere for them. There are other men in his employ now, dangerous men. . . ."

Tonio nodded. But he showed no expression.

429

It was, very simply, as he had hoped. They had fled for their lives. Italy had swallowed them. Someday, somewhere, perhaps, he would catch a glimpse of those faces, and he would take the opportunity when it arose. But they were not important to him. It was not inconceivable that Carlo had found a way to silence them forever.

And it was only Carlo who awaited him now.

"What else can I tell you?" asked Alessandro.

After a pause, Tonio said:

"My mother. Catrina wrote that she was ill."

"She is ill, Tonio, very ill," Alessandro said. "Two children in three years, and the loss most recently of yet another."

Tonio sighed and shook his head.

"Your brother is as unrestrained and imprudent in this as in so much else. But it is her old illness, Tonio"—Alessandro's voice dropped to a whisper—"as much as anything else. You know the nature of it."

Tonio looked away, his head slightly bowed.

After a long pause he asked, "But did he not make her happy!" His tone was softly desperate.

"As happy as anyone could, for a while," Alessandro said. He studied Tonio. It seemed he was weighing both sides of a question.

"She weeps for you, Tonio," he said. "She has never stopped weeping. And when she learned you would perform in Rome, it became her obsession to see you. It is one of my solemn charges that I must bring her the score of the work and as detailed an account of all I saw as I can possibly remember." He smiled faintly. "She loves you, Tonio," he said. And then, his voice dropping so low it was all but unaudible, he said, "Hers is an impossible position."

Tonio absorbed these words silently, without looking at Alessandro.

When he did speak, his voice was strained and unnatural.

"And my brother?" he asked. "Is he faithful to her?"

"It seems he must have as much of life as if he were four men," Alessandro said.

Alessandro's face hardened. "He has done marvelously well in public life, but for his insatiable desires few men admire him privately."

"Does she know?"

"I do not think that she does," Alessandro said. "He is

430

very attentive to her. But of women he cannot get enough, nor of gambling, nor drinking. . . ."

"But these women," Tonio said, his voice a monotone, his fingers touching Alessandro's hand for emphasis, "tell me about them, what sort are they?"

Alessandro was obviously puzzled by the question. He hadn't considered it before. "All sorts." He shrugged. "The best of the courtesans, surely, wives who are bored, girls even now and then, if they are especially pretty and easily corruptible. I think it matters only that they be pretty and that there be no scandal attached to it."

He studied Tonio's face, apparently trying to divine the importance of this to Tonio.

"But he is ever wise and discreet. And to your mother the sun and moon, so small is her world. But he cannot give her the one thing she wants, which is . . . her son Tonio."

Alessandro's face grew pensive and sad.

"She loves him still," Tonio whispered.

"Yes," Alessandro said, "but when had she the slightest will of her own? And I tell you there were times in the past months when she would have left her house on foot to come to you had they not restrained her."

Tonio shook his head; he was suddenly spending himself in a series of little movements as if he could not contain all of this, and did not want to give way to tears, but could not help it. Finally, he settled back in the chair and drank the wine Alessandro had offered him.

When he looked up, his eyes were reddened and vacant and very tired. With his open hand he made a gesture of helplessness.

Alessandro was watching him, and impulsively he reached out and clasped Tonio's shoulder.

"Listen to me," he said. "He is too well guarded! Day and night, inside his house and out of it, four bravos follow him."

Tonio nodded with a bitter twist of a smile. "I know. . . ." he whispered.

"Tonio, to send someone against him might only mean failure, and it would arouse his fear. And there is too much talk of you in Venice now already. There will be more talk after last night's performance. Go out of Italy, Tonio, bide your time."

Again, Tonio gave a slight bitter smile.

"Then you never believed it?" he asked softly.

Alessandro's face became so violent in an instant he seemed not himself. He winced, and his mouth lengthened in a sneer. In a tone full of dark irony, he said: "How can you ask?" Then he drew very close to Tonio. "If I could I would kill him myself."

"No," Tonio whispered, shaking his head. "Leave him to me, Alessandro."

Alessandro sat back. He looked into his wine, and moving the cup ever so slightly to make it swirl, he lifted it to drink. Then he said: "Give it time, Tonio, give it time, and for the love of God, be careful! Don't give him your life. He has taken too much already."

Tonio smiled again and taking Alessandro's hand, he crushed it softly to comfort him.

"I'm there," Alessandro said, "whenever you need me."

A long silence fell between them and it was easy and simple as though they had so long been friends that nothing need be said. For a while, Tonio seemed lost in his memories.

Finally, his face brightened and softened, and some glimmer of well-being returned to him.

"Now," he said, "I want to know how you are, and how it's been with you. Are you still singing at San Marco? And tell me, last night were you proud of your old pupil?"

It was an hour later that he rose to go. The tears came back, and he wanted the embrace to be quick.

But it seemed as their eyes met for the last time, all of Tonio's past thoughts about this one he so loved were revealed to him, the innocent superiority of that boy who had thought Alessandro less than a man, and all the suffering heaped upon those old considerations—all of this visited Tonio as he stood in the door.

And he realized the full measure of what lay unspoken between them, that both were of the same ilk, but neither for the world would say so.

"We'll meet again," Tonio whispered, unsure of his voice. And very unsure of the words he'd just spoken, too, he slipped his arms around Alessandro and held onto him just for an instant before turning and hurrying away.

*   *   *

It was almost noon. He would have to sleep, and yet he could not. And walking on past the Cardinal's house as if he did not even recognize the gates, he found himself finally in one of those many Roman churches he didn't know, full of shadows and the scent and light of hundreds of candles.

Painted saints peered down on him from gilded shrines, black-dressed women moving silently towards the distant crib where the Baby Jesus opened His arms.

And wandering the alcoves, Tonio saw a saint he'd never known. And in the shadows before the little altar he went down on his knees, and then stretched out full length on the stones, burying his face in his arms as he cried and cried, unable to stop himself even for those gentle Roman women who knelt beside him again and again to whisper some small comfort.

17

FOR THE NEXT WEEK, Guido and Tonio lived and breathed opera as never before. All day they went over the "mistakes" and the weaknesses of the previous night's performance, Guido scribbling changes in accompaniment and giving Tonio a refinement of instruction never possible in the past. Signora Bianchi ripped stitches, adjusted panniers, sewed on new lace and paste jewels. Paolo was ever ready for the slightest errand.

Bettichino outdid himself with trills and high notes while Tonio bested his every trick. In the duets, their voices created a singular loveliness unrivaled in the memory of those who heard them, and the theater, silenced over and over by these flashes of brilliance, quickly erupted in shouts and Bravos. A thunderous applause followed every curtain.

Society congregated without cease in the first and second tiers. Foreigners swelled the card games and suppers, and every performance was sold out before Ruggerio even opened the doors.

Each night Guido struggled through the backstage corridors,

pushed and shoved by the crowd, agents at his elbow with offers for seasons in Dresden, Naples, Madrid.

Flowers were brought in, snuffboxes, letters tied with ribbon. Coachmen were waiting for answers. The glum Count di Stefano nodded once again patiently when a firm Maestro insisted Tonio was not yet free for the social whirlwind.

Finally, after the seventh successful performance, Guido sat down in the cluttered dressing room with Signora Bianchi to make a list of those invitations that Tonio must accept first.

For now, he could see Count Raffaele di Stefano any time he wanted. He could go tonight.

Guido had no doubts any longer. His pupil had passed every conceivable test. He had offers from some of the best opera houses in the world. And for the first time, Guido accepted Ruggerio's assurance that the opera would run through the carnival.

But Guido, tired as he was, had not fully felt his exultation until early the following morning when he awoke to see Tonio by his bed, gazing out of the open window.

Count di Stefano had taken Tonio away that evening almost by force. They'd quarreled, made it up, and driven off. And though di Stefano's devotion alarmed Guido somewhat, he had also found it amusing.

He, himself, free of the Contessa, who had gone back to Naples, had spent a delicious four hours with a young dark-skinned eunuch from Palermo. The boy—Marcello was his name—sang well enough for small parts, Guido had told him that frankly.

And then it was lovemaking of the slowest, most rapturous and delicate sort, the young one a master of every sensuous secret. His skin had smelt like warm bread, and he'd been one of those few eunuchs with plump little breasts as delectable and succulent as those of a woman.

He'd been grateful afterwards for the few coins Guido pressed in his hands. And begging to be allowed backstage, had promised to buy a new frock coat with the money Guido gave him.

Guido, realizing these delightful encounters awaited him nightly, was trying to take it in stride and think like a human being.

Now it was almost dawn and a cold wintry light filled the room like a vapor as Tonio turned and approached him.

434

Guido rubbed his eyes. It seemed to him Tonio was cov-- ered with tiny pinpoints of light. He realized that these were droplets of rain, yet Tonio seemed an apparition, the light sparkling on his gold velvet coat, on the white ruffles at his collar, and on his softly mussed black hair. When he sat beside Guido, he appeared full of a shimmering energy as if he had not slept the entire night.

Guido sat up and put out his arms. He felt Tonio's lips brush his forehead, and then his eyelids, and then that close, utterly familiar embrace.

Tonio seemed splendid and almost miraculous to him in this moment, and then Guido heard him say in a low voice:

"We've done it, haven't we, Guido? We've done it!"

Guido sat silently looking at Tonio, a delicious air washing over him from the open window. It was full of the scent of rain. And an odd thought came to him, random, beautiful, that the winter wind smelled as fresh suddenly as if he were far, far away from the decay of the city, in the open hills of Calabria where he had been born.

But in the grip of this moment, with all of his life before him, the past, the future, he could not speak. He had worked so hard, he was so tired. And his mind was too unaccustomed to such happiness.

Yet he knew he was answering Tonio with his eyes.

"We can do it now, can't we?" came Tonio's low whisper. "We can make a life for ourselves if we want it. It's all there."

"If we want it? If, Tonio?" Guido said.

The room was so cold. Guido found himself looking past Tonio, at the milky sky. The gray rain clouds appeared substantial and to have their own luminous, almost silver terrain.

"Why do you say 'if'?" he asked gently.

Tonio's face had become unspeakably sad.

But this may have been an illusion because when he looked up at Guido again he smiled.

His black eyes crinkled at the corners, and there was such a radiance to his expression that Guido found himself feeling an inevitable sorrow: he could never really merge with Tonio and become part of that beauty himself, forever.

"We're going to Florence next." Guido took both Tonio's hands. "And then who knows where we'll go? Dresden, maybe, maybe even London. We'll go anywhere we want!"

And he could feel a tremor passing from himself into Tonio. Tonio was nodding, and it seemed this moment was too perfect really to endure. But Guido was silently and completely thankful for it.

Tonio was now in his own thoughts, and a stillness had settled over him, sealing him off, and what was left to Guido was the vision of his youth and that radiance.

And Guido realized that as he looked at him he was recalling an image of Tonio he had only lately seen, an image painted exquisitely on porcelain which had given him this same overwhelming and almost mysterious sense of Tonio.

He was seized with a small excitement. Almost tenderly, which was not usual for him, he kissed Tonio, and then he rose, and placing his feet on the chill floor, he walked silently across the room and, in the clutter of his desk, found that small porcelain portrait. It was oval in shape, framed in gold filigree, and he could not see it now in the dark. He hesitated, staring at the dim figure on the side of the bed.

And then he put the picture in Tonio's hands.

"She gave it to me days ago to give to you," he confessed, and he did not examine the pleasure it gave him now to present this little gift to Tonio.

Tonio looked at it, his neglected hair falling out of its ribbon so that it veiled his face.

"She's captured you perfectly, hasn't she? And from memory, completely." Guido shook his head.

He stared down at the little image, the white face, the black eyes. It was a white flame burning in the center of Tonio's open palm.

"She'll be angry with me," Guido said, "for having forgotten it."

But he hadn't forgotten it. He had only waited for a moment such as this when all was quiet and still, for once, and he did not know why it gave him this little satisfaction.

"And how has it been with her?" Tonio whispered. It had a thin sound to it as though he had drawn in his breath with the words, rather than letting it out. "Living alone in Rome, painting portraits."

"Oh, she is quite the rage." Guido smiled. "Though lately I think she has been spending much too much time at the opera."

Guido watched as again Tonio lowered his eyes to the portrait.

436

At every curtain call it seemed Tonio looked up to Christina's box and made her a low, graceful bow. And she, bent over the rail, beamed down at him, her hands in a little flurry of clapping.

"But how is it with her!" Tonio pressed. "Does no one look out for her! Does the Contessa not . . . ? I mean . . ."

Guido waited for a moment and then he turned slowly and went to his desk. He sat down, looking off at the window and the sky that was brightening and changing its shape, devoid of stars, yet revealing the sun's first wintry shimmer.

"Has she no family that cares what she does?" Tonio whispered. "And what would they think if they knew she sent such a gift to a . . ." But again he broke off, holding the little portrait in both hands now as if it were dreadfully fragile.

Guido could not help but smile.

"Tonio," he said softly, "she is an independent young woman, and lives her life as we do ours." And softening his tone even more, he asked, "Must I be the one to give you away again?"

At once caught up, it seemed, and joined up to Christmas's box, and made her close the coach low. And she went over the cell, leaning down at her, her face in a muddle flurry of sleeplook . . .

"Bel boy, is it with her," Tinto rocked. "Does no one look out for her? Does the Countess not . . . ? I often . . ."

Tinto stared for a moment and eye to be turned slowly and went to his desk. He sat down, looking off at the window and the sky that was brightening, and observing, he slowly moved . . .

"I am asked spending in am," first softly murmur . . .

"Ha, she no family that obey is to shouldness," Tonto whispered. "And what would stop think? . . . How much she care so to wait to a . . . "Thus much no hope of having . . .

he little trouble in the trouble now, will it work It means to begin.

. . . lookers will not help be upellie . . .

"I only," he said softly, "she is an independent young woman, and have her life as we to him . . . And within this rate even more, he asked . . . Must I be the one to have you anyway about."

PART VI

A S SOON AS HE HAD taken his final bows, Tonio forced his way through the suffocating backstage press to his dressing room and, telling Signora Bianchi to send Raffaele's coachman away with polite regrets, quickly changed his clothes.

He had sent his note to Christina after the second intermission, and the remainder of the performance had been something of an agony for him.

Finally as the last curtain came down, Paolo had put her answer in his hands.

But it was not until he was fully dressed as himself again, his hair still a tangled mess, that he tore open the note:

The Piazza di Spagna, the Palazzo Sanfredo, my painting studio on the top floor.

He was unable to do anything for a moment. It seemed Guido had come in with some momentous news about an Easter season in Florence, and the insistence for the first time that they play every major house in Italy before going away.

"They're going to need an answer very soon on this," Guido said, tapping the scrap of paper in his hand.

"But what is it, why do they need to know now?" Tonio murmured.

Signora Bianchi came in, shutting the door with difficulty. "You must go out only for a few minutes," she said, just as she did every night.

". . . because it's this Easter we're talking about, forty days after we close here. Tonio, Florence!" Guido said.

"Right, yes, I mean of course, we'll talk about it, Guido," Tonio was stammering, trying vainly to comb his hair.

Had he folded her note and put it in his pocket? Guido was pouring himself a glass of wine.

Paolo slipped in, red in the face, and collapsed with exaggerated relief against the door.

"Go out there, Tonio, now, get it over with!" said Signora

Bianchi. And turning him, she shoved him towards the crowd.

Why was this so difficult? It seemed they all wanted to touch him, to kiss him, to talk to him, to take his hand and tell him how much it had meant to them, and there was the feeling with all of them that he did not want to let them down. Yet the more he smiled, nodded, the more they talked, and by the time he had made his way inside again, he was so frantic he took the wine from Guido and drank all of it.

The usual flowers were being brought in, great bouquets of hothouse flowers, and Signora Bianchi whispered in his ear that Count di Stefano's men were outside.

"Damn," he said. He felt Christina's note in his pocket. It had no signature, but he took it out quite suddenly and while Guido and Paolo and Signora Bianchi stared at him as if he were a madman, he burned it completely by the candle flame.

"Wait a minute," she said as he turned to go. "Just where are you off to? Tell me and tell the Maestro before you go."

"What difference does it make!" he said crossly, and when he saw the secretive smile on Guido's face, the feigned superiority to the childish passion, he was silently enraged.

As soon as he stepped into the corridor, he saw Raffaele's men. These weren't servants. These were the Count's bravos.

"Signore, His Excellency wishes to see . . . ."

"Yes, well not tonight, he cannot," Tonio said quickly and started for the street.

For one moment it seemed the men were not going to let him pass. But before he reached for his sword or did anything equally foolish, he made an icy refusal again. Obviously they weren't prepared for this, and confused as to what to do, did not have the courage to force him into the carriage waiting outside.

But as he climbed into his own carriage, he saw they had mounted their horses, and telling his driver to take him to the Piazza di Spagna he made a small plan.

At the Palazzo Sanfredo the carriage slowed to a crawl. It was at the second alleyway beyond that, the little coach all but scraping the walls, that Tonio slipped out, shutting the door quickly, and stood back in the darkness to watch the Count's bravos pass.

Now the moment had come.

He entered the lower door of the palazzo and seeing a torch blazing on the landing, stood still looking up. The stairwell

441

might have been a street, it was so neglected, so cold. And gazing at it, he let his mind empty of thought. He knew what thoughts would be there, too, if he let them in; that for three years, no, four, he had not held a woman in his arms, save this woman. And that he could not escape what lay ahead of him, though in truth he had no idea how it might end.

At one point, he told himself in a low humming inarticulate way that this would be a resolution. He would not find her beautiful; he would not find her sweet. He would be freed of her then.

Yet he did not move.

And he was quite unprepared when the door opened and two Englishmen entered, talking in their native tongue, who immediately greeted him in a convivial way. They seemed positively in awe of his height, though they themselves were slightly taller than Italians tended to be. He was mortified. They stared at him because he was hideous, he was perfectly sure of it, and coldly he watched them go up the stairs.

It occurred to him that if there had been a mirror near about he might have looked in it and found the overgrown child he saw now and then; or perhaps once and for all a monster. He was musing. Sadness was coming over him, weakening him, and it occurred to him that it would be so easy for him to go to the Count tonight and this girl, then finally insulted by him, would shun him from now on.

He was slightly amazed when he put his foot on the first step and went up.

The door to her studio was open, and the first thing that he saw was the firmament, a pure heaven of blackness and vivid stars.

The room itself was vast and barren and unlit, and there were these great windows reaching high above him, straight forward and to his right, and a broad slanted pane of glass set into the ceiling which opened up even more of the night.

His steps sounded hollow; and for a moment he felt himself losing the surety of his balance, as though the sky surrounding this little pinnacle of earth in the midst of Rome were moving as it might about a listing ship.

But the stars were wondrous to him. He could see the constellations in magnificent clarity, and he allowed himself in this long moment to breathe deeply of the cool fresh air which came from all about him, and to turn very slowly under the heavens, as if he had nothing to fear in the world, and he felt himself suddenly small and very free.

It was only after this that the objects of the room revealed themselves, a table, chairs, and paintings mounted on their easels with dark figures described against whiteness, and clusters of bottles and jars, the smell of turpentine cutting through ever so suddenly the deeper more delicious smell of painters' oils.

And then he saw her, Christina, shrouded in shadow as she stood against the farthest corner of the windows, her head covered with the loose folds of a hood.

A fear gripped him, as debilitating as any he had ever known. And all the difficulties he had envisioned came to plague him: what would he say to her, how would they begin, and what was to pass between them, what was taken for granted, why were they both here?

He felt a tremor in his limbs, and glad of the darkness, he bowed his head. Sorrow was coming into this lofty open room; sorrow was walling it up and extinguishing the night itself. It seemed to him then this girl was too innocent and the memory of her beauty collected in his mind to form an almost ethereal shape.

But in reality a dark mysterious form approached him, and out of this hollow place came her voice saying his name.

"Tonio," she said, as though some intimacy already connected them, and he found himself touching his own lip as he heard her speak, her voice low and almost sweet.

He could see her face now under the hood, and the hood itself struck some note of terror as if reminding him of those friars forever accompanying the condemned to the scaffold, and he reached out, easily closing the gulf between them, and pushed the hood down from her hair.

She didn't move away. She wasn't afraid! Not even when his fingers caught in her stiff waves, forcing the gathered strands apart, and closed on the back of her head. She came near.

And suddenly rising on tiptoe, she gave her whole young body to him under its wrapping of thin wool and lace, and he felt the buttery softness of her little chin, her lips so innocent they had no hardness, no skill for the kissing, and then he felt her tenderness dissolved suddenly as her body was shot through with the most palpitating desire.

It invaded him, it infected all of his limbs, his mouth

443

drawing it up out of her lips and the warm sweet flesh of her throat and then from the roundness of the tops of her covered breasts.

He stopped, pressing her head to him so hard he might have hurt her, and then it seemed he buried his face in her hair, lifting it in glancing handfuls that even in this dark wintry room gave off their glints of yellow. He felt the tiny tendrils on his face, and stopping again, he let out a soft sound to the air.

She drew back and, taking his hand, led him to another room.

Even her fingers felt strange to him and precious, sheathed in that soft liquid flesh. He caught her hand and put it to his mouth.

A bed was before them, set against the far wall, a distant jumble of shrouded furnishings surrounding it, as if the room itself were never used.

"Candles," he whispered to her. "Light."

She stood still as if she didn't understand. And then shook her head.

"No, let me see you," he whispered, and drawing her up again on her toes, he tossed her very lightly up and caught her so that he was holding her eye to eye. Her hair fell forward as if to conceal them both and for a moment, he did nothing except feel the trembling inside himself, and her little tremors passing into his own.

Carrying her cradled in one arm, he was barely conscious of latching the door. And finding a small candelabrum, he brought it with him up into the bed itself, which he closed all around, its heavy velvet curtains giving off the thick smell of clean dust. And then as he struck the match and touched the flame to one candle, and another and another, the light filled up this entire little room of drapery and softness, and she was kneeling there in front of him, her face a marvel of lovely contrasts, her eyes that smoky blue with dark gray lashes that were wet as if she'd been crying, and her lips a virgin pink that had never been rouged. And now quite by surprise, he saw her dress beneath the black cloak she wore was that exquisite violet silk casting its ethereal glow on her cheeks, giving her rounded breasts a preternatural whiteness as, mounded above the ruffles of her bodice, they seemed almost to glow. Violet tinged the edges of her, made the palest shadows in her cheeks that were covered with the tenderest white down.

But though he saw all of this in a glance, it was her expression which went to his soul. And it frightened him, quickened his already driving pulse, because he perceived in the flesh a spirit harbored there as steely and as fierce as his own. She was not afraid of him; she was enrapt and brave and full of will, and she reached out now and, catching the candles, implored him with her eyes to blow them out.

"No . . ." he whispered. He reached out and hesitated, wanting to touch her face. How much easier it was to touch the rest of her in the dark; then his fingers felt that faint white down, and the flesh under it which made him grimace as if with pain. And then her face lost its seriousness; the smoky eyebrows, caught in their frown, became long and like strokes of the pencil above her radiant eyes. And the tears rose, blurring and magnifying the blue color and holding it as if afraid to flow.

He snuffed the lights, and drawing back the curtains on the dim illumination of the room, turned to her, made for her, and even as she shrank back, alerted by his urgency, he stripped off her silk and ruffles and saw her breasts fall free.

She gave out a little cry. She struggled against him and again he caught her up and held her with kisses, feeling her teeth suddenly behind her lips, and the melting softness of that flesh just above her lip, turning her, tilting her so that it was not a mouth any longer but some little portal alive with malleable flesh.

Then he let his own clothes drop around him, crushed under them both, and mounting her, lay down low between her legs, his head against her breasts.

Passion was coarsening him, it was driving the sight and scent of her together before him, and as he closed his mouth on her, first one nipple and then the other, he felt her stiffen under him, and pulling up his knees, he pulled her up too, as if trying to keep her safe for the moment from himself.

Her hair fell over his naked shoulders; her forehead was a warm stone against his cheek; and the hotness of her breasts, swollen and melting against him, was all his dreams made material, and it was sweetness, sweetness and yielding that she was, and unable to draw it out, to have her forever in all her secret parts like a flower broken open petal by petal to his fingers, he had to have her now.

445

He felt her struggle as he suddenly pinned her down. She stiffened and he quieted her with his lips, his hand approaching the wet hair between her legs.

And when she cried out very softly in fear, he held back waiting, waiting, touching that secret flesh there and feeling it grow fuller, its pungent smell rising right to his brain.

She was enfolding him with her arms, drowning herself in him and then finally she lifted her hips and he drove into her, feeling that tightness snap against him, his body now beyond his command. And it was then on the brink of his endurance that he felt the barrier of her innocence and went straight to ecstasy.

She was crying. Clinging to him, she was crying, with one small hand lifted to wipe the wet strands of hair from her face. He sat up in the bed, his arm anchoring her, his eyes staring down at her small bent form under the shower of her hair, and he felt as he lifted her face, he would die if she were to pull away.

"I didn't mean to hurt you . . ." he whispered. "I didn't know. . . ."

But her little mouth opened to him as giving as before.

Her naked limbs, helpless, a collection of fragrant shadows and shapes cleaved to him, and there on the sheet lay the dark stain of her virginal blood.

And though he spoke to her again softly, comforting her, enfolding her with language and kisses, he heard these words of his as if they were outside of himself and far far away. He was simply and madly in love with her. She belonged to him. The sight of the blood on the sheets pushed every other rational thought out of his mind. She was his and she had been no other man's before, and he felt madness, he felt lust; he felt the course of his life shaken and obscured like a thin road winding north over an earthquake, and he felt terrified, and that absolutely blind necessity to *make* her feel pleasure came over him as he had watched it come over the Cardinal in those first confusing nights only months ago.

Months ago! It seemed years; that was as distant and fantastical under the moon of time as Venice had become.

He wanted to take her again now. He would show her such skill and gentleness, *now*, that all her pain would melt away like the blood flowing between her legs, he would kiss that spot and all the silky flesh between her thighs and under her

446

arms, and under the heaviness of her white breasts, and he would give her not what any man might give her, but all the secrets of his patience and his skill, the frankincense and the wine of all those other nights spent lapping love for love's sake when there was not this precious one, this trembling one, this vulnerable one in his arms.

Mystery, mystery, he whispered, and the pounding in him commenced.

2

WHEN HE AWOKE at ten in the morning in his own bed in the palazzo, he quickly set to work at warming his voice with Paolo in a series of difficult duets. Then he dressed in his favorite gray velvet coat and tapestried vest, snow white lace, and his heaviest sword, and went immediately to the Via del Corso, where his carriage came up alongside that of Christina and he slipped into her compartment as stealthily as he could.

She was a vision, and he set upon her, kissing her roughly, and would have taken her right there in the carriage if he could have persuaded her.

Her hair was warm, full of a cooked fragrance from the morning sun, and as she squinted ever so slightly, her dark lashes made her eyes seem all the more translucently blue and lovely. He touched the edge of her lashes with the insides of his fingers. He found himself in love with her slightly pouty and full lower lip.

But if he let it, the sadness would come over him again, and when he felt that, he stopped kissing her and just held her. He'd lifted her onto his lap; he cradled her in his right arm; her hair spilled down a shower of corn yellow over him and then her face took on that beguiling look of innocence and seriousness, generously mixed, and he said her name to her for the first time:

"Christina." Mocking, he tried to say it as the English said it, the way she said it, making the sound a solid block, his face scowling, but then he couldn't and he said it as an

Italian, the tongue in the front of the mouth so that all the air passed through the syllables: it sang.

She laughed, the most mercurial laugh.

"You didn't tell anyone I was there last night," he demanded suddenly.

"No, but why shouldn't I tell anyone?" she asked.

The little treble of her voice, demanding such respect, magnetized him. It was almost impossible to pay attention to her words.

"You're young and foolish and don't know the world, obviously," he said. "I won't leave you the worse for it. I couldn't bear the thought of it. And you have no care for yourself."

"And are you leaving me so soon?" she asked.

He felt himself stunned by the question; he wondered if his face betrayed his feeling. But he could concentrate on nothing now except that he was near her, holding her in his arms.

"Then let me frighten you away from me once and for all," she said. "Let me tell you how little I care for the world."

"Hmmmm . . ." He was trying desperately to listen. But she was too totally appetizing and the pertness with which she said her words was so especially delicious. Determination emanated from her as if she were really a human being and not some luscious creature, for surely she couldn't be human, and such loveliness couldn't harbor a brain.

No, this was nonsense, it was only that all of her was so inviting, and yet she was chirping so clearly and fiercely with intelligence.

"I don't care what others want of me," she was explaining. "I've been married. I was obedient. I did what I was told."

"But to a man too old to remember his rights or privileges, I gather," Tonio answered, "and you are young and you're an heiress, and you can marry again."

"I am not going to marry again," she said, her eyes narrowing just a little as the sunlight flickered through the overhanging leaves. "Why must *you* say these things to me?" she asked with genuine curiosity. "Why is it difficult for you to understand that I want to be free and to paint, to have my studio, to have my life as I please?"

"Ah, you say this now," he said, "but you may not say it later, and nothing will harm you more than indiscretion."

"No." She touched his lips with her fingers. "This is not

448

indiscretion," she said. "I love you. I have always loved you. I loved you from the first moment I saw you years ago, and you knew it. You knew it even then."

"No." He shook his head. "You loved what you saw on the stage, in the choir loft. . . ."

She almost laughed. "I loved you, Tonio, and I love you now," she said. "And there is no indiscretion in loving you, and it would not matter to me if there were."

He bent forward to kiss her, believing her for the moment, the sweetness of her youth and innocence alchemized into something stronger and finer that he could feel when he held her.

But still he said softly, "I'm afraid for you. I don't completely understand."

"But what is there to understand?" she whispered in his ear. "Those years in Naples, didn't you see out of the corner of your eye my unhappiness? You were forever watching me." She kissed him and laid her head against him.

"What can I tell you about my life? That I paint from dawn till dark. I paint at night by poor light. I dream of commissions, chapel walls, the walls of great churches. But ever more I find that faces are what I want to paint, the rich and the poor, all those who are making such a fashion of me, and others I find sometimes in the street. Is that so hard to understand? A life like that?"

His hands could not stop touching her, stroking her, drawing back her rippling yellow curls only to have them tumble gently down again.

"Do you know what I am?" she said with the most lovely smile. "I have known such happiness in the Piazza di Spagna, that I have become a simpleton."

He laughed.

But very quickly his expression altered as he became absorbed. "A simpleton," he whispered.

"Yes, an idiot of sorts." She frowned. "I mean that rising I think of painting, and going to sleep I think of painting, and for me there is only the slight difficulty of getting enough hours in the day. . . ."

He understood. In his worst moments, when he could not stop thinking of Carlo and of Venice, when it seemed the very walls of the Palazzo Treschi had descended upon him and the light was Venetian light, he longed for that simplicity of which she spoke. And it would have been his, save for all

449

that. Guido had it, a divine simplicity because music was his consuming passion, his work, his dreams. And in the last seven days as Guido had worked night and day beyond the point of exhaustion, his face, in that simplicity, had been curiously blank.

"But for love and loneliness," she was saying now and her voice had become distant and poignant, ". . . but for love and loneliness, my life as it is would be a gift from God."

"Is love all it takes, then?" he whispered. "Is my love all it takes to make it God's gift?"

She rose up, slipping her arms about his neck and the light flickered behind her, golden and green and then dark, and he shut his eyes, clasping her, holding her all over with his long broad hands and he felt her smallness and her softness and it seemed to him that if he had ever known such happiness before he'd forgotten it, and would never forget this no matter what came after it.

There was a lightness and a swiftness to all they did as the morning moved towards noon.

To a series of shops they went, Christina in search of old paintings for which she bargained as fiercely as any man. She knew the proprietors and in some instances they were expecting her, and through a clutter of dusty treasures she made her way confidently as if she'd forgotten for the moment that Tonio was there.

He was delighted with these dark and crowded places. He looked at old manuscripts, maps, swords. He found a sheaf of Vivaldi's music and other more ancient folios which he purchased at once.

But most of the time, he watched Christina in abject fascination as the art dealers haggled and pleaded with her only to give in finally to her price. She bought fragments of Roman sculpture, which Tonio helped the coachman wrap carefully in old bedding and secure to the carriage, as she explained she would paint from these models. She bought portraits, cracked and darkening, but still full of rich and lively detail.

There was an ease to being with her. Her self-possession excited him; and without realizing it, he loved this sense of her life as full of substance; he listened to her talk of her treasures, how she must learn better to paint hands and feet, how she must study the flowers, the drapery, how this was good and that was poor.

450

He had that wondrous sense of having always known her, been with her, enjoying this gentle companionship with her, and yet she was new to him so that every gesture, every toss of her yellow hair, quietly astonished him.

The carriage moved out of Rome, going south through the open country full of ruins, a great aqueduct here swallowed in vines, and now and then a column standing erect to mark some moldering sight. She talked softly of the beauty of Italy and how it had been the landscape of her dreams when she discovered it, and her husband, ever gentle with her, had taken her everywhere, letting her sketch and paint as she pleased.

For a while Tonio knew where they were, not far from the Contessa's villa, but then they moved on, farther south and towards the sea, and were soon passing down a long avenue of barren poplars that lifted their thin spikes to the blue sky.

A house lay ahead, stretching its long rectangular facade straight to the right and the left, its surface variegated with weather and deep cracks, all of the ocher paint that had once covered it soft now and peeling so that here and there it fluttered like the petals of a vine. Yet it gleamed in the drenching sun, blind windows gaping dark as they neared it. And Christina, taking Tonio's hand, led him through the open front door.

Leaves swept across the dark stones. Rustling came from the shadows as fleet little hens scurried out into the light. And the bleat of sheep could be heard rising hollow and haunting under the high ceilings, and here and there straw was thrown in stacks against painted walls, and a river the rain had made cascaded down through murals to the wreckage of old furniture.

"What house is this?" he asked her. She had wandered ahead of him, her height giving her a majesty as she lifted her skirts just above the floor, the ripples of her hair flowing down her back below her waist.

He stood still. Almost trembling he looked at this vision of ruin and it took him back, back over the years to some sunlit moment in Venice when he had stood in empty rooms such as these, his tambourine in his hand; and the music rose, rhythmic and fierce for the moment, only to die away as he shut his eyes and felt the sun on his eyelids in a melting warmth.

The air was stirring about him. He felt no sorrow, no regret. And when he opened his eyes again he saw the day

451

cutting shafts through the windows, and the earth rising and tilting in the distance, and he felt this place like a great skeleton of a house thrown open to the rains and the breezes and the smell of green things and things growing in the earth.

She was beckoning him from the stairs.

"It's my house," she said as he followed her, her hand resting on his arm, "if I choose. Do you give it your blessing?" She gave him the most innocent and suddenly vulnerable look. "I can go all over Europe painting; I can do portraits everywhere, and maybe even the great church paintings of my dreams; but then I can come back, here, to this house, my home."

He followed her up the stairs, and into a vast salon from which he could look down on the countryside below. The grass grew as high as wheat blowing away from the long gray lattice of the poplar trees. The low-hanging clouds were tinged with gold.

She was standing before him, very still, her face round and small, the cheeks so soft to look at he wanted to hold her face in both his hands.

But he felt her vitality in this moment; he had felt it keenly when only moments ago she had spoken of her dreams. And it struck him now that all around him were men and women, a great society of beings, who knew nothing of such vitality, such dreams. Guido knew, of course; Bettichino knew; all those who worked and lived for music knew. And she knew.

And it separated her from the contessas, the marchesas, from the counts, from all those exquisitely draped and ornamented humans who made up the audience that nightly cheered him and applauded him. And he felt himself on the verge of understanding her, the things she said, the things she did, the sheer force of her, and how she had always seemed so alone to him even when she was dancing years ago in those crowded rooms.

He was looking at her, staring into her darkening and troubled eyes.

And he wondered what he had thought she would be, some carnal loveliness that would give him a great lost strength? And here she stood, that shell of what she had seemed to him—mindless and beautiful and beyond reach—broken open to reveal *her* in her shuddering completeness. And now seeing what seemed sorrow in her face—what must be sorrow—he drew her near to him to take her in his arms.

He held her face; he smoothed the hair back from her eyes, and he gave himself over to her as she surrendered, so that on a bed of hay they made love, bringing to each other their own warmth.

He dreamed of snow.

Not since Venice had he seen snow, and never such heavy snow, blanketing snow, snow that so obliterated everything. Yet he dreamed that he awoke in this very place to find the land covered with it, pure and white for as far as he could see. The naked poplars were glistening with ice, and snow shone in the crooks of their spiked branches. And soft flakes fell, weightless and magnificent, down over the whole world and into those broken windows as well, so that even the floor around him was carpeted with this stunning whiteness.

She was here with him; but not so that he might touch her. And he realized that on the far wall there were a hundred figures drawn whom he had not seen before, archangels with huge wings and flaming swords, driving the damned below, and saints who looked to heaven in constricted agony. Black chalk had formed these impressions which now seemed so swollen with life it was as if her hand had brought them out of the wall where they had lain captive; and he saw their knotted brows, the clouds above their heads boiling in the sky as below the flames leapt up to consume the defeated sinners.

It terrified him, this picture, its immensity, and her small form before it, her hair spilling down her back, her skirt swaying softly as she moved from place to place, her hand outstretched to blur the form of what seemed inevitable and immutable.

But when she turned he saw that she too was touched by the snow, that it drifted through the open windows to bright flecks upon her skirt, her breasts, her sloping shoulders. Her hair was alive with snow, and it blew in gently to cover both of them.

What did it mean, this snow, falling on this unlikely place? Even in sleep, he wanted desperately to know the answer. Why this extraordinary peace, this shining beauty? And then looking out over the rolling land again that lay beneath a pearlescent sky, he thought he was not in Italy at all, but far away from all he loved and feared and counted upon for meaning. Venice, Carlo, the slow progression of his life towards chaos, these things did not exist! He was merely in the wide world and no particular place, and the thin fall of the snow grew thicker, whiter, more dazzling.

He felt her arms around him as he stood there. He felt the angels and saints glowering from the wall, and he loved her and he knew he was no longer afraid of her.

He awoke.

The sun was hot on his face, and he lay in the straw alone and it was the end of the afternoon, and for a long time he did not move, not even to reach for her. Slowly through the shadows he perceived that a great cartoon did cover the wall just as he had seen it in his dream and surely before he'd fallen asleep, though he did not remember it. And she was there too, standing before it.

3

EVERY NIGHT after the final curtain, he rushed out, slipping from his carriage in the Via del Corso so that he might hurry through a muddy tangle of streets to the Piazza di Spagna to meet her in secret, as Raffaele's bravos were still following him.

An old servant, withered and brown, was always scuttling about, dusting and arranging meaningless things, her tiny black eyes scorning Tonio as if he were "men," and at the sight of her he felt an instantaneous fury. But out of the smoky colors of the room, Christina would disentangle herself to slip forward and quiet him. She took his kisses like a drug, her lids half mast, and melted silently to be held for a long time, before she begged to be allowed to paint him.

He was trembling. It seemed his love was an agony. All the pure excitement of the stage fused to make him hungry and desperate.

But he would nod his head. He let her step back and away, and never had he wanted anything in all his life so much as he wanted her and he felt helpless.

The whole studio was soon ablaze with candles, the high windows turned to mirrors by the swelling light, and setting him down in front of her, she took out paper, tacked it to a board, and commenced to draw him in pastel, which she rapidly colored in as her fingertips became covered with it.

He was often lulled by the rhythmic scratching of the chalk while all around faces peered down on him, lush, magnificently fired, some men and women he knew, others spun to mythic size against massive skies and clouds so real they seemed on the very verge of predictable movement. From a distant frame the Cardinal Calvino towered gently over him, vibrant, unmistakably himself, and engraved there with a strength that vaguely tormented Tonio.

Her talent was beyond doubt. Her figures, robust, familiar or strange, closed in on him with irrepressible vigor.

And in the core of it all, she worked, her hair alive and writhing in the light, becoming more and more bizarre to him. He wondered would she be angry if she could guess his thoughts: that she seemed as exotic in this place as a white dove flown down from some lofty height to play with perfect time upon a harpsichord. So sensuous she was, so seemingly desire incarnate. How could her form contain wit and talent and such will? It was tantalizing to him beyond belief.

And feeling himself on the brink of trance, for his own sweet torment, he imagined her reading books, for surely she did all the time, or writing tomes of philosophy, for he wouldn't have put it past her, and then he came round again to her furiously working hand caked with chalk as she broke piece after piece in two to make a small disaster of her workcase. She must have freedom to lay on colors in frantic little strokes, her face shimmering with absorption as he watched dully, wanting only to ravish her.

But there was time enough for making love.

And he feared the moment after, he would feel the pain all the more.

Some dim memory hacked at him of being in a splendid place full of music, and the music suddenly stopped, and fear creeping up to take hold of him. It seemed Vivaldi's music, the racing violins of the *Four Seasons*. And he could feel the emptiness of the air when it was finished.

Finally she completed her picture. For ten whole days he had been in her thrall, given over to the opera and to her, and no one and nothing else.

It was near to dawn, and she held it up to him and he let out a small gasp.

455

Bland innocence she'd captured in that enameled miniature she'd sent through Guido. But in this he sensed a darkness, a brooding, even a coldness that he had never known he revealed.

Not wanting to disappoint her he murmured simple things. Yet he put it aside and came near her, sitting right beside her on the wooden bench and taking the chalk out of her hand.

Love her, love her, that was all he could think or feel or propel himself to do, and once again he had hold of her, wondering on the thin membrane that separated cruelty from overpowering passion.

To love someone like this, it was to belong to that one. All freedom went the way of reason, and happiness had for itself a perfect place, a perfect moment. He held her close, unwilling to speak, and it seemed her soft hot bones, tumbled against him, told him only the most terrifying secrets.

Love, love, the having of her.

He took her to the bed, he unfolded her, and laid her down; he sought to lose himself in her.

And there came that time together he had known so often with Guido in the past, when the body was at last still and he wanted only to be near her.

The table had been draped. The candles brought in. She lifted a dressing gown to his shoulders, and led him there where the old woman had laid out wine, and plates of steaming pasta. They dined on roasted veal and hot bread, and finally when it was all done, and too much, he took her on his lap, and both of them, shutting their eyes, began a small game of hands and kisses.

Soon it worked into this: that while he blindly felt the bones of her small face, she would blindly feel the bones of his; and as he clutched her tiny shoulders, she would hold onto his, and so on until they knew all the parts of each other.

He began to laugh; and she as if given his assent then was laughing like a child, as all the parts of their bodies were contrasted. He felt that silken lower lip, her round smooth belly and the backs of her knees, and picking her up, carried her to the sheets again to find all those moist crevices, those downy folds, those warm and throbbing parts that were hers alone as the morning hovered at the windows.

It was dawn; the sun spilled in. He sat at the window, his hands folded on the sill, and he wondered that he thought silently of Domenico, or Raffaele, of the Cardinal Calvino, who still made pain in him and something like the zing of violins.

He had loved them all, that was the wonder. But nothing in this quiet time remained of those loves that could conceivably torment him. Guido, Guido he loved more now than ever, but that was full and quiet and no longer wanted passion.

And what was this?

He felt half crazed. And the peace of his dream of snow was beyond him.

He looked at Christina.

She lay deep asleep on her bed. He felt himself husband, brother, father to her. He wanted to carry her out of this place and far, far away from here, but to where? To some place where snow fell? Or back to that villa beyond the gates where they could live together forever? A terrible fatality came over him. What had he done in this? What had he truly wanted? He was not free to love anyone, not even to love life itself.

And he knew if he did not get away from her now he would be lost to her always. Yet feeling her unaccountable power he wanted to cry almost. Or to lie beside her again and just hold her.

Any cruelty she wished she could work on him soon, that was how desperately he loved her. And then he saw that in all his loves he'd never been afraid, not even of Guido had he ever been afraid. But he was afraid of her, *afraid* of her, and he did not know why, only that it was a measure of the power she had to wound him.

Yet she would never do this to him. He knew her. He knew her shadowy places. He sensed at the core of her some grand and simple goodness, for which he yearned with all his soul.

And moving swiftly to the bed, he slipped his arms under her and held her until slowly, very slowly, her eyes opened, and blindly she stared upward.

"Do you love me?" he whispered. "Do you love me?"

And as her eyes grew big and soft and full of sadness to see him like this, he felt himself open completely to her.

"Yes!" she whispered, and she said it as if she had just fully come to know it.

Days later, on an afternoon when half of Rome, it seemed, was gathered in her studio, the sun pouring through the naked windows, men and women chatting, sipping wine and English tea, reading the English papers, she bent over her easel, her

457

cheek smudged with chalk, her hair held indifferently by a violet ribbon. And he from the sidelines gazed at her and realized he belonged to her. Such a fool you are, Tonio, he thought, you only add to your own pain. But it had not even really been a decision.

4

GUIDO KNEW that something was wrong, and he knew that Christina had nothing to do with it.

The Roman carnival was almost upon them, the opera had been running successfully for weeks, and yet Tonio would not discuss any future engagements. No matter how Guido pressed, Tonio begged to be let alone.

He claimed exhaustion, he claimed distraction; he claimed that he must go to Christina's. He claimed that with both of them being received at three that afternoon by an electoress, it was impossible to think of anything.

There were excuses without end. And now and then when Guido did trap Tonio in the very back of his dressing room at the theater, Tonio's face would stiffen, acquiring that coldness that had always struck a chord of muted terror in Guido, as he stammered angrily: "I can't think of that now, Guido. Isn't all of this enough!"

"Enough? It's only the beginning, Tonio," Guido would answer.

And at first, Guido did tell himself it was Christina.

After all, never had he seen Tonio as he was now, completely caught up in this love so that it claimed every moment away from the theater.

But when finally Guido went to Christina in the late afternoon, while Tonio was off to a reception he could not avoid, he was not surprised to hear her denials.

Of course she hadn't discouraged Tonio from accepting the Easter engagement at Florence. She hadn't even been told of it.

"Guido, I'm ready to follow him everywhere," she said simply. "I can paint anywhere as easily as here. I need my

458

easel, my colors, my canvases. It's nothing to go anywhere on earth," and then she dropped her voice, "as long as he is with me."

She had only just let her last guests go home. The maids were clearing away the wineglasses and the teacups. And she, her sleeves pinned up, was working with her oils and pigments. There were glass containers of crimson, vermilion, ocher before her. Her fingertips were red.

"Why, Guido," she asked, brushing back her hair, "why won't he speak of the future?" But it was as if she were afraid of Guido's answer. "Why does he insist upon such secrecy with us, with having everyone believe we are only friends? I've told him if I had my way, he should move into my lodgings! Guido, everyone who cares to know, knows he is my lover. But you know what he said? This wasn't very long ago, and it was late, and he'd had too much wine and he said there was no doubt in his mind that for all you'd done for him, you were better for having known him, that you would be all right. 'The wind will fill his sails after this,' he said. But he said I wouldn't be better off if he left me with my reputation ruined, and he couldn't do that for all the world. But why is he talking of leaving, Guido? Until that night, I feared it was you who wanted him to give me up."

Guido knew she was staring at him, imploring him, and though he increased the pressure with which he held her hand, he could not now satisfy her. He was gazing off over the rooftops beneath her high empty windows and feeling the chill of having discovered the old enemy, the old terror.

He said nothing to Christina except that he would talk to Tonio, and then brushing her cheek with his lips gently, he rose to go.

Forgetting his tricorne hat, he went down the hollow stairs and out into the crowded Piazza di Spagna, turning slowly towards the Tiber, his head down, his hands behind his back.

Rome caught him in its winding streets; it led him from one little irregular piazza to another. It led him past great statues and glittering fountains, while his mind seemed to shrink in the face of its perception, only to enlarge with the fullness of realization again.

Hours later it seemed he was wandering the beautiful vari-colored floor of San Pietro's. He was drifting past the majestic tombs of the popes. Skeletons so perfectly made from hard

459

stone, they seemed to have been discovered in it and released from it, grinned at him. The faithful of the world pushed him to and fro.

He knew what was happening to Tonio. He'd known it before he'd gone to Christina, but he had had to be sure.

And the image came back to him, implanted in his less imaginative and literal mind by the more loquacious Maestro Cavalla: Tonio was being slowly torn apart.

It was the battle of those twins he was witnessing: the one who craved life, and the one who could not live without the hope of revenge.

And now that Christina tugged upon the bright twin, now that the opera surrounded him with such blessings and such promises, the dark twin, out of fear, strove to destroy the loving one, for fear if he did not he himself might cease to exist.

Guido didn't fully understand. It was not an easy image for his mind. What he did perceive was that the more life gave to Tonio, the more Tonio realized he could not enjoy any of it until he had settled the old score in Venice.

Guido stood alone in the midst of this endless crowd streaming through the largest church in the world. He knew he was helpless.

"I cannot . . ." he whispered, hearing his own words distinctly against the multitude of sounds about him. "I cannot live without you." The deep shafts of sunlight blurred his vision. No one took notice of him, that he was speaking as he stood there so still. "My love, my life, my voice," he whispered. "Without you, there is no wind to fill my sails. There is nothing."

And that foreboding he had known when coming to Rome— that fear of the loss of his young and faithful lover—was nothing to this ever deepening darkness.

It was a carnival. The nights grew warmer. The audiences were positively mad. The Contessa had returned and gave balls nightly at her villa.

Guido gave up all plans for the spring season. Yet he did not tell the agents from Florence. If only he could force Tonio into one more engagement. Tonio would never go back on his word, and that would give him time. Time was all he could think of.

* * *

But early one afternoon, as Guido was scribbling out a new duet for Bettichino and Tonio to try if they were bored enough—and they were by now—one of the Cardinal's more important attendants came to tell him that Signore Giacomo Lisani, from Venice, was here to see Tonio.

"Who is this?" Guido asked crossly. Tonio was off with Christina in the mayhem of the carnival.

As soon as Guido saw the blond-haired young man he remembered him. Years ago, he had come on Christmas Eve to visit Tonio in Naples.

He was Tonio's cousin, the son of the woman who wrote so often to Tonio. And he had with him a small trunk, more of a casket, that he wished to present to Tonio himself.

He was disappointed to hear that he couldn't see Tonio now. When Guido identified himself, he explained.

Over two weeks ago, in the Veneto, Tonio's mother had died after a long illness. "You see," he said, "I must tell him this myself."

As it turned out, Tonio couldn't be found, and Guido would not have him told just before the evening's performance.

So it was after midnight when this young Venetian who had returned to the Cardinal's house with the casket gave him the message as directly and painlessly as he could.

The look on Tonio's face was something Guido never wanted to see again in his life.

And after Tonio had kissed his cousin and taken the trunk alone with him to his room, and opened it, and stared down into it, he told Guido simply that he wished to go out.

"Let me go with you, or let me take you to Christina's," Guido said. "Don't try to bear this grief without us."

For a long time, Tonio looked at him as if this puzzled him, this statement; and Guido felt the weight of all that separated him from Tonio and always would. That dark life, that secret life of Tonio, connected to those he'd known and loved in Venice, was a life to which he could admit no one here.

"Please," Guido said, his mouth dry and his hands trembling.

"Guido, if you love me," Tonio said, "let me alone now." Even in this there was that gentleness, that half smile, and a hand out to reassure Guido, who watched silently as Tonio withdrew.

* * *

461

The Cardinal soon came into the room.

Guido was alone looking at the objects which Tonio had left open for anyone to see.

And Guido, examining these things carefully, was filled with such a sense of desolation that he could not speak.

The trunk contained many things.

There was music, mostly the work of Vivaldi, in old volumes bearing Marianna Treschi's name in a girlish script. And there were books, French fairy tales, and stories of the Greek gods and heroes of the sort one might read to a child.

But those objects which most surely chilled Guido and caused him to feel the keenest misery were the clothing and effects of a small boy.

Here was a white christening gown, most likely Tonio's, and half a dozen little suits of clothing, all lovingly kept. There were tiny shoes, there were even little gloves.

And finally there were the portraits, enameled miniatures and one very lifelike painting of the exquisite dark-eyed little boy that Tonio had once been.

As Guido looked at these things, he realized they were all those relics of one's life that are treasured by others, but rarely kept by one's self.

And they had been cleared out, packaged up, and sent away to Rome in perfect evidence that no one now remained in the House of Treschi who loved this young man who had once lived there. It was as if Tonio and all those who had once shared his life were dead.

The Cardinal asked again gently if there was anything he might do. He had sent away his attendants and he stood alone, patient, infinitely charitable, waiting upon a musician who had let him linger as if he were a menial at the door.

Guido looked up at him. He murmured some respectful apology for this confusion. And he tried to divine how much this man might care to know of Tonio, and what if anything he did have the power to do.

He watched the Cardinal look at these random treasures.

"Tonio's mother is dead," Guido said softly. But behind those few simple words lay his realization that Marianna Treschi, whom Guido had never seen or known, might have been the very last thing staying Tonio from the inevitable journey to Venice.

5

THE ROMAN CARNIVAL was under way and with it the last, most frenzied nights of the opera. From dawn till dark the narrow Via del Corso was packed with costumed merrymakers, either side of the thoroughfare built up with stands that were jammed with masked spectators. The lavishly decorated chariots of the great families crawled through the street, weighted down with fantastically costumed Indians, Sultans, gods and goddesses. The great Lamberti float had been done on the theme of Venus born from the foam with the little Contessa herself decked out in garlands of flowers as she stood in a great papier-mâché seashell. Behind came the carriages moving inch by inch, their masked occupants showering a confetti of sugared almonds all around while everywhere men dressed as women, women dressed as men, and all manner of costumed anonymities paraded as princes, sailors, the grand characters of the commedia. The same old themes, the same madness . . .

Tonio, masked, his clothes hidden by a long black *tabarro*, pulled Christina beside him, her hair drawn back like a man's, her small body handsomely clothed in an officer's military costume. They ran this way and that, Tonio lifting his draped arm to shelter her now and then from a whirling war of confetti as they ducked and came up to witness the antics of some Pulcinella putting on a wild show, or escaped for a few moments to kiss, to catch their breath, to cling to each other in a church doorway.

But as the day shaded into late afternoon, the crowd was at last cleared for the final exhilarating climax of the race, fifteen horses being led first from the Piazza del Popolo to the Piazza Venezia and back again before being let loose in the former to rush headlong and free toward the latter. It was reckless and full of scintillating danger, the crush of hooves, the inevitable blunders into the throng, the animals finally crashing into the Piazza Venezia for the announcement of the winner.

463

Then as the sun finally set, masks were stripped away, the street emptied, and everyone moved to yet another spectacle—balls throughout the city or the grandest treat of all: the theater.

The opera audience was at its wildest. Though masks were gone, costumes still prevailed, especially the dark and liberating *tabarro*, and the women charmingly turned out in masculine military dress, enjoying the full freedom of breeches, while the opposing camps of Bettichino and Tonio vied in madness to outdo one another.

It seemed the boxes were so burdened they might have actually collapsed, and the theater rocked again and again with generous applause, the cries of Bravo, the stomping, the shouting.

Then all went home—Tonio and Christina in each other's arms—to rise again at dawn for more of the same merriment.

Sometimes in the midst of the crush, Tonio would stand in one spot, his eyes closed, swaying on the balls of his feet, and imagine himself in the Piazza San Marco. The close walls here vanished for the open sky and the golden mosaics shimmering like great unblinking eyes over the multitude. He could almost smell the sea.

His mother was with him, and there was Alessandro, and it was that first glorious carnival when they had at last gotten free, and it seemed the world was nothing but wondrous and full of exquisite marvels. He heard her laughter, felt even the press of her hand in his, and it seemed all his memories of her were complete and untouched by the misery that had come afterwards. They had their life together, and that would remain forever.

He would have liked to believe she was close to him, that somehow she knew and understood all of it.

And if there was any sharp pain now in these days of bitter and secret grief, it was that he had never never been able to talk to her again, to sit with her, her hands clasped in his, to tell her how much he loved her, and how it had all been beyond his power to change.

She seemed as helpless in death as in life.

But when he opened his eyes, when it was Rome again—and the Roman girls ran about tickling those who didn't mask with their wicker brooms, and the men garbed as advocates scolded the crowd, and those the wickedest of all, the young men got up as women baring their breasts and revealing their

464

legs, went offering themselves to others—when he saw all this life around him, he knew what he had always known, there was never ever meant to be a leave-taking of her. Never in his maddest dreams of vengeance or justice had he envisioned even a passing word, an outstretched hand, a sigh of affection. Across a dim vista, he had seen her rather in a widow's weeds, crying among her orphaned children, her husband, the only husband she'd ever really known, murdered, taken from her.

She had been delivered from this. This had been taken away from him. She was not in a widow's black. She slept in the coffin. And it was Carlo who had wept for her. "He grieves as a madman," Catrina had written. "He is beside himself and vows to spare nothing in the care of his children. And though he works harder and harder, swearing he will be mother and father to them, both, he is so stricken he wanders at any hour out of the Offices of State, to roam like a fool in the piazza."

Christina was pressing his hand.

The crowd pushed him here and there, and he struggled for a moment to secure his footing. He saw his mother in the coffin again, and wondered how they had dressed her. Had they put on her those beautiful white pearls that Andrea had given her? He saw the crimson funeral procession moving out over the undulating waves, red the color for death streaming from the black gondolas, and the sea heaving as the soft crying of the mourners was dissolved into the salted wind.

Christina's face was full of love and sadness.

She stood on tiptoe, her arm around him. She was so splendidly real, so warm, as with her lips she sought, ever so gently, to bring him back to her.

They hurried through the Via Condotti. They pounded up the stairs to the studio above the Piazza di Spagna.

And taking deep gulps of wine from the same bottle, pulled the heavy curtains of the bed and made love feverishly and quickly.

As they lay still after, they could hear the distant roar of the crowd, or just below some singular laughter. It seemed to roll up the stone walls and vanish as it reached the open air.

"Tell me what it is," she said. "Tell me what you are thinking."

465

"That I am alive." He sighed. "Simply that I am alive and so very, very happy."

"Come," she said rising suddenly. She tugged at him to bring him up from the warm bed, and threw his shirt about his shoulders. "We have an hour still before you must be at the theater. If we hurry we can see the race."

"That's not very much time." He smiled, wanting to keep her here.

"And tonight," she said as she kissed him once and twice and three times, "we'll go to the Contessa's and this time, you'll dance with me. We've never danced, you and I, for all the balls we attended in Naples . . . together."

When he didn't move, she dressed him as if he were a child, her fingers deftly working his pearl buttons.

"Would you wear that violet dress?" he asked in her ear. "If you wear that violet gown, I'll dance with you."

He was drunk for the first time in a long time, and he knew that drunkenness was the enemy of sorrow. What had Catrina said, that Carlo roamed the piazza like a fool, his wine his only companion?

But the room was crowded and swirling with colors; and the music made a restless rhythm and he was dancing.

He was dancing as he hadn't danced in years and years, and all of the old steps had come back to him magically. Every time he saw Christina's rapt little face, he bent to steal a kiss, and it seemed that this was Naples and all those times he had longed for her.

And it was Venice, in Catrina's lovely house, or it was that long ago summer on the Brenta.

All of his life seemed a great circle suddenly, and here he was, dancing and dancing, turning and bowing in the lively time of the minuet, and all those he loved were around him.

Guido was there, and Marcello, that handsome young eunuch from Palermo who was his lover, and the Contessa, and Bettichino with his admirers.

And when Tonio had come into the room, it seemed all heads had turned; he could positively hear them whispering: Tonio, it's Tonio.

The music floated in the air around him, and when the dancers broke apart, he had a glass of white wine in his hands very quickly and then it was empty.

466

It seemed Christina wanted him now for the quadrille, and gently, he kissed her hand and said that he would watch her.

He wasn't sure quite when he sensed there would be trouble, or when he first saw Guido approaching him.

It seemed since he had come in he had sensed something very wrong in Guido, and he sought now, embracing Guido lightly, to cheer him and make him smile, even if he was resolutely unwilling.

But Guido's face was full of trouble, and there was some urgency to his whispers that Tonio tell the Contessa himself why they weren't going to Florence.

Not going to Florence?

When had they made that decision? It seemed a great darkness came down around the edges of things, and for a long moment it was impossible to pretend any longer that this was Naples or that it was Venice. It was Rome, and the opera was almost finished, and his mother was dead and carried over the sea to be laid in the earth, and Carlo was roaming the Piazza San Marco, waiting for him.

Guido's face was dark and swollen, and he was saying something rapidly under his breath, yes, tell the Contessa, tell her, why we cannot go to Florence.

And it seemed, in that moment, Tonio felt in spite of himself a dark exhilaration. "We are not going, we are not going . . ." he whispered, and then Guido was pulling him down a dimly lit corridor. All these freshly painted walls, panels of mulberry brocade and the fleur-de-lis in gold, and a pair of doors opening.

Guido's voice was all threats and terrible, terrible accusations.

"And what shall we do after that?" Guido demanded. "All right, if we don't go to Florence, then surely in the fall we can go to Milan. They want us in Milan. They want us in Bologna."

And he knew that if he did not stop himself something terrible and final would be spoken. It would come forth out of the darkness where it had waited.

The Contessa was there, and her round little face looked so old. She lifted her skirts with one hand and with the other she was patting Guido's shoulder, almost lovingly.

". . . never intend to go anywhere else, do you? Answer me, answer, you have no right to do this to me." Guido's heart was breaking.

Don't bring it to a head, don't make me say it. Because

once I say it I can't recall the words. It was exhilaration, ever mounting. He felt like one on the edge of a great downward slope. If he took the first steps, he would be unable to control the momentum.

"You've known, you've always known." Was this Tonio saying this? "You were there, my friend, my truest, dearest friend, my only real brother in the world, you were there and you saw with your own eyes, not little boys scrubbed and groomed and marched into the conservatorio like so many capons to market. Guido . . ."

"Then turn your rage on me," he was pleading, "for the part I played in it. I was your brother's tool and you know it."

The Contessa had put her arms around Guido and was trying vainly to quiet him. And far off, he was crying, I cannot live without you, Tonio, I cannot live without you. . . .

But a coldness had settled over Tonio, and all of this remote and sad and unchangeable. He struggled to say you had no part in it. You were but a chess piece moved from one square to another.

Guido cried there had been a café on San Marco and he had been there when the men came and told him that he must take Tonio to Naples.

"Don't speak of all this," the Contessa said.

"It was my fault, I could have stopped it, turn your vengeance on me!" Guido pleaded.

And she, forcing him back, drew Tonio away, her little dark face so very old, and that voice dropping down down for the profession of terrible secrets. The old plea, send assassins, there was no need for him to dirty his hands, did he not know he had friends who could take care of all of it? But say the word and now she guided him to the edges of the room. The moon was out and the garden was alive and far across the garden, he could see the windows of the ballroom they had just left, and he wondered was Christina there? He saw her in his mind dancing with Alessandro.

"I am alive," he whispered.

"Radiant child," she said.

Guido was weeping.

"But he always knew the time would come when he would go on alone. I wouldn't let him go," he said to her, "if he were not ready. They will want him in Milan just as much without me. And you know it. . . ."

And she was shaking her head. "But radiant child, you know what will happen if you go to Venice now! What can I say to dissuade you. . . ."

So it was spoken. It was done. The thing that had waited and waited in the darkness was now free and there was no curbing it.

And again that exhilaration took hold of him. Go to Venice. Do it. Let it happen. No more waiting and waiting in hatred and bitterness, no more seeing all about you life blazing and beautiful yet against this darkness, this fathomless gloom.

But Guido had rushed at him, and the Contessa had thrown all her weight against Guido to hold him back. Guido's face was pure fury.

"Tell me how you can do this to me!" he was crying. "Tell me, tell me, how you can do this to me. If I was just a pawn in your brother's hands, then I took you out of that town, I took you when you were wounded and broken. . . ."

The Contessa, trying so to quiet him, raised her voice.

". . . tell me you wish I'd left you there to die, they would have killed you if I had left you there, and tell me you wish none of this, none of this, had come to pass!"

"No, stop it. . . ." The Contessa flung out her hands.

And now that exhilaration in him was heating itself to anger. He turned on Guido, and heard his own voice, sharp, clear:

"You know why, better than anyone you know why! The man who did this to me is yet alive and unpunished for it. And am I a man, you tell me, am I a man if I can stand for this!"

He felt himself weak suddenly.

He had stumbled into the garden.

At the door of the ballroom, if the servant hadn't taken his arm, he would have fallen.

"To go home . . ." he said. And Christina, her face stained with tears, nodded her head.

It was morning.

It seemed all night they had fought, he and Guido. And these rooms so cold now, were not their bedchambers any longer so much as some dreary battleground.

And somewhere, beyond these walls, Christina waited for him. Awake, dressed, she sat at the window perhaps, her hands under her chin, looking down in the Piazza di Spagna.

469

But Tonio sat still, alone, and far across the void of the room, he saw himself in the dusky mirror, a white-faced specter so seemingly without expression he seemed a demon with an angel's face. And all the world was different.

Paolo was crying.

Paolo had heard all of it. And Paolo had come to him only to be spurned by his silence.

And huddled somewhere off in the shadows, Paolo was crying inconsolably. And the sound, rising and falling, seemed to echo as if through corridors of an immense and ruined house where Tonio shuffled against the wall, his bare feet covered with dust, the tears stinging his face, as coming through the door, he saw his mother bent over the windowsill. Helplessness, terror caught in his throat as he pulled at her skirts, those cries echoing louder and louder. And just as she turned, he covered his eyes so he couldn't see her face. He felt himself falling. His head thumped the walls and the marble stairs, he could not stop himself. And his screams rose above him, and she, her dress billowing out as she came down, took those screams and carried them up in shrieks rising higher and higher.

He stood up. He was standing in the center of the room, staring into that shadowy mirror. Do you love me, he whispered, but without ever moving his lips, and he saw Christina's eyes open like the mechanical eyes of a doll, and Christina's mouth, glistening, formed the one word: "Yeeeeess . . ."

Paolo was near him. Paolo was a sudden heaviness against him causing him to right himself on his feet. From far far away he heard Paolo's crying. Paolo's hands pulled on him till he closed his own long white fingers over them, peeling them off and holding them tight as he stared forward into the mirror.

Why didn't you warn me, he spoke to his reflection, this giant in the black Venetian *tabarro* with such a white face, and this child clinging to him, head bent, his limbs affixed to the black cloth as though he could not be torn off of it. Why didn't you warn me that the time had run out. That it was nearly finished.

And then tugging Paolo with him, he moved clumsily towards the bed. He fell down into the pillows, Paolo nestled close to him, and it seemed Paolo's crying went on and on in his sleep.

470

6

H E WAS STILL TIRED when he reached the theater. He had taken Paolo to a little café where they had both of them eaten too much. He felt light-headed and the world was blazing around him. Colors bled into the rain that sent the maskers scurrying. Paolo wouldn't eat until he saw Tonio eat, and Tonio had given him much too much wine.

It seemed to him that he could not possibly sing. Yet he knew that nothing would keep him from it.

And as soon as he heard the crowd stomping and howling, and caught a glimpse of Bettichino already painted, his body a proud scaffolding of silk and armor, the habitual excitement came to his rescue along with the force of his will.

He took more care than usual with his dress, highlighting his face with white paint as subtly and skillfully as Bettichino always did, and when at last he stepped before the lights, he was his old self again, his voice struggling only a little at first, and then pouring out of him in full strength. He could feel the carnival merriment in the audience, he could hear it in their hoarse and loving shouts of Bravo. For one second he permitted himself the detachment of seeing this entire theater as it rose before him, this smoky wilderness of faces, and he knew this was the night for risks and tricks and all manner of flights of fancy.

Christina came backstage after the first act. It was the first time he had ever let her close to him when he was in female dress, and he put on a jeweled mask before he let her in, and was not surprised to see that his appearance enticed her.

She let out a little gasp, gazing at him. Or rather as she gazed at this woman in plum-colored velvet and white satin rosettes.

"Come here to me, my dear," he said in a mellow whisper just to frighten her. She herself was the little officer complete with epaulettes, her legs shapely in her tight breeches. And she looked more like a timid boychild as she approached him, almost fearfully, and lifted her hand to touch his face. He was smiling down at her, seeing the pair of them perfectly in the mirror, and as he lowered himself into the chair, his skirts spreading out all around him, he placed her on his lap. He saw the taut angular wrinkles of cloth between her legs and wanted to touch them.

He contented himself instead with the silk of her white neck.

She lifted the wine cup and let him taste it, then kissed him eagerly, and he turned her slowly so she could see the vision in the mirror: the tall woman, powdered white with a cat's mask of sequins and red lips, and the young boy with his exquisite face on her lap.

She turned and touched the beauty marks on his face. She pulled away the mask and seeing his painted eyes, let out another half-concealed gasp.

"You frighten me, Signore," he whispered in that same dark feminine fashion; and she, with a little throb in her throat, made as if to assault him.

Her little hand gathered up his skirt, it felt for the nakedness underneath, and finding the hard organ, grasped it cruelly, so that he whispered under his breath, "Careful, my darling, let's not ruin what's left."

She was shocked into laughter. Then pressing against him, she sighed and then lay still. He had never said such a thing to her before, never touched upon what he was with the slightest levity and he watched her now with indulgence as if she were a child.

"I love you," she whispered.

He closed his eyes. The mirror was gone, and so were the garments that covered both of them; or so it seemed to him. And he was thinking dreamily again of how much he'd liked as a child to be invisible in the dark. No one could wound him if he were invisible; and when he looked at her again, she wasn't seeing paint, or wig, or velvet, or satin, but only him, and it was as if they were in that darkness together.

"What is it? What are you thinking when you look this way?" she whispered.

He shook his head. He smiled. He kissed her. And in the mirror saw that shimmering vision of the two of them, lost in disguises, but a perfect pair.

*   *   *

472

But as soon as he reached the studio with her that night, he knew that Guido had spoken to her.

She was ready to leave everything to be in Florence at Easter. All her portraits could be done before the end of Lent, and surely he could wait that long. They could travel to Florence together.

She walked lightly, quickly about the studio talking of how this could be finished, and how that one was almost done. She needed so little to travel; she'd bought a new leather carrying case for her pastels; she had a desire to do many sketches in the churches in Florence; she had never been to Florence, did he know that? She pulled the ribbon out of her hair at just the right moment and let it fall down.

He felt slender and somewhat weightless as he always did after the performance, his masculine clothes so seemingly slight compared to all that Grecian armour, those skirts. And she was still the boy, only now with all this lovely corn-silk hair as if she were a page or an angel in an old painting.

And he stared at her, not speaking, wishing Guido had not told her, and at the same time knowing Guido had somehow made it easier for him. But these last nights with her . . . these last nights . . . what had he wanted them to be?

He could feel nothing wanting now as he looked at her, and she was showing him no sadness, no fear.

He beckoned for her to follow him into the bedroom, and she was in his arms suddenly, letting herself be lifted and carried. "Ganymede," he whispered to her, feeling her voluptuousness through the breeches, and beneath the hard doubled-breasted front of her little coat.

It was as it had been in the café with Paolo; he felt sleepy and yet wildly alive, assaulted by colors everywhere that he looked. He felt the texture of the sheets between his fingers, the moist and warm flesh at the backs of her knees. Her shoulders were bathed, it seemed, in a bluish light from the candles, and gathering her to him, he wondered how long he could sustain it? When would come the awful, wrenching pain?

When she was softened with love, she lit the candles again. She poured the wine for both of them and commenced to talk.

"Everywhere in the world I'll go with you," she said. "I'll paint the ladies of Dresden and London. I'll paint the

473

Russians in Moscow; I'll paint kings and queens. Think of it, Tonio, all the churches, the museums, the castles of the German countries with their multitude of towers and turrets on the mountain peaks. Tonio, have you ever seen those northern cathedrals, so full of stained glass? Imagine it, a church of stone instead of marble with arches rising high and narrow, soaring as if to heaven, and all those tiny fragments of brilliant color made into angels and saints. Think of it, Tonio, St. Petersburg in winter, a new city fashioned after Venice and blanketed with lovely white snow. . . ."

There was no desperation in her voice, but her eyes had a dreamy glitter, and without answering her, he pressed her hand as if to say, Go on.

Guido hadn't really taken these last few blissful hours from him; there was an eerie beauty to understanding everything so clearly.

"We'd go everywhere, the four of us," she was saying. "You, Guido, Paolo, and me. We'd buy the grandest traveling coach and we'd even take that wicked old Signora Bianchi. Maybe Guido would bring that handsome Marcello, too. And in every city we'd get some sumptuous lodging, taking our meals together and quarreling together and going to the theater together, and in the days I'd paint and in the nights you'd sing. And if we liked this place better than another, we'd stay and maybe now and then go off in the country to be alone, all of us, and away from everything, as we grew all the more to love and understand one another. Imagine it, Tonio."

"I should have run away with the opera," he murmured softly. She bent forward, her golden eyebrows knitted in concentration, and when she saw he wouldn't repeat it, she kissed his lips.

"We'd take the villa I showed you only a month ago, and that would be our real home. We'd come back when we were weary of foreign tongues, and how Italy would blaze around us! Oh, you can't imagine how it would be! Guido could write sonatas in the evenings, and Paolo would grow up to be a marvelous singer. He'd make his debut in Rome.

"But we would all belong to each other. No matter what happened, we would have each other, as if we were a great family, a great clan. I've dreamed it a thousand times," she said. "And if life could give you to me after all those dreams of girlhood, then this too can come true.

474

"What was it you said to Paolo when you took him from Naples?" She paused, watching him intently. "Paolo told me the story himself: you said to him that anything can happen, when you least expect it. And his life is like a fairy tale of palaces and riches and endless song. Tonio, anything can happen, you said it yourself."

"Innocence," he said. He bent forward to kiss her. He stroked her face, marveling at that ineffably soft and almost invisible down that covered her cheeks and he touched her lip with the tip of his finger. She could never be more beautiful than she was now.

"No, not innocence," she protested. "Tonio, this is a choice."

"Listen to me, beautiful one," he said almost sharply, his voice a little harder than he wanted it to be. "You love me very much as I love you. But you've never really known the love of men; you don't know their strength, their necessity, their fire. You speak of northern cathedrals, stone and stained glass, of different kinds of beauty; well, I can tell you with men it's the same, a different kind of love. And in time you'll come to know that the wide world holds secrets for you in the ordinary acts that others take for granted, the ordinary strength of any man. And don't you see, when all is said and done, that is what was taken from both of us, that is what was taken from me?

"What do you think it means to me to know that I can never give you what any common laborer might give you, the spark of life inside of you, the child in which we two could be one? And no matter how you protest that you love me now, how can you say the day won't come when you will see me for precisely what I am!"

He could see he was frightening her. He had hold of her shoulders, so fragile and exquisite, and her lips were trembling, her eyes almost incandescent on the edge of tears.

"You don't know what you are," she said, "or you would not say this to me."

"I'm not talking about respectability anymore," he countered. "I can believe you now when you say you don't care for marriage, that it doesn't matter to you if they talk about you, and vilify you for loving a eunuch singer. You've convinced me you're strong enough to turn your back on that. But you don't know what it's like to hold a man in your arms, and do

475

you think I could bear to see the look in your eyes when you were done with me, and ready for others. . . .''

"Is it so wrong of me to find in you a gentleness uncommon in men!" she demanded. "Is it so strange I prefer your fire to another fire that might consume me? Can't you see what it would be, our life together! Why should I want what anyone can give me when I can have you! After you, what will it matter? What will have any value? You are Tonio Treschi, you have the gifts and greatness in you for which others strive all their lives and to no purpose. Oh, you anger me, you make me want to wound you suddenly because you will not believe in me! And you will not believe in what it would be like for us together! And you make this choice for both of us, and I can never forgive you for it. Do you understand! You gave yourself to me for such a little while! I can never forgive you for it!"

She was bent, her naked breasts beneath a veil of yellow hair, her hands covering her face, her sobs short and strangled and shaking her violently.

He wanted to touch her. He wanted to comfort her, beg her to stop. But he was too angry, and too miserable.

"You're merciless," he said suddenly. And when she looked at him, her face tear-stained and swollen, he went on, "You're merciless to the boy I was and the man I might have been. You're merciless because you don't see that every time I take you in my arms I *know* what might have been between us if . . ."

She placed her hands over his lips. He was staring at her in utter perplexity, and then he lifted her hand away.

"No." She shook her head. "We would never have known each other," she said. "And I swear to you on everything I hold sacred, your enemies are my enemies, and those who hurt you hurt me. But you are speaking not just of vengeance but of death. You mean to end your life for this! Guido knows it. I know it. And why! Because *he* must know, isn't it? *He* must know it's you who've come to kill him after all he's done to you. *He* must know it's you!"

"That's right," he said softly. "That's right. You put it better and more simply that I have ever been able to put it."

Long after he'd thought she was asleep, her tears spent, her limbs wound hot and moist with his, he laid her gently back on the pillow and went alone in her studio and sat by the window looking up at the sweep of tiny stars.

The rain clouds were gone on a swift wind, and yet the city glistened, cleansed and beautiful under the slice of moon, a hundred little lights flickering on balconies and in windows, in the cracks of broken shutters throughout all the narrow streets below him under shining roofs.

He wondered would she ever in the years to come understand? If he turned away now, he would be turned away forever, and how could he live with that weakness in himself, that awesome failure, that he had let Carlo so wrench and destroy his life and go on with a life of his own?

He saw his house in Venice. He saw a ghostly wife he'd never known, he saw a host of ghostly children. He saw the lights go out over the canal and the palazzo shimmer and fade as if melting slowly down into the water. *Why was this done to me!* He wanted to cry out, and then he felt her near him, at his side.

Her small head was against him and he saw her eyes, and it seemed somehow surely he had missed the point of all his life, he must have done some terrible evil or this simply could not have happened! Not to Tonio Treschi, who had been born for so many things.

Mad thoughts.

It was the horror of this world that a thousand evils were visited on those who were blameless and no one was ever punished, and side by side with the greatest promise was nothing but misery and want. Children mutilated to make a choir of seraphim, their song a cry to heaven that heaven did not hear.

And he, fallen into it, by some glorious accident in the alleyways of Venice, he had on winter nights sung his heart out under stars such as these.

And yet suppose it was as she said. He stood looking down at her in the dark, the small curve of her head, her naked shoulders above the cover she held loosely around her, and as she lifted her eyes to him, he saw the white of her forehead and the dark configuration of her face.

Suppose it could really be. That somehow on the glittering margin of the world that was their own, they could live and love together, and all the rest that was given to the others be damned.

"I love you," he said. And you almost made me believe in it, too, he thought. His voice trailed off. How could he leave her? How could he leave Guido? How could he take leave of himself?

"But when will you go?" she asked. "If you've made up your mind to do it and nothing can stop you . . ."

He shook his head. He wished she wouldn't say any more. She was not resigned to it, no, not yet, and just for this moment, he couldn't bear to hear her even pretend that she was. The last night of the opera was tomorrow. They had at least that much.

7

I T WAS AFTER the last race; the horses had charged through the press, stomping into the crowds several times to drive spectators underfoot, the air full of shrieks, though nothing stopped their volatile progress towards the Piazza Venezia. The wounded and the dead were being dragged away. Tonio, at the top of the spectators' stand, held Christina close to him, gazing towards the piazza where great cloths were being thrown over the heads of the maddened animals.

Darkness was coming softly over the rooftops. And now commenced the great closing ceremony of these last few hours before the beginning of Lent: the *moccoli*.

Candles everywhere.

They appeared in windows all along the narrow street; they appeared on the tops of carriages; they appeared on the ends of poles, and in the hands of women, children, men seated at the doors, until everywhere there was this soft flickering of thousands upon thousands of tapers. Tonio quickly took a light from the man beside him, touching it to Christina's candle, as there exploded at once the whispered cries, *"Sia ammazzato chi non porta moccolo"*—"Death to anyone who does not carry a candle."

At once a dark figure darted forward blowing out Christina's flame as she tried to shield it with her hand. *"Sia ammazzato la signorina!"* Tonio quickly gave her a light again, struggling to keep his own flame out of the reach of the same rascal, as with a great breath from his powerful lungs he blew out the man's flame with the same curse: *"Sia ammazzato il signore."*

The entire street below was a sea of dimly lit faces, each protecting its own flame while trying to extinguish another: Death to you, death to you, death to you. . . .

Taking Christina's hand, Tonio led her down through the tiered seats, now and then blowing out a vulnerable light as those about him sought to retaliate; and slipping into the very thick of the crowd, he pulled Christina along under his arm, dreaming of some side street where he might breathe for the moment and again commence the little lovemaking with which they had tormented themselves all day long amid wine drinking and laughing and almost desperate gaiety.

Tonight the opera would be brief so that it could end at the stroke of twelve, the commencement of Ash Wednesday, and for now he cared for nothing else but the starry sky overhead and this great ocean of tender flames and whispers enveloping him. Death to you, death to you, death to you. His flame was gone, so was Christina's, who was gasping, but in this moment, elbowed and pushed, he tumbled her against him and opened her mouth with his, not caring that the candles had gone out. It seemed the crowd held them up, moved them along; it was like being in the sea with one's feet in the sand, leaning against the surf and letting it support you.

"Give me your flame." Christina quickly turned to a tall man beside her, and then gave the fire to Tonio.

Her little face was eerie, lit from below, and those soft wisps of her hair were ignited with gold, and she laid her head on his chest, her candle against his so his hands curled to protect both of them.

Finally it was time to go. The crowd was bleeding away, the children still blowing out the candles of their parents and taunting them with the curse, and the parents recriminating, and the madness ebbing into the side streets, and Tonio stood quietly, not wanting to move, not wanting to leave this last remnant of the carnival, even for the last moments of ecstasy in the theater.

479

All the windows were lit still; lanterns hung over the street, and the carriages drifting past were covered with lights.

"Tonio, we have a little time. . . ." Christina whispered. It was so easy to hold her little hand against her will; she tugged on him; he did not move. She stood on tiptoe and put her hand on the back of his neck. "Tonio, you are dreaming. . . ."

"Yes," he murmured, "of life everlasting . . ."

But he followed her towards the Via Condotti. She was almost dancing in front of him, tugging him as if his long arm were a leash.

A little child darted up to him hissing, *"Sia ammazzato—"* But jerking his arm up with a defiant smile, he rescued the flame.

What happened then came so quickly that he could not piece it together afterwards. He was suddenly aware of a figure rising up before him, the face grimacing: "Death to you!" as Christina let him go, and he fell backwards, off balance, as she screamed.

He had his stiletto out just as he felt the cold blade of another knife against his throat.

He shoved it upwards so it scratched the side of his own face, but he had thrust his own weapon forward, driving it twice and then three times into the figure who sought to force him to the wall.

Yet just as this weight sagged against him, he felt another man behind him, and the sudden tightening of the garrote around his neck.

In absolute terror he struggled, his left hand reaching for the face behind his head, his right arm driving that blade down and back into the man's bowels.

The air was full of stomping, shouting, Christina screaming, but he was strangling, the cord was cutting through his flesh, and then suddenly it was gone.

He turned and flew at his assailant only to realize a man had both his arms and was shouting at him, "Signore, Signore, we are at your service!"

He stared forward. It was a man he'd never seen before, and behind him stood Raffaele's bravos, those men who had been following him for weeks, and between them they held Christina not as if they meant to harm her but as if they were guarding her. At his feet lay the body of the man he'd stabbed.

His chest was heaving. He stood against the wall, a cornered animal, not trusting, not believing, trying to understand what he saw.

"We are in the service of the Cardinal Calvino," said the man to him.

And Raffaele's men had *not* attacked him. They were right there.

The crowd pressed in with its hundred of little candles, until gradually it dawned on him what had happened: all of these men had come to his defense.

He stared at the dead man.

A group of little children rushed in only to draw back with a chorus of gasps, their fingers red and transparent about their guarded flames.

"You must come now, Signore, out of here!" said the bravo, and Raffaele's men were nodding. "There may be others who want to harm you," and as they led him away, another bravo had bent over the dead man and opened his coat.

8

HE SAT ON the very edge of the room. The Cardinal Calvino was in a white rage.

And having summoned Count Raffaele di Stefano, he thanked him profusely for the help of his men in protecting Tonio, and Christina, whom they had taken safely to the Contessa's house.

Raffaele was not too pleased that Tonio's attackers had come so close.

But who were these attackers? Both men turned again to Tonio, who had only shaken his head, to say that he knew what they knew:

Both assailants had been common Venetian cutthroats. They carried Venetian passports, Venetian coin. The Cardinal's bravos had cut down one of them; Tonio had killed the other.

481

"Who in the Veneto would want to kill you?" demanded Raffaele, his small black eyes fixed on Tonio. He was maddened by the blank expression on Tonio's face.

Tonio again shook his head.

That he had managed to get to the theater, that he had managed to go on stage, seemed a marvel to him, and that he had managed to do well was the result of habit and skill which he had never fully valued until now.

But this room was more a penance to him than the lighted stage had been, where listening to his own voice at a great remove, he had been swimming in his own thoughts.

Exhilaration had been the feeling, the same exhilaration he had known when he had laid open his soul to Guido two days before, exhilaration that cooled him and hardened him and which the paint and costumery had magnificently concealed.

Now he forced himself to be quiet; to be still. Yet he could not keep himself from feeling the cut on his throat, wondering just how deep the cord would have to go before it extinguished the voice, if not the life.

And the knife had come against his throat as well. Knife, garrote at the throat.

He looked up and fixed his gaze on Guido, who stood watching these proceedings as if he were just as baffled and horrified as the rest.

It was the southern Italian countenance, the know-nothing countenance that reveals itself to no one but its own.

Four bravos would guard Marc Antonio from now on, said the Cardinal. Tactfully, considerately, anger still agitating him, he did not ask Raffaele why Raffaele's men had been there. The Cardinal's bravos had spoken to these men as if they knew them, as if their presence came as no surprise.

And what if none of them had been there? Tonio narrowed his eyes and looked away as Raffaele bent to kiss the Cardinal's ring.

Across the room, Guido appeared defeated behind his mask of innocence. It was as if he'd seen Tonio's body lying slain in the street.

Tonio felt the cut on his throat again. Raffaele was going out. The bravos would stand guard in the very corridors of the house, even as Tonio had seen those bravos of

Carlo making shadows of themselves in the passages of the Palazzo Treschi.

"Go, Guido," Tonio whispered.

Finally he and the Cardinal Calvino were alone.

"My lord," Tonio asked. "Would you grant me another kindness after so many? Could we go alone to your chapel? Would you hear my confession?"

9

THEY WALKED in silence down the hall. And opening the doors found the air warm inside, candles aglimmer before the marble saints, and the golden doors of the tabernacle giving off a faint light above the smooth whiteness of the linen-draped altar.

The Cardinal moved to the first row of carved chairs set before the communion rail and settled himself there, offering the seat next to him to Tonio. There was no need for the men to use the wooden confessional box itself. The Cardinal's bowed head and haggard profile told him he might begin when he wanted:

"My lord," he said, "what I tell you must be under the seal of the confessional and never repeated to anyone."

The Cardinal's brows knit. "Marc Antonio, why do you remind me of this?" he asked.

He raised his right hand and made an efficient little blessing.

"Because I don't ask absolution, my lord, I seek some justice perhaps, some righteousness before heaven. I don't know what I seek, but I must tell you the one who sent men to kill me is my own father, known to everyone as my brother."

The tale came out of him swiftly, cleanly, as if the years had washed the trivia away, leaving only the bones. And the Cardinal's face constricted with pain and concentration. His lowered lids were smoothly rounded over his eyes and he shook his head ever so slightly in eloquent silence.

"What was done to me would have moved others to vengeance long before now," Tonio whispered. "But I know now it was my *happiness* that caused me to eschew my purpose. I did not abhor my life; I loved it. My voice was not only God's gift to me, it was my joy, and all of those around me became my joy, though granted there was lust and there was passion. I can't deny it. But live I do, and sometimes I've felt I was like a glass of water struck by the sun, the light veritably exploded in it until it became a light itself.

"So how could I strike him down? How could I make a widow of my mother once again, and orphans of her children? How could I bring darkness and death to that house? And how could I raise my hand to him when he was my father, and in love for my mother he had given me life? How could I do this when, save for the hatred of him, I lived in the happiness and contentment I had never known as a child?

"So I put off the doing of it. That he must have not one child, but two, I waited. That my mother should finally be released to heaven, I waited. And even then, when nothing remained to prevent me, when I had discharged my duties to those I loved, and nothing stood in my path, it was my *happiness* and the leaving of it that caused me to waver. But more to the point, my lord, it was my happiness that caused me guilt that I should strike him down! Why must he die if I had the world, and love, and all a man could hunger for? These are the questions I asked myself.

"And even on this very day, I wavered, struggling with my conscience and my purpose, the arguments I gave others but arguments with myself.

"But you see, he has been his own undoing! He has sent his men to kill me. He can do it now. My mother is dead and buried, and four years stand between him and the obvious motives that would have proved his death sentence had he done it before when he counted so upon my allegiance to my house, and my name, and yes, even to him, the last of my family.

"And sending these assassins to cut me down, he has sought to snuff out the very life that was luring me away from him, that was saying to me, forget him, let him live!

"But I cannot forget him. Now he has left me no choice. I must go there and strike him down, and there is no reason under God I cannot do this and come back to those I love who are waiting for me. Tell me there is no reason I must destroy myself to destroy this man who has this very day attempted to kill me!"

"But *can* you destroy him, Marc Antonio," the Cardinal asked, "without forfeiting your own life?"

"Yes, my lord," Tonio answered with quiet conviction. "I can do it. For a long time I have known a way to get him in my power with little danger to myself."

The Cardinal weighed this silently. His eyes narrowed as he looked at the distant tabernacle.

"Ah, how little I knew of you, how little I knew of what you suffered . . ." he said.

"An image has come to my mind," Tonio went on. "All evening it has plagued me. It is that old tale told to children and grown men alike of how the great conqueror Alexander, presented with the Gordian knot, cut through it with his sword. For that was what was inside of me, a veritable Gordian knot of wishing to live and yet believing I could not live until I'd destroyed him and thereby proved my own ruin! Well, he has cut the Gordian knot with the knives of his assassins. And often enough tonight when others thought I smiled or talked or even sang on the stage, I was thinking to myself I understand now how fully that old tale has always disappointed me. What wisdom was there slicing through a puzzle which had defeated finer minds? What a brutal and tragic misunderstanding! Yet these are the ways of men, my lord, the slicing through, the cutting away; and it is only those of us, perhaps, who are not men who can see the wisdom of good and evil in a fuller light and be paralyzed by our vision of it.

"Oh, I would spend my time with eunuchs, with women, with children and saints, who shun the vulgarity of swords if I were but free to do so. But I am not. He comes for me. He reminds me that manhood is not so easily dispatched after all, but can be yet summoned from my bowels to stand against him. It is as I always believed it was: I am not a man and yet I am a man and cannot live as one or the other as long as he lives unpunished!"

"Then there is but one certain way out of this difficulty." The Cardinal turned to him at last. "You cannot raise your hand against your father without suffering for it. You have told me so yourself. I need not quote the Scriptures to you. And yet your father has sought to kill you because he is afraid of you. Hearing of your triumph on the stage, your fame, your fortune, your swordsmanship, the powerful men who have befriended you, he cannot but believe you mean to move against him.

"So you must go to Venice. You must get him in your power. I can send men with you, or those of Count di Stefano, however you choose. And then confront him if you will. Satisfy yourself that he has suffered these four years for the wrong he committed against you. *Then let him go*. And he will have the certainty he needs that you will never do him wrong; and you will have your satisfaction. The Gordian knot will be unraveled and there will be no swords.

"These things I don't say to you as a priest, as your confessor. I say them as one who is in awe of all you have suffered and lost and gained in spite of everything. I have never been tested by God as you have. And when I failed my God, you were gentle with me in my sins and showed me no contempt nor monstrous advantage in my weakness.

"Do as I tell you. The man who let you live for so long does not truly wish to kill you. What he wants above all is your forgiveness. And only when you have him on his knees can you convince him that you have the strength to give it."

"But do I have that strength?" Tonio demanded.

"When you realize it is the *greatest* of all strengths, you will possess it. You will be the man you want to be. And your father will bear eternal witness to it."

Guido was not asleep when Tonio came in. He was at his desk in the dark and there came from him the soft sounds of the cup being lifted, of the liquid in it being drunk, and the cup being set down on the wood again almost silently.

Paolo lay curled in the middle of Guido's bed, the moon laying bare his tear-stained face and loose hair, and the fact that he had never undressed and was cold, with his arms close around him.

Tonio lifted the folded cover and laid it over him. He brought it up to his chin and bent to kiss him.

"Are you weeping for me as well?" He turned to Guido.

"Perhaps," Guido answered. "Perhaps for you, and for me, and for Paolo. And for Christina, also."

Tonio approached the desk. He stood before it watching Guido's face slowly reveal itself.

"Can you have an opera ready for Easter?" he asked.

Hesitantly, Guido nodded.

"And the impresario from Florence, is he still here?"

Again, with hesitation, Guido nodded.

"Then go to the impresario and make the arrangements. Hire a carriage large enough for all of you—Christina, Paolo, Signora Bianchi—and go to Florence and take a house for us there.

"Because I promise you, if I do not come back to you sooner, I will be with you on Easter Sunday before the doors of the theater open."

PART VII

1

EVEN IN THIS VEIL of gently driven rain, it was too beautiful to be a real city. Rather it was the dream of a city, defying reason, its ancient palaces sliding up from the battered surface of the leaden water to form, all of a piece, one grand and glorious and continuous mirage. The sun suffused itself through the broken clouds, burnt silver at the edges, the masts of the ships rising sharply beneath the soaring gulls, banners snapped and flapping, explosions of color against the gleaming sky.

The wind whipped the sheet of water that was the piazzetta, and beyond came the bell of the Campanile, caught up in the cold howling so that the sound seemed the dream of itself, like the screaming of the gulls.

Out of the porticoes of the Offices of State there came that ancient and sacrosanct spectacle of the Most Serene Senate, scarlet robes trailing in the damp, white wigs torn by the wind, as the promenade took it to the water's edge, and one by one these men drifted off into those sleek funereal barges of jet black, up the avenue of unbroken splendor that was the Grand Canal.

Oh, would it never cease to astonish, to lay waste the heart and the mind? Or was it only that for fifteen years of bitter exile in Istanbul he had so hungered for it that it would never be enough? Ever tantalizing, ever mysterious, and ever merciless, his city, Venice, the dream made material over and over again.

Carlo lifted the brandy to his lips. He felt it burn his throat, the vision faltering, and then it held firm again, gulls caught in a great upward motion as the wind stung his eyes.

He turned round, almost lost his balance. And saw his trusted men, his bravos, shadows on the edge of the piazza, drawing just a little closer, uncertain whether they should help him, ready to step forward should he fall.

Carlo smiled. He held the flask by the neck. He drank a deep swallow and the crowd became a sluggish mass of color,

490

mirrored in the water, as insubstantial finally as the rain itself which had dissolved into a silent mist.

"For you," he whispered to the air around him, the sky, this miracle of the solid and the evanescent, "for you, any and every sacrifice, my blood, my sweat, my conscience." And closing his eyes, he listed against the wind. He let it ice his skin in this delicious drunkenness, beyond pain, beyond grief. "For you, I murder," he whispered. "For you, I kill."

He opened his eyes. All those red-robed noblemen were gone. And in an instant, he imagined pleasantly, they had drowned one by one in the sea.

"Excellency, let us take you home."

He turned. It was Federico, the bold one, the one who fancied he was servant as well as bravo, and again the brandy to his lips, he felt it in his mouth before he made the decision to drink.

"Soon, soon . . ." He wanted to say the words, but a film of tears had risen to soften his vision, empty rooms, her empty bed, her dresses yet on hooks, and some perfume faintly lingering. "And time blunts nothing," he said aloud. "Not her death, not the loss of her, not the fact that on her deathbed she spoke *his* name!"

"Signore!" And with his eyes Federico exposed a shadowy figure, ludicrous in the manner in which it shrank from sight suddenly, one of those loathsome and inevitable spies of the state.

Carlo laughed. "Report me, then, will you? 'He is drunk in the piazza because underground his wife is hostess to the worms!' " With the flat of his hand he pushed Federico away.

The crowd swelled, a living thing, and broken open here and there only to close again. The rain, twisted by the wind, fell on his eyelids, and on his lips, drawn back in a smile he could feel with his whole face. He stepped to the side, caught himself, and with the next swallow, he said, "Time," aloud again with that recklessness that only drunkenness could give you, he thought, when time gives nothing, "and drunkenness," he whispered, "gives nothing except now and then the strength to see this vision, this beauty, this *meaning* of the whole."

The rain clouds etched with silver, the gold mosaics shimmering, moving. Had she ever had this vision in all that clandestine drinking, when she pulled the wine right out of his hands as he begged her not to, *"Marianna, stay with me, don't drink it, stay with me!"* Unconscious on her bed, did she even dream?

"Excellency," whispered the bravo, Federico.

"Leave me alone!"

The brandy had an exquisite heat to it; it was like liquid fire. He imagined himself threaded with it, its warmth sustaining him, and the icy air about him could not conceivably touch him and it struck him that all beauty was of its greatest use when one was utterly beyond pain.

The rain sprang afresh from the air, slanting and spattering the sheet of water that lay before him. It made a great hissing sound.

"Well, *he* will be with you very soon, my love," he whispered, his lips twisted back in a grimace, "he shall be with you, and you will in the great bed of the earth lie together."

How she had gone on at the end! "I will go to him, you understand me, I will go to him, you cannot keep me prisoner here, he is in Rome, I will go to him." And he had answered: "Ah, my darling, can you even find your shoes or the comb for your hair?"

"Yeeeesss, be together again"—the words left him like a great sigh—"and then, and then, I can breathe."

He shut his eyes so that when he opened them he might see it once more, this loveliness, the sun a sudden burst of silver and the golden towers peaking sharply above those glittering mosaics. "Death, and all my mistakes of the past corrected, death, and no more Tonio, Tonio the eunuch, Tonio the singer!" he whispered. "On her deathbed she summoned you, didn't she? She said *your name!*"

He swallowed the brandy, loving the shudder it sent through him, his tongue gathering the last taste of it from his lips.

"And you will know how I paid for it all, how I suffered, how every moment I have given you has cost me dearly until I have no more to give you, my bastard son, my indomitable and inescapable rival; you will die, you will die so that I can live again!"

The wind whipped back his neglected hair; it seared his ears and cut even to the thin fabric of his frock coat, lashing his long black *tabarro* out and back between his legs.

But even as he listed again, battling the vision of the death room from which not for one moment in these last few weeks had he *ever* been free, he saw moving towards him across the

492

piazza the very real figure of a woman draped in mourning, whom he had seen over and over in the *calli*, on the *riva*, in the *calli*, throughout these last few drunken and belligerent and bitter days.

He narrowed his eyes, his head falling to one side.

Her skirts drifted so slowly above the shimmering water she seemed to move not by human effort but by the effort of his fevered and grieving mind.

"And you are part of it, my dearest," he whispered, loving the sound of his own voice inside his head, though no one else took the slightest notice of him, nor the open bottle in his hand. "Do you know that? You are part of it, nameless one, and faceless one, yet beautiful one, as if this beauty were not enough, you come forth out of the core of it, dressed in death, black as death, moving ever towards me as if we were lovers, you and I, death. . . ."

The piazza tilted and righted itself.

But this was the pinnacle of some miracle of the brandy and the wine and his suffering: this was that perfect moment when it was all bearable: yes; worth Tonio's death, because I have no choice, I cannot do otherwise! And let it dissolve into poetry, if it will, songbird, singer, my eunuch son! My long arm reaches to Rome and takes you by the throat and silences you forever and then, and then, and then, I can breathe!

Under the arcade, his bravos prowled, never very far away.

He wanted to smile again, to feel it. The piazza, shining this brightly, must explode into a formless glare.

But another feeling was threatening him, an altered vision, something dissolving this lovely pleasure and offering him the taste of . . . what was it? Something like a dry scream in an open mouth.

He drank the brandy. Was it the woman, something in the movement of her skirts, her veil blown out behind her so that he could see the shape of her face beneath it, inciting in him some little panic that made him swallow the drink too fast?

She was coming towards him as she had come towards him on the piazzetta earlier, as she had come near him on the *riva* before.

Some courtesan in Lenten black, what was she? And coming so steadily. It seemed from the milling crowd she'd picked him for her destination, yeeesss! Yes, she was pursuing him, and there was no doubt of it. And where were her ladies, her servants? Did they creep on the edges of things, as did his men?

He liked to imagine it for a moment, yes, she was in pursuit of him; behind that black veil she had seen his smile; she was seeing it now.

"I want it, I want all of it!" He clamped his jaw on the words. "I want it and not this suffering, only would you, would you, would they please come and tell me that he is dead!"

He widened his eyes; she was not a human thing at all, but some specter sent to haunt him and comfort him, as he saw the dim oval of her white face, and the movement of those pale hands beneath her floating veil.

She changed suddenly; she turned her back, but she had never ceased her progress. No! It was so remarkable, he moved his head forward slightly, eyes narrowed again, the better to see.

She was walking backwards, letting all those layers of gauze unravel before her face, and her skirts blow out before her. She walked backwards on her heels, never losing her stride, just as a man would do in this wind, to straighten out his gathered cloak, and then she turned back around.

He laughed, softly, unobtrusively. He had never seen a woman do such a thing in all his life.

And when she turned, her garments were looser around her, and on she came with that same eerie weightless motion, and he felt a sharp pain catch at him, in the side.

He let out his breath with a hiss.

Blind, foolish courtesan, widow, whatever you are, he thought, a malevolence seeping into him as if some little dark place had been lanced suddenly so the poison might spread. What do you know of all of it around you, and how you are part of it, beauty, beauty, just part of it, no matter what your own ugly and trivial and inevitably repulsive thoughts!

The bottle was empty.

He had made no decision to drop it and yet it burst on the wet stones at his feet. The thin water moved out in ripples, and the pieces glittered and settled. He stepped on them. He liked the sound of the crunching glass.

"Get me another!" He gestured. And one of the shadows in the corner of his eye moved forward, grew larger, taller.

"Signore." The bottle was given him. "Please, you should come home."

494

"Aaaah!" He opened the bottle. "All men, my friend, give license to those of us who grieve, and have I not cause to grieve today more than any other?" He leered into Federico's face. "He is most likely putrefying as we stand here, and all those women swooning for his voice are now wailing, and his friends, the rich and powerful of Rome and Naples, are even now laying him out in state."

"Signore, I beg you. . . ."

He shook his head. The sick room again, and that . . . what was it? . . . horror that he could almost taste like a coating on his tongue. She sat up suddenly. "Tonio!"

He laid his hand squarely on Federico's chest and pushed him away.

He drank deep, deep, and slowly, beckoning the sadness to come again, that luminous and fathomless emotion that was without turbulence.

And she, his woman in black, where was she gone?

He turned on his heel and, seeing her not ten paces away from him, was certain that she had turned her head to look at him just as he had looked at her!

Yes, she had done that.

She was looking at him from out of that darkness. He despised her, even as he knew his eyes were full of some lustful glitter, as he gave her his slow, his adoring smile. Always the same insolence, this coquetry, this game of cat and mouse while the grief beat inside of him: you think I want you, you think I desire you, drink you down like wine I will, and cast you aside before you even know what happens to you. But her! Now that was love that time could not touch. No, it took *him* to destroy it. "Tonio!" and she did not speak another word until she died.

He took the brandy too fast; it spilt down the side of his face and onto his clothes.

Someone had greeted him, bowed, and moved off hurriedly seeing the state of things. But they would forgive; everyone forgive; his wife dead, the children crying for her, and him crying for her. And somewhere five hundred miles to the south that disgrace, that old scandal. "Ah, Senator Carlo Treschi," they must be saying to themselves, "what he has had to bear."

Something else. Federico at his elbow. He stared at the woman in black. She was definitely attempting to lure him. "I told you to leave me alone."

". . . is in, and no one was on it, Signore."

"On what? I can't hear you."

"The packet, Signore, there was no . . ."

Graceful, feline whore, something unmistakably elegant, the sway of her dress, and the way she bent with the wind. He wanted her, wanted her, and when this was over he would go down on his knees in the confessional: "I killed him, I had no choice, I did not. . . ." He turned round and tried to see Federico more clearly. "What did you say?"

"There was no one on the packet, Signore. There was no message—" and lowering his voice so it wasn't even a whisper—"no message from Rome."

"Well, there will be." He drew himself up. And so the wait goes on, and the guilt with it. No, not the guilt, merely the discomfort, the tension, this feeling of being unable to breathe.

He almost dreaded it finally, the message. They had said, "We will bring you proof," after the first outrage when he had questioned their integrity. "Oh, will you, and what will that be?" he had asked. "His head in a bloodied sack?"

He had laughed, and even they, those assassins, had been aghast, straining to conceal it behind faces that looked as if they'd been carelessly carved out of wood and never polished. "You don't need to bring me proof. You only need to do it. The news will come to me fast enough."

Tonio Treschi, the singer, people actually called him that now, even to Carlo, even to his brother, they dared, Tonio Treschi, the singer!

Years ago, those others had said they would bring proof, and he had dismissed it. And when they put that mess of viscera and blood before him, the linen dried and cracking with it, he had knocked over the chair to get away from them roaring, "Get it away from me, get it away from me!"

"Excellency . . ." Frederico was talking to him.

"I will not go home."

"Excellency, there is still no message and that means there is the chance . . ."

"What chance!"

". . . that they failed."

Just a touch of exasperation in Frederico, and a touch of anxiousness, his eyes darting over the piazza, passing blindly over that dark-clad woman who had suddenly appeared again. You don't see her? I see her. Carlo smiled.

496

"Failed?" He sneered. "He's a Goddamned eunuch, for the love of God. They could strangle him with their bare hands!"

He lifted the bottle, giving Frederico that almost intimate push to move him from this perfect vision. Yes, she was there again. "All right, beautiful one, come to me," he said under his breath, and quickly drank the brandy again.

It was a great swallow this time, cleaning his mouth and his eyes. The rain was soundless and without weight, just a swirling of silver.

And the burning in his chest was luxurious; he hadn't taken the bottle down from his mouth.

In her last days, Marianna ran round and round tearing open drawers and cabinets. "Give it to me, you have no right to take it, I put it here, you won't keep me in this house."

And the old physician warning, She will kill herself, and finally Nina running through the halls. *"She does not speak, she does not move"*—wailing, wailing.

Four hours before she died, she knew it. She opened her eyes and said, "Carlo, I'm dying."

"I won't let you die! Marianna!" he had insisted, and long after, he had awakened at her slight movement, saw her eyes open, heard her say: "Tonio!" She never uttered another word.

Tonio and Tonio and Tonio.

"Signore, home . . . if it was not done as it should have been done, there is a danger that . . ."

"That what? They went to wring a capon's neck. If they have not done it, they'll do it. I don't want to talk of this, get away from me. . . ."

Tonio Treschi, the singer! He sneered.

"There should have been some message on the packet."

"Yes, and proof!" he said. "Proof." His head in a bloodied sack. *Get that away from me, get that away from meeeeee. . .!*

She had never stopped asking him: "You didn't do it, you didn't do it!" He had whispered his denials a thousand times, a thousand times in those early days when everyone was on him like so many birds of prey ready to strip his flesh from him; behind closed doors, she clung to him, making her hands into claws. "My son, my only son, and our son, you didn't do it!"

"So now you say it." He had laughed and laughed. But

497

no, my darling, a thousand times, I could not have done such a thing. In his rashness he did it. And then her face would soften, just for a little while at least, in his arms, she would believe.

". . . no good to mourn like this."

"Who said that?"

He turned around too fast, and saw a pair of figures retreating, the heavy black *vesti patricie*, the white wigs, his unforgiving and ever vigilant peers.

Frederico was far, far away, watching from the arcade, and with him those others. Four good stilettos and muscle enough to guard him against anything save madness, save bitterness, save *her* death, save endless and terrible years without her, years and years. . . .

A sodden loneliness overtook him. Wanted her, my Marianna, how to describe it, even her crying in his arms, her screaming for her wine, and those drunken eyes accusing him, those lips drawn back over the whitest teeth. "Don't you see I'm with you now," he had said to her. "And we're together and they're gone, they can never separate us again, you are as beautiful as you ever were, no, don't look away from me, look at me, Marianna!"

And just a little while the inevitable softness, that yielding: "I knew you couldn't have done it, not to my Tonio, and he is happy, isn't he? You didn't . . . and he is happy."

"No, my darling, my treasure," he had answered. "He would have accused me if I had. You have seen the papers he signed with your own eyes. What would he have to gain by not accusing me?"

Only the time to plot to kill me, that's what he had to gain, ah, but first my sons, my sons for the House of Treschi, oh, yes, all for the House of Treschi, for which he kept his counsel, Tonio, the singer, Tonio, the swordsman, Tonio, the Treschi!

Would the gossip never stop?

I tell you the Neapolitans are positively in fear of him; they do anything to avoid crossing him. They say he was in a fury when the young Tuscan insulted him; he slashed open the boy's throat. And that brawl in the tavern, he slew the other boy, he is one of those dangerous eunuchs, very dangerous. . . .

Where is my whore in black, he thought suddenly, my beautiful lady Death, my courtesan wandering so boldly alone in the piazza? Put your mind on the living, forget the dead, the dead, the dead.

Yes, living flesh, warm flesh, under all that black, you had better be beautiful, you had better be worth every zecchino. But where was she?

And the water, as the wind lifted the rain from the surface, had become a perfect mirror once again. And in that mirror, he saw a great dark dressed form approaching. No, it stood before him.

"Ah."

He smiled, looking down at the reflection. "So my bold little seductive bitch in black, it's come to this."

But the only word his lips formed for her was "Beautiful." Could she see that?

And what if I gather up that veil and throw it back? You wouldn't dare trick me, would you? No, you'll be beautiful, won't you? And simpering, and mindless, with a tongue like brass! A lot of haggling disguised as conquetry, and all the time you think I want you. Well, I have never wanted anyone in all these years save one woman, one beautiful and crazed woman: "Tonio!" and she died in my arms.

She was so close to him now, this anonymous woman in mourning, that he could see the embroidered edge of her veil. Black silk thread, Lenten flowers, beads of jet.

And then some white movement under the veil, her naked hands.

Her face, her face, give me the face.

She stood so still, and so far from him, much farther than he had realized when he had stared at her reflection in the water. She must be a giant of a woman! Or was this just some confusion? Let her turn away again, he wouldn't follow her, not with this much brandy and this much misery. He almost lifted his hand for Federico.

But she didn't turn away.

It seemed her head beneath that long shroud moved gently to one side, and all of her long body seemed to yield to him, and all of his vague and sentimental thoughts were suddenly dispersed by the gesture: yes.

"Yes, my darling?" he whispered, just as if at this distance she might have heard him.

But others were coming, some little knot of men in dark garments plowing into the wind. They divided her from him, never for a second aware of it, but he fixed his eye on the

499

lone enticing figure staring straight at him through that mourning veil.

And just when he felt a little panic that he might lose sight of her, he saw her over the shoulder of the man in front of her, that veil rising in her white hands, and then her face.

He was stupefied for an instant.

She moved away. He knew he was not so drunk he was seeing visions. She was beautiful! She was beautiful as all of this was beautiful, and she had known it, moving towards him. She had come as if conjured by him, never faltering, a face like a magnificent mannequin, a confection, a life-sized doll.

Porcelain, that is what it looked like, perfectly white, and those eyes!

Now it was he who was following, the rain swirling in a silver light so that he squinted and shivered, trying to catch a glimpse of her, as over her shoulder she showed that face again. Yes, after her. After her.

And boldly, splendidly, she now beckoned for him!

Oh, this was rare, and so delicious, and so what he needed, the pain vanquished for just a little while.

She walked faster and faster.

Then when she reached the edge of the canal ahead of him, she turned.

The veil came down slowly.

But that was all right, that was lovely. He overtook her and she was already beneath him by several steps. Her skirts almost touched the water. He fancied he could see the rise and fall of her breath.

"Bold as well as beautiful," he said to her, though she was still just a little too far away to hear him. She turned and gestured for the gondolier.

He saw his men clustering behind him. He saw Federico approach.

And turning, he came down towards her in a rush, stepping heavily and awkwardly into the boat as it rocked under him and all but pitched him down after her into the closed *felze*.

As he slid back on the seat, he felt the taffeta of her dress against him.

The boat moved. The stench of the canal filled his nostrils. And she rose up before him, breathing under that magnificent drapery.

For a moment all he could do was catch his breath.

500

His heart hammered, and the sweat broke out over him, the price of his rushing. But he had her, though he could barely see her in the light of the parted curtains.

"I want to see it," he whispered, fighting an ugly pain in his chest. "I want to see it. . . ."

"You want to see what?" she whispered, her voice husky and low and absolutely without fear. And Venetian, yes, Venetian, how he had hoped for that!

He laughed to himself.

"This!" He turned on her, snatching up the veil. "Your face!"

And he fell forward on her, his open mouth covering her mouth, and forcing her back against the cushions so that her body stiffened and her hands went up to hold him off.

"What did you think?" He righted himself, licking his lips and looking directly into her black eyes that were no more than a gleam in the shadows. "That you could play games with me?"

She had an expression of the most peculiar astonishment. Nothing of coquettish outrage, nor feigned awe. She was merely looking at him, as if she were dimly fascinated by him, studying him, as one might study something inanimate, and she was as perfectly beautiful in this shadowy place as any creature he had ever seen.

Impossible beauty. He looked for the limit of it, the inevitable disappointment, the inevitable flaws. But she was so lovely to him, at least for this instant, that it seemed he had known this beauty always, in some private compartment of his soul where he had whispered lustily and gracelessly to the god of love, "Give me this, and exactly this, and this, and exactly this." And here it was, with nothing in this face alien to him. Her eyes, so black, and those lashes curling upward, and the flesh so tight over the cheekbones, and that long, luscious and exquisite mouth.

He touched her skin, ah! He drew his fingers back and then he touched her black eyebrows, and those bones, and that mouth.

"Cold, aren't you?" He breathed the words. "Now I want you to really kiss me!" It was spoken like a groan coming out of him, and taking her face in both hands he forced her back and took it from her, sucking her mouth hard and then letting it go, and sucking at it again.

It seemed she hesitated. It seemed for one second she was

501

frozen, and then with a deliberation that amazed him, she gave of herself, her lips softening and her body softening, and he felt the first stirring, through all his drunkenness, between the legs.

He laughed.

He sank back on the cushion. The light flashed colorless and dull in the gap between the curtains, and her face seemed almost too white to be human. But she was human, all right, that he could taste.

"Your price, Signora." He turned to her, drawing so close to her that her white powdered hair tickled his face. When she looked down he felt her eyelashes against him. "What is it, and what do you want?"

"What do *you* want?" came that deep, husky voice. It hit a pitch that made a little spasm in his throat.

"You know what I mean, darling . . ." he purred. How much for the pleasure of ripping off your clothes. "Such beauty requires its tribute," he said, brushing her cheeks with his lips.

But she raised her hand. "You waste what you might savor," she answered. "And for you, there is no price."

They were in a room.

They had come up long stairs, up and up, damp stairs, he did not like it, such a neglected place. There were rats everywhere, he could hear them, but she had fed him those succulent kisses, and that skin, that skin, was enough to kill for.

And now they were in a room.

She had been pressing him to eat, and the wine was like water after the brandy.

He didn't know this house.

He knew the district, however, the houses all around, many a warm bedchamber with a courtesan he liked well enough, but this house. . . .

The candles hurt his eyes; the table was crowded with food that was no longer hot, and beyond loomed the frame of a bed carelessly hung, it seemed, with gold-threaded curtains. The heat of the enormous fire was too warm.

"Too warm," he said. She had bolted all the shutters. And something bothered him, or perhaps several things, that there were so many spider webs under the ceiling, and that it was so damp here, it smelled of decay.

502

Yet all these riches in the midst of it, the goblets, the silver plate; there was something about all of it that reminded him of a stage set when you're so close to the stage you can see the rafters and the wings.

But something bothered him, something in particular. What was it? It was . . . her hands.

"Why, they are enormous . . ." he whispered. And hearing the sound of his own voice, and seeing those long, long white fingers had brought him up out of a stupor, anxious suddenly, and pieces of the afternoon were missing.

What had she said? He couldn't remember getting out of the gondola.

"Too warm?" she whispered. That same husky voice that made you want to touch her throat.

And as his vision cleared he saw her, almost as if for the first time. Not her hands, but *her*. If there had been any other moment that he had seen her, he could no longer recapture it, and he thought, out of habit, that surely, surely, his men were nearby.

But her. He was looking at the blurred outline of her, blinking now and then, straining against the drunkenness as he lifted the cup. The Burgundy was delicious though it was weak.

"You will not mind, my dear," he said as he pulled the cork from the flask in his hand.

"You ask me that again and again." She smiled. It was like breath, that voice; it was like part of her, and when had the voice of a woman ever been like that?

She wore a French wig. Flawless, white curls spilling over her shoulders, pearls embedded in ringlets, and oh, she was so young! So much younger than he had imagined her in the gondola where she had seemed ageless or ancient, and unquestionably Venetian, though he did not know why.

"A child," he said to her gently now, his head suddenly pitching forward so that he felt his limits sharply, and with an attempt at dignity brought himself back up. Her lips were not rose, not pink, but some deep natural color. No, there was no paint. In the gondola, he would have tasted it and smelled it. She was just this vision, and those eyes, staring at him.

And the dress with its tight embroidered band across her breasts. He wanted to slide his hand between her breasts and that tight band and tear it loose, just set them free.

503

"Why have you waited all these years to come to me!" He laughed playfully.

But her face suddenly changed.

It was as if all of a piece she had moved. Yet it happened so quickly, he was unsure of his perception. And now she settled back and that long luscious mouth spread easily in a smile that crinkled her black eyes at the edges.

She answered: "It seemed the perfect time."

"Yes, the perfect time," he said. Oh, if you only knew, if you only knew. He held his wife in his arms every time he held another woman, he held his wife closer and closer only for that moment of horror to see it was not Marianna, it was nobody, it was just this . . . just this whore.

Better not to think of all that now. Better not to think of anything.

He reached out and shoved the glaring candle to his right.

"All the better to see thee, my child." He mocked the French fairy tale.

He laughed and laid his head back against this heavy and very high-backed oak chair.

But as she bent forward, bringing her elbows onto the table and her face into the light, he found himself suddenly shocked. He drew in his breath and stiffened, his shoulders rising slightly.

"Do I frighten you?" she whispered.

He didn't answer her. It was absurd to be frightened of her! He felt a little cruelty come into him, remembering that she would disappoint him, that behind this mysterious expression there would lie only the coquetry finally, and maybe vulgarity and certainly greed. He felt so tired suddenly. So weary. And this room was so close. He saw himself slipping into his own bed; he felt the weight of Marianna next to him. He thought slowly and bitterly, she is in the grave.

And he was too drunk for this, he was on the verge of sickness, and he should never have come.

"But why are you so sad?" she asked him in that purring voice. It was as if she truly wanted an answer, and there was about her something so powerful . . . what was it . . . her beauty had a fierceness. She might truly make him . . . but then this was what he always believed in the beginning, and what was it in the end? The struggle between the sheets, some little cruelty slipping out of him, and that haggling afterwards, threats maybe. And he was too drunk for this, much too drunk.

"I must leave . . ." he said, his mouth working reluctantly. He would take out his purse—that is, if he still had it. His *tabarro*, what had he done with it? It lay at his feet. But then she would be a perfect fool to try robbing him. She knew better than that.

It seemed her face was . . . too large. Impossibly large. Yet those wide-set black eyes were astonishing him. He stared at her hands as she played with the white hair at her temples, such an exquisite forehead, rising without the slightest slope to that expensive French hair. But such large hands for a beautiful woman, large hands for any woman, and those eyes. He had a sudden sense of drifting, of disorientation that he remembered now from the gondola, and it had nothing to do with the water, or did it?

He felt the room moving just as if they were still in the narrow boat.

"I must . . . go. I must lie down."

He watched her rise.

She seemed to rise and rise and rise.

"But that isn't possible . . ." he murmured.

"What isn't possible?" she whispered. She stood over him and he breathed her perfume, which wasn't so much the French scent as it was her freshness, her sweetness, her youth. She was holding something in her hands. It looked like a great black loop of something, of leather, a belt with a buckle.

"That you . . . that you could be so tall . . ." he answered. She had raised the loop over his head.

"You've only just noticed it?" she asked, smiling. Exquisite!

It was almost as if he could fall in love with her, imagine it, love her; it was as if there were some substance to her, not the predictable mystery and its inevitable vulgar core, but something infinitely more fierce. "But what are you doing?" he asked her. "What's this . . . in your hands?"

They didn't look human, these hands.

She had dropped this loop of leather belt down over him. What an extraordinary thing to do. He stared down and saw it binding his chest and his arms.

"What did you do with it?" he asked her.

And then when he tried to move, he knew.

She had dropped it over the back of the chair as well, and it

505

was so tight he couldn't move forward, not lift more than his forearms. This was most strange.

"No," he said smiling. He could raise his forearms and he brought them up almost spilling the brandy from the flask. Suddenly he jerked forward.

It was impossible. The chair, immense and heavy, did not move.

"No," he said again smiling coldly at her. "I don't like this." And as if correcting a little child, he gently shook his head.

But she had passed in back of him where he couldn't see her, and as he tried to lift the belt with his right hand, he realized it was too tight.

He grasped it in both hands now, crossing his arms, the brandy fallen over on the table, his fingers wet and slipping on the leather. Something was holding the belt in its place from behind.

She appeared then at his right shoulder.

"You don't like it?" she asked.

Again, he gave her that cold smile. He would when this inanity had reached its conclusion make her pay for this when he had her stripped and helpless and his hand over her mouth. Nothing too cruel, only a lesson of sorts, and he saw himself slipping his fingers inside that flat band of embroidery and pulling it loose.

"Take this off, my dearest," he said coldly, in a voice that was low and full of command. "Take it off me now."

He saw that large hand dangling just before him at her side, the fingers impossibly long and thin and white, even the rings too large: rubies and emeralds, this was one very accomplished woman, rubies and emeralds and those tiny pearls.

And suddenly jerking his right hand to the side he grabbed hold of her wrist and brought her down hard onto his lap.

"I don't like it," he said in her ear, "and I shall snap your pretty neck if you don't reach behind me and release the buckle now."

"Oh, you wouldn't do that to me, would you?" she said without a flicker of fear.

An alchemy was working in him. His mind was clearing as he looked at her, her perfect face, and yet his body was still hopelessly drunk. Dull pain was gathering itself in the front of his head. His arms were so tightly bound that with his left hand he could not possibly reach her neck. But he would

506

break her arm in a moment if need be and force her down, and that would be the end of it. He had been too drunk for this. He should never have come.

"Take the belt from around me," he said. "Now."

She stared at him without answering and then she seemed to grow very soft. He felt her shifting on his lap, just as he saw that in the very center of her black eyes was the faintest glimmer of dark blue. Her face was closing out the light behind her. She was so near to him he felt her breath. It was fresh, untainted, and there rose in him that lust for her that would have existed no matter had she been plain because she was so very fresh, so very young.

Just flesh for an instant. Her lips touched his lips, and he found himself closing his eyes. His hand loosened on her wrist but she didn't move it, and the kiss sent its shock down into him, summoning his passion almost to that point where nothing else was of importance.

But then he stirred, rolling his head on the back of the chair. "Take off the belt," he said gently. "Come on, I want you! I want you . . ." he whispered. "You are a foolish woman to provoke me."

"But I'm not a woman," she whispered, just before he silenced her with his mouth.

"Hmmmmm . . ." He made a small frown. Something dissonant, horridly dissonant in her little jest. His pleasure was sluggish, at war with his drunkenness, and he was vaguely aware that she had laid his hands down again on the arms of the chair, and with her palms she was pressing his hands to the arms of the chair. Gentle, playful, her very touch tantalizing him, but strange.

"Not a woman?" There was something unearthly about the texture of her skin, it was so sweet, so soft, and yet not. . . .

"Then what are you," he whispered, his lips forming a smile even in his kissing her, "if you're not a woman?"

"I'm Tonio," she breathed into his lips, "your son."

Tonio.

He opened his eyes, his body convulsed violently and painfully before he could even reason, a loud noise like a clanging in his head, his hands struggling both to shove her away off him, yet hold her, grab hold of her, and get her off him, away from him, as he felt a hoarse cry rise out of his throat.

She was gone. She was standing before him, towering over

507

him and staring down at him, and in one moment he understood all of it, the disguise, what was happening, and he went wild.

His feet slid and kicked at the floor, his arms tearing at the leather strap, his head thrashing from side to side.

"Frederico!" he roared. "Frederico!" and as he struggled and fought, his roaring continued, without words, his heels trying vainly to dig into the very stones. Suddenly, very suddenly, when he knew the chair had not moved, that he was helpless, that he could do nothing, he went absolutely still.

She was smiling down at him, smiling.

His head lay to one side, his eyes wide glaring at her, and then she was laughing, a low, smoldering laughter, husky and sensual as her voice had been before:

"You want to kiss me again, Father?" she whispered. And that beautiful face, that flawless white face was frozen in the most lovely and serene smile!

He spat at her.

His teeth clenched, his hands out as if he could somehow summon her with his clawing fingers, he spat at her again.

And then he lapsed back, trembling, head to the side once more, and all of it was coming clear to him with a stunning perfection.

The stage, the endless talk of his beauty and his skill at illusion, that he was the woman incarnate before the footlights, and those hands, those horrid and dreadful hands, and the skin!

He felt the nausea rolling up from his stomach. He clenched his teeth against it and exerted all his will not to panic, not to thrash about, not to give her the satisfaction of it. But he couldn't stop the roaring, the moaning, from coming between his teeth.

Her. She! He closed his eyes, shuddering. Sickness overcame him. He swallowed and shivered with it. And when he opened his eyes again it was Tonio, more surely, holding that great French wig of pearls and white hair in his hands.

The smile was gone from his face. His eyes were glassy and wide and amazed.

He pulled off the black bodice as if it were armor. The skirts, untied, dropped to the floor.

And there, in crumpled white shirt and breeches, hair moist and disheveled, stood a giant of a feline man. There

508

was a stiletto tucked in his waist; there were jewels on the handle, and as he stepped out of the discarded taffeta finery, he adjusted that stiletto with one of those long hands.

Carlo swallowed. The taste in his mouth was rank, and the silence shimmered between them now like the vibration of a thin wire.

For a long time, they looked at one another, this cold-eyed demon with the face of an angel and Carlo, who now very slowly gave an ugly, soft laugh of his own.

He passed his tongue over his lips.

Dry, sore, a crack forming down the middle of the lower lip from which he could taste blood.

"My men . . ." he said.

". . . are too far away to hear you."

"Will come . . ."

". . . not for a long, long time."

And it came back to him dimly, those steps going higher and higher. And he had said to her, "But there's water running somewhere, I can hear it, the canal has broken through. . . ." He could smell the canal. And she, the bitch, the monster, the demon, had answered, "It doesn't matter. There is no one living here. . . ."

No, no one in this house to hear him, this great crumbling old house.

And in this room with the fire blazing, he had gone to those windows for air and with his own eyes had seen not the street with his men waiting and watching, but, some four storeys deep, the dark well of an inner court! They were in the heart of it, this building, and she had let him see it step by step!

Oh, it was too perfect, too clever.

Sweat was drenching him. And after this one I sent a pair of crude murderers. The sweat ran down his back and under his arms. He felt his hands moist and slippery though he did nothing with them, save open and close them, open and close them, struggling against the panic again, the urge to struggle when this oak chair would not yield an inch.

And how many times had he instructed Frederico to give him a wide berth with women, how many times had he warned him not to rouse him from any beds?

It had been staged beautifully, and it was no opera. And he had said: "He's a eunuch, they can strangle him with their bare hands."

509

He watched Tonio seat himself at the table opposite, his white shirt untied at his throat, the light playing on the bones of his face, every movement suggestive of the giant cat, the panther, an eerie grace.

He felt hatred in him, dangerous hatred, attaching itself to that face, that perfect face, and to every detail that he saw, to all the things he had ever known and suffered to know about Tonio, the singer, Tonio, the witch before the footlights, Tonio, the young and beautiful one, the famous one, the child reared by Andrea to every blessing and indulgence under that roof all those years while in Istanbul he raged and raged, Tonio, who had all of it, Tonio whom he had never escaped, not for one moment, Tonio and Tonio and Tonio, whose name she'd cried out on her very deathbed, Tonio who had him now, despite the knife and those long weak eunuch limbs, despite the bravos and a life of caution, helpless and captive now.

If he did not let it out in a great roaring cry, this hatred would drive him mad.

But he was thinking, thinking. What his bravos needed was time. Time to realize this house was empty, too dark, time to start prowling about it.

"Why didn't you kill me?" he demanded straining suddenly against the leather, his hands clutching at the air before him. "Why didn't you do it in the gondola? Why didn't you kill meee!"

"Quickly, stealthily?" came the familiar husky whisper. "And without explanation? The way your men came for me in Rome?"

Carlo narrowed his eyes.

Time, he needed time. Frederico had a nose for danger. He would realize something was wrong. He was only just outside this house.

"I want some wine," Carlo said. His eyes moved to the table, the bone-handled knife in the fowl quite beyond his reach, the goblets, the flask of brandy on its side.

"I want some wine!" His voice thickened. "God damn you, if you did not kill me in the gondola, then give me some wine."

Tonio was studying him as if he had all the time in the world.

Then with one of those impossibly long arms he reached out and moved the cup towards Carlo.

510

"Take it, Father," he said.

Carlo lifted it, but he had to bend his head to drink. He sucked up the wine, washing out the rank taste, and as he lifted his eyes he felt the dizziness so strong surely his head must have fallen heavily to one side.

He drained the cup.

"Give me some more," he said. That knife was much too far away. Even if he could somehow have tipped this massive table, heavier than the chair in which he sat strapped and helpless, he could not have caught hold of that knife in time.

Tonio lifted the bottle.

Frederico would know something was amiss. He would approach the door. The door, the door.

As he was mounting those steps ahead of her, he had heard some loud noise echoing through this place like the boom of a cannon, and some thought in his mind that a woman should not have been able to throw a bolt over the door like that.

But that wouldn't stop his men.

"Why didn't you do it?" he demanded suddenly, the cup in both hands. "Why didn't you kill me before now?"

"Because I wanted to talk to you," Tonio answered so softly it was a whisper. "I wanted to know . . . why you tried to kill *me*." His face, which had been smooth and impassive before now, was coloring with the faintest emotion. "Why did you send assassins for me in Rome when I had done you no harm in four years, and asked nothing of you? Was it my mother who had stayed your hand?"

"You know why I sent them!" Carlo declared. "How long did you plan to wait before you came back for me!" He felt his face flushed and wet, the sweat salty on his lips as he licked them. "Everything you did told me you were coming! You sent for my father's swords, you spent your life in fencing salons, not six months in Naples you slew another eunuch, and in the next year, put a young Tuscan to rout. Everyone was afraid of you!

"And your friends, your powerful friends, would I never stop hearing of them, the Lamberti, the Cardinal Calvino, di Stefano from Florence. And then on the stage you dared to use my name, as if throwing the glove in my face! You lived your life to torment me. You lived your life as if it were a blade thrust forward drawing ever closer to my throat!"

He sat back. His chest was a mass of pain, but oh, it felt

good, so good to voice it at last, to feel the words pouring out of him, an uncontrollable stream of poison and heat.

"What did you think? That I'd deny it?" He glared at the silent figure across from him, those long white hands, those claws, playing with the handle of that long bone-handled knife.

"I gave you your life once, expecting you to stick it between your legs and run with it. But you made a fool of me. God, has one day passed that I have not heard of you, been forced to speak of you, to deny this and deny that and swear innocence and feign tears, and declare platitudes and resignation, and lies without end to it. You made a *fool* of me. The sentimental one, afraid to shed your blood!"

"Oh, Father, curb your tongue," came Tonio's astonished whisper. "You are unwise!"

Carlo laughed, a mirthless dry laughter that made the pain in his head throb.

He gulped the wine without realizing it and as his hand strained for the bottle, he saw it slide forward, and then the liquid splashing into the cup.

"Unwise, am I?" He laughed and laughed. "If you want denials from me, if you want begging, then you will be very disappointed! Take that sword of yours, that famous sword of yours, for surely you've got it hidden somewhere, and use it! Shed your father's blood! Show me none of the mercy I showed you!"

And the deep drafts of Burgundy cooled him for a moment, washing over the pain and over the dryness of that laughter that seemed to carry his words along.

He wanted to wipe his mouth with his hand. It was maddening that he could not touch his mouth.

He let the wine lap against his lip as again he felt a shudder and that panic, that urge to struggle again to no avail.

"I didn't want to send those men to Rome!" he said. "I had no choice! If it had worked differently, if they'd come and told me you'd grown meek and diffident, afraid of your own shadow! I've known eunuchs like that, that despicable old Beppo, who hanged himself in his cell after you left, that slinking Alessandro, for all his insolence, absolutely spiritless. There's nothing to fear from a gelding like that. But you, oh, it had not done its work with you! You were too strong for it, too fine for it, too much of my father's mettle, too old for it, perhaps! And there was no end to hearing of you, I tell you it

512

was as if you lay on the very pillow beside me, as if you lived and breathed under my roof! What was I to do! You tell me! I had no choice!''

Through the haze of the smoking candles he saw the distant face still shocked with amazement, but it had become more remote, and almost sad.

"Ah, you had no choice!" Tonio whispered almost bitterly. "And what if you had come to Rome? What if we two had met as we are met now, and discoursed as we are discoursing now?"

"Met? Discoursed?" Carlo demanded disgustedly. "To what end? So that I might have begged your forgiveness for having you gelded?" He almost sneered. "Well, I begged you once over and over again to yield to me, my bastard son! And you refused. You made your fate! It was your decision, not mine!"

"Oh, you cannot believe that!" Tonio whispered.

"I had no choice!" Carlo roared. He bent forward. "Again, I say to you I had no choice! And damn the men I sent after you in Rome, that was nothing. If they prodded you on your errand, so much the better, for you would have come and you know it, and I say to you I had no choice!"

His vision clouded, but oh, that face was so beautiful even now, demon thing, the irony of it, and youth, youth, the thing he lamented most of all.

But he was seeing the bottom of the cup again. He felt the wine running down his chin. He reached for the bottle.

"Met with you, discoursed with you." He sighed, his chest heaving, his eyes half mast.

But what was he doing, what was he saying?

His eyes moved over the distant ceiling, the great shadowy vault that shivered slightly with the flames of the candles, where spiders lived, and the rain, seeping in, shimmered in droplets through hairline cracks.

It was time he needed, time for it to get dark, and what had he been saying, what had he let pour out of him, all the poison from these old sores.

But as he felt his body flooded with the warmth of the wine, and a great soft exhaustion, he did not care!

What he cared about was all the injustice of it, the brutal and relentless injustice of it that had gone on and on for years. Lies and accusations that were never ending, and all that he had paid and paid and paid! That was the mystery of it, that each thing he had sought had cost him so dearly it was not worth it in the end. Oh, what had he ever enjoyed that had not cost him youth, blood, and endless wrangling, and when had there ever been any understanding, any moment when he could lay down the whole of it before any judge?

"What do you know of it?" he demanded. "Of all those years in Istanbul when you were spoilt and pampered and she taken from me, and then to come home and have her accuse me, accuse *me*! She never believed me, you know! It was always Tonio, and Tonio! I begged her a thousand times to put the wine away, I'd bring physicians, nurses. What didn't I give her? Jewels, Paris fashions, servants to wait on her hand and foot, the gentlest nurses to care for our boys, I gave her everything! But what did she want when it was all said and done: 'Tonio,' and the wine, and it was the wine that brought her to her deathbed, and on her deathbed she asked for you!"

He studied Tonio. What was it now? A look of incredulity? Of unwilling pain? He could not tell. He did not care.

"That must give you solace, surely," he said bitterly, again leaning forward, his head too heavy for him now, the wine cool and fresh in his mouth. "And she in those last days! Do you know what she said to me, that I had ruined her, destroyed her, driven her to madness and drink and taken from her her only comfort, our son! She said this to me!"

"And of course you did not believe it, did you?" Tonio whispered.

"Believe it! After what I had suffered for her!" Carlo felt the leather strap against him with a sharp pain, and settling backwards, held the bottle tight in his hand. "After what I had done for her! Exiled for the love of her, and who after all those years in Istanbul, and she in my father's house, would have bothered with her again!

"But I loved her, and it was a passion that endured fifteen years only to be destroyed by what? Not time, mind you, not my father, mind you, but you! 'Tonio' and she died. She would not even look at our children in the end. . . ."

His voice broke. He was startled at the sound of it, and would have rested his head in his hands if he could.

This bondage was unendurable, but it would be worse were he to struggle and feel its limits, and desperately he told himself that, as he sat still, his hands straining to reach his face, his head moving just a little from side to side.

"You ask if I believed her. What right have you to ask me anything! What right have you to sit in judgment on me!"

He reached for the brandy flask, and quickly emptied it into the cup. He drank it down, feeling the sharper, stronger heat of it, delicious, and the whole room seemed to move under him, some convulsion in him rolling upwards until even his eyes rolled up in his head. Some image was before him, tormenting him, of his young and beautiful Marianna when he had first taken her from the convent, when they had come into his lodgings, and when she realized he was not to marry her, and she commenced to scream.

He was shuddering, remembering only the rush of his words as he had tried to comfort her, assuring her it was only time he needed, time to win over his father. "I am his only son, don't you see, he must yield to me!"

But this was not what he wanted now. He was on the verge of delirium, and without words he had some sense of the years before that, when his mother was alive, and all of his brothers, and all the world had been easy and full of hope and full of love. There stood between him and his father a great buffer, and there had been nothing he could not mend, could not make right. But that had been taken away from him, cruelly, just as she had been taken away, and his youth had been taken away, and it seemed now that all he could truly remember was struggle and bitterness that obliterated everything else.

He moaned. He was gazing at the supper table. Dimly, he knew where he was and that it was Tonio who held him here. He felt the strap cutting him, and drifting, he struggled to see clearly, to remember again that what he needed now was time.

The candles were burning low, and the fire on the hearth was a heap of glowing cinders. When he had gone drunk to the Broglio that morning, swearing he would marry her with or without permission, his father had stood over him, turning him back, that horrid countenance: "You dare to defy me!" And she, sobbing across the bed in those filthy lodgings, "O God in Heaven, what have you done to me?"

He must have made some sound again, some moan.

With a start he realized the room had darkened and grown enormous, and Tonio, opposite, stared at him still without expression save for the hardest line to that long mouth.

His black hair was softened now and fallen down more naturally about his face, and what did he look like? Even after

515

the knife there was still the old resemblance, yes, like a dozen portraits painted years and years ago when they were all together, his brothers and he, and his mother, but this was Tonio!

He felt the sickness rising in him again.

"You . . ." He seethed, his body shuddering. "You hold me prisoner here, you sit in judgment on me! Is that what you've come for, judgment on me! You, the pampered one"—he smiled, that laughter commencing again, low, rustling dry laughter that seemed to carry his words along—"the chosen one of my father, and the singer, yes, the great singer, the celebrity in Rome with women pelting his carriage with flowers, and royalty receiving him, Tonio with gold overflowing his purse, and the great Cardinal Calvino doting on his every wish."

There was just a flicker of feeling in Tonio's face.

"Yes, yes." He laughed, his laughter low and dry. "Do you think I don't know the odious fate to which I so rashly and impulsively condemned you, do you think I haven't heard tell of your lovers, your worshipers, your friends? What door is there that has not opened to you? What is there you would have that has been denied you? Eunuch. What in God's name did they hack away from you that you have laid a siege to the beds of Rome as great as that of the barbarian hordes?

"And you come here, rich, young, blessed by the gods even in your monstrousness, so that you seduce your own father, and you sit in judgment on me! Ask me why I did this and why I did that!"

He rested, his fingers trying vainly to wipe at his lips. There was a taste of brandy yet in the cup and it burned him.

"Tell me"—he bent forward again, head cocked to one side—"would you give up all of that if you could have it back, Tonio! Would you give up all of that for the life I've had since!" He leered into Tonio's face. "Think before you answer. Shall I tell you just what it has been! And never mind my wife wailing ever for her lost son, and your cousin, your dear cousin, Catrina, a harpy at me night and day, claws ever and ever deeper, waiting for my slightest slip of the tongue! And those old senators and councilors, his partisans, vultures, that's what they are, ever watching me out of the corner of their eye!

"No, I am talking of Venice now, the life of duty and obligation of which I so cruelly robbed you, Tonio, the

516

singer, Tonio, the celebrity, the castrato. Well, hearken to me.''

He softened his tone as if confiding a secret, his words almost feverish: ''A great moldering palazzo to begin with, that drains your fortune for its countless rooms, its crumbling walls, its rotting foundations, like a giant sea sponge sucking up all that you give to it and ever wanting more, an emblem finally of the Republic itself, that great government which every day of your life summons you to the Offices of State, there to bow, to smile, to haggle, to lie, to plead and preside over the incessant and never-ending cacophonous babble that is the day-to-day workings of this proud and powerless city without empire, without destiny, without hope! Spies and inquisitors and rubrics and tradition and pomp on the verge of madness, your pocket picked for every new spectacle, feast day, anniversary, celebration, and extravagant display.

''And after that, when finally you are quit of those elephantine robes, and mumbling inanities, your feet blistered, the very muscles of your face aching from dissimulation, what then, but that you are free at last for the one hundredth time to lose your money at the Ridotto, or sleep with the same courtesan or the same tavern girl, or the same adulteress with whom you quarreled seven times the week before, the spies of the state ever at your elbow, your enemies ever judging you, your conduct ever under scrutiny, and when you are weary of it, sick of it, suffocated with it, only to turn round and look about you, from one end of this narrow island to the other, and realize that on the morrow it will all begin over again!

''And you have come home to judge me!

''You want it back! You want to take it in place of the opera, you want it instead of your English beauty in the Piazza di Spagna, you want to give up that voice of yours that has made you a god among the people and a nonpareil, so that you can return here but one of a thousand grasping noblemen all struggling for the same few expensive and dreary offices within this Republic all but shrunk to the very walls you saw around you in the piazza when you played your little dance of cunning for me!''

Low laughter. It had its own momentum, good like the words, an outpouring that could not be checked.

''You take the damned stinking house. You take the damned stinking government. You take it all and. . . .''

He faltered.

He stopped.

He stared straight ahead and it seemed for a moment his mind emptied itself, and the surge of energy which had fired him was dissipated, leaving him weak and spent.

His mind was grasping for something, but for what he did not know.

Save that there was a thread to all of it. And if he grabbed hold of the thread and followed it back and back through the labyrinth of his own ravings, he would surely come to the piazza again in the rain, and that moment, that perfect moment with the gulls soaring, and the banners whipped in the wind. He saw that lustrous sadness, whole and complete and at a great remove from him, and that moment when there had been resignation and hope and some glorious gratitude that for one moment it had all of it made sense. If only Tonio were dead, if only Tonio were finally buried, if only . . . and then he could breathe.

He stared at Tonio. It seemed an eternity they had been together in this room.

The candles were sputtering in their wax, and the fire was almost gone, yet the air was still as warm as a noxious liquid, and his head, how his head throbbed.

But something was wrong.

Something was hideously wrong, and it was wrong in his mind. Something was wrong because these were not lies he had been telling, this was not subterfuge and chatter to buy time so that his men would come. This was something else pouring out of him that had the force and the luster of truth to it, only it could not have been truth, not what he was saying, this could not have been his life.

Tonio's face was contorted, that youthful beauty not so much erased as alchemized into something richer and more complex than innocence, a soul seething inside the temptress, the sorcerer.

But Carlo did not care about Tonio.

He was staring into the chaos that his mind had now become. And the horror was very near him, the horror he had tasted in the piazza, and what had he called it to himself, something curled in the mouth like a dry scream!

He wanted desperately to explain something, something that never never had been understood.

518

When had he ever wanted to murder, to castrate, when had he ever wanted to struggle as he had been forced to struggle . . . ?

But his silence terrified him. He was terrified of the stillness, and then, as though by his silence he had failed any longer to prevent it, he realized that Tonio was rising from the chair.

He stared at the long lean arms that reached for those black clothes, bodice, skirts, the wig with its tiny pearls.

And as he watched in horror, Tonio heaped this in the fireplace on the dying coals.

A flame erupted against the blackened tiles, as with the poker Tonio stirred the fire before him, and the great hollow of the wig was filled with smoke.

Its pearls glinted in the light, and then it commenced to collapse upon itself as all at once it ignited with tiny flames. It gave off a crackling as it grew narrow, like a mouth pinched on both sides. And the black taffeta under it had exploded in a blaze.

"But why are you burning those things?" Carlo heard himself ask. Again, he ran his tongue over his dried lips. The flask was empty, the cup was empty. . . .

He had never in his life known the apprehension he knew now. It seemed he must say something, he must commence again, he must find some way to delay, delay until his men could find him but he could not shake this horror. . . .

"Driven to it," he whispered, his voice so frail it was only for himself, "driven to it, all of it, got at such a price finally that what was it worth then, what was it worth?" He was shaking his head, but these words weren't for Tonio, these words were only for himself.

Yet Tonio had heard.

Tonio held the poker in his hand. Its tip glowed red in the shadows, and now with that slow and feline grace he approached Carlo, the poker held at his side.

"But you have left one thing out, Father," he said, and his voice was calm and cold as if he were speaking formally to a friend. "You have told me of the wife who disappointed you, of the government that drains you and oppresses you, of the peers who persecute you, of my cousin who ever accuses you, you have told me of so much that plagues you and makes your existence nothing but a litany of misery. But you have not told me of your sons!"

"My sons . . ." Carlo's eyes narrowed.

"Your sons," Tonio repeated, "the young Treschi, my

brothers. What is it they do to you, Father? Infants that they are, what is it they do to torment you, what is their injustice to you, do they not keep you awake nightly with their wailing, do they not rob you of your well-deserved sleep?"

Carlo made some uncertain sound.

"Come, Father," Tonio said softly between his teeth. "Surely if all the rest is nothing but obligation and drudgery, surely they are worth it, Father, that four years ago you broke the course of my life!"

Carlo stared forward. Then uncertainly he shook his head. He drew himself up, his shoulders lifted, his feet pushing silently on the floor.

"My sons . . ." he said. "My sons . . . my sons will rise up and seek you out and kill you for this!" he shouted.

"No, Father," Tonio said. He turned and with an easy gesture cast the poker into the fire. "Your sons will never know what happened to you here," he whispered, "if you die in this place."

"That is a damnable lie, they will grow up wishing for your death, living for the day when—"

"No, Father, they will be reared by the Lisani and they will never know much of either of us and our old feud."

"Lies, lies, my men will never rest. . . ."

"Your men will fly this city like rats when they learn they have failed to protect you."

"The inquisitors of state will hunt you down and—"

"If they knew I was here they would have arrested me already," Tonio replied softly, "and in the plain sight of many you left the piazza in the company of a lone whore."

Carlo glared upward, unable to speak.

"No one will know what happened to you, Father"—Tonio sighed—"if you should die here."

And turning he crossed the room with several long strides and opened a darkly varnished armoire.

Carlo sat petrified watching him as, with those easy graceful gestures, Tonio drew out a rusty frock coat which he put on, and then a sword which he strapped to his hip. Then he put a cloak over his shoulders, clasping it at the throat as the deep folds of black wool fell down to the floor.

Those long fingers lifted the hood of the cloak, and Tonio's face gleamed white from beneath the dark triangle of cloth.

Carlo struggled. He convulsed, his teeth clenched in the

520

effort, and with all his weight, he tried to pitch the chair over backwards but it did not move.

The figure approached, the black cloak swaying with that same eerie rhythm of those black skirts in the piazza. And Tonio looked down on the ruined supper, and out of the fowl he drew the long-handled knife.

Carlo's eyes, glassed over with tears of rage, did not flinch. It was not over yet. It was not finished. But if he thought for one instant that it was finished, he would start to scream in madness, it could not have come to this, it could not end in the same injustice, the same injustice, and there pounded in his head only hatred for Tonio and the awful regret that he had not killed him long ago.

"Do you know what I always thought I would do," Tonio whispered, "when this moment came?" He held the knife before Carlo. It gleamed with the grease of the fowl and the ebbing light.

Carlo shrank back against the chair.

"I always thought it would be your eyes I would take," Tonio whispered, lifting the knife carefully, "so that you who have loved as I shall never love, you who have fathered sons as I shall never father sons, you would be shut out of life as I was shut out of it, yet living as I lived!"

The glaze in Carlo's eyes broke and the tears slid down his face. Yet his mouth worked silently as he glared at Tonio. And gathering all his saliva, he spat it into Tonio's face.

Tonio's eyes widened.

With an almost involuntary gesture, he lifted the edge of the cloak and wiped the spittle away.

"Very brave, aren't you, Father?" he whispered. "You have such courage, don't you, Father? Years ago, you told me I had courage, do you remember that? But is it courage, Father, that causes you to defy me now when I have over you the power of life and death? Is it courage, Father, that not for your sons, not for Venice, not for life itself will you bow, will you bend?

"Or is it something infinitely more brutal than courage, more base? Is it not pride and selfishness that have made you nothing more than the slave of your unbridled will, so that any opposition to it must be your mortal enemy regardless of the stakes?"

Tonio drew closer, his voice more heated.

"Was it not selfishness, pride, unbridled will that drove

you to take my mother out of the convent that sheltered her, to ruin her and drive her to madness when she might have had a dozen suitors, and married a dozen times over, well and content? She was the darling of the Pietà, her singing was a legend. But you must have her, wife or no!

"And was it not selfishness and pride and will that drove you yet to defy your father, threatening with extinction a family that had endured for a millennium before you were born!

"And when you came home and found yourself still punished for these crimes, what did you do but seek to take what you would have out of pride, selfishness, and willfulness, even if it meant cruelty, treachery, and lies! 'Yield to me,' you said, and when I could not yield to you, you had me gelded, driven out of my homeland and separated from all that I knew and loved. Banished from Venice rather than accuse you, disgraced rather than see you punished and my house endangered, and now you tell me all this, for which you mutilated me and wronged me, is but persecution and burdens and trials!

"Dear God, a house all but destroyed for you, a woman ruined and driven to madness for you, a son gelded and broken by you, and you dare to complain of accusations and suspicions and that you are forced to tell lies!

"What in the name of God are you that your will and your selfishness and your pride demand such a price!"

"I loathe you!" Carlo cried out. "I curse you. I wish to God I had killed you. If I could, I would kill you now."

"Oh, I believe you when you say that," Tonio answered, his voice shaken and frayed. "And you would tell me yourself again, if you were to do it, that in this as in all else you had no choice!"

"Yes, yes and yes again!" Carlo roared.

Tonio stopped. He was trembling still with the force of his own words, and now it seemed he sought to calm himself, to let the silence drain away the anger that had risen, his eyes fixed on Carlo, but without expression, merely innocence again.

"And you would leave me no choice now, would you?" Tonio asked. "You would have it that I must kill you now, this very instant, though every instinct in me seeks to save you even against your own will."

Carlo's face, frozen in fury, underwent the smallest change.

"I do not want to kill you!" Tonio whispered. "For all your hatred, your recklessness, your endless malice, I do not want to kill you! And not out of mercy for you, the miserable man that you are, but for things you have never honored, and never, never understood."

He paused, catching his breath. His face had a sheen to it now that caught the gleam of the fire.

"That you are Andrea's son," he said slowly, almost wearily, "that you are his flesh and blood and my flesh and blood, that you are a Treschi, and master of my grandfather's house. That you have in your keeping my infant brothers whom I would not orphan, that you for all your bitter complaint against it, do in the government of Venice carry our name!

"For all this, I would let you live, for all this I came here seeking to let you live, and for the wretched truth of it that you are my father, *my father*, and I do not want your blood on my hands!"

Again Tonio stopped. He held the knife still, and his eyes grew distant and dim. It seemed a great exhaustion had come over him, a great revulsion suddenly.

And keenly, Carlo marked this, though his face was full of mockery, unwilling to be deceived.

"And maybe, finally," Tonio whispered, "because I will not allow you to force me to do it, I will not stand before God a patricide, whining as you have whined, 'I had no choice.'

"But can you fathom this? Can you accept a wisdom beyond your willfulness, your own pride? Is there no way yet to unravel this knot of vengeance, injustice, blood?"

Carlo had put his head to the side and looked at Tonio through one narrow eye. His hatred for Tonio pounded in him as if it were the rhythm of his heart.

"I am done hating you," Tonio whispered. "Done fearing you. It seems that you are nothing to me now but some ugly storm that drove my undefended bark off course. And what was lost to me will never be retrieved, but I want no more quarrel with you, no more hatred, nor spite.

"Tell me, Father, though you begged for nothing, can you yet accept that I want no more now than your vow? You will not seek my life after this, and I shall leave you here unharmed. I will go out of Venice as I came, and never seek to injure you or those you love. If you do not believe it this moment you will believe it when I leave you, but for that, Father, you must bend just a little. You must give me your vow.

"This is what I came for. This is why I have not killed you before now. I want that it should be finished between us! I want that you should be restored to your house, and to my infant brothers. I want that you should give me that vow!"

Carlo made a slow scowl. In a low guttural voice, he murmured, "You are tricking me. . . ."

A sharp spasm divided Tonio's face. Then it was smooth again, seemingly incapable of malice. He lowered his eyes.

"Father, for the love of God!" he whispered. "For life itself."

Carlo studied him. His vision was clear now, painfully clear, though the room had fallen into darkness, and he felt such pure hatred for the shadowy figure that stood over him that little else filled his mind.

He saw the knife in Tonio's hands move. Gracefully Tonio had turned it and was now holding it so that Carlo could take it by the handle.

"Father, your vow. Your life for my life, now and forever. Say it!" Tonio whispered. "Say it so that I may believe you."

Slowly, Carlo nodded.

"Say it, Father," Tonio whispered.

"I vow . . . I will . . . I will never seek your life again . . ." he murmured.

And he watched in amazed silence as Tonio extended the knife. "Take it, cut the strap with it," Tonio said. "Let us be free of each other once and for all."

Carlo took the knife. He brought the blade up instantly to slash the leather just inside his left arm.

The strap gave with a loud snapping and Carlo's chest and arms came forward. Cautiously, the knife in his hand, he rose to his feet.

Tonio had taken several steps backwards, but his movement was slow. The long cloak floated around him, the fire gilding the edges of it, and giving a glint still to his dark eyes.

Carlo's eyes grew slowly bigger. If only he could see what lay under those black wool folds that shrouded the figure so completely, if only he could better gauge the expression on that face, but all the capacity for reason in him was yielding to that hatred which fed itself upon the long afternoon, its

524

outrages, that Tonio had held him here, Tonio whom he loathed and should have killed a long, long time before now, Tonio, the eunuch who had made a fool of him in this above all.

And in one final act of defiance he let his eyes move slowly, eloquently, up and down the figure before him as his mouth lengthened in a pure contemptuous sneer.

In an instant, he lunged forward, the knife jabbing in front of him, his left hand plunged into that black wool for the frail arm he knew to be there.

But the tall dark draped figure swept back from him as if it were an illusion, the gesture so swift he could not even see it, and turning, he heard the zing of Tonio's sword. A thin streak of light closed the gap between them as the pain shot through Carlo's chest.

The knife clattered on the floor.

His fingers reached for the blade of the rapier, the flash of fire that skewered him, and when he tried to speak his mouth filled with a warm gushing liquid that spilled down his chin.

It is not finished, not finished! But his voice was lost in a horrid gurgling sound.

And as he felt himself slipping down, and the darkness rising about him, and his mind was turned to absolute terror, he saw the glimmer in Tonio's eyes breaking and flowing, and he saw Tonio's face stricken just before it smoothed itself into that innocence once again.

2

FOR TWO HOURS Tonio remained in the room with Carlo. Carlo's body grew cold, and finally all the lights were gone out, the candles melted away, the coals turned to ash in the fireplace. Tonio wanted to cover Carlo with his black *tabarro*. He wanted to gather Carlo's hands closer to his body. But he did not do these things, and when the room was dark, he rose and left the house silently.

If anyone saw him emerge from the side door, he had no sign of it. No footfall followed him through the *calli* he knew so well. No shadow stalked him across the vast emptiness of the piazza.

And when he came to the doors of San Marco and found them locked, he stood as a man in a daze, unable for the moment to understand that he could not gain entrance.

At last he rested back against the columns of the portico, and he looked at the black sky beyond the dim outline of the Campanile.

Only a few scattered lights burned in the Offices of State. Cafés on the piazza now and then opened their doors to the rain. And those who hurried against the wind took no notice of him.

Soon his face and his hands were iced from the cold. Yet he did not move, and the slanting rain gradually soaked through his garments.

The night wore on. The clock struck the hour over and over. The cafés went dark, and even the beggars deserted the arcades as the city went to sleep around him.

And all that was left of civilization here was the tolling of the clock and the uncertain glimmer of a few distant torches.

It seemed his pain and the cold he felt were one. And he could not believe in the rectitude of a single action. He struggled to envision those he loved, to feel their presence. It was not enough to say their names as if they were prayers. He imagined himself with the Cardinal Calvino in some quiet and safe place where he could try to explain what had happened.

But these were dreams.

He was alone and he had killed his father.

And if he were to go on from this moment now, it would be to carry this burden with him always. He would never tell anyone what had taken place. He would never ask anyone for absolution or forgiveness.

And finally, when it was very close to dawn, he pulled up the hood of his cloak to conceal his face, and he walked out into the piazza.

He looked on these monumental buildings that had once seemed to him the very limit of the world, and then he turned his back on Venice forever.

3

FOR DAYS HE TRAVELED south towards Florence. It was winter still, and a light frost lay over the fields. Yet he could not endure the company of others in the post carriages. Rather he took a saddle horse at each stop, and walking it along the edge of the road, was often far from shelter at nightfall.

By the time he reached the city of Bologna, he was on foot. His cloak was caked with mud, his boots worn through, and had it not been for his sword, he would have looked like a beggar.

He was pushed about in the streets, the noises jarring him. He had eaten so little that he was light-headed now and could not trust his senses.

And when he reached the countryside again, he knew he could go no farther. Knocking on a monastery door, he placed half of all the money he possessed in the hands of the father superior.

He was grateful when they put him to bed. They brought him broth and wine, and took away his boots and clothes to be mended. He could see a little sun-drenched garden through the window, and before he closed his eyes, he asked the date of the day and how long it was before Easter Sunday.

Of one thing he was certain. He must be with Guido and Christina before Easter Sunday.

Days passed. They ran into weeks.

He lay on his pillow looking out into the garden. It reminded him of some other time when he had been content, the sun falling on the flagstone walks, flashing suddenly in the water of the little fountain. The cloister was full of tinted shade. But he could not remember anything clearly. His mind was empty.

He wished it weren't Lent so that he could hear the monks singing.

And when the night came and he was alone in this room, he knew a misery so terrible it seemed to him that each year of his life would mean only a greater capacity to feel it. And he would see his mother in her bed of drunken sleep, and it seemed she had known some wise secret.

No change was worked in him. Or so it seemed. Yet he took more food each day. Soon he was rising early to go to mass with the friars. And he found himself thinking more and more of Guido and Christina.

Had they made a safe journey from Rome? Was Paolo worried about him? He hoped Marcello, that Sicilian singer, had come with them, and of course they couldn't have left without Signora Bianchi.

Sometimes he did not think of them so much as he pictured them. He saw them dining together, talking to one another. It annoyed him that he didn't know where they were, really. Had they taken a villa in the hills with a terrace on which they might sit in the evenings? Or were they in the heart of the city, some bustling street near the theater and the palaces of the Medici?

Finally one morning with no decision or plan, he dressed, put on his boots and his sword, and carrying his cloak over his arm, went to take leave of the father superior.

The monks in the garden were cutting down the young palm branches and putting them in a wooden wheelbarrow. And he knew it was the Friday in Passion Week, the Feast of the Seven Sorrows. He had only twelve days until the opening of the opera.

By the time he reached the post house he was hungry. He ate a hearty meal and fell to watching with uncommon interest the comings and goings of other travelers. Then he hired the best horse he could, and rode south towards Florence.

It was just before dawn in the town of Fiesole that he saw the first playbill for the opera.

Old women and laborers were coming out of the early mass on Palm Sunday. They carried their blessed palms, and the open doors of the cathedral threw a warm yellow light on the stones before it.

Tonio was walking his horse through the piazza when on a weather-stained wall he saw his own name SIGNORE TONIO TRESCHI in high letters.

It seemed an apparition. Then he was seized with an irrepressible excitement. And feeling foolish at the same time, he brought his horse up to the wall and peered at the wrinkled paper.

Richly bordered in red and gold, it announced the performance of XERXES at Easter at the Teatro Di Via Della Pergola in Florence. Even Guido's name was included in modest letters. And there was a portrait of Tonio too, an oval engraving very flattering indeed, and in praise of his voice a few florid verses.

He walked his horse back and forth, steadying himself with a hand on the wall. He could not stop reading the poster.

Then he asked the first man who passed how far was it to the city.

"Go up the hill and you will see," came the answer.

The sky was still a dark blue and full of tiny stars when he reached the summit, and the city of Florence lay spread out in the valley before him. Through a mist he saw its bell towers, a hundred flickering lights, and the motionless path of the Arno. It was as beautiful to him as the sleeping Bethlehem of Christmas paintings.

And as he looked on those distant spires, he realized that never in his life had there been a moment such as this one.

Perhaps when he had waited in the wings of the theater in Rome on opening night, he had known something of this mounting expectation. Maybe years ago in Venice, he'd known it when he went out on the water on the Feast of the Senza.

But he did not dwell on those times.

Before the sun rose he would be with Guido and Christina. And for the first time they would truly be together.

AFTERWORD

CRY TO HEAVEN could not have been written without extensive research, and I am deeply indebted not only to many writers of the period, but to the authors of numerous scholarly and popular works on the opera, the castrati, the eighteenth century, art, music, Italy, and the cities of Naples, Rome, and Venice.

In addition much material was consulted on the physical characteristics of eunuchs, and I express my special thanks to Robert Owen, M.D., for helping me make my way through the morass of medical literature on the subject.

I would also like to thank Anne-Marie Bates, who very generously made available to me a tape recording of Alessandro Moreschi, the last castrato to sing in the Sistine Choir, and the only castrato ever to be recorded.

All the main characters in the book are fictional. And though every effort has been made to portray the castrati and the century accurately, some liberties have been taken with persons and time. Nicolino, Farinelli, and Caffarelli were real and famous castrati; however Caffarelli's appearances in the book are invented.

Guido's teaching methods are based upon *Early History of Singing* by W. J. Henderson, and I must bear the responsibility for simplification and any inaccuracy.

"*Baroque Venice,* Music of Gabrieli, Bassano, Monteverdi," recorded by the Decca Recording Company, 1972, with its album notes describing Jean Baptiste Duval's visit to San Marco in 1607, was the direct inspiration for Tonio's first musical experience there.

Alessandro Scarlatti's *The Garden of Love* (Catherine Gayer, soprano, as Adonis, and Brigitte Fassbaender, contralto, as Venus) on Deutsche Grammophon, 1964, was the inspiration for Tonio's duet with the Contessa in Naples, and this was the only portion of the book actually written to music.

Metastasio's *Achille en Sciro*, the libretto that Guido chose for Tonio's debut in Rome, is described in detail by Vernon Lee in her unique *Studies in the 18th Century in Italy*.

And there are many baroque operas on record today which were popular during this period.

However, for a real understanding of the music, I strongly urge the reader to seek those recordings in which female singers take the old castrato roles. The castrati were true sopranos and contraltos. And countertenors or male falsettists can give no true ideal of the beauty of their voices.

BLOCKBUSTER FICTION FROM PINNACLE BOOKS!